Against all Enemies

Tom Clancy
with Peter Telep

PENGUIN BOOKS

PENGUIN BOOKS

Published by the Penguin Group
Penguin Books Ltd, 80 Strand, London WC2R 0RL, England
Penguin Group (USA) Inc., 375 Hudson Street, New York, New York 10014, USA
Penguin Group (Canada), 90 Eglinton Avenue East, Suite 700, Toronto, Ontario, Canada M4P 2Y3
(a division of Pearson Penguin Canada Inc.)
Penguin Ireland, 25 St Stephen's Green, Dublin 2, Ireland (a division of Penguin Books Ltd)
Penguin Group (Australia), 250 Camberwell Road,
Camberwell, Victoria 3124, Australia (a division of Pearson Australia Group Pty Ltd)
Penguin Books India Pvt Ltd, 11 Community Centre, Panchsheel Park,
New Delhi – 110 017, India
Penguin Group (NZ), 67 Apollo Drive, Rosedale, Auckland 0632, New Zealand
(a division of Pearson New Zealand Ltd)
Penguin Books (South Africa) (Pty) Ltd, 24 Sturdee Avenue, Rosebank, Johannesburg 2196,
South Africa

Penguin Books Ltd, Registered Offices: 80 Strand, London WC2R 0RL, England

www.penguin.com

First published in the United States of America by G. P. Putnam's Sons 2011
First published in Great Britain by Michael Joseph 2011
Published in Penguin Books 2012
1

Copyright © Rubicon, Inc., 2011
All rights reserved

The moral right of the author has been asserted

Printed in England by Clays Ltd, St Ives plc

B-format ISBN: 978-0-241-95716-5
A-format ISBN: 978-0-241-96107-0

www.greenpenguin.co.uk

MIX
Paper from
responsible sources
FSC™ C018179

Penguin Books is committed to a sustainable
future for our business, our readers and our
planet. This book is made from paper certified
by the Forest Stewardship Council.

AGAINST ALL ENEMIES

We think Al-Qaeda is bad,
but they've got nothing on the cartels.
—*unidentified senior FBI agent, El Paso, Texas*

Everyone has a price. The important thing is
to find out what it is.
—*Pablo Escobar*

In Mexico you have death very close. That's true for
all human beings because it's a part of life, but in
Mexico, death can be found in many things.
—*Gael Garcia Bernal*

Prologue

===

RENDEZVOUS FOXTROT

0215 Hours, Arabian Sea
5 Miles South of the Indus River
Coast of Pakistan

A DARKENED SHIP *is a burdened ship*, Moore thought as he stood outside the pilothouse of the OSA-1 fast attack craft *Quwwat*. She was indigenously built by the Karachi Shipyard and Engineering Works and based on an old Soviet design, complete with four HY-2 surface-to-surface missiles and two twin 25-millimeter antiaircraft guns. Three diesel engines and three shafts propelled the 130-foot-long patrol boat at thirty knots across waves tinged silver by a quarter-moon shimmering low on the horizon. Running at "darken ship" meant no range or masthead lights, no port or starboard running lights. International Regulations for Preventing Collisions at Sea (COLREGS) dictated that were an incident to occur, *Quwwat* would be at fault regardless of the circumstances.

Earlier in the evening, at dusk, Moore had walked down a Karachi pier with Sublieutenant Syed Mallaah, trailed by four enlisted men, a SPECOPS team from the Pakistan Special Service Group Navy (SSGN), an organization similar to the U.S. Navy SEALs, but, ahem, their operators were hardly as capable. Once aboard the *Quwwat*, Moore had insisted on a quick tour that ended with a cursory introduction to the commanding officer, Lieutenant Maqsud Kayani, who was distracted as he issued orders to leave port. The CO couldn't have been much older than Moore, who was thirty-five himself, but the comparisons stopped there. Moore's broad shoulders stood in sharp juxtaposition to Kayani's lean cycler's physique that barely tented up his uniform. The lieutenant had a hooked nose, and if he'd shaved in the past week, there was no clear evidence. Despite his rugged appearance, he had the twenty-eight-man crew's utmost attention and respect. He spoke. They jumped. Kayani eventually gave Moore a firm handshake and said, "Welcome aboard, Mr. Fredrickson."

"Thank you, Lieutenant. I appreciate your assistance."

"Of course."

They spoke in Urdu, Pakistan's national language, which Moore had found easier to learn than Dari, Pashto, or Arabic. He'd been identified as "Greg Fredrickson," an American, to these Pakistani naval men, although his darker features, thick beard, and long, black hair now pulled into a ponytail allowed him to pass for an Afghan, Pakistani, or Arab if he so desired.

Lieutenant Kayani went on: "Have no worries, sir. I plan to arrive at our destination promptly, if not early. This boat's name means *prowess*, and she's every bit of that."

"Outstanding."

Point Foxtrot, the rendezvous zone, lay three miles off the Pakistan coast and just outside the Indus River delta. There, they would meet with the Indian patrol boat *Agray* to accept a prisoner. The Indian government had agreed to turn over a recently captured Taliban commander, Akhter Adam, a man they claimed was a High-Value Target with operational intelligence on Taliban forces located along the southern line of the Afghanistan-Pakistan border. The Indians believed that Adam had not yet alerted his own forces of his capture; he had simply gone missing for twenty-four hours. Still, time was of the essence. Both governments wanted to ensure that the Taliban was not tipped off that Adam had fallen into American hands. Therefore, no American military assets or forces were being used in the transfer operation—except a certain CIA paramilitary operations officer named Maxwell Steven Moore.

Admittedly, Moore had misgivings about using a security team of SSGN guys led by a young, inexperienced sublieutenant; however, during the briefing he'd been told that Mallaah, a local boy from Thatta in Sindh Province, was fiercely loyal, trusted, and highly respected. In Moore's book, loyalty, trust, and respect were earned, and they would see if the young sublieutenant was up for the challenge. Mallaah's job was, after all, rudimentary: oversee the transfer and help protect Moore and the prisoner.

Assuming that Akhter Adam made it safely aboard, Moore would begin interrogating him during the trip back to the Karachi pier. For his part, Moore would use that time to determine if the commander was indeed an HVT worthy of serious CIA attention or somebody to leave behind for the Pakistanis to play with.

Forward of the port beam, the blackness was pierced by three quick white flashes from the Turshian Mouth lighthouse guarding the entrance to the Indus River. The sequence repeated every twenty seconds. Farther east, nearer the bow, Moore picked up the single white flash from the Kajhar Creek light, and that flash repeated every twelve seconds. The sealed-beam revolving beacon of the often-disputed Kajhar Creek (aka the Sir Creek light) was situated on the Pakistan-India border. Moore had taken special note of the lighthouse names, locations, and their identifying flash sequences from the navigational charts rolled out during the briefing. Old SEAL habits died hard.

With moonset at 0220 and fifty percent cloud cover, he anticipated pitch-black conditions for the 0300 rendezvous. The Indians were running at darken ship, too. In a pinch the Turshian Mouth and Kajhar Creek lighthouses would keep him oriented.

Lieutenant Kayani held true to his word. They reached Point Foxtrot at 0250 hours, and Moore shifted around the pilothouse to the only available night-vision scope mounted on the port side. Kayani was already there, manning the scope.

Meanwhile, Mallaah and his team waited on the main deck, midships, to haul the prisoner across once the Indian vessel came alongside.

Kayani backed away from the night scope and offered it to Moore. Despite the gathering clouds, starlight provided sufficient photons to bathe the Indian Pauk-class patrol boat in a green eerie twilight, bright enough to expose the numerals 36 painted on her hull. Approaching bows-on, at twice the weight of the *Quwwat*, the five-hundred-ton *Agray* carried eight GRAIL surface-to-air missiles and dual RBU-1200 ASW rocket launchers up on her bow. Each ten-tube system was capable of deploying decoys and ASW rockets for surface-to-surface and anti-submarine warfare operations. The *Quwwat* felt diminutive in her presence.

As the *Agray* began to drift down the port side and prepared to come about to make her approach, Moore spotted her name painted in black letters across the stern, rising above the mist agitated by the bow wash. He then glanced through the pilothouse door out to the starboard bridge wing and caught a short-long, short-long light flash. He tried to remember which lighthouse used that light sequence. The *Agray* completed her turn, and Kayani was now busy leaning over the port side, directing the placement of fenders to minimize any hull damage once the two ships came together.

The flashes came again: short-long, short-long.

Lighthouse, my ass, Moore thought. ALPHA-ALPHA was International Morse Code for, in practical terms, "Who the hell are you?"

A chill spiked up Moore's spine. "Lieutenant, we're getting an ALPHA-ALPHA on the starboard side. We're being challenged!"

Kayani charged across the pilothouse to the starboard wing, and Moore hustled up behind him. How many times had they already been challenged? They were in Pakistan territorial waters; what were Pakistan's rules of engagement?

A flare burst overhead, peeling back the night and drawing deep shadows across the decks of both patrol boats. Moore looked across the sea and saw it, a thousand meters out, rising up out of the waves, a nightmare with imposing black sail and dull black decks fully awash as she breached, her bow pointed at them. The commander had brought the sub to the surface to challenge them, then had fired the flare to visually confirm his target.

Kayani lifted the pair of binoculars dangling around his neck and zoomed in. "It's the *Shushhuk*! She's one of ours. She's supposed to be back at the pier!"

Moore's chest tightened. What the hell was a Pakistan Navy submarine doing in his rendezvous zone?

He craned his head to the *Agray*, where he assumed that by now the Taliban prisoner was on deck. According to the plan, Adam was wearing a black jumpsuit and turban, and his wrists were bound. His escorts were supposed to be two heavily armed MARCOS, or marine commandos, of the Indian Navy. Moore spun back to face the submarine—

And then, suddenly, he saw it—a line of phosphorescence

bubbling up in the water and streaking past their stern, heading toward the *Agray*.

He pointed. "TORPEDO!"

In the next breath, Moore came up behind Kayani, shoved him over the side, then jumped himself as the torpedo struck the *Agray* in a horrific explosion whose thundering and flashing was as surreal as it was shockingly close. A blast wave of debris pinged off the *Quwwat*'s hull and rained down to strike the water in dozens of splashes.

Moore's eyes widened as the steaming, hissing sea came up at them, heated now by all the white-hot shards of hull and deck and torpedo that continued to blast off the *Agray*. As he hit the water, narrowly missing a jagged piece of steel, a ball of flames set off the *Agray*'s GRAIL surface-to-air missiles and both clusters of ASW rockets on her fo'c'sle.

Moore sank below the waves, his shoes colliding with something below. He swam back to the surface and jerked his head around, searching for the lieutenant. There he was, just out of reach.

Suddenly, three of the *Agray*'s ASW rockets blew up into the Silkworm missile housings aboard the *Quwwat*. The resulting detonations boomed so loudly and brightly that Moore reflexively ducked back under the water for cover. He swam toward the lieutenant, who was floating supine and appeared only semiconscious, his face bloody from a deep gash along the left side of his head. He must've struck some debris as he'd entered the water. Moore surfaced at the man's shoulder. He splashed salt water onto the gash as Kayani stared vaguely at him. "Lieutenant! Come on!"

Thirty meters away, the sea surface was aflame with burning diesel fuel. The stench left Moore grimacing as for the first time he felt the deep rumble of nearby diesel engines . . . the submarine. He had some time. The sub wouldn't approach the wreckage until the flames subsided.

Other men were in the water, barely visible, their shouts punctuated by more explosions. A strangled cry resounded nearby. Moore scanned the area for their Taliban prisoner, but the twin thunderclaps of another detonation sent him back under the waves. When he came up and turned back, the *Quwwat* was already listing badly to port, getting ready to sink. The *Agray*'s bow was entirely submerged, the fires and deep black smoke still raging, ammunition cooking off with sharp cracks and half-muffled booms. The air grew clogged with a haze that reeked of burning rubber and plastic.

Willing himself into a state of calm as the heat of the fires pressed on his face, Moore removed his shoes, tied the laces together, then draped them around his neck. *Three miles to the beach* . . . but right now, this low in the water, he had no idea where the beach was. With the exception of the flames, everywhere he looked was inky black, and each time he glanced toward the conflagration, his night vision was ruined.

Flash-flash-flash. Wait a minute. He remembered. He started counting . . . one one thousand, two one thousand . . . at nineteen, he was rewarded with three more quick flashes. He had a lock on the Turshian Mouth lighthouse.

Moore seized Kayani and rolled him around. Still drifting in and out of consciousness, the lieutenant took one look at Moore, at the fires around them, and panicked. He reached out, seizing Moore by the head. Obviously the man wasn't thinking straight, and this behavior was not uncommon among accident victims. But if Moore didn't react, the frantic lieutenant could easily drown him.

Without pause, Moore placed both hands on the front of Kayani's hips with the heels of his hands against the man's body, fingers extended, thumbs grasping the lieutenant's sides. He pushed Kayani back toward the horizontal position, using this leverage to loosen the man's grip. Moore freed his head and screamed, "Relax! I got you! Just turn around and breathe." Moore grabbed him by the back of the collar. "Now float on your back."

With the man in a collar tow, Moore began a modified combat sidestroke around the burning debris, the pools of burning diesel beginning to swell toward them, his ears stinging from the continuous thundering and drone of the spitting and whipping flames.

Kayani settled down until they passed through a half-dozen bodies, members of his crew, just more flotsam and jetsam now. He hollered their names, and Moore kicked harder to get them away. Nevertheless, the sea became more grisly, an arm here, a leg there. And then something dark in the water ahead. A turban floating there. The prisoner's turban. Moore paused, craning his head right and left until he spotted a lifeless form bobbing on the waves. He swam to it, rolled the body sideways enough to see the bearded face, the black jumpsuit, the terrible slash across his neck that had severed his carotid artery. It was their guy. Moore gritted his teeth and adjusted his grip on Kayani's collar. Before starting off, he looked in the direction of the submarine. It was already gone.

During his time as a SEAL, Moore could swim two ocean miles without fins in under seventy minutes. Collar-towing another man might slow him down, but he refused to let that challenge crush his spirit.

He focused on the lighthouse, kept breathing and kicking, his movements smooth and graceful, no wasted energy, every shift of the arm and flutter of the feet directing the power where it needed to go. He would turn his head up, steal a breath, and continue on, swimming with machinelike precision.

A shout from somewhere behind caused Moore to slow. He paddled around, squinting toward a small group of men, ten—fifteen, perhaps—swimming toward him.

"Just follow me!" he cried. "Follow me."

Now he wasn't just trying to save Kayani; he was providing the motivation for the rest of the survivors to reach the shore. These were Navy men, trained to swim and swim hard, but three miles was an awful long way, more so with injuries. They needed to keep him in sight.

The lactic acid was building in his arm and his legs, the burn steady at first, then threatening to grow worse. He slowed, shook his legs and the one arm he was using, took another breath, and told himself, *I will not quit. Ever.*

He would focus on that. He would lead from the front,

drive the rest of these men home—even if it killed him. He guided them across the rising and falling sea, kick after agonizing kick, listening to the voices of the past, the voices of instructors and proctors who'd dedicated their lives to helping others unleash the warrior's spirit lying deep and dormant in their hearts.

Nearly ninety minutes later he heard the surf breaking on the shoreline, and with every rising swell he saw flashlights moving and bobbing all along the beach. Flashlights meant people. They'd come down to view the fires and explosions offshore, and they might even see him. Moore's covert operation was about to make headlines. He cursed and looked back. The group of survivors had drifted much farther back, fifty meters or more, unable to keep up with Moore's blistering pace. He could barely see them now.

By the time his bare feet touched the sandy bottom, Moore was spent, leaving everything he had back in the Arabian Sea. Kayani was still going in and out as Moore dragged him from the surf and hauled him onto the beach as five or six villagers gathered around him. "Call for help!" he shouted.

Out in the distance, the flames and flashes continued, like heat lightning that printed the clouds negative, yet the silhouettes of both ships were now gone, leaving the rest of the fuel to continue burning off.

Moore wrenched out his cell phone, but it had died. Next time he planned on being attacked by a submarine, he'd be sure to pack a waterproof version. He asked one of the villagers, a college-aged kid with a thin beard, for a phone.

"I saw the ships explode," the kid said breathlessly.

"Me, too," snapped Moore. "Thanks for the phone."

"Give it to me," called Kayani from the beach, his voice cracking, but he seemed much more lucid now. "My uncle's a colonel in the Army. He'll get us helicopters here within an hour. It's the fastest way."

"Take it, then," said Moore. He'd read the maps, knew they were hours away by car from the nearest hospital. The rendezvous had intentionally been located opposite a rural, sparsely populated coastline.

Kayani reached his uncle, who in turn promised immediate relief. A second call to Kayani's commanding officer would summon Coast Guard rescue craft for those still at sea, but the Pakistan Coast Guard had no air–sea rescue choppers, just Chinese-built corvettes and patrol boats that wouldn't arrive until mid-morning. Moore turned his attention back on the surf, studying every wave, searching for the survivors.

Five minutes. Ten. Nothing. Not a soul. Between the blood and body parts strewn across the water like some ungodly stew, it was a safe bet that the sharks had come. And quickly. That, coupled with the injuries of the other survivors, may have been too much for them.

It took another half-hour before Moore spotted the first body rising up on a wave like a piece of driftwood. Many others would follow.

M ore than an hour passed before an Mi-17 appeared in the northwest sky, its twin turbines roaring, its rotors whomping and echoing off the hillsides. The chopper had been specifically designed by the Soviets for their war in Afghanistan and had become symbolic of that conflict: Goliaths of the sky slain by slingshots. The Pakistan Army had nearly one hundred Mi-17s in their inventory, a trivial detail Moore knew because he'd been a passenger aboard them a few times and had overheard a pilot griping about how he was stuck flying a Russian pile of junk that broke down every other flight and that the Pakistan Army had almost a hundred flying junkyards.

Slightly unnerved, Moore boarded the Mi-17 and was flown with Kayani to the Sindh Government Hospital in Liaquatabad Town, a suburb of Karachi. While en route, the flight medics administered painkillers, and Kayani's wide-eyed grimace turned to a more peaceful stare. It was sunrise by the time they touched down.

M oore stepped out of the hospital's elevator on the second floor and ducked into Kayani's room. They'd been at the hospital for about an hour now. The lieutenant would have a nice battle scar to help him get laid. Both men had been severely dehydrated when they'd come ashore, and an IV drip had been jabbed in the lieutenant's left arm.

"How are you feeling?"

Kayani reached up and touched the bandage on his head. "I still have a headache."

"It'll pass."

"I couldn't have swum back."

Moore nodded. "You got hit hard, and you lost some blood."

"I don't know what to say. Thank you is not enough."

Moore took a long pull on the bottle of water given to him by one of the nurses. "Hey, forget it." Movement in the doorway drew Moore's attention. That was Douglas Stone, a colleague from the Agency, who stroked his mottled gray beard and stared at Moore above the rim of his glasses. "I have to go," Moore said.

"Mr. Fredrickson, wait."

Moore frowned.

"Is there a way I can contact you?"

"Sure, why?"

Kayani looked to Stone and pursed his lips.

"Oh, he's okay. A good friend."

The lieutenant hesitated a few seconds more, then said, "I just want to thank you . . . somehow."

Moore used a tablet and pen on the tray table to scribble down an e-mail address.

The lieutenant clutched the paper tightly in his palm. "I'll be in touch."

Moore shrugged. "Okay."

He headed out into the hallway, turned, then marched forcefully away from Stone, speaking through his teeth. "So, Doug, tell me—just what the fuck happened?"

"I know, I know." Stone had deployed his usual calming tone, but Moore would have none of that, not now.

"We assured the Indians that the rendezvous would be clear. They had to cross into Pakistan territorial waters. They were very concerned about that."

"We were told the Pakistanis were taking care of everything."

"Who dropped the ball?"

"They're telling us their submarine commander never received any orders to remain at the pier. Somebody forgot to issue them. He made his usual patrol and thought he'd sailed into some kind of engagement. According to him, he sent out multiple challenges without response."

Moore snickered. "Well, it's not like we were looking for him—and when we did see him, it was already too late."

"The commander also reported that he saw the Indians taking prisoners on their deck."

"So he was ready to fire on his own people, too?"

"Who knows."

Moore stopped dead in his tracks, whirled, and gaped at the man. "The only prisoner they had was our guy."

"Hey, Max, I know where you're coming from."

"Let's go swim three miles. Then you'll know."

Stone removed his glasses and rubbed his eyes. "Look, it could be worse. We could be Slater and O'Hara and have to figure how to apologize to the Indians while making sure they don't nuke Islamabad."

"That'd be nice—because I'm headed there now."

1

DECISIONS

Marriott Hotel
Islamabad, Pakistan
Three Weeks Later

LIEUTENANT MAQSUD KAYANI'S solution to repay Moore for saving his life came in the form of an invitation for an introductory meeting between Moore and Kayani's uncle, Colonel Saadat Khodai of the Pakistan Army. Upon his arrival in Islamabad, Moore found the lieutenant's intriguing e-mail in his inbox. Kayani's uncle, the same man who had orchestrated their helicopter rescue, had confided in his nephew his ongoing battle with depression triggered by a crisis of personal ethics. The e-mail did not disclose the exact nature of the colonel's crisis, but Kayani stressed that such a meeting might benefit both Moore and his uncle immeasurably.

Over several weeks of meetings and extensive verbal sparring, Moore came to suspect that Khodai could identify key Taliban sympathizers within the Army's ranks. He drank liters of tea with the colonel, trying to convince him to disclose what he knew about the Taliban's infiltration and exploitation of the country's northwest tribal lands, most particularly the region known as Waziristan. The colonel was reluctant to commit, to cross the line. Moore was frustrated. It was a major stumbling block, the crux of their impasse.

The colonel was not only concerned about the possible ramifications to his family, but he now found himself up against his own deeply held personal convictions to never speak out adversely or otherwise betray his fellow officers and comrades, even though they'd broken their oath of loyalty to Pakistan and his beloved Army. His conversations with Moore, however, had ultimately brought him to the abyss. If not him, then who?

Then one evening the colonel had called Moore and said he was willing to talk. Moore had picked him up at his house and driven him to the hotel, where he would sit down with Moore and two of Moore's colleagues. They pulled into the guest parking lot.

Khodai had just turned fifty, and his thick, closely cropped hair was woven with streaks of gray. His eyes appeared worn and narrow, and his prominent chin was dappled by a quarter-inch of snow-white growth. He was dressed in civilian clothes, simple slacks and a dress shirt, but his military boots betrayed his office. His BlackBerry was tucked tightly in its leather case, and he nervously twirled it between his thumb and middle finger.

Moore reached for his door handle, but Khodai raised a palm. "Wait. I said I was ready, but maybe I need more time."

The colonel had studied English in high school and had then attended the University of Punjab in Lahore, where he'd earned a BA in engineering. His accent was thick, but he possessed a wide vocabulary, his tone always impressive and commanding. Moore could see why he'd risen so quickly through the ranks. When he spoke, you couldn't help but gravitate toward him, and so Moore relaxed, removed his hand from the door, and said, "You *are* ready for this. And you'll forgive yourself. Eventually."

"Do you really believe that?"

Moore raked errant locks of hair out of his eyes, sighed, and answered, "I want to."

The man grinned weakly. "The burdens you carry are at least as heavy as mine."

"You assume a lot."

"I know an ex-military man when I see one. And given your current office, you have seen a lot yourself."

"Maybe. The question for you is—which burden is heaviest? Doing something? Or doing nothing?"

"You're still a very young man, but I daresay wise beyond your years."

"I know where you're coming from."

He hoisted his brows. "I have your promise that my family will be completely protected?"

"You don't have to ask again. What you're going to do will save lives. You understand that."

"I do. But I'm not just risking myself and my career. Both the Taliban and my colleagues are ruthless. Relentless. I'm still concerned that even your friends won't be able to help us—despite all your reassurances."

"Then I won't reassure you anymore. It's your choice. We both know what happens if you don't go up there. That's at least one outcome we can predict."

"You're right. I can't sit by anymore. They will *not* dictate how we operate. They can't strip us of our honor. Never."

"Well, let me remind you that the offer to bring your family to the U.S. is still on the table. We can better protect them there."

He shook his head and rubbed the corners of his eyes. "I can't disrupt their lives. My sons are in high school now. My wife was just promoted. She works right there in the tech center next door. Pakistan is our home. We'll never leave."

"Then help us make it better. Safer."

Khodai glanced up, faced Moore, and widened his eyes. "What would you do if you were me?"

"I wouldn't want the terrorists to win by doing nothing. This is the most difficult decision of your life. I know that. I don't take this lightly. You have no idea how much respect I have for what you're about to do . . . the courage it takes. You're a man who wants justice. So, yes, if I were you, I'd open that car door and come up to meet my friends—and let's restore honor to the Pakistan Army."

Khodai closed his eyes, and his breathing grew shallow. "You sound like a politician, Mr. Moore."

"Maybe, but the difference is I really believe what I just said."

Khodai offered a faint grin. "I would have thought you had lived a life of privilege before entering the military."

"Not me." Moore thought a moment. "Are you ready, Colonel?"

He closed his eyes. "Yes, I am."

They got out and crossed the parking lot, heading up the ramp, beneath the broad awnings, toward the hotel's main entrance. Moore's gaze surveyed the road, the lot, even slid along the rooflines of the buildings across the street, but all seemed quiet. They passed the cabdrivers, leaning on the hoods of their cars and smoking quietly. They nodded to the young valets loitering near a small lectern and a box mounted on the wall, within which hung dozens of keys. They moved inside, past the newly constructed bombproof wall, and past the security checkpoint, where they were X-rayed for bombs and weapons. Then they shifted across ivory-colored marble tiles that gleamed and stretched out to the ornate check-in counters, behind which stood dark-suited concierges. A bearded man in a white cotton suit played a soft melody on a baby grand piano positioned off to their left. There were a few people at the counter, businessmen, Moore thought. Otherwise the hotel was quiet, tranquil, inviting. He gave Khodai a curt nod, and they crossed to the elevators.

"Do you have any children?" Khodai asked as they waited for the lift.

"No."

"Do you wish you had?"

"That seems like another life. I travel too much. I don't think it would be fair. Why do you ask?"

"Because everything we do is to make the world a better place for them."

"You're right. Maybe someday."

Khodai reached out and put a hand on Moore's shoulder. "Don't give them everything. That's a decision you'll regret. Become a father, and the world will become a different place."

Moore nodded. He wished he could tell Khodai about the many women he'd been with over the years, the relationships that had all become victims of his careers in both the Navy and the CIA. The divorce rates varied, but some said that for SEALs the numbers reached as high as ninety percent. After all, how many women could marry men they would barely see? Marriage became more like having an affair—and one of Moore's ex-girlfriends suggested that's exactly what they do. She wanted to marry a man while continuing her relationship with him, only because he provided her with the humor and physical thrills that the other man could not, while the other guy provided financial support and an emotional cushion. With a husband in the forefront and a Navy SEAL on the side, she'd have the best of both worlds. No, Moore wasn't willing to play that game. And, unfortunately, he'd bedded too many call girls and strippers and crazy drunken women to count, though in more recent years his life had become a hotel bed with just one pillow ever used. His mother still begged him to find a nice girl and settle down. He laughed and told her that the settling-down part was impossible, which in turn made finding the girl impossible. She'd asked him, "Don't you think you're being selfish?" He told her that yes, he understood that she wanted grandchildren, but his job asked too much of him, and he feared that being an absentee father would be worse than not being a father at all.

She'd told him to quit. He told her he'd finally found a place for himself in this world, after all the pain he'd caused her. There was no quitting now. Not ever.

He wanted to share all of those thoughts with Khodai—they were kindred spirits—but the bell rang and the elevator arrived. They stepped inside, and the colonel seemed to grow paler as the doors shut.

They rode in silence to the fifth floor, the doors opened, and Moore quickly spotted a man silhouetted in the stairwell door frame at the opposite end of the corridor—he was a Pakistani operative from ISI (Inter-Services Intelligence). The cell phone plastered to the agent's ear reminded Moore to reach into his own pocket for his smartphone so he could call the others and tell them they were nearing the door, but then he realized he'd left the phone down in the car, damn it.

They reached the door, and Moore knocked and said, "It's me, guys."

The door swung open, and one of his colleagues, Regina Harris, answered and invited Khodai into the room. Douglas Stone was with her as well.

"Left my phone down in the car," said Moore. "I'll be right back."

Moore started off down the hallway, and now he spied a

second agent at the elevators. Smart move—the ISI now controlled the foot traffic for the entire fifth floor. The elevator man was a short, scruffy-faced dude with large brown eyes and was talking nervously into his phone. He wore a blue dress shirt, brown slacks, and black sneakers, and his features seemed more rodent than human.

When the man spotted Moore, he lowered his phone and started back down the hall, toward the stairwell, and for a second this puzzled Moore. He walked a few more steps, then froze and whirled toward the room.

The explosion tore through the hallway, heaving up a chute of flames and a mountain of rubble that cut off Moore from the elevator and knocked him flat onto his rump. Next came the smoke pouring out of the room and billowing in thick clouds down the hall. Moore rolled onto his hands and knees, gasping curses as his eyes burned and the air grew thick with the stench of the bomb. His thoughts raced, taking him back to every reservation the colonel had mentioned, as though all of those doubts had manifested themselves in the explosion. Moore imagined Khodai and his colleagues being ripped apart, and that image drove him onto his feet and toward the now-empty stairwell—

After the bastard who'd run off.

The chase left no time to feel guilty, and for that Moore was thankful. If he paused, even for a second, to reflect on the fact that he'd convinced Khodai to "do the right thing," only to get the man killed because of his team's lapse in security, he might break down. And that was, perhaps, Moore's greatest weakness. He'd once been described in an After-Action Report as "an immensely passionate man who cared deeply for his colleagues," which of course explained why a particular face from his Navy SEAL past never stopped haunting him, and Khodai's sudden loss only reminded him of that night.

Moore burst into the stairwell and spotted the man charging downward. Gritting his teeth, Moore raced after him, using the railing to take three and four stairs at a time and swearing over the fact that his pistol was still down in the car. They'd been permitted to use the hotel as a meeting place, but both hotel security and the local police had been adamant about their weapons: None would be allowed inside the building. There'd been no room for negotiation on this point, and while Moore and his colleagues had access to a number of weapons that could bypass security, they'd opted to honor the request, lest they risk an already tenuous relationship. Moore had to assume that if the man had made it past the ISI security checkpoint, then he wasn't armed. But Moore had also assumed that their hotel room was a safe meeting place. They'd chosen one of the four vacant rooms on the fifth floor that faced the street so they could observe comings and goings of guests and traffic patterns. Any abrupt changes were early clues that something was about to happen, and they liked to call that an early-warning system for the astute. While they hadn't had access to a bomb-sniffing dog, they had scanned the room for electronic devices and had been using it for a few weeks without incident. That these thugs had managed to get explosives inside was infuriating and heartbreaking. Khodai had passed through screening with no problems, thus Moore had to assume the man had not been wired . . . unless of course the security checkpoint itself was a fake, the man there working for the Taliban . . .

The little guy kept a blistering pace, hit the first floor, and burst out of the stairwell door, with Moore about six seconds behind him.

A couple of breaths later and Moore was out the door, swinging his head left toward the main lobby, then right toward a long hall leading off to the spa, gym, and rear parking lot nestled at the corner of a large wooded area.

Meanwhile, the rest of the hotel was gripped in chaos, with alarms sounding, security personnel screaming, and hotel staff dashing everywhere as the smoke from the explosion began filtering into the air system with the pungent scent of explosives.

Stealing another look over his shoulder, the man sprinted for the door as Moore whirled and bounded after him, drawing the attention of two housekeepers, who were pointing at them and screaming for security. *Good.*

Moore closed the gap as the guy raised both hands and slammed into the rear door, swinging it open before he vanished outside. And three, two, one, Moore hit the door with a gasp, the cooler night enveloping him as he caught sight of the man sprinting toward the same parking lot where Moore had left his car. This was the best exit for him, with the woods beyond, but it would also take them past Moore's car—and his pistol stowed inside.

Moore's anger finally found his muscles. This guy would not get away. This was no longer a decision or even a goal but a cold, hard fact. Moore already envisioned his capture; it was simply time to make it so. As expected, his prey did not have the physical endurance that he did, and the man began to slow as he hit his lactate threshold, but Moore had a long way to go before he reached his . . . and so he darted up behind the man like a wolf and launched himself into a low kick to the guy's left leg that sent him screaming and crashing onto the grass, just before both of them reached the asphalt.

There was an old and very well-known saying about Muay Thai fighting techniques: "Kick loses to punch, punch loses to knee, knee loses to elbow, elbow loses to kick."

Well, this asshat had just lost it all to Moore's kick, and now Moore seized the man's wrists and maneuvered himself on top to straddle and pin him.

"Don't move. You're done!" Moore said in Urdu, the language most frequently used in the city.

The man lifted his head, struggling against Moore's grip, but then his eyes narrowed and his mouth opened in—what? Horror? Shock?

Thunder boomed somewhere behind them. Familiar thunder. Terribly familiar . . .

At nearly the same time the man's head exploded, showering Moore in blood and causing him to react on instinct, all muscle memory, no forethought, just self-preservation driving him away from the man and rolling onto his side.

He gasped, kept rolling, still in full control of his body, the evolutions of SEAL training never forgotten, the body remembering, responding, reacting.

The gun boomed two more times, the rounds burrowing into the dirt not six inches from Moore's torso as he came onto his hands and knees and bolted off toward his car, right there, just ten meters away. That gun was a Russian-made Dragunov sniper's rifle. Moore was certain of that. He'd fired them, watched them be fired, and been shot at by men using them. The weapon had a range of eight hundred meters, and up to thirteen hundred if the shooter was skilled and exploiting his scope. The ten-round detachable box magazine could keep this guy in business for a while.

Another shot punched a hole in the driver's-side door as Moore reached into his pocket, hit his key fob, and the car chirped. He shifted around the vehicle, out of the sniper's line of fire, and opened the passenger's-side door.

The windshield shattered as another round punched through. Out of the glove box came Moore's Glock 30, the word AUSTRIA embossed on the .45-caliber pistol's side. He came around the door, scanned the tree line and hotel beyond, and there he was, leaning forward on the roof of the two-story tech center next door.

The sniper wore a black woolen cap, but his face was clearly visible. Dark beard. Wide eyes. Broad nose. And Moore nodded inwardly over the Dragunov sniper's rifle with the attached scope and big magazine that the sniper lifted higher, balancing it with one elbow propped on the ledge.

Even as Moore spotted him, the sniper saw Moore and fired three shots in rapid succession that hammered the door as Moore rushed back around the car, toward the driver's side.

But then, just as the third shot echoed off, Moore bolted up and, cupping his gun hand in his left palm, returned fire, his rounds drilling into the concrete within inches of where the sniper had been perched, about forty meters away. That was beyond his pistol's accurate range, but Moore figured the sniper wasn't doing any ballistics homework at the moment, only ducking from wild bullets.

Four hotel security guards were already rushing into the parking lot area, and Moore pointed and shouted to them, "He's up there! Get down!"

One guy rushed at Moore while the others darted behind several other parked cars.

"Don't move!" the guard ordered—and then the sniper took off his head.

Another guard began barking into his radio.

When Moore returned his gaze to the building, he spotted the sniper on the far east side using a maintenance ladder to descend to the lot below, gliding swiftly, like an arachnid leaving its nest.

Moore sprinted away and the path grew uneven, the grass

turning to gravel and then back to pavement. A narrow alley between the tech center and a row of small one-story offices behind it led northwest toward Aga Khan Road, the main thoroughfare in front of the hotel. The scent of sweet pork had filled the alley, as the hotel's kitchen exhaust fans filtered in that direction, and Moore's stomach growled even though a meal was hardly on his mind.

Without slowing, he turned left, his Glock leading the way, and there, not twenty meters ahead, sat an idling Toyota HiAce van with two gunmen hanging from the rear driver's-side and rear passenger's-side windows.

The sniper ran toward the rolling van and leapt into the passenger's seat as the gunmen to the rear raised their rifles at Moore, who had the better part of two seconds to lunge down into a small alcove as the bricks above him shattered under automatic-weapons fire. Twice he tried to peer out to get a tag number, but the incoming was relentless, and by the time they ceased fire, the van was turning onto the main highway. Gone.

Moore rushed back to his car, grabbed his cell phone, and, with a trembling hand, tried to make a call. Then he just stopped himself and leaned back on his car as more security guys swarmed him, with their chief demanding answers.

He needed to call in the van, get eyes in the sky on that vehicle.

He needed to tell them what had happened.

Everyone was dead.

But all he could do was breathe.

Saidpur Village
Islamabad, Pakistan
Three Hours Later

Tucked tightly into the Margallah Hills overlooking Islamabad, Saidpur Village offered a picturesque view of the city and attracted a steady stream of tourists searching for what some guides called the "soul" of Pakistan. The guides said you could find it in Saidpur.

However, if the city had a soul, it had just grown darker. Columns of smoke still wafted up from the Marriott Hotel, cutting lines across the star-filled sky, and Moore stood there on the balcony of the safe house, cursing once more. The explosion had not only taken out their room but two other adjacent ones to the right and left, and before others could get near the area, the roof in that section of the building had collapsed.

With the assistance of three other operatives called in to help secure the area, along with a special forensics team and two crime scene specialists, Moore was able to work with private hotel security, the local police, and a five-man Inter-Services Intelligence team even while he fed a steady stream of misinformation to Associated Press reporters. By the time the story hit outlets like CNN, they were reporting that a Taliban bomb had gone off in the hotel and that the terrorists had claimed responsibility because they were seeking revenge for killings by Shiites of members of a Sunni extremist ally of the group known as Sipah-e-Sahaba. A Pakistan Army colonel had been inadvertently caught in the blast. Between the hard-to-remember names of the groups and the vague circumstances, Moore felt certain the story would continue to grow more convoluted. His colleagues in the room had carried nothing that would identify them as Americans or members of the CIA.

He turned away from the balcony and into a voice within his head: *"I can't disrupt their lives. My sons are in high school now. My wife was just promoted. She works right there in the tech center next door. Pakistan is our home. We'll never leave."*

Moore clutched the stone rail, leaned over, lost his breath, and began to vomit. He just stood there, with his forehead balanced on his arm, waiting for it to pass, trying to release it all, though the bombing had, in effect, brought it all back. He'd spent years trying to repress the memories, grappling with them during countless sleepless night, fighting against the urge to take the easy way out and drink the pain away . . . And for the past few years he'd wanted to believe that he'd won.

And then this. He'd met his fellow operatives only a few weeks prior and hadn't made anything other than a professional connection with them. Yes, he felt terrible over their loss, but it was Khodai, the torn colonel, who pained him the most . . . Moore had learned a lot about him, and the loss felt *significant*. How would Khodai's nephew react to his uncle's death? The lieutenant had thought he was helping both men, and while he must have known that Khodai would be endangering himself by talking to Moore, he probably denied any thoughts of his uncle being murdered.

Moore had promised to protect Khodai and his family.

He'd failed on every level. When the police arrived at Khodai's house just an hour ago, they'd found the man's wife and sons stabbed to death, and the agent assigned to protect them was missing. The Taliban were so well connected, so thoroughly wired into the pulse of the city, that it seemed virtually impossible for Moore and his people to get any real work done. That was his depression talking, of course, but the Taliban had spotters everywhere, and no matter how hard he'd tried to blend in—growing the beard, wearing the local garb, speaking the language—they'd guessed who he was and what he was after.

He wiped his mouth and stood taller, glancing back to the city, to the lingering smoke, to the lights twinkling out to the horizon. He swallowed, mustered up the courage, and whispered, "I'm sorry."

A few hours later, Moore was on a video call with Greg O'Hara, deputy director of the CIA's National Clandestine Service. O'Hara was a fit man in his late fifties, with grayish-red hair and a hard, blue-eyed stare magnified by his glasses. He had a penchant for gold ties and must have owned a hundred of them. Moore gave him a capsule summary of what had happened, and they decided they would speak again in the morning, once the other teams had completed their investigations and logged their findings. Moore's immediate boss, the chief of the Special Activities Division, would also participate in the call.

One of Moore's local contacts, Israr Rana, an operative he'd recruited himself after spending the past two years in Afghanistan and Pakistan, arrived at the safe house. Rana was a college student in his mid-twenties, with a keen wit, birdlike features, and a passion for playing cricket. His sense of humor and boyish charm allowed him to gather remarkable amounts of intel for the Agency. That, coupled with his ancestry—his family had become fairly well known over the past century as both great soldiers and cunning businesspeople—made him a near-perfect operative.

Moore plopped into a chair, with Rana standing near the sofa. "Thanks for coming."

"No problem, Money."

That was Rana's nickname for Moore—and it made sense. Rana was paid handsomely for his services.

"I need to know where the leak happened. Did we blow it from the get-go? Was it the Army, the Taliban, or both?"

Rana shook his head and made a face. "I'll do everything I can to get you something. But for now, let me get you a drink. Something to help you sleep."

Moore waved him off. "Nothing will help me sleep."

Rana nodded. "I'm going to make some calls. Can I use the computer?"

"It's over there."

Moore retired to the bedroom, and within an hour he realized he'd been wrong. He drifted off into an exhausted sleep, floating relentlessly on black waves, until his heartbeat, like the thumping of a helicopter's rotors, sent him bolting upright in a cold sweat. He glanced around the room, sighed, and collapsed back onto his pillow.

A half-hour later he was in his car, heading back to the scene. He glanced over at the shattered building, then at the tech center next door. He found a security guard from the tech center and, along with two local policemen, gained access to the building. They went up to the roof, where Moore had already been earlier and from where they'd collected the sniper's shell casings to search for prints on them.

It was a revelation, an epiphany of sorts, that had come to him as his mind had drifted between the conscious and unconscious, because the problem of how their adversaries had gotten the explosives into the room had continued to burn in his head until a very low-tech solution took hold. All he needed to do was find evidence of it.

He walked along the edge of the rooftop, allowing his flashlight to slowly glide over the dust-caked concrete and steel . . . until he found it.

The Special Activities Division, operating within the National Clandestine Service, was manned by Paramilitary Ops officers recruited from the military who conducted deniable covert operations on foreign soil. The division was composed of ground, maritime, and air branches. Moore had originally been recruited for the maritime branch, like most Navy SEALs, but he'd been loaned out to the ground branch and had worked several years in Iraq and Afghanistan, where he'd conducted excellent intelligence operations involving the use of Predator drones to drop Hellfire missiles on numerous

Taliban targets. Moore had not balked at being moved to the ground branch, and he knew that if he was needed for a particular maritime operation, he'd be sent anyway. Operational lines had been drawn by office staff, not field operatives.

SAD consisted of less than two hundred agents, pilots, and other specialists deployed in six-man or fewer teams, with more often than not a solo SAD operative conducting "black" and other covert operations with the assistance of a "handler" and/or "case officer" who often remained out of harm's way. SAD operatives were extensively trained in sabotage, counterterrorism, hostage rescue, bomb damage assessment, kidnapping, and personnel and matériel recovery.

SAD owed its existence to the Office of Strategic Services (OSS), an agency during World War II that was organized under the Joint Chiefs of Staff and had direct access to President Franklin D. Roosevelt. For the most part, the OSS operated independently of military control—an idea that raised brows and drew deep skepticism at the time. MacArthur was said to have been highly reluctant to have any OSS personnel working within his theater of operations. Consequently, when the OSS was disbanded after the war, the CIA was created under the National Security Act of 1947. Missions that could not be associated with the United States went to the paramilitary group of the CIA—the Special Activities Division—a direct descendant of the OSS.

Chief of SAD David Slater, a steel-jawed black man and former Force Recon Marine with twenty years in the military, joined the morning video conference with Deputy Director

O'Hara. The two men stared up at Moore from his tablet computer as he sat in the kitchen of the safe house in Saidpur Village.

"Sorry we couldn't hook up yesterday. I was in the air en route to CONUS," volunteered Slater.

"It's okay, sir. Thanks for joining us."

O'Hara wished Moore a good morning.

"With all due respect, there is absolutely nothing good about it."

"We understand how you feel," replied O'Hara. "We lost some great people and years of intel."

Moore grimaced and bit his tongue. "What do you know so far?"

"Harris and Stone have been recovered from the rubble. At least what was left of them. Gallagher, who was at Khodai's house, is still missing. They must have him in a cellar or a deep cave, because there's no signal from his shoulder beacon. The guy you chased was obviously well trained but still just a low-level guy."

Moore shook his head in disgust. "Do you think Khodai was wired?"

"It's possible," said Slater.

"I thought he was, too. I thought the checkpoint in the lobby was a fake and controlled by them. The X-ray wouldn't pick up anything, even if he was wired. So Khodai came through without triggering the system. Maybe they threatened him, said if he didn't blow us up, they'd kill his family, which they did anyway."

"That's a pretty good theory," said O'Hara.

Moore snorted. "But that's *not* what happened."

"What do you got?" Slater asked him.

"Hotel security is, for the most part, pretty good. I think they used housekeepers to get the bombs in the rooms next to ours."

"Slow down," said Slater. "How'd they get the bombs into the hotel in the first place? They didn't haul them through the main entrance."

Moore shook his head. "They got into the building next door, the tech center, where the sniper was. Less security there, and maybe easier to bribe. The bombs were passed across via a line and pulley from one rooftop to the next."

"You got to be kidding me," said O'Hara.

"I'm not. I went up on the tech-center roof and saw where they'd strung the ropes. Then I went over to the Marriott, found the same signs on the edge of their roof. I'll be uploading some photos I took in a few minutes."

O'Hara's voice lowered in frustration. "That's ridiculously simple."

"And maybe that was our problem: We've got our eyes on the complicated when these guys are using sticks and stones. If they were really daring, they would've tried throwing the bombs across . . ." Moore just shook his head again.

"So those rooms around yours were registered to guests who were never there," O'Hara concluded.

"Exactly. Someone on the inside made sure they looked occupied in the registration system while they remained vacant.

The local cops should be able to nab the one son of a bitch at the front desk who hooked them up. I've got Rana putting out some feelers for me."

"That sounds good," answered O'Hara. "But at this point, we'd like to get you out of there."

Moore inhaled and closed his eyes. "Look, I know you're thinking I let this whole thing go south . . . a lapse in security, but this whole thing was clean. I'd checked everything. I mean *everything*. Now . . . just let me finish this. Please." He wanted to tell them that he needed to do this for the people who died, and he needed to do it for himself, but the words wouldn't come.

"We need you back home."

His eyes snapped open. "Home? In the States?"

Slater broke in. "Yesterday afternoon several officers in Khodai's battalion were photographed with a man we've identified as Tito Llamas, a known lieutenant in the Juárez Cartel. With them were two unidentified men, possibly Taliban. You'll have those photos momentarily."

"So we have corrupt Pakistan Army officers meeting with a drug cartel guy from Mexico and the Taliban," said Moore. "That's an unholy trinity, all right."

Slater nodded. "Max, you know a lot of the Middle Eastern players. You've got the expertise we need. We want you to field-supervise a new joint task force we're putting together."

Moore's brow furrowed in confusion. "Is this like a promotion—after what just happened? I mean, I'm oh-for-two in two weeks . . ."

"We've been discussing this for a long time now, and your

name has always been at the top of the list. That hasn't changed," answered Slater.

But Moore kept shaking his head. "The two guys in the hall . . . I thought they were a couple of ISI agents controlling access to the fifth floor. They were just making sure the bombs went off . . ."

"That's right," said O'Hara.

O'Hara leaned toward the camera. "We need to know the extent to which the Mexican drug cartels are in bed with these Afghan and Pakistani smugglers. If it's any consolation, you'll still be working on the same case—just from another angle."

Moore needed a moment to process all that. "So how do the Mexicans fit in, besides being middlemen and customers?"

O'Hara drifted back into his chair. "That's the real question, isn't it?"

Slater cleared his throat and consulted some notes. "Your primary task will be to learn if this connection between the Taliban and the Mexicans is just to expand the opium market or if it's meant to foster something more problematic, like the Taliban recruiting in Mexico to develop a new base of operations and easier access into the U.S."

"You said joint task force. What other agencies are involved?"

Slater grinned. "The whole alphabet: CIA, FBI, ATF, CBP, and a half-dozen smaller and local agencies to assist."

Moore shuddered as he considered the enormity of what they were asking. "Gentlemen, I appreciate the offer."

"It's not an offer," O'Hara pointed out.

"I see. Look, just give me a couple of days to follow up on Khodai's killers and see if I can get some intel on Gallagher. That's all I'm asking."

"We've already got another team en route," said Slater.

"That's fine. But let me take one more shot."

O'Hara winced. "We all failed here. Not just you."

"They killed the colonel and murdered his family. He was a good man. He was doing the right thing. We owe him and his nephew this much. I can't walk away."

O'Hara mulled that over, then raised his brows. "Two days."

2

MOVEMENT

Somewhere in the Jungle
Northwest of Bogotá, Colombia

JUAN RAMÓN BALLESTEROS cursed through his teeth and reached past his swollen beer gut for the cell phone lodged in the pocket of his cargo shorts. His sleeveless white T-shirt was already soaked in sweat, and the unlit Cohiba Behike jammed between his lips was soggy. It had been a brutal and unforgiving summer, the air so humid that it felt as though he were walking through loaves of warm bread.

Ballesteros was barely forty, but the heavy burdens of his position had drawn deep lines around his eyes, had turned his beard and curly locks gunmetal gray, and had left him hunched over with chronic back pain that struck like blows from a machete.

However, his physical discomforts were the least of his concerns: The four young men with gunshot wounds to their heads had his complete attention.

They'd been lying on the jungle floor for most of the night, and the early-morning dew had left a sheen on their pale bodies. The flies buzzed and alighted on their cheeks, their eyelids, and flew into their open mouths. Rigor mortis had already set in, and their bowels had released. The stench was ungodly and had Ballesteros turning his head away to gasp and swallow back the bile.

The team had come to set up another mobile cocaine lab, which was anything but high-tech and hygienic—only a few homemade tents covering mountains of coca leaves drying on the dirt floor. One tent was used for the production and storage of gasoline and sulfuric acid, among other chemicals necessary to manufacture at least one thousand kilos of paste per week. In years past, Ballesteros had given a few of his more powerful buyers tours of the camps, showing them the exacting and multi-stage process by which the product was produced.

While coca farmers all followed slightly different recipes, Ballesteros's men needed one thousand kilos of coca leaves to get just one kilo of paste, about 2.2 pounds. For the tours they would demonstrate how to make one-tenth of that amount. His men fired up weed whackers to crush one hundred kilos of leaves and add to them sixteen kilos of sea salt and eight kilos of limestone. They would mix those ingredients together by vigorously stomping on them until they created a black, dirtlike mixture that was poured into a large drum. Twenty liters of gasoline were added, and the ingredients were left to sit for about four hours.

The men would turn to another drum that had already been soaking, and this liquid would be drained into a bucket so they could discard the pulp and leaves. The valuable product at this stage was the drug leached from the coca leaves and now suspended in the gasoline.

Next came eight liters of water and eight teaspoons of sulfuric acid, and this new mixture was scrubbed with a plunger for a couple of minutes, then decanted, leaving the sediment on the bottom. Sodium permanganate was added to the sediment, along with caustic soda in no specific amounts, just enough to drown the sediment. The liquid was now a milky white, the paste congealing at the bottom. The remaining liquid was filtered away via a rag, and the paste was left to dry in the sun until it turned a light brown.

The price for Ballesteros to produce one kilo was about one thousand U.S. dollars. When that kilo was processed into cocaine powder and transported to Mexico, the price jumped to $10,000 per kilo. Once that same kilo reached the United States, it sold for $30,000 or more to the street gangs, who then cut it with additives to reduce the purity and get more out of each stash. The gangs sold their product by the gram, and a single kilo could generate a street value of $175,000 or more.

Ironically, a buyer had once asked, "Why do you do this?" Didn't he understand that some teenager in Los Angeles had just died by overdosing on the very substance he produced?

Didn't he realize that he was destroying families and ruining lives all over the globe?

He never thought about it and considered himself a farmer come full circle from his own family's days working on the coffee plantations. He'd grown up in Bogotá, gone off to college in the United States, in Florida, and had returned home with a business degree to try to start his own organic banana farm, which had failed miserably. Some of his friends in the banana business introduced him to several drug traffickers, and as they say, the rest was history. It was, for him, a matter of survival. After twenty long years as a drug producer and trafficker, Ballesteros was reaping the benefits of his high-risk occupation. His family now lived among white Europeans in a wealthy northern suburb of the city, his two sons were doing well in high school, and his wife wanted for nothing, save for more time with him. He was away most of the week on "business" but returned home on the weekends for family gatherings, church, and time to attend soccer games with his sons. In truth, he lived in his jungle house about a quarter-kilometer away from this lab and had, thus far, an excellent relationship with FARC, the Revolutionary Armed Forces of Colombia, a paramilitary group that helped him distribute and export his product. He hoped his men were not killed by FARC members; there had been some tension between himself and a FARC colonel named Dios, a simple disagreement over price. Now Ballesteros's workers had been executed in their sleep with what had to be a silenced weapon.

He speed-dialed Dante Corrales, his contact in Mexico, and waited for the young man to answer.

"You only call me when there is a problem," said Corrales. "But there'd better not be a problem."

"Dios," was all Ballesteros said.

"Okay. Now try not to bother me again."

"Wait, I'm not sure it was Dios, but maybe . . ."

The kid had already ended the call.

Ballesteros had met Corrales only once, two years ago, when members of the Juárez Cartel had come down to both survey his operation and offer security forces and workers to help him increase production. Corrales was an arrogant young man, the new breed of narco-trafficker with no sense of history or respect for those who'd come before him. These young *sicarios* were more concerned with power and image and intimidation than with making money. They had fantasies of being in Hollywood movies, thought they were Al Pacino. Ballesteros had little use for them, but he'd been forced to accept the cartel's assistance when the government had tightened its grip on his operation, and nowadays they were his primary buyers.

After another terse phone call with Corrales the week before, Ballesteros had learned that the cartel boss himself would be in the country very soon and that he should not delay the next shipment. He swore and went running back to his house, where he sent two more of his men back to the lab to collect the bodies.

Four old trucks whose flatbeds were covered with heavy tarpaulins had pulled up outside the house, and another team of men was loading the banana boxes filled with bananas and cocaine onto the trucks.

Ballesteros tried to hide his fury and disgust over the murdered men and shouted to his crew to hurry. The boat had already arrived at the dock in Buenaventura.

They drove over the potholed roads and were thrown hard against their seats in the hot cabs. None of the trucks had a working air conditioner, and it was just as well. Ballesteros didn't want any of his men to get too comfortable. They had to remain vigilant, and Ballesteros himself scrutinized every passing car and pedestrian along the route.

Because this particular shipment was large (seven tons, to be precise), and because his operation had just been struck a blow by the murderers, Ballesteros was wary of another attack and opted to follow this shipment at least until the second or third exchange point.

The crew of a ninety-five-foot Houston shrimp boat hustled onto the dock when Ballesteros and his men arrived. The teams of men began the swift transfer of the cargo, using a gas-powered forklift along with the boat's inboard net boom to move the pallets of banana boxes from dockside to the shrimper's hold.

Not far off, near the end of the dock, stood two FARC soldiers watching the entire operation. One gave a nod to Ballesteros, who hustled up the gangway, much to the surprise of the crew. Yes, he told them. He was coming along. And how far was he going? Far enough.

They headed west for about two hundred fifty nautical miles, nearing Isla de Malpelo, a small island with fantastic escarpments and spectacular rock formations glistening in the sun. They would remain in the area until nightfall, conducting routine "shrimping" operations while tailed by a school of silky sharks. Ballesteros remained quiet for most of the day, still haunted by the images of his men.

Finally, a dark shadow swelled like a whale or great white shark off the port bow. As the shadow drew closer, the men on the deck shouted to one another and got to work readying the lines. The shadow rose from the water, taking on a mottled pattern of blue, gray, and black, and then, with seawater washing off its sides, it fully broke the surface . . .

A submarine.

The vessel glided alongside them, and Ballesteros cried out to the captain, who was rising into the hatch, "This time, I'm coming along for the ride!"

The sub was diesel electric-powered, thirty-one meters long, and nearly three meters high from deck plates to ceiling. It was constructed of fiberglass and could cut through the water via twin screws at more than twenty kilometers per hour, even while carrying up to ten tons of cocaine. The vessel had a three-meter-tall conning tower with periscope and the ability to dive to nearly twenty meters. It was a remarkable feat of engineering and a testament to the creativity and tenacity of the leaders of their operation. The submarine belonged to the Juárez Cartel, of course, and it cost more than $4 million to construct inside a carefully hidden dry dock beneath the triple canopy of the Colombian jungle.

Although two other submarines had been discovered and confiscated by military forces before they could be deployed, the cartel had plenty of money to keep building these vessels, and this was one of four they had in continuous operation.

Ballesteros remembered the days when they'd used slow-moving fishing boats, sailboats, and if they were feeling bold, a few cigar boats here and there. But now they'd made huge strides in payload capacity and stealth. The old semi-submersibles could sometimes be detected from the air, but not this submarine. He was helped onto the deck and would exchange places with one of the sub's crew members. They would rendezvous with yet another fishing vessel about a hundred nautical miles off the coast of Mexico, offload the cargo, then turn back for Colombia. Ballesteros would not sleep until he knew the shipment had arrived. He descended into the submarine and found himself in a narrow but air-conditioned compartment while the men outside began the transfer.

Mexican Border
Brewster County, Texas
Two Days Later

U.S. Border Patrol Agent Susan Salinas had parked her SUV along a small ditch, shielding it from view across the open desert that swept out toward the curving horizon of mountains.

The sun had set about two hours ago, and she and her partner, Richard Austin, had crawled up on their bellies to survey the border with their night-vision goggles, the desert now a fluctuating course of shimmering green. They'd received a tip from one of the local ranchers, who'd seen a truck cutting across the valley, heading toward his land, and that truck had tripped one of the remote electronic sensors put in place by the CBP (Customs and Border Protection).

"Could be those kids four-wheeling again," said Austin, issuing a deep sigh as he panned to the right while she surveyed the southeast side.

"No, I think we're going to score big tonight," she said slowly.

"What makes you say that?"

"Because I'm looking at the bastards right now."

A slight dust trail swirled out from behind a battered F-150 whose flatbed was piled high with banana boxes tied down with bungee cords and partially covered by torn canvas. No, those guys were not transporting produce through the rough and mountainous terrain of Brewster County, and yes, they'd done a piss-poor job of concealing their stash. Either that or they were just too brazen to care. She zoomed in, saw three men jammed into the front bench seat with movement behind them in the cab. There could be as many as six.

She calmed herself. Salinas had been with the CBP for nearly three years now, and she'd caught hundreds of people attempting to illegally cross the border. The truth was, she'd never imagined she'd be out here on line watch and carrying a gun. She'd considered herself a "girly girl" in high school as the captain of the cheerleading squad and had ambled her way through those locker-lined halls with low B's. She'd then wandered her way into community college, where she couldn't get excited about any of the majors. When a friend's brother had joined the Border Patrol, she'd done some research. Now she was twenty-seven, still single, but loving the adrenaline rush of her job.

The position had not come easily. She'd spent fifty-five days in Artesia, New Mexico, taking courses in immigration and nationality law, criminal law and statutory authority, Spanish, Border Patrol operations, care and use of firearms, physical training, operation of motor vehicles, and antiterrorism. And no, they hadn't let her fire a gun at community college. This was by far the most exciting thing she'd done in her short life. And now, as her pulse rose, she had further confirmation of that.

"What did you think? We were the puppy patrol up here?" she asked one *sicario* she'd busted last week. "They just handed me a gun and told me to stop the bad guys?"

Ironically, her mother wholeheartedly approved of her job and expressed how proud she was that her daughter had become a law enforcement officer, especially since, as Mom put it, "There's always been such a fuss about protecting the border."

Her father, on the other hand, was about as thrilled as a football fan without beer. Dad had always been a quiet man who'd spent a quiet life as a tax attorney in a quiet office on the outskirts of Phoenix. He enjoyed quiet weekends and was the antithesis of the alpha male. He just couldn't see his daughter handling a weapon when he never would. At one point he'd even quoted Gandhi and gone so far as to tell her that men would no longer view her as feminine, that she'd have trouble dating, and that some might even question her sexuality. And then, of course, she'd get fat. All cops did. Border Patrol officers included. She had never forgotten those words.

Austin was a lot like her: single, pretty much a loner, with a strained relationship with his parents. He was a workaholic and a by-the-book kind of guy, except when it came to their relationship. He'd already hit on her, but she wasn't interested. His facial features were severe, his body just a bit too doughy for her taste. She'd gently let him down.

"All right," he said. "I'm calling for a second unit. You're right. This could be big."

"Roger that," she said. "Get Omaha involved and the ATVs. Send them GPS." Omaha was the call sign of the Black Hawk helicopter that supported their unit, and the three guys who drove the small, rugged all-terrain vehicles that propelled them at high speeds across the heavily rutted desert.

He rolled over, about to key his handset, when he just bolted up and started running. "Hey, you! Hold! Border Patrol!"

She turned and called after him—

As a gunshot sent a lightning bolt of panic straight through her chest.

She rolled away from the mound, drawing her weapon, and found two men standing near their SUV, both Mexicans clad in denim jackets. One with grizzled hair held a pistol that was probably a Belgian-made FN 5.7, a gun nicknamed the *mata policía*, or cop killer, in Mexico because it fired a round that could penetrate police body armor. The other guy clutched a long curved fillet knife. The knife wielder smiled, flashing a single gold tooth.

The first guy screamed in Spanish for her to freeze.

She was panting.

Austin lay on the ground with a gunshot wound to his chest. His armor had, indeed, failed to protect him against that pistol. He was still breathing, clutching the wound and groaning softly.

The guy with the knife started toward her. She looked at him, then at the man with the pistol, and suddenly fired at him, striking him in the shoulder, even as the pickup truck roared within a hundred yards.

She got to her feet as the guy with the knife went for his buddy's gun, which had fallen to the dirt. She was about to shoot him as the pickup truck drew closer and gunfire flashed from the passenger's side, rounds ricocheting near her boots.

She took off running for the gully ahead, practically diving for it, not looking back, just running, the sound of her own breath roaring in her ears, her pulse thumping hard, her footfalls rhythmic across the rocks and dirt. The plan was to get far enough away, then pause to get on her radio.

But she didn't dare stop now.

A shriek echoed across the valley, and she couldn't help but stop, whirl around, and there he was, the knife man, holding up Richard's decapitated head for the men getting out of the pickup truck to see. They all howled as she swung around and dropped down into the gulley, listening as they got back in their truck.

She hit the dirt, dug herself in deeply behind a shrub, and tucked her warm pistol into her chest. She willed herself to control her breathing and heard her father's voice in her head: "You'll die like a dog out there, and no one will remember you."

But then the sound of hope, the truck engine growing not louder but fainter. A miracle? They weren't coming after her? Had they run out of time? She reached for her radio's handset, and, pricking up her ears once more, keyed the mike.

"Road Runner, this is Coyote Five, over."

"Susan, what the hell is going on out there? No contact?"

"Richard's dead," she whispered.

"I can't hear you."

"I said, 'Richard's dead'!" She hit a button on her wrist-mounted GPS. "I need everyone over here!" Her voice cracked as she fed him the GPS coordinates, and then she turned off the radio and listened once more to the truck engine beginning to fade into the wind.

3

FERTILE GROUND

Nogales, Mexico
Near the Arizona Border

Dante Corrales hated being away from home in Juárez, mostly because he missed his woman, Maria. He kept flashing back to last weekend, to the way she'd lifted her legs high in the air and had pointed her polished toenails, to the purring she'd made, to the claws she'd dug into his back, to the way she spoke to him and the expressions on her face. They'd made love like hungry, violent animals, and Corrales felt dizzy as he relived that moment yet again, standing there, inside the burned-out Pemex *gasolinera*, watching as the men unloaded the banana boxes, removed the blocks of cocaine, and placed those blocks inside their backpacks. There were twenty-two runners supervised by Corrales and five other *sicarios*. Their group was known as Los Caballeros, The Gentlemen, because they had a reputation for being exceedingly well dressed and well spoken, even as they lopped off heads and sent corpse messages to their enemies. They were smarter, braver, and certainly far more dangerous and cunning than the other enforcer gangs attached to the rest of Mexico's drug cartels. And as Corrales liked to joke, they were just polishing their machismo!

Some of the shipment, Corrales knew, had gone up to Texas, moving through Brewster County, and he'd just received a call from his lead man, Juan, who said they'd had trouble. His team had encountered a Border Patrol unit. One of the guys Juan had hired for the run had chopped off a border agent's head.

What the fuck was that?

More epithets escaped Corrales's mouth before he could finally calm down and remind Juan that he was not supposed to hire any outside guys. Juan said he'd had no choice, that he'd needed more help because two of his regulars had not shown up and were probably drunk or high.

"The next funeral you attend will be your own." Corrales thumbed off the phone, swore again, then tugged at the collar of his leather trench coat and picked a few pieces of lint from his Armani slacks.

He shouldn't allow himself to get so upset. After all, life was good. He was twenty-four years old, a top lieutenant in a major drug cartel, and he'd already made 14 million pesos—more than a million U.S. dollars—himself. That was impressive for a boy who'd grown up poor in Juárez and had been raised by a housekeeper and maintenance man who had both worked at a cheap motel.

The burned-out station and the lingering stench of all that soot made Corrales want to leave soon. The place was beginning to smell like another night, the worst night of his life.

He'd been seventeen, an only child, and had joined a gang who called themselves the Juárez 8. Their group of high school kids was standing up to the *sicarios* of the Juárez Cartel, fighting back against their threats and forced recruitment of their friends. Too many of Corrales's friends had wound up dead because of their involvement with the cartel, and he and his buddies had decided that enough was enough.

One afternoon, two boys had cornered Corrales behind a Dumpster and had warned him that if he didn't quit that gang and join Los Caballeros that his parents would be killed. They'd said it very clearly.

Corrales could still remember the punk's eyes, glowing like coals in a fire pit, from the shadows of the alley. And he could still hear the punk's voice echoing through time: *We will kill your parents*.

Unsurprisingly, Corrales had told them to fuck off. And two nights later, after coming home from a night of drinking, he'd found the motel engulfed in flames. The bodies of his parents were recovered in the rubble. Both had been bound with tape and left to burn.

He'd gone crazy that night, stolen a gun from a friend, and driven at high speeds throughout the city, looking for the scumbags who'd ruined his life. He'd crashed his car into a fence, abandoned it there, and just gone running back to a small bar, where he'd passed out in the bathroom. The police took him away and delivered him to relatives.

After going to live with his godmother, and after working as a janitor himself while trying to finish high school, he decided that he could no longer toil away like his parents had. He just couldn't do it.

There was no other choice. He would join the very group that had murdered his parents. That decision had not come easily or quickly, but working for Los Caballeros was his only ticket out of the slums. And because he was much smarter than the average thug, and perhaps more vengeful, he'd risen quickly through the ranks and had learned far more about the business than his bosses were aware of. He'd discovered early on that knowledge is power; thus he studied everything he could about the cartel's business and its enemies.

As fate would have it, the two boys that had killed his parents had been murdered themselves, only a few weeks before Corrales had joined their ranks. They'd been killed by a rival cartel because of their bold and foolish acts. The other Caballeros were glad to see them go.

Corrales shuddered now and glanced over at his team of runners dressed in dark hoodies and jeans and weighed down by their bulging backpacks. He led them over to a rear corner of the convenience mart. He lifted a large piece of plywood from the floor, and the tunnel entrance lay below, a narrow shaft accessible via an aluminum ladder. Cold, musty air wafted up from the hole.

"When you get inside the other house," Corrales began, "do not go outside until you see the cars, and only then you go out three at a time. No more. The rest of you stay in the bedroom. If there is trouble, you come back through the tunnel. Okay?"

They murmured their assent.

And down they went, one by one, a few carrying flashlights. This was one of the cartel's smaller but longer tunnels, nearly one hundred meters long, a meter wide, and just under two meters high, with its ceiling reinforced by thick crossbeams. Because there were so many out-of-work masons and construction engineers in Mexico, finding crews to construct such tunnels was ridiculously easy; in fact, many crews were just standing by, ready to jump on the next project.

Corrales's men would keep close and hunched over as they hurried down the shaft. The tunnel passed directly under one of the checkpoints in Nogales, Arizona, and there was always a concern that a larger vehicle like a bus might cause a cave-in. It had happened before. In fact, Corrales had learned that various cartels had been digging tunnels in Nogales for more than twenty years and that literally hundreds had been discovered by authorities—yet the digging of new passages continued, making Nogales the drug tunnel capital of the world. In recent years, though, the Juárez Cartel had begun to expand its tunnel operations and now controlled nearly all of the most significant tunnels passing into the United States. Men were paid handsomely to protect the tunnels and to stop rival cartels from using them. Moreover, the shafts themselves had been dug deeper so ground-penetrating radar would miss them and/ or agents would mistake them for one of the many drainage pipes that ran between Nogales, Mexico, and Nogales, Arizona.

Some shouting from the doorway behind sent him reaching for his *mata policía* tucked into his shoulder holster. He produced the pistol and walked toward the door, where two of his men, Pablo and Raúl, were dragging in another guy with blood pouring from his nose and mouth. The bleeder struggled against the men holding him, then spat blood, the glob missing Corrales's Berluti loafers by only inches. Corrales was certain that the fool had no idea how much the shoes cost.

Corrales frowned. "Who the fuck is this?"

Raúl, the taller of the two, piped up: "I think we found a spy. I think he's one of Zúñiga's boys."

Corrales sighed deeply, raked fingers through his long, dark hair, then suddenly shoved his pistol into the man's forehead. "Were you following us? Do you work for Zúñiga?"

The man licked his bloody lips. Corrales shoved the pistol harder into the man's forehead and screamed for him to answer.

"Fuck you," the guy spat.

Corrales dropped his voice to funereal depths and got in closer to the man. "Do you work for the Sinaloas? If you tell me the truth, you'll live."

The man's eyes went vague; then he lifted his head a little higher and said, "Yes, I work for Zúñiga."

"Are you alone?"

"No. My friend is back at the hotel."

"On the corner?"

"Yes."

"Okay. Thank you."

With that, Corrales abruptly—and without a second's hesitation—put a bullet in the man's head. He did this so quickly, so effortlessly, that his own men gasped and flinched. The spy fell forward, and Corrales's men let him drop to the dirt.

Corrales grunted. "Bag up this motherfucker. We'll leave this garbage on our old friend's doorstep. Get two guys to the hotel and take that other scumbag alive."

Pablo was staring at the dead man and shaking his head. "I thought you'd let him live."

Corrales snorted, then looked down and noticed a bloodstain on one of his shoes. He cursed and started back for the tunnel, reaching for his cell phone to call his man inside the house on the other side of the border.

Crystal Cave Area
Sequoia National Park
California
Four Days Later

A U-Haul truck had pulled up outside the big tent, and FBI Special Agent Michael Ansara watched as two men climbed out of the cab and were joined by two more who'd come out of the tent. One guy, the tallest, unlocked the back of the truck and rolled up the door, and the men began passing boxes to one another, forming a line toward the tent's entrance. This area was a hub for supply distribution to the groups farther north. That the Mexican drug cartels were smuggling cocaine across the border into the United States was hardly as audacious as the operation that Ansara had been reconnoitering for the past week.

The cartels had established extensive marijuana farms within the rugged hills and backcountry of the Sequoia National Park. While there were many hiking trails, large swaths of land were still off-limits to hikers and campers. Foot patrollers were few and far between, meaning the cartels had at their disposal enormous areas of remote, well-camouflaged land protected from aerial surveillance. They were growing their product on this side of the border with impunity and quickly distributing it to their customers, even as the money got shipped back home to Mexico. Ansara had more than once shaken his head in disbelief over those very facts, but the cartels had been doing this for years.

Audacious? Hell, yes. And more so when you'd spent as much time around the area as Ansara had. He'd already noted the extensive security measures put in place, layers of defense beginning with those areas running parallel to the main trails. Any adventurers who strayed far enough off the path might encounter foothold traps of various sizes all the way up to bear, along with trapping pits dug six feet deep and covered with twigs, leaves, and pine needles. At the bottom of these traps lay two-by-fours impaled with nails. The idea was to injure the curious so they'd turn around and seek medical help. Farther in, Ansara found trip wires that again had unsuspecting hikers falling forward onto hidden beds of nails. While admittedly crude, these means of "discouragement" were just part of a more sophisticated network of defense closer in.

Getting to his current vantage point had required a healthy dose of climbing skill. He'd hiked in with a light pack, scaling hills with grades of more than eighteen percent to navigate his way along several rocky cliffs, slipping at least a half-dozen times in order to beat a path wide enough and remain undetected. Loose rocks, low-hanging limbs, and the sheer grade left him gasping.

About an hour north of the big tent he was now observing, and a two-hour hike away from the nearest road, lay what Ansara had nicknamed "the garden." Shaded by the towering sugar pines were more than fifty thousand marijuana plants, some fanning up to more than five feet tall and planted in neat rows six feet apart. These rows swept up the steep terrain and were planted in the rich soil. Many of the plants lay amid thick brush and near streams that the cartels used for irrigation. Pipes had been buried along the hillside, the streams dammed up, and an elaborate drip-line system complete with gravity-fed hoses was in place so that the plants were not overwatered. This was a professional operation, with no expense spared.

Along the growing area's perimeter lay knots of small tents where farmers and security personnel lived, most of their food stored in large sacks and suspended from tree limbs to protect it from black bears roaming the area. The fields themselves were watched twenty-four-seven by as many as thirty armed men at any one time. Supplies were brought in by those who were presumably not told about the operation, only that food, water, clothing, fertilizer, and other essential items were needed. Harvested plants were smuggled out at night by teams of farmers protected by guards. Teams that worked by day actually rode expensive mountain bikes and moved swiftly and silently through the unforgiving valleys. Ansara guessed that many of the workers were relatives and friends of the cartels, people they could trust. Every main entrance and exit of the park was protected by rangers, and Ansara's surveillance had revealed that at least one night guard had been bribed to allow the entrance or exit of a vehicle between midnight and five a.m., about every ten days or so.

Ansara was no stranger to marijuana farming. He had grown up in East L.A., in one side of a Boyle Heights duplex. His mother's older brother, Alejandro De La Cruz, lived on the other side. During the week, his uncle was a "gardener to the stars" in the affluent community of Bel Air. Nights and weekends De La Cruz grew and sold pot to those very same rich clients. Ansara was his trusted assistant.

By ten, Ansara could spell, as well as pronounce, delta-9-tetrahydrocannabinol (THC), the active chemical ingredient in pot that enabled the user to get high. He'd spend hours scrounging up and prepping foam cups. He'd start by punching drain holes in the bottom, add potting soil, and last inserted, pointy end up, a dark brown seed with mottled-looking marbling. He'd line thirty or forty cups in a flat, which was a tray similar to his mother's cookie pan, and then he'd turn on the heating coils lining the underside of the long benches for bottom heat.

He learned how to transplant the germinated seedling, leaving plenty of soil on its root ball, and about the importance of an oscillating fan running twenty-four hours a day. He skimmed newspapers, especially the inserts and flyers, looking for sales on 600-watt, high-pressure sodium grow lamps.

A marijuana plant's nighttime, or dark period, was equally critical to its growth. Twenty-four-hour timers were a challenge. The grow lamps easily burned out regular timers, so his uncle had taught him that expensive high-power switches known as contactors, or relay switches, were necessary.

The demand for specific amounts of daylight and darkness created two security issues. Covering over windows to facilitate total darkness aroused suspicion from the street. Drug and law enforcement officials looked for it. Chronic above-average residential power consumption could trigger a Southern California Edison heads-up report to those same drug and law enforcement officials. Also, a grow space could become quite humid. Open windows at odd hours, regardless of precipitation or outside temperatures, was risky business.

By twelve, Ansara could recite the top dozen most potent marijuana strains in descending order of their THC content, from White Widow seeds to Lowryder seeds. And during all that time Ansara never once smoked pot—and neither did his uncle, who said they were businessmen supplying an important product. If you sell cookies, he'd told Ansara, you don't sit around eating all the cookies.

It all came to a screeching halt when his mother discovered why he spent so much time with Uncle Alejandro. She didn't speak to her brother for months.

That Ansara had gone on to join the FBI and had already busted individuals who grew pot was one of life's true ironies, and yet another irony was, at the moment, fully alive before his eyes. There were only a handful of drug enforcement agents assigned to police California's twenty million acres of federal forests, and unfortunately Ansara was not one of them. He was up there because he'd been hunting a particular smuggler, one Pablo Gutiérrez, who'd murdered a fellow FBI agent in Calexico and who he believed had direct ties to the Juárez Cartel. During his pursuit of this man, Ansara had found the Oz of pot farms in California—yet he and his colleagues were hesitant to bring down this operation because they hoped to use it to gather more intel on the cartels. It was clear to all that they needed to remove the lieutenants and bosses. If they struck too soon, the cartels would just plant another field a couple miles away.

As security tightened along the U.S.-Mexican border, the cartels expanded their growing operations in the United States. Ansara had spoken to a special agent for the federal Bureau of Land Management, who'd told him that just eight months prior, park rangers had confiscated eleven tons of marijuana in a single week. The agent went on to speculate on how much pot they did not confiscate, how much actually made it out of the fields and was sold . . . Mexican drug lords were operating on American soil, and there weren't enough law enforcement officers to stop them. Like soldiers used to say in Vietnam, *There it is* . . .

Ansara lowered his binoculars and tucked himself deeper into the shrubs. He thought he'd seen one of the loaders do a double take in his direction. His pulse began to race. He waited a moment more, then lifted the binoculars. The men were back at it and had set aside some boxes whose lids were removed. Ansara zoomed in to find packages of toothbrushes and toothpaste, soap, disposable razor blades, and bottles of aspirin, Pepto-Bismol, and cough suppressant. Larger boxes contained small tanks of propane and packages of tortillas, as well as canned goods, including tomatoes and tripe.

A bird flitted through the canopy above. Ansara jolted and held his breath. Once more he lowered the binoculars, rubbed his tired eyes, and listened to Lisa in his head: "Yes, I knew what I was getting into, but it's just too much time away. I thought I could do this. I thought this was what I wanted. But it's not."

And thus another long-legged blonde with a smoky voice and soft hands had escaped from Ansara's clutch. But this one had been different. She'd sworn she could put up with his being away and had made a valiant effort for the first year. She was a writer and political-science professor at Arizona State and had told him that it was good when he was away, that she needed time to herself anyway. In fact, on the night of their first anniversary as a couple, she'd seemed completely in love with him. At a party she'd compared him to film and television actors like Jimmy Smits and Benjamin Bratt, and had once described him on her Facebook page as "a tall, lean, clean-shaven Hispanic man with a brilliant smile and bright, unassuming eyes." He'd thought that was pretty cool. He couldn't use words like that. But absence did not make the heart grow fonder—not when you're under thirty. He understood. He let her go. But for the past month he couldn't stop thinking about her. He recalled their first date; he'd taken her to a little mom-and-pop Mexican place way up in Wickenburg, Arizona, where he'd told her about his own time at ASU and about his work as an Army Special Forces operator in Afghanistan. He'd told her about leaving the Army and getting recruited by the FBI. She'd asked, "Are you allowed to tell me all this?"

"I don't know. Does hearing top-secret stuff make you horny?"

She'd rolled her eyes and giggled.

And the conversation had gotten serious when she'd asked about the war, about his fallen brothers, about him saying goodbye to one too many friends. After dessert, she'd said she had to go home, and the implication was that she wasn't really interested in him but that he should thank his sister for setting them up.

Of course, he'd pursued her like any good Special Forces/ FBI guy would, and he eventually wooed her with flowers and bad poetry written in homemade cards and more late-night dinners. But it'd all gone to hell because of his career, and he was beginning to resent that. He imagined himself as a nine-to-fiver with weekends off. But then the thought of working in a cubicle or having a boss breathing down his neck made him nauseated.

Better to be up in the mountains with a pair of binoculars in hand and surveying some bad guys. Hell, he felt like a kid again.

The men finished their unloading, got back in the U-Haul truck, and pulled away. Ansara watched them go, then a few more men appeared outside and began filling up backpacks with materials they lifted from the boxes. They finished in about ten minutes and headed off in the direction of the garden.

Ansara waited until they were gone, then turned to head off.

Had he not matter-of-factly glanced down, he would be dead.

Right there, off to his right, was a small device with a laser cone jutting from its top. Ansara recognized the unit immediately as a laser trip wire, its companion unit located on the other side of the clearing. If he broke the laser, a silent alarm would go off. Ansara tightened his gaze, lifted his binoculars, and spotted several more laser units at the bases of trees. They came into view only if you knew what to look for, and the Mexicans had actually taped leaves and twigs to their sides to further camouflage them. Conventional trip wires and claymore mines had been set up all around the garden, but this was a new section of the park for Ansara, and he had not seen these detection devices before. Damn, if he came up here again, he'd have to be even more careful.

Shouting came from below. Spanish. The words: *Up on the mountain. East side.* Had they spotted him?

Oh, shit. Maybe he had crossed one of the lasers. He took off running, as the men below came rushing out from the tent.

4

THE GOOD SONS

Miran Shah
North Waziristan
Near the Afghan Border

MOORE AND HIS local contact Israr Rana had driven some two hundred ninety kilometers southwest into North Waziristan, one of seven districts within Pakistan's FATA, or Federally Administered Tribal Areas, which were only nominally controlled by the central and federal government of Pakistan. For centuries, mostly Pashtun tribes had inhabited the remote areas. In the nineteenth century the lands had been annexed by the British, during which time the British Raj tried to control the people with the Frontier Crimes Regulations (FCRs), which became known as the "black laws" because they gave unchecked power to local nobles so long as they did the bidding of the British. The people continued with the same governance, right up through the formation of the Islamic Republic of Pakistan in 1956. During the 1980s the region became much more militant with the entry of mujahideen fighters from Afghanistan during the Soviet invasion. After 9/11, both North and South Waziristan gained notoriety for being training grounds and safe havens for terrorists as the Taliban and Al-Qaeda began entering the region. The locals actually welcomed them because the Taliban appealed to their tribal values and customs, reminding them that they should remain fiercely independent and mistrustful of the government.

All of which reminded Moore that he was heading into a most dangerous and volatile place, but Rana had told him the trip would be worth the risk. They were going to meet a man who Rana said might be able to identify the Taliban in Moore's photographs. This man lived in the village of Miran Shah, which during the Soviet invasion had housed a large refugee camp for displaced Afghans who'd fled across the border from Khost, the nearest village in what was a remote region of the country. In fact, many of the roads leading to Miran Shah were frequently impassable during the winter months, and the only electricity available to its inhabitants came from a few diesel-powered generators. To say they were entering a town stuck in the dark ages was an understatement, yet anachronistic evidence of Western influences took Moore aback as he spied tattered billboards for 7Up and Coke strung between a pair of mud-brick buildings. Dust-covered cars lined the streets, and kids chased one another

executive council, and was known to speak out strongly against the Taliban chiefs in the area. The guard returned to his associate and checked a clipboard, then came back and asked for their IDs. Moore, of course, had expertly falsified documents that described him as a gun maker from Darra Adam Khel, a small town devoted entirely to the manufacture of ordnance. Travel to Darra by foreigners was forbidden, but merchants from the town routinely moved throughout the tribal regions making deliveries. The guard was quickly satisfied with Moore's papers, but after their car was searched, he held up a hand. "Why no delivery?"

Moore grinned. "I'm not here on business."

The guard shrugged, and they were waved through the checkpoint.

"How do you know Wazir?" asked Moore.

"My grandfather fought against the Soviets with him. They both came here. I've known him all my life."

"They were mujahideen."

"Yes, the great freedom fighters."

"Excellent."

"I told you when you hired me that I have very good contacts." Rana winked.

"This is a long drive, and I told you my bosses are only giving me two days."

"If anyone knows who those men are, it's Wazir. He is the most well-connected man in this region. He has hundreds of spotters, even some in Islamabad. His network is amazing."

"But he lives in this dump."

"Not all year. But yes, this 'dump,' as you call it, provides ample cover and limited scrutiny from the government."

The dirt road turned lazily to the right, and they climbed up into some foothills to arrive at a pair of modest-sized brick homes with several tents standing behind them. A pair of satellite dishes were mounted on the roof of the larger structure, and generators hummed from beneath the tents. Farther back were pens for goats and cows, and to the left, in the valley below, lay hectares of tilled fields where local farmers grew wheat, barley, and a Persian clover called *shaftal*.

Two guards appeared on the roof, bringing their AK-47s to bear. *Nice*. Wazir had built himself a protected headquarters here in the hills, thought Moore.

They were met at the front door by an old man whose beard fell in great white waves across his chest. He wore light brown robes and a white turban with matching vest, and he clutched a water bottle in his right hand. There wasn't much remaining of his left hand, the fingers gone, deep, ragged scars stitching across the back of his hand and up his arm, toward the sleeve. Moore checked again and realized that part of the old man's left ear was missing. He'd been caught in an explosion, all right, probably mortar fire. He was lucky to be alive.

The introductions were brief. Moore's cover name was Khattak, a Pashtun tribal name, and with his darker hair and complexion (both inherited from his mother's Italian/Spanish ancestry), he could almost pass for a Pakistani. Almost.

Wazir chuckled when he heard the name. "That is not you, of course," he said in accented English. "You're an American, and that is okay. It gives me a chance to practice my English."

"That's not necessary," Moore told him in Pashto.

"Let me have my fun."

Moore pursed his lips and nodded, then broke into a smile. You had to respect the old man. His weathered blue eyes had most certainly gazed on the deeper levels of hell. Wazir led them inside.

The noontime Muslim prayer, Dhuhr, had just finished, Moore knew, and Wazir would no doubt be serving some tea. They shifted into the cool shadows of a wide living area with colorful cushions arranged around an intricately detailed Persian rug. Three places had been set. The cushions, known as *toshak*s, and the thin mat in the center, a *dastarkhān*, were all part of the "ceremony" that was daily tea. Something was cooking in one of the back rooms, and the sweet aroma of onions and something else wafted throughout the room.

A young boy appeared from a back hall and was introduced as Wazir's great-grandson. He was seven or eight and carried a special bowl and jug called a *haftawa-wa-lagan*. They carefully washed their hands. Then the boy returned with the tea, and Moore took a long sip on his, sighing over the flavor, which always reminded him of pistachios.

"How was the drive?" asked Wazir.

"Without incident," Moore answered.

"Very good. You have the photographs?"

Moore reached into the small pack he'd had slung over his shoulder and withdrew his tablet computer. He thumbed it on and handed it to Wazir.

The old man deftly thumbed through the intelligence photos, as though he'd used such a device before. And Moore asked him about that.

"Let me show you something," he said, then called to the boy, who helped him to his feet.

He led them down the hall and into a back room, an office, that left Moore's mouth hanging open. Wazir had banks of computers, two wide-screen televisions, and at least a half-dozen laptops all running at the same time. His electronic command post resembled the bridge of a starship. News websites and television programs flashed, along with screens showing bulletin boards and social-networking sites. The man was plugged in, all right.

And there, on a nearby table, were several tablet computers just like Moore's.

"As you can see," Wazir said, waving his good hand across the room, "I like my toys."

Moore shook his head in surprise. "I've been here for, I don't know, two, three years? Why haven't I heard of you until now?"

"That was my choice."

"Then why now?"

The old man's smile evaporated. "Come on, let's finish our tea. Then lunch. Then we'll talk."

After they returned to the living area and took their seats, the boy brought in an onion-based *quorma*, or stew, along with chutneys, pickles, and naan—an unleavened bread baked in a clay oven. The food was delicious, and Moore felt stuffed by the time they were finished.

Wazir pierced the silence with a question: "What is the most difficult thing you've ever done in your life?"

Moore glanced at Rana, whose body language said, *This matters.*

With a resigned sigh, Moore faced Wazir and asked, "Is this important?"

"No."

"Then why do you ask?"

"Because I'm an old man, and I'm going to die soon, and I believe that brotherhoods are formed in life's sacrifices. I'm a collector of nightmares, if you will. It's the recounting, in the cool of the day, that allows courage and truth to flourish. So, in the name of brotherhood . . . what is the most difficult thing you have ever done in your life?"

"I don't think I've ever faced this question before."

"Are you afraid to tell me?"

"I'm not afraid, I'm just . . ."

"You don't want to look at it. You've hidden it away."

Moore gasped, and he was unsure if he could maintain his gaze on Wazir. "We've all done many difficult things."

"I need the most difficult. Do you want me to go first?"

Moore nodded.

"I yearned to make my father proud. I wanted to be a good son."

"And how was that difficult?"

Wazir raised his stump. "I got hurt early in the war, and with that the paternal glow of pride, each time I entered the room, was quenched from my father's gaze. His son was a cripple now, no longer a warrior. It was never the same with him after that. And there was nothing harder for me to do than make him proud."

"I'm sure you succeeded."

The old man smiled. "You'd have to ask my father."

"He's still alive?"

Wazir nodded. "He lives about an hour from here by car. He must be the oldest man in the village there."

"Well, I'm sure he's proud of you now. I was not a very good son. And by the time I learned what a fool I'd been, it was too late. My father died from cancer."

"I'm sorry to hear that. All we wanted to be were good sons, yes?"

"It's never that simple."

Moore's eyes began to burn—because he knew the old man was going to press him again. He did.

"The hardest thing?"

Moore glanced away. "I'm sorry. I can't look in there."

The old man sat quietly, sipping on his tea, letting the silence reclaim the room, while Moore forced his thoughts onto deep, dark waves of nothing. And then he looked up. "I guess if I don't tell you, you won't help me."

"If you told me too quickly, I wouldn't believe you. I understand that the pain is so great that you can't talk. I know this pain. And I *will* help you. I must help you."

"I just . . . I once made a decision that to this day I'm not sure was the right one. Every time I think about it, I feel like I'm going to throw up."

Wazir's eyes widened. "Then put it behind you! That was some of my best stew you've eaten!"

Moore grinned over the joke.

"Now, the two men in the photograph. I will find out who they are, but I think they're unimportant. It's the men they work for that you have to stop."

"Do you have names?"

"You've seen my office. I have more than that." Wazir took them back to his computers, where he showed Moore photographs of two men he identified as Mullah Abdul Samad and Mullah Omar Rahmani. Samad was the younger of the two, in his forties, while Rahmani was pushing sixty.

"Are these guys Taliban leaders? I . . . I can't believe I haven't heard of them."

Wazir grinned. "They don't want you to know who they are. The best way to explain it is that there are Taliban within Taliban, the more public figures you are familiar with, and a special group that works as secretively as possible. Rahmani is the leader of that group here. And Samad is his fist. They are the men responsible for killing your friends, for killing the colonel who wanted to help you."

Moore threw a wary glance at Rana, who had told the old

man much more than he should have. Rana shrugged. "I needed to tell him what was happening—in order to get his help."

Moore made a face. "Okay." He regarded Wazir. "Now this man is missing." He handed Wazir a picture of Agent Gallagher, with his long, gunmetal-gray hair and scraggly beard. Gallagher's parents had emigrated from Syria to the United States, where he was born. His real name was Bashir Wassouf, but he went by Bobby Gallagher and had his name legally changed when he was a teenager. He'd told Moore about all the discrimination he'd suffered as a kid growing up in Northern California.

"Leave me a copy of this," said Wazir.

"Thank you. Do you know anything about the other man? The Hispanic guy?"

"He's a Mexican, and they're buying a lot more opium than they used to. They were never very good customers, but their business has increased tenfold in recent years, and as you discovered, the Army has been helping them move their product through Pakistan and out of the country, to Mexico, to the United States . . ."

"Do you know where these men are? I mean right now."

"I think so."

"Wazir, I want to thank you for the tea, for the stew . . . for everything. I mean it."

"I know you do. And when you're ready to talk, come back to me. I want to hear your story. I'm an old man. I'm a good listener."

During the drive back, Moore thought a lot about "his story" and the darker waters he could have tread . . .

Fairview High School, Boulder, Colorado (home of the Knights), was where Moore met a kid named Walter Schmidt during their freshman year. Schmidt was a year older than everyone else because he'd flunked out his first time around. He'd been proud of that fact. He boasted of cutting classes, mouthing off to teachers, and smoking pot on school grounds. He repeatedly tried to get Moore involved, and while the temptation had been great, the thoughts of escaping from the turmoil of his parents' divorce incredibly enticing, Moore had stood firm. Even so, Moore was no scholar himself, barely passing his classes, and watching with some envy as Walter grew more popular, attracted girls who would actually have sex with him, and seemed to wriggle his brows at Moore, as if to say, *You could have this life, too, bro.*

Finally, near the end of the school year, Moore's defenses had weakened. He'd decided to attend a party thrown by Schmidt. He would try pot for the first time because a girl he liked would be there, and he already knew she smoked. As he rode his bike down the street toward Schmidt's house, the flashing lights of police cars quickened his pace, and when he drew closer, he caught a glimpse of Schmidt being shoved out of the house like a rabid dog by two officers. Schmidt battled against the handcuffs, cursed, and even spat in one cop's face.

Moore stood there, breathless, as the rest of the partygoers were arrested and taken away—including the girl he liked.

He shook his head. He'd been that close to getting arrested himself. No, that wasn't a life. Not his life. He wasn't going to waste it like these jerks. He'd turn it all around. His father, a nerd who worked for IBM, was always browbeating him about having no direction, no future.

But that night Moore made a decision. He would finally listen to someone else who'd been trying to inspire and encourage him: his high school gym teacher, Mr. Loengard, a man who recognized in him something no one else had witnessed or discovered, a man who made him realize that his life was worth something and that he could make contributions to this world that were immeasurable. He could rise to the call and become a very special breed of warrior: a U.S. Navy SEAL.

Moore's father had told him that the Navy was for drunks and idiots. Well, he was going to prove the old man wrong. He kept himself on the straight and narrow, graduated high school, and by the end of that summer was up in Great Lakes, Illinois, at the Navy Recruitment Training Command for eight weeks of basic training. Moore had to get through the "confidence course" twice, ship training, weapons training, shipboard damage control, and the memorable "confidence chamber," where he'd had to recite his full name and Social Security number while a tear-gas tablet hissed at his feet.

Upon graduation, Moore slid on his U.S. Navy ball cap and was sent to the Navy Law Enforcement Academy in San Antonio to complete the LE/MA (Law Enforcement/Master-at-

Arms) six-week course. He'd found this interesting and exciting because he'd gotten to play with guns. While he was there, his instructors noted his marksmanship, and finally, after much pleading, he received that highly coveted recommendation. Upon graduation, Moore was promoted to Seaman (E-3) and sent off to Coronado, California, home of the U.S. Navy SEALs.

Blood, sweat, and tears awaited him.

5

FATHER FIGURE

Casa de Rojas
Punta de Mita, Mexico

M ORE THAN TWO HUNDRED guests had gathered at the oceanfront estate in the gated community of the Four Seasons golf course resort. At over twenty thousand square feet, including four master suites, two children's bunk rooms, and a detached villa, the home had easily become the most famous residence in the entire community. From the massive, hand-carved front doors to the extensive stonemasonry and marble work that made the foyer seem more like that of a European cathedral than a private residence, Casa de Rojas took your breath away from the moment you entered. Unsurprisingly, Miguel's girlfriend, Sonia Batista, gasped as he led her past the great stone columns supporting archways of rich granite and toward the infinity pool and expansive stone deck beyond.

"Everyone has secrets," she said, pausing to lean on one of the columns and stare up into the broad skylights. "But this . . . this is just a little overwhelming." She then glanced down at the stone floor, whose intricate patterns had taken the artists and world-renowned architects months to conceive and years to complete. Miguel would tell her about that later, once he gave her the full tour. For now, they needed to get to their seats before his father began the presentation.

However, he couldn't resist stealing one last moment to marvel over her shoulder-length curly hair that caught the late-afternoon sun just right, glistening like black volcanic sand. He stood there, a twenty-two-year-old with a raging libido, imagining what they'd do later on. She was as svelte as any runway model but remarkably athletic, too, and for the past month he had explored every curve of her young body and spent many long moments staring into her deep brown eyes, flecked with a half-dozen shades of gold. He shifted to her, quickly stole a kiss. She giggled. Then he grabbed her by the wrist. "Come on. My father will kill me if we're late."

She nearly tripped and fell as they rushed forward, because she wasn't looking ahead but gaping at one of the three expansive kitchens with bars that could seat twelve and the attached banquet hall, with seating for nearly one hundred. To their right and left shimmered more of the stonework soaring toward twenty-foot ceilings. He would tell her all about the furniture that his father had imported from all over the world, with stories behind many of the pieces. The tour would take several hours, he knew, and he hoped they'd have time to visit the library, gym, media room, and indoor shooting range before re-tiring for the evening. She had no idea of the length and breadth of the home, and yet as he showed it to her, she would not only learn more about him but a lot about his father, Jorge Rojas.

"I'm more than a little nervous," she said, squeezing his hand as they reached the end of the long hall and were about to step outside onto the mottled pavers of the pool deck.

Castillo was standing there, as he always did, a six-foot statue in a dark suit with earpiece and dark glasses. Miguel turned and said, "Sonia, this is Fernando Castillo. He's the security chief for my father, but he still sucks at playing Call of Duty . . ."

"That's because you're a cheater," said Castillo with a slight grin. "You hack all those games—I know it."

"You just need to learn how to shoot."

Castillo shook his head, then removed his sunglasses, re-vealing that he had but one eye; the other was stitched closed. She flinched but still took his hand.

"Very nice to meet you," he said.

"You, too."

"I didn't want to be rude to such a pretty lady," he said, replacing his sunglasses. "But sometimes it's better that I keep these on, huh?"

"It's okay," she said. "Thank you."

They shifted away and began filtering through the knots of people standing around dinner tables that encompassed the pool. Miguel whispered to her, "Don't let him kid you. He sees more with that one eye than most people see with two."

"How did he lose it?"

"When he was a boy. It's a sad story. Maybe I'll tell you sometime, but tonight, we drink expensive wine and have fun!" Miguel wriggled his brows and squeezed her hand.

Four different poolside bars with bartenders manning each kept the wine and champagne flowing, and a banner had been erected between two of the bars, with the calm waters of the northern Pacific and a burnt-orange sky serving as the perfect backdrop. The banner read: WELCOME TO THE JORGE ROJAS SCHOOL IMPROVEMENT PROJECT FUND-RAISER. This was a one-thousand-dollar-per-plate dinner, and it was Miguel's father's biannual way of coaxing his rich friends to part with some of their money for a great cause. The work that had been accomplished by his father's foundation was re-markable. The government of Mexico could not do as much to improve the education system as Jorge Rojas already had done and would continue to do.

"Miguel, Miguel," came a familiar voice from behind them. A tightly bunched crowd of guests parted to allow through Mariana and Arturo González, Miguel's aunt and uncle, both in their late forties, impeccably groomed and dressed, looking as though they were ready for a Hollywood red-carpet appear-ance. Mariana was his father's only sibling after the death of their brother.

"Look at you," said his aunt, tugging at the sleeve of his dark gray suit.

"You like it? My father and I found a new designer in New York. He flew down to meet us." Miguel would never tell Sonia that the suit cost him more than ten thousand American dollars. In fact, he was sometimes embarrassed over his family's wealth and dismissed it when he could. Sonia's father was a successful businessman from Madrid, a Castilian who owned a custom bicycle company (Castile) that supplied race bikes to professional teams of the Tour de France. However, her family could never compete with the kind of wealth that his father had amassed. Jorge Rojas wasn't just one of the richest men in Mexico; he was one of the richest men in the entire world, which made life as his son both complicated and surreal.

"So this is the famous Sonia?" asked his aunt.

"Yes," Miguel said, beaming with pride, and then, as his aunt would expect, his tone grew much more formal. "Sonia, this is my aunt Mariana and my uncle, Mr. Arturo González, the governor of Chihuahua."

Sonia was a perfect lady and greeted them in a tone equally formal. Her radiant smile and the diamond necklace that fell softly across her neck did not go unnoticed by his uncle. As Miguel watched her speak, he no longer heard anything and saw only her actions and reactions, the joy that swept over her face and kept her smiling, the light so intoxicating in her eyes.

Miguel's father had introduced them after having worked on some investments with mutual friends. That she was Castilian was very impressive to his father. That she had a great ass and ample cleavage was more impressive to Miguel, at least during the initial stages of their relationship. He'd discovered that she'd attended the Universidad Complutense, one of the biggest universities in all of Europe, and he quickly learned that there was, indeed, a brain behind all that beauty. "Don't judge me," she'd told him. "I didn't go to some expensive private school, but I did graduate magna cum laude."

The summer after she graduated she spent traveling to New York and Miami and Los Angeles, cities she'd never visited before. She was obsessed with fashion and the movie industry. Her degree was in business management, and she thought she'd like to work in California for a big studio or maybe in New York for a famous designer. Sadly, her father would have none of that. He'd given her a year to find herself, but this fall she would go to work for his company. Miguel, of course, had much bigger plans for her.

"So you're finally back from Spain," said his aunt. "How long were you there?"

He grinned at Sonia. "About a month."

"Your father told me that was a graduation gift," his aunt said, widening her eyes.

"It was," Miguel said proudly. Then he turned to his uncle. "How is it going back home?"

Arturo wiped a hand across his bald pate, then nodded. "We still have a lot of work to do. The violence gets worse."

Mariana waved her hand. "But we're not talking about that now, are we? Not on a night like this, when there's so much to celebrate!"

Arturo nodded resignedly and grinned at Sonia. "Very nice to meet you. And now we'll take you to our table. It's right over there."

"Oh, good, we're sitting with you," Sonia said.

Before they could cross the length of the pool to reach their dining area, Miguel was accosted by at least four other friends—business associates of his father's, guys from one of his old soccer teams at USC, and at least one ex-girlfriend who turned thirty seconds into what felt like thirty hours of awkwardness as they spoke in French and Sonia stood there, looking lost.

"I didn't know you spoke French," she said to him, after he finally escaped from the pushy siren.

"English, French, Spanish, German, and Dutch," he said. "And sometimes gangsta, you know what I'm sayin', G?"

She laughed, and they took their seats around the richly appointed table with some of the finest china and flatware available in the world. His father had taught him never to take anything for granted, and while he'd led a life of privilege, he appreciated even the smallest details, like the material of his napkin or the type of leather used to make his belt. When so many had so little, he needed to be thankful and appreciate every luxury of his life.

A microphone-equipped lectern with a laptop computer stood near a large portable projection screen. As was his father's wish, he'd give his presentation *before* the guests ate, because "swollen bellies have no ears," he liked to say.

Arturo rose and went to the lectern. "Ladies and gentlemen, if you'll be seated, we'll begin in a moment. For those of you who don't know me, I'm Arturo González, governor of Chihuahua. I'd like to introduce my brother-in-law, a man who needs no introduction, but I thought for this particular occasion, I would tell you a little about Jorge growing up, because we went to the same school and we have known each other all our lives."

Arturo took a quick breath and added suddenly, "Jorge was a crybaby. I kid you not."

The crowd broke into laughter.

"Whenever we had homework, he would spend hours crying about it. Then he would come over my house, and I would do the homework, and he would give me some Coca-Cola or gum. You see? Even back then he understood good business!"

More laughter.

"But seriously, ladies and gentlemen, Jorge and I both truly appreciated our education and our teachers, and we would not be standing here without them, which is why both of us feel so deeply about giving back to our children. Jorge will explain more about the foundation's work, so without further ado, I give you Mr. Jorge Rojas!"

Arturo looked toward one of the bars, and from behind it, the man appeared, wearing a suit that matched Miguel's, save for his tie, which was a gleaming and powerful red with gold stitching along the edges. He wore his freshly cut hair gelled closely to his head, and for the first time Miguel noticed the gray hairs sprouting from his temple and from his long sideburns. Miguel had never before thought of his father as old. Jorge was an athletic man who'd played on the USC soccer team when he'd been a student there. He'd even been a triathlete for a few years before hurting his knee. He still kept in excellent shape and was an imposing six feet, two inches tall, unlike

Miguel, who was merely five-ten and didn't seem to be growing anymore.

While Jorge often had a few days' growth of stubble on his chin, which he'd explained away by saying he'd been too busy to shave (and that always drew a frown, because one of the richest men in the world couldn't find the time to shave?), on this evening he was clean-shaven, with the sharp jaw of a movie star. He grinned and waved to the crowd as he literally jogged away from the bar and ran up to the lectern to give Arturo a big hug.

But then he pulled back and began to wring his brother-in-law's neck, drawing more laughter from the crowd. He released Arturo and went to the microphone.

"I asked him to never talk about me crying over the homework, but it's true, ladies and gentlemen, it's true. I guess I've always been passionate about school—in one way or another!"

Miguel glanced over at Sonia, who sat there, rapt. Jorge had that effect on everyone, and while it sometimes made Miguel jealous, he couldn't have been more proud of his father, and he knew Sonia would find him utterly amazing, as most people did.

For the next fifteen minutes they sat, listened, and watched the guided tour of the work the foundation had done to build new schools, to equip classrooms with state-of-the-art technology, to hire the best teachers available from both Mexico and neighboring countries. Jorge even provided statistics and test scores to validate the work they were doing. But the most convincing argument came from the students themselves.

Jorge shifted aside and allowed an entire fourth-grade class to line up behind the lectern, and three of the students, two boys and a girl, spoke articulately about the improvements at their school. They were the cutest kids Miguel had ever seen, and they no doubt tugged heavily on the heartstrings of everyone present.

And when they were finished, Jorge concluded by urging everyone to make further donations before they left. He gestured to the kids. "We must invest in our future," he told them, lifting his voice. "And that continues tonight. Enjoy your dinner, everyone! And thank you!"

As he left the lectern, Jorge was joined by his girlfriend, Alexsi, a stunning blonde who'd been standing by at the bar with him. He'd met her while on a business trip to Uzbekistan, and it was clear to all why he'd been so attracted to her. She had eyes as bright and green as Gula, the Afghan girl who'd famously appeared on the cover of *National Geographic* magazine. Her father was a Supreme Court judge who'd been nominated by the president of the country, and she was an attorney herself who didn't look a day over thirty. Miguel knew his father could not abide a woman with whom he could not have an intelligent conversation. She spoke English, Spanish, and Russian quite proficiently, and she was a student of world affairs. Most surprisingly, she had outlasted all of his father's other female friends. They'd been dating for nearly a year now.

Miguel had been wondering about a collection of seats on the far left-hand side of the yard, and when he looked again, those seats had been filled by a live orchestra, which began to play a subtle Jobim bossa nova.

Alexsi glided over to her chair, which was drawn from the table by Jorge, and she took her seat and grinned at everyone.

"Well, I see the world travelers are finally back from Spain," said Rojas, beaming at Sonia. "And it's very good to see you again, Ms. Batista."

"And good to see you, too, sir. Thank you for the presentation. That was incredible."

"We can't do enough for those kids, can we?" He drifted into a thought. "Oh, forgive my terrible manners," he added quickly, turning to Alexsi. "This is my friend Alexsi Gorbotova. Alexsi, this is my son's friend Sonia Batista."

As the pleasantries were exchanged, Miguel recoiled a bit while waiters came around and filled their wineglasses. He stole a glance at the label: Château Mouton Rothschild Pauillac, bottled in 1986. Miguel loved the wine and knew each bottle sold for more than five hundred dollars. Again, he wouldn't share the price with Sonia, but she lifted the glass to her nose and her eyes grew wide.

Jorge lifted his glass. "A toast to the future of our great country, Mexico! *Viva México!*"

Later, Miguel and Sonia slipped away from the table before dessert was served. His father was in an intense conversation with both his uncle and several other local politicians from the area. They had lit up their cigars, and Sonia had found the stench too powerful, the smoke burning her eyes. They retreated to an empty table not far from the orchestra and listened to a surprisingly good rendition of "Samba de Uma Nota Só." She was impressed that he knew the title of the song. His music education classes weren't just electives; they were intense. She put her hand over his and said, "Thank you for bringing me here."

He laughed. "Do you want the grand tour?"

"Not now, if that's okay. I'd just like to sit here and talk."

In the distance a siren blared, followed by more sirens. A car accident, perhaps, but not the violence that his uncle had mentioned, the violence that had settled on the city of Juárez like a fog clouding men's vision and driving them to kill one another. No, it was just a car accident . . .

Sonia lifted her chin and stared across the deck. "Alexsi seems nice."

"She's good for my father, but he'll never marry her."

"Why not?"

"Because he's never stopped loving my mother. These girls can never compete with her."

"It's okay if you don't want to answer, but you still haven't told me how she died."

He frowned. "I thought I did."

"That was your other girlfriend."

He grinned and pretended to punch her arm; then his expression turned serious. "She died of breast cancer. All the money in the world couldn't save her."

"I'm so sorry. How old were you?"

"Eleven."

She nudged in closer, draped her arm over his shoulder. "I'm sure that was very difficult, especially at that age."

"Yes. I just wish my father had . . . I don't know . . . learned how to deal with it better. He assumed I would freak out. He thought if I hung around I wouldn't be able to deal with the pain. So he rushed me off to Le Rosey."

"But you told me you liked it there."

"I did. But it didn't have him."

She nodded. "I have to be honest. After you told me you went there, I looked it up online. It's one of the most expensive boarding schools . . . I mean, anywhere. And you got to go to school in Switzerland. That's fantastic."

"I guess so. I just . . . I really missed my father, and we were never the same after that. He didn't know how to deal with losing her or with raising me, so off I went. I saw him only three or four times a year, and it wasn't like meeting your dad, more like meeting your boss. I don't resent him for it. He only wanted the best for me. I just wish, sometimes, I don't know what I'm saying . . . Sometimes I think he's trying to help all these schoolkids because he feels guilty for what happened to me . . ."

"Maybe you need to talk to him. I mean, really talk. You keep traveling everywhere. Maybe you need to stay home and get to know each other again."

"You're right. But I don't know if he'd want to do that. He's all over the place, too. When you own most of Mexico, you need to keep an eye on things, I guess."

"Your father seems like an honest man. I think he'd be honest with you. You just have to talk."

"I'm a little apprehensive about that. He's already got my life planned out for me, and if we get into a conversation, he's going to hand me a road map. Really, I'm hoping to take off at least the rest of this summer before he puts me to work. Then in the fall it's off to graduate school."

"You didn't tell me that."

"I haven't told you a lot of things. Remember how you said you wanted to move to California?"

"Yes."

"Well, in the fall, we can move there together. I'll be going to school, and you can be with me, maybe find a job at one of the studios, like you said."

She gasped. "That would be amazing! Oh, wow, I could really find something that—"

She broke off suddenly, and her expression soured.

"What's wrong?"

"You know my father will never let me do any of this."

"I'll talk to him."

"That won't work." She lowered her voice to mimic her dad. "His 'stubborn dedication to quality' is what made him successful—at least that's the way he phrases it. And his stubborn dedication to his daughter is the same."

"Then I'll have my father talk to him."

"What are you saying, Miguel?" She hoisted her perfectly tweezed eyebrows.

"I'm saying that your father wants to make you happy. And trust me—I can do that. I can make you very happy. Well, at least I'll try my best."

"You already have . . ." She leaned toward him, and their kiss was deep and passionate, and it quickened Miguel's pulse.

When they finished, he turned away and found his father staring at them from across the deck. Jorge waved them over.

"Here we go," Miguel said with a sigh. "He's going to ask my opinion on every global crisis—and God help me if I don't have one . . ."

"No worries," said Sonia. "I'll offer mine if you don't."

He grinned and took Sonia's hand. "Excellent."

6

VERSE OF
THE SWORD

Shawal Area
North Waziristan

THE CHIEF of the Shawal tribes had called an important meeting to be held at his mud-brick fort down in the Mana Valley, but Mullah Abdul Samad had no intentions of attending. Instead, while the chief's *misharans* began to gather outside the fort, he remained on the hilltop, crouched beside a stand of trees, along with his two most trusted lieutenants, Atif Talwar and Wajid Niazi.

Samad had detected movement on the opposite hillside, and on closer inspection with his binoculars, he marked two men, one dark-haired and bearded, the other much younger and leaner, his beard thin and short. They were dressed like tribesmen, but one consulted a satellite phone and what Samad assumed was a portable GPS unit.

Talwar and Niazi studied the men themselves, and while both were still in their twenties, nearly half Samad's age, he'd spent the last two years training them, and they both offered the same assessment of their visitors: They were advance scouts for American intelligence, for the Pakistan Army, or even for an American Special Forces unit. The chief's foolish and poorly trained men had not picked up these two, and so his forces would pay the price for their ineptitude.

The chief liked to throw the tribal code of conduct into the faces of government officials. He liked to threaten the Army and point out its losses in South Waziristan as an example of what would happen if they attacked him. He said the government should know that his people would use the tribal codes and councils like the *jirga*s to find answers to their problems and needed the government's help with only the basic necessities of life, not with how to rule their people. He assured them that his people would never harbor criminals, that there were no "foreigners" in Shawal, and that bringing harm to his people and their land was the farthest thing from his mind. But the chief wasn't a very good liar, and Samad would make sure he died for that . . . perhaps not today . . . or tomorrow . . . but soon.

The scouts did not move as they surveyed the surrounding valleys with their own binoculars. They seemed particularly interested in the long lines of apple trees that curved down the hill, toward more rows of apricots. Fields had been hewn into some of the steepest hills overlooking the village, and the trees did make for good cover. These men had indeed spotted a few of the chief's guards posted on the perimeter. But they were hardly paying attention to the spies behind them, and once more Samad could only shake his head in disgust.

The American and Pakistani governments had good reason to believe that the tribes here were sheltering Taliban and Al-Qaeda fighters; the Datta Khail and Zakka Khail tribesmen had been known for hundreds of years for their deep bonds of loyalty and for their land being a natural sanctuary for rebels. The current chief was no exception, except that he'd been receiving a lot of pressure from the Americans now, and Samad thought it was only a matter of time before he succumbed to their force and betrayed him and the forty other men training here on the Pakistan side of Shawal and about ten kilometers away, within the Afghan side of the area.

After September 11, 2001, the Pakistan Army entered the area with a mission to secure the border against Northern Alliance soldiers pushing eastward from Afghanistan. While there could have (and in Samad's opinion, should have) been a confrontation, the local tribes welcomed them, and check posts were established. In the years to follow, the tribal leaders would regret that mistake, as many near and dear to them were killed by American drones and daisy cutter bombs because the Americans suspected there were terrorists in the area. The Americans would offer an apology and pathetic reparations, even as they murdered civilians in the name of justice.

In recent months, however, the tribesmen had come to

their senses and had been refusing requests from both the Americans and the Pakistani government. There had been, for a few years, a tribal *lashkar* formed, and it was this group's mission to arrest all fugitives and resistance fighters within the Shawal area. Only a few days prior, the chief had received word from Islamabad that officials were not pleased with the *lashkar*'s performance and that the Army might need to return in great numbers to the area to weed out the fugitives. Samad and his people, along with their leader, Mullah Omar Rahmani, who was presently in the Afghan area, had struck a deal: If the Army returned, the Taliban and Al-Qaeda forces would equip and reinforce the tribesmen against any attacks. Moreover, Rahmani had assured the chief that he would be paid handsomely for his assistance. Rahmani had no shortage of funds so long as the poppies continued to grow and the opium bricks continued shipping overseas. Their most recent deal with the Juárez Cartel of Mexico would make them the major provider of opium into that country if the cartel was able to crush its enemies. While Mexico had never been one of the major buyers of Afghan-produced opium, Rahmani planned to change that and have his product better compete with South America's cocaine and crystal-meth industries, which provided massive quantities of those drugs to the cartels, who in turn got them into the hands of Americans.

Samad lowered his binoculars. "They'll come for us this evening," he told his lieutenants.

"How do you know?" asked Talwar.

"Mark my words. The scouts are always a few hours ahead. That's all. Never more. Rahmani will call to warn us."

"What should we do? Can we get all the others out in time? Can we run?" Niazi asked.

Samad shook his head and lifted an index finger to the sky. "They're watching us, as always." He stroked his long beard in thought, and within a minute, a plan congealed. He gestured that they move back and away, keeping closely to the fruit trees and using the ridge to shield themselves from the spies.

On the other side of the hill lay a small house and large fenced-in pens for goats, sheep, and a half-dozen cows. The farmer who lived there had repeatedly cast an evil eye at Samad when he brought his troops into the valley nearby for target practice. This was a Taliban training ground, and the farmer was well aware of that. He'd been ordered by the tribal chief to assist Samad in any way he could; he had reluctantly agreed. Samad had never spoken to the man, but Rahmani had and had warned Samad that this farmer could not be trusted.

In times of war, men must be sacrificed. Samad's father, a mujahideen fighter who had battled the Russians, told him that on the last night he'd seen the man alive. His father had gone off to war carrying an AK-47 rifle and a small, tattered backpack. His sandals were falling apart. He'd looked back at Samad and smiled. There was a gleam in his eye. Samad was an only child. And soon only he and his mother were left in the world.

Men must be sacrificed. Samad still carried a photo of his father protected by a yellowing plastic film, and when the nights grew most lonely, he'd stare at the picture and talk to the man, asking if his father was proud of all Samad had accomplished.

With the help of several world-aid organizations, Samad had managed to finish school in Afghanistan, and he'd been handpicked by yet another aid group so he could enroll at Middlesex University in the UK on a full scholarship. He'd attended their Dubai regional campus, where he'd earned an undergraduate degree in Information Technology and further honed his political interests. It was there at Middlesex that he'd met young members of the Taliban, Al-Qaeda, and Hezbollah. These rebellious spirits helped ignite his naive soul.

After graduating, he'd traveled with a few friends to Zahedan, a city in southeastern Iran and strategically located in the tri-border region of Pakistan, Iran, and Afghanistan. With finances from the drug trade and the audacious hiring of demolitions experts from Iran's Revolutionary Guard, they created a bomb-making facility. Samad had been placed in charge of building and servicing the facility's computer network system. They manufactured bombs within cinder bricks, and the bombs were smuggled across the borders into Afghanistan and Pakistan, with all of the deliveries timed, marked, and tracked electronically by the software Samad had created. That was Samad's first foray into the world of terrorism.

Jihad was a central duty of all Muslims, but the definition of that word was widely misunderstood, and even Samad had been unsure about it until he'd been taught its true meaning while working at the bomb factory. Some theologians referred to jihad as the struggle within the soul or the defending of the faith from critics, or even migrating to non-Muslim lands for the purpose of spreading Islam. You were striving in the way of

Allah. But was there really any form other than violent jihad? The infidels must be purged from the holy lands. They must be destroyed. They were the leaders of injustice and oppression. They were the rejecters of truth, even after it had been made clear to them. They were already destroying themselves and would bring down the rest of the world if they were not stopped.

A verse from the Qur'an was forever on the tip of Samad's tongue: *Muster against them all the men and cavalry at your disposal so that you can strike terror into the enemies of Allah* . . .

And no group of people more accurately represented the enemies of Allah than Americans, those spoiled, spineless, godless consumers of garbage. Land of the fornicators and home of the obese. They were a threat to all people of the world.

Samad led his men closer to the farmhouse, then called to the farmer to come outside. The man, who lived alone after his wife had died and his two sons had moved to Islamabad, finally wobbled past his front door, balancing himself on a cane and squinting at Samad.

"I don't want you here," he said.

"I know," Samad answered, moving up to the man. He nodded once more and thrust a long, curved blade directly into the man's heart. As the farmer fell back, Samad caught him, even as Talwar and Niazi helped seize and carry him into the house. They lay him on the dirt floor, and he just stared at them as he continued bleeding to death.

"After he dies, we need to hide his body," said Niazi.

"Of course," Samad answered.

"He'll be missed," Talwar pointed out.

"We'll say he left to visit his sons in the city. But that's only if the tribesmen ask. If the Americans or the Army come, then this is our farm. Do you understand? Fleeing now will only draw more suspicion."

They nodded.

Out near one of the goat pens they found a hole the farmer had been using to pile up the dung. They threw him in there and buried him with more dung. Samad grinned. No soldier would want to go digging through dung to find the body of some worthless farmer. Samad donned some of the old man's clothes; then they sat back in some squeaky chairs, prepared some tea, and waited for nightfall.

M oore and his young recruit Rana had observed three men near a stand of trees on the hilltop, but these men were too low and too far away to see their faces, even with binoculars. Rana assumed that they were Taliban fighters, sentries on the perimeter, and Moore agreed. He and Rana hiked back across the foothills, down into a ravine, then up to high ground, from where Moore made a call with his Iridium satellite phone. The mountainous terrain interfered with reception if he got too deep into the cuts and ravines, but he usually picked up a clean signal from the mountaintops, where, of course, he was more vulnerable to detection. He reached the detachment commander of an ODA (Operational Detachment Alpha) team, one of the Army's elite Special Forces groups. As a SEAL, Moore had worked alongside these boys in Afghanistan, and he had a deep respect for them, even though barbs were traded regarding which group had the most effective and deadly warriors. The rivalry was both healthy and amusing.

"Ozzy, this is Blackbeard," said Moore, using his CIA call sign. "What's up, brother?"

The voice on the other end belonged to Captain Dale Osbourne, a painfully young but exceedingly bright operator who'd worked with Moore on several night raids that had yielded two High-Value Targets in Afghanistan.

"Going for the hat trick tonight."

Ozzy snorted. "You got actionable intel or just the usual bullshit?"

"Usual bullshit."

"So you didn't see them."

"They're here. We got three already."

"Why do you assholes always do this to me?"

Moore chuckled. "'Cause you suckers like to play in the dirt. I've uploaded the names and pics. I want these guys."

"What else is new?"

"Look, if it helps, we've picked up shell casings all over the place. Definitely a recent training ground here. Sloppy bastards didn't clean up their mess. I need you in here tonight for the surprise party."

"You sure Obi-Wan's not lying his ass off?"

"I'd bet my life on it."

"Well, holy shit, then, you got a deal. Look for us at zero dark thirty, baby. See you then."

"Roger that. And don't forget your gloves. You don't want to ruin your manicure."

"Yeah, right."

Moore grinned and thumbed off the phone.

"What happens now?" asked Rana.

"We find a little cave, set up camp, then you'll hear a helicopter coming."

"Won't that scare them off?"

Moore shook his head. "They know we've got satellites and Predators up there. They'll just dig in. You watch."

"I'm a little frightened," Rana confessed.

"Are you kidding me? Relax. We'll be fine."

Moore gestured to the AK-47 slung over his shoulder and patted the old Soviet-made Makarov holstered at his side. Rana was also carrying a Makarov, and Moore had taught him how to fire and reload the sidearm.

They found a shallow cave along one of the hillsides and half buried the entrance with some larger rocks and shrubs. They remained there as night fell, and Moore began to slowly doze off. He caught himself twice falling asleep and asked Rana to remain awake and keep watch. The kid was tense anyway, and was happy to keep an eye out.

The energy bar he'd eaten earlier wasn't agreeing with him, and it brought on some vivid dreams. He was floating on an ink-black sea, crucified against an endless expanse of darkness, and suddenly he reached out a hand and screamed, "DON'T LEAVE ME! DON'T LEAVE ME!"

He shuddered awake as something pushed over his mouth. Where the hell was he? He didn't feel wet. He was panting, couldn't catch his breath, realized that was because his mouth was in fact being covered by a hand.

Through the grainy darkness came Rana's wide eyes, and he stage-whispered, "Why are you yelling? I'm not going anywhere. I'm not leaving. But you can't yell."

Moore nodded vigorously, and Rana slowly removed his hand. Moore bit his lip and tried to recover his breathing. "Whoa, sorry, bad dreams."

"You thought I was going to leave."

"I don't know. Wait. What time is it?"

"It's after midnight. Almost zero dark thirty."

Moore sat up and switched on his satellite phone. A voice mail was waiting: "Hey, Blackbeard, you worthless sack of flesh. We're mounting up. ETA your backyard, twenty minutes."

He switched off the phone. "Listen. You hear that?"

Samad was awakened by a hand on his shoulder, and for a second or two he lost his bearings; then he remembered they were inside the farmer's house. He sat up on the small wooden bed. "There's a helicopter coming," said Talwar.

"Go back to sleep."

"Are you certain?"

"Go back to sleep. When they come, we'll be annoyed that they woke us up."

Samad went over to a small table and tied a rag across his face, suggesting that he'd lost an eye—not an uncommon sight in this war-torn part of the country. It was a simple disguise, and he'd learned during his days as a bomb-maker that the more simple the bomb, the idea, the plan, the greater the chance for success it had. He'd proven that theory to himself time and again. A rag. A war wound. A bitter farmer pulled from his sleep by foolish Americans. That's all he was.

Allahu Akbar!

God was great!

The twelve-man ODA team fast-roped down from the hovering chopper as a translator addressed a few of the tribesmen who'd stumbled half-asleep from their houses to stare up and shield their eyes from the rotor wash. The translator spoke loudly via the Black Hawk's booming public address system: "We're here to find two men, and that is all. No one will be harmed. No shots will be fired. Please help us to find two men." The translator repeated the message at least three times as Ozzy's team hit the deck, one after another, then fanned out in pairs, rifles at the ready.

The drop zone was a clearing near a row of homes about two hundred meters away from the walls of the chief's fortress, and Moore met the young Special Forces captain and his chief warrant officer in an alley between houses. They waited a few seconds until the Black Hawk banked hard and thumped away into the darkness, navigation lights flashing as its pilot steered back for the secure landing zone a few kilometers away, where they'd wait for Ozzy's call to extract them. Landing the chopper in the village and having it remain there while the team went to work was simply too dangerous.

"You remember my sidekick, Robin?" Moore asked, directing his penlight at Rana.

Ozzy grinned. "How you doing, buddy?"

Rana frowned. "My name's Rana, not Robin."

"It's a joke," said Moore. He faced the chief warrant officer, a guy named Bobby Olsen, aka Bob-O, who took one look at Moore and pretended to scowl. "Are you the CIA puke?"

Bob-O wore the same look and asked the same question every time they got together. For some reason he took evil delight in ribbing Moore every chance he got. Moore raised his index finger and jabbed it into Bob-O's face, about to launch his retort.

"Okay, you knuckleheads, we can stow that," said Ozzy. He raised his brows at Moore. "It's your party, Blackbeard. I hope you're right."

Ozzy's team had been well trained in the art and science of negotiating with the tribesmen, and their fieldwork had allowed them to put classroom theory and mock scenarios into practice. They'd learned the language, had studied the customs, and even had small all-weather cheat sheets folded and stored in their breast pockets in case they were caught off guard in a social situation. They were, in their humble opinion, ambassadors of democracy, and while some might consider that notion silly or cheesy, they were the only contact with the Western world many of the tribesmen would ever have.

Moore, Rana, Ozzy, and Bob-O were about to cross a rutted dirt road lying parallel to the mud-brick homes when two salvos of automatic-weapons fire echoed off the mountains. The gunfire struck Moore breathless. Bob-O cursed.

"Raceman, who fired those shots?" Ozzy barked into the boom mike at his lips as Moore and Rana crouched beside the house.

Bob-O was on his radio at the same time, yapping at the other teams, demanding information.

More gunfire resounded, the cadence and pitch notably different. Yes, that fire belonged to Ozzy's people, their Special Forces Combat Assault Rifles (SCARs) sending 5.56- or 7.63-millimeter responses to the enemy's ambush. Two more volleys followed. Then a third. Then five, six, maybe seven, AK-47s answered, the gun battle about a half-dozen houses away.

Moore pricked up his ears. To fire an AK-47 you loaded your magazine, moved the selector lever off the safety, pulled back and released the charging handle, took aim, and fired—quite a few moves to fire a single shot. But if you moved the selector to the middle position, you had full auto and could lean on the trigger until you emptied the magazine. Basic gun operation, but the point was this: During any gun battle, Moore first listened for the enemy's location and then tried to determine if the enemy was trying to conserve ammo. He heard it every time—either full auto, which often meant that each combatant had multiple magazines at his disposal, or single shot, which suggested that the enemy was trying to make every round count. Sure, this wasn't a foolproof assessment, but more times than not his assumptions had been correct.

When a group of Taliban unleashed full automatic-weapons fire, you'd best assume the worst: They were well stocked with ammo.

Moore faced Rana and said, "Don't do anything. Just hold tight here."

Rana's eyes lit up the alley. "Oh, don't worry. I'm not going anywhere."

"Neo and Big Dan, you get up into the hills on the south side. Raceman's got fire over there," Ozzy was saying as he peered around the corner, then gestured for Moore and Rana to follow him. Moore edged up beside the captain. "How's it looking?"

"We got about eight, maybe ten, Tangos so far. I'm calling in for an Apache to give these suckers some pause."

Ozzy was referring to the AH-64D Apache Longbow, the Army's premier attack helicopter armed with an M230 chain gun, Hydra 70 air-to-ground rockets, and AGM-114 Hellfire or FIM-92 Stinger missiles. The mere silhouette of that helicopter summoned up horrific death in the imaginations of the Taliban who'd seen their fellow warriors shredded under its unceasing fire.

Ozzy got back on his radio and talked to the chopper pilot,

requesting that he come to the village immediately and put his chain gun to work on the insurgents.

"We'll get you back to the landing zone right now," said Ozzy.

"You hear that?" Moore asked Rana. "We're heading back. We'll be okay."

Rana clutched his Makarov to his chest. "I don't like this."

"I'm with you, Rana," Moore said. "You'll be fine."

As the words left Moore's lips, he flicked his gaze up toward the opposite end of the house, where a figure had just rounded the corner, and the figure's rifle appeared in the moonlight.

Moore raised his AK-47, set to full auto, and squeezed off a four-round burst that drummed into the man's chest, sending him thrashing and falling into the sand.

Even as that guy fell, Ozzy and Bob-O came under a hailstorm of fire from the other side of the house—at least three Taliban fighters opening up on them and driving them away from the corner. Bob-O stepped in front of Rana to protect the kid while Moore stole one more look back, then spun around and went charging up beside Ozzy.

Two houses lay on the other side of the street, and Moore noted the muzzle flashes before he hit the deck. One guy was on the flat roof, exploiting the calf-high parapet running along three sides. He fired and tucked himself back behind the stone. Another was at the back of the house, where a knee wall afforded him good cover.

And the last one stood inside the house on the left, shifting into the open window to fire, then rolling back. All three knew that the mud bricks would protect them from the ene-my's rounds.

"Rana, stay with them," Moore told the kid. Then he crawled two more meters to get close to Ozzy. "Keep them busy. I'm cir-cling around. I'll start with the guy on the roof."

"Dude, are you nuts?" asked Ozzy. "Let me frag 'em."

Moore shook his head vigorously. "I want one alive. Give me a couple of zipper cuffs."

Ozzy snickered in disbelief but handed over the cuffs.

Moore winked. "I'll be right back."

"Hey, Money," called Rana nervously.

But Moore was already racing out of the alley. Dressed like a tribesman himself and armed with their weapons, if he were spotted, there might be a moment of pause that he'd fully ex-ploit. He charged around two more houses, crossed the dirt road, then reached the back of the house atop which one of the Taliban fighters had carefully positioned himself. The guy had used a rickety wooden ladder, and it was during the next round of gunfire that Moore rushed up that ladder, allowing the racket to conceal his advance.

He came over the ledge and spotted the guy, kneeling down and popping up like a target in a black turban, laying down fire, then snapping back behind the parapet. Bob-O and Ozzy sent their own suppressing fire into the stone, drilling up debris and dust that rose in small clouds along the parapet.

With the Taliban's attention fully directed ahead, he nei-ther saw nor heard Moore's approach. Moore took the Makarov in his hand, clutching the barrel so that the grip extended from the bottom of his fist, forming an L-shape.

Then, after taking a deep breath, Moore broke into a running leap, arcing high above his opponent, shifting into an offbeat combination of Krav Maga and his own improvisation. As the guy turned his head, catching a flash from the corner of his eye, Moore came down on him like some taloned predator, driving his knee into the man's back and forcing the grip end of the pistol into the man's neck, below and slightly in front of the ear. A sharp blow to the side of the neck would cause unconsciousness by shocking the carotid artery, jugular vein, and vagus nerve.

The guy fell back across the roof, and Moore withdrew the zipper cuffs from his back pocket and bound the man's hands behind his back. Then he zipped up the guy's feet and left him there. When he woke up, they'd have some tea and a nice conversation. For now, though, Moore descended the ladder, as once more Ozzy and Bob-O got off some suppressing fire on the other two Taliban.

Moore brushed his shoulder along the wall as he headed back around the next house, reaching the corner where, to his left and about ten meters ahead, the second Taliban fighter was hunkered down at the knee wall. He was armed with a rifle but also had a pistol holstered at his side and wore a heavy pack that Moore assumed was loaded with more magazines. Moore shuddered over the decision: The guy seemed too far away to catch silently from behind. And if Moore ran forward at the wrong angle, he could be caught by Ozzy's or Bob-O's fire. Getting taken out by doing something bold was one thing; doing something reckless and getting shot by his own people was to reach a level of stupidity usually reserved for adulterous politicians.

Since Moore was carrying an AK-47, if he did fire, then the third Taliban might assume that his buddy was responsible for those rounds. But then came an even better diversion: The Apache Longbow and its thundering rotors swooped down, banked hard right, then began to wheel over them. The wind and roar stole the Taliban fighter's attention, as did the powerful spotlight that panned across the alley.

Moore raised his rifle, got off three rounds, punching the guy in the back, blood spraying. Then he whirled and took off along the wall of the next house, within which stood the last guy. Moore got down on his hands and knees and crawled beneath the side window, then came around the front of the house. Bob-O and Ozzy ceased fire, and Moore was able to position himself beneath the open window through which the last guy was firing.

At this point, yes, they could lob a grenade and finish the guy, but Moore was already an arm's length away from the insurgent. He rolled onto his side and strained his neck to peer upward until there it was, the guy's rifle barrel hanging above the windowsill, within reach. Moore grabbed the rifle by the upper hand guard and used it to haul himself onto his knees, just as the guy, screaming in shock, let go of the weapon and reached for his holstered pistol.

By the time he freed his weapon, Moore had thrown down the AK and leveled his Makarov. Three rounds sent the thug crashing onto the floor. Moore had used his own pistol because one of the oldest of old-school combat rules said that only as a last resort should you put your life in the hands of an enemy's weapon.

The Apache was already leaving, called off by Ozzy.

Only the fading whomp of rotors broke across the Mana Valley. Finally, a dog barked, and then someone hollered in the distance. English.

Moore jogged back across the street and down to the end of the alley, where he met up with Ozzy and Bob-O. The stench of gunpowder was everywhere, and Moore found himself shaking with adrenaline as he crouched down.

"Nice job, Puke," said Bob-O.

"Yeah," breathed Moore. "Took one alive up on the roof. I get to interrogate him."

"We killed four more, but the rest fell back into the mountains," said Ozzy, cupping one hand over his ear to listen to the reports from his men. "We lost them."

"I want to talk to Old Man Shah, let him lie to my face about this," snapped Moore, referring to the chief of the village.

"Me, too," said Ozzy, showing his teeth.

Moore drifted over to Rana, who was still sitting in the alley, knees pulled in to his chest. "Hey. You okay?"

"No."

"It's over now." Moore proffered his hand, and the young man took it.

While Ozzy's team policed the bodies of the Taliban who'd been killed (and fetched the prisoner Moore had bound up on the roof), Moore, Ozzy, Bob-O, and Rana reached the mud-brick fort. The rectangular buildings were surrounded by brick walls rising about two meters and a large wooden gate before which now stood a half-dozen guards. Ozzy told one of the guards that the chief of the Shawal tribes needed to speak with them immediately. The guard went back to the house, while Moore and the others waited.

Chief Habib Shah and one of his most trusted clerics, Aiman Salahuddin, stormed out of the gate. Shah was an imposing man of six-foot-five or so, with a large black turban and a beard that seemed more like a bundle of black wires than hair. His green eyes flashed in Ozzy's light. The cleric was much older, perhaps seventy, with an ivory-white beard, hunched back, and barely five feet tall. He kept shaking his head at Moore and the others, as though he could will them away.

"Let me do the talking," Moore told Ozzy.

"Yeah, because I'm about to tell him off."

"Hello, Chief," said Moore.

"What are you doing here?" the chief demanded.

Moore tried to temper his anger. He tried, all right. And failed. "Before we were attacked by the Taliban, we came in peace, looking for these two men." Moore shoved the pictures into the chief's hand.

The man gave the photos a perfunctory glance and shrugged.

"I've never seen them before. If anyone in this village is helping the Taliban, he will suffer my wrath."

Ozzy snorted. "Chief, did you know the Taliban were here?"

"Of course not. How many times have I told you this, Captain?"

"I think this might be the fourth. You keep telling me you don't help terrorists, and we keep finding them here. I just can't understand that. Do they accidentally drop down out of the sky?" Ozzy had clearly damned to hell the "art and science" of negotiation.

"Chief, we'd like to continue our search with your help," said Moore. "Just a few men."

"I'm sorry, but my men are very busy protecting this village."

"Let's go," said Ozzy, turning away and marching off with Bob-O behind him.

The cleric stepped up to Moore and spoke in English: "Go home with your friends."

"You're helping the wrong people," Rana suddenly blurted out.

Moore glared at the young man and put a finger to his lips.

The cleric narrowed his eyes at Rana. "Young man, it's you who are very much mistaken."

I t took another two hours for Ozzy's Special Forces team to comb through the village and surrounding farmhouses, ever wary of another attack.

In the meantime, Moore questioned the man they had captured. "I'll say it again, what's your name?"

"Kill me."

"What's your name? Where are you from? Have you seen these guys?" He shoved the pictures into the man's face.

"Kill me."

And it went on like that, over and over, until Moore got so frustrated that he gave up before he said something he shouldn't have. Moore's CIA colleagues would take over the questioning anyway. Might take a week or more to crack this guy.

When Ozzy's team finally returned to the helicopter, Moore debriefed them before they took off.

"This farmhouse right here," Moore said, pointing to the home on a satellite photograph. "It's pretty far back. Anyone get it?"

"We did," said Bob-O. "Old farmer with one eye there. Couple of sons. Not happy to see us. They didn't fit the description of your guys."

"So there it is," said Ozzy.

Moore shook his head. "My guys are here. They're probably watching us right now."

"And what're we going to do about it?" asked Ozzy, throwing up his hands. "We're between a rock and, well, another rock. And some mountains. And some pissed-off tribesmen. And some dead Taliban. Better tell your boys back home to ship these folks some Walmart gift cards for their trouble."

The surprise visit wasn't a total loss. Moore's bosses had been unsure which way the chief's loyalty was swinging these days, and now they knew. To believe that not a single person in this part of Shawal had seen Moore's targets was ridiculous. They'd seen them, talked to them, perhaps trained and eaten with them. Moore had experienced this time and again, and for now there was nothing else he could do but leave behind the photographs and ask for the chief's assistance.

"Was the mission a failure?" asked Rana.

"Not a failure," answered Moore. "We've just been delayed by some unforeseen weather."

"Weather?"

Moore snorted. "Yeah. A big shit storm of silence."

Rana shook his head. "I don't know why they choose to help the Taliban."

"You should know that. They get more from the Taliban than anyone else," Moore told the young man. "They're opportunists. They have to be. Look where they live."

"You think we'll ever catch those guys?"

"We will. It just takes time. And that's my problem, isn't it?"

"Perhaps Wazir will have some news about your missing friend."

Moore sighed deeply in frustration. "That'd work. Either way, I'll be out of here by tomorrow night, and I just wish I could have some vengeance for what they did to the colonel and his family. If those guys just walk away, that'll never stop burning me." They climbed aboard the chopper and within ten minutes were in the air.

Before they even landed in Kabul, Moore saw that he'd received a phone call from Slater.

The Mexican guy in the photograph, Tito Llamas, a lieutenant in the Juárez Cartel, had turned up in a car trunk with a bullet in his head. Likewise, Khodai's associates who'd been photographed with Llamas had all been murdered. The only guys in that picture who hadn't turned up dead thus far were the Taliban. Moore needed to get back to Islamabad ASAP. He wanted to talk to the local police about Llamas and see if there were any other leads he could gather. He thought he might buy himself a little more time by "accidentally" missing his flight back home.

He didn't reach the city until morning, and he told Rana to go home and get some sleep. He went to the police station, met with the detectives there, and positively identified Tito Llamas's body. The cartel member had been carrying falsified documentation, including a fake passport, and Moore was able to share with the local police what data the Agency had on the cartel member. Needless to say, those detectives were grateful.

A surprise e-mail from the old man Wazir was very welcome—that was until Moore read its contents.

The two other Taliban in the photograph that Wazir had mentioned were unimportant and were actually Punjabi Taliban, named for their roots in southern Punjab. They were distinguishable because they did not speak Pashto and traditionally had ties with groups such as Jaish-e-Mohammed. The Punjabi Taliban now operated out of North Waziristan and fought alongside Pakistani Taliban and Al-Qaeda.

But that history lesson wasn't the important part of the e-mail. Wazir had found the men, but both had been murdered. He said the Taliban had discovered their security leak and had killed everyone associated with it . . . except Moore, of course, and he was no doubt at the top of their hit list.

Maybe it was time to go home.

7

TRAVEL PLANS

Shawal Area
Afghanistan

SAMAD AND HIS two lieutenants had fled the farmhouse before dawn and had made the laborious ten-kilometer hike across the border and into Afghanistan. They chose a well-beaten path and had joined a small group of five merchants so as not to draw any attention to themselves. As Samad had reminded his men, the Americans were watching from the sky, and if they took what seemed like a route with better tree cover, their vibrations might be detected by one of the many REMBASS-II unattended ground sensors that the American Army had carefully hidden along the border. That movement would subsequently trigger one of the Americans' many Kennan "Keyhole-class" (KH) reconnaissance satellites that would begin taking pictures of them. Their images would almost instantaneously flash across screens in Langley, where analysts sat twenty-four-seven, waiting for Taliban fighters like him to make such mistakes. The response would be swift and fatal: a Predator drone piloted by an Air Force lieutenant colonel sitting in a trailer in Las Vegas would drop Hellfire missiles on his target.

Once in the valley, they found Mullah Omar Rahmani seated on a pile of blankets inside one of a dozen or more tents erected in a semicircle beneath several walnut and oak trees, and hidden from the east by patches of lemon vines. The morning prayers were over, and Rahmani was sipping tea and about to have some round sweet flatbread the Afghans called *roht*, along with some apricots, pistachios, and thick plain yogurt (which was a true luxury in the mountains).

Rahmani greeted them with a terse nod, then stroked his beard, which swept down toward his collarbone, terminating in a sharp point. His gaze, slightly magnified by a pair of thick wire-frame glasses, seemed permanently narrowed, which made it difficult to determine his mood. He'd pushed his white turban farther back to expose deep lines spanning his forehead and the lima-bean-shaped birthmark staining his left temple. His long linen shirt and baggy trousers hid his considerable girth, and were he to remove the camouflage-pattern jacket tightly hugging his shoulders, he might seem just a hair less intimidating. That jacket—old, tattered at the elbows—had been worn during his battles with the Russians.

Samad had to assume that Rahmani was not pleased with all the attention recently drawn to the area, although he might commend Samad for his quick thinking and ability to once more fool the Americans.

Rahmani lifted his chin toward them. "Peace be unto you, brothers, and let us thank God that we are here this morning to enjoy this food and to live another day—because the days grow more difficult for us."

Samad and his men took seats around Rahmani and were served tea by several young men attending to him. A chill spread across Samad's shoulders as he sipped his tea and tried to calm his breathing.

It was, admittedly, difficult every time Samad was in the man's presence. If you crossed him, if you dared fail him, he would have you executed on the spot. This was not a rumor. Samad had watched the beheadings with his own eyes. Sometimes the heads would be hacked off. Other times they would be sawed off slowly, very slowly, while the victim screamed, then drowned in his own blood.

Rahmani took another deep breath, set down his teacup, then folded his arms across his chest, his black shirt and scarves pulling tighter across his neck. He studied them for a moment more, sending an icy pang into Samad's gut, then cleared his throat and finally spoke again: "The Army has grown too unstable for us now. That much is clear. Khodai could have caused even more damage, and while I am grateful for the work your men did back in Islamabad, there are now many loose ends— particularly the agent our sniper spoke about at the hotel. We're still looking for him. And now our new relationship with the Juárez Cartel in Mexico has been threatened because we were forced to kill their man. All of this means we must move more quickly."

"I understand," Samad said. "The CIA has recruited many operatives in the area. They pay well. It is hard for young men to resist. I have two men tracking one right now, a boy named Israr Rana. We believe he's responsible for helping to expose the link."

Rahmani nodded. "Some of us argue that patience will triumph. The Americans cannot and will not remain here forever, and when they leave, we will continue to train here, and we will bring Allah's will to the people of Pakistan and Afghanistan. But I do not agree with sitting down and waiting for the storm to pass. The problem must be dealt with at its source. I've been working for the past five years on a project that will soon come to fruition. The infrastructure is in place. All I need now are the warriors to execute this plan."

"We would be honored."

"Samad, you will lead them. You will bring the jihad back to the United States—and you must use the contacts you've made with the Mexicans to do that. Do you understand?"

Although he nodded, Samad grew tense because he knew asking any favors of the Mexicans might both insult and incense them. Yet if he could somehow garner their support, his mission stood a far greater chance of success.

But how?

He would have to resort to *hudaibiya*—lying—as the Qur'an exhorted him to do when dealing with infidels.

"I must caution you and all of your men, Samad," Rahmani

went on. "Nearly one hundred of our fighters have already dedicated their lives to this plan. Some of them have already given their lives. There is much at stake here, and the consequences for failure are great, very great indeed."

Samad could already feel the blade on his neck. "We all understand."

Rahmani's voice lifted as he quoted from the Qur'an: *"Whoso fighteth in the way of Allah, be he slain or be he victorious, on him we shall bestow a vast reward."*

"Paradise awaits us," Samad added with a vigorous nod. "And yet if we die and are martyred, only to be resurrected and martyred again, we will do it. This is why we love death."

Rahmani narrowed his eyes even more. "This is why . . . Now, then, let's eat, and I will discuss all of the details. The complexity and audacity of this mission will impress you, I'm sure. Within a few days, you will be on the road. And when the time comes, you will bring a message from Allah, the likes of which the Americans have never seen."

"We won't fail you," said Samad.

Rahmani nodded slowly. "Do not fail Allah."

Samad lowered his head. "We are his servants."

Gandhara International Airport
Islamabad, Pakistan

Moore was en route to San Diego to meet with his new joint task force, and he was dreading the more than seventeen hours of travel time it would take to get there. As he sat at the gate, waiting for the first flight of his journey, he kept a wary eye on the travelers around him, mostly businesspeople, international journalists (he assumed), and a few families with small children, one of them decidedly British. Occasionally, he consulted his tablet computer, where all of his data was secured behind a double-encrypted password. Any attempt to access his computer without his thumbprint would summarily wipe the hard drive. He'd just pulled up some of the Agency's most recent declassified reports on cartel activity along the border (he'd read the classified ones in a more private location). He was most interested in finding intel on Middle Eastern or Arabic links to that activity, but for the most part, the cases he reviewed were limited to warfare between rival cartels, most notably the Sinaloa and the Juárez cartels.

Mass graves had been turning up more frequently—some containing dozens of bodies. Beheadings and bodies hung from bridges were pointing to a rise in gruesome attacks by gangs of *sicarios* led by former Mexican Airborne Special Forces troopers. Government officials argued that the cartel wars illustrated the success of government policies, which were causing the drug traffickers to turn against one another. However, Moore had already concluded that the cartels had become so powerful that, in effect, they literally controlled some parts of the country and the violence was simply evidence of their gang law. Moore read one report written by a journalist who'd spent more than a year documenting cartel activity. In some of the more rural towns in the southeast portions of the country, the cartel was the only group the citizens could rely on to provide them with jobs and protection. This journalist published a half-dozen articles before he was shot seventeen times while waiting outside a shopping mall for his mother. Obviously the cartels did not like what he had to say.

Another report made a comparison between small towns in Mexico and those in Afghanistan. Moore had seen the Taliban engage in the same tactics and behavior as the cartels did. Both the Taliban and the drug cartels became much more trusted than the government and certainly more trusted than the foreign invaders. Both the Taliban and the cartels understood the power that drug trafficking brought them, and they used that power to enlist the aid of innocent civilians who were simply not supported or were even ignored by their government. For Moore, it was difficult to remain apolitical when you saw first-hand a government that was more corrupt than its enemies you were tasked with killing.

Still, the human atrocities committed by both groups helped Moore keep it all in perspective.

He flipped quickly through some of the crime-scene photos of Mexican Federal Police lying in blood pools, some brutally gunned down, others with their throats slit. He paused to stare at two dozen immigrants who'd had their heads chopped off, their headless bodies piled up inside an old shed, the heads now missing and nowhere to be found. One *sicario* was crucified outside his house, the cross set on fire so that his father and other family members could watch him burn.

The cartels' brutality knew no bounds, and Moore had a sneaking suspicion that his bosses had bigger plans for him than they'd originally suggested. Everyone's worst nightmare was for this violence to find its way across the border. It was only a matter of time.

He checked his phone and stared at the three e-mails from Leslie Hollander. The first was a request to let her know when he'd be back in Kabul. The second was a question about whether or not he'd received her e-mail.

The third was a question about why he was ignoring her, and said that if he replied she'd set up another session in which she would, as she carefully put it, fuck him until he was walking bowlegged like a cowboy.

Leslie worked in the press office of the public-affairs department of the U.S. Embassy, first assigned to the embassy in Islamabad and then to the one in Kabul. She was twenty-seven years old, very lean, with dark hair and glasses. At first glance, Moore had dismissed her as an uptight geek whose virginity would remain intact until some pale-faced overweight accountant (the male version of her) came along and wrested it from her after a two-hour argument in which the process of sex was analyzed and discussed, the position agreed on, the act both clinical and upsetting to both.

But, dear God, once the glasses and the blouse came off, Ms. Hollander revealed the remarkable contradiction between her appearance and what really lurked in her heart. Moore was overwhelmed by their sexual escapades when he could escape to the city for a weekend and stay with her; however, he already knew the ending of this movie, and the screenwriter had run out of ideas: Guy tells girl job is too important and he must break off their relationship. Guy has to leave town for work, doesn't know when he'll return. This will never work out.

Interestingly enough, he'd explained all of that to her during their first dinner together, that he needed her as a source of information and that if anything came out of that, then they could explore the possibilities, but his career at the moment prevented any long-term or serious relationship.

"Okay," she'd said.

Moore had nearly choked on his beer.

"Do you think I'm a slut?"

"No."

"Well, I am."

He'd smirked. "No, you just know how to manipulate men."

"How am I doing?"

"Very well, but you don't have to work so hard."

"Hey, man, look where we are. Not one of the top ten places to have fun, right? Not the happiest place on earth. So it's up to us. We bring the fun."

It was that positive attitude on life coupled with her sense of humor that made her seem much more mature and utterly attractive to Moore. But the credits were rolling. The popcorn bag was empty. The lights were coming on, and their good thing was over. Should he just tell her that in an e-mail, the way he had at least two women before her? He wasn't sure. He felt like he owed her more than that. Some of them were quick flings. And a brief note had been enough. He always took the blame. Always said it wasn't fair to them. He'd go a year without a relationship, even resort to paying for sex because the efficiency and convenience were exactly what a man like him needed. And then, once in a while, a Leslie would come along and make him second-guess everything.

He dialed her at work and held his breath as the phone rang.

"Hey, stud," she said. "No satellite service? You see, I'm trying to let you off here. Feed you an excuse . . ."

"I got your e-mails. Sorry I didn't get back."

"Where are you?"

"I'm in the airport, getting ready to get on a plane."

"To where? The place you can't tell me?"

"Leslie, they're pulling me out of here. I really don't know when I'll be back."

"Not funny."

"I'm not kidding."

Silence.

"Are you there?"

"Yeah," she said. "So, uh, was this sudden? Did you know about it? We could've gotten together. You didn't let me say good-bye."

"You know I've been out of town. There wouldn't have been any time. I'm sorry."

"Well, this sucks."

"I know."

"Maybe I'll just quit my job and follow you around."

He almost smiled. "You're not a stalker."

"Really? I guess you're right. So what am I supposed to do now?"

"We'll stay in touch."

A moment of awkward silence, just the hum from the connection. Moore's shoulders drew together . . . and then it was more difficult to breathe.

He closed his eyes and heard her cry in his head: *"Don't leave me! Don't leave me!"*

"I think I was starting to fall in love with you," she blurted out, her voice cracking.

"No, you weren't. Look, we were just in it for the fun. You wanted it that way. And I told you this day would come. But you're right. It sucks. Big-time." He softened his tone. "I want to stay in touch. But it's up to you. If it hurts too much, then okay, I respect that. You can do better than me, anyway. Get somebody younger, with fewer obligations."

"Yeah, whatever. We played with fire and we got burned. But it felt so good along the way."

"You know, I'm not sure I can do this again."

"What do you mean?"

"Say good-bye, I guess."

"No more relationships for you?"

"I don't know."

"Hey, remember how you told me I was helping you with the nightmares? When I told you the stories of when I was in college while you were trying to fall asleep?"

"Yeah."

"Don't forget that, okay?"

"Of course I won't."

"I hope you can sleep," she said.

"I hope so, too."

"I wish you would've told me what's bothering you. Maybe I could've helped even more."

"That's okay. I'm feeling much better now. Thanks for that."

"Thanks for the sex."

He chuckled under his breath. "You make it sound so dirty."

She breathed heavily into the phone and said, "It was."

"You're a crazy bitch."

"You, too."

He hesitated. "I'll talk to you soon. Take care." He closed his eyes and broke the connection. *I'll talk to you soon.* He wouldn't. She knew that.

Moore gritted his teeth. He should walk away from this gate and go back to her and haul her out of that job and quit his, and they could start a life together.

And in six months he'd be bored out of his mind.

And in eight months they'd be divorced and he'd be blaming her and hating himself all over again.

The boarding announcement came. Moore stood with the other passengers and started halfheartedly toward the agent accepting their tickets.

8

JORGE'S SHADOW

Casa de Rojas
Punta de Mita, Mexico

THE MORNING after the fund-raiser, Miguel took Sonia to the library before breakfast. He hadn't intended to show her the room until after they'd eaten, but en route to the main kitchen they had passed by and she'd caught sight of several framed photographs on the wall and had asked if they could spend a few moments inside.

The stone fireplace with great arch and black-ash burl mantel, along with the floor-to-ceiling bookcases constructed of more exotic hardwoods, took her breath away. Rolling ladders and tracks stood on each side of the room, and Sonia mounted one to take in all one thousand square feet.

"Your father likes to read!" she cried, her gaze playing over the thousands of hardcover texts. No paperbacks. His father had insisted that all books in the library be hardcovers, many of them leather-bound.

"Knowledge is power, right?" he replied with a grin.

A small wet bar stood near the entrance, from where Jorge often served cognac produced by houses like Courvoisier, Delamain, Hardy, and Hennessy. Leather sofas and tiger-skin rugs imported from India formed an L-shaped seating area in the middle, with smaller islands of heavy leather recliners positioned around them. On several broad coffee tables sat magnifying glasses for reading and stacks of old *Forbes* magazines, dog-eared by his father. Beside them, the coasters stacked in their holders were inlaid with eighteen-karat gold.

Sonia climbed down from the ladder and returned to one of the photographs that had caught her eye.

"What was her name?"

"Sofía."

"She's beautiful."

"She was," he said with a slight tremor, imagining what her funeral was like, the one he'd not been allowed to attend because it would have been "too traumatic for him." He wished his father was aware of the guilt he suffered because he was on an airplane while others were paying their last respects to his mother. He'd cried all the way to Switzerland.

The photograph of his mother had been taken on the beach in Punta de Mita, and, with an expanse of turquoise water sweeping out behind her, Miguel's mother stood there in her black bikini, smiling broadly for the camera, looking like a glamorous movie star from another era.

"My father loved this picture."

"And what about this one," Sonia said, drifting over to a smaller photograph of father, mother, and baby wrapped in linen and silk. They stood before a sea of candles and stained glass and icons adorning the walls.

"That's my baptism. And the one over there is my first Holy Communion. Then my confirmation later on."

Sonia stared deeply at the pictures of his mother. "She looks like . . . I don't know . . . She just looks strong."

"No one could tell my father what to do. No one but her. She was the boss. I don't think I told you this, but one time we were in Cozumel on vacation, and she was snorkeling. We were looking at this sunken airplane, and she thought something bit her, and then we lost her and she almost drowned. We think she might've hit her head on some coral. My father went in after her, and he pulled her out and gave her mouth-to-mouth and she came around and spit up water, just like you see on TV."

"Wow, that's amazing. He saved her life."

"When she told him that, he just said, 'No, you saved mine.'"

"Your father is a romantic."

"That's true. He told me that night that if she had died, he didn't know what we'd do. He told me he'd be lost. A few months later they found the cancer. It was like the trip was a premonition or something, like God was trying to prepare us for what would happen. But it didn't work."

"That's just . . . I don't know what to say . . ."

He smiled weakly. "Let's go eat."

They did, and their omelets with salsa, jack cheese, cumin, and garlic powder were prepared by his father's private chef, Juan Carlos (aka J.C.), who'd said that Jorge had gone off to the beach for a run and a swim. Alexsi was at the pool, already into her third mimosa, according to J.C.

When they were finished eating, Miguel showed Sonia their workout facility, which she remarked was better equipped than most five-star hotels. He said his father was very dedicated to fitness and did two hours per day, five days per week, with a personal trainer.

"Only soccer for you?" she asked.

"Yeah. Those metal weights are heavy."

She grinned, and they ventured on to the media room, with giant projection TV and seating for twenty-five.

"More like a movie theater," she remarked.

He nodded. "Now I'm taking you to my favorite place in the entire house. He led her to a door, then down two flights of stairs and into the basement. They passed through a hall whose walls contained soundproofing material, and Miguel had to plug in a series of security codes on the electronic lock mounted on the next door. The door clicked open, and the lights ahead automatically flickered to cast reflections off a glistening white marble floor that unfurled for twenty meters. A rich black carpet divided the room in half, and on each side stood imposing metal display cases and display tables whose lights also switched on.

"What is this? Some kind of museum?" she asked, stepping inside, her heels clicking across the marble.

"This is my father's weapons collection. Guns, swords, knives—he likes them all. See that door over there? Just inside is a shooting range. It's pretty cool."

"Wow, look at this. He's got some bows and arrows. Is that a crossbow?" She pointed to the weapon hanging from a peg.

"Yeah, it's, like, hundreds of years old or something. Come over here."

He led her down toward a table where more modern-day handguns and other assorted weapons were on display. There were AR-15 long guns, MP-5 submachine guns, AK-47s that his father called "goat horns," along with dozens of other handguns, some inlaid with diamonds, plated in gold and silver, and engraved with the family name, collectibles that his father said should never be fired.

"These are the ones we like to shoot," he said, gesturing to a row of Berettas, Glocks, and Sig Sauer pistols. "Pick one."

"What?"

He lifted his brows. "I said pick one."

"Are you serious?"

"Have you ever fired a gun?"

"Of course not. Are you crazy? If my father found out . . ."

"We won't tell him."

She winced, bit her lip. *So sexy.* "Miguel, I don't know about this. Won't your father be upset?"

"No way. We come down here all the time," he lied. It'd been a few years since he'd engaged in target practice, but she didn't have to know that.

"Can we fire fake bullets, like in the movies?"

"You're scared?"

"Sort of."

He pulled her in to his chest. "Don't worry. Once you get that feeling of power in your hand, you'll be addicted. It's like a drug."

"I can think of something else I'd rather put in my hand." She wriggled her brows.

He shook his head. "Come on. We're going to be badasses and shoot some guns."

She sighed and chose one of the Berettas. He picked a similar pistol, then crossed to a cabinet, worked the padlock there, and pulled out some of the magazines. He led her to the back door, plugged in the code, and they entered the range, again the lights automatically switching on. He took her to one of the shooting booths, where he loaded both of their pistols, then handed her the headphones and safety glasses.

"Do I have to wear these?" she asked of the ear protection. "They'll mess up my hair."

He started laughing. "What's more important? Your hair or your hearing?"

"All right . . ." She flinched and slowly donned the headphones.

Once they were ready to shoot, he motioned that he'd go first and that she should really pay attention. He demonstrated how to hold the weapon, showed her the safety, and then he fired two rounds into the target, the shots going a little wide. He was rustier than he'd thought.

Then they moved over to her shooting booth. He got behind her, breathing deeply into her hair, and taught her how to hold the pistol. Then, ever so gently, he released her, tapped her on the shoulder, then signaled that she should fire.

She took two shots. Their targets were the silhouettes of men, the type used by military and law enforcement officers. She scored two perfect headshots.

"Whoa!" he cried. "Look at that!"

She glanced at him, dumbfounded. "Beginner's luck, I guess! Let me try again."

She did, flinched, and didn't even hit the target with her third shot.

"Try again," he urged her.

She complied, but this time she closed her eyes and the shot actually hit his target.

With a groan, she placed the gun on the small table in front of her, then wrung her hands. "The gun's getting hot! And that hurt!"

He took off his headphones and glasses, the stench of gunpowder heavy in the air. "Let me see your hand." He took her palm in his own and worked his thumbs into her soft skin. Then she moved in close, wrapped an arm around his shoulders, and pulled herself tightly against him, rubbing her thigh against his crotch.

At that point, she had him. And within three minutes they were on the floor. Her moans echoed throughout the range, and he kept putting a finger to his lips, frightened that his father might've returned from his run to search for them. Castillo would know they were down there. He knew everything and would report to Jorge; however, Castillo would remain discreet in regard to the exact nature of their visit to the shooting range.

He suddenly broke away from her.

She sat up and pouted. "Did I do something wrong?"

"No, it's me."

"Then we should talk?"

"I don't know . . . it's just . . . the fund-raiser, all these people . . . You know everyone my father hires is afraid to get fired, so they kiss our asses. But do they really like us? Maybe they think we're just a couple of fools. They pretend to respect us, pretend to honor us, when behind our backs they curse us."

"That's not true. Think about what your father said last night. He's a good man."

"But most men still fear him."

"Maybe you're mixing up fear with respect."

"Maybe I am, but the kind of power my father has is a scary thing, even to me. I mean, we can never really be alone."

"Your father is using his position to do good in the world. And why are you even thinking about this now?"

He breathed deeply and finally nodded. He felt guilty as he got dressed. He hadn't told her about the hidden security cameras. Their entire escapade had been recorded, because turning off the cameras would've immediately alerted Castillo. There was no privacy at Casa de Rojas, because its price was too steep.

They spent the day at the beach, swimming, taking pictures, and drinking. Even though Sonia wore a blue bikini, a few of the pics reminded him very much of his mother, since that shot in the library had been taken on the very same beach. Even their names were similar—Sofía/Sonia—and he began to place himself in the context of Greek tragedies.

Although they attempted to remain discreet, two of his father's security men were there with them, seated on chairs about ten meters away, with Castillo not straying far from the pool deck to spy on them through a pair of binoculars.

"Those guys work for your father, too," Sonia said, staring at them over the rim of her sunglasses.

"How can you tell?" he asked sarcastically.

"I guess you're used to this, huh?"

"It was nice when we were in Spain. I think my father had some people there, but I didn't know who they were, so I never really noticed them."

She shrugged. "When you have money, some people hate you."

"Of course. Kidnapping is never far from my father's mind. He has friends who've suffered through terrible ordeals when their loved ones were taken. The police are useless. The ransom money is ridiculously high. You either pay or you never see your family again."

"The gangs from the cartels do that all the time."

"I'm sure they'd like nothing more than to kidnap my father and get a huge ransom."

"I don't know, he's so well protected. I doubt that would ever happen. Besides, he travels so much. It's hard to predict where he'll be. He said something about having to pack."

"Yes, he's taking off again."

"Where? The International Space Station?"

He laughed. "Colombia, probably. I heard him talking about seeing the president and maybe some other friends down there. We own some businesses in Bogotá. He's got a friend who makes him special suits."

"My father met the French president once, at the Tour de France, but it's not like he's friends with presidents around the world like your father is."

"You know what?" he began, brightening over a thought. "Maybe we'll do a little traveling ourselves . . ."

Dinner was served promptly at six p.m., and Miguel and Sonia had showered and dressed for the occasion. Miguel had warned Sonia that his father placed great emphasis on family meals, because they were so few and far between. Dinners at home were precious experiences, and they should be treated with the utmost respect.

Since there would be only four, they dined at one of the smaller tables just off the main kitchen, and J.C. prepared a four-course meal of beef and chicken that had become one of the signature experiences at every Sofía's throughout the world.

The family owned sixteen of the exclusive restaurants, all named after his mother, and they served both traditional and fusion Mexican cuisine, embracing all six regions of the country. Their world-renowned dishes were served in an atmosphere that Jorge had said should suggest the great ancient civilizations of Mexico, from the Olmecs to the Aztecs. Colossal sculptures of heads, fish vessels, and ancient masks were just a few of the art pieces hanging in every dining room. Dinner for two at the Sofía's in Dallas, Texas, set back most patrons nearly two hundred dollars—before ordering the wine.

"Sonia, how are you enjoying your stay here?" Jorge asked, after taking a long sip on his mineral water.

"Well, it's just horrible. I feel like I'm being mistreated, and I'm ready to go home. You people are obnoxious, terrible hosts; the food is just disgusting."

Miguel nearly dropped his fork. He turned to her.

She burst out laughing and added, "No, seriously, I'm only kidding. Of course it's incredible."

Jorge finally smiled and turned to Alexsi. "You see? That is a sense of humor. That is what I'm talking about. You are much too lovely and much too serious."

Alexsi smiled and reached for her wine. "Being lovely requires serious work."

"Ah, and clever," Jorge added, then reached over and gave her a kiss.

Miguel sighed and glanced away.

The conversation throughout dinner was focused on Sonia, her experiences at school, what she thought about the government in Spain, and her opinions about the European economy in general. She held her own as his father continued to interrogate her. When the meal was over, and they were leaning back and trying to breathe past their swelling waistlines, Jorge leaned toward the table and hardened his gaze on Miguel.

"Son, I have great news for you. I've been waiting to announce this, but I think this is as good a time as any. You've been accepted for a summer apprenticeship at Banorte."

Miguel was about to frown but held back the reaction. His father was beaming, his eyes full of a wonder Miguel had not seen in years.

An apprenticeship at Banorte? What would they have him doing? Filing financial records? Would he be working in a branch or a corporate office? What was his father trying to do? Ruin his entire summer?

"Miguel . . . what's wrong?"

He swallowed.

"You're not excited. This will be a valuable experience. You can take what you've learned as an undergraduate and put it in action. Theory can only take you so far. You need to work in the field to see how these things operate. And then you'll return to school for your MBA, knowing full well what is happening at the bank. This kind of experience you cannot get any other way."

"Yes, sir."

"You disagree?"

"Uh, I just . . ."

"If you'll excuse me?" asked Sonia, rising from her chair.

Miguel immediately stood and helped her out. "I need to use the bathroom," she added.

"Me, too," said Alexsi, glancing emphatically at Miguel.

Jorge waited until the women left and the servants had finished clearing their plates. Then he gestured that they should venture onto the deck to take in the moonlit ocean.

They stood there at a railing, his father with a drink still in hand, Miguel trying to muster the courage to decline his father's offer.

"Miguel, did you think you were going to run around all summer and do nothing?"

"No, I did not."

"This is a great opportunity."

"I understand."

"But you don't want it."

He sighed and finally faced his father. "I wanted to take Sonia on a vacation."

"But you're just back from Spain."

"I know, but I want to show her *our* country. I was thinking about San Cristóbal de las Casas."

Jorge's expression began to soften, and his gaze drifted past Miguel and to the ocean. San Cristóbal was a place his parents had often visited, one of his mother's favorite cities in all of Mexico. She loved the highlands of Chiapas and used to talk about the twisting streets, the brightly colored houses with their red-tiled roofs, and the green mountains all around. The place was rich in culture and Mayan history.

"I remember the first time I took your mother there . . ." He took another deep breath and could not go on.

"I think Sonia would love it, too."

He nodded. "I'll call them at the bank. You take the helicopter and spend a week there. Then, after that, you will go to work. If you want Sonia to remain here, that's fine, but you will be working."

Miguel drew back his head in shock. "Thank you."

"You'll have an escort while you're there," his father reminded him.

"I understand. But can they remain discreet, like they did in Spain?"

"I'll make that happen. So what do you think of this girl?"

"She's . . . great."

"I think so, too."

"Of course. You found her for me."

"No, not just that. She's very elegant. She would be a magnificent addition to our family."

"Yes, but I don't want to rush anything."

"Of course not."

"Well, we've stopped by for dessert," called Miguel's aunt from the doorway, with Arturo at her shoulder. "Are we too late?"

"Never too late," said Jorge, giving her a kiss, then shaking Arturo's hand.

While they chatted, Castillo was behind him, lifting his chin at Miguel, who shifted over to the man. "Do you need something, Fernando?"

"Yes, I've been trying to watch the monitors with my bad eye—if you know what I mean."

"Thank you very much."

"I wouldn't do that again, though," he said. "Your father would not appreciate it. He would say you are not treating her like a lady."

"Understood. Thank you, Fernando. That was foolish."

"I was young, too. I did things like that."

Miguel placed a hand on the man's shoulder. "You're a good friend." He then drifted back onto the deck, where he caught his father telling Arturo that he can really make a difference and that they should work together to stem the violence in Juárez.

"I'm only the governor, Jorge. There is only so much I can do. The president's policies are not working. They are only causing more violence. I just received another report today about more killings in the city, and just yesterday I received yet another death threat."

"You are the best and the brightest we have. You know what to do. But above all, don't get discouraged. This violence will come to an end. I'll do everything I can to help."

"Jorge, you may have heard this before, but not yet from me. I must add my voice to the others."

"What are you talking about?"

"You should become the next president of Mexico."

Jorge recoiled. "Me?"

"You have the connections and the finances. You could run a remarkable campaign."

Jorge began laughing. "No, no, no. I am a businessman, nothing more."

Miguel studied his father, the look of incredulity on the man's face, with just a hint of guilt in his eyes, as though he was letting everyone down if he didn't run.

"Did you miss me?" Sonia asked, hooking her arm around Miguel's.

He turned to her and whispered, "I did. And I have a surprise for you."

9

CONFIANZA

Bonita Real Hotel
Juárez, Mexico

HE WANTED to choke her while they were having sex because he'd read about erotic asphyxiation and she'd told him that it was a turn-on to be dominated by him.

But when Dante Corrales wrapped both hands around Maria's neck, while she had her heels firmly planted on his shoulders, he got a little too carried away, and by the time he reached orgasm, Maria was no longer moving.

"Maria! Maria!"

He slid her legs aside and dropped to her, putting his ear to her mouth, listening, his own breath ragged, his pulse still racing, growing more rapid as images of Maria's funeral flashed through his mind.

The panic came in a shudder through his shoulders. "Oh my God. Oh my God."

Suddenly, her eyes snapped away. "You fucker! You could have killed me!"

"What the fuck? You were faking it!"

"What did you think? You think I'd be stupid enough to let you kill me? Dante, you need to be careful!"

He smacked her across the face. "You dumb bitch! You scared the shit out of me!"

She smacked him across the face, and his eyes grew wide, his hand balling into a fist, his teeth coming together.

But then she looked at him. And burst out laughing. He grabbed her, draped her over his lap, her tight, shiny ass facing him. He spanked her till her cheeks glowed. "Never do that again! Never!"

"Yes, Daddy. Yes . . ."

Fifteen minutes later, he'd left the hotel, making sure Ignacio at the front desk had things under control. Several small-time dealers were coming in to pick up some product, and he went over the details of the sale.

Corrales had just bought the hotel a few months prior and was in the process of having it completely renovated—paint, carpeting, furniture, everything. He wished his parents could see him now. *"I don't work here,"* he would have told them. *"I own the place."*

The building was only four stories, and they had only about

forty rooms. He intended to make at least ten of them "luxury" suites, within which he would entertain more important clients. He'd had a little trouble finding engineers, since most of the best ones were being employed in the tunneling operations along the border. He found that ironic. The plumbers and drywallers were already on the job. He hired an interior designer from San Diego, and Maria had talked him into bringing on a friend and real estate agent who practiced feng shui so they could get the "energy" aligned in every room. That made Maria happy, so he'd agreed without rolling his eyes.

He drove out along Manuel Gómez Morín, following the wide road along the border until he reached a small neighborhood of town homes whose driveways lay behind tall, wrought-iron gates and whose windows were protected by similar bars. These were newer homes, with tiled roofs and high-end bulletproof touring sedans parked in the driveways. Most residents were members of the cartel or relatives of members. Corrales reached a cul-de-sac, wheeled around, and waited. Finally, Raúl and Pablo appeared from one doorway and hopped into the Escalade, both wearing tailored slacks, shirts, and leather jackets.

"Let's make a statement tonight," said Corrales. "Are the other four assholes ready?"

"Yes," answered Pablo. "No problem."

"That's what you said last time," Corrales reminded him. He was referring to the hotel in Nogales, where they'd gone after the second of Zúñiga's spies, but the man had escaped. They'd dumped the body of the first on the doorstep of a house they knew Zúñiga owned in Nogales, but they hadn't heard anything from the man since. Ernesto Zúñiga, aka "El Matador," had homes in many cities throughout Mexico, and he'd recently built a ranch house in the foothills southwest of Juárez. It was a four-thousand-square-foot residence with a brick-paver driveway and security gates and cameras, as well as men posted outside and throughout the foothills.

There was no sneaking up on the place, and Corrales didn't care about that. The point was for their rival to know they were there—and to send him an unforgettable message.

Corrales had spent the last few years studying Zúñiga, his men, his operation, and his history. You kept your enemies closer than your friends, of course, and Corrales frequently lectured new *sicarios* about how cunning and deadly the Sinaloa Cartel was and continued to be.

Zúñiga himself was the fifty-two-year-old son of a cattle rancher and was born in La Tuna near Badiraguato, Mexico. He'd sold citrus as a kid, and rumor had it that he was growing opium poppy on his father's ranch by the time he was eighteen. Zúñiga's father and uncle helped him get a job working for the Sinaloa Cartel as a truck driver, and he'd spent the better part of his twenties helping to transport marijuana and cocaine to their destinations within Mexico.

By the time he was thirty, he'd impressed his bosses enough to be put in charge of all shipments moving from the Sierra to the cities and border. He was one of the first men to use planes to transport cocaine directly into the United States, and he coordinated all boat arrivals of coke. He began establishing command-and-control centers throughout the country and often engaged in operations to rip off other cartel shipments en route. The Juárez Cartel had been robbed by his men on no less than twelve occasions.

A massive undercover operation in the 1990s, one spearheaded by the Federal Police, left the Sinaloa Cartel without a leader, and Zúñiga easily filled those shoes. He married a nineteen-year-old soap-opera star, and fathered two children with her, but the boys and wife were executed following his theft of two million dollars' worth of Juárez Cartel cocaine. Zúñiga sent a thousand red roses to the funeral but did not appear himself—and that was a smart decision. He would have been summarily executed by Juárez members waiting near the funeral home and church.

Corrales had dreams of launching a military-style attack on Zúñiga's house with rocket-propelled grenades, machine guns, and a Javelin missile that would race upward like a flare, arc higher, then roll to make a top-down strike on the man's roof, obliterating him and his little palace in one burst, like a star exploding. He'd watched that weapon in use on the Discovery Channel.

However, as his superiors pointed out, Corrales's attacks must remain very small in scale, just enough to give Zúñiga pause until they received permission to make a bold move and attack the man head-on. It was also true that if they took Zúñiga alive, they could more easily confiscate his assets and take over his entire smuggling operation by torturing the details out of him. When Corrales had asked why they couldn't attack yet, all he got were vague replies about timing and politics, so he decided to carry out a few small plans of his own.

Corrales drove his men out to the demolition site of an old apartment building, which now lay in heaps of concrete blocks and stucco, with wooden struts jutting up into the night like fangs. They parked, ventured around the first two piles, and found their four new recruits holding two other men at gunpoint. None of the recruits was older than twenty, all wearing baggy pants and T-shirts, two of them heavily tattooed. The two men they were holding were similarly dressed, and both had thick tufts of hair under their lips.

"Great work," said Corrales to the men. "I really thought you'd fuck this up."

One lanky kid with a giraffe's neck shot Corrales the evil eye. "These bitches were easy to catch. You have to give us more credit, you know."

"Is that right?"

"Yeah," spat the punk. "It is."

Corrales walked up to the man, studied him, then asked, "Let me see your gun."

The kid frowned but handed it to Corrales, who abruptly stepped back and shot the asshole in the foot. He gave a blood-curdling cry, and the other three punks visibly trembled. One pissed his pants.

The two guys they had captured started crying as Corrales whirled to face them and groaned, "Shut up." Then he shot each man in the head.

The impact wrenched them back, and they fell, lifeless, onto the dust-caked ground.

Corrales sighed. "All right, let's get to work."

He faced the kid he'd shot in the foot. "It's too bad you have so much attitude. We could've used you."

Corrales raised the pistol, answered by the kid raising his hand and screaming. The gunshot silenced that terrible noise, and Corrales took another deep breath and raised his brows at the others. "Five minutes."

They drove immediately to Zúñiga's place, reached the front gates, and were about to be accosted by two security men who were approaching. Corrales's remaining recruits dragged the bodies of the captured men and dumped them near the gate. Then Corrales hit the gas and drove back down the dirt road, only to slow a moment as the guards called in backup, and four men opened the gates and shifted out to examine the bodies.

Corrales watched them from the rearview mirror, and once they were in close enough, he lifted the remote detonator and thumbed the button.

His men began hollering as the explosion shook the ground, blew off the front gates, and swallowed the security guys in a fireball that rose like a mushroom cloud.

"We told him to keep his men away from the border, or things would get worse," Corrales said, for the benefit of his group. "You see what happens? He doesn't pay attention. Maybe now he will wake up . . ."

At the bottom of the hill, a dark sedan approached, and Corrales slowed, then stopped beside the car, lowering his darkly tinted window. The other driver did likewise, and Corrales smiled at the leonine man with gray hair and thick mustache who was just lowering a walkie-talkie.

"Dante, I thought we had an agreement."

"I'm sorry, Alberto, but you broke your promise, too." Corrales tilted his head back toward the rising smoke on the mountainside. "We caught two more trying to blow one of our tunnels, and they had to be dealt with. You promised me you would help keep them away."

"This I did not know."

"Well, that's a problem. Are your men too afraid to help now? Are they?"

"No. I'll look into this."

"I hope so."

Alberto sighed in frustration. "Look, when you do this, you make it very difficult for me."

"I know, but this is something that will pass."

"You always say that."

"It's always true."

"All right. Go now, before the other units arrive. How many this time?"

"Only two."

"Okay . . ."

Corrales nodded and floored it, kicking up dust in their wake.

Alberto Gómez was an inspector with the Mexican Federal Police with more than twenty-five years of service. For nearly twenty of those years he had been on the payroll of one cartel or another, and as he neared retirement, Corrales had witnessed him grow more cranky and annoyingly cautious. The inspector's usefulness was drawing to an end, but for now Corrales would use the man because he continued to recruit others within his ranks. The Federal Police would help them finally crush the Sinaloa Cartel. It was good public relations for them and good business for the cartel.

"What are we doing now?" asked Pablo.

Corrales looked at him. "A drink to celebrate."

"Can I ask you something?" Raúl began, nervously stroking his thin beard in the backseat.

"What now?" Corrales fired back with a groan.

"You shot that guy. He might've been a good man. He had attitude. But we all did—especially in the beginning. Is something bothering you?"

"What do you mean?"

"I mean, are you, I don't know . . . mad about something?"

"You think I'm taking out some anger on these punks?"

"Maybe."

"Let me tell you something, Raúl. I'm only twenty-four years old, but even I can see it. These punks today lack the respect that our fathers had, the respect that we should still have."

"But you told us that there weren't any more lines, that everyone was fair game: mothers, children, everyone. You said we had to hit them as hard as they hit us."

"That's right."

"Well, then, I guess I'm confused."

"Just shut up, Raúl!" Pablo told him. "You're an idiot. He's saying we have to respect our elders and each other, but not our enemies, right, Dante?"

"We have to respect how deadly our enemies can be."

"And that means we have to rip their hearts out and shove them down their throats," said Pablo. "See?"

"That guy could've been useful," said Raúl. "That's all I'm saying. We could've used a punk with a big mouth."

"A guy like you?" Corrales asked Raúl.

"No, sir."

Corrales studied Raúl in the rearview mirror. His eyes had grown glassy, and he kept flicking his gaze toward the window, as though he wanted to escape.

Now Corrales lifted his voice. "Raúl, I'll tell you something . . . a guy like that cannot be trusted. If he mouths off to his boss, you know he's always thinking about himself first."

Raúl nodded.

And Corrales let his statement hang. The punk he'd shot was indeed a lot like him—

Because he, too, could not be trusted. He would never forget that while he worked for this cartel, his parents' blood was still on their hands.

10

INDOC AND BUD/S

Naval Special Warfare Center
Coronado, California

O N A COLD NIGHT in October 1994, Maxwell Steven
Moore was lying on his bunk in the special warfare barracks, a few seconds away from becoming a quitter at
a place where men never said "quit." In fact, if the word took
root in your psyche, then you weren't a Navy SEAL in the first
place. Getting through BUD/S (Basic Underwater Demolition/
SEAL) training would forever change the eighteen-year-old's
life. It had meant everything to him.

But he couldn't go on.

The journey had started nearly two months prior when
he'd arrived at the Naval Special Warfare Center to begin the
INDOC course. The class's proctor, the leather-faced Jack
Killian, whose eyes were too narrow to read and whose shoul-

ders seemed molded into a singular piece of muscle, had addressed Moore's class with an oft-heard question at Coronado: "So I heard you boys want to be Frogmen?"

"Hooyah!" they responded in unison.

"Well, you'll have to get through me first. Drop!"

Moore and the rest of class 198, some 123 candidates in all, hit the beach and began their push-ups. Since they were still only candidates, they were not yet permitted to exercise on the hallowed blacktop square of the BUD/S "grinder," where only those who'd made it through INDOC could perform their calisthenics and other assorted forms of physical torture that were part of BUD/S training First Phase—seven weeks designed to test a man's physical conditioning, water competency, commitment to teamwork, and mental tenacity. No man would begin First Phase without passing the two-week-long INDOC course. The initial endurance test included the following:

> A five-hundred-yard swim using breaststroke and/or sidestroke in less than twelve minutes and thirty seconds
> A minimum of forty-two push-ups in two minutes
> A minimum of fifty sit-ups in two minutes
> A minimum of six dead-hang pull-ups (no time limit)
> A run for 1.5 miles wearing long pants and boots in less than eleven minutes

While Moore's upper-body strength still needed work, he excelled in both the swim and the run, routinely beating his classmates by wide margins. It was during this time that Moore was introduced to the concept of a "swim buddy" and the tenet that you never leave your swim buddy alone and that no man, alive or dead, is ever left behind. "You will never be alone. Ever," Killian had told them. "If you ever leave your swim buddy, the punishment will be severe. Severe!"

Moore's swim buddy was Frank Carmichael, a sandy-haired, blue-eyed kid easily mistaken for a surfer dude. He had an easy grin and spoke in a laid-back cadence that had Moore doubting this guy could ever become a SEAL. Carmichael had grown up in San Diego and had traveled a similar path to INDOC as Moore had, going to boot camp, then being recommended for the SEAL program. He said he wished he'd gone to Annapolis and become a member of the Canoe Club, the nickname given to the Naval Academy, but he'd goofed off too much at Morse High School and his grades weren't competitive enough for admission. He hadn't even bothered getting into JROTC. There were a number of other candidates who were officers—Annapolis graduates, guys who'd come out of Officer Candidate School as O-1 ensigns, and even those who'd served in the fleet for a while. BUD/S, however, leveled the playing field—every candidate had to pass the same tests, no special treatment for officers.

Moore and Carmichael hit it off immediately, middle-class guys who were trying to do something extraordinary with their lives. They suffered together through the four-mile beach runs they had to complete in less than thirty-two minutes. Killian seemed to punctuate every command with the phrase "Get wet and sandy." The entire class would rush down into the freezing surf, come out, roll around in the sand, then, standing there like mummies, like the undead, they'd be sent into their next evolution. They learned immediately that you ran everywhere, including a mile each way to the chow hall.

This was 1994, the year *Time* magazine described the Internet as a "strange new world." Moore griped that today's candidates could get on the Web and learn ten times as much about their upcoming training than Moore could back in those days. Today's crop could review websites dedicated to BUD/S, watch streaming videos and slickly produced Discovery Channel specials. All Moore and his buddies had had were the tall tales passed on from previous classes, the rumors and warnings about the unspeakable horrors to come posted on a few newsgroups. Hyperbole? In some cases, yes, but Moore and Carmichael had faced their challenges with hardly as much preparation as the current group did.

Of all the training evolutions they went through during INDOC, Moore enjoyed the swimming work the most. They taught him how to kick, stroke, and glide, and to, above all, make the water his home. This was where the SEALs excelled over other branches of the service. The intel they gathered by being stealthy in the water assisted Marines and many other combatants. He learned to tie complex naval knots while submerged and did not panic when his hands were bound behind his back during the drown-proofing test. He relaxed, swam up to the surface, took his breath, came back down, and repeated the process, while several members of the Canoe Club near him freaked out and DORed right there. Moore's reaction to that was to demonstrate just the opposite to his instructors, who were floating around him in their scuba gear, waiting for him to panic. He lowered himself to the bottom of the pool and held his breath—

For nearly five minutes.

One instructor came up to him with bug eyes enlarged by his mask and motioned for Moore to get back to the surface. He smiled, waited a few seconds more, then swam up and took his breath. He'd learned to increase his anaerobic tolerance by doing running and swim sprints, and he'd felt certain he could hold his breath even longer than that.

Killian learned of the "stunt," and warned Moore not to try that again. But he'd winked when he'd said it.

The underwater fifty-meter swim proved interesting for many guys. Killian concluded his description of the test with the following: "And don't worry—when you pass out, we will revive you." But Moore did the fifty meters and then some, gliding through the water as though he'd always belonged there, a Frogman through and through. Carmichael told him that even a few of the instructors had cursed in awe.

Moore's natural gifts had been discovered by Mr. Loengard when Moore was just sixteen. Loengard was not only a high school gym teacher but also an avid cyclist. He asked Moore to take a test on a cycle ergometer and found that Moore had a VO_2 max of 88.0, which was comparable to many world-class athletes. Moore's resting heart rate was barely 40 bpm. His body could transport and use oxygen much more efficiently than the average person's, and this, said Loengard, was a genetic gift that made him a very lucky individual. And that's when Loengard began to talk to Moore about the military, specifically the SEALs. Ironically, the man had never been in the Navy himself, nor had any of his relatives. He simply admired and respected military personnel and their commitment to the country.

When Moore and his INDOC classmates weren't in the pool, they were back to the beach, the surf, the grit in every orifice of his body. Even the high-pressure, ice-cold showers back at the barracks could not wash out all the sand. The Navy wanted him and the others to literally become one with the beach and the Pacific.

With Carmichael always at his side, they would lie on their backs, legs out, toes pointed, and perform dozens of flutter kicks without allowing their feet to touch the beach. The goal was to move their legs up and down about eight to twelve inches. Everything they did as SEALs would require strong abdominal muscles, and Killian, along with his fellow instructors, had an obsessive-compulsive fascination with exercises like the flutter kick that turned Moore's abs into rails of steel. He continued to work on his upper body as well, because Killian kept warning him about week number two, but he wouldn't say what they'd face.

By the end of the first week, sixteen guys had already dropped from the class. They seemed to have just packed their bags in the middle of the night and left. Moore and Carmichael had not seen them and barely discussed the DORs in an effort to remain strong and positive.

It was 0500 on the first day of the second week that class 198 bade a resigned hello to the O-course, or obstacle course, a gauntlet through hell designed by evil-minded men to welcome others into their most private and elite club.

Twenty obstacles labeled with signs had been erected on the beach, and as Moore's gaze panned over them, each contraption appeared more complicated and challenging than the last. Killian approached Moore and Carmichael. "You gentlemen have twelve minutes to get through my O-course."

"Hooyah!" they cried. Moore took off in the lead, running toward the first obstacle, the parallel bars. He hoisted himself up and used his hands to walk across the steel, his shoulders and triceps on fire by the time he hit the sand on the other side. Already out of breath, he made a quick right turn, lifted his arms over his head, and hopped his way through the truck tires (about five wide, ten deep) and toward the low wall. There were two ascending stumps he used—right foot, left foot—then with a groan he launched himself onto the top of the wooden wall and swung himself over the side, hitting the sand much harder than he'd thought he would. With his ankle stinging, he jogged over to the high wall, maybe twelve feet, but it could have been fifty at this point. He seized one of the ropes and began to haul himself up, the rope digging sharply into his palms.

At the course's start, Killian was barking orders and/or corrections, but it was hard to hear him. Moore's breath and drumming heart led him over to the concertina wire lying across a series of logs, beneath which were two long furrows. He plunged into the first ditch on his left and crawled on his hands and knees beneath the wire. For just a second he thought his shirt had caught on one of the barbs, but it was just hung up on the wood. With a sigh of relief, he finished breaching the obstacle, got to his feet, and muttered an *Oh, shit*.

The cargo net was fastened between two poles that rose to at least forty feet. Moore immediately determined that the net would be more stable near the pole, as opposed to in the middle, so he mounted it near the pole and began his rapid ascent.

"You got it, buddy," Carmichael said, coming up just behind him.

Looking down was a mistake, as he realized there were no safety measures, and as he came over the top, he began to grow dizzy. He couldn't wait to get to the bottom, and he began to rush down the net. And that's when he missed a rung, slipped, and plunged a half-dozen feet until he miraculously caught hold and broke his descent. The entire class had gasped at that, then hooyahed as he recovered and reached the bottom.

He and Carmichael charged doggedly toward the next bit of fun, the balance logs. The name said it all. If they fell off, Killian would make them work off the mistake in push-ups. Moore tensed and glided across the first log, made a short left turn, then headed back on a straight course down the next one, dumbfounded that he didn't actually fall. Carmichael was right on his heels as they hit the hooyah logs, an obstacle made of six logs stacked and bound in a pyramid. With palms clasped behind their heads, they ran up and over the pyramid, then crossed over to the transfer rope. At this point, Moore's cardio endurance was still holding up strong, but Carmichael's breath was nearly gone, his heart rate clearly in the red zone.

"We got this; come on," he urged his buddy, then took up the first rope, climbed about six feet, then swung over, caught a metal rung with one hand, released the first rope, and then swung himself again to transfer to the second rope. Down he went. Carmichael took an extra swing to reach the rung, but he made it nonetheless.

The next challenge was referred to by the sign as the Dirty Name, and one look at it told Moore why: It comprised three *n*-shaped structures made of logs, two shorter *n*'s sitting side by side so that two lines of candidates could tackle the obstacle at the same time. The longer, taller *n*-shaped barrier stood in the back. Moore ran to the log seated before the *n*, leapt onto the first log, and pulled himself up. Then he stood on that one and leapt across to the taller one to repeat the process, swinging around by hooking his legs over the log. The impact on the second log made him utter the notorious dirty name, as did the impact as he hit the dirt.

Another pyramid of hooyah logs waited for him, this one built with ten logs instead of six—steeper and taller. As he came over the top, his boot gave way, and he crashed face-first into the dirt. Before he knew what was happening, he was being hauled to his feet.

Carmichael, bug-eyed, screamed in his face, "Let's go!" Then turned and ran.

Moore set off after him.

What resembled a pair of giant ladders lying at forty-five-degree angles stood in their way. Killian was shouting at them, "This is the Weaver! You weave in and out of the poles!" Moore clung to the first pole, hurled himself around, swung onto the next, and continued the process, like a needle and thread, sewing himself up and down through the poles, growing dizzy as he did so. Carmichael worked the obstacle beside him and was down the forty-five-degree backside a few seconds before he was.

The rope bridge, better known as the Burma Bridge, was a single piece of thick rope on the bottom, with support lines attached to form a *v*-shape. Carmichael had already climbed to the top of the bridge and was out on the rope. Moore took his first step on the single piece of braided line and realized the best place to step was on the sections where the support lines were tied. He moved from knot to knot, the bridge swinging as Carmichael finished his crossing and Moore came up behind him. By the time he reached the end, he'd felt a sense of rhythm that he vowed not to forget for the next time he hit the obstacle.

He and Carmichael ascended one more ten-log pyramid of hooyah logs, then approached the towering platform of the Slide for Life, a four-story affair that had them swinging up onto each platform (no ropes or use of the ladder) until they reached the top. There were two ways to take the obstacle: go to the top and then work your way down the ropes strung at about forty-five-degree angles from there, or simply go to the first platform and work the low ropes, which Killian was saying would burn the forearms but was less dangerous. First time around, though, he wanted them to go to the very top. Once there, Carmichael grabbed the left rope and Moore grasped the right. He leaned forward, hooked his right leg back over the line, and then, with the rope between his legs, he slid down face-forward, using both hands to draw himself across the line. He wasn't even halfway down when all points making contact with the rope began to burn. He beat Carmichael to the bottom, hit the ground, gaining about two seconds on his buddy, then launched himself toward the rope swing that would take him to a log cross, a set of monkey bars, and then one more beam. He seized the rope, hauled himself forward, and missed the log. Carmichael, on the other hand, ran past the rope, grabbed it, then pendulumed himself easily onto the log. Moore did likewise on his second attempt, but now Carmichael was back in the lead.

After navigating a second bed of tires, they reached a five-foot-tall incline wall they hit from the back side and slid down the front. That led them to the Spider Wall, which was about eighteen feet high, with pieces of wood bolted onto its side in two stair-step patterns to form a very narrow ladder. It was all fingertips and toes moving along the stairs to reach the top; then Moore had to shift down sideways, all the while clinging closely to the wall like a spider. With hands still burning from the rope slide, Moore lost his grip on the very last step but hopped off the wall before he fell.

Meanwhile, Carmichael's boot caught one of the wooden steps at a bad angle. He fell and had to start over, losing precious time.

With only a single obstacle and sprint left, Moore dashed on toward the set of five logs lying on their sides and suspended to about hip height. The logs were spaced about six feet apart, and the entire contraption was called the Vault.

"Don't let your legs touch!" Killian warned them. "Only hands!"

Well, that drew a few inward curses as he slapped his palms on the first log and hauled his leg over. Again. And again. Carmichael was just behind him. Moore slipped on the very last log and banged his knee hard. He went down, groaning in pain. Carmichael arrived, dragged him back to his feet, grabbed Moore's arm, and threw it over his shoulder. Together, they finished the sprint (more a fast limping march) to the end.

"You, Carmichael, did the right thing," said Killian. "I saw you guys racing, but you did not leave your swim buddy behind. Not a bad first time." He regarded Moore with a frown. "How's the leg?"

The leg was beginning to swell like a grapefruit. Moore ignored the pain and shouted, "The leg is fine, Instructor Killian!"

"Good, get down to the beach and get wet!"

The O-course was just one of many more evolutions they faced, and even when they weren't training and simply trying to get their barracks ready for inspection, the instructors would come in and tear apart their rooms, testing to see how they handled the setbacks. Moore hung on through it all, through the final part of INDOC, where they trained with their IBSs (Inflatable Boat, Small). The boats were thirteen feet long and weighed about 180 pounds. Working in seven-man boat teams, the crews learned how to paddle, how to "dump" the boat by flipping it over, and how to carry the heavy bitch on their heads. They were told that once they were in BUD/S, they went everywhere with their boat. They engaged in a series of races, and even did push-ups with their boots up on the rubber gunwales. Carmichael, despite being somewhat lanky, was a remarkable paddler, and with his help, their crew often won races. Winners got to rest. Losers dropped to the beach for push-ups. All of them were taught how to read the surf and when to make a mad dash into it so they could get their boat past the breakers before it capsized.

By the end of the second week, twenty-seven men from Moore's class had dropped. They were good men who'd chosen something else. That's what Killian told them in a warning tone that implied the DORs were not to be mocked.

But the fact remained that they would not receive their Naval Special Warfare Classification (NEC) Code, a great honor but proof positive that an operator had survived the ultimate test of one's physical and mental motivation. A sign at the center reminded them all of the SEALs' motto: "The Only Easy Day Was Yesterday."

At their final briefing of INDOC, Killian gave Moore a firm handshake and said, "You got a lot of talent. I want you to make a name for yourself. And don't you forget—you're one of *my* recruits. Do me proud."

"Hooyah!"

Moore and Carmichael sang to themselves while they moved their gear into the Naval Special Warfare barracks. They weren't visitors anymore. They were real candidates.

The jubilation didn't last long.

Thirty-one guys dropped in the first hour of BUD/S. They rang the bell outside the CO's office, then placed their green helmets with white class number in a neat row outside his door.

In that initial hour, the instructors had wrought sheer chaos on the group with repeated wet and sandy evolutions, followed by huge workouts on the grinder, followed by men throwing themselves into rubber boats filled with ice water. Guys were shaking, crying, suffering hypothermia, passing out.

The instructors were just getting started.

Four-mile runs on the beach were frequent and brutal. Seven-man teams were introduced to the new evolution of log PT. The eight-foot-long log weighed about 160 pounds, but some logs were a little lighter, some a lot heavier. Teams were stuck with the one they could grab first. They dragged the log into the surf, got it wet and sandy, carried it around, marched miles with it, and all the while they were being checked, scolded, and harassed by their instructors, especially the shorter guys, who could more easily dump their load on the taller ones. Moore and Carmichael hung on and were even able to keep their log from falling when, during one evolution, the man at the back of their team had lost his balance and fallen into the surf.

Nine more men dropped by the end of the first week. Class 198 had 56. The line of helmets outside the CO's door had grown at an alarming rate, and Moore gazed on it every day with equal parts determination and foreboding.

It was during breakfast at the end of the first week that Carmichael said something that resonated deeply within Moore: "Those guys that dropped? I think I know what tipped them over the edge."

"What do you mean?"

"I mean, one minute they're in it, hard-core, the next they're out. Like McAllen, for example. Good guy. No way would he drop. He had no intention of quitting, and then the next minute he's running up the beach to ring the bell."

"So you know why he quit?" Moore asked, with a dubious look.

Carmichael nodded. "I know why they all quit—because they didn't take it one hour, one evolution at a time. They started thinking too much about the future and how many more days they had to suffer, and that drove them over the edge."

Moore sighed. "You could be right."

During week three the class was introduced to rock portage, an evolution that had them landing their inflatable boats on an outcropping of rocks. The surf was beating down on the stones like a heavy-metal drummer, the spray shooting into their eyes, as Carmichael got out with the painter tied around his waist. He got up on the rocks, found good purchase with his boots, then leaned forward to be sure the boat didn't slip back into the ocean. It was Moore's job to grab the team's paddles, jump out, swim onto the rocks, climb out of the surf, and store their paddles on dry ground. After he'd climbed out, the others followed, each man trying to haul himself out of the rising and falling water, waves slapping at their faces.

Then Carmichael shouted that he was moving up, and Moore raced back to help him guide the boat up and over the rocks, as the others finally came out of the surf to assist.

When they were finished, they all stood there up on the outcropping, gasping for breath, the wind whipping the seawater from their faces as their instructor shook his head and shouted, "Way too slow!"

Fourth-week assessment was a painful time for both the men and the instructors. Guys who'd stuck it out, tried their best, would not drop, ever, had to be cut from the class because they simply lacked some of the physical qualifications necessary: the stamina, endurance, times on the O-course, and so on. These were men who truly had the hearts and souls of Navy SEALs, but their bodies could not carry the burdens of the position.

Moore and his swim buddy Carmichael survived those fourth-week tests and were preparing themselves for the notorious, the legendary, the dreaded Hell Week, five and one-half days of continuous training evolutions, during which time they were allowed a total of only four hours sleep. Not four hours of sleep per day but four hours of sleep over the entire five days. Moore wasn't even sure that the human body could remain awake for that long, but he'd been assured by his proctor and instructors that "most" of them would manage.

Moore was chosen as a team leader for his continued and exemplary prowess in the water and during the runs. He'd already proven he could hold his breath longer than anyone else in his class, could swim harder and run faster. On the Sunday afternoon before Hell Week was to begin, they all waited inside one of the classrooms, locked down. They were fed pizza and pasta, hamburgers and hot dogs, Cokes. They watched some old Steven Seagal films on videotape and tried to relax.

At about 2300 someone kicked in the classroom door, the lights went off, and gunfire popped and banged everywhere. The "breakout" had begun—simulated combat chaos. Moore hit the deck, trying to convince himself that despite the racket, those men were firing blanks. One instructor had a fifty-caliber machine gun, and the weapon was thundering so loudly that Moore could barely hear a second instructor yelling, "Hear the whistle? Hear the whistle? Crawl toward the whistle!" He and Carmichael did, making it out of the room and out onto the grinder, where they were hit with fire hoses for fifteen minutes and given no orders. All they could do was raise their hands to shield their eyes and try to run out of the blast. Finally they were ordered down to the surf. Instructors continued firing guns, and Moore saw that there must have been more than two dozen instructors brought in to help challenge them for Hell Week.

You must have a never-quit attitude, he told himself. *Never quit.*

The evolutions came fast and furious: workouts in the surf followed by log PT, and they were even tasked with carrying their boat as a team across the O-course. They faced repeated drills of rock portage, followed by carrying their boats to chow after nearly ten hours of hard work on the very first day.

Because they were too excited to sleep the day before, and they had trained throughout the night, by morning of the first day sleep deprivation was already taking its toll. Moore's brain had become fuzzy. He'd call out for Instructor Killian, and Carmichael would remind him that they weren't in INDOC anymore, that this was the real deal, it's Hell Week. They were all heavy-eyed, saying things that made no sense, having weird conversations with ghosts in their heads.

This was a major problem, especially for team leaders who had to pay close attention to their instructors—because the instructors would deliberately leave out directions for a task to see if team leaders were still on the ball. If team leaders caught the error and brought it to the attention of their instructors, their team's task could become much easier—or they might even be allowed to skip the task altogether.

But Moore had been too exhausted, ready to pass out, and certainly not ready to carry a heavy log with the rest of his team.

"Grab your logs and get ready!" came the order.

Most of the men rushed back to their logs, but several team leaders remained behind. Moore was not one of them. Over his shoulder, he heard one of the other team leaders say, "Instructor, don't you mean you want us to grab our logs and get them wet and sandy?"

"Yes, I do! Your team sits this one out."

Moore's shoulders sank. He'd screwed up, and the entire team would pay for his mistake.

That evening, during a rare one hour and forty-five minutes of rest, Moore draped an arm over his eyes. Carmichael had been right. Moore couldn't stop thinking about all the pain and suffering to come and the pressure of being responsible for the others. They'd given him a leadership position, and he'd failed.

"Hey, bro," came a voice from the darkness.

He removed his arm and saw Carmichael leaning over him. "You fucked up. So what."

"You were right. I'm ready to quit."

"No, you're not."

"I failed. Let me quit now so I don't drag down the rest of the team. I'm making it harder for all of us."

"Maybe we needed to carry the log."

"Yeah, right."

Carmichael's eyes grew wider. "Here's the deal. Our training will be even harder than everyone else's. When we get through this, we got bragging rights to say we took on every challenge, and we did 'em the hardest way possible. We weren't looking for the easy way out. We're the best team."

"They haven't said it, but I know the other guys are blaming me for this."

"I talked to them. They're not. They're as strung-out as you are. We're all zombies, man, so get over it."

Moore lay there, just breathing a moment, then said, "I don't know."

"Listen to me. You keep paying attention—but even if the instructor leaves out an order, don't say anything."

Moore shivered. "You're crazy, man. We won't survive."

And Moore wasn't kidding. It was the end of the first day of training, and more than half the guys were gone.

Carmichael's voice grew more stern. "We'll make a bold statement. A few weeks ago they asked us to commit to the warrior's life. You remember that?"

"Yeah."

"We came to fight. And we're going to show them how hard we can fight. Are you with me?"

Moore bit his lip.

"Don't you remember the quote they told us? We can only be beaten in two ways: We either die or we give up. And we're not giving up."

"Okay."

"Then let's do this!"

Moore balled his hands into fists and sat up in his bunk. He looked at Carmichael, whose bloodshot eyes, battered and sunburned face, blistered hands, and scab-covered head mirrored his own. However, Carmichael still had a fire in those eyes, and Moore decided right then and there that his swim buddy was right, had always been right. One evolution at a time. No easy way out. No easy day.

Moore took a long breath. "I screwed up. It doesn't matter. We're not taking the breaks. We're kicking ass and taking names. Let's rock-and-roll."

And by God they did, crawling under barbed wire on the O-course with simulated charges going off and smoke pouring in from everywhere.

Covered in mud, his heart filled with sheer terror, Moore talked himself through it. He would not give up.

Then the time came when the instructor left out a command prior to one of their four-mile runs. The other team leaders caught it.

"Missed it again, Moore?" cried the instructor.

"No, I did not!"

"Then why didn't you say anything?"

"Because this team is not looking for a free pass! This team came here to fight harder than any other team! This team has the heart to do so!"

"Dear God, son, that's impressive. That takes courage. You've just doomed your entire team."

"No, Master Chief, I have not!"

"Then go show me!"

They charged off with their team. It was the fifth day of

Hell Week, the last, and they were running on four hours of sleep, running on a sense of sheer willpower none of them knew they possessed until now.

In fact, the intestinal fortitude displayed by Moore and his team was awe-inspiring, he later heard. They powered their way through more runs, rock portages at night, an "around the world" paddle covering the north end of the island and then back to San Diego Bay and the amphibious base. They cast themselves into the scummy muck of the demo pits and clawed their way out, looking like brown mannequins with flashing eyes.

"In the unlikely event you actually make it through the next two days, there will be a nice meal waiting for you," shouted one of the instructors.

"We got one day left!" cried Moore.

"No, you've got two."

The instructors were lying to them, messing with their minds, but Moore didn't care.

They were held in the freezing-cold surf until they were mere minutes away from hypothermia. They were pulled out, given warm soup, then tossed back in. Guys passed out, were revived, and returned to the water. Moore and Carmichael did not falter.

When the final hour arrived, when Moore and Carmichael and their classmates felt as close to death as ever, they were ordered to haul themselves from the Pacific and roll themselves in the sand. Then came a cry from their proctor to gather around. And once they were huddled up, he nodded slowly.

"Everyone, look around the beach! Look to your left. Look

to your right. You are class 198. You are the warriors who've survived because of your teamwork. For class 198, Hell Week is secured!"

Moore and Carmichael fell to their knees, both teary-eyed, and Moore had never felt more exhausted, more emotionally overwhelmed, in his life. The hooting, hollering, and hooyahing that came from just twenty-six men sounded like a hundred thousand Romans ready to attack.

"Frank, buddy, I owe you big-time."

Carmichael choked up. "You owe me nothing."

They burst out laughing, and the joy, the pure unadulterated joy that he'd actually made it, swelled in Moore's heart and sent chills rushing up his back. He thought he might collapse as the world tipped on its axis, but that was only Carmichael helping him to his feet.

Later, Moore became class 198's Honor Man because of his ability to inspire his classmates to keep on going when they were ready to quit. Carmichael had taught him how to do that, and when he told his swim buddy that it was *he* who should've been named Honor Man, Carmichael just smiled. "You're the toughest guy here. Watching you got me through it."

11

JOINT TASK FORCE JUÁREZ

DEA Office of Diversion Control
San Diego, California
Present Day

B Y THE TIME Moore exited the 15, drove down Balboa, and reached the DEA office on Viewridge Avenue, he was already twenty minutes late for the meeting. His hair hung in his eyes, and his beard still reached down to his clavicle—two years' worth of growth that would soon come off, and thankfully so, as a few gray hairs had appeared near his chin. As he navigated down the long hall toward the conference room, he stole a quick look at his Dockers, the fabric now a relief map of wrinkles. That he'd spilled coffee down his shirt didn't help. He'd blame that on the lady with the three kids who'd failed to note that the enormous cement truck in front of her was rapidly slowing. She'd braked hard, so had Moore, and his coffee obeyed the laws of physics. While his appearance did bother him, it wasn't on the forefront of his mind.

A new e-mail from Leslie Hollander contained a cell phone picture of her terrific smile, and Moore had difficulty purging that image as he simply opened the door and barged into the room.

Heads turned to him.

He sighed. "Sorry I'm late. I've been in the boonies on piggyback tours. I'd forgotten about the traffic around here."

A small group manned the sides along a conference table the length of an aircraft carrier. The table looked long enough to support a steel-deck picnic, touch-and-go landings, and maybe a couple of Harriers. Five individuals had clustered chairs near the head, and a man with a crew cut, his hair glistening like steel shavings under the fluorescent lights, turned away from a dry-erase board, where he'd been writing his name: Henry Towers.

"What do we have here?" asked Towers, using his marker to point out an empty chair. "Are you man? Or beast?"

Moore cracked a grin. The hair and beard did suggest that he'd spent the night in a refrigerator box. With a little grooming, though, Moore would be back to his old self, and it'd be nice to actually feel his cheeks again. He drew back his head. "Where's Polk? They told me the NCS would be heading up this task force."

"Polk's out, I'm in," snapped Towers. "You guys just got lucky, I guess."

"And who are you?" Moore asked, shifting around the table, a portfolio in one hand, his coffee in the other.

Towers eyed him with a crooked grin. "Not much of a reader, are you?"

A lean Hispanic man who had to be Ansara (based on the picture and profile Moore had reviewed) turned to Moore and began laughing. "Relax, bro, he's done this to all of us. He's cool. Just trying to lighten the mood a little."

"That's right, I'm cool," said Towers. "We need to loosen up around here—because what we're about to do will be tense. Very tense."

"What agency are you from?" Moore asked.

"BORTAC. You know what that is?"

Moore nodded. The U.S. Border Patrol Tactical Unit (BOR-TAC) was the global special response team for the Department of Homeland Security's (DHS) Bureau of Customs and Border Protection (CBP). BORTAC agents deployed in more than twenty-eight countries around the world to respond to terrorist threats of all types. Their weapons and gear were comparable to those of SEALs, Army Special Forces, Marine Corps Force Recon, and other special operations units. BORTAC teams worked alongside military units in Iraq and Afghanistan to help find, confiscate, and destroy opium and other drugs being smuggled across the border. They had earned an excellent reputation in the special operations community, and Moore had on several occasions shared intelligence with BORTAC operators who exhibited the highest level of professionalism.

The unit was founded in 1984, and within three years it was already engaged in counter-narcotics operations in South America during Operation Snowcap between 1987 and 1994.

BORTAC agents were tasked with helping to disrupt the growing, processing, and smuggling of cocaine in a long list of countries, including Guatemala, Panama, Colombia, Ecuador, and Peru. Agents worked alongside the DEA and the U.S. Coast Guard's Interdiction Assist Team.

In more recent years, BORTAC teams had taken on a broader array of responsibilities, to include Tactical Relief Operations (TRO) during hurricanes, floods, earthquakes, and other natural disasters. They provided personnel support, equipment assistance, and training to local law enforcement agencies.

Moore would later learn that Towers had more than twenty-five years with BORTAC. He'd been deployed in Los Angeles during the riots that had broken out in the wake of the Rodney King trial. He'd also participated in Operation Reunion, in which BORTAC raided a home in Miami, Florida, in order to safely return refugee Elián González to his father in Cuba. Following the World Trade Center attack, Towers was sent overseas to assist Army Special Forces personnel during some of the first attacks in Afghanistan. In 2002, he worked with the United States Secret Service to secure sports venues at the Salt Lake City Winter Olympic Games.

"I head up the San Diego sector," Towers went on. "But the deputy commissioner wanted me to work with you gorillas for this operation. In my humble opinion, I'm uniquely suited for this job because our mission involves both exposing and dismantling the Juárez Drug Cartel and exposing their relationship with Middle Eastern terrorists, which I'll remind you is Mr. Moore's area of expertise."

"Reporting for duty as ordered—*sir*," Moore said with a mock scowl.

"Now you're playing along," Towers said with a genuine smile. "Welcome to Joint Task Force Juárez. And as a matter of fact, I've been asked to make you our field team leader."

Moore chuckled under his breath. "What crazy drunk suggested that?"

"Your boss."

That drew some laughs from the table.

"All right, team, in all seriousness, we've got a lot to cover here. I heard you guys love PowerPoint presentations, so I've got a few of them. Just give me a minute to load them up."

Ansara groaned and turned to Moore. "Good to meet you. They didn't put much in your file."

"They never do. Just your friendly neighborhood spook is all I am."

"And you were a Navy SEAL."

"With a little help from my friends."

"You've been doing some good work over in Afghanistan and Pakistan. Not sure I'd last five minutes."

Moore smiled. "Maybe ten."

Ansara was a damned fine FBI agent with numerous successful operations under his belt. More recently, he'd been performing recon operations in Sequoia National Park, where the cartels were growing marijuana and where he'd been tracking the *sicario* who'd murdered one of his associates. He was, in Moore's estimation, a bit too handsome for his own good, but his welcoming smile and tone suggested they'd become friends.

Seated beside him was Gloria Vega, a thirty-two-year-old CIA agent like Moore who would be embedded with the Mexican Federal Police. She was a broad-shouldered, no-nonsense Hispanic woman with black hair pulled tightly into a bun. According to a few of Moore's colleagues, she was appreciated and feared because of her exacting nature and utter dedication to the job. She was a single woman and an only child whose parents had already died. The Agency was her life. Period. Her scrutinizing glance when Moore had entered was probably just the beginning of her interrogation of him. That the Federal Police were aiding and abetting the cartels in Mexico was old news; that an American CIA agent would be working alongside them would be as dangerous as it might be enlightening. The NCS had been working directly with Federal Police authorities to establish a relationship that would grant Vega full access while also protecting her identity. That sounded fine in theory; however, Ms. Vega was being dropped into a pit of rattlers, and Moore was glad he didn't have her job.

The man seated across from her was David Whittaker, a special agent with the Bureau of Alcohol, Tobacco, Firearms, and Explosives (ATF). He had thinning gray hair combed straight back, a graying goatee, and wire-frame glasses. He wore a blue polo shirt with his agency's patch on the breast and a badge hung loosely from a chain around his neck. He rose from his chair to hand Towers a USB key, which probably contained his own presentation. According to his file, Whittaker had been working for several years on the cartels' gun-smuggling operations and had more recently helped organize ten-member teams based in seven border cities to address the problem. The cartels were recruiting "straw buyers" in the United States, who made purchases of firearms on their behalf and then paid people to bring the weapons across the border. In one of his reports, Whittaker noted that the Juárez Cartel had created an elaborate network based in (of all places) Minnesota to have weapons smuggled down into Mexico. Because law enforcement efforts had been doubled and redoubled in states such as California, Texas, and Arizona, the cartels had resorted to more extreme measures and remote locations to serve as hubs for transport. Whittaker's contacts also led him to believe that military-grade weapons from Russia were being smuggled up through South America. Going after the cartels' gun-smuggling operations was at least as difficult, dangerous, and frustrating as was trying to bring down their drug operations, and Whittaker's report ended on an ominous note: He wasn't sure the cartels could ever be stopped, only delayed, slowed, temporarily dismantled . . .

Moore caught the gaze of the man near the head of the table, Thomas Fitzpatrick, who, despite his surname, could easily pass for a Mexican *sicario*. His father was half Irish, half Guatemalan, and his mother was Mexican. He'd been born and raised in the United States and been recruited out of community college to join the DEA. Eighteen months ago he'd been sent into Mexico to penetrate the Juárez Cartel, but as happenstance would have it, he'd more easily penetrated and become a trusted member of the Sinaloas. He worked for a man named Luis Torres, who was Zúñiga's right hand and head of his enforcer gang.

Fitzpatrick, whose sinewy arms were covered in tattoos depicting Catholic imagery and whose head was shaven, narrowed his gaze and spoke rapidly in Spanish: "What's up, Moore? I hope your Spanish is good, because these guys will lay you out in a second if you don't sound legit. And to be honest, my cover right now is more important than you, so you'd better brush up and forget about all those terrorist languages you've been speaking. You running with the big dogs now."

Moore's Spanish was excellent, although his knowledge of gang and cartel slang was admittedly lacking. He would, indeed, have to brush up on them. He answered in Spanish: "No worries, *vato*. I know what I need to do."

Fitzpatrick, who went by the nickname Flexxx, reached across the table and made a fist, three of his fingers sporting thick gold rings. He banged fists with Moore, then settled back into his seat.

Gloria Vega glanced over at Moore and asked in Spanish, "Take a shower lately?"

"Yeah, but . . . yeah . . . I'm still jet-lagging."

She rolled her eyes and faced the projector screen being lowered by Towers.

Moore squinted at the intelligence photograph of two young Hispanic males.

"I assume you've all seen this?" asked Towers.

"Yeah," Moore began, hoping to demonstrate to the others that he wasn't a total slacker. "The guy on the left is Dante Corrales. He's the leader of the cartel's enforcer gang. They call themselves The Gentlemen, if I recall. The guy on the right is

Pablo Gutiérrez. He killed an FBI agent in Calexico. Mr. Ansara would like to get his hands on him."

"You have no idea," said Ansara, with a hiss of anger.

Towers nodded. "Our boy Corrales is a very clever young man, but he keeps hitting the Sinaloas head-on. We don't think his superiors approve of this."

"Why?" asked Moore.

Towers looked to Fitzpatrick, who cleared his throat and said, "Because of Escuadrón de la Muerte, the Guatemalan death squads. They're back in action after a two-year hiatus. They've reorganized, and they're killing members of Guatemala City's meth labs and maritime exporting ops out of Puerto Barrios and Santo Tomás de Castilla in the Caribbean. They've also taken out cartel members at the Port of San José and Port of Champerico on the Pacific side."

"And let me guess, they're only hitting the other cartels. The Juárez Cartel has not been touched."

"Exactly," said Towers. "So if they want to terrorize the Sinaloas, why not use Los Buitres Justicieros? That's what their most prolific hit team is calling themselves . . . the Avenging Vultures."

"And we think at least a dozen of their members are now in Juárez," said Fitzpatrick. "If you think the regular *sicarios* are hard-core, these guys are insane."

"Sounds like a powder keg," said Moore.

"Torres and Zúñiga know these guys are in town, and they're concerned," said Fitzpatrick. "There's talk of hitting the Juárez guys again, but Zúñiga's more concerned about securing a tunnel, and he's unwilling to pay the Juárez Cartel for the rights to use one of theirs."

"Why doesn't he dig one of his own?" asked Vega.

Fitzpatrick snorted. "He's tried. And every time Corrales and his boys come down and kill everyone. They have a lot more money than we do. They've got spotters everywhere. A huge network. Corrales has also paid off most of the engineers in town, so they'll never work for Zúñiga. That little bastard has got the whole place locked up."

Towers pointed at the photograph. "All right, our problem is this. Corrales is, at this moment, the highest-ranking member of the cartel we've identified, and in this case old-school conventional wisdom holds true: If we can identify and take out the leader, in most cases the cartel will fall. These are complex and sophisticated operations, and they're not run by dummies. I'd daresay it takes a freaking genius to pull off some of the stuff they do. Whoever our guy is, he's masked himself awfully well, and his organization has become the single most aggressive cartel in Mexico."

"Persons of interest?" asked Moore.

"Not many," said Towers. "We've investigated the mayor, chief of police, even the governor. You know less-educated guys like Zúñiga keep a higher profile, which satisfies their egos, but this guy is extremely well insulated."

Towers brought up a color-coded flow chart representing the various facets of the Juárez Cartel's operations. He continued, "The bottom line is this—we need to identify links the Juárez Cartel might have to terrorists in Afghanistan and Pakistan, to meth and coke labs in Colombia and Guatemala, and we need to positively link them to their gun-smuggling operations in the U.S. We also need to identify and attempt to expose the cartel's contacts within the local and Federal Police forces. That's phase one. Phase two is simple—we take 'em out."

Ansara began to shake his head. "We have a lot of homework. And I hate homework."

"Question," Moore began. "Has Zúñiga ever been openly approached about helping to bring down the Juárez guys? Maybe he knows who's running their operation."

"Whoa, hold on there, dude," Towers said, raising a palm. "You're talking about the United States government entering into a partnership with a Mexican drug cartel."

Moore beamed. "Absolutely."

"Sounds like business as usual," said Vega. "We get in bed with one devil to take out another."

"Are you being sarcastic?" Moore asked her.

"You have a keen eye for the obvious. You're right. It doesn't thrill me."

"Well, it's not pretty, but it works."

"I have to assume we wouldn't get authorization to do that," said Towers. "You'll be able to recruit informants from both cartels, but I warn you those people don't usually live very long."

Moore nodded. "I've got a few ideas. And Fitzpatrick, I'll need you to keep your ear to the ground. Any sign of Middle Eastern activity, Arabs, what have you, and I need to know about it."

"None so far, but you got it. And if you've read my report, you know I haven't met Zúñiga yet, so I can't tell you if he knows who's running the cartel. I've asked Luis, but he doesn't know."

"Okay," answered Moore.

Since Fitzpatrick had already done an excellent job of penetrating and reconnoitering the Sinaloa Cartel, he took over for a few minutes, describing that cartel's operation, its assets, and its desire to usurp the Juárez Cartel and its stranglehold on the more desirable border crossing areas. But this was information already contained within his report, and he was embellishing as he went.

"Mr. Moore, we don't know much about your ops in Pakistan," said Towers, after Fitzpatrick had taken his seat. "They've given us the file on Tito Llamas, the guy who turned up in a trunk in Pakistan."

"I saw that," answered Moore. "He's our first link. The cartel's buying more opium from Afghanistan, but we're not sure why Llamas was sent there. His death might've put a dent in their relationship."

"Let's hope so."

"I can't imagine any cartel willing to let terrorists cross the border into the United States," said Vega. "Why would you let them kill all your best customers and risk massive retaliation from the U.S.?"

"What about Zúñiga?" Moore asked, turning to Fitzpatrick. "You think he might want to help Taliban guys get through, just to hurt the Juárez Cartel?"

"No way. From what Luis has said, this has been discussed at length. I don't think any member of any cartel would aid or abet known terrorists. It'd have to be an independent coyote group, guys just in it for a quick score. Something like that. But the cartels have a good handle on those guides. They usually don't make a move without the cartel knowing about it."

"Well, then, I can go home," said Moore with a slight grin. "Because the cartels are protecting our borders from terrorist threats so we can keep buying their drugs."

"Whoa, slow down there, dude," said Towers, grinning over the irony. "So the cartels might not willingly help, but the Taliban or Al-Qaeda could enter by force."

Fitzpatrick sighed in frustration. "All I can say is they'd better bring some big guns—because every time the Sinaloas get into it with the Juárez guys, we always lose."

"Don't kid yourselves. The terrorists are already here. They're all around us. Sleeper cells are just waiting to strike," said Vega.

"She's right," said Fitzpatrick.

"Oh, happy day," said Moore, with a grunt.

"All right, people, we'll take it one step at a time. I've got some big assets to call in if we need them; otherwise, our limited size and scope is what gives us the advantage. Ansara, we'll start you off in Calexico. See if you can win over some mules for our team. Agents at the checkpoint there confiscated nearly one million dollars' worth of coke and marijuana just last week. The cartel hid the stuff in a secret compartment built into the dash, probably the most sophisticated thing we've seen. You needed a remote and an access code to open the secret panel. Pretty amazing stuff. They even wrapped the drugs in a layer of hot sauce to try to throw off the dogs. That's the level of sophistication we're dealing with here. Vega, you're going in deep. You know the drill. Flexxx, you just get back home to Zúñiga. Whittaker, you're heading back home to Minnesota. And that just leaves you, Mr. Moore."

He grinned. "Let's lock and load. Next stop: Mexico."

12

ALLIES AND ENEMIES

Aéroport Paris–Charles de Gaulle
Terminal 1

AHMAD LEGHARI was a member of the Punjabi Taliban, and he was scheduled to meet up with Mullah Abdul Samad in Colombia. Leghari was twenty-six and dressed in conservative slacks, a silk shirt, and a light jacket. He had one carry-on backpack and had already checked through one other suitcase. He carried nothing suspicious in his luggage. His credentials had been in order, and no one had confronted him thus far. The woman at the check-in desk had actually been friendly and had tolerated his rudimentary French, even after he'd been warned about the airport's reputation for overworked and rude employees. Moreover, there was no reason to believe he was on

America's no-fly list. His confidence in this regard was justified. The list of roughly nine thousand names was publicly criticized as costly, riddled with false positives, and easily defeated. Numerous children, many under five and some under one, appeared on the list. Conversely, the list had failed to detect terrorist Umar Farouk Abdulmutallab, the NWA flight 253 bomber, and Faisal Shahzad, the Times Square car bomber, in a timely manner. The most notable false positive was the late Senator Edward "Ted" Kennedy. The listing "T. Kennedy" caused the politician considerable inconvenience and aggravation when flying. The fact that "Ted" was a nickname, not the senator's real name, didn't seem to matter. Kennedy finally got relief by going directly to the director of Homeland Security, an option not available to the average citizen, and a fact publicly noted by the senator himself.

How people got on the list was supposed to be a closely guarded secret, with only pieces of information revealed during American congressional hearings. However, the Taliban had pieced together a working analysis of how some of their people wound up on that list. A first step might be having law enforcement or an intelligence agent glean information and submit it to the National Counterterrorism Center in Virginia, nicknamed Liberty Crossing, where it was entered into a classified database known as the Terrorist Identities Datamart Environment (TIDE). That information was then data-mined to connect dots and hunt for names and identities. If that process yielded more results, then the intelligence would be passed on to the Terrorist Screening Center, also in Virginia, for more analysis. Each day more than three hundred names were sent to the center. If, at that point, a suspect's information caused a "reasonable suspicion," he might wind up on the FBI's terrorist watchlist used by airport security personnel to add extra screening for some travelers, but yes, he could still fly. The Taliban had discovered that in order for someone to get on the actual no-fly list, authorities had to have their full names, their ages, and information that they were a threat to aviation or national security. While the Taliban couldn't confirm it, they'd heard that the final decision for adding a name to the list rested with six administrators from the Transportation Safety Administration (TSA). Even if placed on the no-fly list, some suspects were still permitted to travel with escorts, and unless wanted for a specific crime, many on the list who attempted to fly were simply stopped at the gate, quarantined, questioned, and ultimately released.

Suspects might also be placed on the "selectee list," which automatically had them passing through extra screening measures if they met certain criteria that might include booking a one-way flight, paying cash for tickets, making reservations on the same day as their flight, and flying without an ID.

Leghari had been training for this trip for nearly nine months, memorizing the layout of the terminal, considering what people would say to him and how he would react. He'd spent the better part of his life in Dera Ghazi Khan, a poverty-stricken frontier town in the Punjab Province with a growing phalanx of hard-line religious schools.

His parents were veterans of Pakistan's state-sponsored insurgency against Indian forces in Kashmir until pressure from the United States forced then-president Pervez Musharraf to withdraw support for the Punjabi group. His parents were forced to flee to the tribal areas, where they deepened their ties with the Taliban and Al-Qaeda. Leghari was left behind with relatives.

This, more than anything else, drove the embittered boy to the local madrassa led by Muhammad Ismail Gul, a recruiting center for the banned Punjabi Lashkar-i-Jhangvi Taliban group.

Leghari took a deep breath and stepped into the hexagonal-shaped millimeter wave full-body scanner. The airport had been testing the controversial technology for months on all passengers of United States–bound flights but had more recently broadened its scope of use. Leghari was instructed to raise his arms, then moving plates simultaneously beamed extremely high-frequency (EHF) radio waves at the front and back of his body. The reflected energy produced an image interpreted by security. He was, of course, not carrying liquids, sharp objects, or anything that would trigger an alarm.

However, as he was shifting down a corridor of polished steel and glass and following large yellow signs, he was accosted by two men in dark blue uniforms, along with the friendly check-in agent from the desk.

"Is that him?" they asked her in English.

"*Oui.*"

The taller man said something to him that Ahmad did not fully understand, but a few words chilled him: U.S. Customs and Border Protection Immigration Advisory. One of the patches on the man's uniform displayed the American flag.

He took a step back and swallowed. American security here? His trainers had not anticipated this.

Suddenly, he couldn't breathe.

They spoke to him again, more slowly, and the woman told him in French that he would have to go with the men.

Ahmad gasped. And then, without thinking, without any forewarning at all, he ran. Straight ahead. Down the corridor. The men shouted after him. He didn't look back.

As he wove his way past travelers dragging suitcases on rollers or carefully balancing their coffee cups, he sloughed off his own backpack, which was weighing him down. He left the pack in his wake and broke into a full-on sprint.

The men shouted again.

He didn't stop. He wouldn't. He reached an intersection, ducked around the right corner, and an alarm began to blare inside the terminal and voices rattled through loudspeakers.

A male French voice finally ordered all passengers to remain at their gates.

Ahead lay a bank of glass doors, but beyond was a maintenance area with baggage trucks lined up in neat rows. The sign said something about restricted access. He didn't care.

Outside. He needed to get outside.

But then he nearly ran head-on into an airport security officer. He tried to shift around the portly man, but the guy tackled him, and Ahmad dropped to the ground, his hands fumbling for and finding the man's pistol. He got it, wrenched himself away, and fired two shots into the man's chest. He sprang to his feet, and people screamed around him and cleared away, the shots still echoing, the Americans behind him hollering—and then a crackling like fireworks . . .

Sharp, stabbing pain woke in his back and drove him down to the tile once more. Suddenly, he was choking—on his own blood, he knew. He dropped, rolled onto his back, and envisioned himself dropping into the open arms of thousands of virgins. *Allahu Akbar!*

They reached him and kept screaming, the Americans' faces twisted into ugly masks, their weapons pointed at him, as the world grew dark around the edges.

Jungle House
Northwest of Bogotá, Colombia

Samad wiped the sweat from his brow and turned away from the laptop computer screen, where he'd just watched an Al Jazeera video news report of the shooting at Paris–Charles de Gaulle.

Of the fifteen Taliban who were coming to Colombia, each using a different route, only one had been caught—of course the youngest and most inexperienced. Ahmad Leghari had failed to realize that the Americans had no authority to arrest him in Paris. They were there only in an advisory capacity. His paperwork and passport were flawless. He would have been detained, questioned, and most likely released. Instead, he'd panicked. Still, the question remained of how he was identified. Again, the Americans were paying handsomely for tribesmen to spy on Taliban operations, and Samad had to assume that was what had happened. He could only sigh deeply and shake his head at Niazi and Talwar, both seated across from him and sipping on small bottles of Pepsi, since their barbaric host had no tea.

As he took a pull on his own soda, Samad once more heard Mullah Omar Rahmani's words ring in his head: *"You will lead them. You will bring the jihad back to the United States—and you must use the contacts you've made with the Mexicans to do that. Do you understand?"*

Samad could only glare at the fat pig who entered the house with the unlit cigar dangling from his lips. If Juan Ramón Ballesteros had bathed in the last week, he would still need an attorney to prove it. He removed the cigar, stroked his silver beard, and said in Spanish, "I'll help get you to Mexico, but the submarine will not be available."

"What?" cried Samad, practicing his own Spanish. "We were promised, and you've been well paid for this."

"I'm sorry, but we'll have to make other arrangements. The sub will be overloaded with my product—and yours—and the other two are being serviced right now. When we agreed on this arrangement, I was very careful to tell Rahmani that once the opium reaches Colombia, I am in charge of shipment. You have a much better chance of success this way. Do you understand?"

Samad gritted his teeth. Their collaboration was unprecedented but a work of genius, according to members of the Juárez Cartel. Instead of having Ballesteros and his cocaine compete with the opium being smuggled in, why not partner up to streamline and expedite the shipping process? Bonuses would be paid by the Juárez Cartel to both organizations for playing nice and getting along. It was a unique relationship, and they hoped it was unforeseen by the Americans. Ballesteros had already established a dozen separate smuggling routes via land, sea, and air, and Rahmani had seen the wisdom in this and been willing to pay for access to those routes and for couriers.

"The rest of my group will be here soon," Samad told Ballesteros. "How do you expect us to get to Mexico? Walk?"

"I'm looking into a plane that will get you as far as Costa Rica. But don't worry about that now. We'll need to go to Bogotá soon. Perhaps tomorrow. Look, let's agree that we do not like one another, but our employer has paid handsomely for this, and so we will be tolerant."

"Agreed."

"You must also promise never to tell anyone about how I've helped you with, shall we say, your travel plans. Not our employer. Not anyone."

"I have no reason to discuss this with anyone but you," Samad lied. He already knew that the head of the Juárez Cartel could help him and his men gain safe passage into the United States, and he had every intention of seeking out that man's help. Sure, Ballesteros the pig could help him get to Mexico, but once he was there, it would be difficult to cross the border without help.

Ballesteros turned toward the door and cursed over the heat.

That's when gunfire suddenly ripped through the walls and windows, glass shattering, men outside screaming, more gunfire echoing the first wave.

Samad hit the floor, along with his lieutenants, and Ballesteros was there as well, unhurt but grimacing as another salvo of gunfire stitched through the walls, splintering wood and sending dust motes swirling up toward the ceiling.

"What is this?" cried Samad.

"We all have enemies," Ballesteros said with a grunt.

Islamabad Serena Hotel
Islamabad, Pakistan

Israr Rana had not been very receptive to being recruited by the CIA. It had taken Moore nearly three months to finally persuade Rana that not only could this work be thrilling and lucrative, but Rana could be doing something for the greater good and helping to keep his own nation safe. Going to college was supposed to be his priority, but as Rana had been trained by Moore and sent off to gather information, he found the work very exciting. He'd seen every James Bond film and had even memorized some of the dialogue, which he'd used during conversations with Moore, much to the man's chagrin. In fact, Rana had perfected his English through American cinema. Unfortunately, his wealthy parents would never, ever approve of him doing this kind of work, and so he thought he'd have some fun—at least for a little while—until he grew bored. It was true that Moore could have resorted to other means to recruit him—less-than-ethical means, such as blackmail, and Moore had even described how that worked—but he'd said that he wanted to create a real apprenticeship founded on trust, and Rana respected that so much that it made him work even harder at gathering information for his friend and mentor.

At the moment, he was tucked tightly into a ditch along the foothills overlooking the hotel, and his pulse rose as he thumbed a text message to Moore:

LOCATED GALLAGHER. SERENA HOTEL.
ISLAMABAD.

Rana was about to tell Moore that their dear colleague was as dirty as they came. Gallagher was working with known Taliban lieutenants now and had been meeting with several of them the hotel. Rana thought that he may very well have killed Khodai's family—when in fact he'd been charged with protecting them. Every man had a price, and the Taliban had met Gallagher's.

Rana did not hear them come up from behind. A hand suddenly wrenched the phone out of his hands, and as he turned back, a club came down as an echoing blow knocked him into unconsciousness.

R ana's head hung toward his chest, and a deep throbbing emanated from the back of his neck and across the side of his face.

He opened his eyes to find only curtains of grainy blue and green—and then suddenly a bright light was in his eyes.

"You are the traitor who is working for the Americans, are you not?"

The man who'd posed that question was nearby, although Rana still could not see him. The blurriness persisted, and it felt as though he had little control over his head.

Judging from the sound of his voice, the man was young, no older than thirty, and probably one of the lieutenants Rana had already observed.

"I'm sorry, poor boy," came another voice, and this one he knew. Gallagher. His accent was unmistakable.

And now Rana couldn't help but try to talk, his lips feeling strangely numb. "What are you doing with them?"

"Moore sent you after me, huh? He couldn't leave well enough alone. You're a good boy."

"Please, let me go."

A hand fell on his cheek, and he finally mustered the strength to tilt his head back and look up. Gallagher's wizened face came in and out of focus, and Rana realized they were not in a hotel room but in a cave somewhere, perhaps the Bajaur tribal area northwest of the hotel, and the blue and green he'd seen earlier were part of Gallagher's tunic and trousers.

"All right, we will let you go, but first we're going to ask you some questions about what you've been doing and what you and Moore have learned here in Pakistan. Do you understand? If you cooperate with us, you will go free. You will not be harmed."

Every part of Rana's being wanted to believe that, but Moore had told him that that was exactly what they'd say if he was ever captured. They would assure him freedom, make him talk, then kill him once they learned what they needed to know.

Rana realized with a chill that he was already dead.

And so young, too. Not even out of college. Never married. No children. So much of life waiting for him—but he would never arrive at that stop.

His parents would be heartbroken.

At that, he gritted his teeth and began to pant in anger.

"Rana, let's make this easy," said Gallagher.

He drew in a deep breath and spoke in English, using words that Moore had taught him: "Fuck you, Gallagher, you fucking traitor. You're going to kill me anyway, so get on with it, you scumbag."

"Some bravado now, but the torture will be long and terrible. And your friend, your hero Mr. Moore, has left you here to rot. You're going to remain loyal to someone who has abandoned you? I want you to think about that, Rana. Think very carefully about that."

Rana knew that Moore had not intentionally left Pakistan. He was called away, and that was the nature of his job as an operative. He'd mentioned that several times and had explained that other agents might contact him and that his relationship with the Agency was very important to them.

But Rana was not sure he could deal with the torture. He imagined them chopping off his fingers and toes, attaching battery cables to his genitalia, and pulling out his teeth. He imagined them cutting him, burning him, putting out one of his eyes, and allowing snakes to bite him. He saw himself lying in the dirt, hacked apart like a lamb, and bleeding until the cold consumed him.

He tugged against the bindings around his wrists and ankles.

His vision finally cleared. Gallagher stood there with the two Taliban lieutenants behind. One of the men clutched a large knife, while the other was leaning on a large metal pipe, using it as a cane of sorts.

"Look at me, Rana," said Gallagher. "I promise you, if you tell us what we need to know, we'll let you go."

"Do you think I'm that stupid?"

Gallagher recoiled. "Do you think I'm that ruthless?"

"Fuck you."

"All right, then. I'm sorry." He glanced to the men. "You are going to cry like a baby, and you are going to tell us everything we want to know." Gallagher gestured to the man with the knife. "Cut his bindings. And then we'll start with his feet."

Rana trembled. Held his breath. And yes, he wept like a child now.

The sheer panic came on in quakes throughout his chest

and gut. Maybe if he did talk, if he did tell them everything, they would free him. No, they wouldn't. But maybe they would? There was nothing left to believe. Now he shook so violently that he was about to vomit.

"Okay, okay, I will help you!" he screamed.

Gallagher leaned in closer and smiled darkly. "We knew you would . . ."

13

WHERE WE BELONG

Bonita Real Hotel
Juárez, Mexico

ALL OF THE high-tech devices in the world could not replace old-fashioned boots on the ground gathering Human Intelligence (HUMINT), and that, Moore often mused, had kept him gainfully employed all these years. When the engineers invented an android that could do everything he did, he might be forced to hang up his balaclava and turn in his spy card—because, in his humble opinion, the world would soon be coming to an end as the machines took over. An age-old theme in science fiction would become reality, and Moore would watch it all unfold in the grandstands, with, he prayed, a hot dog in one hand and a beer in the other.

However, he still marveled over all the highly encrypted

data he could view on his smartphone. At the moment, he was watching real-time streaming satellite images of the hotel so that he could observe the comings and goings of everyone outside, even while tucked nicely into his bed, feet propped up, the TV morning news humming softly in the background. The spy satellites used to feed him that intelligence were operated by the National Reconnaissance Office (staffed by DoD and CIA personnel) and hung in low-earth orbits to optimize their resolution for several minutes before each handed off the job to the next satellite in line in a sophisticated relay of data transfer.

He was also receiving text alerts from the analysts back home who were watching the same images and could draw his attention to anything they noted. Other windows would show him the GPS locations of all other JTF members, and yet another window displayed more photographs of other targets in the city, such as cartel leader Zúñiga's ranch house. Indeed, it was a complex and aggressive overwatch campaign by geeks sipping on lattes half a world away.

Moore had checked in to the hotel owned by Dante Corrales (noted by Towers as the most senior-ranking member of the cartel that authorities had identified thus far). Like all good drug pushers, Corrales was beginning to surround himself with legitimate businesses, but even so, mistakes would be made, money laundered, and the poor honest folks he did employ would either be implicated in his crimes or simply lose their jobs as his operations were shut down and he was arrested.

However, he would not be apprehended anytime soon.

They needed him running wild in order to help identify the lord of the operation himself, and Corrales seemed like just the kind of loose cannon who could do that.

The bio they had on him was fragmentary, gleaned from street informants and personal documents they'd been able to obtain. That his parents had been killed in a hotel fire and he'd turned around and bought one was interesting. His hubris was well appreciated by the Agency and could be exploited. His penchant for showy cars and clothes made him ridiculously easy to spot around town. The guy probably had a *Scarface* poster hanging above his bed, and in some ways, he resembled a seventeen-year-old Moore—combative, full of bravado, with little sense of how the choices he made now would affect his future.

Moore rose, set down the phone, and pulled on a polo shirt and expensive slacks. His hair had been trimmed and pulled back into a ponytail, and his closely cropped beard was a far cry from the lobster bib he'd sported in Afghanistan and Pakistan. He'd donned a fake diamond earring to give him an edge. He picked up a leather briefcase and headed for the door. His Breitling Chronomat read 9:21 a.m.

He took the elevator down from his fourth-floor room to the first floor, and the man at the front desk whose badge read *Ignacio* gave him a polite nod.

Standing behind him was an absolutely stunning young woman with long, dark hair and vampire's eyes. She wore a silver-and-brown dress, and a gold crucifix dangled down into

graffiti-laden walls still standing but not much else. Between the stretches of broken glass and the gray haze that had permanently settled around the lots and spilled past the broken chain-link fence, Moore couldn't help but grimace. He took out his phone and snapped a few pictures. And then he forced a broad grin and said, "Mrs. García, I appreciate you showing them to me. Like I told you on the phone, we're scouting properties all over Mexico to build assembly plants for our solar panels. Our assembly plants will be here, while our administrative, engineering, and warehouse activities will remain in San Diego and El Paso. I'm looking for land just like this, with excellent access to the highways."

Moore was simply referring to an operation known as a maquiladora, named after a U.S.-Mexican program allowing low duties on goods assembled in Mexico. Literally thousands of maquiladoras operated on both sides of the border.

In fact, Moore had had dinner with an old SEAL buddy who'd gone to work for GI (General Instruments), a telecom company. His buddy had become the general manager of GI's maquiladoras, and when it was time to move raw materials from the United States to Mexico, he'd hit a snag. All goods for manufacturing had to originate from Mexico and could not be currently owned by GI. Moore's buddy had devised a clever solution: He sold the goods to a third-party Mexican trucking firm that drove them into Mexico, and once there, he bought them back at cost plus *mordita* (a bribe), as goods originating in Mexico. To quote his buddy, "Mexico runs on *mordita*." The memory of that dinner had helped Moore devise his initial cover while in Juárez.

As the real estate agent smiled, Moore looked past her at the two punks parked across the street. They were shadowing him, and that was fine. He would not have expected anything less. He only wondered if they were from the Juárez or Sinaloa cartels.

Or worse . . . they could be Guatemalans. Avenging Vultures . . .

Moore raised his brows. "I think this land would work out perfectly, and I'd like to meet with the owner to discuss his price."

The woman winced. "I'm afraid that's not possible."

"Oh, I'm sorry, why?" Moore tempered his curiosity because he already knew why: The land was owned by Zúñiga, leader of the Sinaloa Cartel.

"The owner is a very private man, and he travels a lot as well. All of this would be handled through his attorneys."

Moore made a face. "That's not the way I like to do business."

"I understand," she said. "But he is a very busy man. It is rare when I can get him on the phone."

"Well, I hope you will try. And I hope he will make an exception in my case. Tell him it'll be well worth his time and money. Now here . . ." Moore reached into his briefcase and withdrew a portfolio filled with marketing materials regarding his fictitious company. Embedded in the portfolio was a wafer-thin GPS beacon. Moore hoped she'd actually give the materials to Zúñiga and that he would actually follow up and check out his company, only to realize it was fake.

You didn't just walk up to a cartel leader's front door, ring the bell, and ask if he'd like to cut a deal. You would never get that meeting. You had to "inspire" his curiosity first, make him become so curious, in fact, that he'd demand to see you. This was a game Moore had played many times with warlords in Afghanistan.

"Here, please share this with the owner."

"Mr. Howard, I'll do my best, but I can't make any promises. I hope that no matter what happens, you'll seriously consider this land. Like you said, it's perfect for your new operation."

She'd barely finished her sales pitch when automatic-weapons fire echoed in the distance. Another volley split the morning silence, followed by a police siren.

The real estate lady smiled guiltily. "This is, uh, okay, this is, you know, maybe the rougher part of town."

"Yes, no problem," Moore said, dismissing the gunfire with a wave of his hand. "My new operation will require a lot of security, I know that. I will also require a lot of help and good information—that's why I would like to talk to the owner myself. Please let him know that."

"I will. Thank you for looking at the properties, Mr. Howard. I'll be in touch."

He shook her hand, then headed back to his car, careful not to look in the direction of the men watching him. He took a seat, lowered the window, and just waited there, checking the most recent photos of the hotel's exterior and the cars parked there. The men remained. He glanced back, saw that he couldn't get a tag number, so he started his car and drove off, heading straight for his hotel. A billboard in Spanish touted greyhound racing at a track in the city, with legal betting on the races.

Many years ago Moore and his parents had made a trip to Las Vegas that his father had been dreaming about. The ride had seemed interminable to the ten-year-old Moore, and he'd spent most of his time playing in the backseat with his G.I. Joes and baseball cards. His mother relentlessly complained about the ride being too long and costing too much, while his father retorted with arguments about how it was worth the drive and that he had a system for winning and that numbers were his business. If she would just believe in him for a change, they might have some luck.

There'd been no luck. His father had lost big-time, and there hadn't been any money for lunch because they needed to fill up the gas tank in order to drive back home. Moore had never been hungrier in his life, and it was then, he thought, sitting for hours in that hot car whose air conditioner had broken, that he began developing a deep hatred for numbers, for gambling, for anything that his father liked. Numbers had, of course, come in handy in his mathematics courses later in life, but back then, money and accounting represented evil obsessions that made his mother cry and made Moore's stomach ache.

And whenever the teenage Moore watched the film versions of Dickens's novella *A Christmas Carol*, he always pictured his father in the role of Scrooge, counting his pennies.

His adolescent rebellion, he knew now, was just his way to strike back at his father for not being the superhero Moore wanted him to be. He'd been such an imposing and opinionated man before the cancer had reduced him to a frail shell, then a bloated, drug-filled victim who'd passed away on Christmas Eve, a last laugh against a family who'd ridiculed him.

Moore wished he'd had a father who'd taught him how to be a man, who'd reveled in the pleasures of hunting and fishing and sports, not a pencil-pushing middle manager with a comb-over and a sagging gut. He wanted to love his father, but first he had to respect the man, and the more he reflected on the man's life, the harder that became.

And so Moore had found not a father figure but a sense of brotherhood in the military. He'd become part of a storied organization whose very name inspired awe and fear in all those who heard it.

"Oh, what did you do in the military?"

"I was a Navy SEAL."

"Holy shit, really?"

After BUD/S, Moore, along with Frank Carmichael, had been selected for SEAL Team 8 and sent to Little Creek, Virginia, to begin platoon training, what operators called "the real deal," training for war. He'd spent twenty-four months moving from the workup phase to actual deployment and then to the stand-down phase. He was promoted to E-5 petty officer second class, and by 1996 had received three Letters of Commendation, enough for his CO to recommend him for a slot in Officer Candidate School. He spent twelve long weeks in OCS and graduated as an O-1 ensign. By 1998 he'd become a lieutenant (jg) O-2 with another Letter of Commendation and a Secretary of the Navy Commendation Medal. Because of his exceptional performance, he was deep-selected for early promotion, and in March 2000 became a lieutenant O-3.

Then, in September 2001, all hell broke loose. Moore's SEAL team was sent to Afghanistan, where they were deployed on numerous Special Reconnaissance missions and earned a Presidential Unit Citation and the Navy Unit Commendation for operations against Taliban insurgents. In March of 2002, he participated in Operation Anaconda, an ultimately successful operation to remove Al-Qaeda and Taliban forces in the Shahi-Kot Valley and Arma Mountains in Afghanistan.

Even Moore himself had difficulty believing that he'd matured so much from his days as a high school punk.

There were, of course, many punks to be found here in Juárez, Moore thought. He pulled into the hotel's parking lot and snapped off some pictures of the tags of every other car in the lot. He forwarded them to Langley, then went inside and fixed himself a cup of coffee in the lobby while Ignacio watched him. Hammers, saws, and the shouting of construction workers resounded from outside.

"Did your business go okay, señor?" the man asked in English.

Moore answered in Spanish. "Yes, excellent. I'm looking at some very nice properties here in Juárez to expand my business."

"Señor, that is a great thing. You can bring your clients

here. We will take very good care of them. Too many people are afraid to come to Juárez, but we are a new place now. No more violence."

"Very good." Moore headed up to his room, which Ignacio had told him would be "cheap, cheap," because the hotel was still being renovated. Moore had not realized how loud the racket would be since he'd left before the workers had begun their hammering and sawing.

Back in his room, he received all the information the Agency could find on the dark-haired woman, Maria Puentes-Hierra, twenty-two years old, born in Mexico City and girlfriend of Dante Corrales. They didn't have much else on her, except that she'd spent about a year stripping at Club Monarch, one of the few remaining adult bars in the city. Most of the others had been either closed down by the Federal Police or burned by the Sinaloa Cartel. Monarch was run by the Juárez Cartel and was well protected by the police, who the report indicated were frequent patrons there. Moore assumed Corrales had met the young beauty while she was clutching a tacky metal pole and swimming in disco lights. Love had blossomed among watered-down drinks and cigarette smoke.

After finishing up with that report, Moore checked on the status of his fellow task force members.

Fitzpatrick had returned to the Sinaloa ranch house after his "vacation" in the United States. He and his "boss" Luis Torres were plotting an attack on the Juárez Cartel in retaliation for the explosion at the ranch house that had killed several of

Zúñiga's men and caused more than $10,000 in damage to his main gate and electronic security and surveillance system.

Gloria Vega would begin her first day on the job as an inspector for the Federal Police in Juárez. Moore assumed she'd get an ear- and eyeful.

Ansara checked in to say he was already in Calexico, California, which bordered Mexicali in Mexico, and he was working with agents at the main checkpoints to identify mules and recruit one for their team.

ATF Agent Whittaker was back in Minnesota and on the job, already reconnoitering several storage rental facilities being used by the cartel to stash weapons.

The real estate lady was at her office and making phone calls, which analysts at Langley listened to and interpreted.

And Moore was ready to lie back down on the bed, sip some coffee, and take a little break until they came for him . . .

As he was grimacing over the coffee grounds on the bottom of his foam cup, he received a text message from a surprising source: Nek Wazir, the old man and informant from North Waziristan. The message unnerved Moore. It simply said: PLEASE CALL ME.

Moore had the man's satellite phone number, and he immediately dialed, not giving a second thought to the time difference, which he estimated at more than ten hours, so Wazir was texting him at around eleven p.m. his time.

"Hello, Moore?" Wazir asked.

There weren't many people who knew Moore's real name,

but given Wazir's considerable skills and contacts, Moore had trusted him with that most sacred piece of information—in part as a way to seal their trust, and in part to tell the man that he wanted, truly wanted, to be his friend.

"Wazir, it's me. I received your text. Do you have something for me?"

The old man hesitated, and Moore held his breath.

Moore spent the next hour on the phone with Slater and O'Hara, and it wasn't until after he'd vented his anger and frustration to his bosses and took a long moment to stare out the window of his room that his eyes finally burned with tears.

The sons of bitches had killed poor Rana. He was just . . . just a smart boy who'd done a stupid thing: He'd agreed to work with Moore. And not for the money. The kid's parents were already rich. He was an adventurer who'd wanted more out of life, and somehow, there was a bit of Moore in him, and now they were carrying his body down from the Bajaur tribal area, wrapped in old blankets. They'd cut and burned him for what little he knew. Wazir said he had probably lasted ten, fifteen hours at the most before he'd died. Rumors of the torturing had reached Wazir's men, who'd gone up to the caves and had found the body. The Taliban had left Rana as a message to any other Pakistanis who chose the "wrong" path of justice.

Moore sat on the bed and let the tears flow. He cursed and cursed again. Then he rose, whirled, drew his Glock from its shoulder holster and aimed it at the window, imagining the heads of the Taliban who had captured Rana.

Then he holstered the pistol, caught his breath, and returned to the bed. Oh, hell, if it was time to feel sorry for himself, he might as well get through it now, before the guys tailing him came knocking.

He sent Leslie a text message, told her he missed her, told her to send him another picture of herself, that things weren't going so well and he could use some cheering up. He waited a few minutes, but it was late over there, and she didn't reply. He lay back on the bed and felt overwhelmed by that same feeling he'd had during BUD/S, that suffocating desire to surrender and accept defeat. He wished that Frank Carmichael were with him now, to convince him that Khodai's death and the kid's death meant something and that walking away was far worse than anything else he could do. Yet another voice inside, a voice that seemed far more reasonable, told him that he wasn't getting any younger, that there were far less dangerous and lucrative ways to make money, as, say, a consultant for a private security firm or as a sales rep for one of the big military and police gear manufacturers, and that if he remained in his current position, he would never have a wife and a family. The job was always fun and exciting until someone you knew, someone you had fostered a deep relationship with, a relationship built on profound respect and trust, was tortured and murdered. Every time Moore let down his guard and allowed himself to truly feel for someone, that relationship would be wrenched away. Was this how he wanted to live the rest of his life?

Back in late 1994, Moore and Carmichael were in a bar in Little Creek, Virginia, celebrating the fact that they were about to become counterterrorism specialists with their new SEAL team. They were talking to another SEAL, nicknamed Captain Nemo, a gunner's mate second class who was assigned to Task Unit BRAVO as the SEAL delivery vehicle pilot and Ordnance Engineering Department head. During a proof-of-concept full-mission rehearsal in which Nemo was piloting the SDV, one of his fellow operators had accidentally drowned. He'd refused to go into the details of the incident, but both Moore and Carmichael had heard about it before meeting the guy, who they learned was ready to leave the SEALs. He felt responsible for what had happened, even though the investigation had cleared him of any wrongdoing.

There they were, Moore and Carmichael, getting ready to embark on their careers as SEAL operators—and Nemo was putting a real damper on their celebration.

Again, good old Carmichael had stepped in with his words of wisdom: "There's no way you can quit," he'd told Nemo.

"Oh, yeah, why?"

"Because who else is going to do it?"

Nemo smirked. "You guys. The new guys, the ones who are too naive to realize that it's just not worth it."

"Listen to me, bro. That we're here is a gift. We answered the call because deep down—and I want you to think about this—deep down we knew beyond a shadow of a doubt that we weren't born to live ordinary lives. We knew that when we were kids. And we know it now. You can't escape that feeling. You'll have it for the rest of your life, whether you quit now or not. And if you quit, you'll regret it. You'll look around and think, *I don't belong here. I belong there.*"

Moore stood up from the bed in his hotel room, whirled around, and muttered aloud, "I belong here, damn it."

His phone beeped with a text message. He checked it. Leslie. He sighed.

14

A SANGRE FRÍA

Delicias Police Station
Juárez, Mexico

GLORIA VEGA HOPPED into the passenger's side of an F-150 4x4 with the words *Policía Federal* emblazoned across the doors. She wore full tactical gear, including a Kevlar vest, a balaclava pulled over her face, and a helmet secured tightly by its chinstrap. She carried two Glocks holstered at her hips and a Heckler & Koch MP5 nine-millimeter submachine gun whose barrel she held up near her shoulder. That a police inspector had to don this kind of gear and arm herself for bear would be a real eye-opener for some of the detectives back home, she thought. Those slackers could arrive at a crime scene in plainclothes with just a single sidearm, no vests, and doughnut powder staining their lips.

The graying man at the wheel, Alberto Gómez, was dressed

similarly to Vega and had warned her that visiting the crime scenes "after the fact" could be as dangerous as the initial incidents themselves. Bodies were all too often used as bait to lure in police so the *sicarios* could blow them up, taking police with them. Sometimes, if the bodies weren't booby-trapped, snipers would be posted along the rooftops, and again, the police would be set up for a mass killing.

And so the days of operating in plainclothes were over for the inspectors, Gómez had told her with a shrug. He'd scrutinized her with eyes so weary that she wondered why he hadn't retired already.

Well, then again, she knew why. She hadn't been paired with him by accident. While the Federal Police had no definitive proof, Gómez was at the top of their list of inspectors with ties to the cartels. Sadly, he'd had so many years on the job and so many "successful" busts that no one wanted to implicate the old man. There was an implicit understanding that he would finish out his few years and retire, and that no one should interfere with that. He was a real family man, with four kids and eleven grandchildren, and he volunteered at the local schools to teach the kids about crime and safety. He was an usher at his local Catholic church and a well-known member of the Knights of Columbus who had risen up to the role of district deputy. He volunteered at the local hospital, and if he could, he would spend weekends helping old ladies cross the street.

All of which Vega suspected was an elaborate cover, a false life that made him feel better about being on the cartel's payroll.

Senior-ranking members of the Federal Police, particularly the newer administrators and hires, had a much more aggressive and zero-tolerance policy for corruption, while the local districts too often looked the other way—out of respect, seniority, and, most of all, fear. And so it was that Vega was seated beside a man who could be one of the dirtiest in all of Juárez.

"We have three bodies. When we get there, say nothing," Gómez told her.

"Why not?"

"Because they don't need to know anything from you."

"What is that supposed to mean?"

"It means that I don't care how many years you spent in Mexico City. I don't care about your long and impressive record. I don't care about your promotion or about all the kind words your colleagues have said about you in your file. All I care about now is helping you to stay alive. Do you understand me, young lady?"

"I understand you. But I don't understand why I'm not permitted to talk. I'm not sure if you realize this, but women in Mexico are allowed to vote and run for public office. Maybe you haven't picked up a newspaper in a while."

"You see? *That* is your problem. That attitude. I suggest you put that into your purse and never take it out, so long as you are here, in Ciudad Juárez."

"Oh, let me see if I can find my purse. Oh, all I have are these big guns and extra magazines."

He smirked.

She shook her head and gritted her teeth. Eight years in

Army Intelligence and four years as a seasoned CIA field officer had led her to this: sitting in a car and taking machismo crap from a broken-down and corrupt Federal Police inspector. The miscarriage, the divorce, the alienation of her brothers and sisters . . . and for what? This? She turned to Gómez and burned him with her glare.

They listened to the other units over the radio, and within ten minutes rolled down a street lined with pink, white, and purple apartment buildings, the alley between them festooned with laundry. A few lanky boys of ten or twelve stood in the doorways, watching them and making calls on their cell phones. They were the cartel's spotters, and Gómez marked them, too.

At the end of the street, near the next intersection, three bodies blocked the road. Vega yanked a pair of binoculars from the center console and dialed to focus.

They were all young males, two lying prone amid blood pools, the third facing up with a hand clutching his heart. They were dressed in dark jeans and T-shirts, and if they'd been wearing any jewelry, it'd already been stolen. Two police cruisers were parked about twenty meters away, the officers crouching down behind their doors. Gómez parked behind one cruiser and widened his eyes. "Say nothing."

They got out, and Vega's gaze swept across the rooftops, where at least a half-dozen men were just sitting up there, watching, a few talking on more cell phones. She clutched her rifle a bit tighter, and her mouth went dry.

A van rolled up behind them, and out came two more officers with a pair of bomb-sniffing dogs. As they shifted by,

Gómez's cell phone rang, and he drifted to the back of the truck to take the call. What Vega noted, though, was that the old man carried two phones; this was not the phone he'd used to call her cell, thereby giving her his number. This was a second phone. *Interesting.*

She couldn't hear what he was saying over the shouting from the officers ahead. The canine team moved in slowly, and once they swept the area and the bodies, one man gave a wave and a shout. All clear.

He took a sniper's round from the rooftop to their left, and most of his head came off.

Just like that. Without warning. Broad daylight. Civilians watching from the balconies of the apartments.

And as the others screamed to get down, the second canine officer was shot in the neck, the round hammering him from the back and exploding from beneath his chin.

A new wave of automatic-weapons fire came in from AK-47s that ripped through the bodies in the street and cut into the dogs, both of which fell while Vega crawled forward on her chest, keeping tight to the truck's front wheel. She lifted her rifle and returned fire at the rooftops, her bead spraying along the ledge and chiseling away at the stucco.

"Hold your fire!" cried Gómez. "Hold your fire!"

And then . . . nothing. A few shouts, the stench of gunpowder everywhere now, and the heat of the asphalt rising in waves up into Vega's face.

Brakes squealed, stealing her attention. At the next cross street sat a white pickup truck missing its tailgate, and from one of the back alleys came three men armed with rifles—AR-15s and one AK-47. They ran toward the truck and leapt onto the flatbed. Several of the officers ahead opened fire, but the truck was already hightailing it away. As a matter of fact, the rounds from those officers seemed perfunctory at best—not a single one struck the truck.

Vega bolted to her feet and ran around to the passenger's side, where Gómez was hunkered down and shaking his head.

"Come on!" she urged him. "Come on!"

"I'll call for the backup. Other units will pursue them."

"We go now!" she cried.

His eyes widened, and his voice lifted sharply: "What did I tell you?"

She inhaled, bit back a curse, then rose and spun toward one of the rooftops, where the sniper who'd killed the two canine cops had her dead in his sights.

"Oh my God," she gasped, a second before the killer disappeared behind the rooftop parapet.

She blinked. Breathed.

And was back in the moment.

"He's right there," she shouted. "Up there!"

The other officers remained behind their car doors, shaking their heads and gesturing for her to get down, take cover.

She went back to Gómez and crouched down beside him. "We're letting him get away."

"The other units will find him. Just wait. We didn't come here to fight them. We came here to investigate the crime scene. Now *shut up.*"

Vega closed her eyes, and it hit her—right there and then. She was going about this all wrong. She needed to get close to this guy, gain his trust, not turn him into the enemy she already presumed he was. She needed to be his daughter, allow him to teach her about the city, and as he grew to like her, perhaps even respect her, he'd lower his guard enough for her to strike.

But her ego had gotten in the way, her exacting nature, and she'd admittedly screwed up.

They remained there for another two, maybe three, minutes, and then, finally, the officers up front began to slowly move toward the bodies, even as residents in the apartments came back out onto their balconies to watch the show.

"Is she your new partner?" one of the officers asked Gómez.

"Yes," he answered curtly.

"She'll be dead by the end of the week."

Gómez looked at Vega. "Let's hope not."

She gulped. "I'm sorry. I didn't realize it would be like this . . ."

Gómez cocked an eyebrow. "Maybe you should pick up a newspaper."

Club Monarch
Juárez, Mexico

Dante Corrales was in the mood to kill someone. Three of his *sicarios* had been gunned down in Delicias, and Inspector Gómez had called to say that he was worried. The Federal Police were watching him more closely now and had assigned to him a female inspector who was probably working with the president's office. She couldn't be trusted, and he had to be much more careful now that he was being watched.

Moreover, an American had checked into the hotel, a Mr. Scott Howard, and Ignacio had learned that the guy was scouting properties for his businesses. Corrales didn't quite believe that and was having the man followed, but thus far his story had checked out.

While Raúl and Pablo were making a large cash delivery to a contact they simply referred to as "the banker," Corrales was headed over to the Monarch for lunch and *cervezas*. En route, his phone rang: Ballesteros calling from Bogotá. What the hell did that fat bastard want now?

"Dante, you know the FARC guys hit me again? I'm going to need some more help."

"Okay, okay. You can talk to them when they get there."

"When?"

"Soon."

"Have you heard about Puerto Rico?"

"What now?"

"Haven't you been watching the news?"

"I've been busy."

"The FBI pulled off another inside operation. Over one hundred police arrested. Do you know what that's going to do to me? We counted on them. That's a whole shipping route I've lost in a single day. Do you know what this means?"

"Shut the fuck up and stop crying, you fat old fuck! The boss will be there soon. Stop fucking crying!"

With that, Corrales hung up, cursed, and pulled into the club's parking lot.

There were only two strippers onstage, day workers who'd had children and weren't shy about revealing their cesarean scars. Two other patrons sat at the main bar, old men wearing wide-brimmed hats, thick leather belts, and cowboy boots.

Corrales went to a back table, where he met his friend Johnny Sanchez, a tall, long-haired Hispanic-American screenwriter and reporter who wore tiny glasses and a UC Berkeley college ring. Johnny was the son of Corrales's godmother, and he'd gone away to the United States and received his education, only to return to contact Corrales because he wanted to write some articles about the drug cartels in Mexico. He'd never accused Corrales of working for the cartels. He'd said only that he guessed Corrales knew a lot about them. And they'd left it at that.

For the past few months, Corrales had been talking to the man, helping him develop a screenplay that would chronicle Corrales's life. Their lunch meetings were often the best part of Corrales's day, when he wasn't having sex with Maria, of course.

With Corrales's permission, Johnny had just had an article published in the *Los Angeles Times* about cartel violence along the border. The article focused mainly on how police corruption was so widespread that authorities could no longer tell the good guys from the bad guys. That was exactly how the Juárez Cartel wanted it.

"The article was very well received," Johnny said, then took a long pull on his beer.

"You are welcome."

"It's a pretty exciting time for me," he said.

They spoke in Spanish, of course, but once in a while Johnny would break unconsciously into English—like he just did—and he would lose Corrales. Sometimes that would annoy Corrales to the point that he'd bang his fist on the table, and Johnny would blink and apologize.

"What did you say?" Corrales asked.

"Oh, sorry. I received over a hundred e-mails about the article, and the editor would like to turn it into a series."

Corrales shook his head. "I think you should focus on our movie script."

"I will. Don't worry."

"I'm talking to you because you are my godmother's son, and because I want you to tell the story of my life, which would make a very good movie. I don't want you to write any more articles about the cartels. People would become very upset. And I would be afraid for you. Okay?"

Johnny tried to repress his frown. "Okay."

Corrales smiled. "Good."

"Is something wrong?"

Corrales traced a finger along the sweat covering his beer bottle, then looked up and said, "I lost some good men today."

"I didn't know about it. There was nothing on the news."

"I hate the news."

He glanced at the table. The Juárez Cartel had their hands firmly planted on the shoulders of the local media outlets, which sometimes defied them, but the more recent murders of two well-known field reporters who'd been beheaded outside their TV news stations had resulted in some significant "delays" and omissions of stories altogether. Many journalists remained defiant while others feared reporting on anything related to the cartels and cartel violence.

"I want to talk about the day those *sicarios* threatened you," Johnny said, trying to lighten the mood. "That would be a very good scene in the movie. And then we would show you falling to your knees outside the hotel, with the fire raging in the background, and you . . . there . . . weeping, knowing your parents are dead inside, their bodies burning because you stood up to the cartel and refused to give in. Can you see that scene? Oh my God! What a scene! The audience will be crying with you! There you are, a poor young boy with no future who just wants to stay out of a world of crime, and they punish you for it! They punish you! And you're left with nothing. Absolutely nothing. And you need to rebuild from the ashes. You need to rise up again, and we're rooting for you all the way! And then there really is no choice. You're trapped in a city with nothing to offer, with only one true business, and so you do what you must because you need to survive."

Johnny always whipped himself up into a fit of passion as he discussed the film, and Corrales couldn't help but become infected by the writer's enthusiasm. He was about to comment on Johnny's suggestion that he was in fact in a cartel—but

Johnny turned his head, focusing on something out near the main bar.

"Get down," he screamed, as he dove across the table and knocked Corrales onto the floor, just as a gun boomed from that direction, followed by at least a half-dozen more shots that pinged into the table and thumped into the wall behind them. The strippers began hollering, and the bartenders were shouting about no shooting, no shooting.

Then, as Corrales rolled onto the floor, it was Johnny who shocked the hell out of him and returned fire with a Beretta clutched in his right hand.

"Is this what you want?" Johnny screamed in Spanish. "Is this what you want from me?"

And the gunman near the bar spun around and sprinted off as Johnny emptied his clip into the man's wake.

They sat there, just breathing, looking at each other.

Then Johnny said, "Motherfucker . . ."

"Where did you get that gun?" Corrales asked.

It took a moment before Johnny answered. "From my cousin in Nogales."

"Where did you learn to shoot?"

Johnny laughed. "I only shot it once before."

"Well, it was enough. You saved me."

"I just saw them first."

"And if you hadn't, I'd be dead."

"We'd both be dead."

"Yeah," Corrales said.

"Why do they want to kill you?"

"Because I'm not in the cartel."

Johnny sighed. "Corrales, we're like blood. And I don't believe you."

He slowly nodded.

"Can't you tell me the truth?"

"I guess maybe now I owe you that. Okay. I'm the head of the Juárez Cartel," he lied. "I control the entire operation. And those guys were from the Sinaloa Cartel. We're at war with them over the border tunnels and their interference with our shipments."

"I thought you were maybe a *sicario*. But you are the leader?"

He nodded.

"Then you shouldn't be out in public like this. It's foolish."

"I won't hide like a coward. Not like the other leaders. I will be out here in the street, so the people can see me. So they can know who their true friend is—not the police or the government but us . . ."

"But that's very dangerous," Johnny said.

Corrales began to laugh. "Maybe this can go in the movie, too?"

Johnny's expression shifted from a deep frown into his more wide-eyed stare, as though he were already staring through a camera's lens. "Yeah," he finally said. "Yeah."

15

THE BUILDER AND
THE MULE

Border Tunnel Construction Site
Mexicali, Mexico

PEDRO ROMERO estimated that within a week they would finish their digging. The home they'd chosen in Calexico, California, was in a densely populated residential district of lower-middle-class families whose breadwinners worked in the nearby retail businesses and industrial parks. The Juárez Cartel had already purchased the home at Romero's suggestion, and he had carefully gone over his plans for the tunnel's construction with the cartel's youthful "representative," Mr. Dante Corrales, who had recruited Romero off another engineering project he'd been doing in the Silicon Border area, where most recently some of his colleagues had been getting let go from their jobs. As the economy had tightened, so had corporate expansion and the jobs created by those projects.

Romero shifted down the tunnel with two of his diggers behind him. The shaft was nearly six feet tall, three feet wide, and when complete would be nearly 1,900 feet long. It had been dug at a depth of only ten feet because the water table was frustratingly shallow in this area, and twice, in fact, they'd had to pump water from the tunnel when they'd accidentally gone too deep.

The walls and ceiling were reinforced with heavy concrete beams, and Romero had set down temporary tracks for carts loaded with dirt to be hauled out by the workers. The dirt was loaded onto heavy dump trucks and hauled away to a secondary site some ten miles south, and would be used on another project.

In order to remain silent, the digging had begun with shovels and continued that way throughout the entire operation. Romero had teams of fifteen working around the clock to drive them forward. While they were ever wary of cave-ins, they'd lost four men in a most unexpected way. It had been about 2:30 a.m. and Romero had been awakened by a phone call from his foreman: a huge sinkhole nearly two meters wide had opened up in the tunnel floor, had swallowed four men, and then its sides had collapsed. The hole was nearly ten feet deep, its bottom filled with water. The men had been forced under the water by the collapsing sand and had drowned or suffocated in the heavy mud before they could be rescued. While the entire crew had been unnerved by the accident, the work, of course, went on.

The Mexican side of the tunnel began inside a small warehouse within a major construction site for a Z-Cells manufacturing facility. Five buildings were being constructed for the photovoltaic cell builder and the dump trucks coming and going from the job helped disguise the ones leaving from the tunnel operation. This was not Romero's brilliant idea. Corrales had revealed that it had come down from the cartel's leader himself, a man whose identity remained a mystery for security reasons. The "regular" construction workers on the Z-Cells site never questioned the tunneling operation, which made Pedro believe that everyone was on the cartel's payroll—even the CEO of Z-Cells. Everyone knew what was happening, but so long as they were paid, the wall of silence would not come down.

According to Romero's blueprints, the tunnel would be the most audacious and complex dig ever attempted by the cartel, and because of that, Romero was being paid the equivalent of one hundred thousand U.S. dollars for his services. He had been skeptical of working for the cartel, but that kind of money, paid upfront and in cash, had been too hard to resist—more so because Romero was nearing forty and the oldest of his two daughters, Blanca, who'd just turned sixteen, had been suffering from chronic kidney disease to the point where she would now require a transplant. She'd already been treated for anemia and bone disease, and was going through very costly dialysis. The money he earned from this operation would surely help to pay for their mounting medical costs. While he'd shared those facts with only a few of his workers, word spread quickly, and Romero had learned from one of his foremen that every man on the job would work his hardest in order to help save his daughter. Suddenly, Romero wasn't a thug taking a bribe from the cartel; he was now a family man trying to save his little girl. The men had even taken up a collection for him and had presented the money, along with a thank-you card, to him at the end of the previous workweek. Romero had been moved, had thanked them, and prayed with them that they would finish their work and not be caught.

In point of fact, disguising all the dirt they were removing from the tunnel wasn't their only challenge; there was another very serious concern: Both the Mexican and American governments employed ground-penetrating radar (GPR) to detect the cavities associated with a digging operation. Again, the adjacent construction site would help mask most of their initial excavation sounds, which were also detected by remote REMBASS-II sensors adapted from military operations and monitored by the Border Patrol. Additionally, the tunnel itself had been constructed in a series of forty-five-degree angles instead of simply a straight line heading due north. Its shape would help mask it as a fragmentary section of drainage pipes. Romero knew that all the seismic data was being recorded at the same time, even if the computers being used were looking at only one spot. Border Patrol agents could examine a set of seismic-event-density maps in an attempt to discern traffic patterns and other activity in and around the site. The tunnel itself would affect the seismic field as it absorbed sounds passing through it and sometimes delayed the passing of that information, creating an echo or reverberation that would appear as a "ghost" on the agents' detection equipment. To address that issue, Romero had ordered and received thousands of acoustical panels that lined the tunnel walls to not only help absorb much of the sound of their digging but to try to mimic the natural surroundings as best they could. He'd even brought in a seismic engineer he knew from Mexico City, who'd helped him brainstorm and implement the plan. But soon it would all be over, the job complete, Romero issued his last payment in full. With God's help, his daughter would have her transplant.

Romero consulted with one of his electricians, who was in the process of extending the power cables into the newer section of tunnel, even as two other men worked on hanging some air-conditioning ducts. His diggers had asked if they could set up a small shrine just in case of an accident—at least they'd have somewhere to pray—and Romero had allowed them to carve out a small side tunnel where they'd set up candles and photos of their families, and where the men did, in fact, come to pray before each shift. These were hard times, and they were engaged in hard work that could ultimately result in their arrests. Praying, Romero knew, gave them the strength to go on.

Romero slapped his hand on the electrician's shoulder. "How are you today, Eduardo?"

"Very well, very well! The new lines will be finished this evening."

"You are an expert."

"Thank you, sir. Thank you."

Romero grinned and shifted farther into the tunnel, careful not to trip over the tracks. He fired up his flashlight and began to smell the cool, damp earth being removed by his men with only shovels, pickaxes, and all the power they could muster in their backs and shoulders.

He tried to deny the tunnel's use, the millions of dollars' worth of cash, drugs, and weapons that would move through thanks to him and his team, the lives that would be affected in both unbelievable and tragic ways. He told himself he was a man with a job, and that was all. His daughter needed him. But the guilt clawed away, stole hours from his sleep, and made him shudder at the thought of being arrested and sent to prison for the rest of his life.

"What will you do when this is over?" asked one of the diggers following him.

"Find more work."

"With them?"

Romero tensed. "Honestly, I hope not."

"Me, too."

"God will protect us."

"I know. He already has by making you our boss."

"All right, enough of that," Romero said with a grin. "Get up there and get back to work!"

Calexico–Mexicali Border Crossing
East Station—Northbound

When the main Calexico-Mexicali station got very crowded, and the delay was going to last more than one hour to pass through the checkpoint to enter the United States, seventeen-year-old American high school student Rueben Everson had been instructed to drive the six miles east of the main crossing in order to use the alternate port of entry, the one that handled the spillover during overcrowded times and was known mostly by the locals, not the tourists.

Rueben had been a "mule" for the Juárez Cartel for nearly a year. He had made more than twenty mule runs and had grossed more than $80,000 in cash—enough to pay for all four years of college at the state university. He had spent only about $1,500 of the money so far and had banked the rest. His parents had no idea what he was doing and were certainly unaware of his bank account. His sister Georgina, who'd just turned twenty, suspected something was going on, and she repeatedly warned him, but he just blew her off.

Rueben had first learned about becoming a mule from a friend at a party, who'd responded to an ad in a Mexican newspaper promising well-paying jobs with benefits. Rueben had met with a man named Pablo, who had "interviewed" him and given him about two thousand dollars' worth of pot to carry on foot across the border. After that job had gone well, they'd supplied him with a Ford SUV whose dashboard and gas tank had been modified to hold huge stashes of cocaine and marijuana. The dash had a secret code you typed in via a remote, and the center console where the radio and A/C controls were located would pop open and rise on motors to allow access to a secret compartment that extended all the way to the firewall. Rueben couldn't believe how sophisticated the operation was, and because of that, he'd built up the courage to take on larger shipments. The car's gas tank had been cut in half so that the side facing the car could carry blocks of drugs while the bottom masked the scent of the drugs with gasoline. The tank had then been sprayed with mud to disguise it from the border agents, who used mirrors to check for recent work to the underside of any car. Twice Rueben had been pulled off the line, his car inspected, but during both times he had not been carrying any drugs. That was part of the operation as well—establish a frequent traffic pattern that some agents became familiar with, and a solid alibi, like a job in Mexico while you lived in California. The cartel had covered that part for him, and many of the Border Patrol agents remembered him and his car, so more often than not, he glided on through, just another high school kid who'd found some part-time work in Mexicali.

But today was different. They'd pulled him off the line, and he drove to the secondary inspection area. There he saw a tall, lean Hispanic man who looked like a movie star and whose eyes would not leave him. Rueben parked the car and stepped out to speak with one of the Border Patrol agents, who checked his license and said, "Rueben, this is Mr. Ansara with the FBI. He'd like to talk to you for a few minutes while we check out your car. No worries right now, okay?"

Rueben did as always: He pictured happy thoughts with his girlfriend, eating out, kissing her, buying clothes with the extra money he made. He relaxed. "Sure, man, no problem."

Ansara narrowed his gaze and simply said, "Follow me."

They went into the crowded station, where at least fifteen people in dusty clothes sat in chairs, their expressions long.

Rueben immediately concluded that they'd all been trying to sneak through the checkpoint and had probably been caught at the same time. Perhaps they'd been hiding within a tractor-trailer's load or other such large shipment. A mother and two small girls were sitting there, and the woman was sobbing. Six or seven Border Patrol personnel manned positions behind a long counter, and one agent was trying to explain to an old man that anyone carrying as much cash as he had needed to be searched and detained, the money declared.

Rueben steeled himself against the scene and hurried after Ansara down a long, sterile-looking hall. Rueben had never been inside the facility, and his pulse began to mount as Ansara opened the door to what was a small interrogation room where another young man about Rueben's age sat at the table, brooding. He was a white kid with brown hair and freckles. His arms were covered in tattoos, and he wore a skull earring made of gold.

Ansara closed the door. "Have a seat."

Rueben complied, and the other kid just kept staring through the table.

"Rueben, this is Billy."

"What's up?" Rueben asked.

"Dude, you have no fucking idea," the kid groaned, still not bothering to look up.

Rueben looked his question at Ansara. "What's going on? Am I in trouble or something? What did I do?"

"I'll cut to the chase. They recruit you kids out of the high schools, so we always start there. A couple of your friends tipped us off because they're afraid for you. I also made a promise to your sister—but don't worry . . . she won't tell your parents. Now, I brought Billy down here to show you something. Show him, Billy."

The kid suddenly shoved his chair back and propped both of his bare feet up on the table.

He had no toes.

Every one of them had been hacked off, the scars still fresh and pink, and so ugly that Rueben tasted bile in the back of his throat.

"I lost a load worth fifty thousand. I'm only seventeen, so they worked it out so I only got probation. Doesn't matter, though. They came across the border for me. Caught me one day after class. Threw me in a van. Look what those fuckers did to me."

"Who?"

"Your buddy Pablo, and his boss, Corrales. They chopped off my toes—and they'll do it to you, too, the moment you fuck up. Get out now, bro. Get out right fucking now."

A knock came at the door. Ansara answered and stepped outside to speak to an agent.

"They really did that to you?"

"What do you think? Fuck, dude, you think I'll ever get laid again? You think any woman is going to be attracted to a guy with these fucking feet?" He threw back his head and started crying, and then he began screaming, "Ansara! I want out! Get me the fuck out of here! I'm done!"

The door opened, and Ansara appeared, waving Billy outside. The kid rose and hobbled to the door, carrying a pair of odd-looking boots under his arm.

The door closed again.

And Rueben sat there alone for five, ten, fifteen minutes, his imagination running wild. He saw himself in prison, being trapped in the shower by fourteen potbellied gang members who wanted him as their little bitch—all because he wanted to go to college and make some extra money. He wasn't a rocket scientist. The scholarships wouldn't help very much. He needed the cash.

Abruptly, Ansara returned and said, "Your car has a very unique dashboard and gas tank."

"Fuck," Rueben said and gasped.

"You think because you're not eighteen you'll just get released or put on probation?"

Rueben couldn't help it. He began to cry.

"Listen to me, kid. We know the cartel's spotters are out there, watching all of this. We made it look like we didn't find anything. You'll finish your run today. You'll deliver the drugs. But now you work for me. And we have a lot to discuss . . ."

16

BACKSEAT DRIVER

Bonita Real Hotel
Juárez, Mexico

T HE ONLY WAY Moore could stop thinking about Rana's murder was to focus on the moment, on the two men who had been following him. They were now parked across the street from the hotel. *They must be bored out of their minds*, he thought. They'd been sitting there for two hours, just playing with their cell phones and watching the front door and parking lot. While some aspects of the cartel were highly sophisticated, others, like human surveillance, were crude and rudimentary. A few times they even got out of their Corolla (with a front quarter-panel that was red, although the rest of the car was white) and leaned on the trunk, smoking cigarettes and repeatedly looking in the hotel's direction. These young studs were geniuses, all right, and Moore could see why they'd been given the flunky job of tailing him. Any *sicario* worth his salt would never entrust money, guns, or drugs to a couple of stooges like this. When he'd returned, Moore had observed two spotters on the hotel's roof, both dressed like construction workers, but they were security to alert Corrales and his cronies of any attacks on the hotel itself. Whether they were in contact with his tail Moore wasn't sure.

Moore had photographed the two punks by the car several times already and sent the pics back home, where analysts identified them and searched Mexican police files for more data. Both men had records, mostly petty stuff—burglary and drug possession—thus neither of them had done any serious time. They were marked in their police files as "suspected cartel members." Somewhere out there was a Mexican police detective with a keen eye for the obvious.

Moore sent a text message to Fitzpatrick, who replied and said they were not members of the Sinaloa Cartel and most assuredly worked for Corrales.

That was a disappointment, and a problem, because he was trying to goad the Sinaloas into a meeting via his real estate inquiry, but Fitzpatrick said neither he nor Luis Torres had been given orders to pick up the American at the hotel.

Moore pondered that before answering a call from Gloria Vega.

"I'll make this fast," she said. "We engaged some cartel members. Fitzpatrick confirmed they were Zúñiga's boys. Three

Juárez guys killed. The police are scared, and Gómez is in deep. He might be the key player and best link to the cartel. He's carrying two phones, and the read I get from the others at the station is that he's a god there. I think the best I can do is gather enough evidence on him, then flip him and see how many more he'll hand us. As far as I'm concerned, there's no way around it. We'll have to cut a deal with him."

"Don't feel bad about that."

"I don't. I just feel bad because he won't hand us everyone, and this just slows them down. That's all."

"Whatever we can do, we do it. Without exception."

"Yeah, I get that. Or at least I'm trying to."

Her cynicism was understandable but taxing, so he changed the subject. "Hey, you hear about that big bust in Puerto Rico?"

"Yeah, another huge score for the Bureau."

"Our time will come, trust me. Just hang tight."

"That's not easy. Gómez is a male chauvinist pig. My tongue's already sore from biting it."

Moore softened his tone. "Well, if anybody can get it done, you can."

She snorted. "How the hell do you know?"

"Trust me, pretty lady, your reputation precedes you."

"Okay, talk soon." She hung up.

Their call was, of course, encrypted and would not show up on her phone, the bill, or anywhere else, for that matter. If the Agency wanted a communication record to go away, it went away. Period.

Moore got an alert from Towers about a shooting at the Monarch strip club, where their bestest buddy Dante Corrales liked to hang out. Local police had arrived. No one injured, just shots fired, and the gunmen had fled. He mused that in the city of Juárez the TV stations needed to start reporting on the day's shootings, as though they were temperature and humidity levels.

After checking the window once more to see that his two super-thugs were still down there, Moore slipped on a baggy hoodie to conceal his Glock and shoulder holster, then left his room. He figured he'd drive across town to the V Bar. Fitzpatrick had said that the Sinaloa *sicarios* often hung out there.

As Moore drove into the parking lot, his thoughts took him back to Rana and the cheesy Batman joke. He'd introduced Rana to the Special Forces guys as his sidekick, "Robin," and the kid's frown warranted an explanation, but Moore had forgotten all about that.

As he stiffened and tightened his fists, imagining his young friend's murder all over again, he wasn't aware of the man behind him until he felt something blunt and solid—the barrel of a pistol, presumably—jammed into the back of his head.

"Easy," said the man in English, his voice deep and burred, as though from a lifetime of tobacco use. "Raise your arms."

Moore rarely disconnected from his immediate surroundings; such a lapse could wash him out of the Special Activities Division, possibly the Agency itself. But losing Rana was like losing a kid brother, and giving in to his frustration and anger had—just that quickly—derailed his focus.

The man checked Moore's hips, then reached up and almost immediately felt the shoulder holster. He tugged down the hoodie's zipper, threw back the Velcro strap on the holster, and removed Moore's Glock.

"Now get in and start it."

Moore gritted his teeth, cursing himself for the error and feeling his pulse rise against the unknown. He wasn't sure what the guy had done with his gun, but he could still feel the other one on his head. Too close. Too risky to make a move. He could knock one gun away only to find the other pointed at his chest. *Boom.* Shot with his own Glock. "You're the boss," he said. He slowly climbed into the car, and the man quickly wrenched open the back door and hopped into the seat behind him, pressing the gun once more to the back of Moore's head.

"Do you want the car?" Moore asked. "My money?"

"*No ese.* Just do what I say."

Moore pulled out of the parking lot, and in the rearview mirror he spotted the two guys in the Corolla hopping in their heap to follow.

He also caught a glimpse of the man in the backseat, his beard graying, his curly hair gone to ash. He wore a blue sweatshirt and jeans, and had a gold hoop earring in his left ear. His eyes remained narrow in a permanent squint. He was a far cry from the punks in the car behind them, and his English was surprisingly good. Those fools were already tailing them, though Moore wasn't sure if they could see he was being abducted, and he wasn't sure if his abductor was aware of them yet, either.

He drove on for another minute, made a right turn as ordered, then said, "There's a car behind us, the Toyota with the red panel. Two men following. Are they with you?"

The man in the backseat whirled, saw the car, and cursed in Spanish.

"What do we do now?" Moore asked.

"Keep driving."

"I guess they're not your friends?"

"Shut up!"

"Look, if you don't want the car or my money, then what's the deal here?"

"The deal is you drive."

Moore's cell phone began to ring. *Shit.* It was tucked into his front pocket, and the guy had failed to find it.

"Don't even think about it," warned the man.

The ringtone indicated that Fitzpatrick had sent him a text message, and if that message had anything to do with Moore's passenger, then Fitzpatrick was a day late and a dollar short with his warning.

"Throw that fucking phone out the window."

Moore reached down into his pocket, set the phone on vibrate by holding down the side button, then threw the phone's leather slipcase out of the window before the guy could get a good look at it.

"Where are we going?" he asked, sliding the phone back into his pocket.

"No more questions."

Moore checked the mirror once more, while his abductor stole a look back at the punks following them.

————

The car tailing them began to accelerate, and the gap narrowed to within two car lengths. The man in the backseat grew more agitated—shifting forward and tossing repeated looks out the rear window. He was panting now, his pistol still trained on Moore's neck. He'd tucked Moore's Glock into his waistband. Moore slowed as the light ahead turned red. He glanced around: Wendy's, Denny's, McDonald's, Popeyes, and Starbucks. All five of the food groups. For a moment, he thought he was back in San Diego, with the smog and stench of gasoline and exhaust fumes finding their way inside the air-conditioned car. Bad part of town. Bad guy in the backseat. Just another day on the farm.

"Why are you stopping?" shouted the guy.

Moore gestured with a hand. "Red light!"

"Go, go, go!"

But it was too late. The car behind them rushed up, and the two guys leapt out and began firing.

"No, no, no!" Moore shouted as he hit the gas and squealed away into the intersection, burning rubber and narrowly avoiding a pickup truck whose tailgate was nearly dragging along the ground.

The two clowns behind them were intent on emptying their magazines, the shots thumping into Moore's trunk as the back window shattered, along with the rear driver's side, and Moore's passenger released a strangled cry.

Moore glanced back and wished he hadn't. The man lay there with gunshot wounds to his head and shoulder.

The man wasn't moving. Blood pooled onto the seat. Moore cursed.

A quick glance to the rearview mirror showed that the guys had rushed back to their car, jumped in, and were continuing after him. They'd bridged the intersection and were weaving around two small sedans.

Ahead lay another cross street, and farther out, the "better" part of the barrio, with tin roofs held down with nails instead of old truck tires. Moore wasn't sure where he was now, and had planned to use his smartphone's GPS to get him to the bar. No time to program that info into the phone now . . .

But he tugged out the device anyway and thumbed a direct-dial number to Langley. A familiar man's voice answered on the speakerphone: "Three-two-seven here. What do you need?"

"Get me to the V Bar. Update Fitzpatrick."

"On it. Hold on . . ."

Moore checked his rearview mirror once more, while the two fools chasing him swerved in front of a step van, and the driver floored it toward the next intersection.

Just as Moore's car passed through the intersection, the light turned red behind him.

An old man rode into the street on a bike fitted with baskets fore and aft. The baskets were piled high with blankets and plastic bottles and several backpacks. He was in the cross-

walk, along with several pedestrians shifting a few meters behind him.

The idiots tailing Moore could not stop in time.

The man and the bike arced up and over their car like toys
flung in the air, and their car's hood folded in like a taco, but they
kept on, the man and bike clattering out of sight behind them,
the other pedestrians screaming and running back toward him.

A voice buzzed from the phone's speaker: "Next left. Make
it. Then third light, right turn. I'll call the local police and see if
they can run some interference for you. I've got eyes in the sky
on your position now. See your tail."

"Thanks." Moore jammed his foot harder onto the accelerator as the next light ahead turned yellow. He'd already noticed that in Juárez, red, yellow, and green lights were mere
suggestions to drivers. Many only slowed down for red lights,
then just blew on through them—even if they weren't involved
in car chases. He made the left turn as instructed.

The street sign read *Paseo Triunfo de la República*, and the
bus stops, billboards, and clean sidewalks of this business district made Moore feel a bit more at ease. Pedestrian traffic was
fairly heavy, and he thought the rocket scientists behind him
might think twice about pulling any stunts in this area.

He scanned the side streets as he raced by, noting how they
were lined on both sides by parked cars. You could travel only
in one direction, but there were no signs to indicate that the
roads were one-way.

The knuckleheads behind him were gaining, and the passenger slid out onto the windowsill and leveled his pistol.

That was it. Third light. "Three-two-seven? I won't need you anymore, thanks."

"Are you sure?"

"Roger that. I'll check in later."

Holding his breath, Moore hung the hard right down the next side street and floored it. He gasped as he rocketed down the alley, turned another hard left, careened off a Dumpster, and kept on moving. He was coming up behind the V Bar, which would be on his left-hand side.

He checked his six o'clock—clear for now.

A car shot across the intersection ahead and turned head-on, and with a start he realized it was the punks following him. They'd anticipated his move. They were supposed to be dummies. What was wrong with them? Why had they gone smart? Now they were playing chicken, and Moore had nowhere to go.

He reached into the backseat, tried to grab one of the guns—the guy's on the floor or the Glock tucked into the dead man's waistband—but both were still out of reach.

Then he slowed, was about to throw it in reverse, when another car raced up behind him, an older Range Rover with a huge Hispanic male at the wheel—big as a sumo wrestler or Samoan warrior—and Moore's colleague and fellow JTF team member Fitzpatrick was riding shotgun. Were they the cavalry or the execution squad? Either way, Moore was sandwiched between members of rival cartels with a body in his backseat.

Consequently, he did what his training dictated. He prepared to abandon ship. He threw the car in park, whirled back and seized his Glock, then tossed himself out the door, rolling across the pavement to the cover of two parked cars. The driver's door turned into a pincushion for small-arms fire.

God helps those who help themselves. Time for Moore to help Moore.

He crawled around to the back of the car, stole another look to the street, and saw that the two men following him were dead, their backs peppered with gunshot wounds.

Since Fitzpatrick was with the rest of the Sinaloas, Moore decided that if he surrendered, his colleague might be able to better control the situation—at least get them all talking instead of shooting. If Moore decided to bolt, he might not only draw their fire but be back to square one: still trying to get a meeting with the boss. Of course, getting the cartel's attention like this was not what he'd had in mind.

His name was Scott Howard. What would a solar-panel businessman do, a guy whose most dangerous moments came on the golf course, not the mean streets of Juárez?

He thought a moment more, then shouted in Spanish to the men from the Range Rover. "I'm an American. Here on business! I was kidnapped!"

"Yeah, you were kidnapped by us," answered a man who was definitely not Fitzpatrick. Moore peeked around the car.

A leather-clad gangster with a hoop in his nose kept tight to the back door of the Range Rover and tugged free an empty magazine from his pistol.

"Those guys shot at us. Killed the guy in my backseat," Moore explained.

Another voice now: "We know. Come out here!"

As Moore slowly rose with his hands in the air, the gun in his right hand clearly visible, two men with shaved heads broke off from the group near the Range Rover. They carried the bodies of the two punks back into the Toyota with the red panel, then one guy jumped behind the wheel and drove off. Moore watched this as three other men surrounded him, including the tattooed guy with the nose ring. Fitzpatrick was with them and would not meet his gaze. *Good.* Another guy got in Moore's car, backed out, and vanished.

The fat driver of the SUV weighed in at four hundred pounds, Moore estimated, with a belly that shifted in great waves, even as he breathed. Here was the infamous Luis Torres, leader of the Sinaloa Cartel's enforcer gang and Fitzpatrick's "boss." He wore a black baseball cap turned backward, and a lavish pattern of lightning-bolt tattoos seemed to crackle up and down his massive arms. On one biceps he sported the intricate likeness of a skeleton dressed in flowing religious robes. This was Santa Muerte, the saint of death worshipped by drug traffickers. On a stranger note, his eyelids had been tattooed with pictures of another set of eyes, so when he blinked, it still appeared he was staring at you. The image was nearly as unnerving as the man's face—so thick, so round, so cherubic that he strained to see past the folds of fat framing his eyes. And the teeth . . . the rotting and yellowed teeth, destroyed by a junk-food diet, no doubt, were enough to make Moore grimace.

But he didn't. He sighed . . . At least they'd stopped shooting. For now.

Okay. He'd been captured by the Sinaloa Cartel. *Check.*

Don't get yourself killed, he thought. *And don't let them see you shaking.*

Torres pursed his lips and frowned at Moore's gun, the long hairs on his chin sweeping forward like a broom. "What're you doing with this?" His nostrils flared as he now spoke in English.

"I told you, I'm an American here on business."

"So am I."

"Really?"

Torres snorted. "I was born in South Central L.A."

"I'm from Colorado," Moore said.

"So you're on business? What kind of business?"

"Solar panels."

"And you're carrying a gun?"

"I took it from the guy in the backseat."

Torres's gaze grew harder, and he snickered. "And you always wear a shoulder holster just in case you find a gun?"

Moore realized only then that his hoodie was still unzipped.

"You're already dead. You know that? You're already dead."

"Look, I don't know who you are, but you guys saved my life. I'll pay you for that."

Torres shook his head. "You're full of shit."

A couple of blocks over, a police siren resounded. Ah, the local guys Moore's pal back at Langley had called in, but neither Torres nor his cronies reacted to the sound.

"I'm sorry you don't believe me. Maybe I can talk to some-body else?"

Torres swore under his breath. "Take this prick inside."

Moore was ushered into a second-story office over the club's dance floor, and he sat there in a metal folding chair, frowning at the 1970s brown paneling on the walls and the heavy steel desk positioned near the window. A bookshelf behind the desk buckled from the weight of dozens of binders, and harsh fluorescent lights buzzed overhead. The only thing modern about the room was the iPad glowing on the desk. Fitz-patrick, two other thugs, and Torres remained in the room, and Torres lowered himself into the desk chair like an old walrus testing the water before sliding into the surf. In his case, the fat man was making sure said chair did not collapse under his im-posing girth.

"What are we doing now?" Moore asked, drawing the grin of every man in the room.

"Listen, motherfucker, you start talking, otherwise, *el guiso* for you. Do you understand?"

Moore swallowed and nodded.

El guiso, or "the stew," was a well-known execution method employed by the cartels. They put you in a fifty-five-gallon drum, poured gasoline or diesel fuel all over you, then burned you alive in a human stew. The drum made the cleanup and dis-posing of your body nice and tidy.

Torres folded his arms over his chest. "Are you working with the Federal Police?"

"No."

"Local?"

"No."

"Then why the hell are you poking around those old properties?"

"I was hoping to meet the owner. So you sent that guy to kidnap me?"

"Yeah, I did," said Torres. "Talk about a botched job."

"Not really. I still wound up here," said Moore.

"Who are you?"

"All right. Here's the deal. I'm someone who can help your boss. I need to sit down and talk with him, mano a mano."

Torres chuckled under his breath. "Not in your lifetime."

"Luis, listen to me very carefully."

His gaze tightened. "How do you know my name?"

"We know a lot more than that, but I'll cut to the chase. I work for a group of international investors. We're based in Pakistan, and we were doing some very lucrative opium business with the Juárez Cartel until we were screwed over. My employers want the Juárez Cartel out of business. Period."

"So why do we care?"

"Because I've been sent here to assassinate the leaders of that cartel. And you're going to help me."

Torres cracked a huge grin and addressed the others in Spanish: "Do you hear what this gringo is saying? Do you believe it?"

"They should believe it. Give me my phone. I'll show you some pictures."

Torres turned to Fitzpatrick, who'd been the one to confiscate Moore's smartphone. He tossed it to Moore, and Torres leaned in toward him.

"If you make a call or send out some warning," Torres began, "we'll shoot you now."

"You don't want to kill me. I'm going to be your new best buddy." Moore thumbed through screens on the phone and arrived at his photo gallery. He scrolled to a pic of Dante Corrales. "Is this one of the fuckers you want dead?"

"Corrales . . ." Torres breathed.

"I need to talk to your boss. I'll pay fifty grand for the opportunity."

"Fifty grand?" Torres was taken aback. "You're not here alone, are you?"

Moore almost looked in Fitzpatrick's direction. Almost. "We don't care about you guys. We might even strike up a new deal with you. But first, it's *el guiso* for Corrales and all his friends . . ."

Torres leaned back, the desk chair creaking loudly. And then, after a tremendous breath, he began to nod. "Where do you have the money? At the hotel?"

"Electronic transfer."

"I'm sorry, gringo. Cash only."

"I understand. I'll get you the cash. You get me the meeting with your boss. And you're right. I'm not here alone."

17

SOME HAVE MONEY
AND GUNS

Rojas Boeing 777
En Route to Bogotá, Colombia

JORGE ROJAS stared absently through the oval-shaped window and sighed. They were at 41,000 feet now and his Boeing 777's Rolls-Royce Trent 800 engines had been reduced to a purr by the well-insulated cabin. That was quite remarkable, since the 777 had the largest-diameter turbofan engines of any aircraft—and it should have big engines, he mused, given its cost. He had spent nearly $300 million on this VIP airliner, the world's largest twin jet and often referred to as the "triple seven." He could fly nearly halfway around the world before they had to land for refueling. If he was in a hurry, his pilot and copilot, veteran and distinguished officers of the Mexican Air Force, could get him there at .89 mach. The jet, like his many homes, was a testament to his success and a magnificent retreat. He'd taken delivery of the plane and had it flown from the Boeing plant in Seattle to the Lufthansa base in Hamburg, where it was furnished with an entirely customized cabin that followed his very specific and ambitious requests. While he could fly up to fifty passengers in a first-class seating area, most of the plane had been converted into his airborne home and office, complete with a master bedroom suite trimmed in knotty, warm tones of black-ash burl. The travertine-stone bathroom had a six-head shower and sauna for up to four, along with a jet tub. The adjoining office had been furnished with antique French pieces secured to the floor. Even his bookcases had little racks that protected the volumes from sliding off. While the furniture was old, the technology was state-of-the-art: printers, scanners, computers, Wi-Fi networks, webcams, and anything else his onboard information-technology expert thought he needed. Opposite his desk was a conference table with a flat-screen television and computer display projector, along with posh, heavily padded leather seats that his guests repeatedly sighed into and admired. Outside the office was a media room with yet another widescreen television and full-size sofas and recliners, along with a full-size wet bar manned by Hans DeVaughn, a World Class–winning international bartending champion that Rojas had recruited while in Spain. The World Class competition was recognized as the Oscars of the bartending industry, and Hans—with his knowledge, skill, and creative flair—had beaten more than six thousand bartenders from more than twenty-four different countries. In fact, all

of his precious Sofía—would now become the center of the boy's life. Rojas smiled inwardly. He was simply feeling the pain of a father coming to terms with his son's independence. That was all. Logic needed to trump emotions. Easier said than done, though. When he saw them together, looking so young and vibrant and beautiful, he could not help but see himself and Sofía. He was jealous, of course, jealous of his son's youth and the fact that he'd found someone to love when Rojas had lost the love of his life. Was it right to feel that way? To envy your own son?

Across the cabin sat Jeffrey Campbell, an old friend from USC who'd founded Betatest, a company involved in the early stages of applications for several cell-phone platforms. Campbell had made millions and was expanding his business into South America with Rojas's help. They'd both played on the soccer team and had once dated twin sisters, which became quite a sensation on campus, as those two young vixens were well sought after by legions of students.

"You look a million miles away," said Campbell.

Rojas smiled weakly. "Not quite a million. How're you feeling?"

"I'm all right. I always thought I'd go before him. It's not easy to bury your kid brother."

That last sentence stung Rojas. "Of course not."

Campbell's brother, also a college athlete, who had never smoked a single cigarette in his life, had contracted lung cancer and suddenly passed away. He was thirty-eight. His doctors suspected that he'd been exposed to depleted uranium when his M1A1 Abrams tank had struck an IED while in Iraq, but proving that and trying to gain reparations from the military would be difficult.

Rojas's older brother had died when he was only seventeen and Rojas had been fifteen. They'd grown up in Apatzingán, then a much smaller town in the state of Michoacán in southwest Mexico. Their father had been a farmer and rancher who on weekends repaired farming equipment and the taxis for a company that operated in some of the cities. He was a broadshouldered man with a thick mustache and tan felt hat that some people joked he wore to bed. Their mother, whose large brown eyes and thick brows could form an expression that chilled Rojas to the bone, toiled endlessly on the farm and kept their home impeccably clean. His parents had instilled in him a work ethic that tolerated no distractions, one that also gave him little patience for those who chose to shuffle nonchalantly through their lives.

The night had been cool and crisp, the wind sweeping down from the mountains and swinging the fence gate to and fro, since the latch had rusted off. The three gangsters were standing there, backlit by a waning moon, waiting for Rojas's brother, Esteban, to emerge and confront them. They were dressed in dark clothes, with two wearing hoods like grim reapers. The tallest stood farther back, like a sentinel charged with recording the incident for eyes more powerful than his.

Rojas came out onto the porch and grabbed his brother's wrist. "Just give it back to them."

"I can't," said Esteban. "I already spent it."

"On what?"

"On fixing the tractor and the water pipes."

"That's how you got the money?"

"Yes."

"Why did you do this?" Rojas's voice was beginning to crack.

"Because look at us! We're peasants! We work all day, and for what? Hardly anything! They work for the cartel and in five minutes they make what we have in a month! It's not fair."

"I know, but you shouldn't have done it!"

"Okay, you're right. I shouldn't have stolen their money, but I did. And now it's too late. So now I have to talk to them. Maybe they will let me work it off."

"Don't go."

"I have to get this over with. I can't sleep anymore. I have to make a deal with them."

Esteban yanked his arm free and started down from the porch, heading across the dirt trail toward the fence.

Rojas would watch him make that walk over and over in his nightmares. He marked every footfall, every shifting shadow edging across his brother's corduroy jacket. Esteban was tugging nervously on the sleeves of that jacket, pulling the fabric deeper into his palms. Rojas had always looked up to his older brother, and never once had he seen him afraid.

But those hands tugging on the sleeves . . . and his gait, carefully measured but the boots dragging deeper than they usually did . . . told him that his hero, his protector, the boy who had taught him how to fish, skip rocks, and drive a tractor, was very much afraid.

"Esteban!" Rojas cried.

His brother spun and raised a finger. "Stay on the porch!"

Rojas wanted nothing more than to either accompany his brother or run back into the house and alert his parents, but they had gone into the city to celebrate their wedding anniversary, and Rojas's father had boasted about saving up enough money to treat his wife to an expensive meal.

One of the gangsters said something to Esteban, who fired back a retort, his voice rising. Esteban neared the gate, and oddly enough, the gangsters refused to come past it, as though there were some force holding them back.

It was not until Esteban pushed past the gate and stepped into the dirt road beyond that they surrounded him. Rojas thought of the shotgun their father kept under his bed. He thought of rushing out there and blasting each of those evil boys in the face. He could no longer watch his brother being accosted by these *cabrones*.

He remembered the candy that Esteban had brought home last week, a real luxury to them, and he realized that even that had been purchased with the stolen money.

"Here," Esteban had said. "I know how much you love chocolate."

"Thank you! I can't believe you got some!"

"I know. Neither can I!"

And after they'd finished eating all the chocolate and were lying in their bunk beds, staring up at the ceiling, Esteban had said, "You should never be scared of anyone, Jorge. People will try to intimidate you, but no one is better than anyone else. Some have money and guns. That is the only difference. Don't be scared. You need to be a fighter in this life."

"I don't know if *el padre* would go along with that," he'd said. "He told us to be scared of the gangs."

"No! Never be scared."

But Rojas was scared, more than ever now, as he'd watched the gangsters begin shouting at his brother.

The shortest one shoved Esteban, who returned the shove and screamed, "I'll pay back the money!"

And then the tallest one, the sentinel who'd remained a few steps behind and had not said a word, reached into his jacket and produced a pistol.

Rojas gasped, tensed, reached out—

The gunshot made him flinch and blink as Esteban's head snapped to one side and he dropped to the ground.

Without a word, Rojas ran into the house, into his father's bedroom, and snatched up the shotgun. He rushed back outside. The three gangsters were already sprinting across the field, toward the moon hanging low on the horizon. Rojas banged past the gate and screamed after them. He fired the shotgun twice, the boom echoing off the house and hills. The gangsters were well out of range. He cursed, slowed to a halt, and struggled for breath.

Then he turned back to his brother, lying motionless in the dirt. He rushed to his brother's side, and the shotgun fell out of his hands. The gaping hole in Esteban's head sent shudders through him. His brother stared back with a weird reflection in his eyes, and later on, in the dreams and nightmares, Rojas would see the moon in those eyes, and against that moon, cast in silhouette, stood the sentinel, raising his pistol. Rojas would struggle to see the boy's face, but he never could.

He put his head down on his brother's chest and began to cry. Neighbors found him there a few minutes later, and eventually his parents arrived. The wailing of his mother carried on throughout the night.

That was another lifetime, thought Rojas, running a finger along the burled-wood arm of his seat. The rags-to-riches story was a cliché, he'd been told, yet he defied anyone to classify his present life as a cliché. As much as he still loved and admired his brother, Rojas understood now that Esteban had made a grave and foolish mistake. Rojas had spent nearly half of his life searching for the boy who had killed Esteban, but no one had come forward to help.

"Well, Jorge, I can't thank you enough for this. For all of this. I mean, I've never actually met the president of a country before."

"I've met many of them," Rojas said. "And you know what? They are just men. People will try to intimidate you, but no one is better than anyone else. Some have money and guns. That is the only difference."

"Some have private jets, too," Campbell added with a grin.

He nodded. "I like to travel."

"I'm sure you've been asked this question before, but I'm

always intrigued by people like you. What do you think contributed the most to your success? Was it discipline or just smarts? Luck? A little bit of everything? I mean, you've told me the story of the small town where you grew up. And now you're literally one of the richest people on the planet. That article in *Newsweek* said your estimated worth is at least eight percent of Mexico's gross domestic product. It's just . . . staggering. Who would've thought this in college, right?"

"You've done pretty well, too. Don't sell yourself short."

He nodded. "But nothing like this. So, as I look around your beautiful jet, I ask you, how'd you get here?"

"Buying businesses, making wise investments . . . I don't know, really. Friends helped the most."

"Don't be coy."

"I'm serious. The friendships I've made are what's become most important, and you'll see that when we get to Colombia."

Campbell considered that and finally nodded, and it seemed Rojas had successfully ducked the question. But then Campbell said, "Do you think it was school? Doing well in school?"

"Sure, that's it. Friends and school."

"But that doesn't answer the *real* mystery."

Rojas frowned. "Oh, what's that?"

"How so many of your companies have been able to weather this economic downturn. If memory serves, not a single one of your companies has had to file for bankruptcy. Given this volatile market, that's incredible."

Rojas allowed himself a faint grin. "I have good people

working for me and an army of lawyers to protect me and my investments."

"The Subways you have in Mexico are making more money than those in the United States, yet the people in Mexico have less disposable income. How do you do it?"

He began laughing. "We sell a lot of sandwiches." And then he cast his mind back to a board of directors meeting he'd had in the previous month, where his team had presented on the year's earnings for the chain of car dealerships he owned with locations throughout all of Mexico. Many people were unaware that the country often had the largest car production and sales in the world. The numbers, however, had been disappointing, yet Rojas had been able to assure his people that dealer incentives would not only remain but increase tenfold.

"But how can they do that with this tremendous drop in sales?" asked his CEO. It was a fair question, and the dozen or so people seated at the long conference table focused their attention on Rojas, who stood at the head and said, "I've been in direct talks with the manufacturers, and I promise you that your incentives will increase."

They shrugged in disbelief. But Rojas made it happen. And the calls and e-mails flooded in: "Thank you! Thank you!"

One manager even remarked that Señor Rojas "has a magical vault filled with magical money that saves lives and protects families and schools."

The truth was, indeed, often said in jest, and the vault contained within the mansion at Cuernavaca just outside Mexico

City was, in fact, piled from floor to ceiling with dollars and pesos. Walls and walls of cash. Millions and millions—money that would be deftly laundered through the networks and the shell companies and deposited in overseas accounts in addition to bolstering Rojas's legitimate businesses, his dealerships and restaurants and cigarette manufacturers and telecom companies.

Because the one business that not only weathered rough economic times but even flourished was the drug trade. At times Rojas wished he could detach himself from the business that had helped build his empire. It had been a painstaking challenge to keep his identity and involvement in the cartel a secret. Neither his wife nor his son knew anything about the Juárez Cartel and how Rojas, then a senior in college, had become involved with the business.

Rojas had met a grad student named Enrique Juárez, who his colleagues and professors said was a genius in recombinant DNA gene technology and the insulin manufacturing process. Juárez wanted to establish a pharmaceutical company in Mexico to take advantage of the cheap labor. So impressed was Rojas by the business proposal that he invested a huge portion of his life savings (nearly $20,000) for a partnership in the company. GA Lab (Genetics Acuña) was established in Ciudad Acuña (population 209,000) along the banks of the Rio Grande, south of Del Rio, Texas. Juárez had explained the process of their operation: The first contract was to produce the A chain with twenty-one amino acids and the B chain containing thirty amino acids as the precursor to the synthesis of human insulin.

Once the A and B amino-acid chains were grown, GA would ship the material back to the United States, where it would be stitched into circular DNA strands called plasmids, using special enzymes to perform molecular surgery, the next step in the insulin manufacturing process.

The contracts came in. The business took off, and during the next five years both Rojas and Juárez drew six-figure salaries. Rojas clearly saw the advantage of owning a pharmaceutical company with a legitimate front, and he began to hire people behind Juárez's back to produce black-market versions of drugs such as Dilaudid, Vicodin, Percocet, and Oxycontin, all of which produced more money than the insulin side of the business.

One Friday night, over a long dinner and even more heated debate, Juárez stared at Rojas through his thick glasses and said, "Jorge, I don't like the direction you are taking our company. There's too much at stake now. Too much to lose. I don't care how much we make on the black-market drugs. If we get caught, we lose everything."

"I know what you're saying. That's why I'm prepared to buy you out of the business. You can take the money and start up a new venture. I'll make you a very generous offer. I don't want to see you unhappy. We started this with some great ideas and a lot of praying. Let me free you up to do something else."

"I created this business. It was my brainchild from the start. You know that. I'm not going to hand it over to you. We were partners, but you've never consulted me on any of this. You've gone behind my back. I can't trust you anymore."

Rojas stiffened. "You'd be nothing without my money."

"I won't sell you this business. I'm asking you to stop risking everything."

"You need to accept my offer."

"No, I don't." Juárez rose, wiped his mouth, and stormed away from the table.

The next morning he attempted to fire all of the scientists and lab personnel Rojas had hired.

Rojas told him to go away, take a week off, go skiing in Switzerland. He was not thinking clearly. Juárez finally resigned himself to the pressure and took the vacation. Unfortunately, while there he died in a terrible skiing "accident," and had left all of his money and property to his elderly mother, who immediately struck a most agreeable deal with Rojas.

The Juárez Cartel had been unofficially named after the city where the operation did most of its business, but the striking irony was that the man responsible for its birth also bore the same name. Rojas had begun with a small pharmaceutical company, which he expanded into many more businesses, which in turn helped him to create companies that could help launder money while purchasing huge swaths of real estate that cut through some of the most populated cities in Mexico.

He recognized that the quickest way to achieve expertise in new enterprises was to bypass time-consuming learning curves and buy up successful preexisting companies in that market. His understanding of finances and how to move and sell product led to the rapid—even extreme—growth of his empire. However, his organization was not without problems. Three of the cartel's highest-ranking members began running the drug-smuggling operations into the ground based on their egos and hubris, thus he'd been forced to "remove" them from power. The decision—like the one concerning Juárez—still haunted him, but he knew if he didn't act swiftly, the operation would go down, and he along with it.

In more recent years he'd purchased land in New York City and made millions by flipping such parcels. He bailed out book and magazine publishers and bought stock in them. He often flirted with the idea of simply handing over the entire cartel and its businesses to Fernando Castillo, who would provide stable and keen leadership. Rojas had been ready to make a clean break, but then the world's economy had nose-dived, and he'd been forced to reinforce his companies and build back his earnings by remaining the clandestine leader of what now had become the most profitable and powerful drug cartel in Mexico.

How did he do it?

He thought of leaning toward Campbell and telling him the truth. *"Jeffrey, this world is unfair. This world took my dear wife from me. And because of that, I can't play by the rules. I have to take chances like my brother did. So I'm doing what I have to do. Doing what good I can in the world, but I know that other lives are being ruined, that good people are dying, but many more are being saved. This is the ugly truth of me. The terrible secret. At least you don't have to live with it . . . Only I do."*

J.C. arrived with their dinner—freshly made fajitas that

filled the cabin with an aroma that made Rojas dizzy. He thought of Miguel, who'd soon be heading off with his young lady for a short vacation.

What would that day be like? The day his only son learned the truth?

18

THE SLEEPING DOG

Casa de Nariño
Bogotá, Colombia

THE PRESIDENTIAL PALACE of Colombia had been named in honor of Antonio Nariño, born 1765, who'd been one of the political and military leaders of the independence movement in Colombia and who'd built his own home on the same site. Four pairs of round columns rose up to a stunning archway at the palace's entrance, and as Rojas passed into the shadows of that magnificent work of art, he thought that yes, it would be nice to live in a house with as much history and tradition as this one. Jeff Campbell came up behind him, and President Tomás Rodriguez was already there, beaming at them. He had a thick shock of dark brown hair and wore a black suit, white dress shirt, and gold silk tie that gave Rojas pause. He'd never seen material as smooth and glistening, and he made a mental note to ask the president about it.

The introductions were brief, with the president making direct eye contact and giving both Rojas and Campbell firm handshakes, following up with an *abrazo* for Rojas and a firm pat on the shoulder. "It has been too long, my friend."

"I apologize for our late arrival," said Rojas. "But after that madness in Paris, passing through customs was nearly a three-hour ordeal."

"I understand the delay," said Rodriguez. "Now, I've set us up in the library. I won't turn in until ten this evening, so we have plenty of time. We can also move to the observatory, if it's not too cold. I'm sure you'll chew my ear off with the reports on your holdings, more than I'd ever want to know about petroleum, coffee, and coal . . . I want to tell you that we're doing much better than the last time we talked."

"Yes, we are," said Rojas, his tone brightening.

The president started off.

Campbell turned to Rojas and grinned. "This is incredible."

"Of course," said Rojas. Then he added in a whisper, "And when we're finished, you're going to have a government contract, trust me."

"Excellent," Campbell said with a gasp.

They shifted past the entrance foyer, whose walls displayed fine pieces of framed art, including several paintings of Antonio Nariño himself, along with ornate furniture dating back several hundred years. This kind of history and opulence no longer moved Rojas to an outward reaction, but he enjoyed watching Campbell's eyes grow even wider the farther they ventured into the palace.

His phone vibrated. He checked the text message from Fernando Castillo: I'm here now with Ballesteros.

Rojas nodded inwardly. Ballesteros had been having a very rough time of it, and Rojas was glad they were here now in the country to help his loyal supplier. Ballesteros's enemies were about to suffer the full wrath of the Juárez Cartel.

FARC Base Camp
Somewhere in the Jungle
Near Bogotá, Colombia

Colonel Julio Dios of the Revolutionary Armed Forces of Colombia, the largest and oldest insurgent group in the Americas, settled down onto his cot inside the tent. This was his fiftieth birthday, and he'd spent the day drinking and celebrating with his men. Ah, the word *men* was being too generous. Most of his force was comprised of boys, really, barely eighteen, some only fourteen or fifteen, but he had trained them well, and they were fiercely loyal to him and his mission to further squeeze the cocaine producers for more money so they could expand and better equip their force. They were hardly ready for a military coup against the government of Colombia, but Dios speculated that in several years, FARC forces could rise up and attain a decided victory. They would finally bring down the corrupt president and his intolerable regime. For now, though, they would increase their funding by more heavily taxing the drug producers. The relationship he had with one producer in particular, Juan Ramón Ballesteros, had been an ad hoc alliance of convenience, with Ballesteros often trading cocaine for weapons. FARC made sure to steer itself clear of any involvement in the actual production and transportation of the drugs, and he provided Ballesteros with the added security he needed to the keep local and federal law enforcement authorities off his back.

But while Ballesteros was expanding his business, Dios and his comrades were being aggressively hunted down, their numbers beginning to dwindle, their fate seemingly tied to the generosity of Ballesteros and other drug traffickers like him. That, Dios had decided, needed to change, and so he had been putting more than a little pressure on the drug man, whose stubbornness would soon get him killed.

Dios cupped his head in his hands. He was ready to enjoy a long and restful night.

He neither heard nor saw the man enter his tent, only felt the hand go over his mouth and the white-hot pain flood into his chest. When he finally looked up through the grainy darkness, he saw only a figure dressed in black, the face covered by a balaclava with only one eye cut out—or was that a patch lying beneath the other eyehole?

"Ballesteros sends his regards. You don't fuck with us. Ever. Your boys will know that now . . . Go see God . . ."

The man punched him in the chest again, more white-hot pain, and suddenly Dios had no control over his arms and legs.

He wanted to cough. Couldn't. He started to take a breath. Couldn't. And then . . .

As he left the tent with blood-covered gloves, Fernando Castillo thought about the other men who were being killed at the exact same moment, six other high-ranking FARC leaders who would all be murdered with notes pinned to their chests "asking" for their renewed cooperation and "patience." The Juárez Cartel had spoken.

Private Mansion
Bogotá, Colombia

"You will lead them. You will bring the jihad back to the United States—and you must use the contacts you've made with the Mexicans to do that. Do you understand?"

Those were Mullah Abdul Samad's orders, and every decision he made was directed toward completing that mission. No matter how much he loathed what he was about to do, he would not forget Mullah Omar Rahmani's words.

Samad had traveled alone in the black Mercedes limousine. Niazi and Talwar were watching Spanish soap operas back at the Charleston Hotel, where Ballesteros had put them up in suites— all seventeen of them. Fourteen of Samad's fifteen fighters had arrived in the city, and it was Allah's will that he, Niazi, and Talwar had escaped from that jungle house after the attack by FARC paramilitary troops. Thus far there had been only one setback: the death of Ahmad Leghari in Paris. That Ballesteros could not use the submarine to get them into Mexico was an issue that could be addressed, but most crucial was the border crossing into the United States. If Samad could strike a deal now with the Juárez Cartel, then the most challenging leg of his journey would be addressed. If not, there would be other plans set into motion, and Rahmani had said that he was already in contact with at least one other cartel. He'd feared that contacting several cartels at once might alert Rojas, and so they would advance slowly, subtly.

The limousine driver, a young man no more than twenty-one, took him up across the broad cobblestone driveway and toward the entrance of a spectacular colonial-style mansion set into the foothills and overlooking the entire city. This, Ballesteros had said, was yet another of his boss's vacation homes, worth millions in a good real estate market, and Samad, being a man of simple means and simple resources, could not help but despise the ostentation of it all, from the dozens of dormer windows to the six different fountains set across the circular driveway to the marble statues that suggested he'd arrived at a museum rather than a private residence. They stopped before a pair of wooden doors hand-carved with leaf patterns accented in gold and finished in a deep walnut. The driver stepped out and opened the door for Samad, who slid outside. He would be unrecognizable to even his trusted lieutenants, were they to glimpse him from afar. The beard and hair had been severely trimmed, and he'd purchased a very Western business suit along with a leather attaché. He was, to any Colombian, a successful-looking foreign businessman who on the weekends enjoyed the outdoors, as suggested by his rough-and-tumble beard and lean frame.

A slightly hunchbacked man with gray mustache and dressed in a butler's uniform met him at the door and led him onto a back terrace, where the man Samad had come to see was alone before a wrought-iron table, reading the daily edition of *La República Bogotá*, a glass of orange juice waiting at his side.

"Señor Rojas? Your guest has arrived," said the butler in Spanish.

The newspaper lowered to reveal a man shockingly young for his position. Samad tried to hide his surprise as the man rose, raked fingers through thick black hair with the barest touch of gray, then reached out to offer Samad a firm handshake.

"*Buenos días*. Please, have a seat."

"*Gracias*," Samad said, assuming they would speak in Spanish. "It's a great honor to finally meet you in person. Mullah Rahmani has shared many great things about you."

"Well, I appreciate that. Your breakfast will be here shortly."

"Excellent."

"Señor Ballesteros tells me you have a rather large party accompanying you."

"That's true."

Rojas made a face. "That troubles me. And I already expressed my concern to Mullah Rahmani."

"Then you understand our dilemma," said Samad.

"I'm afraid I don't. He didn't tell me the reason for your

visit, only that you were coming and that it was extremely important that we talk."

"Well, before we discuss that, I would like to assure you that the mistakes made in Pakistan will not happen again. The CIA has put a lot of pressure on us, but we've recruited an operative on the inside. He's given us a few names. With his help, shipments will resume as usual."

Rojas hoisted one of his brows. "I'm sure they will, otherwise I'll be forced to find another supplier. Many warlords in the north have been knocking on my door. And as I've made Rahmani very much aware, we are the only cartel with whom you will do business."

"Of course."

"Mark my words. If I learn that you're not happy with us and sell your product to perhaps the Sinaloa Cartel or another one of my competitors, there would be grave consequences."

While Samad could not hide his disdain over being threatened, he remained keenly aware that he would not leave these grounds alive were he to cross this man. "We understand very clearly that our arrangement is exclusive. And we're very happy to be working with you and for you to take such care in trying to expand the reach of our product, which has, in the past, been largely ignored by the cartels. In fact, we are so grateful for your help that I've brought some gifts."

Samad caught Rojas staring at his briefcase. "Oh, no," Samad added with a grin. "They're not in here. They are much larger, shall we say."

"I think I know what you have in mind."

"Yes. Something for your enemies."

Back at Ballesteros's jungle house were two trucks loaded down with sophisticated improvised explosive devices manufactured in Samad's factory in Zahedan. Along with the hundreds of bombs were twenty-two crates of Belgian-made FN 5.7 pistols, which Samad knew were a favorite among the Mexican drug cartels, who used the *mata policía* against police wearing body armor. The pistol's rounds often penetrated that armor, and Samad assumed a gift like this would most assuredly please Rojas and his *sicarios*.

Samad removed from his briefcase an inventory sheet and showed it to Rojas, whose gaze widened. "Excellent."

"I'll have them delivered this afternoon."

"Not here. I'll have Fernando call you to make arrangements for that. So I'm to assume you didn't come all this way to deliver arms or to apologize for what happened in Pakistan?"

"No."

"You're looking for a favor."

Samad sighed deeply. "One of our dear friends, a revered imam, has been stricken with lung cancer and needs to enter the United States for advanced medical treatment. He's traveling with us, along with his two sons, two nephews, and a group of acolytes. I assure you he is no terrorist, only a poor dying soul who needs the best medical help we can find for him. The university in Houston has the number-one-ranked cancer center. We want to bring the imam there. But we need your help. You see, because of his religious beliefs and questionable funding from Arab states, his name is on the U.S. terrorist list and also on the international no-fly list. If you would help us get him and his party to Houston, we would be eternally grateful."

Another servant appeared at the table and set before Samad a tray with some toast, jam, breakfast cereal, and coffee. The interruption was awkward, as he was trying to read the reaction on Rojas's face.

Samad thanked the woman, then glanced up at Rojas, who was staring hard at his glass of orange juice. He leaned toward the table and said, "I can't help you."

"But señor, this is a matter of life and death."

"Indeed, it is."

Rojas pushed back his chair, stood, walked away from the table, then returned, scratching his chin in thought. When he finally spoke again, his tone had grown much darker: "Can you imagine what would happen if your party were caught? Can you imagine that?"

"But we would not be caught, because we would rely upon your expertise to get us there."

Rojas shook his head. "The United States is a sleeping dog. And as they say, we must let sleeping dogs lie. If we awaken that dog, then both you and I will suffer his wrath. We could be arrested, and our businesses would be ruined. I've made this very clear to Rahmani. You cannot use us to fight your jihad. You will never be able to use us for safe passage into the United States. I will never do anything to threaten the demand for our product, and both you and I understand that Americans are the number-one consumers of our product."

"The imam will surely pass away without your help."

"There's too much to risk. The United States is already allocating millions more to protect its border. The drones that cause you so much trouble in Waziristan? Well, they're flying them along the border, too. You have no idea how difficult it is for us right now, the length and breadth of our operation to evade them—and all of this while the dog is still asleep."

Rojas's expression neared implacable. There would be no changing his mind. Samad knew better than to push the issue now. "I understand your concerns. I'm disappointed by your decision, and we will have to tell the imam that we must look elsewhere for treatment."

"That much I can help you with. I'll have my office make some calls, and we'll find you a cancer center that should meet all of the imam's needs."

"Thank you very much, señor."

Rojas excused himself to take a phone call, and Samad sampled his breakfast. When the man returned to the table, he took a long pull on his orange juice, then said, "Samad, I'm still very troubled by this visit. I'm concerned that you and your group might do something rash. I'm going to call Mullah Rahmani and tell him the same thing I'm about to tell you—if you try to gain entry into the United States, our deal will be off. No one in Mexico will buy any of your opium. No one. I will shut down your business. In fact, when I'm finished, no one in the world will buy from you. I want you to think very carefully about that. What we have at this moment is something special.

Ruining that to save one man is foolish. I don't want to sound coldhearted. These are the facts."

"Trust must be earned," said Samad. "And I have not earned yours yet. But I will. You'll see. So, please, do not worry about this anymore."

"Good. Now, then, do you have a wife? Any children?"

"No."

"I'm sorry to hear that, because that call I just received was from my son. He's off to a vacation with his girlfriend, and recently he's been making me feel very old." Rojas grinned, then took another pull on his juice.

Back at the Charleston Hotel, Samad met with Talwar and Niazi and gave them a summary of the meeting. They wore the same expression when he was finished.

"Ballesteros is loyal to Rojas. I don't think he can be bought. So we're going to cancel our plans to travel to Mexico with his help."

"But Mullah Rahmani has ordered us—"

"I know," Samad said, cutting off Talwar. "We're still going to Mexico, but we need to get there without Ballesteros or anyone else associated with the cartel knowing what we're doing now. I really thought we could get Rojas's help, but I was wrong."

"You said he threatened to end our arrangement."

"He did, but I spoke to Rahmani on the way back here, and he told me he doesn't care about Rojas or the Mexicans anymore. There will always be new buyers. If the Mexicans cannot help us with the jihad, then they, too, should be considered expendable."

His lieutenants nodded, and then Niazi said, "We have a friend, I think, who can fly us to Costa Rica. Do you remember him?"

Samad grinned. "Very good. Yes, I remember. Call him now."

They were going to the United States.

And Rojas had been right: They must let the sleeping dog lie . . .

So they could put a knife in its heart.

19

NEW ALLIANCES

Sacred Heart Catholic Church
Juárez, Mexico

MOORE SAT in the last pew on the right side, staring up at the stained-glass windows depicting images of Jesus and the Virgin Mary. Beams of light twinkling with dust motes shone down across the six-foot-tall brass crucifix that stood atop a marble pedestal. Sacred Heart was a modest-sized church in a run-down neighborhood on the outskirts of the city; it stood like an oasis of hope in a genuine slum of rusting cars and graffiti. The red carpet unfurling toward the candlelit altar had dark stains here and there, and Moore imagined those had come from blood and that the cleaners had been unable to remove them. There was no sacred ground, no line that could not be crossed. And it was no secret that the cartels had been blackmailing the local churches, extorting money and using priests and pastors as message bearers to their congregations: "This Sunday night all residents are urged to remain home. Do not go out on the street." A hit was going down. Only two weeks prior, a grandmother who lived a mere three blocks from the church had thrown her sixteen-year-old grandson a birthday party. She had chosen to have the party at her house and not at the church or community center in the interest of safety. What she hadn't known was that her grandson had ties to the Sinaloa Cartel, and that they had put a target on his back. Four gunmen from the Juárez Cartel had arrived at the party and begun firing. Thirteen had died, including an eight-year-old boy.

As Moore's uneasiness grew, the icons that adorned the church's back wall began to morph into images of demons, and now he imagined two men standing at the altar: a bearded man with a black turban, clutching an AK-47, and a shorter Mexican getting ready to pull the pin on a grenade. He closed his eyes, told himself to calm down, that the Agency knew exactly where he was, that Fitzpatrick had his back, and that these Sinaloa thugs were still as wary of him as he was of them. A knot began to twist in his stomach.

Earlier in the day, fat man Luis Torres had accompanied him to the bank, where he'd withdrawn another $50,000 in cash and had delivered it to him on the spot. The thug had been quite impressed, and it was amazing how his attitude changed in the face of bundled cash. The meeting with Sinaloa Cartel leader Zúñiga had been arranged, and Moore had been driven out to the church and told to wait for the man inside.

How many meetings like this had Moore attended? There was that night in Saudi Arabia when he'd spent thirteen hours waiting for an informant. He'd lived in a ditch in the Helmand Province for over a week in order to spend five minutes talking to an Afghan warlord. He'd spent nine days in the Somali jungle waiting for an Islamic militant to return to his jungle hideout. Too much waiting. Too much to ponder. He began thinking about God and the afterlife and Colonel Khodai and his young operative recruit, Rana, and all the other friends he'd lost. He thought of praying for their forgiveness. The mottled carpet in his mind's eye turned to tile, and the candlelight dissolved into the harsh glare of the old briefing room aboard the aircraft carrier *Carl Vinson*. American flags and seals of the U.S. Navy rose behind their commander.

"We will engage in a hydrographic recon of the Al Basrah Oil Terminal. The information we gather will be vital in the planning of tomorrow's attack."

Moore had become the Officer in Charge (OIC) of a SEAL platoon, with Carmichael as his assistant OIC, despite Carmichael's identical rank of O-3, superior knowledge, and tenacity. The advantage Moore had in physical ability Carmichael made up for in tactical skills. He could memorize maps, mission plans, anything he viewed or read. He could get you in and out swiftly, safely, without ever consulting a GPS. They'd become a formidable pair, with reputations that preceded them.

"No glory in this one," Carmichael said. "We go in and take pictures of an Iraqi oil platform. Whoop-dee-do."

"Frank, I'm counting on you for the usual."

He frowned. "Dude, you have to ask? I've had your back since BUD/S. What's wrong?"

The knot twisted tighter in Moore's stomach. "Nothing."

"Mr. Howard?"

Moore snapped open his eyes and turned toward the church's center aisle.

Ernesto Zúñiga was much shorter and slighter than his photographs led one to believe. His thinning hair was gelled straight back, and his sideburns were white at the roots. He had an unfortunate complexion, scarred heavily by acne, and the deep line from an old wound ran down from his left cheek and across his jaw. He was missing one earlobe. The file had said he was fifty-two, but Moore would have put him closer to sixty. He'd either dressed down so that he wouldn't be noticed or simply wore polo shirts and jeans as a course of habit, but Moore grinned inwardly over how he stood in sharp juxtaposition to a narcissist like Dante Corrales from the Juárez Cartel. You could mistake Zúñiga for a guy selling bagged oranges on the street corner—and that might be how he preferred it.

"Señor Zúñiga, I appreciate you coming."

"Don't get up." Zúñiga blessed himself, genuflected, and slid into the pew next to Moore. "The people pray every Sunday for an end to all the violence."

Moore nodded. "That's why I'm here."

"*You* can answer their prayers?"

"We both can."

He chuckled under his breath. "Some say I'm the cause of the problem."

"Not you alone."

He shrugged. "It's my understanding that you want to work out a deal."

"We have the same goal."

"You paid a lot of money for this meeting, so I suppose I will listen to you . . . for a few minutes."

Moore nodded. "The Juárez Cartel is crushing your business. I know what they've done to you."

"You know nothing."

"They murdered your wife and sons. I know you've never gotten revenge for that."

He grabbed Moore's wrist and squeezed. "Do not talk about revenge in the house of God."

"Then I'll talk about justice."

"What do you know? Have you ever lost anyone close to you, a young man like yourself? Do you know what real pain feels like?"

Moore braced himself, then finally said, "I'm not that young. And you have to believe when I say I *know* how you feel."

Zúñiga made a face, then snorted. "You come here with your bullshit story about buying my property for your solar-panel company, and then you tell Luis you are an assassin, but you are just another scumbag DEA man from California or Texas trying to flip me. I have been doing this my entire life, and you try to play me for a fool? We will mail them your head, and then we'll be done with this."

"You're wrong about me. If we work together, I promise you that neither you nor anyone in your operation will be touched. My group is much more powerful than any of your enemies."

"There is nothing you can say, Mr. DEA Man, that will get me to help you. And leaving this church alive is going to cost you yet another fifty thousand."

Moore smiled. "I don't work for the DEA, but you're right. I'm not interested in your properties, only your enemies, and I can promise you that the group I work for will not only pay you well, but we can establish a new joint venture for opium transport—just like the Juárez Cartel is doing now. Let's be honest. People are not lining up in this church, reaching out a hand to help you—and it's clear to us that you need help."

"You tempt me with your lies, you really do, but I'm afraid you're wasting your time, because neither your group nor I will ever bring down the Juárez Cartel."

Moore frowned deeply. "Why do you say that?"

"I thought your people knew everything."

"If we did, I wouldn't be here."

"Very well." Zúñiga gathered his breath, and what he said next sounded somewhat rehearsed, as though he'd given this speech to his men to put their actions into perspective. "I'll tell you a story about a man who grew up very poor, a man who watched his brother die before his eyes, a man who saved up enough money and went to America for his education, then returned to Mexico to start many businesses. This is a man who used drug trafficking to help support and finance those businesses, a man who over the years became one of the richest men in the world. This is the man you want to bring down, the Caesar you want to overthrow, but his resources are endless, and all we can do now is fight small battles in a war we lose."

"What's his name?"

Zúñiga began to chuckle. "Are you serious? If your group is so powerful, they should already know."

"I'm sorry, we don't."

Zúñiga made a face. "Jorge Rojas."

Moore nearly fell out of the pew. He knew the name well. "Rojas is the leader of the Juárez Cartel? He's always been a person of interest to us, but there's never been any real evidence to pin on him. How can you be sure?"

"Oh, I'm sure. He's threatened me personally. And he's buried himself behind a wall of beautiful lies so that no one can ever touch him. He has the audacity of Pablo Escobar and the resources of Bill Gates. He is the smartest and most powerful drug trafficker in the history of the world."

"Do your men know this? Are they aware of how powerful their enemy is?"

Zúñiga shook his head. "They don't need to know that. It's too depressing to discuss with them, so we don't talk about it . . ."

Moore slowly nodded. That explained why Fitzpatrick hadn't come to the joint task force earlier with the knowledge that Rojas was the cartel leader. "If he's got so much money, why would he continue to run a drug cartel?"

Zúñiga's eyes widened. "Why not? People have questioned why during such tough economic times his businesses never fail.

It's because they are helped by drug money, always helped. This is all Rojas knows, but now he is far removed from the daily operation and his lieutenants do all the work. I really believe he is living in denial now. Truly living in denial. He puts his name on schools and calls himself a saint, while he employs demons to do all his dirty work."

"Dante Corrales."

Zúñiga recoiled at the sound of the name. "Yes. How do you know that name?"

"I told you we know a lot—but not everything."

"What else do you know?"

"We know they control the border tunnels, and they rip off your guys. We've heard they disrupt and steal your shipments, and use the Federal Police to kill your men while their boys are left alone. We know the Guatemalans are hunting you now. I can get you access back to the tunnels and get the police and the Guatemalans off your back. We can work together, and we'll find a way to bring down Rojas."

Zúñiga's lips curled in a dubious grin. "A ridiculous dream. I'm sorry, Mr. Howard. Luis is going to take you to the bank. And you're going to give him another fifty thousand dollars. Then we'll decide whether you live or die."

Moore's voice turned softer, more emphatic. "Ernesto, I didn't come here alone. You don't need any more enemies. You have enough already. Let me go, and I will earn your trust. I promise you. Give me a number that you and I can use to talk directly."

"No."

"You have nothing to lose. In fact, you'll have more to lose if you don't do something soon. Even if you don't believe who I say I am—and you still think I'm DEA, what's the difference? I'm telling you, we won't touch you. We want the Juárez Cartel. We want Rojas."

"You're a very persuasive man, Mr. Howard. You seem almost too comfortable, as though you have done this many times before."

Zúñiga was very observant and certainly correct, although the last time Moore had been in a house of worship it had been a chapel, and he'd dismissed the Navy chaplain with a wave of his hand.

"You cannot abandon your faith," the chaplain had said. "Not at a time like this, when your faith is what will carry you through. You will overcome."

"I want to believe that, Father. I really do . . ."

Moore narrowed his gaze on Zúñiga. "I'll give you the money. You let me go, and while you consider my offer, I'll see what I can do to help your business. I think you might be very surprised."

"They're going to say I'm crazy for trusting you."

"No need to trust me yet. I told you I will earn it. Will you give me that opportunity?"

Zúñiga frowned. "I didn't get where I am by taking the easy or the safe road. I told my dear wife to take a chance on me, and she did. And now I know how she feels."

"Thank you, señor." Moore proffered his hand, and after a moment's hesitation, Zúñiga took it—

And then he squeezed the hand firmly and tugged Moore toward him. "Do the right thing."

Moore's voice did not waver. "I will."

Consulado Inn
Juárez, Mexico

It was nearly ten p.m., and Johnny Sanchez was alone in his hotel room, typing furiously on his notebook computer after having just inhaled two cheeseburgers and a large order of fries, the grease-stained wrappers and containers lying on the desk near his mouse. The city's lights were gleaming, and the U.S. Consulate was just five hundred yards off and clearly visible through his window. He pushed back his desk chair and reread what he'd just written:

```
EXT. BURNING HOTEL — NIGHT
As Corrales falls to his knees in the street, the
fires raging skyward: an inferno of an old life
turning to ashes. The boy looks skyward, the flames
reflected in his tear-filled eyes, and he rages
aloud against the heavens. We cry with him . . .
```

"That is fucking beautiful," Johnny shouted at the computer screen. "Fucking beautiful! Who's the man? You the man, Johnny! This bitch is going to sell big-time!"

A slight click came from the hallway, and as Johnny looked up, the front door opened. Johnny bolted from his chair and gasped at a man dressed in dark slacks, a black shirt, and a leather jacket. The man was over six feet, with a closely cropped beard, an earring, and long hair pulled back into a ponytail. He appeared either Arabic or Hispanic, Johnny wasn't sure, but he felt pretty certain about the make of the pistol in the man's hand. It was a Glock, all right, most certainly loaded, and pointed at Johnny's head. Attached silencer. Johnny's pistol was in the nightstand drawer, out of reach, damn it.

"What the fuck is this?" Johnny asked in Spanish.

The man answered in English. "This is me saying, 'Hi, Johnny. I read your article. Good stuff. You're a good writer.'"

"Who the fuck are you?"

The man's expression twisted. "Didn't your mother ever teach you to respect a man who's got a gun to your head? These are those little life lessons she should've taught you."

"Are you done with your alpha-male bullshit? What the fuck are you doing here?"

"How long did you think it would take? Did you think you could come down here to Mexico and hang out with a drug cartel and not gain anyone's attention?"

"I don't know what you're talking about. I'm an investigative journalist. I report on criminal activity. You read my fucking article. You think I'm in bed with them? You're fucking nuts. And I'm calling the police."

The man shifted up to him, raising the pistol even higher. His playful tone vanished. "Sit down, motherfucker."

Johnny returned to his chair. "Jesus Christ . . ."

"The wheels are spinning now, huh? You're thinking, *Holy shit, what have I gotten myself into?* Well, you should've thought about that before you started working with Corrales. Blood might be thicker than water, but as I like to say, lead will always get you dead."

"Look, asshole, all I'm doing is writing. I'm not hurting anyone. I'm not taking from anyone."

"But you're not helping anyone, either."

"Bullshit I'm not. I'm taking the American public into the trenches of the drug war here. This is a behind-the-scenes tour into hell, into how screwed up this community has become."

"That sounds pretty fucking dramatic, and I guess it is, since you've got a gun to your head right now. Are you going to put me in an article?"

"Who the fuck are you?"

The man widened his eyes. "I'm your last friend in the whole wide world. Now show me your hand."

"What?"

"Show me your hand."

Johnny extended one palm, and the man used his free hand to grab Johnny's and turn it backside up.

"Here, hold this," said the man, offering Johnny the gun.

"What the fuck?" Johnny cried.

"Oh, don't worry. It's not loaded."

The man shoved the gun in Johnny's free hand, then reached into an inner breast pocket and produced a large syringe that he shoved into the soft tissue between Johnny's thumb and fore-finger. The pain was sharp for a second, and Johnny screamed and demanded to know what was happening. The man released him and said, "Gun?"

"Are you for real?"

The guy made a face. "Gun?"

"What did you do? Poison me?"

"Easy, Shakespeare. It's just an implant. GPS. So we can keep you safe."

"Who's 'we'?"

"There are a lot of letters in the alphabet, Johnny, and I'm betting as a writer you can figure that out."

"DEA?" Johnny asked. "Oh my God."

"Sorry," said the man. "I'm afraid you've just climbed into bed with the United States government."

Johnny's shoulders shrank. "This cannot be happening."

"Look, you can't talk. It's already too late for that. If you go to Corrales and tell him we're here, you'll die. We won't kill you, he will. Like I said, I'm your last friend. You won't make it out of Mexico alive without me."

Johnny's eyes began to burn, and he was fast running out of breath. "What do you want? What am I supposed to do?"

"The Juárez Cartel is being led by Jorge Rojas."

Johnny burst out laughing. "Is that what you dumbass Feds think? Oh my God . . . stupidity run amok!"

"I got that from Zúñiga."

"Are you kidding me?"

"Then you know who he is, and I'm sure Corrales can confirm that Rojas is his boss. I need you to pump Corrales for everything you can get on Rojas."

"Do I have to wear a wire?"

"Not right now. But we'll see."

Johnny stiffened. "I won't do it. I'm leaving Mexico tonight; you Feds can go fuck yourselves."

"Yeah, and the moment you step off the plane in California we'll place you under arrest."

"For what?"

The man eyed the junk-food wrappers on the desk. "For failing to eat a balanced diet."

"Dude, you'd better leave now."

"You are the son of Corrales's godmother. He trusts you like you were blood. And you feed his ego. That's very important to us, and you can do the right thing here. You might be afraid now, but I need you to think how many people will be saved because of your help. I can sit you down and spend a week showing you how many families have been ruined by drugs."

"Spare me the bleeding-heart bullshit. People choose to buy and use drugs. Corrales and the cartel are just the suppliers. You want to talk politics, then let's talk about the Mexican economy."

The man waved Johnny off and pulled a business card from his pocket and handed it to him. The guy's name was Scott Howard, and he was president of a solar-energy company. "So you're Mr. Howard? Yeah, right."

"My number's there. You let me know the next time you're going to make contact with Corrales."

Howard—or whatever his name was—pocketed his "empty" weapon and moved swiftly to the door.

Johnny sat there as a shudder ripped through his shoulders. What would he do?

20

DIVERSIONS

Border Tunnel Construction Site
Mexicali, Mexico

I T WAS SEVEN A.M., and Dante Corrales was not in the mood to wait for a man who was supposed to be working for him, a man who answered to him, a man who knew better than to disrespect him like this. Corrales had yet to have his morning coffee, and he'd wanted to get this meeting over within five minutes, but the workers in the tunnel had told him that Romero had still not arrived and that he usually didn't show up until eight a.m. What kind of bullshit was that? The man was being paid good money to get the job done, and he thought he could float in every morning at eight? Did he think he was a banker? Hell would be paid—with interest—and his failure to answer his cell phone was salt in the wound.

And so Corrales waited for him inside the warehouse, listening to the clunks and roars of heavy construction equipment being used next door. The vibrations worked their way up into his legs and back. Those guys got to work at dawn and finished at dusk. They didn't stroll in at eight. They had a sense of urgency that Romero needed to learn.

"Go get me some goddamned coffee," Corrales finally shouted at Raúl, who was loitering near the metal roll-up door with Pablo.

Raúl shook his head, muttered something under his breath, then headed outside, the sky washed pink by the rising sun. Pablo shifted up to Corrales and said, "Are you okay?"

"This fucking guy won't be here till eight, you believe that shit? And why isn't he answering his phone?"

"Something else is bothering you," said Pablo. "You want to talk about it?"

"What're you, my shrink?"

"You still upset about the two guys we lost at the V Bar? Don't be. Those assholes screwed up the job big-time. I told you from the get-go they were *cabrones*."

"I don't give a shit about them. It's the American I'm worried about. Can't find him now. He could be working with the Federal Police, who knows . . ."

"Aw, that dumb shit probably just got scared off. He didn't look like a Fed. Just some asshole business guy who thought he could come down here and get some Mexican slaves for his company, the fucker . . ."

"No, there's something happening, and if we don't keep our eyes wide open, this . . . all of this . . . is going to come tumbling down, and the boss will make sure you get buried right here."

Corrales sighed and waited another five minutes for his coffee. Pablo continued to make small talk, most of which Corrales ignored. Raúl finally returned, and Corrales practically wrenched the cup from Raúl's hand and took a long sip. His nose crinkled. This was hardly as good as the Starbucks he'd get on the other side of the border, but he'd drink it anyway, and as he reached the bottom of his cup at exactly 7:39, Pedro Romero dragged himself into the warehouse. He shoved his glasses farther up his nose and tugged at his jeans, which were dropping below his potbelly. He frowned at Corrales and the others and lifted his voice, "*Buenos días.*"

"Where the fuck you been?" Corrales asked, marching up to the man, whose gaze widened.

"I was at home, then I came here."

"You don't know how to answer your cell phone?"

"My battery died. I was recharging it in the car. Did you try to call me?"

"Uh, yeah. They told me you come in at eight a.m. Is that true?"

"Yes."

Corrales smacked the man hard across the face. Romero recoiled and raised a palm to his cheek.

"Do you know why I did that, old man? Do you? Because you are a digger! You are *not* a fucking banker! You get here when the sun comes up, and you leave when the sun goes down. Do you fucking understand me?"

"Yes, sir."

"You want to save your daughter?"

"Yes, sir."

"You want to collect your money?"

"Yes, sir."

"Then you get here when I say! Now, tell me right here, right now, that we have broken through to the other side and will be ready to begin shipping tonight."

"I need a few more days."

"What? 'A few more days'? What the fuck is that?"

"I will show you how far we are, but we've had some trouble. As I told you in the beginning, the water table is very shallow here, and we've had to pump water out of the tunnel quite a few times already. It is a complicated operation."

"Maybe if you got to work earlier, this wouldn't be a problem."

"Señor Corrales, I want to assure you that my being here one hour earlier would not make a huge difference. It takes all night to pump out the water, and we cannot dig while that's happening."

"Don't challenge me, old man. You better make me a believer. Let's go."

"All right, but you must know that these men are working as hard as they can. I have two shifts, as you ordered, but I cannot remain here around the clock. I have my family to take care of, and my wife needs help."

"Then you'd better find her some help, because I want this tunnel opened up and ready to go by tonight."

"Tonight? There is too much dirt and rock left to remove. It is physically impossible."

"No, it's not. You're going to make it happen. Trust me."

Corrales's smartphone rang. Fernando Castillo was calling. "Hello?"

"Dante, the boss has another job for you. We need you back right away."

Bell 430 Helicopter
En Route to San Cristóbal de las Casas
Chiapas, Mexico

Miguel Rojas and Sonia Batista sat in two of the three backseats of a twin-engine corporate helicopter whose cabin boasted utility seating for up to seven passengers in addition to the pilot and copilot. The helicopter was one of several Jorge used for short business trips, and while it was merely a corporate transport and not armed like a military craft, his pilots always carried pistols. As with all of Jorge's other means of transport, no expense had been spared in regard to accents and trim: rich Italian leather and exotic hardwoods, along with small flat screens and headphones to watch corporate presentations and/or movies. Miguel and Sonia had forgone the idea of watching a film in favor of taking in the views. They had donned their headsets and microphones so they could hear and speak to each other over the drone of the aircraft's powerful Rolls-Royce engines.

In front of them were the dour-faced bodyguards/ chaperones they'd been forced to drag along: Corrales, Raúl, and Pablo. *Well, it could be worse*, Miguel thought. Jorge had said he was sending a team of twelve men to travel with them, and some members of that team would arrive ahead of them. They would rent four SUVs to move in a caravan everywhere they went. Miguel had pleaded against this. He wanted a nice, intimate vacation with Sonia—not a security spectacle/parade everywhere he went. Besides, per his father's insistence, he'd kept a low profile for most of his life, and the average citizen in Mexico could not identify him the way they could identify Jorge. There was no reason to believe they needed such a big team, which would, in fact, call a lot of attention to themselves and perhaps even invite criminal activity as local citizens pointed their fingers and said, "There he goes, the rich guy with all his bodyguards." Jorge had finally agreed to send along three men, and Miguel thanked his father profusely for reaching a compromise. What Miguel hadn't counted on was Corrales's attitude. Miguel had made it quite clear to the man—the most arrogant of the bunch—that he needed to keep his distance and stop ogling Sonia. Even Corrales's simple "Yes, señor" sounded sarcastic. Miguel was certain that the man hated the fact that he'd worked for nothing, been handed everything on a silver platter—while Corrales had probably been a street punk who'd been lucky enough to get a job working for Jorge Rojas.

"How long will it take to get there?" Sonia asked, staring out the window.

"About three hours or so," Miguel answered. "But we have to make one stop to refuel. Have you ever been on a helicopter before?"

"A few times with my father. There was this famous cyclist—I can't even remember his name, because I was only ten or eleven at the time—but he's like a living legend and had his own helicopter. He took us on a vacation."

"I'll tell you something funny. There's a big nut on top of the rotor, and you know what the pilot calls it?"

She shook her head.

"He calls it the Jesus nut, because if that nut falls off, then you better start praying to Jesus . . ."

"Gee, that makes me feel better," she said, rolling her eyes.

"Are you scared?"

She shook her head, her hair gleaming in the light filtering in through the window.

"It's worth the flight, trust me," he told her. "And we'll be getting there during a special carnival they put on for tourists. You're going to love this place."

She grabbed his hand and squeezed it. "I know I will."

Consulado Inn
Juárez, Mexico

It was pretty damned obvious that Moore, aka Scott Howard, couldn't return to the hotel owned by Dante Corrales, as he'd have some explaining to do about why the men following him had been killed. He'd smiled inwardly over actually going there anyway, walking nonchalantly past Ignacio, who might ask, "How was your day, señor?"

"It was great. I got kidnapped by this *sicario* from the Sinaloa Cartel, but thank God Corrales's two boys were following us, because they killed my kidnapper, but then they got killed by more guys, so maybe it wasn't so great—because I was really hoping to be kidnapped by the Sinaloas. Long story short, it all worked out. Have I received any calls or packages? And also, I'd like the maid to leave me some extra towels."

Instead Moore chose the safer and far less audacious route of finding another hotel, but why scour the streets for a nice one when Johnny Sanchez had found himself a little slice of heaven right near the U.S. Consulate? Thus Moore got a room three doors down from Johnny's and rented himself a new car. Johnny wasn't happy with the arrangement and threatened to check out. Moore warned him about that.

JTF leader Towers sent a text message: Rojas's son, Miguel, had just left with his girlfriend, in a helicopter heading westward. Dante Corrales and two others were with them.

That Rojas's son was fraternizing with a known cartel member did "seem" to link Rojas to the cartel, but that evidence was, at the moment, purely circumstantial.

Yet something about that bothered Moore. A lot. Their joint task force had already received intelligence that identified Dante Corrales as a cartel member. This intelligence had been gathered well before the joint task force's formation. It was reasonable to assume that the Agency had kept their electronic and human eyes on Corrales since first identifying him as a player. Moore would have to check the file to see how long ago that had occurred—because if Rojas was involved, then it was reasonable to assume that this wasn't the first time Corrales had been around the family, in which case the Agency would have more clearly identified Rojas as more than a "person of interest."

Or maybe this was the first time Corrales had been seen with the family? Moore still had a difficult time believing that. So what was happening now? Where were they going? Moore leaned on Sanchez, and the writer called Corrales, who'd said he couldn't work on the screenplay for a week because he'd be in San Cristóbal de las Casas on a babysitting job.

Bingo.

Moore called Towers with a plan. Rojas made only rare public appearances and was otherwise never seen. Moore had a plan to draw him out, and when he finished going over it, Towers gave him the blessing.

An hour later, Moore was sitting in the backseat of Luis Torres's Range Rover. The fat man was at the wheel, with DEA agent Fitzpatrick riding beside him.

"You guys need to fly down there and kidnap the son and his girlfriend. You'll have some great leverage if you can do that. We'll draw out Rojas, and I'll take care of the rest. You bring this plan to Zúñiga and see what he says. And tell him he needs to start returning my calls."

"He doesn't trust you, Mr. Howard. And I doubt he'll start trusting you anytime soon."

"I've got intelligence photos of them leaving on the chopper. I've got an informant who personally spoke to Corrales and confirmed they'll be there for a week. You go down there, you kill Corrales and the other bodyguards, you kidnap the kid, and you've got Rojas by the balls. Which part are you failing to understand? I'm going to help you take out your main rival. Your enemy is my enemy. How many other ways do you want me to spell it out?"

"You could be setting us up, getting us to go down there so you and your little overseas group can take us out. Maybe you work for Rojas."

"Dude, if we wanted you dead, there'd already be weeds on your grave. Don't be fools. You *need* to do this. Tell Zúñiga this is the plan."

"I think he's right," said Fitzpatrick, trying not to make his endorsement too obvious. "Let's look at what he's got, and then Señor Zúñiga can make a decision."

"Don't waste too much time." Moore opened the back door and got out. "You need to be on an airplane today."

Moore walked across the alley to his rental car, climbed in, and drove off.

Miguel Rojas's little vacation with his girlfriend was an excellent lead and opportunity, and Moore had already shared the news with FBI Agent Ansara, who was working with his new mule/informant to penetrate one of the Juárez Cartel's primary smuggling routes.

Fellow CIA operative Vega was still keeping a close eye on inspector Alberto Gómez, the legendary veteran of the Federal Police who'd been dirty since his rookie year. However, Vega had shared some troubling news. Gómez, along with several other inspectors, was trying to "expose corruption" by setting up another inspector to take a fall, thus pointing the spotlight elsewhere. Vega suspected that he knew he was being watched, so this ploy was his answer.

ATF agent Whittaker reported that a large shipment of guns might be coming down from Minnesota very soon. Cartel members up there were amassing what he contended was their largest cache to date.

Fitzpatrick called later on in the day to confirm that Zúñiga was still mulling over the intel photos and plan, but he also said that the Sinaloa Cartel had just picked up some information from a spotter about a sizable shipment coming up from the south, and their spotter believed that this group of mules would use one of the cartel's smaller tunnels that ran for about 130 feet under a concrete-lined section of the Rio Grande near Juárez and the Bridge of the Americas.

Moore sent a message to Fitzpatrick: Tell the Sinaloa boys to stay away from the tunnel and go after Miguel Rojas. Moore would personally intercept that shipment and deliver it to Zúñiga as a clear sign of his willingness to help. That Moore would take out one set of drug smugglers to help another was the price they paid in order to catch the biggest fish of all. He'd done likewise in at least four different countries and no longer questioned the moral or ethical implications of his actions. It was the only way to fight an asymmetric enemy with no rules. He contacted Ansara and told him to have a Border Patrol force waiting at the predesignated storm drain in El Paso. Ansara was on it and would be ready with the net.

Moore was a bit surprised that JTF leader Towers himself met him in a parking lot about three blocks away from the drainage ditch. Moore's watch read nearly 1:08 a.m., and according to Towers, the mules would arrive within fifteen minutes in a white cargo van.

"They're not only moving drugs," Towers said, "but women and children. Big-time coyotes employed by the cartel. These guys might have a deal with a group of snakeheads in China—because the young girls we saw were all Asian. They bring them over here as sex slaves."

"Damn, it's just keeps getting uglier. Drugs, human trafficking . . ."

"Just stick to the plan."

"I will. So what brings you to this beautiful part of town?" Moore figured he'd pose the question, since the assumption had been that Towers would remain back in San Diego.

"I'm a field officer. They knew that when they hired me. Did they think they could get me to sit behind a desk the whole time? Hell, no . . ."

"I hear you."

"All right, then, buddy, let's get you ready."

Moore grinned and began to suit up in nondescript black fatigues, Kevlar vest, and balaclava. He was wearing nearly the same clothes as the two guards the Juárez Cartel had posted at the tunnel entrance.

His inventory included two Glock 21 .45-caliber pistols with attached wet/dry suppressors whose inside chambers had already been greased up to get the ultimate sound attenuation. He also grabbed a couple of smoke grenades and a couple of flash bangs, in case the group was not as "cooperative" as they could be. He slipped on an earpiece with attached boom mike, and took off running across the parking lot, with Towers's voice in his ear: "Next left and the ditch will be straight ahead. Good cover along the south-side wall. Once you get in past the big grating, your two buddies will be just inside."

An automotive junkyard's chain-link fence lined the left side of the street, with a row of ramshackle buildings collapsing to the right, all of them unoccupied—abandoned machine and tool shops, judging from the faded placards above their doors. Even the graffiti that slashed across some of the crumbling walls looked washed out. It was difficult to see much more detail, since the streetlights that towered overhead were all dark, their bulbs either shot out or burned out. Flickering light came from the block next door, and Moore wasn't sure of its source.

He reached the meter-high concrete wall along the south side of the ditch and kept tight, shifting hunched over until he found the two main grating plates lying on the opposite side of the ditch, about ten meters away: the main entrance to the storm drains and smaller tunnel inside. It'd been a considerably dry season, with only a few shallow puddles dotting the ground and a carpet of weeds spreading up to the grating. He grimaced over a faint sewage smell that he hoped would not get stronger once he crossed the ditch.

"ETA on the truck: five minutes," said Towers.

That wasn't much time. Moore tugged from his hip pocket a portable night-vision monocular. He raised the device to his right eye and zoomed in on the grating. Through the cross-hatched pattern he spotted one of the two guards sitting beside a circular hole burrowed in the side wall, the shadows beyond it fluctuating like pale green heat waves. The guard was about five feet tall, no mask—just a shaved head with tattoos forming a talon across his neck. Moore imagined a perfectly placed sniper's round sailing through one of the grating holes and taking out the man where he sat. Moore was a good shot, but hell he wasn't that good . . .

After a deep, calming breath, he pocketed the monocular and took off running across the ditch. He reached the grating and knew that lifting the door would cause a commotion. There just wasn't a way to sneak up on these guys. A section of the grating had been cut out to form a one-meter-by-one-meter hatch. Moore gave it a tug. Locked. *Shit.* He told Towers, who said, "Well, fuck it, dude, get them to open it."

"Hey," shouted one of the guards from inside. "You're here already? You're early."

"Hurry up!" Moore answered in Spanish. "We have a big shipment here!"

Moore raised one of his Glocks and waited for the man to unlock the grating. Despite the suppressor, his shot would hardly be silent. Even though his bullet would exit the barrel at subsonic speeds—which would help in the suppression of the sound—the Glock's slide would still make a loud enough click to alert anyone within the immediate area, most notably the other guard. The word *silencer* implied a blowgun-like thump, but that was a misnomer. Moreover, when you saw guys "limp-wristing," or one-handing a suppressed pistol and firing it, the kinetic energy from the slide would transfer to their wrists and not only make the shot go wide but possibly injure them, so you always held the pistol tightly with both hands, as Moore did.

Some might argue that the more silent way to kill the guard would be with a knife, but again, killing someone with a *single* knife blow was exceedingly difficult. After the first blow, you more often than not still had a struggle on your hands and several more blows to deliver while you tried to gag the guy. The whole affair was sloppy and much more dangerous—and Moore knew this firsthand from his SEAL training and from taking out several pirates in Somalia who'd each needed a half-dozen blows from his knife before they properly died. Moore preferred to take his chances with the clack of the slide and the assurance that one round would finish the job without him having to lay a hand on the man.

A lock clicked from inside, followed by the rattle of a chain. The grating squeaked upward, and the man thrust out his head and faced Moore.

His eyes widened first on Moore and then on the suppressor attached to Moore's Glock. He opened his mouth to scream.

Moore fired, the round hitting the guard just above his left eye and booting him back past the grating.

Before the brass casing from Moore's round could hit the dirt, he was on the move, lowering himself past the grating and down into the wider storm-drain conduit, a rectangular shaft of concrete about seven feet high by nearly fifteen feet across. He had to climb over the first guard's body and peer into the darkness, searching for the second guard.

Where was the son of a bitch? Surely he'd heard that round—and damn, there wasn't time to waste looking for him.

"I had to kill one of the mules!" Moore shouted, his voice echoing off into the conduit as he lifted the night-vision monocular to his eye. "He tried to steal from us."

Movement ahead.

Moore threw himself forward into a puddle spanning the floor. A shot rang out, striking the water at his elbow. He rolled away, onto his back, realizing that if he didn't sit up and return fire in the next two heartbeats, he was dead.

21

BULLETPROOF

Al Basrah Oil Terminal
Persian Gulf, Iraq
March 19, 2003

FOR JUST A SECOND, while he was lying in that puddle of water, staring straight up into the darkness, Moore took himself back to 2003 when he was also lying on his back but submerged to twenty feet and observing the silhouettes of two immense concrete pilings that grew thicker, like the muscular legs of a giant standing in knee-deep water. The oil platform's security lights transformed the surface into a rippling mirror of yellow-edged flashes that faded to a deep blue on the periphery. Within those dark expanses hovered four more shadows, like a pod of whales bobbing slowly on the current. An eerie calm settled over him as he floated there, his LAR V

Dräger closed-circuit gear emitting not a single bubble, his breathing controlled and rhythmic and allowing his thoughts to clear so he could focus on the task at hand. The digital camera worked effortlessly, capturing images so they could mark the positions of the platform's own underwater security cameras which he and the rest of his team had carefully evaded.

Moore, Carmichael, and the other SEALs organized into two four-man teams had used several Mark 8 mod 1 SEAL Delivery Vehicles—small manned submersibles—to arrive at the oil terminal's southern platform. The whole affair resembled a trampoline suspended high above the water by dozens of crab-like legs. Sweeping antennae and broad satellite dishes had been mounted atop the superstructure, along with a geodesic dome and perches for lookouts. Guards patrolled the railings on all four sides of the tower.

"No glory in this one. We go in and take pictures of an Iraqi oil platform. Whoop-dee-do."

Indeed, this was a by-the-numbers picture-taking recon operation that within a few minutes would be over and they'd be cracking open some beers for breakfast. While Moore got the underwater shots, the other three men in his charge were photographing what they could near and on the surface, marking the positions and courses of Iraqi patrol boats and gun emplacements on the platform.

At the moment, four tanker ships were simultaneously docked at the platform and having oil pumped into their holds. During the briefing Moore had learned that eighty percent of

Iraq's gross domestic product passed through the terminal, about 1.5 million barrels per day, which of course made Al Basrah a vital part of the country's economy and had warranted an unusual presence there, as noted by Carmichael over the radio: "Team Two, this is Mako Two, listen up. The regular garrison is gone. They've got Revolutionary Guard up there manning the lookouts. They've brought in the big guns, and they're armed for bear now."

"Roger that," answered Moore. "Everyone look for signs."

"We're on it, Mako One," answered Carmichael.

Moore had just ordered Carmichael's team and his own to search for signs of underwater demolitions and evidence of charges set up top, along the exterior of the platform. The Iraqis would rather destroy their oil terminal than have it fall into enemy hands, and knowing them, Moore figured they'd use C-4 but probably weren't clever enough to rig it to blow inward, nor were they even aware of expansion products such as Dexpan that would allow them to crack apart the platform's pilings in a much safer and more regulated way. If they had C-4 charges set below the surface, there was a good chance they'd hit the panic button and not only take out the structure but kill any SEALs in the water because those explosions would blow outward.

"Team Two, this is Mako Two, again. Got signs up top! Repeat! Got signs—charges rigged beneath the railing on south and east sides . . ."

But now that was not Carmichael's voice in Moore's ear; it was JTF leader Towers. "The van is pulling up outside! Moore, did you copy that? The van is there!"

Storm Drain
Near Bridge of the Americas
Juárez, Mexico
Present Day

Moore was still lying on his back, staring up at the ceiling. Towers shouted again, and reality came in a hard shudder through his shoulders. He sat up and rolled to his right, just as a beam of light struck his eyes and a gunshot pinged off the wall behind him, fragments of concrete striking his neck where the balaclava failed to reach. He lifted the monocular, spotted the second guard crouched about three meters away from that circular hole cut into the wall, and without hesitation returned fire, squeezing off four rounds until a faint cry came from ahead and a lit flashlight rolled across the floor. A glance through the monocular showed the second guy lying on his stomach, blood leaking from his mouth.

Cursing, Moore whirled back and bolted to the entrance. He seized the first guard's body and dragged it away as fast as he could, panting and finally reaching the second guard's position. He looked around.

No, this wasn't good: The conduit stretched out for about thirty more feet, then terminated in a solid stone wall. Even if he dragged the two guards all the way to the end, the simple flick of a flashlight would expose them.

Every good ambush always included a plan for hiding the bodies of the guards you killed—thus Moore decided at that moment that this wasn't a very good plan.

He jogged back toward the grating as voices sounded from outside. They'd driven the van right into the drainage ditch and parked outside the grating. These guys were even higher-ranking geniuses than the two who'd been following him outside Corrales's hotel. Or maybe they felt safe enough to make such a bold move—driving right up to the grating? After all, who would stop them? The local police? The Feds? That they operated this audaciously was unsettling, but to make himself feel better, Moore decided they were idiots, and even though his plan wasn't very good, it'd be enough to bring down these fools.

He climbed out past the grating and lifted his suppressed Glock at the group. He counted six young females, all Asian, as Towers had indicated, along with four boys no more than sixteen or seventeen, each one wearing a heavy backpack presumably jammed with bricks of marijuana and cocaine.

Two men in their mid- to late twenties and wearing New York Yankees jackets had AK-47 rifles slung over their shoulders and held pistols on the group as they all stood there, balancing themselves on the grassy slope. The men were the *sicarios*, of course, with thick eyebrows, multiple piercings, and permanent scowls on their pockmarked faces. They'd employed the skinniest kids they could find to slip through the narrow tunnel while pushing their backpacks of drugs ahead of them. They couldn't wear the backpacks and still fit through; they'd escaped an arduous passage by Moore's intervention. He had read the files of other tunnel operations that included small carts on tracks (like mining carts) with attached ropes that were used to pull drugs through the tunnels without ever having to send mules through the passages.

"Who the fuck are you?" asked the taller of the two *sicarios*.

"I'm a Boston Red Sox fan," Moore answered, then shot the guy in the face. There had been no guilt, no hesitation, nothing but action and reaction. If Moore felt anything, it was utter repulsion for these scumbags who'd stooped to this level. To aid and abet an organization involved in the enslavement of other human beings was to reserve for yourself a special hotel room located in the deepest pit of hell. The taller punk had already slid his door key past the electronic swipe and now inhaled fire.

As the women screamed and the boys darted back for the van, Moore turned his Glock on the second guy, who had a room reserved next to his buddy.

The punk raised his gun.

Moore pulled his trigger.

And the *sicario* fired a half-second afterward.

But Moore was already jerking back as the second guy spun sideways and collapsed, only to go rolling down the ditch and back toward the van. He'd taken a round in the head.

Towers, who was presumably watching it all go down from the other side of the ditch, spoke rapidly over the radio: "Get the women to go through the tunnel. We can't do anything to help them till they get to the other side. I'll get down there and take care of the bodies."

"Okay," grunted Moore.

"Get those backpacks loaded into the van," he ordered the boys. "Right now! Then I want all of you back here! I'm a good guy. I'm sending you through the tunnel! I'm a good guy. Let's go!"

As the boys rushed back to the truck, Moore began collecting the weapons from the two *sicarios*, lest any of his captives decide to do the same. The girls hurried up and past the grating and began to climb down into the storm drain. They all wore the same style of cheap, white tennis shoes you could buy at Walmart, probably given to them by the *sicarios*.

With the backpacks returned to the van, Moore shouted for the boys to follow the girls, and he directed them from the rear, heavily weighed down by two AKs, extra pistols, and his own weapons. Once they were all inside, Moore picked up one of the *sicarios'* flashlights and shone it in the hole.

He glanced back at the group and said one word in English: "America."

The girls, a few of whom were crying now, shook their heads in fear, but one, the tallest and perhaps the oldest, shoved her way from the back and pushed herself into the tunnel. She screamed back at the other girls, her Chinese coming in the rat-tat-tat of a machine gun. Seeing her courage and hearing her admonishments, the others came forward, one by one, and eased themselves into the narrow hole.

"When you get to the other side, you will have help. I don't want you to ever work for the cartels again," Moore told the boys. "No matter what they say. No matter what they do. Never work for them again. Okay?"

"Okay, señor," said one boy. "Okay."

Within a minute all of them were in the tunnel and Moore was on the phone with Ansara. "They're heading your way, bro. They're all yours."

"Roger that. We'll take 'em quietly so they don't try to back out."

The girls would be processed and deported back to China—unless some humanitarian group was able to intervene on their behalf. The boys would no doubt be processed, and if there weren't any warrants on them, they, too, would be deported back to Mexico, which was why Moore implored them not to return to working for the cartels. The sad thing was, most of them would ignore him, especially once they understood how the process worked. They'd take the risk again.

Moore then called Luis Torres. "I've got an early birthday present for your boss."

"How much?"

"A very nice load."

What Torres, Zúñiga, and the rest of the Sinaloa Cartel didn't know was that Moore and Towers would inject each brick with a GPS beacon so that once those bricks were smuggled across the border, they'd be immediately located and confiscated by authorities. Moore's bosses would never allow him to know-ingly let the drugs pass into the United States without some way of retrieving them, and that was certainly understandable. How-ever, as tiny as the injection holes would be, Moore was certain that Zúñiga and his cronies would carefully scrutinize each brick for any signs of tampering. Moore and Towers would have to carefully choose their injection sites along the seams in the tape used to seal the bricks.

"Okay, we're good to go out here," said Towers.

Moore's phone rang again: Ansara. "First few girls have come through. Took them nice and quiet. Excellent work, boss man. Score one for the team."

"Dude," Moore said with a sigh of exhaustion. "We're just getting started. It's going to be a very long night."

"And when in our business were they ever short?" Ansara pointed out.

Moore grinned and hustled off for the van.

Somoza Designs International
Bogotá, Colombia

Before leaving Bogotá, Jorge Rojas had scheduled a final visit with his old friend Felipe Somoza, who had called to say that he had a very special gift for Rojas. At ten in the morning, Rojas and his old college buddy Jeff Campbell, who'd struck a lucrative cell phone deal with the Colombian government, arrived outside the block-long, two-story shop and attached warehouse. They were greeted by Lucille, a dark-haired woman in her fifties who had been working as Somoza's receptionist for the past ten years and was, like all of the man's employees, fiercely loyal, treating Somoza more like a family member than a boss, to the point of handling his dry cleaning, the oil changes on his vehicles, even handling his personal schedule for attending his three sons' college soccer games.

Rojas and Campbell were escorted through the shop floor and tailoring area, where dozens of women from eighteen to nearly eighty wore blue uniforms and sat diligently behind sewing machines, producing cold, warm, wet, formal, and casual wear for both men and women.

However, they weren't making "normal" clothing.

Somoza was known as the "Armored Armani," and his bulletproof clothing was world-renowned. His business had flourished since 9/11, after which he had focused his attention on private security and bodyguard companies. He expanded to supply clothing to diplomats, ambassadors, princes, and presidents of more than forty nations and was now popular with individuals and with more than two hundred private security firms, as well as local police throughout the Americas. What set him apart from other bulletproof manufacturers was his attention to comfort and fashion design. He wasn't just making ugly militarylike vests; his clothing ranged from bulletproof suits to dresses to even socks and ties. He even had a boutique in Mexico City on the same street as such names as Hugo Boss, Ferrari, BMW, and Calvin Klein. He was planning to open a new shop on Rodeo Drive in Beverly Hills, California, so he could supply both celebrities and their bodyguards with some of the most stylish yet "safe" clothing in the world.

The bulletproof panels themselves were carefully concealed within the garments. Each panel was designed from sheets of plastic polymers composed of many layers. Kevlar, Spectra Shield, or sometimes Twaron (nearly identical to Kevlar) and Dyneema (similar to Spectra) became part of the process, depending upon the garment's target weight and available materials. Kevlar thread was used to sew together layers of woven Kevlar, while the Spectra Shield was coated and bonded with resins such as Kraton before being sealed between sheets of polyethylene film.

"Now, Jeff," Rojas whispered as they neared Somoza's office near the back of the shop, "he's going to have a little fun with us, and you need to play along."

"What do you mean?"

"I mean, don't insult him. Just do whatever he says. Okay?"

"You're the boss, Jorge."

Campbell had no idea what was about to happen, and Rojas chuckled inwardly.

Somoza was already at the door as they reached it. Barely fifty, with a thick shock of black hair dappled with a few patches of gray, he was an imposing figure of six-foot-two with broad shoulders and a belly that betrayed his addiction to sweets. In fact, four glass candy jars the size of one-pound coffee cans were lined up on his broad mahogany desk, standing in sharp juxtaposition with a large placard hanging on the back wall. This was the company's logo—a pair of crossed swords behind a black shield with a superimposed silver bullet that suggested a combination of medieval armor and modern-day technology.

Somoza trundled forward in a pair of tight designer jeans and a long-sleeved shirt that offered a light level of protection against long-range fire. He always wore his own products: nothing but . . .

"*Buenos días*, Felipe," Rojas cried as he embraced the man. "This is my friend, Jeff Campbell."

"*Hola*, Jeff. Very nice to meet you."

Jeff shook hands with Somoza. "It's an honor to meet the famous bulletproof tailor."

"Famous? No," said Somoza. "Busy? Yes, yes! Come inside, gentlemen. Come inside."

Rojas and Campbell sank into plush leather chairs opposite Somoza's desk, while he slipped outside for a second, calling after Lucille to bring him the present. Off to their left hung dozens of pictures of Somoza with movie stars and dignitaries, all wearing his clothing. Rojas pointed to the photos, and Campbell's mouth began to open. "This is quite an operation he's got here. Look at all the movie stars."

Rojas nodded. "I'll show you the warehouse before we leave. It's a very ambitious business. I'm very proud of him. I remember when he was just starting up."

"Well, it's a much more dangerous world."

"Yes, the one we leave our children." Rojas sighed deeply, then turned his head as Somoza entered the room carrying a black leather trench coat.

"For you, Jorge!"

Rojas stood and took the coat. "Are you kidding me? This is not bulletproof." He ran his fingers across the material and the flexible plates behind it. "It's much too light and thin."

"I know, right?" agreed Somoza. "It's our latest design, and I want you to have it. It's your size, of course."

"Thank you very much."

"We just finished showing it at our annual fashion show in New York."

"Wow, a fashion show in New York for bulletproof clothes?" asked Campbell.

"It's very popular," said Somoza.

Jorge glanced at Campbell, then faced Somoza and winked. "Are you sure it'll stop a bullet?"

Somoza reached into a desk drawer and withdrew a .45-caliber revolver, which he placed on the desk.

"Wow," cried Campbell. "What're we doing now?"

"We need to test it out," said Somoza, his eyes growing devilishly wide. "Jeff, I want you to know that I give all of my employees the test. You can't work here unless you're willing to put on the product and take a bullet. You need to know what that feels like, and you need to trust in the product and in your work. This is why my quality control is so good: I shoot all of my employees."

Somoza said this so matter-of-factly, so coolly, that Rojas couldn't help but burst out laughing. Rojas then handed the jacket to Campbell. "Put it on."

"Are you serious?"

"It's no problem," said Somoza. "Please . . ."

Campbell's eyes glassed up, and he sat there, perched on a cliff between offending Somoza and obeying Rojas's warning about playing along. Rojas had known the man for a long time, known him to be a risk-taker, so he was surprised when Campbell said, "I'm sorry, I'm just, uh, I wasn't expecting this."

"Lucille?" called Somoza.

The woman arrived in the doorway just a few seconds later.

"Did I shoot you?" asked Somoza.

"Yes, señor. Twice."

Somoza faced Campbell. "You see? The lady gets shot? You are too afraid?"

"All right," Campbell said, struggling to his feet and wrenching the jacket away from Rojas. "I can't believe I'm saying this, but you can shoot me."

"Excellent!" cried Somoza, who whirled around in his chair and reached into a cabinet to produce three sets of earphones.

Once Campbell had wormed his way into the trench coat, Somoza carefully buttoned it up and placed a round sticker on the jacket's left side, near the abdomen.

"So that's your target," said Campbell.

"Yes, I need this because I am not a very good shot," Somoza said in a deadpan.

Rojas chuckled again.

"Go ahead and laugh," said Campbell. "You're not getting shot!"

"He takes the bullet all the time," said Somoza. "Jorge? How many times have I shot you?"

"Five, I think."

"Look at that. Five times," said Somoza. "Surely you can take one bullet."

Campbell nodded. "My hands are shaking. Look." He held them up, and yes, he was involuntarily trembling.

"It's okay; you're going to feel fine," said Somoza, sliding a pair of earphones over Campbell's head.

Rojas donned his own pair, as did Somoza, who then produced a bullet from the drawer and loaded the gun. He moved Campbell to a position away from the desk and held up the pistol point-blank to Campbell's chest.

"That close? Are you nuts?" asked Campbell.

"Okay, listen, this is the way it goes. You take a deep breath and hold it. You count one, two, three, and I shoot. There it is again. One, two, three, BOOM! Okay?" Somoza had raised his voice so they could hear him despite the earphones.

Campbell swallowed and glanced over at Rojas, his eyes pleading.

"Look at me," said Somoza. "Take a deep breath. Ready? One, two—"

BOOM!

Somoza fired after two, and that was how he always did it with new people who would tense up too much during the moment they expected to hear the boom. He fired early, when the participant was still relaxed.

Campbell hunched over slightly and tugged off his earphones, as they all did. "Wow," he said and gasped. "You tricked me! But it's okay. I didn't feel anything, maybe a little pressure."

Somoza unbuttoned the trench coat and tugged out Campbell's shirt to prove to him that he'd not been injured. Then he dug into the coat and produced the flattened piece of lead. "Here you go. A souvenir!"

Campbell took the piece of lead and smiled. "This is pretty amazing."

And then he held his mouth, raced over to the wastebasket, and retched.

At this, Somoza threw back his head and cackled until his ribs probably hurt.

Later, over coffee, Rojas spoke alone with his old friend, while Campbell was given a more in-depth tour of the facility by Lucille. Rojas shared his feelings about his son. Somoza talked about his own sons, who were growing up too fast as well and were destined to work in the business with him.

"Our boys are a lot alike," said Rojas. "Children of privilege. How do we keep them . . . I don't know . . . normal?"

"This is difficult in a crazy world. We want to protect them, but there is nothing you and I can do except teach them to make the right choices. I want my sons to wear bulletproof suits. Yes, I can protect them from the bullets but not from all the bullshit life is going to hand them."

Rojas nodded. "You are a wise man, my friend."

"And good-looking, too!"

They laughed.

But then Rojas sobered. "Now, Ballesteros has been having some problems again, and I want you to take care of him and his people. You send me the bill. Whatever they need."

"Of course. A pleasure doing business, as always. And I want to get some measurements of your friend, Señor Campbell. We're going to make him a trench coat like yours—for being such a good sport."

"I'm sure he'll really appreciate that."

"And one more thing, Jorge." Now it was Somoza's turn to grow serious, his voice burred with tension. "I have been thinking about this for a long time. We are both at the stage in our life where we no longer need to associate with the trade. My business is legitimate and booming now. Of course I will help our friend Ballesteros, but for me, this has to be the last deal, the last connection. I'm very concerned. The mess in Puerto Rico has us all concerned. I want you to understand that I still work for you, but I must cut connections here, and honestly, Jorge, I think you should pull out. Turn it over to someone else. It's time. As you said, your boy is moving on. So should you."

Rojas thought for a long moment. Somoza was indeed speaking to him as a dear friend, and he was talking sense—but his words were born of fear, and Rojas could see that fear etched in the man's eyes.

"My friend, you should never be scared of anyone. People will try to intimidate you, but no one is better than anyone else. You need to be a fighter in this life."

"Yes, Jorge, yes. But a man must be wise enough to pick his battles. We are not young anymore. Let the boys fight this battle, not us. We have far too much to lose."

Rojas got to his feet. "I'll think about it. You are a good friend, and I know what you are saying."

22

TAKING THE FALL

Zúñiga Ranch House
Juárez, Mexico

AT ABOUT ELEVEN A.M. the next morning, Moore, Zúñiga, and six more cartel members assembled in Zúñiga's four-car garage with the doors cracked half open. Moore delivered the drug shipment he'd seized and watched as Zúñiga's men inspected the bricks and did not find anything suspicious—notably, the tiny injection holes made by Moore and Towers as they'd planted the GPS beacons. The Sinaloa Cartel was powerful but not quite as sophisticated as the Juárez, who Moore believed would have X-rayed the bricks and possibly found the trackers.

As Moore had hoped, Zúñiga seemed very pleased with the "gift" and most assuredly had plans in motion to move the stuff before nightfall. He nodded over the bricks, then faced Moore. "Your enemy is my enemy, it seems."

"When one cartel becomes too powerful, it is everyone's enemy."

"I agree."

"All right. I would like to continue to help. Let me take a few of your men. We'll all go kidnap Rojas's son. Like I told you, we're in this together," said Moore.

"Mr. Howard, maybe I am crazy enough to believe you now. Maybe I'm going to say okay."

"It'll take most of the day to fly down there in one of your planes, so maybe we should leave now?"

"Maybe I haven't made up my mind."

At this Moore snapped, and he probably shouldn't have, but he hadn't gotten much sleep. He raised his voice to a near shout. "Señor Zúñiga, what else do you need? One hundred and fifty in cash, a huge drug shipment stolen from Rojas? What else? My bosses are growing impatient."

Torres, who'd been standing nearby, waddled up and raised his own voice. "Do not speak to Señor Zúñiga that way! I will twist off your head!"

Moore glared at the man, then faced Zúñiga. "I'm tired of playing games. I've made a good offer. Let's get this done."

Zúñiga gave Moore one final appraising look, then reached out his hand. "I want you to kill Rojas."

Two hours later, Moore, Torres, and Fitzpatrick, along with a pilot and copilot, were packed into a twin-prop Piper PA-31 Navajo on a southeast track toward San Cristóbal de las

Casas. The weather was clear, the views spectacular, the company miserable, because Torres got airsick and had twice vomited into his little white sack. If it had been a long night, it was going to be an even longer day, and Moore looked across the cabin at Fitzpatrick, who rolled his eyes over the fat man's inability to handle air travel. Torres apparently had a massive but delicate stomach, and Fitzpatrick had chided him before they'd boarded the plane about them being unable to lift off because of the "added cargo." Torres's revenge for that remark was potent, and currently in the form of a foul-smelling bag of vomit seated between his legs.

Moore closed his eyes and tried to steal an hour or two of sleep, allowing the hum of the props to draw him deeper into unconsciousness . . .

The lights on the oil platform winked out, and suddenly Carmichael cried, "We've been spotted!"

Moore shook hard and sat forward in the airplane seat.

Torres looked back at him. "Bad dream?"

"Yes, and you were in it."

The fat man was about to say something, then put his hand to his mouth.

Border Tunnel Construction Site
Mexicali, Mexico

High school student Rueben Everson had thought that working for the Juárez Cartel and smuggling drugs across the border was at first a pretty scary proposition. But then they had shown him all the money he could make, and over time, he'd grown used to the whole operation, even carrying large shipments while wearing a mask of utter calm. He'd been clever, all right, not making the stupid mistakes that had cost some of the other mules their freedom. He'd always been smooth when talking to the officers, and he never carried statues or cards of all the saints those fools prayed to in order to keep them safe during a run. La Santa Muerte was the most popular among some thugs, who even built shrines to her. Making the skeletal image of the Virgin of Guadalupe seem like some savior when she looked like pure evil was just kind of stupid to him. Then there was Saint Jude, the patron saint of lost causes, and one fool had even tried to stuff thirty pounds of pot inside a statue of Jude and walk across the border with it. What a jackass. One lesser-known saint was Ramón Nonato. The legend said that he had his mouth padlocked shut to prevent him from recruiting new followers. The thugs liked this idea, and prayed to him so that others would keep silent about their crimes.

Some of Rueben's colleagues relied heavily on other kinds of good-luck charms: sentimental jewelry, watches, pendants, rabbits' feet, and other types of talismans, as well as *Scarface* movie posters. The one lucky charm that made Rueben laugh was the yellow bird Tweety from the Looney Tunes cartoons. At first he hadn't understood why so many mules and other drug traffickers found the bird so popular, but then he'd realized that Tweety never gets caught by Sylvester the cat, so the little bird had become a hero among thugs. The irony, of course, was that they called themselves "mules" while a bird was their mascot.

At the moment, though, no manner of magic or religion could save Rueben. He'd been caught by the FBI, had met a kid who'd had his toes chopped off over a bad run, and was now forced to work for the government if he was going to avoid jail time. The easy-money runs to save up for college were gone forever. Agent Ansara had been very clear about that. They'd injected him with a GPS tracker and had turned his cell phone into a listening device via the Bluetooth earpiece. He was a dog on a leash.

Earlier in the day, he'd been called by his cartel contact and told to report to Mexicali, where a car was being loaded for him, and while he was standing there, inside the warehouse, a middle-aged man with glasses and hair covered in dust walked over to him and asked in Spanish, "Are you the new one?"

"I guess so. But I'm not new. I just haven't worked over here before. They usually have me pick it up someplace else. What are you guys doing in here? Digging another tunnel?"

"That's none of your business, young man."

Rueben thrust his hands into his pockets. "Whatever."

"How old are you?"

"Why do you care?"

"You're still in high school, aren't you?"

"Are you my new boss?"

"That doesn't matter."

Rueben frowned. "Why do you care?"

"How are your grades?"

Rueben snorted. "Are you serious?"

"Answer the question."

"They're pretty good. Mostly A's and B's."

"Then you need to stop doing this. No more. You will either die or get arrested, and your life will be over. Do you understand me?"

Rueben's eyes burned. *I understand you more than you know, old man. But it's too fucking late for me.* "I'm going to go to college, and this is how I'll pay for my tuition. As soon as I have enough money, I will quit."

"They all say the same thing. I need money for this and for that, but next week I will quit."

"I just want to go now and get this over with."

"What's your name?"

"Rueben."

The man proffered his hand, and Rueben reluctantly took it. "I'm Pedro Romero. I hope I do not see you here again. Okay?"

"Wish I could help you out, but you *will* see me again. It's just the way it is."

"You think about what I told you."

Rueben shrugged and turned as one of the loaders marched up to him and said, "Ready to go."

"Think about it," Romero urged him, sounding very much like Rueben's father.

I wish I had, old man. I wish I had.

Rueben drove the car across the border and surrendered the car to a team of Ansara's men without incident. They dropped him off at a rental-car office, and the man there gave him a ride home in the airport bus. A black Escalade was parked across the street from his house, and Rueben climbed into the backseat once the bus had left his street. FBI agent Ansara was at the wheel.

"Good work today, Rueben."

"Yeah, whatever."

"The old man was right, wasn't he?"

"Yeah, okay, he was. I should've quit before you busted me, but now I'm fucked."

"No, you did great. You got me some good pics and audio of that man. Now we can ID him and see what's going on at that warehouse."

Rueben closed his eyes. He wanted to cry. He could barely sleep now. He dreamed they would come for him during the night, dressed as skeletons armed with knives for carving up his heart. He watched his parents attend his funeral, and while they were leaving, a carload of *sicarios* raced by and unleashed machine-gun fire on the crowd, killing his parents, both shot in the head and gazing skyward to whisper, "You were such a good boy. What happened to you?"

Delicias Police Station
Juárez, Mexico

As a CIA agent, Gloria Vega had worked in more than twenty-six countries, performing missions as brief as eight hours and as long as sixteen months. She'd witnessed her share of bloodshed and corruption, and had been prepared to witness more of the same when she'd joined JTF Juárez and realized she was being sent into a city known as the murder capital of the world. However, what she hadn't expected was that the bloodshed would occur between members of her own force.

The shouting had reached her desk only five minutes ago, and they'd all rushed to put on their armor, grab their rifles, and get outside. Inspector Alberto Gómez had pulled on a balaclava to conceal his own identity and stood beside her. Each end of the street had been cordoned off by Federal Police vehicles, and Vega estimated that a crowd of at least two hundred officers in black uniforms and balaclavas had gathered and were shouting and screaming to "Bring out the pig!"

And then, before Vega, Gómez, or anyone else could stop them, a half-dozen officers rushed inside the station, and the crowd roared once again. This time Vega heard a name: Lopez, Lopez, Lopez!

She knew that name, all right, and her blood felt as though it'd turned to ice. Lopez was one of Gómez's colleagues, an inspector with nearly as many years on the force. Vega's own investigation had concluded that Lopez was clean and trying to do the right thing; he was the man Alberto Gómez should have been. On the flip side, Gómez's phones had been tapped, he'd been followed by two other spotters that JTF leader Towers had provided to Vega, and she had gathered enough evidence to present to Federal Police authorities to bring down Gómez for corruption and indisputable ties to the Juárez Drug Cartel. Towers, however, wasn't ready to pull the trigger on that operation, because Gómez's arrest would tip off the cartel. All the dominoes needed to be knocked over simultaneously.

And so with time to spare, Gómez had turned the situation around before Vega could react. As she whirled toward the entrance door, six men dragged Lopez out of the building, one of them gripping the old man by his shock of gray hair. Once Lopez's clean-shaven face was spotted by the crowd, the screaming grew louder, and some hollered, "Kill the pig!" The officers surrounded Lopez, and at least two reared back and began pummeling the old man.

"They're teaching him a lesson before they arrest him," shouted Gómez in her ear. "He's been taking money from the cartels and serving as an informant for them. Children have died because of him. And now he needs to pay."

You fucking hypocrite is what Vega wanted to say. "They can't do this. They can't beat him up!"

The group broke into a chant: "Lopez is the devil and must go down! Lopez is the devil . . ."

The chant continued, and Vega flinched as another officer with biceps the size of her hips struck a hard blow to Lopez's cheek.

That was it. Gloria Vega, former Army Intelligence officer and CIA operative, now embedded with the Mexican Federal Police, had seen enough.

She raised her gun into the air and fired off a salvo, the rat-tat-tat silencing the crowd. Before she knew what was happening, a hand wrapped around her neck, other hands had wrenched the gun from her grip, and still more hands were dragging her back into the police station. She screamed and tried to writhe out of their grip, but it was no use. They dragged her inside, and there she was immediately released as Gómez passed in front of her and tugged off his balaclava. "What the hell are you doing?"

"It's not right. What evidence do they have? They can't beat up the old man like that!"

"He's in bed with scum. So *he* is scum!"

She bit her tongue. Oh, God, how she bit her tongue.

"I told you I would try to keep you alive," Gómez added. "But you make that very hard when you do something like this! Now, listen to me. Lopez isn't the only one. The other commanders are dirty as well. Today we are going to clean up this house, and you're either going to help or I'm going to put you in a jail cell to keep you safe."

She wrenched off her own mask as the shouting outside seemed to reach a fever pitch. "You'd better lock me up for now. I can't watch this anymore."

Vega rubbed the corners of her eyes, the frustration burning so deeply that she thought she might vomit. How much more could she take? How long would they have to wait before she could slap cuffs on Gómez and be done with it? He was the proverbial wolf in sheep's clothing who needed to swallow a bullet. She imagined herself shooting him right there, cutting off one vein of corruption but realizing that the network was so complex that his death wouldn't make a difference. No difference at all. Her heart began to sink.

"Gloria, come with me," he ordered.

She followed him into his small office, where he closed the door so they were out of earshot of the other inspectors and officers. "I know how you feel," he said.

"Really?"

"I was your age once. I wanted to save the world, but there is too much temptation all around us."

"No kidding! They pay us nothing. That's why we can't do anything. It's just a crazy game, and we're all wasting our time here. Wasting our time. What else can we do?"

"The right thing," he said. "Always the right thing. This is what God wants."

"God?"

"Yes. I pray to God every day to save our country and save our Federal Police force. He will do it. We must have faith in him."

"There has to be a better way. I need to make more money than this. And I need to work with people I can trust. Can you help me do that?"

He narrowed his gaze. "You can trust me . . ."

Montana Restaurant and Bar
Juárez, Mexico

Johnny Sanchez had parked his rental car on Avenida Abraham Lincoln, which was just five minutes from the Cordova Bridge, in order to take his girlfriend, Juanita, to his favorite restaurant in Ciudad Juárez. The Montana's Southwest-style interior featured dining on two levels and rich wood accents throughout. White linen tablecloths and scented candles did not go unnoticed by his date, and Johnny made sure they got a table near the gas fireplace. *El capitán de meseros* (the captain of the waiters) was a young man named Billy, and Johnny had become good friends with him and tipped Billy's team of waiters quite generously. In exchange, Billy slipped Johnny mixed drinks and oversized portions when he ordered. Johnny asked for his usual, the New York club steak, while Juanita, who'd recently dyed her hair blond and gotten a rather aggressive boob job, would have a taco salad.

As they waited for their entrées, Juanita tugged nervously on the straps of her red dress and asked, "What's wrong?"

"What do you mean?"

"You're not here. You're out there somewhere." She lifted her chin toward the window and the bridge beyond.

"I'm sorry." He wouldn't tell her that his mother's godson was a *sicario* and that he was now working for the CIA. That would probably ruin their dinner.

She frowned and blurted out, "I think we should leave Mexico."

"Why?"

"Because I don't like it here anymore."

"You just got here."

"I know . . . I came for *you*. It's always about you and your writing. But what about me?"

"You said you were going to dance."

"You want me to show my body to other men?"

"You paid enough for it."

"That's no reason."

"No, but if it makes you happy . . ."

She leaned forward and grabbed his hand. "Don't you understand? I want you to say no. I want you to be jealous. What's wrong with you?"

"I can't think straight anymore. And you're right. We need to leave Mexico." His voice cracked. "But we can't."

"Why not?"

"Señor Sanchez?"

Johnny turned at the approach of two men wearing expensive silk shirts and pants. They were both in their mid-twenties, neither more than five feet tall, and if Johnny had to guess at their nationalities, he would say Colombian or Guatemalan.

"Who are you?" Johnny asked.

One man lowered his voice and gazed unflinchingly at Johnny. "Señor, we need you to come with us. It's a matter of life and death." That was not a Mexican accent. These guys were definitely from South America, somewhere . . .

"I asked you a question," Johnny repeated.

"Señor, please come now, and no one will be hurt. Not you. Not her. Please."

"Johnny, what the fuck is this?" asked Juanita, lifting her voice and thrusting out her chest—which drew the attention of both men.

"Who do you work for?" asked Johnny, his pulse beginning to race.

The man looked at him. "Let's go, señor."

Oh, no, Johnny thought. *Dante must already know I've been tapped by the CIA. They've come to kill me.*

Johnny's gun was back in the hotel room. He looked to Juanita, then leaned over and gave her a deep and passionate kiss.

She pushed him away. "What's going on?"

"Come on, baby. We need to go with them." He stood, trembling, as the waiter came over with his steak. "I'll take that to go," he said.

The two men nodded at him.

And that's when Johnny grabbed Juanita's hand and made a mad dash for the door.

He expected to hear some shouting and/or the sound of gunfire as the men who'd wanted to abduct them decided they would have to die instead.

But he and Juanita made it outside and into the parking lot, and when he whirled around, they were *not* being followed.

"Johnny!" cried Juanita. "What do they want?"

Before he could open his mouth, two small sedans roared up and cut them off. More men—at least six—got out, all similarly dressed, all about the same height and age.

Johnny lifted his palms. It was over. *I'm sorry, Dante.*

They took Juanita by the throat and shoved her into one car, grabbed him and threw him into the other. Johnny's head hit the backseat as the driver screeched off, and sometime after they left the parking lot, perhaps a minute or two later, he had become so nervous that he simply fainted.

Johnny awoke some time later, his arms and legs bound against some kind of a pole that he realized was part of a car lift. He was inside an auto-body shop, surrounded by vehicles in various stages of assembly and repair. Dim light filtered in from a bank of windows to his right, with two large steel garage doors rising directly ahead.

The two men who were in the restaurant stood before him, an HD video camera clutched by the slightly leaner man. Johnny sighed. They'd just kidnapped him and were holding him for ransom. He'd make the video. Corrales would pay. Everything would be all right.

"Okay, okay, okay," he said through another sigh. "I'll say whatever you want. Where's Juanita? Where's my girlfriend?"

The camera guy glanced away from the tiny screen he'd been studying and shouted across the room, "Are you finished yet?"

"Yes!" came a voice.

And then Johnny saw them: two more men wearing black protective jumpsuits, the kind used while painting cars, although they hadn't donned the headgear. The suits were stained darkly on the arms and hips. One man carried a yellow power tool with a narrow blade extending from the front, a reciprocating saw. Johnny had been to many accident scenes as a local newspaper reporter a few years back, and he'd become familiar with the tools first responders used to extricate people trapped in their cars.

The man with the saw revved the tool's engine, and as he stepped closer, Johnny realized that the saw was stained with . . . blood.

"Look, no need for threats. I'll do what you say."

With a snort, the guy with the saw rolled his eyes and moved forward.

"Wait!" Johnny cried. "What do you want from me? Please!"

"Señor," said the man with the camera. "We just want you to die."

23

BUITRES
JUSTICIEROS

Villas Casa Morada
San Cristóbal de las Casas
Chiapas, Mexico

MIGUEL ROJAS was awakened at 6:41 a.m. by an aching desire. He rolled over and let his hand move slowly up Sonia's leg. She stirred and whispered, "Always in the morning with you. Wasn't last night enough?"

"It's nature," he said.

"No, it's just you."

"I can't help it. It's your fault, really. I can't stop thinking about, you know . . ."

"Well, there's more to life."

"I know, I know."

"Good. I understand how men are, and it's okay, but I worry about you losing respect for me."

"Never."

"You say that now." She draped an arm over her head. "Sometimes I wish . . ."

He frowned at her. "What?"

"I wish everything in my life had been different."

"That can't be true."

"You might be the perfect man for me. But life is complicated, and I just worry for us. I wish everything had been different before I met you."

"What was wrong with your life before that? You have great parents who love you very much. You've done very well."

"I don't know what I'm saying, really."

"Is it the money? Because—"

"No, it has nothing to do with that."

He tensed. "Then what is it? Another guy back home? That's it. You're still in love with another guy."

She began to laugh. "No."

He gently grabbed her by the chin. "Do you love me?"

"Too much."

"What does that mean?"

She closed her eyes. "It means that sometimes it hurts."

"Well, it shouldn't. What can I do?"

"Just kiss me."

He did, and one thing led to another. He wondered if Corrales and the others in the next room could hear them. She groaned softly, but they tried their best to remain discreet.

They hadn't done much during their first day in the old city, spending most of their time around the villa and getting accustomed to the area. Miguel had chosen to stay in a new place and to live like a tourist, rather than exploit his father's connections and stay in the same old boring mansions. He'd found them a quaint, European-run boutique hotel, and their first-floor villa had a kitchen, dining table, sitting area, and bedroom with bath. Murals and Mayan textiles adorned the walls, with a wood-burning fireplace opposite their bed. While the room had no air conditioning, they didn't need it. Outside was a veranda with chairs, so they could sit and watch people in the lushly landscaped courtyard, where a hammock lay beneath the long limbs of a shade tree. A young couple had been lying on the hammock and kissing deeply. That image had been enough to drive him and Sonia back into their bedroom for a quick round of sex only hours after they'd arrived.

As Miguel rolled off of Sonia, the cockerels began their morning announcements: Indeed, the sun was rising. It felt as though they were on a farm, but Miguel enjoyed their racket. This was semirural Mexico, and it was just he and Sonia and this beautiful little city to explore. The concierge had told them that many writers, artists, academics, and archaeologists stayed at the hotel and spent their days both exploring the city and driving out thirty minutes to the ancient Mayan city known as Palenque, where the ancient temples and palaces with their broad staircases and partially crumbling walls drew thousands of visitors each year. Miguel had been to the ruins only once, as a boy, so he thought he'd like to explore them again.

First, however, they'd go shopping, which he knew would make Sonia very happy. They were only a ten-minute walk down the hill to the louder central streets. Miguel rose and moved to the window, staring out past the courtyard at the highlands, draped in long shadows, the green mountains still dark and forming a moonscape along the horizon.

Farther away, the streets seemed to writhe their way along the hillsides, and the brightly colored houses—some green, purple, and yellow, and all with red tiled roofs—lay in tight clusters along those narrow paths. Beyond them, seated atop a great shoulder of rock, was an ornate cathedral painted in gold, and several mansions whose towering wrought-iron gates lifted to some four meters. Sonia had remarked that the city seemed more like a theme park than a real place because it was so brightly colored and impeccably clean. Miguel had told her that the people here were exceedingly proud of their Mayan heritage, and you could find Mayan influences throughout everything in the city: from the architecture to the food to the interior design. Miguel's father often said that San Cristóbal reminded him more of Guatemala than of Mexico.

"When is Carnival?" asked Sonia, sitting up in the bed.

He smiled at her. "They'll start tonight. But we have to go to the village of San Juan Chamula first. I want you to see the church there. Then tomorrow, the ruins."

A knock came at the door.

Sonia frowned, and Miguel crossed the room and leaned toward the door before opening it. "Who's there?"

"It's me, sir, Corrales. Is everything all right?"

He swung around, faced Sonia, and nearly burst out laughing, as did she.

"Yes, Corrales, we're okay. Go back to bed. We'll be having breakfast at eight a.m., thank you."

"Okay, sir. Just checking."

Miguel rushed back toward the bed and took a flying leap onto it, nearly knocking Sonia off the other side. She began giggling as he swung her around and kissed her deeply.

From the balcony of a hotel room around the corner, Moore watched Rojas's son kiss his girlfriend. The kid had pushed open the curtains and given him a clear view of their naked forms splayed across the bed.

Moore lowered his binoculars and turned back to Fitzpatrick and Torres. The fat man was lying in his bed, fast asleep. Fitzpatrick was typing fiercely on his laptop computer, sending an e-mail to Zúñiga.

"Must be nice to be young," Moore said, sighing over his own lost years.

"They're pretty horny, huh?" said Fitzpatrick. "So what do we got in the way of security? Corrales and his two flunkies? That's it?"

"I don't see anyone else. He'll stay close and leave the other two to trail. We need to take them out first. I want Corrales alive—and there's no negotiation there. We have to take him alive."

"Agreed." Then Fitzpatrick cocked a thumb over his shoulder at Torres. "What about him?" he whispered.

"Be cool. He's the least of our worries right now . . ."

Moore's smartphone vibrated with a text message from Gloria Vega:

```
We found Sanchez and his girlfriend outside
the Monarch strip club. They were
butchered. Gomez thinks the Sinaloas are
responsible because of where we found the
bodies. Can you follow up?
```

He thumbed in a reply: I'm on it.

Then he shared the news with Fitzpatrick, who shook his head. "No way. We would've known about that hit."

"Let me call Zúñiga."

Torres stirred and looked up at them. "Why are you two bastards up this early?"

Moore chuckled. "Because, fat boy, we're on a mission to do more than puke in a bag."

Torres made a face. "My stomach still hurts. But when I feel better, I'm going to sit on you."

"Hey, dude," called Fitzpatrick, gaining Torres's attention. "We need to make our move today. Let them settle in, get comfortable, get complacent, then bam. So you'd better get going."

"Exactly," said Moore. "I think we'll do it at their villa. Nice controlled environment. We track 'em throughout the day, and then when they get back home, all tired and ready to bang, we take Miguel and the girl—but we need to get Corrales and his boys first."

"Listen to me, gringo," said Torres. "I'm in charge here. But I like your plan. However, once we get the boy and his girl, we will kill the girl in front of him. This way he knows we mean business."

Moore looked to Fitzpatrick, who said, "We might get more money if we have both of them. And we can negotiate with Rojas to open up the tunnels."

"We're here to kill Rojas and everyone around him. Señor Zúñiga made this very clear to me—and I'm making it very clear to you . . ."

Fitzpatrick glared at him.

"No," said Moore. "We keep the girl for extra leverage. Now what about the other guys? Are they coming down?"

Torres cleared his throat. "They should be in Guadalajara by this afternoon."

"Good." Moore dialed Zúñiga but was sent straight to voice mail. "Call me back, señor."

"Hey, let's get cleaned up and get outside," said Fitzpatrick. "They might be leaving soon."

Corrales sat at the breakfast table with Raúl, Pablo, Miguel, and Sonia, and he couldn't take his eyes off of the woman. She was the sexiest woman he'd ever seen, much more so than his Maria, and while he knew that staring would get him in trouble once again, he no longer cared. It was clear that the two of them had been loud for his benefit, and so he wouldn't make it easy for them.

"Thank you for checking on us this morning," said Miguel, between bites of his cereal. "It's good to know you're providing such good security."

"*Gracias*. That's our job."

"Is it your job to stare at my girlfriend's tits?"

"Miguel," Sonia said, and gasped.

"Well, look at him. He's drooling like a fucking thug over there." Miguel rose from the table, crossed around it, then came up behind Corrales and growled in his ear, "You better keep your distance today. I don't want to see you once. Not once. You protect us; that's fine. But I don't want to know you are there. Do you understand me, you fucking pig?"

Corrales tensed and shook with the desire to reach for his pistol and cap this spoiled bitch. But he sat there and took it. "Yes, señor. You won't see us, but we'll be there . . ."

"You like your job, right?"

"Yes."

"Then do what I say and you'll keep it."

Miguel moved back to his seat. "I'm so sorry, Sonia. I didn't want you to see that."

"It's okay. Corrales," Sonia said, pursing her lips, "I know you're trying to do your job. I am sorry about all of this."

He smiled at her: a wolf's grin.

Within an hour they were walking the streets of San Cristóbal, with Corrales ordering Raúl and Pablo to fan out and keep a half a block away. Pablo called on his cell phone to say, "This is not good. If something happens, we are too far from them."

"You know what, Pablo? At this point—"

Corrales did not finish his sentence. Another call was coming in from his friend Hernando Chase, who managed the Monarch strip club. "Dante, some very bad news. Johnny was killed. They killed his girlfriend, too. They dumped the bodies outside the club. They must have tortured them, then chopped them up with a saw. They left a note, and I got it before I called the police."

"Fucking Zúñiga," Corrales said through his teeth.

"No, I don't think it was the Sinaloas," said Hernando. "I asked around."

"What's the note say?"

"Just two words: Buitres Justicieros."

Corrales tensed. Avenging Vultures. Fucking Guatemalans— who were supposed to be working for the Juárez Cartel, not executing its allies.

However, Corrales knew exactly why they'd killed Johnny. And it was all his fault.

Taliban Safe House
Near San José
Costa Rica

As instructed by Rahmani, Samad had ordered the Anza MKIII (QW-2), which was considered the Chinese equivalent of the U.S. FIM-92E Stinger missile. Thank Allah he'd also received free shipping—even without an online coupon! His lieutenants had appreciated that joke, and in reality, it wasn't too far from the truth. Their weapons deal had been finalized through an encrypted website and with electronic payment; moreover, their Chinese allies had been able to smuggle the weapons into Costa Rica via container ship without incident.

Samad and his entourage had left Colombia aboard a small cargo plane and been flown to Costa Rica by an ally who'd delivered them to a Taliban safe house in a canton called Uruca on the outskirts of the country's capital. It was there, inside the small two-bedroom home that reeked of mothballs and bleach, that they took delivery of the man-portable surface-to-air missile launchers, six in all, packed in Anvil cases fitted with backpack-style harnesses for easier carrying. And it was there that Talwar and Niazi once more questioned the details of their mission.

"When can you tell us what will happen?" asked Niazi.

"When we arrive in the United States."

"How will we do that without help from the Mexicans?" asked Talwar.

"When you build a plan, you must build three other plans, so as each falls you turn to the next."

"And when you run out of plans?" asked Talwar.

Samad raised his brows. "You either succeed or die."

"So what is your plan to get us into the United States?"

"Patience," Samad told Talwar. "We have to get to Mexico first. And when we arrive there, you'll see. We have friends who have been keeping a careful watch on the border. We are not alone. Mullah Rahmani has taken very good care of us."

"Samad, I am worried about some of the others. They are very young and impressionable. I fear that once we reach America, some will leave when they see the kind of life they can have there—McDonald's and Burger King and Walmart."

"How can you doubt their faith now?"

Talwar shrugged. "It is one thing to have faith in the valley. It is another to have faith in the palace. I am here as a warrior, but I am concerned."

Samad put a hand on his lieutenant's shoulder. "We will shoot any man who deserts us. Do you understand?"

Talwar and Niazi nodded.

"Then we've nothing left to discuss. We have the missiles and launchers. Let's get the trucks loaded and get back to the airport."

They would lift off from Costa Rica and fly to a private airport with a dirt strip about one thousand miles south of Mexicali and literally in the middle of nowhere. Trucks and drivers were already waiting for them to complete the last leg of the journey northward, toward the border.

Samad's excitement was beginning to mount. If they could just make that border crossing, the rest of his mission would unfold as precisely as Mullah Rahmani had described it to him. Years' worth of planning and the dedication of many warriors of Allah would all come to fruition.

Samad could not feel more proud. He carried the will of

Allah in his heart, and the fire of jihad in his hands. Those were all he needed.

San Cristóbal de las Casas
Chiapas, Mexico

It wasn't until now that Moore had been able to get some digital pictures of all three of the "bodyguards" that Miguel and his girlfriend had following them. And when he'd sent back the photos to Towers, the results were impressive. Not only was Corrales a High-Value Target, but so was Pablo Gutiérrez, who'd killed an FBI agent in Calexico. In fact, Agent Ansara from Moore's own task force had followed a few leads on Pablo that had taken him up into the Sequoia National Forest. Consequently, they could now, as Towers had put it, nab two major scumbags with one stone.

"Three," Moore had corrected. "Don't forget about the big dog himself, Rojas . . ."

"Trust me. I haven't forgotten about him," Towers had said. "But let's be patient."

Tailing Miguel, his girl, and their three bodyguards was a bigger challenge than Moore had thought. They had, of course, packed clothes so they'd resemble tourists, with cameras dangling from their necks, but Torres had a physique and face you didn't easily forget, and Moore had questioned him thoroughly: "Will Corrales know who you are if he sees you?"

"No, he won't," said the fat man. Neither he nor Fitzpatrick had ever had any direct contact with the man, but that didn't mean Corrales hadn't seen pictures of them. Corrales's spotters seemed to be everywhere in Juárez.

With that in mind, Moore argued for Fitzpatrick and Torres to hold even farther back and not take any chances. Torres had protested, saying that Corrales had probably seen pictures of Moore, since he'd stayed in the hotel. While that might be true, Moore could blend in far easier than the others. He was wearing a floral-print shirt, a photographer's vest, and an awestruck grin on his face: classic dumbass tourist. The vest did a nice job of hiding his pair of suppressed Glocks. Fitzpatrick and Torres would take out Corrales's two puppies, but Moore was intent on nabbing Corrales himself. Once they dealt with those three, they would move on to Rojas's son and his girl, and all of them would be flown to a safe house in Guadalajara. From there Zúñiga would take over the negotiations with Rojas. While Torres had wanted the girl killed, Moore told him innocents would be left out of the equation. Period. Torres thought about it, figured an extra hostage wasn't a bad idea.

With his own two accomplices sifting through the crowded street much farther back, Moore was shadowing Miguel and Sonia. They had stopped at one of the dozens of makeshift booths set up by native women to sell their wares: brightly colored belts and dresses, and children's dolls made of wood. A few of the dolls surprised Moore, as they'd been fashioned to resemble soldiers with guns and wearing woolen balaclavas. That was an interesting message to send to the children in this city: Your heroes wear masks and carry guns . . .

Farther down the street lay the more densely packed booths

of the market, where a wide variety of fresh fruits and vegetables were stacked neatly in pyramids and sold out of wicker baskets. There were more booths selling rice and fish, others featuring beef and chicken, and even one with a big banner advertising locally grown coffee beans, since the valley was one of Mexico's premier areas for the crop.

Moore shifted to within a few feet of Miguel's girlfriend, who was holding up a dress to the light and studying its rich yellow-and-red floral pattern. She was lean and athletic, wearing an oversized pair of black sunglasses.

"What do you think?" she asked her boyfriend.

Miguel glanced up from his smartphone. "Oh, Sonia, that's much too loud for you. Keep looking."

She shrugged and handed the dress back to the old lady who owned the booth.

"Men don't know how to dress women," said the old lady. "This one is perfect for you. He doesn't know what he's talking about."

Sonia (Moore liked that name) smiled. "I agree, but he is a very strong-willed man."

At that, Moore frowned. He would have told Sonia that the dress was beautiful and that she smelled so very sweet, and that she was so fresh and young and sexy that it was easy to forget that his friends wanted to kill her.

Well, he would have told her some of that.

"Come on, Sonia, let's keep going," said Miguel.

Moore pretended to look at a wallet on a table nearby. As they were about to leave, he glanced up, over the rim of his sunglasses, and there he was, the little son of a bitch, Dante Corrales, standing across the street in the alcove of a small building, staring at them, arms folded over his chest.

Watching the boss's son, huh, buddy? Can't wait for you and I to sit down and have coffee . . . I'm hoping you'll have a lot to talk about.

Moore had barely finished that thought when a hand wrapped around Corrales's mouth, and suddenly two men were on him, dragging him back into the building. Moore immediately got on his cell phone to Fitzpatrick, and said, "A bunch of guys just grabbed Corrales."

"No shit. We just lost the other two guys. What the fuck is going on?"

"Get up here. They pulled him into the pink building on my left. I'll stay with Miguel and the girl."

But when Moore turned around, both the young man and his lovely companion were gone.

24

HE THAT DIES PAYS ALL DEBTS

San Cristóbal de las Casas
Chiapas, Mexico

MOORE SWUNG AROUND, his gaze probing the throngs of tourists, sweeping from left to right, then farther down the street toward the more crowded market.

Between all the colors worn by the vendors and the shifting about of the pedestrians, Moore realized, in the mere instant he'd taken his eyes off Miguel and Sonia and looked to Corrales he'd lost the couple. That fast. A few heartbeats. They must've been approached by gunmen and quietly ushered away.

It wasn't exactly panic that set in but a kind of electricity that coursed through Moore's veins, humming in tune to the rapid beating of his heart.

A car engine fired up, the sound originating from the next corner. Moore bolted off, weaving his way through the shoppers and reaching the corner, where at the foot of a steep hill Miguel and Sonia were running across the street to the next alley. They were being pursued by two short men dressed like local farmers, who just happened to be carrying pistols. Maybe they had been led away—but they'd made their break.

The lead guy fired two shots at the couple, but the rounds were clearly warning shots that burrowed into the whitewashed walls behind them as they disappeared into the alley. The guy could have easily killed them both. So these men, whoever they were, wanted prisoners as well.

They weren't members of the Sinaloa Cartel. The question was, how many other groups had Corrales and his cronies pissed off? Damn, they were probably lining up to take potshots at the punk from the all-powerful Juárez Cartel, and now Moore swore under his breath. The mission was difficult enough without competition.

He fell in behind them but was trying to keep a safe-enough distance to avoid detection. He jogged into the narrow alley, and the rear guy must've heard Moore's footfalls, because he stole a look back, then slowed—turning to fire.

Throwing himself toward the wall and reaching for his pistol, Moore evaded the first round by perhaps a meter before he had his pistol free from its holster, and returned two suppressed rounds, the cap-gun-like pop echoing off the walls.

The guy did likewise, diving for the wall.

Moore's first shot missed the guy's head by mere inches,

but the second caught him in the shoulder, and with a half-strangled cry he dropped hard to the dirt.

Wishing he had time to call Fitzpatrick and Torres, Moore charged past the fallen guy, kicking his weapon away, turned right at the end of the alley, then found himself on another steep cobblestone road, with cars lining both sides.

Miguel and Sonia were on the sidewalk and struggling up the hill, with the lone guy still behind them. Their pursuer fired another warning round that shattered the rear window of a small pickup truck beside them. Then he screamed in Spanish for them to stop running.

Moore bounded forward as a car engine roared behind him. He craned his neck at the dark blue sedan as it rushed past—a rental car, no doubt, the windows lowered, two men in the front seats, the passenger's arm hanging over the door with a pistol in his grip. Christ, how many were there? Moore ducked behind two cars as the passenger opened fire on him, and those were not warning shots.

As the car mounted the hill, Moore sprang up and fired another pair of rounds, the first punching the rear window and striking the passenger's head, the second going wide as the driver cut the wheel hard, out of Moore's bead.

Miguel and Sonia ducked into an alcove and once more vanished.

The remaining guy on foot steered himself into the same alcove as the car pulled to a stop.

Bad move, guys, Moore thought, because the kid and his

girl were going into a three-story hotel, and they would probably be trapped inside.

Miguel kept cursing and trying to keep up with Sonia, who
rushed past the hotel's front desk, where the elderly
woman working there gaped at them. They left her calling after
them and bounded into the stairwell.

"Where are we going?" he cried.

"Just keep going!"

Where had she found this bravery? He was supposed to be
the man and protect her, but she'd spotted Corrales being abducted, had seen the approach of two other men, and had kicked
off her heels and gotten them out of there before these idiots
could kidnap them. But now there was still at least one bastard
on their tail (who knew what happened to the other one), yet
Sonia seemed to have a plan.

"We can't go to the roof," he shouted back. "We'll get stuck
up there!"

"We're not going to the roof," she said, arriving on the next
landing. She opened the door to the second floor, waved him
on. Then they waited there, just panting, taking in the stale air
as they listened for the footsteps of the guy chasing them. He
arrived on the landing but kept on going up to the third floor.

Miguel breathed the deepest sigh of relief of his life. He
glanced over at Sonia, still struggling for breath. He looked down,
and in her hand was a small knife whose blade curved into a hook.

"Where'd you get that?"

"From my purse. My father gave it to me. It's really just a good-luck charm, but my father taught me how to use it."

"Fernando is very strict about us having weapons."

"I know. I didn't want to tell you, but he let me keep it. I have to protect myself."

Miguel frowned—

Just as the door swung open.

"Don't move," said the guy who'd been chasing them, his gun leveled on Miguel. "All you have to do is come along. There's a car outside."

Miguel thought he was dreaming as Sonia screamed, reared back, and slashed open the guy's throat, the blood coming in a great fountain across the wall.

"Get his gun!" she hollered.

He stood there, stunned. Who was this girl he'd fallen in love with? She was remarkable.

With his phone vibrating and yet another car arriving outside the hotel and at least three more guys rushing inside, Moore figured that if he walked in there, he'd be either captured or just shot for being in the wrong place at the wrong time. He crouched low behind a car and tugged out the phone: Fitzpatrick's number had come up while he'd just missed a call from Towers. He answered Fitzpatrick's call. "Where are you? We still can't find the other two guys, and no sign of Corrales."

"Damn, we need to find them," Moore said. "But yeah, I'm near this hotel a couple of blocks down. The road is real steep. The kid and the girl are inside, but these other guys are coming in to grab them."

"Who the fuck are they?"

"Don't know yet. But sure as shit we'll find out. Get the car and meet me over here!"

"Dude, how the hell did this go south so fast?"

"I don't know. Just get here."

That they'd come up from behind him and had managed to drag him into the building was very disappointing to Corrales. He'd prided himself on being very in tune with his senses, with his environment, always aware of any danger, reaching out with an extrasensory perception, as though he could read the thoughts of his actors before they drew close, feel their body heat from meters away, and know ahead of time what dark intentions lay in their hearts.

But that was bullshit, and he'd fucked up—because he'd let his guard down and forgotten that in this business there were people who wanted to kill you every day.

So these light-footed bastards had managed to drag him into the shop, which had turned out to be an old clothing store under heavy renovation, with construction materials all around them.

While they'd managed to disarm Corrales, they hadn't

been able to get a firm grip on him, and he slithered like a snake out of the first guy's grip, turned, and took a round point-blank in his shoulder before ripping his gun back from the guy who'd seized it.

Before either of the guys could react, Corrales put a bullet in each of their hearts.

And then he fell onto the floor, gasping, the blood pouring from his shoulder. He cursed and cursed again. He'd been shot before, but only minor flesh wounds, nothing like this.

He fumbled for his cell phone, dialed Miguel, waited. No answer. He called Pablo. Nothing. He sat there, bleeding. He called Raúl. Voice mail. Police sirens rose in the distance, and out behind the dust-caked windows of the shop, the tourists turned their heads as a police car rumbled past them.

Those bastards would no doubt capture Miguel and Sonia. How would he explain this to his boss, Castillo? That one-eyed fool would be outraged, and Corrales's failure would result in his execution unless he was able to link back up with the boss's son and the girl.

Castillo would ask, "Why did the Guatemalans attack you? I told you to hire them and have them make some hits on the Sinaloas."

But Corrales would be unable to answer. He could not tell Castillo that the money he'd been given to pay off the Guatemalans and use them as assassins had actually been used to help finance Corrales's hotel restoration and that he'd lied to the Guatemalans about payment. He'd given them twenty percent down, they had completed a half-dozen killings, but then Corrales had screwed them out of their money. They were, to put it delicately, fucking pissed. They'd killed Johnny and had followed Corrales here. He hadn't realized how relentless the little fuckers were, and now everything was falling apart.

Damn, he needed to get to a hospital.

Miguel clutched the pistol and shook his head in disbelief at Sonia. Her arm was covered in blood, but she was unfazed by that. Their would-be kidnapper lay on the ground with a geyser still erupting from his neck.

She wrenched open the door, but the sound of men running up the stairs sent them back inside, down the hallway.

"This way!" she cried.

They hung a sharp left and found another stairwell. This time he tugged open the door.

Others were charging upward.

"How many are there?" he asked, dumbfounded.

"Too many," she answered.

"They're going to trap us," he said.

She bit her lip, turned back, then went running toward the nearest hotel-room door and gave it a sharp kick with the bottom of her bare foot. She cursed in pain. The door did not give.

"Get back," he cried, then fired two rounds into the doorjamb, shattering some of the wood. He wrenched the door back and kicked it open. They hustled inside.

The tiny room reeked of cleaning products, the bed perfectly made. No suitcase. *Empty room. Good.*

"They'll see the door," she said, rushing to the window.

"Sonia, you're amazing. You're not hysterical."

"I am. I'm just hiding it," she said, trying to catch her breath. "Come on, we have to get out."

"You killed a guy back there," he said.

"Oh my God, I know." She tugged back the long curtains, threw open the window's latch, then slit open the screen with her knife. They looked down into the alley below, about a five-meter drop.

"Tie the sheets!" she shouted. "Come on! Tie the sheets."

"We're not going out that way," he said. "I have a gun, come on."

"Forget it. There's too many of them. We have to keep moving," she said.

He shook his head.

And just as she rushed toward the bed to tug away the bedspread, the door burst open.

Miguel fired at the first guy who entered, striking him in the stomach, but the second guy moved in very fast and held his pistol on Sonia. "Shoot again, señor. And she dies."

The gunfire coming from within the hotel, and the police sirens from not one, not two, but at least three units, drove Moore farther back from the hotel and toward the corner, where he huddled behind an old Volkswagen Beetle and returned the cell-phone call to Towers.

After Moore had given the man a ten-second capsule summary of what was happening, Towers swore under his breath and said, "I've got bad news for you, buddy. Very bad news . . ."

That was exactly how Moore's Navy SEAL buddy Carmichael had put it only seconds after the platform's lights had gone dark. He'd shouted, "We've been spotted!" Then had added, "Very bad news! We've been spotted!"

Carmichael had taken his three other SEALs up and onto the platform to try to defuse the explosives that the Revolutionary Guard troops had rigged there. Moore's men were hanging beneath the pilings, and Moore knew that he needed to send off those guys already in the water. He ordered them to take the SDV and get out, which they reluctantly did. Then he called to his task-unit commander to get an RHIB (rigid-hull inflatable boat) sent from the Iraqi patrol boat that was in truth being operated by the SEALs. The Zodiac would carry them out of there much faster than the SDV. Only problem was, they'd need a diversion to keep the troops on the platform busy while they took off.

"Mako Two, get your team in the water! Drop!"

"Roger that!" hollered Carmichael, the sound of gunfire cracking between his words.

Moore watched and waited as one man hit the waves, then a second.

Where were the others? "Mako Two, only see two guys?"

"I know! I know! Six has been hit. I gotta get him out!"

Many voices broke over the radio, and more gunfire crackled through, like static punctuating the fear voiced by his men, and then, for a moment that seemed like all the years he spent grieving, there was only the sound of Moore's breathing. And then . . .

Towers was still talking to him. "Moore, are you there?"

"I'm here."

"Listen to me, and listen good. Seems your agency has always had a keen interest in Mr. Jorge Rojas—so much so that they've had an agent working deep cover for over a year now. It's a classic case of the right hand not knowing what the left hand is doing."

"Wait a minute. What the hell are you saying?"

"I'm saying it's the kid's girlfriend, bro. She's CIA. Recruited in Europe a long time ago. She's a blue badger like you. And now you're telling me you've just lost her to some other guys?"

Moore gritted his teeth. "Holy shit. But no, no, no. We haven't lost them yet. I'll get back to you."

Surprised? Moore wasn't. Annoyed? Frustrated beyond belief? Ready to kill someone who sat behind a desk and had failed to tip off his bosses? Of course. Task Force Juárez's mission file had been either ignored or not delivered to the right desk to allow for a coordinated and concerted effort on behalf of all agents working on the case. This wasn't the first time late or fragmented information resulted in a communication breakdown in one of Moore's operations, and it certainly wouldn't be the last. Breakdowns between agencies such as the FBI and the CIA were far more common, which made this revelation all the more aggravating.

He hung up as Fitzpatrick and Torres turned the corner in their little white rental car. He climbed onto the backseat. "See the blue car up there. Hold back. If they're not dead, they'll be coming out the door right there."

Lo and behold, they did, both Miguel and Sonia, escorted by a pair of men holding them at gunpoint. They climbed into the sedan, and the car sped off.

"I'll wait a few seconds, then follow," said Fitzpatrick.

"Keep your distance," Moore warned him.

"Corrales has a lot of enemies," Torres said. "His enemies need to be our friends, but they're not. They've stolen our cash cow!"

"Yeah, ain't that our bad luck," said Moore.

"We've got nothing," Torres spat. "What the hell will I tell the boss?"

"Easy does it, big boy. I told you the group I work for is very powerful, much more powerful than a bunch of fucking punks with guns."

Moore looked at Fitzpatrick, who almost cracked a smile.

"If we lose them, someone will have to pay for this," Torres warned. "And it won't be me."

Moore snorted. "If you don't shut up, I'm going to kick your fat ass out of this car and make you walk . . . *tough* guy."

Torres smirked and leaned forward. "Just don't lose them," he told Fitzpatrick.

———

Look, I demand to know where you're taking us," said Miguel. "If this is just a simple kidnapping, my father will pay the money and we'll be done with this by the end of the day, all right?"

The driver, whose dark complexion was hard to read as they passed into the shadows of the taller buildings, glanced back and smiled. "Okay, boss, whatever you say."

"Who are you guys, and where are we going?"

"If you keep talking, we will put a gag in your mouth," said the driver.

Sonia put a hand on Miguel's, while the guy in the passenger's seat kept his pistol aimed at her. Another carful of men had joined them, and they were following.

"Miguel, it's okay," Sonia said. "They won't tell us anything, so don't waste your energy. Let's focus on staying calm. Everything will be all right."

"How do you know?" he said, tears welling in his eyes. "They're going to torture us and kill us. Fuck this shit! Fuck it. We need to get out!"

"No," she said, squeezing his hand. "Don't do anything stupid. We'll be okay. They just want money. This is just what your father was afraid of. I just wish Corrales had done a better job."

"I'm going to kill him when I see him."

She shrugged. "He might be dead already."

———

Corrales had managed to call the hotel and got Ignacio on the phone. Ignacio, in turn, had run off from the front desk and had found María. Corrales babbled somewhat incoherently to her, told her he needed her and some guys to come down and pick him up. Said he was going to find a hospital, that he'd been shot.

He staggered out of the building, walked about a block, then didn't remember anything else.

"There you go, Dante. There you go," said Pablo.

He flickered open his eyes, realized he was back in his hotel room, and there was a man he didn't recognize standing at Pablo's side. This man had long gray hair, a thin beard, and thick glasses.

"This is going to be very expensive," said the man.

"Dante, he's a doctor, and he's going to get the bullet out of your shoulder—no questions asked."

"How did you get away?"

Pablo breathed deeply. "I got one of them. I don't know what happened to Raúl. Then I found you on the street, just in time, too—but don't worry about that now. He's going to give you some drugs to put you out. Then you'll feel better. I talked to María and some of the boys. They're flying down to get us like you asked."

"We can't leave. We lost the boss's son!"

"Easy, easy. We'll find them."

"No, we won't. The fucking Guatemalans have them!"

Pablo recoiled. "Why?"

"Because I didn't pay them, and now I have to tell Castillo what's happened. He'll have me killed."

"No, don't tell him anything. I'll take care of it. Rest easy now, my friend. Everything will be okay."

But it wouldn't, and as the old man put a mask across Corrales's face, Corrales saw the fires of his youth rage once more, and his parents, their faces burning, the skin melting off, walked out of their old hotel, and his father raised a finger at him and said, "I told you never to join the cartel. They killed us. And now they will kill you."

25

IF I RETREAT, KILL ME

San Juan Chamula
Chiapas, Mexico

Moore, Fitzpatrick, and Torres followed the blue car and a green-and-white van that seemed to be leading the car, out of San Cristóbal de las Casas and into the foothills, toward the small town of San Juan Chamula, about ten kilometers away. It was there, Moore had read, that the indigenous Tzotzil Mayan people were preparing for an early-summer carnival that attracted tourists. Dancing, singing, live music, fireworks, and a long parade through the village would not only entertain visitors but bring much-needed revenue into the otherwise poor town.

Torres repeatedly ordered Fitzpatrick to get closer, and Moore struck down those commands, saying that if they were spotted, the hostages could be killed—and there'd be no cash cow for Señor Zúñiga, nor any negotiations to open up border tunnels for use by the Sinaloas.

What neither Torres nor Fitzpatrick knew was that Miguel's girlfriend, one Sonia Batista (whose real name was Olivia Montello), had a chip embedded in her shoulder that would allow the Agency to track her position. Moore needed to find a moment away from Torres when he could fill in Fitzpatrick on what was happening; for now all these two guys needed to know was that they should keep their distance. In the meantime, Towers and the rest of the Agency were doing everything they could to positively identify these men, yet Moore and Towers agreed that they were more than likely Avenging Vultures, the Guatemalan death squad that had, for some reason, double-crossed the Juárez Cartel. Moore and the others were, after all, just a few hundred kilometers from the Guatemalan border, and the relationship between the Guatemalans and the Juárez Cartel was well documented. What had soured between the groups Moore did not know, but these guys weren't your young, dumb, off-the-shelf thugs. Back at the first briefing, Towers had said these guys made the *sicarios* look tame. Many of them were ex-military and/or had been members of a Guatemalan Special Forces group known as the Kaibiles, whose motto was: *If I advance, follow me. If I stop, urge me on. If I retreat, kill me.*

Even more notable was their ability to exercise great reserve. They dressed like civilians, carried only pistols, and had kept their operation simple thus far. But that wouldn't last,

Moore assumed. Not now, when they were ready to negotiate and expected retaliation. That thought chilled Moore as he considered Sonia being touched, abused, and tortured by them. He shuddered.

Moore tugged out his smartphone, and within a minute he was studying a satellite image of the town with Sonia's GPS beacon marked as a slowly shifting blue dot superimposed over the road.

"You looking at maps now?" asked Torres, leaning over Moore's shoulder.

"No, porn."

"Why do you have to be such a wiseass?"

Moore snorted. "Don't make me answer that." The fat man was already taxing his patience.

Another data screen on the town indicated that Chamula had its own police force and that no outside military or law enforcement were allowed inside; moreover, tourists were, for the most part, forbidden to take pictures while visiting. Very strict rules indeed, but what if the Vultures had a deal with the local police? What if they'd planned this capture all along and now had a perfect safe house from which to conduct their kidnapping negotiations? That they were not driving back toward Guatemala made that even more probable.

Fitzpatrick guided them along a poorly paved road that snaked its way up near the church of San Juan, a modest structure of dusty white walls, green parapets, and an ornate tile archway. Moore told Fitzpatrick to park along a row of tourist cars and taxis opposite fifty or more booths shaded by colorful umbrellas. Overhead flapped long lines of pennons that swooped down from the church's steeples. This was the marketplace, and several hundred people were weaving their way through the maze of tables. Here much of the fruit was stacked on blankets spread across the grassy field, with piles of citrus lined up like bowling pins.

"We can't park now," barked Torres, pointing at the fleeing cars. "We'll lose them!"

"I'm tracking the car, asshole," said Moore, showing him the smartphone. "GPS beacon. I planted it on them."

"When did you do that?"

"Before you got to me," Moore lied. "Now shut up. Let's get out. Behind the church is a graveyard. We're going into the hills out back." Moore used his thumb and index finger to zoom in on the touch screen. The kidnappers came to a stop outside a small cluster of houses just west of the graveyard. The hills would make for a perfect observation post.

"Hey, why you go along with him so easy?" Torres asked Fitzpatrick.

"Because he's good. He tracked them. Did you? Without him, we would've lost them already."

Torres muttered a string of epithets, then heaved himself out of the car. He lifted his camera, thinking he'd pretend to do the tourist thing, when Moore slapped down his hands.

"What the hell?"

"No pictures here—I told you. They don't like it. Let's move."

From the trunk they retrieved three heavy backpacks bulging with gear that included three sniper rifles disassembled and stowed in their cases.

They hiked up a narrow rocky trail with deep cuts from the summer rains. Torres tripped twice over these cuts as they began to take in the graveyard with its white, blue, and black wooden crosses flanked by lanky pines and the T-shaped power and phone lines. Below lay the ruins of San Sebastián Church, whose steeples were long gone and whose yellowed and crumbling walls were spanned by deep cracks like veins. The upper edges near the rooftops were draped in moss and mold.

Once they reached the summit of the tallest hill, Moore led them to a cluster of pines, where they crouched down. He activated his smartphone's camera and thumbed on the ARS (augmented reality system) app that would turn the phone into a computer-enhanced imaging device by superimposing wire frames over the images and displaying data boxes that indicated the size and range of various structures and targets within his field of view. Additionally, the system tapped into real-time streaming data on the house where they'd taken Sonia and Miguel. Moore knew the geeks back home were all focusing on that house as well, and within thirty seconds he'd have that imagery. He clipped a Bluetooth receiver into his ear, then switched it on.

"Torres, you see that blue house down there, the one right next to the taller beige one?" Moore asked.

"Yes."

"That's where they have Miguel and Sonia. Looks like they're trying to do the same thing we planned, so we don't have much time. They might be on the phone with Rojas right now."

"Then it's over. How can we say we've taken his son hostage when these guys have already done it?"

Moore grinned crookedly. "I guess we shouldn't worry about that until we rescue the hostages—so we can kidnap them ourselves."

"Why don't we just wait for Rojas to show up?" asked Fitzpatrick.

"There's no guarantee he will. Our negotiations are contingent upon him making a personal appearance, but who knows what these guys want," Moore pointed out. "Could just want the money and don't care who brings it." He looked to Torres. "You got the binoculars in your pack? Just keep an eye on that house for now. Flexxx?"

Fitzpatrick hoisted his brows at the sound of his nickname.

"I want to set you up on the east side over there so you can keep an eye on their little police station. I'll show you a good spot."

Moore waved over the man, and they hiked between the trees for a minute until they were out of Torres's earshot.

In a rapid-fire report, Moore told the DEA agent everything.

"Holy shit," Fitzpatrick said through a gasp.

"My words exactly."

"So this *really is* a rescue operation."

Moore nodded. "And now I'm not sure what to do with Torres."

"He could be a huge problem—no pun intended," said Fitzpatrick.

Moore gave a little snort over the joke. "Well, I guess we need him now. I'm just worried he'll kill Sonia. He's already said it. He thinks the boy will be demoralized. He could wind up shooting her when we make our move."

Fitzpatrick shrugged. "We'll just stress the point for now—unless you want him to get caught in some crossfire—"

"Or we send him on a suicide mission."

"Yeah," said Fitzpatrick, his eyes lighting over the idea. "We just make the fat boy think he's a hero."

"Great minds think alike, bro."

Fitzpatrick nodded. "No problem. I've thought of offing the bastard many times, so we'll come up with something."

Moore stopped and stared at the marketplace partially obscured by the ruins. "Carnival starts at sundown. Gunfire, fireworks, they all sound the same—and that's about the only bit of luck we've had so far."

"I'll take it. So if we manage to get back Miguel and the girl, what do we do with them?"

Moore laughed. "You know what? I never even asked . . ."

"I mean, if we've already got a deep-cover agent close to Rojas and the family, do we still need to hold them hostage? Maybe the original plan has gone to shit. The deep-cover team she's working with needs to start talking to us."

The question hung as Moore called back Towers, filled him

in, and got the official orders from the Agency: Rescue Sonia Batista but in no way interfere with her mission, which Moore and Towers interpreted as letting them go.

The fat man Torres would not like that. No, he would not like that at all.

In fact, speak of the devil, Torres was calling Moore. "What?" Moore asked.

"Another car just pulled up. They got one of Corrales's guys. They're bringing him into the house now."

"Which guy is it?" Moore asked. "Raúl or Pablo?"

"I think it's Raúl."

"You sure they only got one?"

"Positive."

"I'll be right up."

Miguel winced at the laundry line they'd used to bind his hands behind his back. Still more of that coarse, weather-beaten twine had been used to bind his legs, and they'd forced him to sit on the old wooden floor in a corner near the back window. Sonia, who'd been bound as well, was sitting on the floor opposite him, leaning forward, staring blankly into space.

There were six of them altogether, and none would answer any of his questions. Both he and Sonia had stopped talking about ten minutes prior, and they listened as the tallest of the group, a man with a gray crew cut and narrow eyes who the others addressed as Captain Salou, spoke in murmurs on his cell phone, both his accent and his fast speech making it very difficult to discern anything.

The depression had already made breathing difficult and had knotted Miguel's stomach. He had failed his girlfriend and his father, and had disgraced the memory of his dear mother. He had allowed himself to be used as a pawn, and it was quite clear that if these men did not get what they wanted, he and Sonia would be murdered. The only thing they could pray for now was a quick death.

But judging from the salacious looks on their faces, these men would have none of that. Sonia was dinner.

How the hell had this happened? Because his father had hired a bunch of dolts as security men. Then should he blame his father for this? Perhaps Fernando had hired these men. Maybe he was to blame. His incompetence had led to this . . .

Sonia glanced up at him, her eyes creased in pain.

"Don't worry," he said, barely able to speak, his mouth gone dry. "My father will deal with these dogs. He will deal with them swiftly."

She looked at him, then over at the window, then back toward the small wooden table and chairs, where two men sat, drinking bottles of Coca-Cola. A third man came into the room, carrying several olive-drab backpacks with patches depicting a blazing sword. He dropped the backpacks to the floor and said, "Everyone wears a radio now. Captain's orders."

The front door opened, and three more men shuffled into the room. Miguel's eyes widened on one of Corrales's stooges,

Raúl, who'd also managed to get himself caught. He'd already been tied and gagged, and Salou turned to them and asked, "He is your employee?"

"Yes," answered Miguel. "My bodyguard. He did a very good job, didn't he . . ."

Salou and the others broke into laughter, and then, as Raúl was shoved into the living room, Salou's expression grew serious. "All we want is our money."

"I don't know what you're talking about. Who are you?"

Salou glanced back at the others, as though looking for some approval. He crinkled his thin nose, as though he didn't like the stench coming from Raúl, then said, "We are soldiers of justice. And we want you and your lovely companion to understand that. We want you to know that we are men of our word. And we will show you."

Two men shoved Raúl onto the floor, facedown, between Miguel and Sonia. One man sat on top of Raúl, another pinned his legs to the floor, while a third grabbed Raúl's head by the hair.

Miguel craned his neck as one of the men from the table disappeared into the kitchen, only to return with a long hatchet.

"No, wait a second, we don't have to do this," said Miguel. "My father's got money. You want money? We'll give it to you. There's no need for any of this!"

Salou accepted the hatchet and tested the edge with his thumb.

"We believe you," said Sonia. "We believe you'll kill us. You don't have to show us. We know."

"This isn't just for you," said Salou. "It's for all the men who've deceived us and used us." He glanced over his shoulder at another of his men, who'd drawn a small HD video camera from one of the backpacks, its LED recording light flashing steadily.

Raúl began screaming against his gag and writhing left and right to free himself. But it was no good. The three men held him to the floor as Salou came around them and began taking practice swings with the hatchet.

"Don't look," Sonia said. "Just don't look."

Miguel closed his eyes, but then he couldn't bear that any longer, and the moment he opened them, Salou brought down the ax in one great arc.

Aw, fuck, they killed him," said Torres, lowering his binoculars.

Moore grabbed the binoculars and watched through the window as the hatchet man, who appeared to be the leader and oldest guy, reached down and lifted up something. That's when Moore realized what it was, and he recoiled.

A fellow agent was a hatchet stroke away from death, and he and these two guys were all that stood in the way. The weight of that responsibility felt suffocating and familiar, and he didn't want to believe that history was repeating itself, but it was, and it would again, because the universe had a very dark sense of humor, and he always bore the brunt.

He closed his eyes and listened to the disembodied voices in his head:

"Zodiac's on the way! Thirty seconds. Getting two right away. Mako One, we need you up top, now!"

"On my way. Mako Two, let's roll!"

"Negative, negative. Still can't get to Six."

"Mako One, this is Raptor. I am taking fire. Can't hold this bird for much longer. Get your people out of the water and off the platform NOW."

Another voice now, female, soft, calm: "But you understand that what happened cannot be changed, no matter how many times you remember it? You understand that your memory will not change the outcome. You can't reimagine what happened."

"I know."

"But this is what's happening. You're playing it over and over again because deep down you still believe you can change something. But you can't."

"No one gets left behind."

"Do you know who's been left behind? You. The world's passing you by because you can't come to terms with this. So you're living in Purgatory, and you think that you're not allowed to be happy because of what happened."

"How can I be happy? How can I enjoy this life? You're the shrink. You have all the answers. Tell me how I'm supposed to be fucking happy after what I did! After what I fucking did!"

Moore opened his eyes as Torres tugged the binoculars out of his hands and once more stared down through the window. "I see some military backpacks inside. This is much worse than I thought."

After a deep breath, Moore gritted his teeth. "We're getting that kid and his girlfriend out of there. We're not going to lose them."

"They got seven guys so far. Just saw two more leave. Who knows how many back at San Cristóbal."

Moore considered that. "I saw them grab Corrales. He might be already dead, since they didn't bring him here."

"Maybe he got away. He's a slippery little fucker."

Moore rose and walked away from Torres. He called Towers, told him to keep eyes in the sky on the town for Corrales and Pablo. Then he told Towers about the execution and the military backpacks.

"Well, there you have it. Avenging Vultures double-crossing the Juárez Cartel, and we're caught in the middle."

"Listen, I need a lot from you, and I need it fast," said Moore.

"Talk to me."

"Looks like they're going to start communicating by radio. I need a tap in and a translated feed back to me."

"Not easy."

"No shit."

"What else?"

"Can we tap Rojas's communications?"

"Deep-cover team says they've been trying to do that for months, but he's got electronic countermeasures and hackers who do nothing but sweep for leaks, so our guys have had no luck."

"What about Corrales's phones?"

"If we picked up anything good from him, I would've come

with that a long time ago. Truth is we've intercepted his calls from the start, but he's very good about who he calls and what he says . . . He knows we're listening."

"Well, see if you can confirm now if he's still alive. And Pablo as well."

"Anything else?"

"Yeah," Moore said and grunted. "A SEAL team would be nice."

"I'll give them a call."

Moore thumbed off the phone and returned to Torres's side. "What's happening now?"

"It was gross, dude. They wiped blood all over the girl's face."

"But they didn't hurt her."

"Not yet."

"How many we got?"

"Six or seven. Looks like four guys posted outside. They got a fifth guy sitting in the van down the street. Not sure how many else inside."

"All right, Luis. If we're going to make this happen, I need you to take on the toughest job of all."

"Look at me," said Torres, his voice filling with bravado. "You think those little pussies scare me?"

Moore grinned. "All right. Listen up."

26

ATTEMPTS

La Estancia Apartments
Juárez, Mexico

GLORIA VEGA HAD LEARNED from Towers that the Sinaloas were not responsible for the murder of Johnny Sanchez and his girlfriend. Towers had confirmed via Moore, who was now in southeast Mexico, that members of that Guatemalan death squad, the Avenging Vultures, had killed the journalist.

When Vega had mentioned that she thought the Guatemalans might be responsible for the murder, Inspector Gómez had dismissed her with a flagrant wave. "Johnny was reporting on the cartels, and he paid the price. The Sinaloas did this. There is nothing more to it."

But the old man's face had grown pale, and he'd given her

a long, troubled look before telling her he was going home and that she should do the same.

After the riot outside the station, Vega had told Gómez that she would trust him, that she was afraid that everyone around her was corrupt, and that all she wanted to do was the right thing.

"What if the right thing is to look the other way?" he'd asked her. "What if you realize that nothing we do will change anything and that sometimes we must fight fire with fire?"

She'd just stared at him.

He'd grabbed her hands. "You've seen what I've seen. And now you know what I know." And then he did something that shocked her. He released her hands and gave her a deep hug. When he was through, he pulled back with tears in his eyes. "I am sorry that you've come to see the truth of this. It is a bitter truth, but we must accept it."

She put the key in her apartment door, but something wasn't right. The key did not slide into the lock as smoothly as it usually did. This was something that the average person might dismiss as an annoying inconvenience, but Vega was keenly aware of her surroundings, especially now, in Juárez, and missing even the slightest detail could result in death. She took a deep breath and wondered if someone had tried to pick the lock.

Drawing her weapon, she opened the door and stepped inside.

A shuffle of feet, and then—

He came at her from behind, a male voice coming in a deep groan as he tried to get the wire around her throat, but her hand was already there, coming up reflexively before the wire could touch her throat. It sliced into her palm as she swung around, dragging him with her.

The foyer was still dark, and she couldn't turn back to see him, could only bring her arm around her side and fire once, twice, until the wire went slack and she screamed and rushed forward to whirl back and fire again.

A shaft of light came in from the living room window, and she saw him, barely her height, dressed in jeans and a gray sweatshirt, a balaclava over his face. He lay there with gunshot wounds in his chest.

Despite her heavy breathing, the stench of gunpowder, and the saliva filling her mouth, she still detected movement from the bedroom. A second one? There it was: a window latch thrown, something trying to get out.

"Don't move!" she screamed, and rushed into the bedroom, in time to see another man dressed similarly to the first trying to slip away through the window. He'd been the backup man but had chickened out, and Vega was so pumped with adrenaline and so fearful that he'd turn back with a weapon that she emptied the rest of her magazine into the punk, who fell back into the bedroom. Reflexively, she ejected the magazine, jammed in a fresh one, then chambered a round, all in a matter of seconds.

She rushed to the light switch, threw it on, then swept the rest of the apartment, the walk-in closet, the bathroom. *Clear.* They'd sent two punks, thinking it'd be an easy job to off one lady cop. She stood there, just breathing.

And then she cursed. Because in that moment as she tried to regain her breath, she began to cry.

She reached for her cell phone, dialed Towers. "I want off this fucking case. I want out of here. Right now."

"Whoa, whoa, whoa, slow down. Talk to me."

She hung up on him, waited another moment, then dialed the police. *I'm not a quitter*, she told herself. *No matter what comes out of my mouth.*

She made the report as a knock came at her front door, probably the landlord or a concerned neighbor.

Her phone rang: Towers calling back. She answered, "Two punks just jumped me in my apartment. I killed them both."

"Then we'll pull you out of there."

"No."

"But you just said—"

"I know what I said. I'm going to finish this. I'll arrest Gómez myself."

"All right, just hang in there. I'll have some sensors put in place in the apartment. This won't happen again."

"I don't know about that. Gómez sent these bastards to kill me. He knows . . ."

"You need to hang tight for now, because when we bring him down, the rest will follow. Big bust, just like in Puerto Rico, but we can't rush into it, not yet . . ."

"Just hope I live long enough," she spat. "Now, I have to go. They're banging on my door, and a couple of units are on the way . . ."

San Cristóbal de las Casas
Chiapas, Mexico

The image of his father, backlit by the burning hotel, still haunted Dante Corrales as he lay there in the bed, his shoulder heavily bandaged, his left arm in a sling. He dialed the number and listened to the unanswered ring. There was no voice mail, only the endless buzzing.

"He still doesn't pick up?" Pablo asked, sitting on a chair near the doors leading out to the veranda.

"What if they're trying to call Miguel? What if they already know something's wrong?"

"If you call Castillo and you tell him the truth, you know what he's going to say . . ."

"He'll expect me to run. They'll hunt me down and kill me. I can't do that."

"Dante, why are you so scared? I've never seen you this way. Come on. We can beat this."

"Why am I scared? Do you have any fucking idea what'll happen now?"

"No."

He swore in his head, then aloud. "Shit. I should've just paid that scumbag Salou, but he's a sloppy bastard, and he's lucky he got the down payment at all."

"Do you have the money?"

Corrales shook his head. "Long gone."

"You didn't think they'd come after you for the rest?"

Corrales almost smiled. "I knew they would, but I figured by then I'd have a few extra bucks from the shipments. But we got screwed there, too . . ."

Corrales's phone rang—a number he didn't recognize. "Hello?"

"Corrales, my friend, I noticed you've been trying to call me. I'm so happy we finally have your attention."

He stiffened. It was Salou, and the bastard was practically singing with bravado. "Be careful what you say," Corrales told him. "A word to the wise."

"I'm disappointed."

"I know. Let me make it up to you."

"Three times my original estimate."

"Done. And you know what I want."

"Of course."

"Where are you?"

"Oh, Corrales, you know that's impossible. Tell me where you are, and I'll send a car."

"This will take time. Twenty-four hours, at least."

"I'm sorry, Corrales, but I am supposed to trust you now, after what you did? So no, I don't have twenty-four hours. I have until midnight. Okay?"

"I can't do that."

"Sure, you can. We can take care of this electronically. I have all the information you need."

But that was not how Corrales wanted to pay off the man. He wanted to get cash so he could bury the money, hide it from

Castillo. That kind of money would require him to draw from one of the cartel's operations accounts, and Castillo would be tipped off by such a withdrawal.

"I will come with the cash," Corrales said. "By midnight."

"No, like I said, we'll send a man for you when you're ready. No more games, Corrales."

"I understand."

"I hope you do. This is your last chance. I know that you are very sorry for your mistake, and I am willing to help you one last time, because I will profit from it. Otherwise, God help you . . . God help you . . ."

Corrales hung up and looked to Pablo. "We need a lot of cash here as fast as you can. Contact Héctor and tell La Familia that we need a loan."

"Now we're borrowing money from another cartel?" asked Pablo.

"Don't question me! Just do it!" Corrales winced as the throbbing in his shoulder became a knifing pain.

Jorge Rojas Medical Institute
Mexico City

A crowd of about two hundred people had gathered in the parking lot of a brand-new five-story office complex. Jorge Rojas straightened his shoulders at the lectern and smiled once more at the board of directors, the senior-level administrators, and at the dozens and dozens of office workers who'd been hired to help spearhead this ambitious endeavor. A handful of local media had also arrived to cover the historic ribbon-cutting ceremony.

Rojas had made a surprise visit to the ceremony (he'd originally bowed out of an appearance because of travel plans), but he'd returned early from Colombia and had decided at the last moment to accept the security risk and speak at the event.

He'd arrived in a convoy of six bulletproof SUVs, and his team of twenty men, dressed discreetly in Somoza's suits and well armed, had secured the perimeter. He was just finishing up his remarks: "And as I've said, the current medical model is flawed. It's our hope to focus on preventative medicine through promotion and greater access to services. This is a patient-centered approach rather than a health-care-system-centered approach. We hope to encourage all citizens of Mexico—and everyone in Latin America, for that matter—to take a more proactive role in their health care. We'll do this by helping other nonprofit organizations and by providing grants for students, professors, researchers, and other health-care professionals. I founded this institute with one purpose in mind: to help people live better and longer. Now, then, can we cut this ribbon? Because over there, I think they have churros and coffee for us all!"

The audience laughed as Rojas stepped off the podium, accepted the oversized pair of scissors, and did the honors, to great applause. He wished he could have turned to stare into the glistening eyes of his wife, but instead there was Alexsi, always stunning in her designer dresses and jewelry but a mannequin and hardly the conversationalist his wife had been. Beside her stood Castillo, putting a hand to his Bluetooth receiver and speaking softly to the rest of their security team.

Before Rojas could turn away so that they could hear a few words from the new institute's director, a reporter from XEW-TV, Inés Ortega, a middle-aged woman who had interviewed Rojas several times before and whose questions repeatedly annoyed him, pushed herself to the front of the group and thrust a microphone in his face.

"Señor Rojas, you are one of the richest men in the world, and your influence is seen everywhere. I can talk over my Rojas-operated cell phone while shopping at a supermarket you own with money I keep in one of your banks. When I'm finished, I can go buy a cup of coffee at a restaurant you own. You're hard to escape."

"I'm happy to help people," he said, waving his hand at her. "If you don't have any questions—"

"Actually, I do. How do you respond to people who call you greedy? Much of the nation starves, and you become richer because your businesses never seem to fail . . ."

"I respond like this," he said, gesturing back to the medical complex. "We're doing everything we can to give back to the community. There will always be critics, but the facts speak for themselves. If you want to talk about wealth, then I believe it must be protected to benefit future generations—that's why it's important for my businesses to do well. I'm not here to make myself rich anymore. I'm here to help our people and our president address this country's needs—and if people want to call that greedy, then that is a misinterpretation of what's in my heart."

A crack—not much louder than a firecracker—resounded from the back of the group, and almost immediately a thud like a punch struck Rojas's chest and knocked him off balance. He reached out toward the staircase railing behind him, missed, and collapsed onto the steps, his elbow crashing hard onto the concrete.

Pandemonium swept through the crowd, the screams coming in waves as some fled toward the parked cars while others simply hit the ground, all of them seeking cover except Fernando Castillo, who spotted the lone gunman at the back of the crowd and gave chase as the rest of the security team began to swarm around their prey.

From the corner of his eye, Rojas watched as Castillo ran but twenty steps before opening fire and hitting the man, who dropped before he could reach a pickup truck parked at the back of the lot, beneath two large oak trees. Castillo sprinted to the fallen shooter and put two more bullets in the man's head, much to Rojas's chagrin. It might've been useful to question the man, but then again, a public figure as prominent as himself had many enemies. This could have been a troubled citizen who just snapped one day and decided to kill someone he'd read about or seen on TV.

Both Alexsi and the reporter, Inés, were at Rojas's side as he dug into the inside pocket of his suit jacket and wriggled out the round that had lodged in the flexible plate. He lifted it up and showed it to the two women. "Thank God for protection," he said.

"You will have to call Felipe in Colombia and tell him," said Alexsi.

They helped him back to his feet as more people, including his board of directors, approached and asked if he was all right.

He returned to the lectern as the sirens grew in the distance. "I'm not dead," he cried. "And neither is the dream we've built here!"

With that, the crowd began to cheer.

Afterward, in the backseat of his armored Mercedes, Rojas watched the TV footage captured by the news crew. The story was being picked up by all the major news networks and newswires: the Associated Press, BBC News World, Reuters, and United Press International. Every major network in Mexico and the United States was either covering the story or about to cover the story, Rojas knew.

He tried once more to call Miguel. No answer. Voice mail.

"Nothing from my son. Nothing from Sonia," he told Castillo.

"Nothing from Dante, either, but give them some time," said Castillo. "Maybe there's trouble with the towers—that would explain why none of them are answering us."

"You're right. I shouldn't be worried, but if Miguel sees the news of what happened, he'll be worried, I know."

"He'll call you," Castillo assured him. "Now, sir, are you sure you don't want to go to the hospital?"

"Just take us home."

Alexsi put her hand on his and said, "Everything is fine, my love. Thank God you are so careful. I won't complain about you going to Colombia again."

He grinned faintly and tried to calm himself.

She frowned. "Why do you think that madman wanted to kill you? Just jealousy? After all you do for the country? I just can't believe there is so much hate in the world."

"Believe it," he said, turning his attention to the darkly tinted window. They were merging back onto the highway, heading toward Cuernavaca and his mansion in the suburbs. He suddenly yelled, "I want to know who that guy was!"

"Of course," said Castillo. "I'm already working on that. The detectives will call me as soon as they know."

"Okay, excellent," he said, catching his breath. And then a deep sigh of relief: a text message from Miguel.

He thumbed on the message, which had no text, only a video attached. He double-tapped the video icon, turned his phone horizontally, and watched in widescreen as the camera panned, revealing Sonia . . . and then Miguel . . .

Rojas began to lose his breath. "Fernando! Pull over! Pull over!"

A man came into view carrying an ax.

"Don't look," Sonia said. "Just don't look."

And Rojas's hands began to tremble. "No!"

Private Airstrip
Approx. 1,000 Miles South of Mexicali, Mexico

It was nearly dusk by the time they finished transferring their gear and all of their personnel onto the trucks, both of which were step vans, one belonging to a plumber whose logo was emblazoned across the side of the vehicle. The other was a seafood-delivery vehicle whose bay reeked of fish and crabs. Samad and his men could only grimace and climb aboard. These trucks were all they had, and he was, despite their confines, grateful to Allah for them.

Samad estimated it would take them about eighteen hours of drive time, averaging fifty-five miles per hour, and so he'd warned his men that the next two days on the road would be long and arduous. Talwar and Niazi, who were in the other van, said they would do their best to keep the men calm and remind them that refueling points were their only chance to use the bathroom facilities. With a group as large as theirs, that would become a serious consideration.

They were but twenty miles into their journey when the other truck pulled to the side of the road with a flat tire, and this made Samad throw his hands up in frustration. Yes, they had a spare; yes, they could fix it; but many, many others already in the United States were waiting for them, and the delay caused his stomach to knot and his hands to ball into fists. The drivers, both Mexicans, were yelling at each other in Spanish as they fixed the flat, and Samad was beginning to realize that the driver of his truck might be having second thoughts. He shifted up to the man, hunkered down, and said in Spanish, "We trust you to deliver us to our destination. That's all you need to do. To get paid. To stay alive. Do you understand me?"

The man swallowed and nodded.

A commercial airliner cut across the sky in the distance. Samad turned up toward the plane and watched it vanish into a raft of pink clouds.

27

AL RESCATE

San Juan Chamula
Chiapas, Mexico

DEEP SHADOWS HAD FALLEN across the graveyard, and the rows of crosses now stood in silhouette against the moldy walls of the abandoned church. Down below, past the church and the marketplace, Moore, who was lying on his belly, scanned the large crowds of locals and tourists gathering around and lining the streets of the main road, where the parade and fireworks show of Carnival would soon commence. Troupes of dancers were already shifting and whirling across beds of burning embers whose sparks rose around them.

Moore panned to the right with his night-vision scope and back to the house where the small blue car and van were still parked. Torres had fetched their rental car and had moved it up behind the pair of smaller houses at the bottom of the road. He'd left the car there with the keys under the mat.

After another long breath, Moore adjusted his grip on the weapon in his hands, one of the Mark 11 Model 0's, which had earned the nickname "Pirate Killer," based on their use by Navy SEALs to rescue captured sailors from Somali pirates. Fitzpatrick had feigned surprise over Moore toting them, and Torres had grilled Moore about how he'd acquired such powerful military-issue weapons. "Like I told you," Moore had said, "the people I work for are very well connected."

Indeed.

The Mark 11 was a twenty-round semiautomatic rifle equipped with a biped. The rifle's magazine held twenty 7.62x5-millimeter NATO rounds, and Moore liked to joke that if you needed twenty bullets to hit your target, then you'd best get into politics and out of soldiering. When Moore fired the Mark 11, the round would streak off faster than the speed of sound, creating a small sonic boom that would dissipate as the round slowed to subsonic speeds. At about six hundred meters out in places such as the mountains of Afghanistan, a sniper could shoot and remain silent to his target; however, in more urban environments such as San Juan Chamula, Moore and Fitzpatrick, who also lay on his belly on the other side of the hill, needed the KAC suppressors that would help conceal and confuse the source of their ordnance. If Moore were to take his shot beyond eight hundred meters, he could fire at will without the enemy ever detecting his location. Of course, as Murphy's Law would have it, the math was not in their favor.

Range to the house and the four guards positioned there was only 527 meters. Current wind was NNE at nine miles per hour. Elevation was 7,410 feet, and they were approximately 29 feet higher than their target with a grade of nine percent heading up into the hills. Between the wind, the calculations for bullet drop, and their current positions, the shots would be difficult but not impossible. They would certainly be heard, and the only thing to help mask them would be the fireworks echoing from town. As Moore had earlier remarked, that was their only stroke of luck, and they'd need a lot more than luck, because the real test would occur after they brought down the guards . . .

Moore called Towers, who was monitoring the Avenging Vultures' radio channel. "Anything?"

"Still running through the cell-phone calls. That'll take a while. Just the usual small talk on the radio. They're calling one guy Captain Salou, and I pulled up what we have on him: Guatemalan Special Forces, twenty-year veteran before he re-tired and turned mercenary. In technical terms, he's a mean-ass motherfucker."

"And handy with an ax," Moore added darkly.

"Something else is going on, though, down in Cristóbal. Local police are on high alert, and from what we can tell, they're searching for missing persons."

"No surprise. Maybe Daddy found out that his little boy's been kidnapped and put in some calls."

"Well, if he did, then you need to extract them and get the hell out of there before Rojas's team arrives."

"I hear that. I'm just waiting for the party to begin . . ."

Moore closed his eyes, trying to purge all the extraneous thoughts and simply focus on the shots, on the moment. But his conscience wasn't cooperating because of how similar this moment was to the past. He unwillingly took himself back to the beach at Coronado and stood there, watching the tide roll in, watching as out there in the dark sea, a hand rose above the waves . . . and a voice that was really his own came in a bellow, *"Don't leave me! Don't leave me!"*

"We have to go back!"

"He's taking off! We can't!"

"Don't do this, Max! Don't do it!"

"No choice! Shut the fuck up! We're leaving!"

Moore shuddered violently over those voices.

And then another one: *"You are class 198. You are the warriors who've survived because of your teamwork."*

Not anymore. He'd tricked the Navy into thinking he was worth it, but he should have never become a SEAL. He had broken the most basic rule, and should have been punished for his actions, and because he wasn't, he thought he should take on that job himself. He didn't deserve a real life after what he'd done. No, he didn't.

During a time when he was feeling most depressed, he'd tried to lift his spirits by literally launching himself into the air, but not parachuting, no. He'd talked to a few buddies and found something much more exotic in the Romsdal Valley of Norway. Within two days of his arrival, he was wearing a wingsuit and jetting through the air at 150 miles per hour. He dove down into the valley, taking advantage of the favorable winds during the summer solstice. The wingsuit allowed him to soar like a bird, with the fabric fanning out beneath his arms and legs like webbing. This was not free fall but a very fast, very dangerous form of gliding. All Moore had to do was lean to the left or to the right to steer himself within a meter of the cliff walls beside which he raced.

He came whipping around one corner, close enough to reach out and grab the rock face, then he rolled to the left and plummeted at a forty-five-degree angle, the wind now roaring across him. Death was very close, whispering in his ear, and he began to find peace with himself, with the wind, the valley, and for a few seconds, he just closed his eyes, knowing he should pull his rip cord but waiting to see how long he would wait, how long, just a few more seconds, the euphoria mounting as he imagined the mottled rock face below.

He pulled the cord. *Boom.* The chute blossomed; the cords tugged. It was over.

The group roared from somewhere behind him.

Of the fifteen people in his extreme-sports posse who'd come from all over the world to do this, Moore's flight had been the fastest, the longest, without question the most dangerous of all, like something out of an action film and not a tourist's joyride. He hadn't realized what he'd done until the others gazed on him in awe, as though his temples had gone gray and he'd seen the maker.

Afterward, their Norwegian guide, Bjoernolf, took them all out for lunch, and over *smørrebrød* topped with smoked salmon and cups of dark-roast coffee, he pulled Moore aside and, in his heavily accented English, simply asked, "Why do you want to die?"

"Excuse me?" Moore replied, lowering his mug.

"I've done this thousands of times with many, many clients. No one has ever flown like that. Not even *me*. And you flew only three practice runs and then did that?"

"I told you I was in the Navy."

He shook his head. "Doesn't matter. You came much too close to the mountain. You waited much too long to pull your cord. I'm sorry, but I won't take you up there again."

"Are you kidding me? I've already paid for two more days."

"I'm sorry, Mr. Moore. I can only work with people who want to come back. I don't know what your problem is, but I won't let you become mine. I'll return your money."

"I don't believe this."

"Look, you are not the first one who's come here looking for more than I can give. Get some help. Whatever is bothering you, I think you can get through it. This is not the way. I'm sorry."

Moore thought of bolting to his feet and letting the cocky long-haired asshole have it, but there was nothing but concern in the man's eyes—and the guy wasn't a kid, either, probably Moore's age, and he probably had seen his share of emotionally damaged thrill-seekers also attempting to punish themselves.

"How do you learn to forgive yourself?" Moore asked, realizing that he was speaking to a hillside in San Juan Chamula and not to a Norwegian daredevil.

"When you're ready to talk, come back to me. I want to hear your story. I'm an old man. I'm a good listener."

Maybe the old man Wazir, tucked tightly away in his compound in the tribal lands, did have an answer . . .

The first booms from the fireworks were met by a roaring crowd, the crackling and popping like corn, as even then, at that precise moment, Moore's cell phone rang.

"Ready when you are, boss," said Fitzpatrick.

"Whoa, whoa, whoa, hold on," Moore said, shifting his rifle slightly to the right and watching as the front door opened and the older guy Moore assumed was Salou ventured out.

"Maybe he wants to see the show," said Fitzpatrick.

"He needs to close that door; otherwise, we're screwed."

Salou stood there, reached into his pocket, and pulled out a pack of cigarettes. He lit one, took a long drag, then stood there, staring off at the lights of the parade beyond.

"Come on, come on," Moore said, as another salvo of firecrackers exploded and echoed off the hillside. A few suppressed cracks from sniper rifles would easily be lost in the racket, but this fool was wasting the moment.

"Oh, shit. You see him? You see Torres? What the fuck is he doing?" asked Fitzpatrick.

Torres had rigged the two cars to explode and was supposed to detonate the explosives just after Moore and Fitzpatrick took out the guards with their sniper rifles. But now the fool was marching toward the front door of the house. A curious Salou took one last pull on his cigarette, then stepped down from the porch.

"What the hell is he thinking?" asked Moore.

"Wait a minute," said Fitzpatrick, as Torres actually shook hands with Salou. "Son of a bitch. I think Torres knows this guy! Holy fucking shit. I think this might be a setup!"

"Fuck this, then, fire, fire!" cried Moore, as Salou threw his arm over Torres's shoulders and wheeled him around toward the house. That fat bastard had played them all, all right, and now he was going to tip off the Guatemalans. Maybe he, Zúñiga, and Salou had all struck a deal, cutting Moore's group out of the negotiations.

But then again, would Torres be stupid enough to act friendly when he knew Moore and Fitzpatrick were watching? Maybe he didn't care anymore.

Well, Moore would never find out—

Because the fat man was the first guy he targeted, and the round took off the back of Torres's head and sent him twisting around like an oil drum toppling off a cargo ship. He crashed to the ground and was lost in the darkness.

Moore switched aim to his first guard, who was already on the move, rushing forward from a tree on the north side and scanning the hills. Moore had to track down, readjust his aim yet again, and finally fire, hoping the guy would literally run into his shot. *Bingo.* The round punched him squarely in the chest, the blood spraying as he was knocked onto his back—all within the span of a heartbeat.

Meanwhile, Fitzpatrick's rifle cracked despite the suppressor, and then it sounded once more. The DEA agent's aim had better prove true, because they were not going to lose Sonia.

They would *not*.

Moore would die first. The decision had been made.

True, he didn't know the woman, but he could not bear what losing her represented. He reasoned, perhaps illogically, that, if he saved her, he saved part of himself. If he failed, he wasn't sure what could be salvaged.

Still holding his breath, he found his second guard and shot him twice as he was running alongside the house, back toward the front door.

Just then, and without any explanation, since Torres had been the one carrying the remote detonators for the two cars, they exploded in succession, their front ends rising a meter off the ground, the fireballs mushrooming up into the night and casting the house in a flickering otherworldly glow.

Whether Torres had remained alive long enough to blow the cars or had set them for remote timer, Moore wasn't sure. He didn't think the fat man was smart enough to deal with the timers and had shown him only the most rudimentary of setups, C-4 here, wire, remote here. *Take your fat-ass thumb and push this button. Got it, knucklehead?*

Whatever the case, they needed those cars taken out, and the job was complete.

"Let's go!" Moore shouted across the hillside, drawing his pair of Glocks and breaking into a full-on sprint down the hill, with Fitzpatrick falling in beside him.

They had changed into black utilities—pants and long-sleeved shirts—and now wore balaclavas and Kevlar vests, the latter of which Torres had balked at because he'd been unable to pull his protection over his massive man-boobs.

As Moore hit the bottom of the hill, he saw Salou rushing back outside with a rifle in his grip. Behind him were Sonia and Miguel, whose legs had been freed but whose arms were still bound behind their backs. They were each being dragged by a pair of men, all armed with pistols. Without transportation and with the car fires raging and drawing attention away from the parade down below, Moore figured, the Guatemalan had only one avenue of escape: up the narrow road running directly east and away from the marketplace.

Indeed, the group turned in that direction as Salou glanced back over his shoulder, spotted Moore, and shouted to his men.

But Moore was already in the air, leaping toward a dirt mound ahead and firing with both pistols, the stench of gunpowder both familiar and welcome and making him grimace tightly. Salou had detached himself from the group, which was his final mistake. Even as the old Special Forces veteran leveled his AK-47 on Moore, he took two rounds in the chest, one in the neck, and a final one in the thigh that brought him to his knees, his rifle twisting to one side, his rounds stitching into the ground ten meters ahead of Moore.

Whether there were any more men inside the house, Moore wasn't sure, but they needed to know. "Take the house!" he told Fitzpatrick, as the two men holding Miguel shoved him toward

Sonia, broke away, and dropped to the deck so they could return fire.

The incoming drove Moore deeper into the mound before he could roll to his right and answer their shots. His first three rounds all missed. *Shit*. That's what he got for firing with one hand, even though his first attack on Salou had been deadly accurate. He sat up a bit more, took aim, and hit the guy on the right, whose muzzle flash easily betrayed him—but he, too, got off a shot, which thumped barely six inches below Moore.

Music from the parade wafted up from the valley, heavy drums and guitars and trumpets amid more pops and booms of fireworks, and for a few seconds, Moore wasn't sure if the guys ahead were still firing at him.

Either way, he launched himself up from the ground and began running toward the house, dropping in behind Fitzpatrick, his boots heavy on the earth, his breath uneven and raging in his ears.

Miguel, Sonia, and the three guys left were hustling up the back road, as Moore had anticipated. He bolted around the house while Fitzpatrick rushed inside.

Gunfire rattled and glass shattered. *Damn it*, Salou had left some men in the house. Fitzpatrick was on his own now. Moore came charging up the road, where the group was now darting toward another house near the top of the hill. Two old cars were parked along the street, and as Moore came rushing up along a rotting old fence, he heard Sonia begin to scream and curse at the men. The cars blocked Moore's view.

That was it. All he needed to hear. He couldn't change what had happened that night on the oil platform, but maybe he could prevent the same thing from happening again. Sonia would not be left to die.

Tensing with an anger that had been simmering since that fateful night, and with a heart swelling with rage over his inability to forgive himself, Moore charged at full tilt up the hill, toward the sound of the screaming, with the breath of a ghost on his back.

As he rounded the cars, he saw that Sonia had broken away from one man and was being held only by a single guy, who now spotted Moore and put his pistol directly to Sonia's head.

The other two guys had their guns pointed at Miguel's chest, and the young man was now crying and begging for his life.

This wouldn't be a standoff, a negotiation, a moment where he talked the men into surrendering because their boss was already dead and they had nothing left to gain, no. The deal-making was over, the bets off.

With the adrenaline pumping through his veins like molten lava, and with the years of training and experience he'd earned as both a Navy SEAL and a CIA operative—the hundreds of hours spent listening to instructors shout at him and direct him and reward him—Moore took in the entire situation in the better part of one second and reacted like the man he was: a combatant with the muscle memory for killing.

Gritting his teeth, striking out at the guilt now personified as three members of a Guatemalan death squad, he looked at the guy holding Sonia and cried, "Hey!"

The guy widened his eyes.

Bang! Moore shot him in the head.

That the other two guys would probably kill Miguel was of no concern. It was all about Sonia.

That the Guatemalans decided to engage Moore instead of killing the kid was the kid's good fortune.

Moore fired his pistols, hitting each man in the chest. They staggered away from the kid, even as Moore nearly tripped back. He recovered his balance enough to lean forward, step toward the two thugs, and finish them with another round each. As his Glock went silent, police sirens clashed with the trumpeters of Carnival, and for just a few seconds, Moore paused, his head spinning, the adrenaline now making him feel as though his chest would explode.

"Who are you?" cried Miguel.

Moore answered him in Spanish: "I work for your father." He reached into his hip pocket for a karambit, a hawk-billed blade whose edge curved like a slice of melon. He hurriedly cut Sonia's bonds, then Miguel's, then waved them over. "I have a car down below. Keys under the mat. It's right down there. You get it. You take it. You get out of here and don't look back. Go to the airport. Fly out. Now!"

"Let's go!" Sonia shouted to Miguel, then led him away.

Moore stood there for a few seconds to regain his breath, then he holstered his pistols and raced back toward the house, leaping over Torres's body to enter the living room, where he found Fitzpatrick lying on the floor with two gunshot wounds to his head.

"Aw, fuck . . . Buddy, no way . . ."

He dropped to his knees, but it was damned clear that the DEA agent was dead. He ripped off his balaclava and just remained there.

A phone was ringing somewhere outside. Moore rose, shifted over to Torres's body, and withdrew his cell from the fat man's hip pocket. It was Zúñiga calling.

"Hello?"

"Luis, is that you?"

"No, Señor Zúñiga, this is Señor Howard. I have very bad news. Luis and Flexxx are dead. Rojas's son and his girl got away . . ."

"What is this?" Zúñiga shouted. "You told me your group was very powerful!"

"I'm coming back to Juárez. I need to meet with you."

"If you're smart, you will not do that, Mr. Howard. You would not survive that meeting."

"Listen to me. We're not done yet. I'll call you when I get back up there." Moore hung up, pocketed Torres's phone, then jogged over to Salou's body and fetched his phone as well. As he headed back into the house, he dialed Towers, told his boss what had happened.

"I need to get the fuck out of here with Fitzpatrick's body."

"Get up into the hills, due north. I've got an extraction team on the way."

He sighed. "Thank you."

Moore reached down and picked up Fitzpatrick's body in

a fireman's carry. His eyes began to burn. "Hang on," he whispered. "I'll get you out of here."

He shifted outside and around the house as the damned sirens quickened his step. A car came roaring up, and two teenagers jumped out, gaping at the bodies.

"I need help!" Moore cried, then reached into one holster and drew his Glock. "Which means I'm taking your car."

They lifted their palms and backed away. Moore opened the sedan's rear door and lowered Fitzpatrick onto the seat. The boys could have jumped him then, but they were wise enough to read their futures in his expression. "Don't worry," he assured them. "You'll get your car back." He hopped in and floored it, the little engine whining and struggling to get them up the hillside road.

28

INSOMNIO

Villas Casa Morada
San Cristóbal de las Casas
Chiapas, Mexico

THE LOCAL POLICE had thoroughly searched the hotel for Miguel and Sonia. They'd received digital pictures of the two, had printed them out, and had been questioning the hotel staff and guests. Dante Corrales had watched them from the car across the street, and he'd sent one of the four men who'd come with María into the hotel to learn more.

"Have you seen these missing tourists?" they'd demanded.

"No," Corrales's man had lied.

Pablo was now seated to his right, María to his left, and his arm and shoulder were still throbbing as he ordered the driver to pull away.

"Dante, if you won't talk to Fernando, then I'm not sure

what to do. They'll hunt me down and kill me, too, along with those men."

"I'll talk to him," Corrales lied. "Don't worry. Fernando has never had contact with them, so I'll take care of everything."

"What are you going to do?" asked María.

"Just like I said. We'll get the money from La Familia, and then we'll call Salou. He has them. We'll get them back, and all will be well."

"How will you explain it to Castillo?"

"I'm thinking about that, but I'm sure he's busy trying to figure out how he screwed up and let a shooter get so close to the boss."

Abruptly, the driver, who'd been listening to an AM news station, turned back and said, "Big shooting up in San Juan Chamula. Whole bunch of bodies up there."

"Do you think it's them?" asked Pablo.

Corrales's heart sank. He checked his watch. "We have time to find out." He called out to the driver, "Take us up there. Now!"

The situation could not have become more confusing. When Corrales and his party arrived in the small town, they sent out another of the men, who returned with his report: It appeared military rebels had been killed. The police had cordoned off the area.

"I looked for Raúl, like you said," his man reported. "They pulled out a decapitated body, and the pants were khaki-colored, like you said. I think it was Raúl."

Corrales gritted his teeth and thumbed off his phone. Salou was not answering and might very well be among the dead. Had Castillo's men arrived and attacked Salou? If so, then why hadn't he called Corrales?

Now Corrales might need to call back La Familia, tell them he didn't need the loan—which would piss them off even more than his original call had. He really did need to call Castillo, to at least get some closure on the situation.

But not now. Not yet. He still hadn't thought of what he'd say . . .

"They'll expect us to go to the airport," he finally told the group. "Let's get out of here. I don't care if we drive all night. Head up north, up to Villahermosa. There's another airport we've used in the past."

"I'm scared, Dante," said María. "I'm very scared. I just want to go back home."

He wrapped his good arm around her and whispered, "I know, but I told you, this will all pass."

Corrales's phone rang. Incoming call from Castillo. He should take it, find out the truth, and answer Castillo's questions with lies: They attacked, and I don't know why. Instead, he hid the screen from María and ignored the call.

He closed his eyes and threw his head back on the seat. Those car fires outside the house up in Chamula had struck a chord, but now all Corrales wanted to do was sleep, sleep away all of his problems.

The phone rang again. Castillo. He turned it off.

So here they were, all because of a grave error: Corrales had assumed that Salou would be too intimidated to stand up to the all-powerful Juárez Cartel. Salou would allow himself to be ripped off and not retaliate for fear of a response. But Corrales was no veteran and had not accounted for the resolve of military men, a resolve he'd become excruciatingly familiar with now.

During the drive back down from Chamula, Miguel had argued with Sonia that they should go directly to the police, but she worried about those officers being in bed with the men who'd captured them. She said they should do what his father's soldier had told them and head to the airport. Their cell phones had been confiscated by their kidnappers, and Miguel thought the least they should do was stop so that he could call his father.

But Sonia would have none of that. She was behind the wheel, racing down the narrow street, the headlights barely picking out their path until the small yellow sign on the side of the road finally indicated a left toward the San Cristóbal de las Casas Airport.

Once they reached the modest main terminal, only then did Sonia park and say, "Okay, we'll call your father. I think we are okay now . . ."

Miguel raked his fingers through his hair and rubbed his tired eyes as they strode into the terminal and found a pay phone that accepted only phone cards. They swore and ran over to a small shop, where they were able to purchase a card for thirty pesos.

With an unsteady hand he reached his father's personal voice mail. Of course the man wouldn't pick up; he wouldn't have recognized the number.

The message was frantic, fragmented, enough to allow his father to know he was still alive and that he and Sonia were unharmed. He had no idea what had happened to Corrales and the other two but was thankful his father's men had arrived, although he wasn't sure why they'd been left to escape on their own and had not been escorted.

When he hung up, he looked into Sonia's eyes and shook his head in disbelief. "You are the strongest woman I know. Stronger than my mother was—and that's saying a lot."

"Do you mean to say you can't believe how strong I am—even though I'm a woman?" She raised one brow.

He grinned. "No, what I mean to say is . . . *thank you*." He leaned over and kissed her.

"You're welcome," she said.

"How could you stay so calm? I thought I was going to pass out."

"I didn't think they'd kill us. We were worth too much to them, so I decided to be strong . . . for you."

"But still . . ."

"Well, sometimes I just get more mad than scared."

"I hope that someday you can teach me how to do that. I want to learn from you."

She breathed deeply and glanced away, her lip trembling as though she was about to cry.

"What's wrong?"

"Nothing."

Miguel glanced up at a flat-screen TV, where news footage showed a crowd scattering and the caption read: ASSASSINA-TION ATTEMPT ON JORGE ROJAS.

He gasped.

Rojas Mansion
Cuernavaca, Mexico
56 Miles South of Mexico City

Jorge Rojas had built his main home in a world-renowned center for the study of Spanish. Cuernavaca was equally famous for its lush parks and gardens, its charming zocalo, or town center, with historic colonial architecture and numerous restaurants and street cafés, and its university, which attracted artists and intellectuals from all over the world. The Rojas mansion—all 7,800 square feet of it, based on sixteenth-century architectural designs—overlooked the town and was even more well decorated and audacious than his vacation residence in Acapulco, with library, home theater, game room, gym, and all the other amenities one would expect in a residence owned by a man of his stature. His wife had dubbed it La Casa de la Eterna Primavera and had decorated it, along with a team of designers. After she'd passed away, he had not changed a single thing. This place was his safe haven, his Shangri-la that he longed for every time he traveled. In Cuernavaca he was surrounded by his family and the memories of his dear wife, and there'd been months in the past when he'd worked from home and had rarely left its confines. The vacation home in Punta de Mita was a great place for parties and fund-raisers, but it never made him feel quite as warm.

Presently, he stood in the library, near one of the sliding ladders before a wall of more than two thousand books. He was in his silk robe and on his cell phone, listening to the message from his son. He'd been pacing the room for the past hour, beating a deep path in the burgundy carpet, and he'd been on and off the phone for nearly twice as long. He turned to Castillo and nearly fainted as he listened to his voice mail. A call had come in, a number he hadn't recognized, while he'd been talking to one of his pilots who'd called regarding a maintenance issue with one of his aircraft. "They're okay, thank God. They were rescued by our men."

"That's not possible," said the one-eyed man. "Our team just got there."

Rojas drew back his head and frowned. "Maybe my son is confused, but it doesn't matter. Thank God he's safe. Send the team to the airport right away. I'm calling him back now."

"Yes, señor."

But Castillo did not move. He just frowned deeply, trying to work something out.

"What's wrong, Fernando?"

"I've lost contact with Dante and his team. I wonder if maybe they were able to help?"

"No, I think my son would've mentioned that. He said they

hadn't seen Dante and the team since they were in the town, when it all started."

"Then something is not right here, señor. Miguel is a smart man. I don't think he was confused."

"Well, I'll leave you to figure out what happened. Just get my boy and his girlfriend."

Rojas turned his head as Alexsi appeared in the doorway, out of breath. "They found them?"

He nodded.

She ran to him, fell into his arms. "Thank God . . ."

DEA Office of Diversion Control
San Diego, California
Two Days Later

Moore, Towers, and FBI agent Michael Ansara were seated at the conference table. Vega was still on the job and remaining close to Inspector Gómez, and they didn't want to risk blowing her cover. Fitzpatrick's death was carefully concealed from the media, and he was already being flown home to Chicago for burial. ATF Agent Whittaker was still in Minnesota but following up on a very disturbing piece of news: A U.S. military weapons cache had been purportedly smuggled out of Afghanistan and sold to cartel buyers outside of Minneapolis. Some of the initial evidence indicated that the cache had been moved and sold by—Moore had gasped—a U.S. Navy SEAL. He didn't want to believe that, refused to acknowledge that one of his own brothers could be corrupted in that way. Ansara had just shrugged and said, "If they paid those guys what they're really worth, they wouldn't be tempted to do something like that."

"It's not about the pay," said Moore.

Ansara nodded. "Just saying."

"Don't say. I just can't believe it."

Towers shrugged.

"So where are we at, boss?" Moore said, hoping to change the subject.

Towers glanced up from his notebook computer. "Our boy Corrales still hasn't turned up. And after almost getting whacked, Rojas went back to his mansion in Cuernavaca. We've got boots on the ground and eyes in the sky watching the place."

"Anything on the shooter?" Moore asked.

"Nothing yet, but the way it was carried out . . . . I doubt it was a rival cartel hit. Just some random asshole wanting to kill a rich guy."

"What about the son and our girl?"

"Sonia and Miguel were flown there by some of Rojas's security guys, and they're all still there, no change."

"Any word from her?"

"Not yet. The Guatemalans took her surveillance watch and her phone, but she knows where the dead drops are and how to get word out to cover her tracks. She will."

"So do we wait on her?" asked Moore. "Or what?"

Towers shook his head. "We've got some spotters up in Sequoia. The cartel's getting ready to move one of their biggest harvests ever. You guys are going up there and following the distribution and money trails, which should take you right back into Mexico. I want to follow that trail all the way down to their *sicarios* making the deposits into the banks and/or laundering the money through Rojas's businesses. This is a perfect opportunity for us to do that."

"I'd love to pick up some credible witnesses along the way who can definitively, without question, pin this whole thing on Rojas."

Towers grinned. "Dream on, buddy. Meanwhile, we need to attack this bastard from every angle—with Sonia, with the Sinaloas, with his ties to the Federal Police, and with following the money. And speaking of the Sinaloas—"

Moore snorted and cut him off. "I promised Zúñiga we would do something, but he just screamed at the top of his lungs, told me I'd pay for the deaths of his men, and that he was going to hunt me down till the day he dies."

"That sounds about right," said Towers, with a grin. "But we need to stay in touch with him."

"I think he'll keep taking my calls, probably more out of curiosity." Moore's voice began to crack. He'd been unable to sleep for the past two nights as a familiar face once more appeared in his mind's eye. "I want you guys to know that Fitzpatrick was an ace out there. A fucking ace. I wouldn't be sitting here if it weren't for him."

The air in the room seemed to escape. And both Towers and Ansara took a second or two to reflect on that.

They always die. They always would. There wasn't any

easy way to get over it or past it. Moore was supposed to simply acknowledge that and move on. For the mission. For his country. He'd made the pledge, taken the oath.

"His family knew how dangerous his job was," said Towers. "They didn't take it well, but they weren't surprised, either." He slapped shut his laptop and rose. "All right, then, gentlemen. You guys need to get up north, ASAP."

"You're going to love this, Moore," said Ansara. "They got the whole place rigged with booby traps and electronic surveillance. Should be a nice party." He winked.

Moore sighed. "Couldn't we just do a little wine tasting and call it a day?"

"Detour to Napa, huh?" asked Ansara. "I don't think so."

Taliban Safe House
Casa de la Fortuna
Mexicali, Mexico

"Everything we've gathered so far is on this flash drive," the man said to Samad, handing over the USB key with attached lanyard.

His name was Felipe. He was fifty years old and had been hired, according to him, two years ago to become a spotter for Mullah Omar Rahmani. Felipe was extremely well paid, had established a safe house in Mexicali, and had been informed that Samad and his group were coming. He worked with a crew of five other men, all loyal and sworn to secrecy, and he said that the intelligence they had gathered would be very useful.

Because they were so well paid, they had been able to avoid the temptation of joining one of the cartels. In fact, when they encountered *sicarios*, many assumed they were part of some other group, and not, as Felipe referred to his men, "independent contractors."

"Thank you for this, and for all of your other help," said Samad, accepting the key and plugging it into the notebook computer sitting on the kitchen's small bar. He climbed onto the stool and sat there, clicking open the files, which contained hundreds of photographs.

Felipe nodded and said, "Señor, we know what it is you plan to do."

"Really?"

"I've been to the United States three times in my life. I've been banned for five years for trying to smuggle money out of the country. I haven't seen my wife and daughters in all that time. I know you are going to cross. I will pay you anything if you will take me."

Samad thought about that. It'd be very useful to have a local guide, someone expendable as well. "You've done enough already. I will take you. But only you."

"Will you talk to Mullah Rahmani for me as well?"

"Of course."

He gasped and cried, "Thank you, señor! Thank you!"

Samad nodded and refocused his attention on the computer screen.

They'd finally made it to Mexicali, despite the flat tire and their less-than-agreeable drivers. His men had marveled over how densely populated the city was and had found it ironic that there was, in fact, a small but bustling Chinatown district. In fact, one of Felipe's men, Zhen, had been born and raised in Mexicali and was the descendant of Chinese immigrants who'd gone to work for the Colorado River Land Company, which had come to the area in the early twentieth century to build an extensive irrigation system in the valley. Samad knew this because Felipe was a man who loved to talk, to the point of utter annoyance.

Samad continued reviewing the photographs and reports while the rest of his men were eating, changing, and chatting within the small three-bedroom home. Yes, they were jammed into the house like canned fish, and Samad was determined that they wouldn't spend more than a few days here. Felipe had already briefed him regarding his group's findings: They were certain that the Juárez Cartel was involved in a major tunneling operation at a construction site for a new Z-Cells production plant. The photographs depicted five buildings in various stages of construction and a small warehouse within the facility that had already been finished. Interestingly enough, large quantities of soil had been moved out of the warehouse and loaded onto dump trucks. Moreover, Samad noted the presence of work crews coming and going at regular intervals and in shifts that kept teams working twenty-four hours a day, seven days a week. And Samad knew that where there was a major tunneling operation, there was always a foreman and/or engineer who controlled the operation. Of all of the men who'd been photographed, one in particular stood out because he was older and better dressed than most of the crews and because, according to Felipe, he arrived in the morning and left in the evening, although his schedule had more recently changed, moving up his arrival time to the wee hours of the morning. He had never been followed home, though, and so Samad made that a priority.

Within an hour, Samad, Talwar, and Felipe were sitting in a beat-up Honda Civic driven by Felipe. They waited until the first crew left the warehouse. Their man did not yet leave. They waited until sunset, and then, finally, Samad spotted him, climbing into a black Kia as old and battered as their car. They followed him away from the site and south, past the city and toward the suburbs along the southeast corridor.

Within twenty minutes they'd located the man's house and watched him park, and then, with a call made by Felipe, they had a man placed outside the residence to alert them when he thought that everyone had left in the morning.

"He will help us cross the border. He doesn't know it yet, but he is a servant of Allah," Samad said.

Talwar, who'd been working on his smartphone, looked up and said, "If the information is still good, this house belongs to Pedro Romero. I Googled him, and he was an engineer, but the company he worked for went out of business."

"Construction has been very tough here," said Felipe. "I know many good men who are out of work."

"Well, he found a good job, didn't he?" Samad said. "He's

our man. But we need to move very carefully. We need to make sure he is very cooperative, so we need to know everything about Señor Pedro Romero."

Rojas Mansion
Cuernavaca, Mexico
56 Miles South of Mexico City

Rojas lay in his bed, staring up at the crown molding that spanned the far wall, long lines of expensive hardwood extending off into the shadows. The ceiling fan whirred, the blades turning slowly, the moonlight coming in from the window cutting through those blades and casting a flickering shadow across his bedspread and across Alexsi's cheek. She slept soundly beside him, and Rojas closed his eyes once more, then snapped them open and looked at the clock: 2:07 a.m.

His emotions had wreaked havoc with him during the past twenty-four hours. An assassination attempt, a kidnapping attempt of Miguel and his girlfriend . . . he decided he needed an immediate vacation from his real life.

With a shudder he rose, donned his robe, and, using his cell phone as a flashlight, ventured down the stairs in the cool darkness. He entered the kitchen, switched on a light, and crossed to one of three stainless-steel refrigerators to fetch some milk, which he planned to heat up and sip slowly, a regimen that often helped him sleep.

By the time he had the pot on the gas stove and had poured the milk, a tiny voice came from behind him. "Señor Rojas?"

He turned to find Sonia standing there, her black negligee covered mostly by her own silk robe. He had to blink because he thought he had imagined her.

"Señor Rojas, are you okay?"

"Oh, I'm sorry, Sonia, I'm still half asleep, I guess. What are you doing up now?"

"I heard someone down here. Miguel took the pills like you said, and he is sleeping very well. I don't like to take any medication, and now I can't sleep. I keep seeing what they did to that man over and over."

"I'm so sorry. Tomorrow I will make some calls and we can help you with some therapy."

"Thank you, señor. I don't know if there's a way to forget that. They wiped his blood on my face."

He nodded, pursed his lips, then blurted out, "Do you want some milk? I'm just heating it up."

"That would be nice. Thank you." She moved into the kitchen and slid effortlessly onto one of the stools. "I guess you couldn't sleep, either, after what happened to you."

"I've been expecting something like that for many years. That's why I've taken so many precautions, but you never know how you'll react when the day comes. You can never plan everything."

"That's very true."

"Sonia, I love my boy very much. He's all I have left in this world, and I can't thank you enough. He's told me how strong you were. He couldn't believe it. But you know something? I could. When I first met you, I could see something powerful in your eyes, that same light I saw in my wife. You were very brave."

She lowered her head and blushed.

He'd gone too far, he knew, and his tone was a little too alluring.

"I just wanted to thank you," he suddenly added.

"I think the milk is boiling," she said, lifting her chin at the stove.

He whirled and lowered the heat, but the milk foamed over the pot, and he cursed and brought it off the flame, the milk hissing and spitting.

"Señor Rojas, may I ask a very personal question?" she said, after he'd gotten the milk under control and had fetched two mugs from a cabinet.

"Sure, why not?"

"Are you entirely honest with your son?"

"What do you mean?"

"Does he know everything about you and your companies? I mean, would he be able to step into your shoes if something were to happen?"

"That's a rather morbid question."

"If we stay together, and we decide to get married, he would need to know everything."

"Of course."

She had trouble now meeting his gaze. "He just seems rather naive about some aspects right now."

"And with good reason," said Rojas, growing a little suspicious of her prying. "Some of my businesses are too petty for his concern. I have people running them and reporting weekly or monthly to me. When he's ready, I will teach him everything."

"Would you teach me everything, too?"

He hesitated. Indeed, she was a powerful woman, perhaps too powerful, and he had never allowed his dear wife to know even five percent of exactly what he did. "Of course I would," he lied, handing her a mug of steaming milk. "I would expect you and Miguel to be the heirs—if you are one day married."

"I don't mean to sound like a gold digger, señor. I am just worried about Miguel. I know you want him to work at the bank this summer, but I am worried that he'll hate it. And if he is miserable, we both will be miserable."

"What do you suggest?"

"Teach him about how you operate your businesses. Let him be your right-hand man. He is your son, after all."

Rojas thought about that. She was right. Miguel was the heir to his empire, and the boy knew so very little. Rojas could have been killed, and Miguel would hardly understand the enormity of his father's world. But Rojas would never reveal the ugly truth of the cartel—not to Miguel, not to anyone, ever . . .

Suddenly, Alexsi appeared in the doorway. "What's going on here?" she asked, staring accusingly at Sonia.

"Do you want some warm milk?" asked Rojas, ignoring her question. "I have some more."

"All right."

"I couldn't sleep. Not after what's happened," said Sonia. "I heard Señor Rojas come down, and so I thought I'd join him."

Alexsi's expression softened. "I understand."

Rojas stared at Alexsi. If she could read his mind, her bags would be packed within the hour.

And if Sonia could read his mind, she would be joining Alexsi in a taxicab that would take them very far away from his world.

29

THE ONLY
EASY DAY

Al Basrah Oil Terminal
Persian Gulf, Iraq
March 19, 2003

MOORE HEAVED HIMSELF UP and into the black Zodiac to join the other two SEALs who'd jumped from the platform. They were still waiting on Carmichael and one of his guys, Mako Six, who'd been hit. Moore tugged off his mask and took in a long breath of the salty air. Out to the west, across the charcoal-colored waves and beneath a mantle of clouds, hovered the CH-47 Chinook helicopter, it's rear ramp lowered, its pilot perched precariously over the water. The tandem rotors created a wash that lifted high into the night and drew a pale white vortex over the gulf, while the chopper's turboshaft engines roared. That pilot, Moore knew, was battling fiercely against the wind.

An onslaught of small-arms fire erupted from the platform, most of it directed at the chopper itself, while Moore was on the radio, trying to call in fire support from the patrol ship; however, the request was denied and he was ordered to extract immediately.

The chopper pilot echoed those orders: "Mako One, this is Seabird, taking fire, taking fire! Need you out of there NOW, over!"

"Roger that, Seabird. Roger that!"

The Chinook's fuselage came alive with the flashes of ricocheting rounds that were quickly lost in the mist. Moore turned back toward the platform and saw Carmichael at the railing with Electronics Technician First Class Billy Hartogg, Mako Six.

"Frank, we're running out of time here, buddy!" Moore reminded his friend.

But Frank Carmichael understood that in life or in death no man should be left behind. He and Moore had learned first-hand that that wasn't some jingoistic cliché uttered in war movies. It was truth, and Carmichael's actions reflected the kind of steel he had in his back and the quality of his character. He picked up the lifeless form of Electronics Technician First Class Hartogg and was determined to bring the SEAL home.

SEALs like Carmichael did not take the easy way out, not during INDOC, not during BUD/S, not anytime. The only easy day was yesterday. However, before Carmichael could make it over the edge, gunfire ripped across the railing, pinging and sparking, driving him back and away.

And then more salvos punched into the water between the Zodiac and the platform, and Moore found himself looking up into the eyes of two guardsmen, now leveling their rifles on him.

Gunfire boomed from behind him as his men lifted their own rifles and took out the two Iraqis, who fell back and out of sight onto the platform.

A loud splash stole Moore's attention. Carmichael and their fallen colleague had dropped ten meters off the platform and had hit the waves—

But they were on the other side, near one of the largest pilings, some twenty meters away.

A hand rose above the waves . . . and a voice that was only in Moore's mind echoed: *"Don't leave me! Don't leave me!"*

"We have to go back!" shouted Gary Brand, the platoon's leading petty officer, seated in the Zodiac beside Moore.

Moore looked at Carmichael, then back at the helicopter.

"Mako One, this is Seabird! I cannot wait for you any longer!"

Moore cursed and shook his head. "You wait for me! You will wait!"

"Damn you, Mako One!" cried the pilot. "Thirty seconds!"

The gurgling outboard that had been resting in idle wailed as Moore speeded off after Carmichael, telling his men to get ready on the rope.

Moore then took a deep breath and held it.

All Carmichael had to do was catch the line and slide the loop up his arm. They'd drag his ass onto the Zodiac if it was the last thing Moore did.

He steered them closer to Carmichael, who was trying to hang on to Hartogg's body. They motored up beside him—

The rope went out.

Carmichael had only one good arm to make the catch.

He missed. *Shit!*

Moore turned the boat so tightly that it felt as though the craft were on rails. He believed he had time for another pass. Then he looked back at the Chinook.

Seabird was beginning to pull away.

And suddenly seconds were years. There was no noise save for Moore's heartbeat, no sensation save for salt water in his mouth.

Carmichael bobbed up and down near the piling.

The chopper's ramp sent a waterfall back into the gulf as the pilot throttled up.

"Don't you remember the quote they told us?" Carmichael had asked. *"We can only be beaten in two ways: We either die or we give up. And we're not giving up."*

A fresh volley of fire wrenched Moore out of his daze and sent his gaze back to the chopper. "He's taking off! We have to go!"

He wasn't sure who replied, the voice distorted by the wind, the gunfire, the rotor wash, but he heard enough: "Don't do this, Max! Don't do it!"

But he realized in that moment that he couldn't save them all. Not all of them. Not Carmichael. "No choice. We're leaving!"

When he looked back at the platform, Carmichael was still there, waving not for help but signaling for them to go.

Save yourselves.

Gunfire ripped across the side of the Zodiac, and that was it. Moore wheeled the boat around once more and throttled up the outboard, sending them skipping across the wave tops and toward the chopper.

"Seabird, this is Mako One. We're on our way!"

"Roger that, Mako One. Move it!"

The Chinook descended, its ramp once more awash.

"Don't leave me!"

But Carmichael had never shouted that. He'd urged them to leave. He knew he must remain behind.

Moore took the boat at full throttle toward the Chinook, whose pilot now descended a few more feet, the ramp perfectly aligned, the incoming fire still pinging all around them, until—

The Zodiac, under Moore's determined guidance, streaked right up the ramp and came to a skidding, colliding halt inside the chopper.

Before Moore could even throttle down, the Chinook's pilot pitched the bird up, and they thundered away from the platform, leaving the waves and incoming gunfire behind.

After switching off the engine, Moore sat there. When he looked up, it was into the eyes of his fellow SEALs, all staring at him, as though waiting for an excuse, something they could cling to that would justify what had just happened. We left a man in the water to die.

But all Moore could do was close his eyes, look away, and stiffen against a breakdown.

And then his men went back to work, tugging off their

gear, now back in the groove, as though nothing had ever happened. The training had kicked in, the countless hours of training, of routine, of not even remembering they'd finished the mission and had packed up the gear and somehow had made it to the bar and were already on their third round. The blur. The fog. The blinding intensity of combat sapping away senses that would return in time.

Within two hours the single largest operation in the history of the U.S. Navy SEALs was launched. Much to Moore's frustration, his team had been held back in reserve.

SEALs, along with Royal Marines, had attacked the pumping locks for each terminal and platform; however, intel had failed to note the concertina wire surrounding those locks, so SEALs got caught up in that obstacle and took fire from the platform's garrison until they were able to secure the area. Not soon after, they took fire from an Iraqi armored vehicle, but their embedded Air Force Combat Controller had been able to call up an Air Force A-10 Warthog whose Weapons System Officer summarily identified and destroyed the vehicle with a 670-pound AGM-65 Maverick air-to-surface missile.

Still more assaults were launched by SEALs on the refinery and port on the Al-Faw peninsula, while U.S. Marines from the 5th Regimental Combat Team of the 1st Marine Expeditionary Force attacked targets farther north in the Rumaila oil fields. Moore had listened to his commander complain that the ground looked unstable out there, too unstable for their standard rear-wheel-drive Desert Patrol Vehicles (DPVs). The SEALs' fears were confirmed when they arrived and their DPVs became trapped in desert sand soaked with oil. They'd been forced to move out on foot to face more than three hundred entrenched Iraqi solders and armored vehicles. With the assistance of close air support called in by their combat controllers, the SEAL teams battled their way through the enemy positions until dawn, killing several hundred Iraqis, capturing nearly one hundred more, and destroying all of their armored vehicles until they were relieved by the 42 Commando of the British Royal Marines.

Following the operation, Carmichael's body was recovered. He'd been shot by the Iraqis on the platform and bitten by yellow-bellied sea snakes that had been stirred up by the outboard motor's wash. The snakes were common to the gulf, their venom more toxic than that of the cobra or the krait, paralyzing the victim's respiratory system. Hartogg's body had also been recovered, although he had drifted nearly a quarter-mile away from the platform.

At Carmichael's funeral in San Diego, Moore, along with more than thirty other SEALs who knew Carmichael and had served with him, lined up on both sides of the pallbearers' path, with the coffin emerging from the hearse and carried between them. As the coffin passed each SEAL, he removed the golden Trident, aka "Budweiser," from his uniform. With the Trident's heavy pin sticking out from the bottom, he slapped the pin onto the coffin, embedding it in the wood. One by one, as the pallbearers waited, the SEALs plunged their Tridents into Carmichael's casket so that by the time it reached the grave site, a pair of golden inlays had been drawn across each side. This was the least Moore and his colleagues could do—a final tribute to one of their brothers.

Moore, being Carmichael's closest and best friend, was last to drive home his pin, and that had been too much. He'd broken down for just a few seconds, but the stoic faces born of the extreme discipline of his peers motivated him to hang on. He would get through this. He looked to Frank's young wife, Laney, now the widow, sobbing into her tissue, her black mascara running across her cheeks, as dark as her dress. Telling her he was sorry was a joke, a terribly bad joke. She had lost her husband because of him. The frustration of being unable to help was maddening, and he balled his hands into fists.

A few hours later at the wake, held at a big Italian restaurant called Anthony's, Moore took Laney aside and tried to explain to her what had happened. She'd been told only a very broad-stroke account of the incident, and nowhere in the report did it say that Moore had made the decision to leave Carmichael and take the rest of the team back to the helicopter, only that the SEALs had taken heavy fire and Carmichael had been killed.

"The truth is, Laney, it's all my fault."

She shook her head and pushed him away. "I don't want to hear it. I don't want to know. Nothing will change. I'm not stupid, Max. I knew this was a possibility, so don't think I'm some poor and shocked widow and try to give me someone to blame. You can apologize if it makes you feel better, but you don't have to. I took on the responsibility of marrying a Navy SEAL, and I'd be a goddamned fool if I didn't think this day might come. You know what's weird? When you guys were last deployed, I had this feeling . . . I just knew . . ."

"I don't know what to say."

"Frank died doing what he loved. And he loved you guys. It was his life. That's the way we'll remember him."

"But he didn't have to die. And I just . . . I wouldn't even be here if . . ."

"I told you—no apologies."

"I know, but—"

"Then just forget it."

"Laney, I don't expect you to forgive me." Moore choked up. "I just . . . There wasn't . . . He tried to tell me to go . . ."

"Stop it. Don't say anything else."

"But I have to."

She put a finger to his lips. "No. You don't."

Moore abruptly turned away and rushed out of the restaurant, feeling the gazes of every other SEAL burn into the back of his head.

Crystal Cave Area
Sequoia National Park
California

"Just five," whispered Ansara as he stared through his binoculars. He was lying on his belly, shoulder to shoulder with Moore, who confirmed the same from behind his own binoculars.

In a clearing about fifteen meters below, five Hispanic men were loading a fourteen-foot-long nondescript truck with brick after brick of dried marijuana. Ansara had already given Moore the tour of a place he called "the garden," where beneath the extensive cover of sugar pines the cartel had established a sophisticated growing operation whose expansive and clever irrigation system left Moore stunned. He had witnessed the growers' tents, and the other much larger and longer tents where the harvested plants were hung from twine and carefully dried over a three- to four-day period, with the growers carefully checking each plant to be sure it had not contracted any mold. Once dried, the bundled plants were moved to yet another tent, where a team of sixteen women (Moore had counted them, and some appeared as young as fifteen or sixteen) did the weighing, bundling, and taping of each brick. They'd left the tent's side flaps open, and through those openings Moore had been able to photograph the entire operation, itself under surveillance by a collection of battery-operated cameras mounted within and around the tents. Ansara, who'd already performed excellent reconnaissance of the operation, knew every guard post, and every weak section in the farm's defenses.

"I wanted to bust these guys the last time I was up here, but the Bureau wouldn't have it," he'd told Moore. "Probably the right decision."

"Yeah, because in a week they'd set up another shop. We need to shut them down back in Mexico and break the chain of command."

"Why is it all you ex-military boys talk about the tactics, techniques, and procedures and refer to a bunch of drug dealers as having a 'chain of command'?"

"Because we're not ex-military. We are always military. And because that's exactly what it is."

"I'm just busting your balls."

Moore smiled as he remembered the conversation and now glanced back at the laser trip wire they'd marked with a small piece of duct tape on each tree. Those were the areas through which they could not pass, and Ansara had twice prevented Moore from slipping up and breaking a beam. He'd taken a little baby powder between his fingers to show Moore exactly where the laser traversed, dusting the beam ever so slightly with the powder.

A camera mounted on top of the tent from within which the men were moving the bricks panned toward the hill, then tilted up, toward Moore and Ansara, who dug deeper behind the log they were using for cover. At that precise moment, footfalls and the crunching of leaves came from behind them, the southeast. Guards on patrol. Voices. Spanish. Something about bear tracks.

Bears? Not good.

Ansara gestured to him. *Wait. They'll pass.*

The men below finished their loading, and just three of them climbed into the truck's cab, and the driver started the engine.

Moore and Ansara needed to get back down into the valley, where they'd retrieve their full-suspension mountain bikes and ride soundlessly down to the main roads to their 4x4 pickup truck. The cartel truck would have a significant lead on them, but it would be tracked by satellite, those feeds piped directly to Moore's smartphone. Somewhere along the line Moore would need to get close, to plant a GPS tracker on the vehicle, which would provide more accurate data on the truck's location. The satellite feeds were often interrupted by the weather and terrain, and this was one truck they *did not* want to lose.

Once the voices of the guards grew faint, Ansara led the way through knots of pines and across the beds of needles crackling under their boots. It was 11:35 a.m.

By the time they reached their bikes, they heard the truck lumbering slowly down the dirt road, a single narrow path that had been cleared by cartel workers and lying about twenty meters east of their location. Ansara mounted his bike and took off. He was an experienced bike handler, having trained extensively with his buddy Dave Ameno, who'd taught him to navigate some of Central Florida's most technical trails. Ansara's skills annoyed Moore, who could barely stay on his wheels as he leapt over roots and made small jumps. Ansara knew exactly when to come out of the saddle and throw his weight back, while Moore got thrown around on the bike like a rag doll whose wrists had been duct-taped to the handlebars.

That Moore fell only twice before they reached their truck was sheer luck. That he hadn't broken anything or drawn blood was the miracle they needed. They threw their bikes in the back of the pickup and took off, heading southwest down Sierra Drive, with Moore studying the map and the superimposed blue blip that represented the truck.

"How far up are they?" Ansara asked.

"Three-point-four-five miles."

The FBI agent nodded. "Remind me when this is all over to teach you how to ride a mountain bike. I can see that wasn't part of your extensive training."

"Hey, I made it."

"Yeah, but you looked real tentative through those whoop-de-doos. I told you to relax and let the bike tell you where it wants to go."

"I don't speak bike."

"Obviously."

"The bike wanted to go in the trees."

"You must become one with the machine, grasshopper."

"Yeah, whatever."

Ansara laughed. "Hey, you got a girlfriend?"

He grinned crookedly at the man. "You always talk this much?"

"Hey, we're following a truck."

"That's right. So let's stay on it. Signal's still good. Any speculation on their first stop?"

"Well, if they get onto 198, then I'm thinking Porterville. There's been some trafficking through there before. DEA scored big a couple of years ago, I think."

Moore was about to broaden his view of the map when he turned to Ansara and said, "And to answer your question, I don't have a girlfriend. I was with a very nice lady in Afghanistan, but I'm not sure when I'll ever get back."

"A local?"

"Oh, that would go over well, eh? They'd string me up by my you-know-whats, so no, she's an American. She works for the U.S. Embassy."

"She hot?"

Moore grinned. "No."

"Too bad." Ansara's cell phone rang. "Oh, this is a call I need to take."

"Who?"

"Rueben. The kid I recruited. What do you have for me, young man?"

Moore picked up only bits and pieces of the kid's voice on the other end, but Ansara's reaction filled in the blanks: The cartel had completed some kind of extensive tunnel running between Mexicali and Calexico. Rueben was one of about ten young men who were going to begin making major shipments through the tunnels, probably cocaine from Colombia and opium from Afghanistan. This was a brand-new avenue of approach for the cartel, and after the call, Ansara said that the mules had already made several dry runs. Now they felt certain the passageway was clean and undetected, thus the real product would begin moving north, while the money and weapons flowed south.

The cartel truck moved at no more than forty-five miles per hour through the winding roads, and Ansara's guess had been right. They'd driven directly into the small town of Porterville, California, population about fifty thousand, and headed straight for the Holiday Inn Express, where they parked in a space behind the three-story building.

Moore and Ansara watched them from the parking lot of the Burger King across the street. All three men remained in the cab, nixing Moore's plan to affix his GPS tracker to the underside of the vehicle. They dared not get any closer.

"You want a cheeseburger?" asked Ansara.

Moore looked at him in mock disgust. "Well, the In-N-Out Burger is the best burger on the West Coast, in my humble opinion, because it is one hundred percent pure beef. And their fries are cooked in one hundred percent pure cholesterol-free vegetable oil."

"Are you serious? You want a burger or not?"

"Get me two."

And by the time Ansara returned with their food, another vehicle had pulled up beside the cartel truck. This second one was a white cargo van with tinted windows.

Staring through the long lenses of his digital surveillance camera, Moore nearly choked on his cheeseburger as he watched the men transfer at least forty cinder-block-size bricks from the cartel truck to the van—in broad daylight.

The driver of the van, another Hispanic man wearing a denim jacket and sunglasses, handed the cartel men a backpack, assumedly bulging with cash.

"I can't believe they're this bold."

"Believe it," answered Ansara. "Hi, there. Here are your drugs. Thanks for the money. Have a nice day."

The van left, and while the Agency would track it via satellite and Moore's photographs of its tag number, intercepting it might result in a call back to the cartel guys in the truck, who would panic and not complete their distribution, so the van would be left alone. The truck pulled out of the parking lot and headed west, back out toward 65. Ansara kept well behind them, and by the time they merged onto the highway, heading south, the cartel truck had a two-mile lead.

"So this girlfriend of yours," Ansara said out of nowhere. "You still talking to her?"

"Why do you ask?"

"I don't have much luck with women."

"Because of this."

"The job? Hell, yeah . . ."

"Well, I'm the wrong guy to ask for advice."

Ansara cracked a grin. "Maybe one day I'll find a guy who knows how to do it. I'd forgotten you were a SEAL, so that pretty much dooms you."

"Hey, I knew some guys with families."

"They're the exception, not the rule. Women nowadays want too much. I think some think we're selfish for spending so much time away. When I was in the 'Stan, I didn't know any-one on any of the ODA teams who wasn't either single, di-vorced, or going through a divorce. It was kind of pathetic."

"I'd forgotten you were Special Forces. I thought you were just an ex–mountain biker looking for fame and fortune."

"Yeah, that's why I joined the FBI—so I could work ridicu-lous hours and get underpaid while people try to kill me . . ."

"You love it."

"Every minute."

Moore glanced down at the map. "Hey, bro. They stopped. Gas station. Near Delano."

"Could be just to refuel—but if it's another exchange, we need to boogie, otherwise we could miss it."

Moore was about to zoom in on the image when the satellite feed froze up. "Shit. Lost the signal."

30

DEAR LADY

Bonita Real Hotel
Juárez, Mexico

GLORIA VEGA was sitting in the unmarked sedan across the street from the hotel. Inspector Gómez was at the wheel. At Gómez's request, they were dressed in civilian clothes but wearing their Kevlar vests. The desk clerk at the hotel, a man named Ignacio Hernández, had been found dead the night before, shot once, execution-style, in the forehead. The owner of the hotel, Mr. Dante Corrales, was nowhere to be found, and neither was his girlfriend. Gómez had contacted several other employees of the hotel, along with construction workers involved in a renovation project, and he and Vega were going to interview them today.

"You see them up there," said Gómez, referring to the two men sitting on the hotel's roof. "They're spotters, but not the usual ones. These men I haven't seen before."

"Maybe Corrales killed his desk clerk and took off," said Vega.

"Why would he do that?"

She shrugged. "He was stealing."

"No. It's a lot more complicated than that."

"How do you know?"

He faced her and snapped. "Because I've been doing this for most of my life. Wait here until I come back for you."

With a little snort, the old man levered himself out of the car, slammed the door shut, and ventured across the street, toward the hotel's main entrance. Vega watched as the spotters marked his every move.

When would the hammer fall? Everything had to be carefully timed and planned, Towers kept telling her. In point of fact, she was running out of time, and being careful was a hell of a lot harder now. Could she survive another attempt on her life? Was any of this even worth it anymore?

She looked to the hotel.

The spotters were focused on something else.

She heard the engine first. Then a dark blue sedan came barreling around the corner with two men hanging out the passenger-side windows. They wore T-shirts, jeans, and balaclavas over their faces.

Vega bolted out of the car as their shotguns swung around,

toward her. She was already returning fire as they opened up on her, their guns booming, buckshot ripping into the car.

But their shots were accompanied by two more, and her gaze flicked up to the rooftop of the hotel, where both the spotters were now holding rifles and firing at her.

A breath later, a needling pain woke in her neck, and two more needles pierced her shoulders as blood began pumping onto the pavement. Her hand went reflexively for her neck, which was now bathed in blood. She shuddered, wanted to scream, opened her mouth, but her vocal cords no longer worked. She collapsed behind the car as the other vehicle screeched to a halt, and Vega barely turned her head in that direction as one of the men approached her, lifted his shotgun, and fired point-blank into her face, which was already going numb.

It might've been a minute or two, or just a few seconds, she wasn't sure, but she looked up with one good eye and through a haze of blood and saw Gómez leaning over her.

She should be dead already. She knew that. But her body was as stubborn as her spirit.

"I'm sorry, dear lady," said Gómez. "I'm so sorry . . ." He reached into her pocket and fished out her cell phone. "I've been doing this for too long to let myself get caught. You know that. And I know they sent you to find a rat. It's a terrible business. Terrible, terrible, terrible."

He rose and turned back to another man. "Pablo? What are you doing here? Where's Dante?"

"He's safe. We had some trouble with the Guatemalans."

"What can I do?"

"Dante sent me with a message: Leave Zúñiga alone. Don't touch him."

"Zúñiga? Are you crazy? He's the one we need to kill."

Vega tried to listen, wished she could contact Towers, and then her thoughts broke off from their constricted orbit and floated away to her dead parents. She wanted to see them, to see the light, but for the time being there was only a numbing darkness.

And from that void came a final exchange of voices.

"Dante is making a horrible mistake. Tell him I want to speak to him before he does anything."

"I will, señor. I will."

And now the cold set in, pushing back the numbness. She shivered violently. There it was now, a pinprick at first and then a glorious beam of light as hot and warm as the summer sun. This was not God, some argued, only a reaction of the brain. But Vega knew better. She knew . . .

Chevron Gas Station
Delano, California

Despite losing the satellite signal, Moore and Ansara went to the truck's last known location at the gas station, and by the time they arrived, Moore had reacquired the satellite and confirmed that the truck had not moved. Sometimes they picked up a little luck in their travels, most times not.

A surprise phone call from ATF Agent Whittaker as they were nearing the station left Moore's breath shallow.

"You're looking for a silver Honda Odyssey van," the man said. "Should be reaching your location pretty soon. They'll pull out back behind the car wash, I think. Towers says we let 'em make the exchange."

"Roger that," said Moore. "And you're sure those are the same weapons that SEAL smuggled out of the 'Stan?"

"Oh, I'm positive."

"Jesus . . ."

"Yeah, well, he'll be going down—because that's only part of the shipment on that van. The rest of it is still up in Minnesota, and that's the evidence I'll be collecting. Glad they weren't stupid enough to try to smuggle it all in one shipment. Their attempt to be smart works in my favor. We should have him and the weapons in custody by tonight."

"Well, thanks for the heads-up," said Moore, as Ansara pulled into the parking lot of a transmission shop next door to the station. They had a clear, unobstructed view of the truck, which had, in fact, parked out back behind the car wash.

Moore called up one of Whittaker's reports on his smart-phone and scanned the inventory list of items purportedly stolen and smuggled by that Navy SEAL:

14 M4A1 rifles with SOPMOD accessory kits
11 M14 sniper rifles (7.62mm)
9 MK11 Mod 0 sniper weapon systems
2 HK MP5 submachine guns

6 Benelli M4 Super 90 shotguns
14 M203 grenade launchers

Moore gave Ansara a description of the Honda, and the words had barely left his mouth when the van pulled into the station, its rear end sagging slightly from the weight of its cargo.

"You know, at least in Afghanistan the bad guys tried to act like bad guys," Moore said. "They smuggled opium and weapons at night. They used the caves. They tried to remain out of sight . . . but these guys . . . damn . . ."

Ansara nodded and lifted his camera. "Act like you're doing nothing wrong and no one will think you're doing anything wrong. The thing is, they know we're looking for them at night. They know we'll raid their houses in the early morning, when everyone is supposed to be sleeping, so a lot of them do business in the early morning, sleep all afternoon, then stay up all night."

Moore nodded. "You've seen that inventory list, right?"

"Yeah."

"Then you know we can't let those weapons get into Mexico."

"Whoa, whoa, whoa, hang on there, cowboy. The money trail's more important than the guns—you know that."

"I know, but I just can't bear the thought of a gun that once belonged to a SEAL being in the hands of some cartel scumbag."

"Maybe they're all new guns," said Ansara.

Moore snorted and began taking pictures himself as a collection of black Anvil cases was hauled from the van and into the back of the truck. The cartel truck's driver handed a brown-paper shopping bag to the van's driver, a tall, wiry guy with wispy black hair extending down to his shoulders. He looked more Native American than Mexican.

The exchange took no more than five minutes, with the men performing their loading operations smoothly, even routinely. The van drove off. The cartel guys climbed into the cab but waited a few moments. Moore zoomed in with his camera. The driver was on the phone.

Moore's own phone vibrated. Towers. Just three words to make Moore's heart sink: "Vega is dead."

"How?"

Towers explained. Then added, "I just got word. After they shot her, they rigged her body with C-4. When EMS and the local police arrived, they detonated the charges. You believe that?"

"Who rigged her? Gómez or the cartel?"

"Not sure. We had a feed on the area but lost the signal when we switched from one satellite to another."

Moore spoke through clenched teeth: "I'll bet it was that fucker Gómez. He had her killed, and he set it up to look like the cartel."

"She was our best link to him. I've got a few spotters of our own out there, and some pretty good civilian informants, but this is still a major setback."

Moore closed his eyes. "She didn't die for nothing. We'll make sure of that."

After he got off the phone with Towers, he and Ansara sat in silence, watching as the cartel truck left the station and got back on the road. They fell in behind them, allowed several cars to get in front, and continued on with a good satellite signal. A message from Langley indicated that they'd identified the cartel truck driver's cell phone and had hacked into its operating system to turn on its GPS signal—so now they were tracking the truck via visual images from a satellite and by using the GPS signal emitted by the driver's cell phone. According to the message, signal interruption should not happen again. Moore wasn't buying that and was looking for any chance he could get to plant a good old-fashioned beacon on the truck, which they could track locally.

"And five are now three," Moore said, breaking the silence in the cab.

"Yeah," answered Ansara. "I've only lost two close buddies over the years. Even after all my time overseas. Only two. Both FBI agents. All my close buddies in the Army made it through— at least so far. How about you?"

"We don't want to go there."

"That many, huh?"

"It's not a numbers game."

"I know you were there with Fitzpatrick. And I agree. He was an ace. I hope you're not blaming yourself."

Moore sighed. "You think about how you could've set it up differently and how your buddy might still be alive. I sent him into the house to clear it. He got ambushed and died. I can let myself off the hook, or I can take responsibility for the orders I gave him."

"Dude, if you go through life like that, you'll be miserable."

"Yup. I know . . ."

For a few seconds Moore closed his eyes and sat down at a table with Frank Carmichael at the head. Beside him were Rana, Colonel Khodai, and Fitzpatrick. Vega sauntered into the restaurant, which turned out to be the Italian place where they'd had Carmichael's wake. The feisty woman *tsk*ed at them, as if to say they were fools for allowing themselves to be killed. Then she faced Moore. "You know what to do."

He nodded.

About an hour later they reached Bakersfield, where they drove for a few minutes through the city and noted that the truck had pulled into the alley behind José Taco, a well-known Mexican restaurant, according to online reviews. On one side of the alley stood a row of businesses, including the restaurant, and on the other was a long brick wall cordoning off the business district from the six-story buildings of a low-rent apartment complex.

"Shit, this won't be easy," said Ansara, driving past the alley and heading farther down the cross street.

"We need to get out," said Moore, gesturing to a line of empty parking spots to their right.

Ansara agreed, took them into a spot, and they both hustled out of the truck and sprinted toward the apartments.

"This way," said Moore, running behind the first building and toward a bank of low-lying shrubs planted along the
brick wall.

They turned the corner, and directly ahead, no more than
thirty meters, was the truck, its rear door open, the men loading blocks of marijuana. Moore saw that if they edged up closer,
remaining behind the bushes, they could reach two Dumpsters
to the left whose black plastic lids hung open. From behind
them they'd have a better view of the exchange.

Hunched over, he led them forward, up to the Dumpster,
where they slipped around the side, and there, squatting in the
shadows of some palm trees behind them, he began taking his
pictures while Ansara did likewise from the other corner. The
sour stench emanating from the trash left him with a tight
grimace.

The other vehicle was a black BMW 650i two-door sport
job whose trunk was being filled with bricks. The driver was a
gray-haired Hispanic man in an expensive-looking suit and
wearing gold cuff links. In Moore's estimation, once you got into
the world of cuff links, you could be into some serious money
for clothes. The frame around the BMW's tag indicated that the
vehicle had come from a dealership in Santa Monica, and there
was little doubt as to the destination of his newly acquired precious cargo. Again, he didn't come in a big truck to pick up his
drugs; rather, he took his expensive business machine and
would carefully drive the speed limit all the way back to La-la
Land so that his shipment could receive white-gloved distribution to Hollywood's elite, who had the means, the access, and

the desire to get higher than the hills on which they'd constructed their mansions.

The driver shook hands with the cartel guys, handed over two thick envelopes to the driver, then climbed into his car and whirred off. Moore and Ansara were prepared to leave when another car rumbled into the alley, sending them crouching even tighter against the Dumpster. The vehicle was a Toyota Tacoma pickup truck, an older model, with a roll-lock cap and tinted windows. Two men climbed out dressed like wannabe Mexican gangsters, with baggy pants, and wallets affixed to chains that dangled from their hips. One guy, the fatter one and driver, shook hands with the cartel guys, and once again, more bricks were loaded into the back of their truck.

When they finished, the cartel guys got in their truck and pulled out. Moore and Ansara were waiting for the two guys in the Toyota to leave, but they just sat there in their idling vehicle. Then one climbed out, banged on the back door of the restaurant, and yelled something about their food taking too long. Moore almost laughed. They'd ordered takeout as part of the drug-buying operation.

The man who answered the door was not Mexican but Chinese, although he wore a José Taco apron. He shouted at the guy in broken English, told him to be patient, then slammed the door in his face.

As the thug whirled back toward his car, he looked over at the Dumpsters.

Moore froze.

"Oh, shit," Ansara whispered.

The thug frowned, took another step toward them. He suddenly jogged to one side, spotted them.

His eyes bugged out.

He whirled around, screaming at the guy in the Toyota.

Moore had already shoved his camera back into a side pocket and had drawn his suppressed Glock.

He was on his feet as the guy looked over his shoulder and saw Moore sprinting toward him, with Ansara now right behind. The thug reached into his waistband and drew the pistol he'd stored there. He swung the gun back at Moore, who fired two rounds into the guy's chest before the thug could fire.

The guy in the pickup, seeing what was happening outside, must have slid into the driver's seat. The engine roared, and the truck began to pull away.

Shots rang out behind Moore—and that was Ansara, firing at the truck's rear wheels, his aim pinpoint-accurate. The left tire popped and blew out, followed by the right, rubber flapping loudly now against the asphalt. The truck slowed enough for Moore to reach the back and make a flying leap onto the rear bumper. He latched a hand onto the tailgate and held on as the driver tried to steer them out of the alley on two flat tires.

Moore leaned out to the side and fired two rounds into the driver's-side window, shattering it. He still couldn't get a direct bead on the driver. In the mirror, he saw the guy bringing his cell phone to his ear.

With a curse, Moore fired a third round into the back window, but the shot must've missed the guy, who just ducked and kept on driving.

Now Moore leaned out even farther to his left, getting the angle he needed. He fired once more, a direct headshot, and the truck veered to the right and plowed into the brick wall, just as Moore jumped off, hit the ground, and fought to keep balance. Out of breath, and with Ansara on his heels, he rushed up to the cab and wrenched open the door. The driver leaned over and fell out of the truck. There, on the center console, was a heap of cocaine, a few joints, one of them still burning in the ashtray, and a few more bags of coke sitting inside the open glove compartment.

Moore reached down and grabbed the man's cell phone, checking to see if he'd made that call. No, the call had never gone through. *Thank God.*

He didn't realize he was just standing there, looking at all the drugs, until Ansara nudged him aside and said, "Whoa, look at that. But hey, come on, let's go! We'll have to call this in. I got the other guy's cell. Moore? Are you listening to me?"

He faced Ansara, stared through him as though the man were on a movie screen, then blinked and said, "Yeah, come on!" They raced through the alley, and by the time they turned the corner and Moore stole a look back over his shoulder, the Chinese guy with the José Taco apron was coming outside, carrying two bags of takeout.

Within five minutes they were in the pickup, back on the

road, and back on track, following the cartel truck, which An-sara predicted was heading down into Palmdale. Moore re-ported what had happened to Towers, who wasn't happy, but at least the thugs hadn't alerted the cartel guys. Local police were en route to the scene.

31

RITES OF PASSAGE

Rojas Mansion
Cuernavaca, Mexico
56 Miles South of Mexico City

IGUEL SWAM DOWN to the deepest part of the pool and remained there, wondering what it might feel like to hold his breath until he lost consciousness. That he was having such morbid thoughts was due in part to his failure to act more bravely during their kidnapping. Sonia had been the strong one, and while he loved her deeply, he found it increasingly hard to accept how scared he'd been and how he'd failed to protect his woman, as any good man should. At one point, he'd even begun to cry, and it'd been Sonia who'd talked him through it. He cursed himself for that.

His father had touched on the subject over breakfast, even suggesting that Miguel should return to practicing the martial arts he'd studied during his preteen years. He'd even said that Fernando could show him a few new moves, and he'd even pay for a trip to Thailand so that Miguel could study with some Muay Thai masters there. Miguel had politely declined. And then he'd excused himself and retired to the pool, where he'd remained for most of the day, with Sonia sprawled across a lounger in her bikini and reading a Spanish soap-opera magazine.

He hadn't discussed with her what Raúl had said, and he wondered if she'd even noticed it. In fact, he'd tried to repress it himself but he kept coming back to the poor man's last words, his pleading to the Guatemalans that the "cartel will pay you anything" and that "Dante will do whatever you ask."

Over the years, Miguel had overheard many conversations between his father and his father's associates, and the words *cartel* and *drug dealers* and *sicarios* were often used by them. His father had always emphasized that he was trying to run legitimate businesses in the face of organized crime and police corruption. The cartels were the mortal enemies of the Rojas empire, and at first Miguel had assumed that Raúl might have been a former cartel member employed by his father. That, too, was not uncommon. Over the years, Fernando had rescued and recruited many young men from the slums of Mexico and turned them into security personnel and bodyguards. Dante Corrales was a shining example of that, and had become Fernando's right-hand man.

So why, then, would Raúl—a man who answered directly to Corrales—call upon the help of "the cartel," and why, then, would Corrales do "whatever you ask"? Why would the cartel be willing to pay ransom for Raúl if he was not one of them? And if he was, then were Fernando and Miguel's father aware of that? Was Corrales also involved? How had the kidnappers known where they'd be? Miguel had assumed that their vacation was known by only close family members and bodyguards. There was definitely a rat in the organization, and Miguel assumed his father and Fernando were trying to weed him out.

Miguel didn't want to believe it, but there had always been—deep down—a gnawing suspicion that something wasn't exactly truthful about his father's businesses. He wouldn't go so far as to say that his father had direct ties to any of the cartels, but perhaps bribes were paid, thugs kept quiet, so that operations could go on. That was understandable and did not make his father a criminal. This was business in modern Mexico. But what if he was wrong about everything? What if his father was in bed with all of them? What if the man who had tried to kill his father wasn't just some nutjob bent on revenge? What if he'd been a professional assassin hired by a drug cartel?

Miguel swam straight up and exploded out of the water, shook his head, and swam over to the pool's edge.

"You were down there for a long time," Sonia said, staring over the rim of her sunglasses.

"There are places in this house that we are not allowed to go," he said.

"What?"

"Locked doors leading to the basement. No one is allowed behind them."

"Is that what you were thinking about?"

"My father has secrets."

"All men do."

"And not women?"

She feigned innocence. "Of course not."

"He says the only thing down there are the vaults. He says he has art and other collectibles and doesn't want anyone damaging those pieces."

"Sounds like you don't believe him."

"I don't."

"Why not? What do you think he's hiding?"

Miguel began to feel heartsick. "I don't know."

"So why don't we ask him to go down there and just look at the stuff? He can come with us . . ."

"He won't agree."

"Why?"

"I don't know."

"Would you like me to ask him?" She smiled coyly. "I'm pretty sure he likes me."

Miguel sighed. "Of course he likes you, but it won't matter."

She wriggled her brows like a little girl. "Do you want to sneak down there?"

Miguel snickered. "He's got a guard standing at the door twenty-four-seven."

"Maybe he's got some jewelry down there, too. More expensive stuff he's really worried about, so he has a guard. I don't see why any of this is so odd to you. These are dangerous times, and possessions must be protected."

"I want to tell you something, but I'm afraid."

She rose and crossed to him, took a seat on the ledge, and dunked her legs in the water. He pushed himself beside her, and she placed a hand on his cheek. "You can tell me anything you want."

"Do you remember what Raúl said before they killed him?"

She grimaced. "Do we have to talk about that?"

"Please . . ."

She sighed deeply. "I don't remember what he said. I only remember the screaming. And . . . all the blood . . ." She put a hand to her own cheek, clearly remembering how they'd wiped Raúl's blood across her face.

"He said the cartel would pay anything. Let me say that again. He said *the cartel* would pay. Why would he say that?"

"Maybe he was working for a cartel, too, and never told Fernando. Who knows? Maybe that's why we got into trouble in the first place. Why is that bothering you?"

"It's just . . . nothing."

"You said there's a guard outside the door to the basement. I haven't seen him."

"We haven't been to that side of the house."

"Maybe we can bribe him."

"Won't work."

"We don't know till we try. Come on. It'll be fun. It'll take your mind off all of this."

She picked herself up and turned back toward Fernando, who'd come onto the pool deck and who was lowering his cell phone. "Better get showered and ready," he said. "We'll be joining Señor Rojas for dinner soon . . ."

"We want to go down to the basement first."

He frowned at her and looked to Miguel. "I'm sorry, but only Señor Rojas is permitted there."

Sonia softened her tone and edged up to him, thrusting out her chest. "Come on, Fernando. Take us for a little tour."

"That's not possible."

She pouted like a schoolgirl. "Okay, then. We'll go get ready for dinner. Come on, Miguel. I'm getting burned, anyway . . ."

She helped him out of the pool, and he accepted a towel from her, then stood there, being scrutinized by Castillo. "Fernando, is something wrong?"

"No, señor."

The suspicion hung heavy in the bodyguard's tone.

Private Residence
121 South Broad Street
Palmdale, California

The cartel truck backed into the driveway of a two-story private home in a suburban neighborhood of southeast Palmdale. The truck sat there in the driveway, just idling, with Ansara and Moore parked about fifteen houses away, down the street, sandwiched between two other cars. Palmdale was a city in the high desert, separated from Los Angeles by the San Gabriel Mountains and exceedingly hot in the summertime. It was a well-planned community of suburbs with the tiled roofs of thousands of houses forming terra-cotta ribbons across the otherwise drab mountains. More than 150,000 people called Palmdale home, and bike trails, parks, theaters, and a new regional medical center attracted young families who deemed the city a great place to raise kids. Moore had been there once before, visiting a SEAL buddy's parents who worked for the largest employer in the area, Lockheed Martin. The seedy underbelly of Palmdale and its neighboring city Lancaster was much more apparent at the hotels and motels that had sprouted up along the freeway, where prostitution and drug deals ran rampant.

While they waited, Moore contacted Towers, who had another bit of news to share. They'd reestablished contact with Sonia, who'd reached one of the many dead drops the Agency had established for her around Rojas's mansion in case she got into trouble. Hidden at each drop were a pistol and a satellite phone. The dead drop she'd used was at a restaurant not far from Rojas's mansion. While Miguel waited, she'd gone to the ladies' room and, once the room was empty, she'd retrieved the phone from a small box tucked deeply beneath the far-right sink and made the encrypted call to her handler. She was demanding to know who'd saved her, and trying to find out why a joint task force had been assigned to her case without her knowledge.

"Did you tell her we had the same question?" Moore asked, chuckling sardonically through his words.

"Are you kidding? I can't talk to her directly. This comes to me from your bosses."

"Oh, well, tell them I said she owes me a cup of coffee."

"Yeah, right, I'll do that. She does offer some news. Dante Corrales is missing. Off the grid. His girlfriend with him. Vega confirmed that before she was killed. They murdered the desk clerk at Corrales's hotel. That tells me they're looking for Corrales."

"Maybe he screwed over the Guatemalans, and now he's on the run from them and from his own cartel."

"That's what I've been thinking."

"Hey, I know where he'd go."

"Are you serious?"

"Yeah. Hang on now. I'll call you back." Moore lifted his camera and zoomed in.

Two motorcycles pulled up and parked across the street from the truck. A tall man got off the first one, and a slightly shorter man swung off the second. They wore jeans, leather jackets, and expensive basketball sneakers. They both had athletic builds, and once they removed their helmets, it was clear neither man was over thirty-five. Moore got some good pictures of their faces and immediately uploaded them to the satellite so Langley could begin working on their identities.

They crossed the street and had a conversation with the driver of the truck, who did not get out of his vehicle, and neither did his two accomplices. After two minutes of that, one of the men opened the garage door with a remote, and the men inside the truck climbed out and got to work. What appeared to be the final shipment of marijuana bricks was transferred into the garage and packed into cardboard moving boxes. The weapons remained onboard the truck.

By the time the cartel men were finished unloading and the two men were getting ready to rumble off on their bikes, Towers had called to confirm that the bikers were local sheriff's deputies. Moore could only shake his head. American law enforcement officers were as susceptible to temptation as the Mexican local and federal authorities. When there was this much money at stake, men barely making $50,000 per year—men who could make that much in a weekend doing the cartel's bidding—found it excruciatingly difficult to remain honest. While Moore hardly agreed with that, he understood it. And hated it.

"Let's bust these bastards right now," he muttered. "They take an oath . . . and then shit on it."

"I'd love to," said Ansara. "But it's not over yet. There they go."

The truck pulled out of the driveway and started down the street. Towers had sent over more information on the vehicle's registration, which Moore had reviewed. The truck was registered to Roberto Guzman of 14818 Archwood Avenue, Van Nuys, California. Guzman owned a produce distribution company in Los Angeles. He'd already been brought in for questioning and claimed he didn't know anything about his truck being used to pick up, transport, and distribute marijuana. According to him, the driver of the vehicle worked for him and had taken the truck home for the weekend to perform some minor repairs in order to "save the boss some money." That was bullshit, of course. Guzman had been bought, his truck borrowed, his ass now in a sling for helping the cartel.

They drove for another hour, still heading south, when the truck exited the freeway and pulled into a gas station. All three men got out. They entered the convenience store, where two slipped down a back hall, presumably to use the bathroom, and the third, the driver, went over to the soda-and-beer case.

Moore instructed Ansara to park at the pump behind the truck, and within two minutes he had placed the GPS transponder beneath their bumper and was back to pumping gas into their own pickup truck. He tugged down the baseball cap he'd put on before getting out, and he kept his head low as the men returned, climbed into the truck, and pulled away.

They had redundant systems of surveillance now, and Moore felt very confident that they would not lose the truck again. They had them by video streamed from the satellite, by the driver's cell phone, and now by Moore's GPS transponder. If these guys escaped, Moore would retire on the spot. Then again, he'd better not make that promise. Stranger things had happened.

"They bought some Corona and limes," said Ansara. "They're celebrating already."

Before Moore could answer, Ansara reached for his vibrating cell phone. "Yeah? Really? Okay. We'll be on it. Thanks, kid . . ."

He looked at Moore. "My mule says he's making a run

through the new tunnel tonight, and afterward, he's been told to stick around to do some heavier moving."

"Well, isn't that convenient," Moore said.

"These guys are going to Calexico. I'd bet anything on that."

"If you're right, it'll be dark by the time we get there. Going to hit some traffic as we get through San Bernardino."

"Only there?" Ansara asked. "We'll be sitting in traffic for most of the way."

Moore sighed and glanced out the window at the cars passing them, at another pickup truck with a couple of dirt bikes lashed to the truck's bed. He grinned to himself. If he tried riding one of those, he'd definitely kill himself.

Romero Residence
Mexicali, Mexico

Pedro Romero had twice tried to call his wife, Cecilia, but she had failed to answer her cell phone. Then he'd tried Blanca's number, but his sixteen-year-old daughter did not answer her cell, either. María, the twelve-year-old, did not have a phone but liked to call their home land line her own. And no, she didn't answer, and the answering machine did not pick up. Maybe they'd gone shopping? The cell-phone network was down? Romero had called them only to say he'd be late, and now he was beginning to worry.

Yet when he pulled into the driveway, his wife's Corolla was parked on the street and the lights were on inside the house. This was very strange, indeed.

He opened the front door and shifted inside, into the entrance foyer. He called out to his wife. No answer. He moved farther down the hall and into the living room.

What he saw felt like a curved blade plunged deeply into his spine to send out bolts of white-hot pain. He could not speak. He could not breathe. He could only stand there, in shock, in sudden fear, as in the next second he shuddered and widened his eyes.

Blanca and María were sitting on the sofa, hands behind their backs, their mouths covered by silver duct tape. Their eyes were red, their hair disheveled. Seated beside them was his wife, she too gagged and taped. And on either side of them were two men, olive-skinned and dressed in jeans and flannel shirts, like migrant workers, although they were anything but. They had long beards and held pistols on his family.

Another man came out of the kitchen, sipping a cup of tea, the bag's string dangling from his mug. He was dressed like the others, bearded as well but a bit older. He narrowed his gaze on Pedro and spoke in accented Spanish. "We've been waiting a long time for you, Señor Romero. Was that you trying to call to say you'd be late?"

Romero began to pant in fear and in anger. More in fear. "Who are you?"

"We understand you are building something—a tunnel, perhaps?"

As an engineer, as a man who'd been trained to construct and deconstruct situations for the better part of his life, he knew immediately what was happening. These were Arabs.

Terrorists, more than likely. They wanted safe passage into the United States, and they'd kill his family if he didn't comply. No other words needed to be spoken.

"I understand," said Romero.

The tall man widened his gaze. "You do?"

"Of course. I can make a call and let them know we're coming. I'll get you through. And you will release my family."

"Señor Romero, you are a very brave and smart man. You do as we ask, and all will be well."

"Is it just you three?"

The man shook his head. "No, we have fourteen more. Seventeen of us in all."

"Seventeen?" Romero said and gasped.

"Why are you so worried? We won't hurt your family."

"But the men I work for will—if they learn I've allowed so many of you to go through."

"They won't find out."

"That will be difficult. I'll have to evacuate the tunnel before you arrive and have the cameras turned off. Will you have someone to pick you up on the other side?"

"I will arrange that. I will need the address."

The toilet flushed in the other room, and then a Mexican man appeared, about Romero's age. He frowned at Romero, then shrugged, as if to say, *I'm sorry.*

"This is Felipe. He'll remain here to make sure we get through to the other side. If I call him and tell him that, your family will be released. If he doesn't receive that call, he has instructions to kill them."

Romero spoke rapidly to Felipe, hoping the sheer speed of his words would confuse the Arabs. He could tell they were translating in their heads as he spoke. "Señor, why have you gotten in bed with these terrorists? They want to kill the Americans, who are the cartel's best customers. If that happens, we'll both be killed. You are playing with fire, my friend."

Felipe made a face. "They pay better than the cartel."

The backpack rose higher than his head and extended down past his rump. The thing weighed a ton, and Rueben Everson was supposed to be back home, doing his math assignment. Instead he was about to enter a three-thousand-foot-long tunnel with about twenty-five kilos of cocaine strapped to his back. He, along with ten other guys of various ages, some Mexican, some American, had arrived at the warehouse and were loaded up by a team from the cartel.

They were supposed to deliver their backpacks to a room inside the house on the other side. Once there, they would wait for another delivery to arrive, and that second delivery would be carried back down the tunnel. This was the heavy-lifting part the *sicarios* had mentioned. After that, he and the rest of the mules would be transported from the warehouse via vans. Rueben had his doubts that he'd actually get a ride all the way home, but he took the cash ahead of time and figured he could use a few bucks of the thousand they'd given him to pay for a taxi.

The tunnel entrance inside the warehouse had been carefully concealed within a narrow electrical maintenance room. There was a four-foot-by-four-foot hole cut into the concrete, with a wooden staircase leading down to the dirt floor. Rueben carefully descended the stairs, following the heavyset man in front of him, then turned to his right, staring down the seemingly endless shaft. The ceiling rose to nearly six feet, and his backpack didn't even brush along the sides of the tunnel, which he thought were at least three feet apart. LED lights had been strung across the ceiling, as though the cartel had decorated the place for the holidays. Rueben also noticed ventilation pipes and electrical wires, along with a piece of PVC piping that ran along the right side of the floor. As they got farther into the tunnel, the walls and ceiling became covered in strange white panels that he overheard one of the guys behind him say were being used to absorb sound.

The Bluetooth in Rueben's ear began to itch. The FBI guys listening to his every move were losing their signal now, and even his GPS transponder was failing, he knew.

He began to grow claustrophobic and tried to steal a glance behind him as those panels on the walls seemed to close in. The long line of men kept coming, and the gap between himself and the fat man in front of him was widening.

"Come on, move it!" cried the guy behind him.

Rueben hustled up, reached the man, and began to breathe deeply, trying to calm himself. Even if the police were waiting to bust all of them on the other end, it didn't matter. He'd walk. He'd already been turned, made his deal with the devil, and there was no going back. This is what it was to be a man, to take responsibility for his actions, and he hated it.

The man behind him grunted and said, "Welcome to America," because someone had painted a line on the ceiling and written *U.S.* on one side, *Mexico* on the other, demarcating the border. Rueben just shrugged and moved on. A secondary tunnel shifted off to the right, where he noted a small sanctuary with burning candles. He wished he had time to say a prayer for himself and his family. He wished everything had been different. He thought of the boy with no toes . . . and shivered.

32

PAWNS IN THE KINGDOM OF HEAVEN

En Route to Border Tunnel Site
Mexicali, Mexico

Pedro Romero overheard one of the Arabs call the tall man "Samad," and so he began addressing the man as such, just to unnerve him. *I know your name.* That was petty power but all Romero had for the time being; still, he was biding his time, because he hadn't truly surrendered. Not yet.

There was a scintilla of hope.

He'd phoned the *sicarios* in charge of the cocaine shipment, and the newest lieutenant, José, a kid who used to work for

Corrales and who now wanted to be called El Jefe, though he was barely twenty-two, began screaming at Romero that he could not get everyone out of the tunnel.

"These orders come down from Corrales himself."

"Where is Corrales? Where has he been? No one has seen or heard from him. That's why I've been put in charge of this shipment. This is my operation right here."

"Shut up and listen to me. I want all those men out of the tunnel and out of the house within ten minutes. If you don't get that done, Corrales will come for you."

"I don't believe you."

"If you want to take a chance, then okay. But you will die, young man. You will definitely die."

The kid swore, hesitated, then finally agreed.

Three vehicles had been used to carry Romero, Samad, his two men, and the other fourteen Arabs to the tunnel site. Romero was driving his own car, with Samad seated next to him and the two lieutenants in the backseat. Behind them, in his wife's car, were five other men, and behind them, crammed into an old Tropic Traveler van, were the other nine, along with six rather large traveling bags whose long rectangular shapes left Romero shaking his head. Bundles of rifles? Missiles? Rocket launchers? It was safe to assume they weren't toting camping gear.

As they neared the site, Romero considered what might happen once the Arabs reached the end of the tunnel. He asked God for his salvation and prayed that his family be spared.

These men did not want witnesses, and they would murder him once they got what they wanted out of him. He could no longer deny that. He'd been around evil men long enough to understand how they reasoned.

He also wondered what they would do once they reached the United States, how many people they would kill, how much property they would destroy. He hated them as much as the Americans did, and they thought he was powerless against them.

But as he'd noted, hope was not entirely lost.

What Samad and his fanatical followers did not realize was that the tunnel had been rigged with C-4 charges so that it could be destroyed at a moment's notice, even timed in such a way as to bury anyone within it. This was made very clear to Romero during the early stages of construction. Corrales had told Romero that his bosses feared the tunnel might be used by their enemies or even terrorists one day, and so a fail-safe would be put in place. Inside a construction trailer on the opposite side of the site were three *sicarios* whose job it was to monitor the tunnel's security cameras. There were nine men in all who worked in three shifts. They were also in possession of the primary set of wireless electric detonators, although they would not blow the tunnel without direct orders from Corrales or one of the other bosses. The backup set of detonators was on the top shelf of a locker inside the maintenance room. Romero need only retrieve one of them before taking the Arabs into the tunnel.

And then he would make his move.

Rueben sloughed off his heavy backpack and let it drop to the floor, and the other men did the same. Before they could sit and wait for the shipment bound for Mexico to arrive, the *sicario* who demanded they call him El Jefe had come up from the tunnel and told them they needed to leave right away. The orders had come down.

"What about the other shipment?" Rueben asked. "I thought they needed our help. They said we'd get a bonus."

"Forget it. Go."

Rueben's frown deepened. "What about our backpacks? Who's coming to take them?"

"I don't know."

"Is something wrong?"

"Look, I need to evacuate this place now! Those are my orders. That's what's happening."

"Then I'm coming back through the tunnel with you," said Rueben. "My ride's waiting for me out there."

El Jefe shook his head. "Get the fuck out. You figure out your own ride home."

One of the other mules, probably the oldest, with a streak of gray hair near his left temple, lifted his voice: "We can't all leave at the same time. That draws too much attention. They told us that."

"The fuck you can't! Go!"

The other men began filing past Rueben, heading for the front door. The oldest mule held them back.

El Jefe rushed up to the mule and jammed his pistol into the man's forehead. *"¡Váyanse!"*

The man gave the young punk the evil eye for a few seconds, then nodded slowly and turned back for the door. The mules began filing outside after him.

"Well, I'm taking a piss first," said Rueben, crossing to the bathroom. He went inside, shut the door, and waited. The house grew silent. He turned on the faucet and called Ansara, who'd been updated and knew what was happening.

"What do I do now?"

"Go back in that tunnel. See if you can find out what's going on."

"Are you nuts?"

"Tell them you can't find your phone. Just get back down there. They evacuated the place for a reason. The big shipment is only about a half-hour away. Do what I say. Remember what I told you."

Rueben left the bathroom and found El Jefe waiting for him.

"Who were you talking to?"

"My ride."

"Go."

Rueben shrugged, went outside, then made a quick turn left and darted back into the bushes beside the house. He remained there for a few minutes, then carefully moved back up to one of the windows. *Damn, blinds closed.* He shifted around the house to the front door, put his ear to it. Nothing. He grabbed the handle, pushed open the door, then crossed to the back bedroom, where the tunnel entrance was located inside the master closet. El Jefe and his cronies had already gone back down and were headed to the warehouse. Rueben wrung his hands, paced back and forth in front of the dark square cut into the floor and the ladder leading to the bottom. He should just walk away, call it too dangerous. But would they really hurt him for going back to look for a lost phone?

Wait a minute. How could he use that excuse? El Jefe had heard him speaking on his cell. *Shit*. He needed another story. He could say he thought the cops were outside, and so he came running scared into the tunnel. That was it. That would take the focus off him. He descended the ladder, turned, and hurried across the damp earth, following the strings of LED lights. And now he really had to use the bathroom.

While driving to the tunnel, Romero had explained to Samad that the three *sicarios* in the trailer would be watching via battery-operated security cameras around the warehouse and the tunnel. They'd tested wireless cameras, but the signals had been too weak to be read on the surface. Two things needed to happen at once: The power would need to be cut to the monitors of those cameras, and the *sicarios* would need to be "separated from their phones," as Romero had put it.

Romero had the keys and access to the electrical terminals and could turn off the power, so long as Samad's men could deal with the *sicarios*. They parked their vehicles on the south side of the site, shielded by heavy earthmovers and bulldozers, and hustled out. Samad sent six of his men to deal with the surveillance guys while he and his two lieutenants accompanied Romero to an electrical terminal located behind the warehouse. Though he was primarily a construction engineer, he'd worked closely with the electrical engineers on the site and been shown emergency procedures for cutting the power.

As they neared the terminal, they were forced to take cover behind some drainage pipes to watch as three young *sicarios* left the warehouse's main door and climbed into an SUV. Romero recognized one of them as the kid El Jefe. *Good boy.* He didn't realize it yet, but he'd just saved his own life by following instructions.

When both groups were in position, Romero opened the access panels with his key and tugged down the main breaker, which thumped, and a few of the parking-lot lights went dark. Simultaneously, Samad gave the orders to take out the men inside the trailer. Then he regarded Romero. "Let's go."

Romero led the Arabs inside via the light from their cell phones, then paused before the maintenance room and looked back at the group. "Wait here."

"Why?" asked Samad.

"Because I need to get the remote."

"For what?"

"To switch off the battery backups for the cameras and the recorders; otherwise they'll monitor the downloads and see that we've been through here."

"Very good," said Samad. "But I come with you."

Romero shrugged. "Okay."

He took the man inside the room and led him past the heavy pumps they'd been using to remove water from the tunnel and toward the bank of lockers. Meanwhile, Samad's phone rang, and he spoke quickly to his men, then announced, "Very good. The men in the trailer are gone. No phone calls were placed."

Romero used a key from his heavy ring to open the locker, then reached up and snatched the wireless detonator before Samad could get a close look at it. The detonator was about the size of a walkie-talkie, with a small rubber antenna. Very simple, old-school, and effective. He pretended to push several buttons, then shoved the remote in his pocket. He fetched a pair of flashlights from the locker, took one, handed the other to Samad. "Okay, we can go through now. I hope you will keep your promise. When you are on the other side, you will call Felipe and tell him to release my family."

Samad grinned. "Of course."

The rest of the Arabs arrived, and Romero led them down the staircase, the plywood creaking and covered in dirt. Samad was just behind him, a pistol in hand. They walked about five hundred feet, made the first two ninety-degree turns—a hard left followed by a hard right—and then, far ahead, a tiny light woke in the distance. As the light grew brighter, a silhouette appeared behind it. The figure was coming straight at them.

"Stop. Who is that?" Samad demanded, halting the entire group.

"I don't know," said Romero. "The tunnel was supposed to be clear. Could be one of the mules." He lifted his voice. "Who's that?"

"Uh, sorry, yeah, it's me, Rueben! I think the cops are outside. I had to come back down here."

Romero hustled forward and reached the kid. "Are you sure about the police?"

"Not really."

"Why are you trembling?"

Rueben lifted his cell phone, the light playing over the men behind Romero. They were dark-skinned and bearded, but they were definitely not Mexicans. One man in the back barked something to the others behind him. That was *not* Spanish, and Rueben had killed enough "digital" terrorists in video games to believe these guys were Middle Eastern, maybe even terrorists themselves.

"*Yalla*, let's go," the man in the back said.

Now, Rueben knew that word, *yalla*. That was Arabic.

With a deep sigh, Romero bit his lip, then turned back to Samad. "He's one of the cartel's mules. He got scared, thought he saw something outside. Maybe the police, but he's not sure . . ."

"I don't think he saw the police," said Samad, sounding oddly confident about that. "Let me have a word with him."

Romero shifted aside and let Samad squeeze by.

In one moment Samad was speaking softly to the boy, the

words almost inaudible, and in the next moment Rueben was flailing at Samad's face and neck as the man slipped behind him and plunged a blade into the boy's chest. Rueben fell to the dirt, his face twisted in agony, blood spurting from his chest as he then coughed and reached up to clutch the wound.

"He was just a boy!" cried Romero.

"And you're just a man who will join him."

"I'm sorry," Rueben said and gasped. "I didn't want to do anything wrong. I don't want to die. Don't leave me here. Oh my God . . . Oh my God . . ." He began to sob.

Romero couldn't help himself. He kneeled beside the young man and took his hand. "Lord Jesus, take him into your bosom and protect him from all evil."

"Let's move," said Samad through his teeth as he handed the boy's cell phone to one of his men. "Pedro, you lead the way." He pushed back past Romero, then drove his pistol into the nape of Romero's neck.

Swallowing deeply, Romero released Rueben's hand, then rose and stepped over the dying boy to forge on, his eyes burning. He'd told the kid to get out. He'd tried.

They reached the little sanctuary, where Samad shook his head at the flickering candles and crucifixes and pictures of the families of the mules and diggers.

Romero stole another look back over his shoulder. Samad and his Arabs were monsters, and Romero knew now that the time had come. He stopped and dug into his pocket for the detonator. And then he held his breath.

———

As Rueben lay there on his side, bleeding to death, something shimmered in the dirt near his hand. He thought it might be an angel, come to life from the dirt to rise up and save him. He reached out toward the tiny sparkle and trapped it between his fingers. It was too dark to see the object clearly, but it felt like a pendant, with smooth curves and a large eyelet. He remembered feeling a chain snap between his fingers as he'd fought against the Arab's grip. He tucked the pendant deep into his palm, closed his eyes, and asked God to save him.

En Route to Border Tunnel House
Calexico, California

The cartel truck was about five or six cars ahead, and Moore estimated they were about twenty minutes away from the house. Towers had just called to say they'd lost contact with Ansara's mule. The kid might be dead. Towers had five spotters watching the house from all angles, and thus far they'd reported the exit of a mule team but had not seen the boy. The Mexican Federal Police were supposed to have more spotters watching the warehouse in Mexicali, but thus far they had failed to answer any of Towers's calls, their cooperation suddenly becoming nonexistent. Towers had several civilian spotters in the area who'd reported the arrival of several cars and more men who looked like mules, and that it appeared the construction site had lost power. Unfortunately, the civilians' observation posts were not close enough to positively identify any of the mules.

Nevertheless, another group was definitely moving through the tunnel, and Moore assumed they were additional mules come to help transport the weapons.

Ansara was visibly moved by the news, gritting his teeth and swearing under his breath. "I didn't think it'd come to this," he eventually said, his voice cracking. "I was hoping to clean him up, set him back on the straight and narrow. He showed a lot of promise."

"We don't know what happened yet."

"He must've choked."

"He wasn't wired, was he?"

"Just his Bluetooth. Nothing they can detect there. He might've panicked, said something. I don't know yet. Towers was on another call when it happened."

"Just clear your head, buddy, all right?" Moore asked. "It's going to get hot real soon."

Border Tunnel Site
Mexicali, Mexico

"I want you to call Felipe right now and tell him you're safely across. Tell him to release my family."

Romero began to hyperventilate, and he fought to keep his hands from trembling. His thumb rested gently on the detonator's main button, and a small status light glowed green. The red light would illuminate the moment he pushed the button. And about two seconds later, vengeance would be his.

"Pedro, what are you doing?" asked Samad, his gaze focusing on the detonator.

"I'm saving my family."

"And you think this is the way?"

"I know it's the way."

"I don't believe you."

"Did you think the cartel would build a tunnel like this without a way to destroy it? They don't want their enemies taking advantage of all their hard work. Let me show you." Romero shifted over to the wall and removed one of the acoustical panels to reveal several bricks of C-4 explosives. "There are fourteen charges. I supervised their installation myself. They will detonate in succession, sealing the entire tunnel. If we're not killed in the blast, then we'll be buried alive and suffocate before we're rescued."

Samad's eyes widened. "You want to die? You're ready to meet your God?"

Romero steeled his voice. "I'm ready—but I know you're not; that's why you *will* release my family."

"I thought you would be much wiser than this. You're a smart man, an engineer."

"Call Felipe."

"I would have released all of you anyway—did you know that?"

Romero held up the detonator. "I'm ready to do this."

Samad sighed deeply. "You should have trusted us. All we wanted was safe passage into the United States." He lowered his pistol and slipped his cell phone from his pocket. He dialed a number. "Hello, Felipe? Yes, hold on. I want you to talk to Señor Romero and tell him you are releasing his family. Let him talk to them if he'd like . . ."

Samad proffered the phone, and Romero carefully accepted it. "Felipe, please, release my family."

"Okay, señor. Okay. Those are my orders."

Romero took a few breaths, then heard his wife's voice, and his shoulders shrank in relief. He kept the phone to his ear.

Samad pointed to the detonator and gestured for Romero to hand it over.

Romero looked at him. "What are you going to do when you get to the United States?"

Samad began to chuckle. "We're going to eat cheeseburgers and french fries."

"Maybe I shouldn't let you go."

"Do you think Felipe is the only one I've left back at the house? Again, you have to consider the complexity of what I'm doing. Now stop wasting my time. Give it to me."

Romero thought for a few seconds more, then complied. Samad found the power switch, slid it off, then pocketed the detonator and gestured for them to continue. Romero stayed on the phone with Felipe and heard the voices of his daughters as well. They were all right but crying, begging him to come back home.

His wife got on the line. "Pedro? Are you there?"

"I'll be home soon. Let me speak to Felipe." Once the man was on the other end, Romero told him, "You leave my house now. You get out—and take anyone else with you."

"If it is okay with Samad."

"It's okay," said Romero, raising his voice. "Leave now!"

"All right."

Samad raised a pistol to Romero's head. "My phone."

Romero returned the phone and walked on.

They reached the end of the tunnel, and Romero mounted the ladder and emerged inside the master-bedroom closet. There, he shifted back and waited as the Arabs rose, one by one, into the bedroom.

Romero was about to tell Samad he was leaving when a hand suddenly wrapped around his mouth and a low voice came in his ear, "Shhh shhh shhh . . ."

He didn't realize a knife was being driven into his heart until it was already too late: A quick punch and the needling hot pain came quickly, radiating out from his chest.

"Shhh shhh shhh . . ."

He was lowered to the ground and released. He stared up at the dark ceiling until Samad leaned over him. "You've done Allah's work, and you will be rewarded for it. *Allahu Akbar!*"

Romero closed his eyes. He did not want the last thing he saw in this world to be the face of a monster. He imagined his beautiful wife and daughters, knew that his ailing child would receive all she needed, that there was enough money and that he had provided a better life for them. He cried inwardly over having to leave them and over the pain his death would cause.

They were strong women and would continue to fight in this life, as he had. Now he would build himself a new house, engineered using beams of light in the Kingdom of Heaven. And from there, he would wait for them.

Samad turned away from the dying Mexican and faced his group, gesturing to the floor as his phone began to vibrate. "These backpacks will come with us, but leave them on the floor with the launchers for now."

Niazi and Talwar began helping the men slip off the backpacks containing the launchers. The man on the other end of the line was an ally from Afghanistan who said only two words in Pashto: "Two minutes."

"We're ready."

Samad had left one of his men down in the tunnel to be sure they weren't being followed. The man called up to say everything was clear thus far.

His group stood in line, hands clasped behind their backs. They fidgeted nervously, but Samad had faith in their training and in their resolve.

The sirens grew louder, and Samad went to the window and finally spotted the two Calexico police cars, followed by a pair of police vans, lights flashing as they rolled up, and eight officers, weapons drawn, got out and stormed the house.

"Okay, everyone," he began calmly. "We are all under arrest—in the name of Allah."

The front door swung open, and in burst two officers, their

beards closely cropped and their skin as dark as Samad's. "All right, listen to me," the cop said, once more in Pashto. "We wait another minute. Then we march outside with your hands clasped behind your back, as though you are handcuffed. We will take the bags."

"Excellent," said Samad. They were putting on a good show for any of the cartel's spotters, who were most certainly watching the house. Of course, there could be others: enemies of the cartel that included rivals and federal authorities from both countries.

"Moving out now to the vans," said the officer after two more of his colleagues had entered the home from the rear door.

Samad nodded, called down to his man still in the tunnel, then he and the others left with their hands held tightly behind their backs. They were escorted at gunpoint across the street and were helped into the waiting vans. His gaze scanned the rooflines and shrubs of the neighboring homes, and several people stood near their front doors to shake their heads at the "big arrest" on their street.

Next came the backpacks bulging with drugs, and then the six launchers. Within three minutes they were roaring away from the house, with Samad closing his eyes and balling his hands into fists. They'd made it. The jihad had returned to America.

33

HE MUST NEVER
LEARN ABOUT
THE CARTEL

Border Tunnel House
Calexico, California

OORE AND ANSARA parked their pickup truck around the corner from the tunnel house. Before they headed out, Moore received a call from Towers. "Big bust by local Calexico police at the house. Mules taken out, along with what spotters are saying was a huge shipment of drugs. This confirms Rueben's reports. Still following up, but local police deny any involvement. Trying to track the vehicles, but they've all disappeared. Either the Calexico police are in bed with the cartel or this is some pretty damned elaborate shit to rip off those drugs."

"I don't know what to tell you," said Moore. "But we're going in after these guys. Just keep everyone away from this place. I'll call you back."

He and Ansara stole their way around the rows of shrubs and arrived beside the house across the street from the target home. They crouched behind two palm trees. The cartel truck had been backed into the driveway, and one man remained in the cab while the other two had presumably gone inside.

They'd have to enter the house from the back to avoid detection by the guy in the truck. For now, Moore indicated to Ansara that they'd wait. He continually reminded himself that their job was to follow the guys, follow the money trail, not intercept them, even though he and Ansara were champing at the bit to do so, Ansara more so because they'd lost contact with his informant.

They waited five more minutes before the garage door finally opened and the two men appeared in the dim light of a single bulb. The guy who Moore recognized as the driver worked the lock on the truck's back door. The man in the cab climbed out and joined the other two as they transferred the Anvil cases into the garage. Once the truck was unloaded, they tugged down the door.

How long should they wait? Those guys couldn't move all of those weapons in one trip. Five minutes? Ten? It looked as though the blinds had been drawn on the windows.

Ansara signaled to Moore. *Let's move in*. Moore hesitated, then finally nodded.

Rojas Mansion
Cuernavaca, Mexico
56 Miles South of Mexico City

Fernando Castillo entered Señor Rojas's home office, an intimidating monument to the man and his influence, which fell on Mexico like the weather. The people . . . the government . . . All they could really do was adapt to him and his decisions, as Castillo had, although he felt a fierce sense of loyalty to the man who had rescued him from poverty, given him a life of unimaginable wealth, and treated him with more dignity and respect than his own family had.

Castillo stole a glance up at the bookshelves rising more than twenty-five feet and spanning the entire forty-foot back wall. In their shadow rose Rojas's gargantuan mahogany desk, atop which stood no less than four computers whose twenty-seven-inch flat screens formed a half-circle. The desk was, in effect, a cockpit of information flowing in to the man who was leaning back in the plush leather chair he'd bought in Paris and sipping on a glass of Montrachet. Along the left side of the room was a bank of LED TVs permanently tuned to cable financial networks from around the globe. Castillo had recently supervised the installation of those screens, and although that was hardly part of his job as security chief, Rojas had in recent years trusted him with many of his personal tasks and decisions, especially those concerning Miguel.

Rojas raked his fingers through his hair, then finally looked up from one of his screens.

"What can I do for you, Fernando?"

"Sorry to bother you, señor, but I wanted to discuss this in person. Dante's body has still not been found, and the murder at the hotel failed to draw him out. And if you recall, Pablo is also missing, and so is Dante's girlfriend, María."

"Yes, I know, I know—what are you worried about? And why are you bothering me with these trivial details? I pay you very well to handle these things. Find him. He knows he failed to protect my son. He knows the consequences."

"Yes, señor, but this is important, and you should know. We've had trouble at the new tunnel. Another shipment has been stolen."

Rojas drew back his head and frowned. "We lost another one? Are you kidding me?"

"We lost everything. The mules, the police cars, the entire shipment."

"Slow down. Police cars? What are you talking about?"

"Our spotters tell me it looked like a raid on the house by Calexico police, but no one ever saw the police vans arrive at the station. They disappeared while en route."

"That's ridiculous. They switched cars. Who was in charge of following them? I want him killed."

Castillo sighed. "It gets worse. Pedro Romero, our chief

engineer on the project? His family was killed, and we found him dead inside the house, along with another mule in the tunnel. The weapons shipment from Minnesota arrived there, and it was that team that found them. They're getting the weapons through the tunnel right now, but the power was cut."

Rojas rubbed the corners of his eyes, cursed under his breath, then asked, "What do you think?"

Castillo closed his eyes and took a deep breath. "When you got back from Colombia, you told me about your meeting with Samad and what he wanted."

"No, that's not possible," Rojas said quickly. "I warned them, and they'd be fools to test us. Either Dante or Zúñiga stole from us."

"Señor, it's very possible that this Samad used our tunnel to get into the United States."

"I don't believe it."

Castillo grew more emphatic. "When the police carried out the backpacks, the spotters counted six extra bags. The spotters are sure they were not the usual packs—and I'm sure those packs weren't stored in the house by anyone else. They had to come through the tunnel."

"I'll call Samad right now."

"If it's him, he won't answer."

"Then Rahmani must answer for this."

"And if he denies everything?"

Rojas bolted up from his chair, his voice lifting: "Then everything we've built together is in danger."

Castillo recoiled as a chill struck him.

Rojas winced. "Fernando, I'm sorry for shouting. It's just . . . you know I've thought of putting an end to all this. Walking away from it all—and if what you're saying is true . . ."

"I understand, señor. I would still call Rahmani to let him know that he must pay if Samad has entered the United States. Any threat to the cartel must be neutralized."

Rojas stood there, his gaze going distant, as though he were imagining mushroom clouds rising over every major American city. "Our Calexico informants are well paid. Lean on them hard. Find the drivers of those police cars. I want to be certain before we act. Am I clear?"

"As always, señor."

Castillo left the office. He'd planned to share with Rojas one other bit of news, but the man already had enough on his mind. Miguel was doing some probing around the house and on the Internet, and of course this wasn't the first time that he'd tried to spy on his father. Occasionally a news report would come out that attempted to link Señor Rojas to investment fraud or real estate scams or even vote tampering during several elections, and while Miguel would always openly stand behind his father, Castillo knew that the young man still had his doubts. The recent attempt on his father's life had probably rekindled his curiosity. Castillo would have a long talk with Miguel to once more allay his suspicions. On this point, Señor Rojas had been adamant.

He must never learn about the cartel.

Border Tunnel House
Calexico, California

Moore's senses were already reaching into the house as he opened the back door as silently as he could and stepped into a small washroom. Beyond it was a narrow hall with two bedroom doors and a third door farther up. Ansara moved ahead, pistol drawn, and turned left down another hall, toward where the garage door should be. Meanwhile, Moore searched the first two bedrooms for the tunnel entrance. Just some cheap put-together Walmart furniture and old mattresses standing atop stained carpeting. Ansara met him back in the hallway to say, "They've only moved half the cases so far. They'll be coming back for the rest."

He'd barely finished when the sound of footfalls came from the master bedroom.

They ducked back into one of the smaller rooms and stood there, behind the door, not daring to breathe, as the men shifted across the hallway and back out toward the garage door.

Moore was back in a zone of calm, standing there behind the door, just looking at Ansara, who'd given up on holding his own breath. The man's chest rose and fell, his breath coming louder. Moore raised a palm, as if to say, *Take it easy*.

Ansara nodded quickly.

The men lumbered back from the garage with the rest of the cases and crossed into the bedroom. The sound of shuffling feet and metal buckling tightened Moore's frown.

He held up a finger. *Wait . . . wait . . .* He lifted his smartphone and sent off a text to Towers: In house, about to enter the tunnel. Weapons moving through. Stand by . . .

A sharp nod to Ansara said it was time to go. They shifted gingerly out of the bedroom and crossed into the master, where, near the closet door, they found a man lying on his back, his shirt soaked in blood. Ansara leaned over him, then drew back his head and whispered, "I know this guy. I mean, I know who he is. Pedro Romero. He was the engineer on this project. He had contact with my mule." Ansara's expression grew darker. "Dude, we got some wild-card shit happening here. Sinaloas . . . who knows . . ."

Why they'd killed the engineer remained to be seen. While Ansara took pictures of the dead man and messaged them back to Towers, Moore inspected the tunnel entrance set into the closet. They would gain access via an aluminum ladder someone had picked up at the local Home Depot for $89.99 plus tax (the sticker was still affixed to the top).

Ansara motioned that he'd go first. The ladder protested, and Moore winced. He reached the bottom some eight feet below. Moore followed, and together they started down the shaft. Despite the rather crude entry, the shaft itself was an engineering marvel. Using penlights they'd drawn from their breast pockets and keeping their pistols at the ready, they picked up the pace. Moore rapped a knuckle on one of the acoustic panels and grew further impressed. They had strung up LED lights, which were now dark, had hung ventilation and electrical pipes, and what could be a drainage pipe ran along the floor, which was still dirt but swept and leveled with great precision. The tunnel was, Moore speculated, one of the most complex and audacious smuggling operations that had ever been constructed by any cartel.

Flickering light came from ahead, and for a few seconds Ansara froze, believing the light was headed toward them, but they resumed their pace and shifted left to find what Moore interpreted as a makeshift chapel built within a shallow side tunnel that terminated in a wall of wooden trusses bound together by aluminum straps. The candles and crucifixes and photographs stole his attention away from the floor, where Ansara was first to spot the body.

"It's the kid," he gasped, just as Moore noted a pair of furrows in the dirt caused by the kid's heels as he'd been dragged from behind.

Ansara dropped to his knees and directed his light at the boy's eyes. Damn, the mule was young. Stabbed. His life snuffed out in an instant.

Suddenly, Ansara put his ear to the boy's mouth. "Shit, he's still breathing!"

"Yeah, but buddy, we can't stay," Moore insisted. "They could be gone already. And all we got is one guy's cell to track. He turns off that phone, and we're screwed."

Ansara nodded, then faced Rueben. "I know, I know, but look, he's trying to say something. Who did this to you, Rueben? Who did this?"

Moore slid up beside Ansara and watched as the kid, his eyes narrowed to slits, moved his mouth, but he couldn't muster the words.

"Hang in there, kid," said Moore. "We'll come back for you, I promise."

The kid reached up and grabbed Moore's wrist.

"Just relax, don't strain yourself," said Ansara. "You don't worry."

Moore pulled free and started off. A look back told him Ansara was right there, though his eyes were glassy, his breathing even more labored. Ansara wore the guilt on his face, and Moore knew exactly how he felt.

Rueben was screaming in his mind, but he lacked the strength to convert those thoughts to sounds that the FBI agent could understand: *They blackmailed Pedro. Arabs came through the tunnel! Terrorists! And they stabbed me! They stabbed me! Now they're in the United States. They made it. Don't leave me here. I'm going to die.*

The thoughts were too quick, too disorganized, too erratic, for him to dwell on any longer. He heard Ansara telling his mother that he'd been killed.

"I'm so sorry about your son."

His death would be enough of a shock, but add to that his involvement with a drug cartel and the FBI? He wasn't sure his mother could survive that news.

And that was all he could think about now, not even realizing that he was no longer breathing and that the candlelight had gone dark.

———

The man had not identified himself on the phone, but José understood what was happening, and the sudden arrival of four more cars and at least a dozen more *sicarios* told him that whoever this guy was, he had his connections and that José had best listen to his orders.

"But remember," José told him. "I am El Jefe. Corrales is gone now."

"Yeah, okay, kid, fine. Now you do exactly as I ask. You're inside the trailer, right? Do you see the safe under the desk?"

"Yeah, I see it."

"Get down in there. Hit the power button. Type in 43678009, then hit the pound key. Got it?"

Jose did as he was told, screwed up the number, had to ask for it again, then finally got it right and heard a click. The safe opened, and he gasped as the light of his phone revealed its contents. The top shelf was crammed with bound stacks of U.S. dollars in denominations of twenties and fifties. He began stuffing them into the pockets of his leather trench coat, the one he'd bought after seeing how cool Corrales looked in his.

"Are you done stealing the cash yet?"

José shuddered. "I haven't touched the money."

"Okay, I believe you," said the man with a snort. "See the walkie-talkie in there?"

"Yeah."

"That's not a walkie-talkie. Once the weapons team gets

the guns through, you send them back into the tunnel, then you blow it while they're still inside. Just power on and jam down the big red button. Can you do this for me, José? Are you fucking smart enough? Because if you are, you can keep all the money."

"I'll get it done. But who are you?"

"I'm Fernando. I am your boss. I work for Los Caballeros. And you are a gentleman just like me. That's all."

A wooden staircase constructed of two-by-fours and plywood lay at the far end of the tunnel, where the sound-dampening panels broke off and the ground rose about two feet. Dim light flickered from above, from either flashlights or something else. Moore thought he heard voices, faint but there, and the sound of a metal door clinking steadily as it was rolled open.

Holding his breath once more, and with Ansara still at his back, he slowly ascended the stairs, peered up past the ledge that was in effect the floor, and realized the entrance had been set within some kind of maintenance/electrical/plumbing room lined with pumps and lockers and other construction and custodial equipment. The door ahead was open, allowing him to gaze farther out into a large warehouse with at least a twenty-foot ceiling. Pallets of construction materials—cinder blocks, bags of concrete, stacks of rebar—were lined up in long rows to the right and left, but dead ahead stood a group of men and the

Anvil cases containing the weapons, which were being loaded into the back of a Ford Explorer.

Moore turned back down to Ansara, widened his gaze, and motioned for him to hold.

And when Moore turned back, lifting his head just a little higher to get a better view, a thug with a goatee and sideburns that formed a chinstrap suddenly turned into the room—

"Hey, what the fuck?" he shouted, gaping at Moore. "Who are you?"

"We're with those guys," Moore answered quickly.

"Bullshit!" The guy spun back toward the others. "José!"

Just then Moore's phone began to vibrate, and Ansara shouted, "Towers called. They've got a big group outside!"

Moore put two rounds in the screamer's back, then faced Ansara. "Run!"

José broke away from the group as his man Tito collapsed onto his belly. Beyond him was the tunnel entrance, and he couldn't see who'd shot his man but guessed it was someone who'd come up from the tunnel.

Breaking into a sprint, he hollered back to the three men who'd delivered the weapons, then burst into the maintenance room, searching the areas behind the pumps until he reached the tunnel entrance and the others arrived breathlessly behind him.

José gestured with his pistol. "Get down in there. Clear it out. I want the fucker who did this."

All three were armed with their *mata policías* and hustled down the stairs.

His heart racing, José ran back to the others and screamed for them to hurry loading the weapons and that he'd join them in a minute.

Catch your breath, he ordered himself, as he shifted away from the SUV and turned his back on the group. He pulled the detonator from his pocket and switched on the power. The green light cast a glow across his face, and for a few seconds he just stared at it, hypnotized by the light.

And then, imagining that the weapons team was now about a thousand feet into the shaft, he began to chuckle, heady with the power in his hands.

Rojas Mansion
Cuernavaca, Mexico
56 Miles South of Mexico City

Sonia waited at the door while Miguel entered the office and cleared his throat. His father glanced up from the desk and said, "Miguel, I'm sorry, I'm working late tonight and I'm extremely busy right now. Is there something wrong?"

"I want to see the vaults in the basement," he blurted out.

"What?"

"Take me to the basement right now. Show me what you have in the vaults down there."

His father finally glanced up from his computer screens and frowned. "Why?"

Miguel could not bear to utter the truth. "I just . . . I've never been down there. I thought I'd show Sonia. But you have a guard there—all the time."

"Fine, then. Let's go now."

"Are you serious? You always say no. How many times have I asked you? At least twenty times over the years?"

"Okay, so now I'll show you." He bolted from his chair and stormed past Miguel, wrenched open the door, and startled Sonia, who was texting her father on her smartphone.

"Did you want the tour as well?" his father snapped.

"I'm sorry, señor. We didn't mean to disturb you."

His father raised a palm and stormed down the hall.

Miguel gave Sonia a worried glance, then hustled after the man.

They reached the twin doors leading to the broad staircase, and his father ordered the guard to unlock the doors and allow them to pass. "Turn off the alarms as well," he said.

He tossed a glance back at Miguel. "I know what this is about. And I'm disappointed."

Miguel bit his lip and averted his gaze. His father stomped past the door held open by the guard, and Miguel and Sonia got on his heels.

The staircase was heavily carpeted in a deep burgundy and turned onto two separate landings before reaching the bottom. Lights set into the ceiling controlled via motion sensors automatically clicked on as they shifted ahead across an ornately tiled floor. Behind them was a garage that again Miguel had never seen. There were at least ten antique automobiles and a lift to carry them up to a ramp leading outside. Miguel thought it amusing and not surprising that the basement of their house was as well decorated as the rest of the mansion.

Two vaults like the ones you'd find in neighborhood banks stood side by side on the far end. Both doors were shut. His father approached a control panel to the right side of one vault. He typed in a code, rested his hand on a dark piece of glass. A light shone in his eye; then he moved his hand to another device, where he inserted his index finger. A computer voice said, "Sampling." He withdrew the finger, now spotted with blood, and licked it.

The vault door thumped several times, then hissed open, as though propelled by air.

"Go on in. Have a look, while I open the other one," his father said.

Miguel motioned to Sonia, and they shifted past the giant door and into the vault, which stretched back at least twenty meters and was equally wide. Hundreds of pieces of art stood in rows on the floor or on easels, while in the far corner were at least twenty, perhaps even thirty, pieces of handmade furniture, desks and chests of drawers and armoires Miguel remembered seeing his father purchase but had forgotten about. More guns like the ones he collected in the vacation house were sitting on two long tables, with others tucked tightly in their cases stacked on the floor beside them. From a series of long poles to their immediate left hung twenty or more exotic rugs his father had no doubt purchased in Asia, the documentation for each still pinned in the corners. Still another series of humidity-controlled

glass cases held collections of his father's rarest pre-1900 litera-
ture, first editions that Miguel knew were worth a fortune.
Sonia gazed in wonder at the items while Miguel turned back
to the door, where his father had appeared.

His father's tone turned accusatory. "What were you expecting?"

"I don't know."

"You don't trust me anymore, do you?"

"Um, if you'd like me to leave, can I go into the other vault?"
asked Sonia, shifting her weight awkwardly from side to side.

"No, that's okay, you stay," said Miguel, hardening his tone
just a little. "I think maybe the issue is that you don't trust me.
If you've had nothing to hide, then why didn't you show me this
place years ago?"

"Because I wanted you to trust me. You have no idea how
important that is. Don't dismiss it. Do you want to see the
other vault?"

"It's just more of the same, huh?"

"I need another house to display all of this. Your mother
always said my eyes were too big for my stomach, and that ap-
plies to my purchases as well."

Miguel realized at that moment that he'd been wasting his
time. If his father really wanted to conceal something from him,
he wouldn't have done it as obviously as saying *No, you can't see
what's in the vaults*. Moreover, he only incited the man. But he
still had his doubts. "I'm sorry."

"Miguel, I want nothing but the best for you. There's nothing illegal about what I do. The newspapers will print anything

to sell copies and sell advertising. They've called me a criminal for years, but you've seen what I've tried to do in our country, how much I've tried to give back. I am sincere about that. Your mother taught me more than you know about how to open my heart."

Miguel looked to Sonia, who was pursing her lips and nodding.

"Then I have to ask you something. Before they killed Raúl, he begged them, said the cartel would pay anything. If he worked for us, then why would he ask the cartel to pay?"

His father shrugged. "I don't know. Fernando recruits many of those people himself. I have no doubt that some may have once belonged to the cartel, and we save them from that life."

Miguel took a deep breath. "If I ask you something, will you promise to tell me the truth?"

His father nodded.

"Are you doing business with the drug cartels?"

His father grinned weakly and looked away. "No, of course not."

"All right, then. I'm sorry."

His father began to choke up. He moved suddenly toward Miguel and hugged him deeply. "You are my only son. You are my world. You have to believe in me."

The lie caused a deep and terrible pain to wake in Rojas's heart, and that pain took him to a place where his murdered brother stared back at him with a weird reflection in his eyes and his wife lay motionless in her casket, her beautiful skin now alabaster and lifeless. The lie was death itself.

As he embraced his son, he fought to leave that place, tried to convince himself that he was not, in a sense, murdering them both by keeping the secret, that it was all for the boy's own good.

But the pain was so great that he wished he could take Miguel and Sonia to the back of the vault, open the well-disguised panel doors there, and show his son the second vault—the vault within the vault—where millions in American dollars were waiting to be laundered . . .

He should be the one to confess his sins. Miguel should not have to learn from a second party.

But another part of Rojas argued staunchly against that. Everything should be as always. His wife had never learned the ugly truth, and neither should his son.

Rojas released his son and stared deeply into the boy's eyes as a chill rippled across his shoulders.

Yes, the lie was death.

34

THE HAND
OF FATIMA

Border Tunnel
Calexico–Mexicali

I T WASN'T THAT Moore regretted his decision to flee back into the tunnel. After all, he'd received two simultaneous pieces of information and had reacted to them in an instant: (1) they'd been spotted, and (2) a large group was inside the warehouse.

Fight or flight.

What frustrated him most was that the mission to follow the money was over. The trail had ended the second that punk had spotted them. He tried to convince himself that there was nothing they could've done differently. It was simply a matter of bad timing (flashback to Somalia and that fiasco, wherein they sent him in a few days late and a dollar short). Sure, he and

Ansara would tell Towers about the Ford Explorer, and they'd track the vehicle with their eyes in the sky and Towers's civilian informants, perhaps even get permission to intercept it and seize the weapons and maybe even confiscate the cash, but Moore had been counting on identifying a much more definitive link between the cartel and Jorge Rojas, at least via one of Rojas's businesses.

Ansara was sprinting up the tunnel, increasing the gap, but Moore was beginning to slow as he heard the thundering boots of men coming down the staircase behind them. He stopped, spun around, and dropped onto his belly as, lit by the flickering light from the tunnel entrance, a figure rushed forward, arm extended. For just a heartbeat Moore glimpsed his assailant's face: the cartel truck's driver.

Propped up on his elbows now, Moore fired once into the figure's chest, the round booting him sideways into the panels before he fell onto his back.

From behind him came two more men, the rest of the weapons-transfer crew, their Belgian-made cop-killer pistols flashing, the shots booming through the tunnel as one 5.7x28-millimeter round struck the pipe near Moore's elbow.

Their winking muzzles betrayed their positions, and drawing deeply on decades of experience—and his rage—he targeted the first man, delivered a pair of rounds into his chest, then panned slightly to the right and unloaded his magazine into the second guy, who staggered backward as though he were being electrocuted.

As Moore ejected his magazine and scrambled to his feet,

about to turn back toward Ansara, the far end of the tunnel vanished.

Just like that.

That faint beam of shifting light that had fallen on the wooden staircase had been extinguished in a nanosecond, replaced by a huge wall of earth and dust, accompanied by an explosion that originated from both sides of the wall, sending a blast wave of dirt and rocks and pieces of support beams boomeranging through the shaft.

Moore was intimately familiar with the sound of cyclotri-methylene trinitramine, or C-4 plastic explosives, and as the debris began to pelt him, a second explosion hammered behind him, this one much closer, the ground rumbling more violently, and then a third explosion thundered through the first two, this one even closer, as he whirled back and sprinted, echoing his first admonishment to Ansara: "Run!" That cry was all reflex and reaction; Ansara didn't need any more motivation.

Even as he shifted past the turns, believing that each ninety-degree angle would further protect him, more detonations tore apart the tunnel, timed to blow in succession and drawing nearer. Up on his right lay the little sanctuary flickering in candlelight. As he passed, he saw Ansara trying to lift Rueben into a fireman's carry.

Moore cursed but kept running. "Forget him! We gotta go!"

"He's still not dead!"

The next explosion occurred so closely that Moore thought

his eardrums had been blown out. The dust clouds and debris wave filled the tunnel now, dousing the candles and cutting off Ansara as he begged for another second.

Gasping and blinded, Moore ran forward, unsure if his partner was behind him. He banged straight into the ladder as an explosion near where the acoustic panels terminated loosed a wall of dirt that collapsed around him, the musty earth hissing like a chorus of snakes and burying him up to his waist as dust clouds billowed into his face.

He took a breath, tasted the gritty dirt, coughed hard, then tried to breathe again, blinking hard against the burn in his eyes. He tried to turn around, but his legs were pinned by the dirt. He screamed Ansara's name, but there were easily thousands of pounds of debris between him and his colleague. He screamed again, beat his fists into the fresh piles of sand, knowing that Ansara and the kid were suffocating and there wasn't a goddamned thing he could do about it. He dug past the dirt and into his pocket, barely noticing the blood dripping down his arm. He took hold of his smartphone, but his hand trembled so badly that he dropped it. Fighting for breath and coughing yet again, he picked up the phone and dialed Towers. "They blew the fucking tunnel. Ansara's buried. I'm stuck in here, too. Do you hear me? They blew the tunnel . . ."

"I hear you. A team's coming."

"Fuck. They spotted us."

"They get off with the weapons?"

"I think so. Black Ford Explorer. Probably leaving the warehouse. Check with your spotters."

"Got it. Now, Moore, you just sit tight. Help's on the way. And I'm coming down there myself."

It took him another five minutes to free one of his legs, and by the time he was able to lift that leg in an attempt to wriggle out of the hole, he heard a group moving into the bedroom and a voice he didn't recognize shouting his name.

"Down here!" he cried.

A flashlight blinded him for a second until the man holding it doused the beam.

Moore glanced up into the eyes of a guy wearing the black helmet and black fatigues of an FBI task force. The guy shouldered his rifle. "Holy shit!"

Moore just looked at him. "Hurry up. My buddy's down here with a kid. He's buried. They can't breathe."

"Aw, Jesus . . ."

Within ten minutes Moore was free and climbing the ladder, groaning over the pain in his arm as he tried to cling to the rungs. Metal fragments from one of the trusses had torn through his shirt and lodged themselves in his biceps. The wound was nothing. He couldn't take his mind off Ansara, and as he stood there in the bedroom, pacing, wanting to get back down there and dig through the sand with his bare hands, one of the task force members came back up the ladder and said, "We'll need a goddamned Bobcat to get them out."

Moore leaned back on the bedroom wall, cursing and grimacing again over the dirt in his mouth. He held his breath and took himself back into the tunnel, through all that dirt and into a tiny depression where Ansara lay, taking his final few breaths. Moore shuddered. Wanted to scream. Then he just stormed out of the house, slamming the door behind him.

Maybe he was just cursed. That was it. If you hung around him long enough, you'd wind up dead. How much more of this could he take? How many ghosts could populate his head?

He found Towers getting out of an unmarked car across the street. "Let's get you out of here."

Moore glanced back at the house. "Not till they get him out."

"All right, just take it easy."

Moore turned away and marched back toward the house. Other units were arriving, and the entire street would be cordoned off. Welcome to the circus, a police and first-responder big top lorded over by spotters from the FBI and the drug cartels, along with nosy neighbors, kids running around in diapers, and a host of stray cats and dogs.

Moore and Towers returned to the bedroom, where down in the tunnel several agents were clearing away debris with their hands and the butts of their rifles until an excavation crew could arrive.

"He was going to teach me how to ride a mountain bike, did you know that?" Moore asked Towers. "He told me I really sucked."

Towers shook his head. "Don't do it, buddy. Don't torture yourself."

"He's dying in there right now."

Towers hardened his tone. "Are you listening to me?"

The excavation team didn't reach Ansara and Rueben until nearly one p.m. the following day, and while Moore had been coaxed away from the scene by Towers and had gone to a hotel to take a shower and get some fresh clothes, he'd returned and waited there until both his colleague and the young mule were taken out and set down on the bedroom floor. Ansara's face and most of the left side of his body had been peppered with shrapnel, so there was a good chance he'd died in the explosion. Rueben, meanwhile, had probably been shielded by Ansara and had only his major stab wound.

One of the kid's hands was balled tightly in a fist, while the other was limp, and that struck Moore as a little odd. He dropped to his knees and delicately pried open the kid's hand to find a gold pendant covered in dirt.

Moore breathed another curse, because he knew exactly what he was looking at: an eighteen-karat-gold Hamsa, a Middle Eastern symbol also called the Hand of Fatima, named after the daughter of the prophet Mohammed. The pendant was shaped like the back of a human hand and included delicate filigree work that suggested lace. It was worn by Muslims to ward off the evil eye.

The tunnel had been dark. Moore and Ansara had never noticed Rueben's other hand. He'd grabbed Moore and had been desperately trying to tell him something, perhaps give him something.

Moore closed his eyes and squeezed the pendant tightly between his fingertips.

Farmacias Nacional
Avenida Benito Juárez, near the Santa Fe Bridge
Juárez, Mexico

Pablo Gutiérrez had murdered an FBI agent in Calexico during a mission to help Pedro Romero scout out homes for the workers on the Juárez Cartel's new tunnel project. The agent had confronted them, pretending to be a *sicario*, but he hadn't realized that his cover had already been blown and that Pablo knew exactly who he was. While Romero watched, Pablo had duct-taped the man to a chair inside one of the houses the cartel owned near the border fence.

The agent had been full of bravado and had pretended that he did not work for the U.S. government, even after Pablo removed both of his pinkies with a pair of hedge clippers he'd found in the garage. The blades were caked with rust and dull. After two more fingers were removed from the federal agent's right hand, he began to babble like a little boy, confessing all he knew about the cartel's operations in the area—or at least his story sounded good enough. Pablo didn't care either way. His job, according to Corrales, was to kill, not interrogate, the man, but he thought he'd have a little fun first. Pablo thanked the agent, then lifted an ax to the man's neck and made a few practice swings while Romero turned away and put a hand to his face.

The agent released a bloodcurdling cry as Pablo raised the ax and told him to be still.

It took five solid blows before the man's head toppled to the floor. Pablo had never before seen that much blood, and there was a strange odor coming from the body, almost like raw seafood.

He ordered Romero to help him carry the chair and body out to the curb as though they were putting out the trash and recyclables. He pinned a sign on the headless corpse: *FBI Agents Leave Calexico Now.*

They mailed the head to the J. Edgar Hoover Building in Washington, D.C., the headquarters of the FBI, but it wouldn't arrive for three to five days. However, less than an hour later, neighbors coming home from work spotted the grisly sight at the curb, and within minutes after Pablo left, units were on the scene.

That night, Pablo had laughed his ass off as he'd watched the story on CNN, with tickers flashing ridiculously obvious statements, such as "Trending: Mexican drug war crosses border into the United States." Did they think it would never happen? What kind of fantasy land were the Americans living in? *Dumb fuckers.*

That was the night that Pablo had become a wanted man in the United States because a teenage boy had photographed him near the house and had surrendered that picture to the American authorities (Pablo had killed that kid as well). Now he realized that those were the good old days, and that his involvement with Corrales and Los Caballeros and the cartel tore at him from both sides.

He'd agonized over where his loyalty should lie: to Corrales, his immediate boss, the man who'd taught him everything and had made him a trusted right hand, rescuing him from a life of mowing lawns as an eighteen-year-old illegal immigrant in Las Vegas . . . or Fernando Castillo, the man whose identity Pablo had only recently learned and who had been repeatedly calling Pablo. That he'd finally decided to answer one of the calls was a well-kept secret from Corrales, who had cloistered all of them away in a pair of apartments above Farmacias Nacional.

Corrales had said that the cartel would not find them because they were unaware of his friendship with the apartment owner, and Pablo believed him. The owner of the pharmacy, also one of Corrales's friends, ran a prescription-drug-smuggling operation to foil U.S. customs regulations that stated you could carry only the amount of a prescription for personal use back into the United States and that you needed a copy of the prescription. The pharmacist had partnered with a doctor, and together they wrote and sold thousands of dollars' worth of falsified prescriptions that moved across the border. They were small-time smugglers but proud of their business, and thus far not a single one of their mules had been caught—a remarkable record. Corrales had laughed at them, because what the cartel smuggled was worth millions.

Dante Corrales wouldn't be laughing for much longer, though.

"Where are you going?" the man asked, sitting on the sofa in a tank shirt and jeans, a bottle of Pacífico propped on his knee. He'd been on that sofa for the past few days, watching soap operas, going into rages, then calming down. His left arm was still in a sling, the bandages on his shoulder changed daily.

"I'm going to get some lunch," Pablo told him.

"Get enough for all of us, okay?"

"Okay."

Pablo shuddered and headed out into the hallway. He entered the stairwell, reached the first floor, and when he opened the back door leading into the alley behind the pharmacy, Fernando Castillo's men were already waiting. Three of them. They wore long jackets to conceal their weapons.

"He's up there?" asked one of them, a young punk named José who had once challenged Corrales during a smuggling run in Nogales and who Castillo said was now taking over the gang.

Pablo nodded. "There are two cameras. Look for them. And God forgive me."

"God has nothing to do with this," said José. "Nothing at all . . ."

Pablo walked away and dialed the number. "It's me."

"Are they going up?" asked Castillo.

"Yes."

"Good. Remember. I want to see a picture of the body."

"You don't even want to talk to him?"

"What good would that do?"

"Maybe he's sorry. Maybe he'll pay you back."

"Oh, he'll pay us back. With interest. Right now."

Corrales rose and went to the bedroom, where María was still lying sideways across the bed, still wearing her negligee and reading one of her fashion magazines. Her panties rode high up her ass, and for a second or two, Corrales thought of jumping on her, but she'd fight him off, piss and moan like the depressed bitch she'd become, and he'd tell her once more to be patient, that Zúñiga would come around, that he'd take them in as allies and finally be convinced that he could help them. They had plenty of money to live off for now, but they wouldn't dare go near the hotel to get any more out of the safe there. Those fuckers had already killed Ignacio, and Castillo was watching the place twenty-four-seven for Corrales's return.

Corrales saw no way to survive other than to join the rival cartel. He needed protection, because Fernando had the manpower and the money to hunt him no matter where in the world he chose to hide. Deep down he knew he would one day turn his back on the cartel that had murdered his parents. He had used it for all it was worth. His reckless decision to use the cartel's money to finance his hotel restoration instead of paying off the Guatemalans was probably born in his subconscious. He wanted to get caught. He wanted things to go south so that he'd be forced to get out. That's why he'd prepared for this day by spending years gathering crucial information: the identities of suppliers and smugglers around the world, including their main contacts, Ballesteros in Colombia and Rahmani in Waziristan; bank account numbers and deposit receipts; and recordings of phone calls and copies of e-mail messages that could incriminate both Castillo and Rojas himself. Corrales would offer Zúñiga inside information on the workings of the Juárez Cartel so that he could help the man he once hated take over operations in the city.

But Zúñiga had thus far failed to answer any of his calls. Corrales had even sent Pablo to his house, and the man would send out his thugs and tell Pablo to leave or suffer the consequences.

Corrales had set up two wireless battery-powered surveillance cameras around the apartment and pharmacy: one in the hall outside their apartment door, the other in the main stairwell leading up from the back alley door. The small monitor that sat on the bar near the kitchen sink showed static, and Corrales caught that screen from the corner of his eye. He swore and dragged himself from the sofa to investigate the problem.

That his FN 5.7 pistol was lying on the counter beside the monitor was the only reason why they didn't kill him immediately.

A shuffle of feet just outside the front door caught his attention. He reached for the gun.

José, the little rat that Corrales had trained himself, kicked in the door and leveled his gun on Corrales, who was already bringing his pistol around.

There was a half-second of recognition and an almost guilt-stricken sheen appearing in José's eyes before he yelled Corrales's name.

Corrales fired once—a lightning-fast headshot—as two

more bastards rushed in behind José, but Corrales was already ducking away, behind the bar, taking good cover. José hit the floor, a gaping wound above his left eye.

María screamed from the bedroom, and one of the guys broke off and ran down the hall.

Corrales hollered her name, drawing fire from the other guy, who'd dodged into the living room and thrown himself behind the sofa. Corrales burst from behind the bar, and releasing a cry that came from deep within his gut, he rounded the sofa and came face-to-face with the punk, who took one look at him and lifted his gun in surrender.

He was sixteen, if that. Corrales shot him twice in the face. María screamed his name.

Two shots rang out. Corrales bounded into the bedroom, just as the last *sicario*, a heavily tattooed guy with a potbelly whom Corrales had never seen before, turned toward him.

It took but a fraction of a second for Corrales to see María splayed across the bed with blood seeping through her negligee. She mouthed his name.

Then two things happened at once.

The guy cried, "Fuck you, *vato*!" and lifted his pistol.

Corrales opened his mouth, rocked by the sight of his woman lying there, dying, as he jammed down the trigger of his pistol while rushing toward the guy, thrusting the gun into the guy's chest as though it were a sword, the last two rounds muted as they slammed into his flesh, the muzzle burning the guy's shirt even as he fired two rounds into the ceiling. The guy crashed backward into the flat-screen television, knocking it onto the floor as he tumbled and landed facedown on the carpeting. The stench of gunpowder and burned fabric and flesh was enough to make Corrales gag.

Shouts came from the hallway outside, Paco the pharmacist, along with his wife, screaming for their two sons to get out of the apartment next door.

Corrales stood there, his chest rising and falling, the very act of breathing almost too painful to bear. He choked up, and tears that had been held back for years finally stained his cheeks as he climbed onto the bed and put his hand on María's face. He was trembling now, lip quivering, his thoughts swirling in a vortex of anger as he flicked a glance at the dead *sicario* and fired three more times, but his pistol clicked uselessly. What now? Another magazine. There could be more of them outside. He tore off his sling and, with a dull ache in his shoulder, raced back into the kitchen, reloaded his gun, then returned to scoop María into his arms and carry her out of the apartment, the shoulder now on fire, his pistol clenched in his hand.

The pharmacist was screaming at him as he hit the stairwell and made it outside, but when he turned back to where he usually parked his car in the alley, he found it there—with Pablo leaning on the hood.

"We just got hit!" he cried. "Get in the car! We have to leave now!"

But Pablo just looked at him, stunned, then reached back into his waistband and drew his pistol.

No, Corrales hadn't seen this coming, and the betrayal robbed him of breath. He turned away, back toward the door, while trying to get his arm high enough so he could fire at the young man he'd called a trusted friend.

Pablo got off the first round, but it struck María; then Corrales fired two shots as Pablo started around the car, trying to duck behind the trunk. One round caught him in the abdomen, the other in the arm. He slumped to the ground, groaning, lifting his pistol again, and Corrales squeezed off two more shots that drummed into Pablo's chest. He staggered to the car, reached it, set María on the ground, and, weeping once more, he opened the back door and strained to drag his dead girlfriend into the backseat. Once he got her inside, he climbed into the driver's seat and fired up the engine. The sirens were wailing in the distance as he left rubber on the pavement and a cloud of exhaust fumes pouring over Pablo's body.

Zúñiga Ranch House
Juárez, Mexico

Spotters from the Juárez Cartel were watching Corrales drive up the dirt road toward Zúñiga's house, and there wasn't anything he could do about them. The two men had been posted in the small apartment complex where the turnoff toward the dirt road began, and he noted them on the rooftop. They, in turn, were being watched by Zúñiga's men, who were no doubt positioned along the fence perimeter, in a dirt parking lot beside a detached shed on the north side of the house.

With a dust trail clearly marking his path, Corrales roared up to Zúñiga's newly repaired front gates—the ones he'd blown up that night to send a message to his rival. He rushed out of the car, grabbed María, and carried her toward the gate, looking up into the security camera and screaming, "Zúñiga! They killed my woman! They killed her! You have to talk to me. Please! You have to talk to me!"

He fell to his knees and began to sob into María's bloody chest.

And then something thumped and motors began to whine. He looked up through the tears as the wrought-iron gates parted, and up ahead, far down the long paved driveway, came Zúñiga himself, flanked by two guards.

35

REVELATIONS AND RESERVE

DEA Office of Diversion Control
San Diego, California

MOORE WAS SITTING in a cubicle he'd borrowed from one of the diversion investigators who was in a meeting. Moore had never been in this area of the building, where the special agents, chemists, pharmacologists, and program analysts had set up shop. Their mission was extensive, to coordinate operations with Homeland Security and the DEA's own El Paso Intelligence Center. Computerized monitoring and tracking of the distribution of controlled substances was all in an effort to provide tactical intelligence to their partners. They even drafted and proposed congressional legislation from this location. It was an impressive collection of experts—an office bustling with round-the-clock activity because, as Moore had overheard one analyst say, "The cartels never sleep."

And neither did the Taliban.

The pendant Moore had taken from Rueben's hand had already been turned over to one of the Agency's mobile labs, which had arrived thirty minutes prior. The techs inside the step van were using a new rapid DNA analysis platform that was fully automated; it had been developed by the Center for Applied NanoBioscience and Medicine at the University of Arizona College of Medicine. The techs were running the samples through multiple national databases, including the DEA's and the FBI's, as well as international lists such as Interpol's (whose members included Pakistan and Afghanistan), so that within a few hours they'd have results—instead of the weeks or months sometimes required in the past. A new security consortium established through the European Commission's Seventh Framework program (which, among many other things, bundled together all research related to European Union initiatives) was helping to fund the project, which could, in turn, lead to the creation of an even more accurate and comprehensive criminal database.

And therein resided the problem. DNA analysis would reveal his prints, Rueben's, but he doubted that any of the terrorists that he suspected had passed through the tunnel would have samples on record. The techs said they could run an "ancestry test" developed by DNAPrint Genomics of Sarasota, Florida, that would examine tiny genetic markers on the DNA molecule that were often common among people of certain groups. If they had a good sample, they said, they could tell if a suspect's heritage was Native American, Southeast Asian, sub-Saharan African, European, or even a mix of those. Traits such as skin pigmentation, eye color, hair color, facial geometry, and height could be predicted through analysis of DNA sequences.

Moore had argued with Towers, who'd told him that the pendant alone was not enough proof that terrorists had passed through and that perhaps Rueben had bought it from someone and had been using it as a good-luck charm. He'd been stabbed and perhaps held the pendant in his hand to try to ward off death. Towers had gone on to point out that lots of young Mexicans (and young Americans along the border, for that matter) had a keen fascination with terrorists and terrorism. Some mules had even shown up in jail with tattoos in Farsi on their forearms, though investigations to try to definitively link them to terrorist organizations such as Hezbollah and others repeatedly turned up empty. They were just kids who'd turned from *Scarface* to an even more ruthless "hero."

Moore had told him that if Ansara was still alive, he'd agree that terrorists had come through the tunnel. Ansara knew the kid. There was no fascination with Middle Eastern thugs. Somehow the kid had acquired the pendant, whose bail contained scratches, as though it had been hung from a chain and been wrenched from someone's neck. That was Moore's belief, and he called Deputy Director O'Hara at the Special Activities Division to share his thoughts. O'Hara said he'd take it as high as the President if Moore was that certain, but at the very least Homeland Security's four mega-centers in Michigan, Colorado, Pennsylvania, and Maryland (whose analysts were already monitoring the joint task force's activities) had been alerted of the possible breach. The threat level for all domestic and international flights was already at orange/high, and O'Hara would argue to have the national threat level raised from yellow/ elevated to orange as well.

Search teams from both the FBI and the CIA had already been deployed to find those police cars and vans. Meanwhile, Moore said he'd call his best contact in the tribal lands to see what the old man in North Waziristan knew.

He was about to do that when he received a text message from Leslie. She wanted to know why he hadn't replied to several of her messages. He just sighed. If he chatted with her now, his depression would seep through, and he'd rather have no contact than bad contact at this point. He accessed his address book to find Nek Wazir's number, which he had coded as nw33. The old man picked up after the third ring.

"Moore, it is good to hear your voice. And this is something, because I was going to call you tomorrow."

"Well, then, I beat you to it. And I'm glad you're still awake. It's good to hear your voice, too."

Indeed, it was. Something had happened between them. Wazir was not just another paid informant introduced to Moore by Rana; they now shared something—mutual grief over Rana's murder, and a question that Moore had yet to answer: *"What is the most difficult thing you've ever done in your life?"*

Wazir hesitated, then said, "I wish I could bring good news."

Moore tensed. "What is it?"

"I've received information about your man Gallagher, the one you said was missing."

"Is he dead?"

"No."

"Then they've got him. How much do they want?"

"No, Moore, you don't understand."

"I guess I don't."

"I'll send you some pictures I received yesterday. They were taken about a week ago. They show your friend Gallagher up near the border. He is meeting with Rahmani."

"I'll have to check on that. He could be deep cover."

"I don't think so, Moore. I don't have evidence. I only have the word of the men I pay, but they tell me they heard that the American, Gallagher, is the one who killed Rana. Again, I have no evidence. Only rumors. But if this is true, then he is not your friend, and I worry about the damage he could do to you and the wrath he could bring upon this country."

"I understand. Where's Gallagher now?"

"I don't know."

"Can you find him for me?"

"I will press my people harder."

"Thank you. I'll be waiting for the pictures."

"Of course. If there's nothing else?"

"Actually, there is. I was calling because I think we've had a breach. The Taliban might've moved through a tunnel from Mexico into the United States; they came from a city called Mexicali into California, a city called Calexico."

"I am familiar with those cities."

"I think one of them was wearing a pendant, the Hand of Fatima. I'll send you a picture. I know this might not mean anything, but could you review the intel you have to see if any of the Taliban in your intel photographs is wearing the same pendant?"

Wazir chuckled under his breath. "Don't look now, my friend, but your biases are showing. What if it was a party of Jews running late for a bris?"

"What am I missing here?"

"The Sephardic Jewish community calls that very same pendant the Hand of Miriam."

"Aw, shit. Am I in over my head here?"

"Not as long as you have an *educated* Muslim for a friend. Most likely your first instincts are correct. I will look into this. And I'll send those pictures of Gallagher now."

"I'll take care of the compensation."

"Thank you, Moore. Try to be safe. I will call you as soon as I know something."

Moore thumbed off the connection, then immediately uploaded the picture of the pendant he'd taken with his smartphone. He sat there at the cubicle, trembling over the news about Gallagher. He waited for Wazir's message that would contain the pictures of . . . a possible traitor.

Towers came rushing over. "We found the police cars!"

At the same time, Moore's phone rang.

He recoiled at the number: Zúñiga. He motioned for Towers to hang on, showed the caller ID screen to his boss, who nodded and waited, eyes widening.

Moore answered in Spanish. *"Hola, Señor Zúñiga."*

"Hola, Señor Howard," he answered, using Moore's cover name. "As much as I want to kill you for what you've done to me, for the losses I've incurred because of you, I have a very lucrative proposition."

Moore's phone beeped with an incoming message: Wazir's e-mail. He winced and said, "Go ahead, señor."

"Sitting in my living room right now is Mr. Dante Corrales. He tells me the cartel killed his woman and that he wants to join me. He says he has secrets about the cartel. He says he can help me undermine them and bring down Rojas. He says he has the evidence to do that."

"Then he's a very valuable asset—to both of us."

"Ah, more so to you. I will deliver him to you under two conditions. In this economy, I think he's worth about one million dollars. And I want the assurance that neither myself nor my people or organization will be touched."

Moore held back his grin. No way in hell was the American government going to hand over $1 million to a Mexican drug cartel. At this point Moore would determine if Corrales was worth anything, and if he was, then other arrangements would be made to extract him from Zúñiga, a thug who'd already been paid well enough.

"Señor, that's a lot of money, and we don't really know how useful Corrales will be, so here's what I suggest: a meeting between the three of us. We need Corrales to prove his value to us, and I have several methods we can use to better vet him. If all goes well, I will arrange payment and take possession of the man. If we both agree that he is not as useful as we thought, then we might turn him over to the authorities and consider new plans to take down the Juárez Cartel. What happened in San Cristóbal was nothing we could have anticipated. You need to believe that."

"I'll decide what I need to believe. And I want to remind you that we can't turn over Corrales to the Federal Police. He has too many allies there."

"We'll turn him over to the Mexican Navy. I've heard they're the only ones who can be trusted."

Zúñiga chuckled. "I've heard that, too. How soon can you be here?"

"By tonight. Let's say eight p.m. I'll meet you at the usual place for the transfer. Their spotters will still be watching us."

"Very good, señor. I'll have my people meet you there."

Moore thumbed off the phone. "Corrales went to Zúñiga. We might have a deal—and a key witness."

"Excellent."

"Let me finish before you tell me about the cars. Better yet, let me show you something."

Moore opened up the message and enlarged one of the photographs taken with a long lens and clearly showing Gallagher sitting outside a tent in the hills of Waziristan beside Rahmani. Wazir's people had gathered remarkable intel, all right, and the image sent chills through Moore, who'd known Gallagher for years and had even run a few joint operations with him, including their mission to take Colonel Khodai into their protection. Wazir had said that Rahmani's people were responsible for murdering the colonel; consequently, Moore might've been set up from the beginning by his "buddy" Gallagher.

"The guy on the left is a colleague of mine. I need to send this to O'Hara. This guy might be dirty, and if that's the case, he's got access to our intel. Not sure how much he's feeding them, but this is . . ." Moore gasped as the enormity finally hit him. "This is fucking huge."

Towers swore to himself in disbelief. "Send those pics up the pipe, then we'll talk about your meeting with Zúñiga."

"The cars?"

"We think they split up after leaving the house, but they all wound up heading south, got onto Second Street, then drove to the airport. We found all four vehicles inside a hangar on the southeast side. They're not registered to Calexico police. They were all stolen and repainted professionally to resemble police vehicles. The paint was still tacky on a couple of them. Employees have no idea how the vehicles got there and didn't see anyone. We'll be hitting up all the auto-body and paint shops in the area."

"Records of flights out?"

"We'll get 'em, but the FAA only has docs on two-thirds of all small planes—and you know that if our boys flew out of there, it was on a plane whose registry we can't track."

"Right . . ."

"I want to believe you're wrong. This is a bunch of mules

with a good escape plan. They've stolen the drugs and are trying to sell them. It's nothing more than that."

"We'll see what the DNA says."

"I hope it's negative."

Moore snorted. "Otherwise we've let a group of terrorists
slip right past us, and they're now in the United States, which,
in my humble opinion, is a slightly bigger problem than taking
down Jorge Rojas."

Towers leaned in closer to Moore. "May I remind you that
you're the counterterrorism expert. So I want to know, then,
who the hell those bastards are and what they're doing right now."

"I'm already on it. And maybe our boy Corrales knows
something."

Towers's phone rang. Moore listened in and heard enough:
big shooting at a pharmacy in Juárez. Local police IDed one of
the bodies as Pablo Gutiérrez, the scumbag who murdered that
FBI agent who was a friend of Ansara's.

"So they got Pablo," said Moore. "Who do you think did it?"

"I think his own people. They're on the hunt for Corrales,
and Pablo was with that gang of *sicarios*."

"Well, you know how you find out?" Moore asked. "Everyone around Corrales dies as they home in on their target."

Within thirty minutes Moore had a video conference with
Chief Slater and Deputy Director O'Hara regarding
the photos of Gallagher, who they confirmed was not working

any deep-cover operation and had, for all intents and purposes, gone rogue. Whether he was on the Taliban's payroll, the cartel's, or even the Pakistan Army's remained to be seen, but operatives there were issued orders to capture or kill him. All of his access codes to the Agency's databases had been erased within twenty-four hours of his disappearance, but Gallagher was an accomplished hacker, who not only knew his way around the Agency's computer and communications systems but may not, as Slater had speculated, have been working alone.

The DNA results had come back and had identified Moore and Rueben, but DNA from a third subject had been detected, possibly Middle Eastern or sub-Saharan African. While standing inside the step van, Moore showed one of the techs some of the pictures that Wazir had sent to him.

"Probably this guy," said the tech, tapping his finger on the photo of Mullah Abdul Samad. "He'd fit pretty closely." Moore stared hard at the picture for any sign of a necklace or pendant, although the necklace might've been tucked under Samad's shirt.

He turned to Towers. "You're still not buying this?"

"All right, I'm buying. And now excuse me while I go throw up."

Moore sighed and said, "Mind if I join you?"

They left the van and headed back into the office building, where ATF Agent Whittaker was waiting for them.

"Back from Minnesota with good news," he began. "The other part of the weapons cache was seized."

"Excellent," said Towers; then he read something from his

smartphone. "And I just got some intel right here. Juárez police captured the second cache from the Ford Explorer, and they busted three *sicarios* and killed two."

"Did they recover the money?" asked Whittaker.

"I'm not sure. Two guys fled on foot. Money could be with them. They're still looking for them."

"You think if the Juárez police bust them with the money we're going to get it back?" Moore asked.

Whittaker gave a resigned sigh. "Good point. This ain't Kansas, and it ain't Minnesota."

Delicias Police Station
Juárez, Mexico

It was five p.m., and Inspector Alberto Gómez had just left the station. He was walking toward his sedan in the dirt parking lot out back. He'd just received a call on his second line from Dante Corrales, who said he was at Zúñiga's ranch house, that the cartel knew he was there, and that he feared an attack. He wanted Gómez's federal troops to be put in place to aid Zúñiga's security team. Gómez had felt torn over that decision but had decided to dispatch two units to the perimeter, four men in all.

The cinder-block wall to his left, repainted last week to cover the splotches of graffiti, had once more been stained by young thugs with their spray cans. He shook his head in disgust, opened the car door, then climbed inside.

He reached down to put the key in the ignition when a

hard tap came on the glass. He glanced over and saw a gun, a Glock with a suppressor attached, pointed at his face.

"Open the window," ordered the man outside, who was dressed in black jeans, a black shirt, and a long leather jacket. Gómez could not yet see his face.

He inserted the key in the ignition, thought of firing up the car and screeching out of there, but a scintilla of curiosity nagged him—that and the fear of being shot in the head. He hit the button, and the window scrolled down, allowing his assailant to press the gun deeper into his head. "You know this is a police station, right?"

"I know. But what I got in front of me is hardly a policeman. Hardly. Your weapon."

Gómez turned his gaze higher. The man was in his forties, with slightly dark skin, unshaven, with thick black hair pulled into a ponytail. His Spanish was good, but he was not Mexican. A weird light burned in his eyes.

"That's it," said the man. "Very slowly take it out and hand it over to me."

Gómez complied, and the man tucked the pistol into his waistband.

"Open the back door."

Again, Gómez complied, and the man climbed into the backseat and shut the door. "Drive."

"May I ask where we're going?"

"Just pull out of the parking lot and get on the road."

"And if I refuse?"

The man's voice turned dark. "Then I'm going to blow your brains out all over this car, and I won't think twice about it. Do you understand?"

"Yes."

Gómez pulled out of the lot and headed down the street, into very light traffic.

"I'm going to ask you a simple question: Did you order her death?"

"Whose death?"

"Gloria's."

"I'm not telling you anything."

"You will. To save your family."

Gómez stiffened. "Who are you?"

"Just tell me that you ordered her death, and your family lives. It's as simple as that. It's too late for you, but I'll spare them. You've spent your entire life providing for them, protecting them, pretending to be a model citizen, when you've been in bed with the Juárez Cartel for many, many years."

Gómez couldn't help himself. He screamed, "Who the fuck are you?"

"DID YOU ORDER HER DEATH?"

"It doesn't matter!"

The man fired his pistol just over Gómez's shoulder, the round punching a neat hole in the windshield, the crack still loud enough to make Gómez wince, his ear now ringing in pain.

"DID YOU ORDER HER DEATH?"

"If I admit that, you'll leave my family alone?"

"I promise."

"Then okay, I ordered her death. It was me." Gómez began to choke up.

"Pull over."

He did, and something white flashed in his rearview mirror. A van. Men wearing black fatigues and helmets and carrying high-powered rifles were already flanking the car, their weapons trained on him. They weren't Federal Police. No patches of any kind.

"Who are you?" Gómez asked again.

"I'm a friend of the lady you had killed. She was an intelligence agent of the United States of America."

Gómez closed his eyes, and his shoulders slumped. He raised his palms in the air. "It's much worse than I thought."

"Oh, yes," said the man. "Much worse."

M oore climbed out of the car as the men behind him cuffed Gómez and escorted him toward the van. Towers was waiting for him, his gaze sweeping the rooftops for spotters. Moore unclipped the digital recorder from his inside breast pocket and handed it to his boss. "This, along with the evidence that Gloria gathered, should be more than enough. How many do you think he can hand us?"

"I think he's a talker," said Towers. "I think he's going to do very well for us. And I appreciate you exercising so much reserve. I would've shot the motherfucker myself."

"Look at this," Moore said, holding up his trembling hand. "This is me still wanting to shoot him."

Towers slapped a palm on his shoulder. "We needed some good news today. Now you can get something to eat before your big meeting." He checked his watch. "Damn, we need to move."

Cereso Prison
Juárez, Mexico

Prison Director Salvador Quiñones missed the phone call from Fernando Castillo because he'd been down in the courtyard, making sure none of his guards shot any of the rioting inmates there. As skirmishes went, this one had been small, only a dozen or so inmates involved, one of whom had murdered Felix, the ice-cream vendor, a fifty-nine-year-old father of three who did nothing more than make broken men happy with cold treats. One of the newest punks had stabbed him. Damned shame.

When you attempted to house three thousand men in a facility capable of holding only fifteen hundred, tempers would flare on a daily basis. In order to address that—and the facility's reputation for violent uprisings—Quiñones had allowed his inmates to buy a little comfort. They could rent cells with their own toilets and showers, buy small refrigerators, stoves, fans, and TVs, and even receive cable by paying a monthly charge. A few cells came equipped with air conditioners. Prisoners had conjugal visits in special cells they could rent for $10 per night. In fact, Quiñones had helped build a small prison economy in which privately owned stores participated and inmates without funds could earn money by doing odd jobs or working in the shops. He tried to stress the humanizing factors of his facility, but in the end, he knew his efforts might very well be forgotten or taken for granted. Moreover, his salary as director of the entire facility, which rose up from the concrete like an alabaster behemoth cordoned off by fence and barbed wire, was hardly enough to put his two sons through college in the United States.

And so, when Fernando Castillo had offered a particular "arrangement" and had thrown around numbers that had Quiñones's mouth falling open, he'd jumped at the opportunity.

"Hello, Fernando. I'm sorry I missed your call."

"That's all right. I need six men to go over to Zúñiga's house and kill Dante Corrales. He's there right now."

"I'll take care of it."

"Please do. I sent my own men to do the job, and Dante killed them all. Your boys had better have more luck."

"Oh, don't worry, Fernando, when Dante sees who's coming after him now, he's going to wet his pants."

The six men Quiñones already had in mind for the job were members of the Aztecas gang, and within ten minutes all of them were standing in his office, their arms sleeved in tattoos, their heads shaven, their scowls growing even tighter as they suspected that something bad was going down in the prison.

"Not at all," he told them. "I have a job for you. The pay is more than any of you would earn in a year. I will provide all the weapons and the cars. You just need to get the job done, then return to the prison."

"You're letting us go?" asked the shortest one, whom the others simply called Amigo.

36

ZONA DE GUERRA

En Route to Zúñiga Ranch House
Juárez, Mexico

THE ONE-STORY COMMERCIAL building that housed Border Plus, an electrical supply company owned by Zúñiga, had a rear loading dock and pit to accommodate tractor-trailers, and beside the dock stood a secondary entrance with a concrete ramp large enough to permit a car. One of Zúñiga's *sicarios* was already waiting for Moore as he drove up the ramp. The rolling door was open, and the guy, a gaunt-faced kid with a tuft of hair under his lip and a gray hoodie over his head, waved him through. Inside, Moore parked his car, was patted down for weapons by another *sicario* with the requisite body art and piercings, then got into the backseat of the same Range Rover that the fat man, Luis Torres, had once driven. The car chilled Moore as he reflected on Torres's death back in San Juan

Chamula. The Rover's windows had been newly tinted, and inside were three more men he did not recognize. The guy beside him pointed his pistol at Moore and said, "*Hola*." He smiled, as though this was his first big mission and he was enjoying the hell out of holding Moore at gunpoint.

Zúñiga liked to use the facility as a transfer-and-exchange point to keep the Juárez Cartel's spotters guessing. They'd watch the Range Rover pull inside, and they never really knew how many people would leave or how many were in the car. Sometimes the exchanges involved as many as four vehicles. It was a basic but generally effective method of concealing who was actually visiting Zúñiga's ranch and how much product was being transferred in and out.

Moore assumed the Rover was well known by the Juárez Cartel, and it was probably still being used as the primary transfer vehicle to make the spotters believe that Zúñiga and his people were unaware of their presence. Whatever the case, Moore sat back to enjoy the ride.

They'd allowed him to keep his smartphone, which unbeknownst to the thugs permitted Towers to listen in on his every move. That, coupled with the GPS beacon embedded in his shoulder, was supposed to make him feel more secure. Sure, you could lower yourself into a pit of snakes with a bottle of antivenom in your pocket, but the bite was still going to hurt.

He glanced over at the *sicario* holding the gun on him. The kid was eighteen, if that, with a skull earring in his right lobe. "What's new, bro?"

The kid began to laugh. "I like you. I hope he lets you live."

Moore hoisted his brows. "He's a pretty smart man."

"He's always sad."

Moore snorted. "If you had your wife and sons murdered by your enemies, you'd be sad all the time, too."

"His family was killed?"

"I can see you're a new guy."

"Tell me what happened," the kid demanded.

Moore gave him a lopsided grin and left it at that.

Within fifteen minutes they reached Zúñiga's gates and rolled up the driveway to turn into the four-car garage. Moore was led into the living room, which Zúñiga had had professionally decorated in a southwestern theme. Crosses, quivers of arrows, multicolored geckos, and pieces of sandstone art hung near an impressive gas fireplace whose flames illuminated the granite mantel. Across the broad room lay Navajo-patterned rugs, and pigskin-covered furniture was arranged around the hearth.

Dante Corrales was seated on one sofa, wearing a black silk shirt, his arm bound in a sling. His eyes were bloodshot, and he had trouble getting to his feet as Moore approached.

Zúñiga loitered behind the sofa, a beer in hand. He sighed deeply and said, "Señor Howard, I've just had a big dinner, and I'm already beginning to fall asleep. So let's get down to business."

"Who is this guy?" asked Corrales.

"He is a business associate," Zúñiga snapped.

Corrales's frown grew more sharp. "No, no, no. I told you why I'm here and what we're going to do together—just the two of us, no one else."

"Dante, if you're as valuable as you say, then I'm selling you to him." Zúñiga began to chuckle.

"Selling me? What the hell?"

Moore held up a palm. "Relax. We're all here to help each other."

Moore's smartphone began to vibrate. He winced and decided to ignore the call.

And then, before anyone else could speak, gunfire boomed from somewhere outside, drawing their gazes toward the bay windows along the front of the house.

Dollar Tree
Sherman Way
North Hollywood, California

Samad, Talwar, and Niazi each had a basket in hand as they strolled through the aisles of the store, trying to keep their reactions in check. The other shoppers at the Dollar Tree paid little attention to them. They were dressed like Mexican migrant workers, in jeans, flannel shirts, and ball caps. They spoke Spanish to one another, and repeatedly Talwar shouldered up to Samad and expressed his disbelief over the prices: "One dollar? For everything? Just one dollar?"

He held up a container of jalapeño cheese spread, along with a bag of Burger King Onion Rings.

Niazi snorted, then eyed him emphatically. "One dollar." He gestured with his bag of beef jerky, which included "50% Free" and said, "See? One dollar. And more free."

Talwar lingered there in the aisle, his eyes welling with tears. "Everything in America is amazing. Everyone has so much. You can buy this stuff cheap. They don't know what it's like for us. Even water is a luxury. They have no idea. Why have they been given these gifts and we have not?"

Samad squinted through a deep breath. He'd known his men would react this way, because they had never been out of their country. What they'd seen of Mexico was not unlike the slums of the Middle East. But this part of America was radically different. During the drive through Los Angeles, they had cruised up Rodeo Drive, with its designer shops—Chanel, Christian Dior, Gucci, Jimmy Choo, and Valentino, among the dozens of others—and they had witnessed a culture of covetousness that for his men must have been mind-boggling. They'd stared openmouthed at the mansions—palaces, really—and Samad had appreciated the irony of how those with money resided in the highlands while those less fortunate lived below in the valley. The cars, the clothes, the fast food, and the advertising were extremely attractive to them, while he found it all utterly repellent—because he'd seen it all before in Dubai during his college days and understood that beneath the veneer of wealth were people who were, more often than not, morally bankrupt.

Wealth was not something that good Muslims should love, but rather they should love Allah and manage their wealth according to the injunctions of Allah and use their wealth as a means to worship Him.

Samad hardened his voice. "Talwar, do not put your worth in material things. This is not what Allah would have for us. We are here for a purpose. We are the instruments of Allah's will. All of this is only a distraction."

After a moment to consider that, Talwar nodded. "I can't help but envy them. To be born into this . . . to be born and not have to struggle your entire life."

"This is what's made them weak, what's killed their god and poisoned their hearts and minds—and stomachs, for that matter. But for now, if you want to sample their junk food and drink their soda, then go ahead. Why not? It will not corrupt our souls. But you will not lose sight of our mission, and you will not envy these people. Their souls are black."

His men nodded and continued down the aisles. Samad poised before some bags of plastic action figures, forty-eight-count, with brown, green, and black soldiers in various poses. He marveled over how the Americans portrayed their forces to their children, immortalizing them in plastic. One soldier held a rocket launcher on his shoulder, and Samad could only snicker over the irony. He decided to buy them. One dollar.

When their baskets were full of junk food and toiletries and whatever else struck their fancy, they got into their Hyundai Accent and drove back toward Studio City, where they had been put up in a second-story apartment on Laurel Canyon Boulevard. Rahmani's team here in Los Angeles—four men who'd been in the United States for the past five years—had welcomed them with open arms. They had laughed and eaten and discussed the group's escape from Mexico during that first night in the city. It was Rahmani's American friend, Gallagher, the one he had recruited from the CIA, who had orchestrated the pickup in Calexico and had arranged for the vehicles to be painted, the escape team to be dressed like local police. It was a sophisticated maneuver that had afforded them secure passage to the Calexico airport. From there, they said their good-byes to the rest of the group. And it was then that Samad had begun to inform his lieutenants about the larger plan, growing more comfortable in the fact that at this point, they might not be captured and questioned. Rahmani had been adamant about telling the teams only at the very last minute exactly what was happening—in case any of them were captured. They'd be in-structed not to be taken alive . . .

There were supposed to be eighteen of them in all, six teams of three men each. But that fool Ahmad Leghari had not made it beyond Paris, leaving them with one team of only two members. Leghari would be replaced as soon as that pair reached their destination city of San Antonio.

Six teams. Six missile launchers.

"What are the targets?" Talwar had kept asking, since he was the one who had received extensive training in the opera-tion and firing of MPADs (Man-Portable Air Defense Systems). He'd been taken under the Pakistani Army's wing, along with five other men, and ushered out to the semidesert region near

Muzaffargarh, where he'd spent two weeks firing practice missiles at fixed targets. Rahmani had paid the Army handsomely for that instruction.

"So are we going to shoot federal buildings? Schools?" Talwar added.

As they had climbed into their single-prop Cessna, about to fly up to Palm Springs with a pilot who was, of course, working for Rahmani, Samad had grinned and said, "Oh, Talwar, our plan is a little more ambitious than that."

Now as they continued back toward the apartment in Studio City, Samad went over the details in his head. He'd memorized the timetable, and his pulse became erratic the more he thought about the days to come . . .

Zúñiga Ranch House
Juárez, Mexico

Moore rushed to the front window and drew back the blinds. Zúñiga had powerful, motion-activated floodlights mounted outside the house, and in all that glare that pushed back the twilight came two white pickup trucks barreling toward the front gates. The trucks were painted with the livery and logos of the Juárez police, but the pairs of men seated in each of the flatbeds were dressed in plainclothes, and one guy in each truck held a weapon that caused Moore to gasp: an M249 light machine gun capable of belching out 750 to 1,000 rounds per minute. Those M249s, still referred to by many as Squad Automatic Weapons, were reserved for military operations.

How these "cops" had acquired such weapons was a question Moore summarily dismissed, because they were directing fire on two more black trucks giving chase, and those vehicles belonged to the Mexican Federal Police. Why the hell would the local cops be firing on the Feds?

The answer came in the next few seconds.

Moore would bet his life on the fact that those local cops weren't cops at all, and as they crashed through the gates, he felt even more certain. They all had shaved heads and arms crawling with tattoos. They'd either stolen the vehicles or been given them by corrupt officers.

Zúñiga's security detail, about six guys who were positioned along the perimeter of the gate, with two guys up on the roof, opened fire on all the trucks, and the popping and booming of all those weapons sent Moore's pulse racing.

Corrales arrived at Moore's side and cried, "The Feds are trying to protect me!"

"Why would they do that?" Moore asked sarcastically. "Because your buddy Inspector Gómez sent them?"

"What the fuck? How do you know him?"

Moore grabbed Corrales by the neck. "If you come with me, I'll offer you full immunity. No jail time. Nothing. You want to bring down the Juárez Cartel? So do I."

Corrales was a young man who—when faced with certain death—did not quibble over details. "Okay, whatever. Let's get the fuck out of here!"

The truck came bouncing forward toward the bay windows, its driver showing no intention of stopping. Even as Moore and Corrales bolted away, the truck plowed through the front of the house, cinder blocks and drywall and glass exploding inward as the pickup's engine roared and the guys on the flatbed screamed and ducked away from the falling debris.

A couple of Zúñiga's guys who'd been inside and in another part of the house rushed toward the truck, which was now idling in the living room. Zúñiga's fresh troops traded fire with the guys in the flatbed. Moore hazarded a look back as the driver of the truck opened his door and thrust out an AK-47. He fired haphazardly but managed to hit one of Zúñiga's men in the shoulder.

Moore and Corrales continued on toward Zúñiga himself, who was already in the kitchen and seizing a Beretta from the countertop.

Outside and visible through the gaping hole in the wall, the second police truck cut left, heading around the side of the house, toward the garage, with the two Federal Police trucks following. "If they cut off the doors back there, we won't get out!" shouted Moore, his phone once more vibrating. That'd be Towers calling to warn him about the attack, a warning he was pretty sure he no longer needed.

Zúñiga's men in the living room—one okay, the other shot but still clutching a rifle—began firing at the pickup's driver, who was returning fire, along with the guys on the flatbed, the walls bursting apart under the fire.

And the second that machine-gunner opened up, rounds chewing into the fieldstone fireplace, Moore, Corrales, and

Zúñiga burst down a hallway, heading toward the back of the house. Moore cursed. You didn't need any more motivation than that.

Between the gunfire thundering in the living room and the shots booming outside, Moore had a flashback to Forward Operating Base Pharaoh in Afghanistan, where the gods of thunder and lightning had warred with each other all night. The news media had been calling Juárez a war zone for years, but Moore hadn't fully appreciated that label until now.

"Give me a fucking gun!" screamed Corrales. "I want a fucking piece right now!"

Zúñiga ignored him, and they raced into the master bedroom, replete with a four-poster bed the size of a swimming pool. Here the walls were adorned with the framed silhouettes of nude women and fantastic art deco pieces depicting South American landscapes that must have cost Zúñiga a fortune. Moore had the better part of two seconds to appreciate those pieces before he spotted another pistol, this one the requisite Belgian-made police blaster, sitting atop a chest of drawers. He grabbed it, flicked off the safety, and spun back toward the sound of heavy footfalls in the hallway. One of the guys from the pickup had escaped from Zúñiga's men and was running straight toward them, both arms raised, pistols in his fists.

Moore got off two shots, hitting the guy in the left breast and groin before rolling out of incoming fire, which must've gone high and thumped into the bedroom ceiling, as dust trickled down into his eyes.

"Holy shit," cried Corrales, staring wide-eyed over Moore's marksmanship.

"Go!" Moore ordered him.

Zúñiga was waving them on into the master bath, where a closet to his left opened into a massive wardrobe at least thirty feet wide, with a dressing table in the center. He shoved a key in the lock of a pair of tall wooden cabinet doors, swung them open, and grabbed a rifle, which he shoved into Corrales's hands. Then he fetched another and thrust it toward Moore, who cursed in surprise.

"Where the hell did you get these?" Moore cried.

"eBay, gringo. Now come on!"

Moore could only shake his head in astonishment as he adjusted his grip on the Colt M16A2 with thirty-round magazine, standard U.S. Marine Corps issue and simply a larger, heavier version of the M4A1 carbines he'd used as a SEAL operator.

What was Zúñiga going to show them next? An M1A1 Abrams Main Battle Tank parked in a secret subterranean garage?

Moore thumbed the rifle's selector lever, which included the safety and the semiautomatic options as well as a three-round burst option that saved you ammo. He chose semiautomatic, then leaned over toward Corrales. "Here, dumbass, the safety's here." He threw the lever and flashed a sarcastic thumbs-up.

The kid returned a middle finger.

And in that second, Moore swung his rifle up, past Corrales's face, and shot the heavyset guy who'd just appeared in the doorway, holding his pistol with both hands.

Corrales screamed, cursed, then swung around and watched as the guy collapsed in a bloody heap.

"What the fuck?" Corrales said with a gasp. He raced over to the guy and hunkered down, examining a tattoo on the guy's biceps: the circular image of an Aztec warrior with his pierced tongue extended. "They're not Fernando's regular guys," said Corrales. "He's Azteca. From the prison. An assassination squad."

"Hired by your old boss?" asked Moore.

"No time!" cried Zúñiga. "Come on!"

Corrales rose and started toward Moore. "We're fucking dead, dude. We are *dead*."

"I don't think so."

They followed Zúñiga toward the other side of the closet, where he fumbled nervously with a key and finally opened another door. He reached in and threw a light switch.

"Where to now?" asked Corrales.

"Up," answered Zúñiga.

"Up? Are you kidding me? What the fuck, old man! How're we getting out!"

"Shut up!" Zúñiga faced Moore. "Now, Señor Howard? Lock the door behind us!"

Moore did so.

Zúñiga led them down a narrow hall, with their shoulders brushing the walls as they reached a metal staircase with about a dozen steps up to another door. Moore understood now. They were going to the flat roof above the garage and could find cover behind the surrounding parapet and drainage lines. *Clever bastard*. Zúñiga must know his Sun Tzu's *Art of War*: "Never launch an upward attack on the enemy who occupies high ground; nor meet the enemy head-on when there are hills backing him; nor follow on his heels in hot pursuit when he pretends to flee."

The door swung open, and across the rooftop was Zúñiga's two-man security detail crouched along the parapet and exchanging fire with the men below. The second white pickup truck had parked outside the garage doors in an attempt to block at least two of them, while the two Federal Police trucks had stopped about thirty yards back, the cops there hunkered down behind their pickups and triggering off volleys of fire when they could to pin down the others. From somewhere in the distance came the rhythmic and approaching drone of a helicopter's rotors.

Corrales rushed to the edge of the parapet, and, one-handing his M16, cut loose a volley on the truck below, where the machine-gunner had positioned himself behind the back wheel.

Moore slung his arm beneath Corrales's chin, choking him and forcing him back from the ledge as the gunner's response chewed into the parapet and through Corrales's ghost. "Stay the fuck back!" Moore screamed. The stupid punk would get himself killed before he had a chance to talk. And that, Moore knew, would be just his luck.

Zúñiga shouted to his men to cover him, while he ran beside the parapet to the other side of the roof, facing the back of the house, where the drainpipe ran down the wall to the ground. "Here!" he cried. "We can climb down here!"

Moore nodded his okay, was about to turn to Corrales—

When the door leading out onto the roof swung open, and one of the Aztecas, his face cast in half-shadow, lifted an AK-47 and let loose a vicious spray that tore into Zúñiga's chest and sent him staggering back toward the parapet.

Moore was only a half-second behind in his reaction, but he couldn't save the man. He squeezed off at least ten rounds into the Azteca, drumming the guy back into the door, where he slumped, leaving a blood trail above him.

And by the time Moore turned his head, Zúñiga was already gone, having tripped over the parapet to vanish over the edge.

Moore rushed over and leaned out for a look. Zúñiga lay there, crucified against the dirt, his shirt still blossoming with blood.

"Have you ever lost anyone close to you, a young man like yourself? Do you know what real pain feels like?"

Zúñiga had asked Moore those questions back at the Sacred Heart Church. They both knew real pain, and now one of them had finally found relief.

Corrales joined Moore, took one look at Zúñiga, then cursed at the guys below and ran forward to the front ledge. There, he cut loose with his rifle before Moore could stop him. He'd removed his sling but was still favoring his right arm and swinging the weapon wildly.

Gritting his teeth, Moore rose and sprinted toward the idiot, who was still firing and drawing the return fire of everyone below. Moore tackled Corrales, wrenched away his rifle, then rolled him over and delivered a roundhouse squarely into the kid's jaw. "I'll fuck you up even more if you do that again! You hear me?"

Corrales looked odd.

And Moore realized he'd screamed in English.

"You *are* a fucking gringo! Who are you?"

The whomping of that approaching helicopter, along with its lights, caught their attention—and the notice of the gunmen below, who switched fire on the bird as it thundered overhead, searchlight panning across the house. The pilot wheeled around and descended toward the backyard, where he had a wide-enough and level-enough swath of land to set down. There was no mistaking the bird's insignia: POLICÍA FEDERAL, the words lit by the ricocheting rounds sparking off the fuselage.

But were these Corrales's allies come to pick him up? If so, Moore wasn't sure he'd be welcome to tag along. He fished out his smartphone, checked the most recent message from Towers: I'm in the chopper. Get to it.

That'll work, Moore thought.

"Aw fuck, look at that," said Corrales, shifting his head to spot the helicopter. "It's over. We're all going to jail."

"No, those are my guys," Moore told him.

"You're a gringo who works for the Federal Police?"

"We're just borrowing their ride. Stick with me. My deal with you is much better than the one you had with him. You'll see."

Moore rose and shouted to the guys on the roof to cover them once more, but the guys told him to fuck himself and ran off, through the rooftop door and back into the house.

As Moore helped Corrales to his feet and over to the ledge and the drainage pipe, muffled gunfire came from inside the house. Zúñiga's men had been met by more Aztecas, no doubt, and it was safe to assume they'd lost that debate and that the Aztecas were coming up.

"I can't climb down that," cried Corrales, the rotor wash whipping in their faces now, as the chopper was a few seconds from touching down.

"GET DOWN THAT PIPE!" Moore screamed, summoning up a fiery tone from the past, echoing one of his own instructors from BUD/S. He repeated the command two more times.

Shuddering, Corrales climbed over the parapet and set his shoe on the first support strap. The straps would serve as rungs of a ladder down, but admittedly, Moore wasn't sure that Corrales, with his bad arm/shoulder, could make it.

"No, no way," said Corrales, trying to lower himself to the next rung.

Moore screamed at him again.

The rooftop door swung open.

"GO!" Moore hollered, craning his head toward the banging door.

Two Aztecas appeared, one armed with a rifle, the other with a machine gun.

They didn't see Moore at first, because all the rotor wash forced them to squint and Moore had dropped to his rump, shoved his back up against the parapet, and kept low, with the stock of the M16 jammed squarely into his shoulder. It really was a beautiful piece of steel and felt perfect in his hands. For just a few seconds, he was back in the SEALs, and Frank Carmichael was still alive.

Then, either out of nervousness or gut instinct, he reached back, thumbed the selector to three-round bursts, and shifted his aim to the machine-gunner.

The first triplet of fire kicked the bastard sideways, away from his buddy, who swung toward the sound of Moore's weapon. That the Azteca had turned was his final mistake, as Moore now had a clear bead. All three rounds pierced the guy's left breast. If he still had a heartbeat as he hit the ground, then you could chalk that up to a miracle.

As Moore turned back to see how Corrales was doing, the dumbass kid lowered himself to the next support strap, lost his grip, and plunged the remaining ten feet to the ground. His feet struck hard, then he fell back, landing across Zúñiga and letting out a cry. Then he wailed in pain.

Good. Dumbass was still alive.

Two Federal Police officers from the chopper were already rushing over in full combat regalia, letting their Heckler & Koch MP5 nine-millimeter submachine guns lead the way. Moore shouted down to Corrales, "Go with them! Go with them!"

He wasn't sure if the kid heard him or had been knocked unconscious, but he wasn't moving.

The two cops dropped to the dirt as gunfire came from the corner, at least two muzzles flashing. Moore rose and rushed along the parapet to the corner of the roofline, looking directly down on the two Aztecas who'd pinned down the cops. They never knew what hit them—that is, until they were lying in pools of their own blood and staring up at the sentinel, who shifted away from the roofline. The last image they'd ever see.

"You're clear, go!" Moore shouted to the cops. Then he raced once more along the opposite edge of the roof, toward the garage doors, where he spotted three more Federal Police cars heading up the dirt road, with lights and sirens.

"Hold it right there! Don't move!" came a voice from behind him.

He thought of turning his head slightly to identify his assailant, but then again, he already knew. The Aztecas weren't taking prisoners, so they wouldn't have ordered him to halt. And that voice . . . familiar?

"Señor, I'm Federal Police, just like you," Moore told the guy.

The rifle was removed from Moore's hands, as was the pistol from his waistband. Moore didn't raise his hands. He just whirled around, surprising the guy, because no one in his right mind would make a sudden move like that, not with a weapon on him. The guy was neither Federal Police nor an Azteca.

It was the young kid from the Range Rover, the one who'd said he'd hoped Zúñiga would let him live, the kid with the skull earring in his right lobe.

"You brought this on us," cried the kid. "I saw him down there. My boss is dead because of you!"

In one fluid movement, Moore drove the heel of his hand up into the kid's nose. An old myth persisted that you could kill a man this way. Nonsense. Moore had wanted only to stun the kid. Besides, his face was far too pretty for his own good, anyway. As the kid shifted back, about to scream, Moore wrenched back the rifle, then drove the stock into the kid's head, knocking him to the roof. *Sicario* down for the count.

Moore rushed back to the drainpipe, shouldered the rifle via the sling, then climbed over the parapet. He was about halfway down the pipe when the straps buckled under his weight and the whole damned pipe pulled away from the wall. Only a six-foot drop but enough to stun his legs as he hit the ground. No time for delays, though, as more Feds were pulling into the driveway. He rolled, rose, and with the needles still rushing up and down his thighs, he bounded for the chopper, reached the bay door, and was hauled inside by Towers. Corrales was already there, his eyes narrowed in pain. One of the officers slid shut the bay door, and the chopper's nose pitched forward as they took off.

Towers cupped his hand around Moore's ear and said, "All I can say is, this kid had better be loaded with secrets."

Moore nodded. With Zúñiga dead, the Sinaloa Cartel's operations would be disrupted—at least for a while, and they'd be vulnerable to further attacks and to a takeover by the Juárez Cartel. If that happened, then the joint task force's mission to dismantle the Juárez Cartel would have not only failed but would've caused Rojas's criminal empire to grow even stronger.

37

TWO DESTINIES

DEA Office of Diversion Control
San Diego, California

I T WAS NEARLY eleven p.m. by the time they made it back to the diversion control office and took Corrales into the conference room. He'd already received attention from a medic onboard the chopper, who repeatedly assured him that he hadn't broken both of his legs and that his right ankle was only sprained. He still had full range of motion. Moore and Towers told him they would get him to a hospital if he insisted, but he needed to talk first.

Corrales had refused.

And so they had decided to simply take him back to the office for some persuading. During the ride over, Moore had told Corrales the bad news. He and Towers were gringos all right, big badass gringos from the United States government. Corrales had demanded to know what agency.

Moore had grinned darkly. "All of them."

Now, as Corrales accepted a foam cup of coffee from Towers, he leaned forward on the table and rubbed his eyes. He uttered a string of curses, then said, "I want it in writing that I have total immunity. And I want a lawyer."

"You don't need a lawyer," said Moore.

"I'm under arrest, right?"

Moore shook his head, and his tone turned grave. "You're here because of what happened to María. We found the body back at Zúñiga's place. What happened? Did Pablo kill her?"

"No, the other fucking bastards did. They killed my woman. They won't survive that."

"Who's your boss?" asked Moore.

"Fernando Castillo."

Towers nodded emphatically. "Rojas's security guy. He's got a patch. One eye."

"They all like to pretend they are not part of the cartel. Los Caballeros. That's bullshit!"

"So what were you giving Zúñiga?"

"I've got names and locations of suppliers and transporters from all around the world. People in Colombia, Pakistan . . . I got shit you stupid cops wouldn't believe. I got bank account numbers, receipts, recordings of phone calls, e-mails; I got it all . . ."

"Well, we got it all on you, too, Corrales. We know what happened to your parents and when you joined the *sicarios*," said Towers. "So it's not only about María. It's about revenge for them, too, huh?"

Corrales took another sip of his coffee, his breath growing shorter, then he slammed his fist on the table and cried, "They're all going down! All of them! Every last one!"

"They killed Ignacio at the hotel, too," said Moore. "He was a nice guy. I liked him."

"Wait a minute. It's you," said Corrales, his eyes growing wider. "You're the guy my boys lost. Your name's Howard."

Moore shrugged. "Small world."

Corrales cursed and said, "Solar panels, my ass . . ."

"So where's all this information you claim to have?" asked Towers.

"It's all on a flash drive. And I've got two more copies in safe-deposit boxes. I'm not an idiot—so stop talking to me like I am."

Moore tried to hold back a chuckle. "Then we need to hit the bank, huh?"

Corrales shook his head and reached down into his black silk shirt. He withdrew a wafer-thin flash drive that hung from a thick gold chain. The drive itself was gold-plated, made by "Super Talent," 64 GB. "It's all right here."

Los Angeles International Airport (LAX)
Cell-Phone Waiting Lot
9011 Airport Boulevard

Samad and Niazi were in the Hyundai Accent and following Talwar, who was driving a DirecTV satellite van given to them by Rahmani's men in Los Angeles. They followed the blue signs and pulled into the seventy-nine-space lot, which was located five minutes from the Central Terminal Area and accessible from the north and east via La Tijera, Sepulveda, Manchester, and Century Boulevards. They had considered using long-term parking lot C directly south and still within their launch radius, but they'd learned that at least two LAPD officers on motorcycles checked the cars daily with the intent of finding vehicles without front license plates so they could issue tickets. The only security in the cell-phone waiting lot was the "airport puppy patrol," as one of Rahmani's men had told them. Those guys checked only for unattended vehicles. No worries there, my friends.

There'd also been some discussion about parking in Inglewood or Huntington Park, northeast of the airport, to avoid running any further security risks, but Samad had argued for the cell lot location, which would allow the team more time to acquire their target, as the plane would lift off, head out over the Pacific in a "Loop Five" departure as part of the airport's noise abatement procedures, then return and be vectored along V-264, passing over their heads and on toward Inglewood and Huntington Park. It was clear to Rahmani and even American authorities that it was absolutely impossible to secure the ground beneath airplane flights, so the teams had free rein to select the best possible locations.

Samad got the chills every time he thought about it. The absolute brilliance and audacity of the jihad on September 11,

2001, would return to American soil as promised, only this time Allah's wrath would fall on Los Angeles, San Diego, Phoenix, Tucson, El Paso, and San Antonio.

Six planes. Six airports. June sixth.

While some of his Muslim colleagues disagreed, Samad firmly believed that 666 was the Qur'an. It was Allah. It was not Satan or the number of the beast, as many Christians believed. It was the perfect number.

And so, too, should be the mission—perfectly executed, precisely timed, the planes carefully chosen after months of research and observation by Taliban and Al-Qaeda sleepers working inside and around each airport, all coordinated by Rahmani himself, who'd spent hundreds of hours downloading documents via the Internet, all readily accessible to him: FAA layouts of the airports, plane departure routes, everything freely and easily accessible by anyone with a connection to the Web. He'd enlisted the help of several computer engineers, who'd created three-dimensional models to simulate each of the six attacks, models that allowed him to plug in various launch coordinates and determine launch radii.

With that data, and with the might of Allah fueling their hearts and minds, the destruction they wreaked would be simultaneous and complete.

The target in Los Angeles was Delta Airlines flight 2965, departing on Sunday, June 6, at 5:40 p.m. for New York's JFK airport. Equipment: Boeing 757 passenger plane, two engines, one on each wing. Wide-body large aircraft; 202 passengers, in addition to pilot, copilot, and attendants. The Sunday-night flights tended to be full, with many business folks and vacationers heading back east to be ready for work on Monday morning.

The capabilities of the weapon had been the first consideration and had dictated both their target selection and location. The MK III missile's guidance system was a dual-band infrared homing seeker, a "fire and forget" system that allowed the operator to launch even if he wasn't pointing at the target. The MK III did more than just chase the target, though; it was a smart missile that would choose the shortest path, cruising at six hundred meters per second. Its warhead contained 1.42 kg of HE fragmentation that would thoroughly destroy the plane's engine, which was mounted on a pylon under the wing but located fairly close to the fuselage. Residual damage to hydraulic lines, electrical systems, control surfaces, and fuel tanks could also occur—and those issues could result in a catastrophic failure.

In November 2003 a DHL A300 was struck in the wing by a missile while taking off from Baghdad. The pilot was able to limp back to the airport, as only the wing had been hit. Samad felt certain that none of his teams would fail in that way, as the MK IIIs would most assuredly find the hottest heat source as the 757 ascended slowly on full power and with full fuel tanks. Not only were commercial airliners most vulnerable at that moment, but once struck, they would go down over heavily populated areas, allowing thousands of gallons of jet fuel to burn, causing maximum damage and loss of life.

While the MK III's range was 5,000 meters, or 16,400

feet, the goal was to be in a location to launch while the target was still below 10,000 feet. This not only increased the likelihood of a good hit but decreased the time the crew had to save the aircraft, which would roll from lift from the undamaged side toward the damaged side. Best-case scenario was that the engine would explode, shearing off the entire wing, in which case the plane and its crew were doomed from that second on.

Indeed, all of these scenarios assumed that only one missile had been launched—when Samad and his teams had two MK IIIs, and the teams had every intention of launching both of their missiles.

One driver. One shooter. One assistant to help reload the weapon. Total time to launch both missiles and get out of there: thirty seconds. Should anyone attempt to stop them after the first launch, the assistant was armed with two Makarov semi-automatic pistols, an AK-47, and six fragmentation grenades. The driver was equally armed. A second car with a backup driver would be stationed just ahead of them.

How could any of the citizens waiting in the cell-phone lot stop them? Most were probably armed only with cell phones and bad attitudes. Perhaps a couple of gangsters from South Central would be there, waiting to pick up one of their fellow thugs from Oakland or Chicago, but even so, they would drop quickly to the asphalt in a barrage of fire.

Samad and his men could thank the United States government and the airlines for doing nothing to thwart their plans. Equipping all commercial airliners with military-style counter-measures, such as white-hot flares (chaff) and/or infrared jammers, high-powered lasers to burn out the seeker heads on missiles, or using fighter planes to escort jets in and out of the highest-risk areas, were all extremely cost-prohibitive in view of what government officials called a "lack of actionable intelligence." The Federal Aviation Administration did state that the government provided some "war risk" insurance to the airlines, but they were unclear if the program accounted for surface-to-air missile strikes. Samad could only chuckle to himself. While five-year-olds were being patted down at airport security checkpoints, nothing—absolutely nothing—was being done to secure planes against such missile strikes.

Allahu Akbar!

The Israelis had not allowed themselves to be caught in the legal and political quagmire concerning this subject, in part because they knew they would forever have targets on their backs. They had equipped their El Al planes with sophisticated antimissile systems that had already proven themselves in one notable case of a 757-300 managing to evade not one but two missiles. The Israeli government denied that the plane was equipped with any countermeasures, although it was the same one often used by the Israeli prime minister.

They drove toward the northeast end of the cell-phone lot. Their Hyundai had a wide-enough trunk to accommodate both the launcher and missiles if they were loaded at the correct angle. They pulled into a space where just ahead to the northwest lay the soccer and baseball fields of Carl E. Nielsen Youth Park. To their right stood a residential neighborhood that abutted the park. Samad got out and stood there, taking in the cooler night air.

Talwar parked the van a few spots down, got out, and joined them.

"The journey here was far more difficult than the actual mission will be," said Niazi.

Samad grinned. "Look around. These people won't even react. They'll stay in their cars, and pretend they're watching this all on TV."

"Someone will have a phone camera on us for the second launch," said Talwar. "And then we will be on CNN. And they can watch it all again."

A car came around the row—airport security—and Samad quickly lifted his cell phone and pretended to talk.

The car paused before them, the window going down. "You need to get back in your vehicles," said a bored-sounding black man.

Samad nodded, smiled, waved, and they headed back.

They'd return tomorrow evening for a true dry run, and then, the following night, the phone calls would be made, the teams positioned, and their destinies would unfold before them.

DEA *Office of Diversion Control*
San Diego, California

Towers turned over the flash drive to analysts at the office and was eager to remain with them to study Corrales's purported evidence against the cartel. Moore told the man that the spirit was willing but the flesh had been shot at a bit too much, and he was happy to return to the hotel for some shut-eye. He didn't actually fall asleep until nearly two a.m., and when he did, he found himself back on Zúñiga's roof, watching as bullets riddled Frank Carmichael's chest and he plunged to the dirt. Sonia kept telling Moore to stop weeping and that he had a mission and that he'd saved her life and that had to account for something. Not everyone died around him. Not everyone.

She was a stunning woman, and he felt guilty over feeling that way, as though he were betraying Leslie. But Leslie was so far away, and they both knew in their hearts that what they had was no more than a fling, two desperate people trying to find happiness in a land with so much misery and death. He could easily fall in love with Sonia, her youth very much appealing to a man his age, and he hadn't realized until now that saving her really did mean much more than completing a mission objective.

Towers called him at 7:30 a.m. "How're you doing?"

"I'm doing."

"I need you to get down here."

"You sound exhausted."

"I've been here all night."

"Hey, you know, I appreciate that."

"Just get here."

Moore climbed out of bed, pulled on some clothes, and hopped in the rental car.

The girl at the Starbucks counter asked him if he was all right.

"Just had a bunch of people trying to kill me last night," he quipped.

"My boyfriend does that all the time," she said. "Stays up all night playing Call of Duty, and then he's a grumpy asshat all day . . ."

Moore accepted his coffee and handed over his credit card. "Thanks for the tip. I'll try not to be a grumpy asshat today." He winked and rushed out.

At the office, he found Towers—who looked like death warmed over—sitting with a group of analysts. He rose, tucked a folder under his arm, then gestured that they head back into the conference room. Once they were inside, Moore asked about Corrales.

"We put him up in the same hotel, got a couple of people running security. We think we got a couple of Juárez spotters watching this place now, too."

"No surprise."

"Got some news about those police cars and vans from Calexico. They found the kid who did the painting. One of your guys was there to question him. He IDed your buddy Gallagher."

"What's Gallagher doing? Working for the cartel, the Taliban, or both?"

"You'll find out. For now you boys have a major breach."

"I just . . . they told me I could trust that guy, a good guy, a case officer for a lot of years. What happened?"

"Money," Towers said curtly.

"I hope they're paying him a fortune. He'll need it to hide from us. Now, what about Rojas?"

"I don't know where to begin." Towers rubbed his eyes and glanced away. "The situation is . . . complicated."

"What's wrong? Corrales didn't give us anything?"

"Oh, no, he's got some great stuff. We've IDed the cartel's main supplier in Bogotá, guy named Ballesteros. We're already working with the Colombian government to lock him up, but the timing is crucial. Corrales even got some intel on Rahmani's location in Waziristan."

"Nice."

"We're following up on that, too."

"Then what's the problem?"

Towers pursed his lips and hesitated again. "Let me take it from the beginning. Jorge Rojas is one of the richest men in the world, and one of the most famous men in Mexico. He's done more for the Mexican people than the government has. He's a celebrity, a saint."

"And he's financed it all with drug money. His companies stay afloat with drug money. Thousands have died because of him and his drug money."

Towers waved off the arguments. "Do you know who Rojas's brother-in-law is? Arturo González, the governor of Chihuahua."

"Cut to the chase."

"Rojas is also in bed with the chief justice of Mexico's Supreme Court. He's gone on vacations with the attorney general and is godfather to the man's oldest boy."

"So what? I'm sure he hangs out on weekends with the president of Mexico. He's still a fucking drug dealer."

Towers opened the folder he'd taken along and riffled through some documents. "Okay, I had them do some research for me on the Mexican government, since I'm a layman. Listen to this: According to the Constitution of 1917, the states and federation are free and sovereign and have their own congresses and constitutions, while the Federal District has only limited autonomy, with a local congress and its own government."

"So the states have a lot more power. Why do we care?"

"Because there's enough right here to keep Rojas from ever seeing justice. The governor of Chihuahua—Rojas's brother-in-law—has sovereign power and would never give him up to the federal court system. And even if he did, with the chief justice and attorney general in his pocket, Rojas would walk. On top of that, capital punishment was abolished in 1930, except for crimes against national security, so he'd never get the death penalty."

"Let me understand this. After losing three good people, there's not a damned thing we can do? Corrales has the evidence. Let's turn it over to our court system. Get Rojas put up on federal narcotics trafficking and conspiracy charges."

Towers raised his palms. "Slow down. Think about your leak with Gallagher. He's talking to Rahmani, and Rahmani's talking to Rojas. It'll take two to three weeks to process this evidence, and then we have to hope that the judge finds Corrales credible, even though he's clearly out for revenge—which doesn't help our case. And during all that time, we need to hope that your buddy Gallagher doesn't send word back that we're trying to indict Rojas, because if he gets tipped off, he'll disappear. I'll bet he's got properties all over the world that no one even knows about. He'll drop off the grid, and it'll take years to find him, if ever."

"We've got Sonia on the inside. He can't go into hiding."

"There's no guarantee Rojas will take her along. He's kept his involvement in the cartel a secret from his own son. That's made Sonia's operation extremely difficult. She's tried repeatedly to gather evidence, get into his computers, but she's come up short every time. He's got electronic sweepers throughout the house, so we can't even wiretap him without him knowing about it. You see, Moore, when we got into this, we had no idea it'd all lead back to a guy like Rojas. I mean, look at Zúñiga. He's much more typical and easy to indict."

"Like that guy Niebla up in Chicago. They held him in Mexico for eleven months, then we got him extradited."

"Yeah, because the Mexican government thought he was a bad guy. He had no friends there. He was working with Zúñiga, so of course Rojas leaned on his friends to get rid of the guy. But Rojas . . . Jesus . . . He's got the world by the balls. He's the saint of Mexico, and they all love him."

Moore threw his hands in the air. "So it was all for nothing?"

"Look, I've got fourteen different agencies working on this. We can turn over the evidence to our people and hope for the best."

Moore closed his eyes, thought a moment, then said, "No, we're not doing that. No way. We need to move now, and we can't wait for Rojas. That assassination attempt has him laying low. If we start busting his smugglers and suppliers, he'll realize what's happening. We need to get him first."

"How do we do that and maintain deniability?"

"Let me make a call. Give me a few minutes."

"You want coffee?"

Moore gestured to the cup in his hand.

Towers gave a snort. "I didn't even notice that. I am *really* tired. I'll be right back."

After speed-dialing a number, Moore got past Chief Slater's assistant and finally had the man himself. "Sir, it's my understanding that you were a Force Recon Marine."

"You say that in the past tense."

"Hooyah, sir. Once a Marine, I know. We've got a terrible situation here, and I would appreciate you thinking about this more like a soldier than a spy, if you catch my meaning." Moore went on to explain the details, and by the time he finished, Slater himself was cursing.

"So, sir, I think you know what I'm asking."

"We need to be very clever about this. Very clever. It'd be easier if we could use the Sinaloas or the Guatemalans, but we can't trust those bastards."

"Can't trust anyone in Mexico except for the Navy—that's why I need you to make that call."

"I know you trained with those guys, and so did I. They're good people. There's at least two commandos there who owe me big-time—if they're still active-duty. I'll make the call."

"Thank you, sir." Moore thumbed off the phone and set

down his coffee. He closed his eyes again and asked the universe to grant him a molecule of justice.

Towers returned, still long-faced, and inhaling the steam from his coffee.

"Good news," Moore said, drawing Towers's interest. "Slater's calling in some favors from the Mexican Navy."

"So what do you have in mind?"

Moore took a deep breath. "Obviously, we can't get the American or Mexican governments involved in any of this. Our President needs deniability, and Rojas would be tipped off if we tried to negotiate formally with his government. However, we might be able to do some business with the Mexican Navy's Special Forces guys. Basically, we hire ourselves a platoon or two that won't tip off their government. Those guys are gung-ho and would like nothing more than to take down a scumbag drug smuggler. They'll get onboard so that when word gets out, it appears the Mexican Navy did the job. Our President can stand at the podium and say we had nothing to do with this."

Towers smiled. "We just turn their Special Forces guys into mercenaries."

"I'm telling you, they'll do it. They'll say they had to act on their own because of corruption in their government. So, we go down there at the invitation of those guys, we set up a raid on Rojas's mansion, and we get the bastard. We let Slater pay off the Navy and let them confiscate everything else."

"You'll need to get Sonia out of there first."

"Absolutely."

"What about Rojas? What do we do with him if we actually capture him?"

"What do you mean *capture*?"

Towers raised his palms. "Hey, slow down. He's the only guy who knows how all the pieces fit together."

"Let me ask you something—are we getting enough from Corrales to bring down the cartel?"

Towers squinted to process that. "The little runt knows a lot more than I thought. We've got enough to cause major damage."

"Then fuck Rojas. I'm not worrying about capturing him. My plan is to take him out."

"He's more valuable alive, but I'll concede that keeping him alive would be a security threat and a logistical nightmare. If we turn him over to the Navy, they'll have to cap him anyway—otherwise, he'll walk."

"Don't overthink it."

Five minutes later, Moore's phone rang. Slater. "Good news," he said. "We just hired some Special Forces from the Mexican Navy. Hooyah."

38

BY INVITATION ONLY

Rojas Mansion
Cuernavaca, Mexico
56 Miles South of Mexico City

ALL THE FINANCIAL NEWS that reached Jorge Rojas's desk that morning should have lifted his spirits. The Dow, the NASDAQ, and the S&P 500 were all up, and the IPC of the Bolsa Mexicana de Valores, which represented thirty-five stocks and was the broadest indicator of the BMV's overall performance, was looking excellent. The IPC was especially important, because Rojas's companies represented forty-three percent of that statistic. Indeed, his investments were earning solid returns and his companies were reporting increased profits for the quarter.

Why, then, was Rojas staring bitterly into his morning cup of coffee?

Because of so many things . . . because of the lie he'd been telling his son . . . because of the loss of his wife that pained him every day . . . because of this new threat to the business that he both loved and loathed . . .

What had happened to him? He hadn't built his empire on tears but on sweat. He hadn't crushed his opponents by weeping when they struck. He always struck back tenfold.

He had the money. He had the guns. But no, he wasn't any better or different from them, from the scumbags who sold drugs on the playgrounds, from the gangsters who stole from their grandmothers to feed their addictions. He was already a corpse in a bulletproof suit, sitting in a mansion and feeling sorry for the loss of his soul. While he never shared his secrets with Alexsi, she saw his pain and often suggested he seek professional help. Rojas would have none of that. He needed to thrust out his chest and move on, as he always did, even after staring into his brother's lifeless eyes.

He checked his smartphone once more. Nothing. Rojas had been trying to contact Mullah Rahmani, but the man had not returned his calls. Samad's number had been disconnected. Castillo had told Rojas that the police cars in Calexico had been driven by Arabs and that a local kid had been hired to paint the cars. Rojas had already concluded that Samad and his entourage had murdered Pedro Romero and gained access to the tunnels. After ordering his men to destroy the tunnel, Castillo said, Romero's family had been found dead in their home, all shot in the back of the head, execution-style. Corrales was still missing, although Fernando had believed that he'd gone to Zúñiga's ranch house. A gunfight there had left Zúñiga dead. Spotters reported that a woman's body had been brought out of the house. She may have been Corrales's girlfriend, María, but none of the spotters had identified Corrales. Federal agents who may have been acting as spies had fled in a helicopter. The spotters could not get a good look at them. Rojas feared that Corrales had gone to the authorities, either Mexican or American. And worse, Fernando had reported that their best contact with the Federal Police, Inspector Alberto Gómez, had disappeared.

It was time to start closing out accounts, moving money, emptying drawers, and switching locks. He'd become an expert at concealing his ties to the cartel through legitimate businesses and fiercely loyal employees who had never once threatened to expose him. Everything was different now.

His phone rang, and the number caused him to jolt in his chair. "Hello?"

"Hello, Señor Rojas." The man spoke in Spanish, but Rojas winced over the accent.

"Rahmani, why haven't you returned my calls?"

"I've been traveling, and the cell-phone reception has not been good."

"I don't believe you. Where are you now?"

"Back home."

"Now, before you say another word, you listen to me very carefully. Samad came to me in Bogotá with some long sob story about a sick imam. He was looking for safe passage into the United States. He tried to bribe me with IEDs and pistols."

"Which I understand you took."

"Of course, but you know where I draw the line—we must not wake the sleeping dog."

"Señor, please accept my apology. Samad is a rogue and I've lost communication with him. Honestly, I'm not sure if he's in the United States or not. I specifically instructed him to stay away and never jeopardize our relationship, but he is a brash young man, and I will have to make him pay for his mistakes."

"If he's in America, then you and I are finished. I'll not only stop importing and moving your product, I'll make sure you can't move any of it into my country ever again. I will cut you off at the knees. I warned Samad of this, and I tried to warn you earlier when I was in Bogotá, but you never answered my calls. Do you understand me?"

"Yes, I do, but not to worry. I'll do what I can to eliminate any problems that Samad may pose to you or your business."

Rojas's tone turned more harsh, the words clearly a threat. "I look forward to hearing from you very soon."

"You will. Oh, and one more item. We have a valuable intelligence asset that might be of interest, an American CIA agent who now works for us. I'll be happy to provide any information he gathers that might affect our businesses. In the meantime, I implore you to keep the product flowing. Do not do anything rash. The dog, as you say, is still asleep, and we will keep him that way."

"Find Samad. Then call me." With that, Rojas thumbed off the phone and looked to the doorway, where Fernando Castillo was waiting.

"Good morning. J.C. has breakfast ready."

"Thank you, Fernando. I didn't realize you were the house butler, too."

"No, sir. I actually came for something else—two things, in fact . . ." He took a deep breath and his gaze found the rug.

"What?"

"There was an explosion down in San Martín Texmelucan."

"The pipeline?"

He nodded. "About fifty people killed. The Zetas ignored our warnings again, and they're still at it."

The Gulf Cartel's gang of *sicarios*, Los Zetas, had been engaged in tapping into and stealing oil from Pemex, the state-owned and state-run petroleum company. The president of Mexico had come to Rojas for advice and assistance, and while Rojas denied having any direct contact with the cartel, he'd donated money to help bolster local law enforcement and Pemex security in the most vulnerable areas. Meanwhile, Rojas had Castillo contact the Zetas and warn them about further taps. In the current year alone they'd stolen more than nine thousand barrels, enough to fill more than forty tanker trucks. They sold the fuel through their own gas stations and trucking firms, which they'd already established to launder money, as well as selling it on the international black market. Much of that fuel ended up in the United States. Sometimes they mixed stolen fuel with legitimately purchased product to make extra profit. Castillo had often spoken about taking over the Zetas' operation and enjoying some significant cash flow. While it was true that Rojas gave to the government with one hand and stole from it with the other, jeopardizing the financial stability of the country's main oil supplier was shortsighted and reckless. Moreover, the operation was much too risky and sloppily run. The current explosion only underscored his reservations.

Rojas swore and glanced away in thought. "Call your friend. Tell him if the Zetas don't stop their taps, then we're coming to secure the pipeline on behalf of the government."

"I will," said Castillo.

"Now, what about the tunnel we lost?"

"We'll fill in the hole from our side, deny any knowledge of it being in the warehouse, and set up one of the subcontractors to take the fall. I'm already searching for a new engineer and a new tunnel site, but we lost a lot of money there. I hope you understand that destroying it was the right thing to do."

"Of course, Fernando. You've never let me down."

Castillo grinned mildly, then walked over to Rojas's desk and slipped a small digital voice recorder from behind one of the many framed photos there. "I received an alert about an unauthorized device in your office. This is the other reason why I'm here."

"Miguel?"

Castillo nodded.

Rojas mulled over what to do, then blurted out, "Just erase it. And leave it there . . ."

With a hollow feeling in his stomach, Rojas left the office and padded in his robe toward the kitchen, where at least one thing brought happiness: the sweet aroma of huevos rancheros.

———

Sonia was staring through the bedroom window, out across the stones of the mansion's driveway and toward the street below. Miguel came up behind her and slid his arms around her waist. "You smell good," he said.

"So do you. Are we going to the waterfall today?"

"I'm not sure."

"You promised. And I was thinking about that resort and spa you told me about—Misión del Sol. We could get massages, and I want to get a pedicure. Then we could stay overnight, do something really romantic. I think we need that."

Miguel felt the tension pass into his shoulders, as though someone were fastening heavy leather belts around him and tightening them slowly, one hole at a time. "I'm not feeling so good."

She pulled out of his grip to face him. She studied his eyes, placed her palm on his forehead, and stared at him with pouty lips, a sad little girl. "No fever."

"It's not that. Look at this." He pulled the device from his hip pocket.

"A new phone?"

"It's a digital voice recorder. I put it in my father's office last night and I just went in there and got it out. He always makes a lot of calls in the mornings. You know, I've thought about doing it for years. He lied to me when we were down in the vault. He lied. I know it. And he doesn't want me to know, because he's afraid of what I'll think of him."

"Have you listened to it yet?"

"No. I'm afraid."

She crossed over to the bedroom door and shut it. "It's okay. You want me to be with you?"

"Yeah."

They sat on the bed, and he took a deep breath. He hit the play button. Nothing.

"Is it broken?"

"No. And it worked. I know it did."

"Maybe he found it."

"Yeah, and if there was anything on there, he erased it, because he doesn't want to confront me on this."

"I'm sorry."

Miguel's breath quickened. "He has to be hiding something."

Sonia made a face. "Your father's not a drug dealer. You keep forgetting all he's done for Mexico. If he has to deal with the drug cartels—you know, manipulate them, navigate around them—then you should understand that."

"I don't think he's manipulating the drug cartels. I think he *is* them."

"You're not listening to me. My father has to do very similar things in his business. There are dealers and manufacturers that are always giving him trouble. Cyclists who take drugs and get busted for that, sponsorships that my father has to cancel. This is the world of business, and you should accept that sometimes things need to be done—because one day you'll inherit much more than the money. You'll inherit the commitment, and that, I'm sure, is what your father wants. Maybe he's trying to protect you from the dirty side of things, but business nowadays is not clean. It's not."

"You talk a lot today."

"Only because I care."

"You don't have to tell me that."

"So what if you're right? What if your father is the cartel? And then they arrest him. What will you do?"

"Kill myself."

"That's not the answer, you know that. You'd go on because you're a much stronger man than you know."

Miguel took the digital recorder, opened a dresser drawer, and tossed it inside. "I don't know what I am."

She rolled her eyes at his gloomy tone and remark, glanced away, then faced him once more. "So next week you'll start your summer job at Banorte. That'll get your mind off all this."

He sighed. "I don't know. Maybe."

"Oh, just do it. We'll move together to California in the fall, and everything will be perfect."

"Now you sound almost sad about that."

Her lips tightened. "I'll just miss my family."

He pulled her into his chest. "We'll visit them as much as we can . . ." Miguel's phone vibrated. "That's a text from the kitchen. J.C. says the eggs are getting cold. Are you hungry?"

"Not really."

"Neither am I. Let's leave now. We'll get some coffee on the road. I don't feel like looking at my father right now."

Gulfstream III
En Route to Mexico City

Moore and Towers sat aboard the twin-engine jet, going over the PDF file that contained the floor plans of Rojas's mansion in Cuernavaca. The home was nearly eight thousand square feet, comprising two stories with a multilevel garage, a full basement, and stonework to make it resemble a sixteenth-century storybook castle built on a hillside overlooking the town. The residence had been featured in a magazine article in which Rojas's late wife, Sofia (whose name was uncannily similar to that of Sonia, their agent), had taken the editors on a grand tour of the home and accompanying gardens. She had dubbed the place La Casa de la Eterna Primavera.

The Agency had been surveying the house with human spotters since the perimeter was equipped with bug detection, and, in fact, Towers and Moore had a detailed report on the number of Rojas's security personnel, their positions, and further analysis of the home's electronic surveillance and security equipment. Rojas owned several security companies in Mexico and in the United States, so it was safe to assume he protected his home with the best that money could buy: hidden cameras that operated on backup power and whose software could be "trained" to set off alarms based on electronic analysis of "interesting" objects, such as the silhouettes of people, animals, or anything else you taught the system to detect. He also had motion and sound sensors, lasers, interior and exterior bug sweepers, all part of a virtual catalog of detection equipment monitored by a guard seated in a well-protected basement bunker. The article included photos of Rojas's antique furniture and book collections, which the author stated were carefully protected within home vaults. Moore concluded that those vaults were located in the basement.

Towers had already picked out a rear sundeck on the second story in the southwest corner of the house. Perfect entry onto the second floor. He double-tapped on that spot on his iPad's screen and placed a blue pushpin icon there.

"He's got an exit here from the main driveway," Moore said, pointing at the screen. "And if he gets desperate, he can come out through that ramp in the garage and try to crash through the brick wall here . . . and here . . . There's this secondary garage here. He could have a vehicle waiting there."

Towers looked at Moore. "If he gets outside, then we should both retire."

"I'm just saying."

"Don't say. That won't happen on my watch."

Moore smiled. "So, you never told me . . . How'd you get permission to come?"

"I didn't. They think I'm back in San Diego."

"You're shitting me."

He grinned. "I am. I've got a good boss. And he respects what I do. I've never lost so many people on one operation. I'm going to see this through to the end. Slater backed me up, too. He didn't want you going in alone. Apparently, they like you."

"I'm shocked."

Towers cocked a brow. "I was, too. And by the way, the list Gómez gave us checked out. He's named ten key players within the Federales, plus the assistant attorney general, and the minute we're through with this operation, I'm pulling the trigger on that one. I don't care if we have to arrest the entire force in Juárez. They're all going down."

"I'm with you, boss. At least now we'll get to work with some real hard-core operators. These FES guys are awesome, and they throw a great party. I'm pretty happy we got an invitation."

Moore was being coy, of course. Slater had relied on his own contacts and Moore's experience as a Navy SEAL to hire the Fuerzas Especiales (FES), a special-operations unit of the Mexican Navy that was established in late 2001. Moore thought of them as Mexico's version of Navy SEALs, and he had indeed spent four weeks training with them at Coronado not long after the group was formed. Their motto was simple: *"Fuerza, espíritu, sabiduría"*—force, spirit, wisdom. The group of nearly five hundred men grew out of the Marine Airborne Battalion of the 1990s. While their primary task was to carry out amphibious special operations, they were well trained to independently conduct nonconventional warfare in the air, sea, and land using all means available. They were experienced divers and parachutists, and were well versed in vertical descent, urban combat, and sniping. Like any good naval commandos, they also had a healthy interest in things that went boom. The group was divided into Pacific and Gulf units and participated in a fifty-three-week-long training program that left only the strong men standing. They'd already made significant contributions to the Mexican government's war on drug traffickers through their well-planned and highly aggressive tactics, techniques, and procedures—the good old TTPs, as Moore knew them.

One of the FES's more notable operations came on July 16, 2008, when they were operating off the southwest coast of Oaxaca, Mexico. FES teams rappelled from a helicopter onto the deck of a thirty-three-foot-long narco-submarine. They arrested four men and seized 5.8 tons of Colombian cocaine.

In a somewhat notorious cable leaked by U.S. diplomats, the Mexican Army was described as closed-minded, risk-averse, and much too territorial after agencies like the DEA and CIA attempted to work with them to combat drug runners; in contrast, Mexican Navy officers had been working with their U.S. counterparts for years and had already earned their trust. The level of cooperation between the Navy and the American agencies was unmatched. Understandably, the DEA had always been squeamish about working in conjunction with any Mexican force after the now famous kidnapping of one of their most successful agents, Enrique Camarena, who back in 1985 was abducted by corrupt police, tortured, then brutally murdered.

Captain Omar Luis Soto was Moore's contact with the FES, and that was no accident, because they knew each other from Coronado. Soto was in his late thirties by now, with an easy grin, broad shoulders, and a nose that he referred to as "Mayan architecture." While his stature was less than intimidating, his marksmanship made him the most memorable guy in the Mexican group. When asked how he was able to make so many kill shots with so many different weapons, he only smiled and said, "I want to live." Moore had later learned that Soto's passion was target shooting and he'd been honing his skills since childhood.

Moore thought it would be great to see the man again, though he wished it was under different circumstances. And to be clear, as Slater had put it, the United States had nothing to do with the raid on Jorge Rojas's mansion. For its part, the FES was being paid very well to keep the entire operation under wraps so that the Mexican government was none the wiser.

As Slater had learned and Moore had suspected, Soto's team was trembling with the desire for a raid and were thrilled to be working alongside two Americans with good intelligence.

Campo Militar 1
Mexico City

Moore and Towers landed in Mexico City by mid-afternoon, rented a car, and drove out to a military installation between Conscripto and Zapadores Avenues and the Belt Freeway. It was the only military base Moore had ever seen with pink walls and black wrought-iron fencing. They showed their IDs to the guard at the main gate, who made a call and checked their names off a list, and then they were waved on through. They reached a single-story administration building where they'd been told they would meet up with Soto and the rest of his team. The conference room was being loaned to the Navy by the camp's administrators, and Soto had apologized in advance for traffic and less-than-stellar accommodations.

A few seconds after Moore guided them into a parking space, the twin doors opened, and Soto appeared, dressed in jeans and a sweatshirt. He grinned and shook Moore's hand vigorously. "Good to see you again, Max!"

"You, too." Moore introduced Towers, and they quickly followed Soto into the building. They reached a conference room after navigating three hallways that had not seen a janitor's mop in some time. They stepped inside, where about twelve men all dressed in civilian clothes like Soto had clustered around a long table. Much to Moore's surprise there was a projection unit at the back of the room where they could plug in their computers and iPads to display images. They had requested the equipment but weren't sure the FES would come through.

Soto took his time introducing them to each and every operator, all seasoned Navy personnel turned Special Forces operators. Two of the men were pilots. Once the introductions were finished, Towers switched into briefing mode, cleared his throat, and in Spanish said, "All right, gentlemen, what we're about to do will make headlines. Jorge Rojas isn't just one of the richest men in the world. He's one of the most significant drug cartel leaders in history, and tonight we're going to take him down and dismantle his cartel."

"Señor Towers, our group is used to making history," said Soto, eyeing his team with a healthy dose of admiration. "So you can count on us."

Moore glanced around the room. The men were beaming with anticipation, and seeing that, Moore's pulse began to race.

He thought once more of Khodai, Rana, Fitzpatrick, Vega, and Ansara, and how tonight he would ensure that none of them had died in vain.

Towers raised his voice. "Gentlemen, we have the blueprints to Rojas's mansion, and we're going to go over them very carefully, but we have to assume that not everything is on here. After that we're going to analyze the entire neighborhood and fine-tune our attack plan. Once again, I need to emphasize that this entire operation is highly classified. We cannot, under any circumstances, allow the government to know this operation is taking place."

Soto nodded. "We understand, Señor Towers. All the arrangements have been made . . ."

39

THE FIRE
IN THEIR HANDS

Los Angeles International Airport (LAX)
Cell-Phone Waiting Lot
9011 Airport Boulevard

I N TIMES OF WAR, preparations must be made.

Men must be sacrificed.

And Allah's wisdom must not be questioned.

When Samad was a boy growing up in Sangsar, a small village on the outskirts of Kandahar in southern Afghanistan, he'd stare up at the snow-covered peaks and watch as planes cut across them. He would imagine the pilots making sharp turns and landing their aircraft directly on top of the peaks so that passengers could come outside and take pictures. Samad and his friends would meet them up there and sell them souvenir postcards and jewelry to commemorate their extraordinary trip. Samad had never figured out exactly how he and his friends were supposed to climb the mountains, but that wasn't important. Sometimes he imagined himself flying aboard one of those planes to some place where they had candy—chocolate, to be more precise. He dreamed of chocolate . . . every day . . . for years. White, milk, sweet, semisweet, and dark were all his favorites. He'd come to learn a few names of the manufacturers, too: Hershey's, Cadbury, Godiva, and he had even watched a black-market videotape copy of the movie *Charlie and the Chocolate Factory* on TV in the back of a rug salesman's booth at his local bazaar.

As he sat there in the idling van, with Niazi in the passenger's seat and Talwar shouldering the missile launcher in the back of the van, he reached into his pocket and withdrew the picture of his father, wearing that broken-toothed grin, his beard like steel wool, his face blurred by the yellowed plastic. He reached into his other pocket and withdrew a Hershey's Kiss—he'd bought a package at the Dollar Tree. He unwrapped the candy and placed it in his mouth, letting the chocolate melt across his tongue.

I'm not an evil man, he'd told his father. *The infidels have brought this upon themselves, and I am Allah's instrument. You have to believe that, Father. You can't doubt it for one second. Please . . .*

He checked his watch, pocketed the photo, then told Talwar and Niazi to wait as he stepped out of the van.

The text messages from their team inside the airport had already been pouring in:

From 8185557865: The flight is pulling
away now.

From 8185556599: Taxiing to the runway.

From 8185554590: Lifting off.

Each three-man team outside the airport was supported
by another three-man team inside; these inside teams were
from sleeper cells planted in the country years prior. They
worked as custodians or baggage handlers or at any of the dozens of businesses located inside the terminals. They were simply spotters with good intel that supported the flight data
Samad could view on his computer. Their job was to watch,
report, and, above all, not be identified or captured.

He stood near the van's hood and tapped on his iPhone
to bring up the Airline Identifier application that he'd down-
loaded from iTunes for $4.99. He pointed it at the plane flying
just overhead, one that had taken off before their target, and
the application correctly identified the airline, the flight number, the speed, the destination, the distance from Samad, and
more. While the software wasn't always accurate, and while
Samad felt certain that the next flight coming would be theirs,
he'd instructed all the other teams to be doubly sure that they
had the correct flight. Rahmani had been very specific about
that, because at the designated time, a sleeper agent aboard
each plane—a man who was going to martyr himself—would

read a statement to the passengers. These men didn't need to hide explosive liquids inside travel-sized containers while trying to comply with the 3-1-1 rule for liquids. They could board the plane completely naked and still deliver their message. The Department of Homeland Security's Transportation Security Administration (TSA) was powerless to stop them while they had Allah's will on their side. Moreover, the sleepers would instruct passengers to turn their camera-equipped cell phones back on and record what happened. That video would be released to the American public, either through e-mail, streamed directly to the Web, or after being recovered from the wreckage.

Samad squinted into the distance, heard the deep baritone of approaching jet engines, then rapped twice on the van's hood. The back doors opened and Talwar came out, although the missile launcher was still inside. Talwar held up his cell phone, as though talking, but he was, in truth, getting into his firing position. The plane's flashing lights appeared in the distance, and then finally the fuselage came into view and streaked past them as Talwar pivoted toward it.

"Three, two, one, fire," Samad whispered.

"And three, two, one, reload," Talwar answered.

Niazi shifted beside his friend and nodded. "Reloading in three, two, one. Ready to fire."

"Ready to fire. Three, two, one, fire," said Talwar.

Samad counted another five seconds to himself, then said, "Let's go." He took one last look at the plane and then consulted the iPhone app, which correctly IDed it as Delta flight 2965.

He climbed into the van, then glanced around at the other drivers around him. Not a single person had looked up from his or her cell phone. Wouldn't it be ironic if Talwar had been wrong? Perhaps these Americans were so hypnotized by their technology that not even a shoulder-fired missile launch right beside them would be enough to pry them away from their apps and games and YouTube videos and social-networking sites. After all, they strolled through shopping malls like zombies, staring blankly into the tiny screens clutched in their hands, never looking up, never considering that the fire that would burn their souls forever was already in their hands.

"I don't see any problems," said Talwar, reinspecting the Anza launcher from the back of the van. "The battery is still fully charged."

Samad nodded. *"Allahu Akbar."*

The men echoed. And as they drove away, Samad remembered a question that Talwar had asked him. "What will we do when it's all over? Where will we go? Back home?"

Samad had shaken his head. "We can never go home."

Rojas Mansion
Cuernavaca, Mexico
56 Miles South of Mexico City

The clock read 1:21 a.m., and Jorge Rojas grunted, threw an arm over his forehead, and closed his eyes. Again. Alexsi lay beside him, sleeping quietly. Somewhere in the distance, Rojas thought he heard the sound of a helicopter—another police chase, to be sure. He cleared his mind and let himself drift further into the darkness.

Misión del Sol
Resort and Spa
Cuernavaca, Mexico

Miguel rolled over and discovered that Sonia was gone, but a thin wedge of light came from the door leading into the bathroom of the posh villa they had reserved for the night. He reached for his phone to check the time, but it wasn't on the nightstand where he thought he'd left it. Hmmm. Probably still in his pants pocket, then. The bathroom light flickered, shadows shifted. Perhaps she wasn't feeling well. They'd had a pretty good day together, although he was still depressed and she seemed distant. Neither had been in the mood for sex, so they'd just talked for a little while about the restaurant and the waterfall, and then they had returned to the hotel, toured the magnificent gardens that were alive with the fragrance of tropical flowers, then went inside for their massages and a quiet dessert. He'd called his father to let him know where they were, pretending that he hadn't noticed his father's two bodyguards tailing them.

The bathroom light went off. He heard her padding toward the bed and pretended he was asleep. She slid in next to him and pushed herself up close against his back.

"Are you okay?" he whispered.

"Yes. Just a little stomachache. Let's go back to sleep . . ."

Rojas Mansion
Cuernavaca, Mexico
56 Miles South of Mexico City

Fernando Castillo always kept three things on his nightstand: his phone, his eye patch, and the Beretta his father had given him when he'd turned twenty-one. Set into the Beretta's grip was a golden cowboy that resembled his father, a rancher, and Castillo had only fired the weapon once or twice per year to be sure it was in good working order.

He wasn't sure which had woken him up first: the thumping of the helicopter, the vibrating of his phone, or the faint hissing from somewhere outside. With a chill, he bolted upright, answered the phone, a call from his guard monitoring the cameras in the basement.

Even as he listened to the report, he went to his closet, where in the back stood a large gun safe, large enough for dozens of rifles or weapons even more powerful.

Mexican Navy UH-60 Black Hawk
En Route to Rojas Mansion
0131 Hours Local Time

Given the assumption that Rojas had the most complex series of redundant security measures found anywhere in the world, and given the fact that cordoning off the house and its environs was a top priority and would be completed before they initiated the raid, the decision had been made to go in as a team and go in hot, without cutting power to the entire neighborhood, which they'd originally considered. Attempting to bypass each security measure so an agent could slip inside and locate Rojas would be too time-consuming and pit one man against an unknown number of combatants inside. They needed to minimize the risk, maximize the chances of getting Rojas, and create an opportunity to capture or kill any of his other people—lieutenants, *sicarios*—who might also be inside. This was not the time or place for single-handed heroics or the time to cause anything that the home's occupants might view as out of the ordinary, such as a power failure.

Moore, a man who had once believed only in himself but had been taught teamwork by Frank Carmichael and the Navy SEALs, wholeheartedly agreed with that assessment.

Yes, they would strike in the wee hours as a team, and they would do it now, while, Sonia had assured them, the man would be home. Every time she called her father in Spain, that call was rerouted to Langley, and her two most recent reports indicated that Rojas was on edge and might be planning to travel soon.

Neutralizing the twenty-two guards that Rojas had posted around the home, throughout the two-acre gardens, and along the brick walls that encompassed the grounds was already in progress.

A Ford F-250 series "minicommando" truck had pulled up across the street from Rojas's main gate, a ten-foot affair of iron with ornate leaf patterns, attached to a pair of stone columns standing at least fifteen feet high. The truck was manned by three of Soto's men, who immediately got to work before Rojas's security teams could react. Mounted on a railing fixed to the truck's flatbed was a CIS (Chartered Industries of Singapore) 40-millimeter automatic grenade launcher capable of dispensing 350 to 500 rounds per minute, with a muzzle velocity of 242 meters per second. The launcher came equipped with a folding leaf sight, and its feed system was a linked belt of 40x53-millimeter grenades that were not fragmentary but instead carried a modified and less-than-lethal version of Kolokol-1, an opiate-derived incapacitating agent developed in a military research facility near Leningrad during the 1970s. The drug would take effect within only a few seconds, leaving Rojas's exterior security force unconscious for two to six hours. According to intelligence sources, Spetsnaz troops had employed a more unstable version of the gas during the Moscow theater crisis in October 2002, resulting in the deaths of at least 129 hostages. While Moore, Towers, and the rest of the FES forces were not particularly concerned if one of Rojas's security men accidentally succumbed, the thought was to limit the number of fatalities to Rojas's staff (maids, cooks, etc.), which the Mexicans agreed would earn them even more glory.

Thus, as one of Soto's men began launching the cylindrical gas grenades onto Rojas's property, the hissing ordnance arcing over the gate and landing in strategically placed locations as close to the guards as possible (and within the weapon's 2,200-meter range), another operator armed with an M240 machine gun stood on the flatbed and guarded him from any attacks outside the gate. A driver sat at the wheel, waiting to bolt as soon as they came under heavier fire.

Meanwhile, following Soto's plan, a much larger force of nearly one hundred operators were cordoning off every street leading up to the neighborhood. For this job they employed more commando pickup trucks and several Russian-made BTR-60s and -70s, eight-wheeled armored personnel carriers whose presence would immediately strike fear into the hearts of the local residents, if not any of Rojas's forces who spotted them.

Moore sat beside Towers inside the UH-60 Black Hawk with the word MARINA painted across the helo's fuselage and underside between the landing gear. The Mexican pilot, the co-pilot, and two crew chief/gunners manning the 7.62-millimeter miniguns with Gatling-style rotating barrels were waiting for the good-to-go signal from Soto's lieutenant on the ground.

Soto, who sat beside Moore, was in close contact with his ground team. Mission time was 0134 hours. They reported that some of the guards were fleeing back toward the house before they succumbed to the gas. That was not unexpected, and the assault team would keep them busy once the first-floor entrances were breached. The team planned to gain access through a kitchen door, a door leading into the master bedroom, the living room's sliding glass doors, the garage doors, and the main entrance doors. Explosives and battering rams would take care of those obstacles.

"All right, all right, we're good to move in!" Soto cried over the intercom. He removed his helmet and tugged on his gas mask, as the others had already done.

The Black Hawk banked hard, causing Moore to tighten his grip on the edge of his narrow seat. The three FES troops seated directly across from him, their knees nearly banging against Moore's, grew wide-eyed. In addition to their alien-looking masks, they wore black combat helmets and matching fatigues, with heavy Kevlar vests beneath their shirts and the tactical web gear that covered their chests with pouches for knives, spare ammo, grenades, zipper cuffs, flashlights, compass, and canteens, and beneath that they wore their heavy pistol belts. Moore was dressed similarly, with patches on his shoulders, back, and chest that IDed him as "Marina." His two trusted Glocks were tucked into a pair of TAC SERPA holsters at his hips, though he'd detached the suppressors. He had also been given a choice of an AK-103, an M16A2, or an M4 carbine. Did they have to ask? Of course, he chose the M4A1 with SOPMOD package, including Rail Interface System (RIS), flip-up rear sight, and Trijicon ACOG 4x scope. SOPMOD stood for Special Operations Peculiar Modification, and Moore considered himself a peculiar kind of guy, well suited to such a weapon. Besides, the rifle was exactly the type he'd often fielded on SEAL missions, and while the M16 he'd fired on Zúñiga's roof had felt like home in his hands, the M4 felt like a million bucks. Now, with the gun balanced between his legs and his breath coming hard through the mask, he waited as they wheeled around once more and began to descend, the chopper's engine revving.

At the far south side of the gardens and higher up the hill-side stood a smaller building, a two-car detached garage that served as both a lawn and maintenance equipment storage facility and an armory for the guards.

A few of them were dashing toward the building when the pilot pulled back up and called out the targets to the crew chiefs, both of whom unleashed hell, their barrels rolling, the guns booming, tracers lashing out like red lasers toward the building, which began to shatter under the barrage of 7.62-millimeter fire. The portside gunner jerked his rifle to the left and cut down three guards. They were nearing the garage, just as motion-activated lights above the doors clicked on to reveal their bodies, bloody and still writhing.

Before Moore could fully take in that scene, the pilot cut the stick once more and descended sharply, bringing them in over that second-story sundeck at the southwest corner of the house.

The crew chief on the starboard side slid his arm under the first of two fast ropes attached to a support arm extending from the chopper's open bay door. Each rope had been created out of a four-strand round braid that reduced kinking, created an outer pattern that was far easier to grip than any smooth rope, and allowed operators to better control the speed of their descent through a towel-wringing motion as they slid down. Each rope had been coiled into a loop with the diameter of a truck tire, and the crew chief sent the first one flying over the side, followed by the second.

Moore wasn't just a little experienced with fast-roping out

of a helicopter. He'd spent entire weekends doing it over and over and over again until he could fast-rope in his sleep. When the Navy was dropping you off somewhere, there was never any time for long good-byes or thanks for the hospitality. They booted your ass out of a helicopter, and down you went. As many a crew chief had advised him: *Be ready.*

"Ropes out," the chief hollered in Spanish, then glanced over the side. "Ropes on the deck. Ropes clear and ready. Go, go, go!" He pointed at Moore and Towers, who threw off their safety harnesses and got to their feet.

Moore slid the M4 over his back, making sure the single-point storm sling was secure, then he shifted over to the rope on the right side, while Towers took the one on his left.

"One more radio check," said Towers.

"J-One, this is J-Two, gotcha," Moore answered. A toothpick-thin boom mike ran down the side of his cheek and was attached to an earpiece even smaller than the average cell phone's Bluetooth headset.

"This is Marina One, I got you, too," Soto added over the channel.

"All right, this is J-One. We are good to go!"

Moore braced himself, making sure his heavily padded gloves felt secure on the line. He leaned forward, then swung himself out of the chopper, beginning his descent, the rope firmly guided between his boots. He glanced over and saw Towers on his line, just a meter above. Allowing himself to slide a little faster, Moore craned his head down to better judge his speed and approach.

And that's when something struck the helicopter with a muffled thud, followed by an ear-shattering explosion that sent Towers and Moore sliding wildly down the ropes.

Moore could barely see what was happening above him, but he felt a rush of heat and suddenly the rope was dragging him away from the sundeck and toward the lawn.

When he glanced up, he saw only smoke and flames.

Fernando Castillo lowered the rocket-propelled grenade launcher from his shoulder, then rushed back into the house, through the sliding glass patio doors. He began to cough, to feel sick to his stomach, because he'd breathed in a bit of the gas before putting on the gas mask and fetching the RPG from his closet.

As Jorge Rojas's right-hand man and chief security man, Castillo had planned for every scenario his imagination could muster, and an assault using tear gas—or whatever kind of chemical agent the Navy was using against them—was not very creative.

He'd already called his boss, ordered him to go to his own closet gun safe, arm himself, and don his own gas mask. He would get down to the basement, where they would go through the vault within the vault and take a tunnel that led back up the hillside to the two-car garage, where inside was parked Castillo's armored Mercedes. Castillo would try to hold off the attackers for as long as he could.

Beyond the doors, the helicopter plummeted in a great

conflagration, crashing onto the hillside beside the garage, the rotors snapping off as though they were made of plastic, the secondary explosion and burning fuel igniting across the slope and creating walls of flames.

Castillo had but another second to turn away, drop the RPG, and lift his rifle. Waves of gunfire tore through the windows and, as he hit the deck and hunkered down behind a sofa, another volley blasted through, followed by the heavy footfalls of approaching soldiers.

After hearing the gunfire, the hissing of gas, and the much louder droning of the helicopter, Jorge Rojas had gone to his window and had spotted the truck across the street with the soldier launching grenades onto his property. Then Castillo had called.

God, it seemed, had come for Rojas.

And Rojas wished he had the courage of his brother to simply go out there and face his attackers, confront them head-on, but he had to escape. That was everything.

So he'd donned his bulletproof trench coat over his silk pajamas, fetched an AK-47 and spare magazine from his gun safe, along with the gas masks that Castillo had insisted they wear, then told Alexsi to meet him in the basement. She was frightened out of her mind, of course, and twice he'd had to scream at her: "Get to the basement!" She tugged the mask on and dashed off.

Rojas reached for his phone and speed-dialed Miguel. His son did not pick up, and the call went directly to voice mail.

Then what sounded like a great thunderclap came from the backyard, rattling the walls and throwing Rojas off balance.

Moore and Towers had dropped some three meters onto the lawn, hitting the grass and rolling as the chopper had come spinning erratically behind them. They buried their heads as the helo hit the ground, and the explosion ripped across the gardens, flames shooting from the helo's fuel tanks, the heat billowing in greater waves, the bird's engines still wailing as the fires began to engulf the chopper.

"Oh my God," Towers said over the radio, and groaned. "Soto and the rest of them."

Gunfire boomed from inside the house, multiple weapons, Soto's men, and an AK-47, at least one.

Moore cursed. "We need to move!" He bolted to his feet, bringing his rifle around. "Now!"

Towers fell in behind him, rifle at the ready. Still fighting for breath, they charged toward the sliding glass doors, which had already been blown in by the first assault team, whose job was to secure the first floor.

Moore didn't see him at first, only heard the rat-tat-tat of his rifle, and when he turned in that direction, he spotted the bare-chested figure wearing a gas mask and driving the stock of an AK-47 into his shoulder. Moore wasn't certain, but he thought he saw an eye patch, and if so, then this was Fernando Castillo, Rojas's head of security.

In that instant, as Moore was about to return fire, Towers cried out and fell to the carpet near Moore's boot.

Repressing the desire to look down toward his fallen boss, Moore fired, his salvo piercing the air where their assailant had been.

Leaping on top of a coffee table, then throwing himself toward the sofa, Moore opened fire again, believing the man had ducked down behind the sofa, but as he hit the carpet there, he saw the guy was already darting down the adjoining hall.

"Max," Towers called over the radio. "Max . . ."

As if on cue, automatic-weapons fire echoed loudly throughout the house, coming from the front. Glass shattered. Unfamiliar voices lifted, punctuating the rounds with curses in Spanish.

As Rojas rushed into the basement, breathing steadily through the gas mask, he spotted a soldier leaning over his fallen comrade in the living room. And then, beyond them, past the blown-out back doors, he saw more gunmen rushing toward the house. Who were these bastards? And why had no one called to warn him? Heads were going to roll.

40

CHANGE OF PLANS

Rojas Mansion
Cuernavaca, Mexico
56 Miles South of Mexico City

TOWERS HAD BEEN SHOT in the right biceps and had taken a round in the shoulder that had pierced his Kevlar vest. The shot in the arm had grazed him, but the round to his shoulder had left a nasty exit wound.

"If he gets away now, we'll lose him forever," said Towers. "Get moving!"

"Not before I get you a medic." Moore reached down and tapped the remote on his belt. "Marina-Two, this is J-Two, over?"

Moore's earpiece crackled with static, then a voice came through, "J-One, J-Two? This is Marina-Two. Lost contact with Marina-One. Are you there, over?"

It was Soto's lieutenant on the ground, a guy named Morales.

"Marina-Two, this is Moore. I need a medic in the living room for Towers. We lost Soto in the crash, over."

"Roger, J-Two. Medic on the way."

Moore sighed in relief as from the corner of his eye he spotted movement near a pair of doors on the other side of the living room. One door was wide open, revealing a broad stairwell beyond. A figure wearing a gas mask and trench coat raced into the stairwell, setting Moore's feet in motion. He wasn't sure, but the height, hair, and build were similar to Rojas's.

Somewhere on the second floor, Soto's men traded fire with at least two more of Rojas's guards as Moore hit the stairwell and charged down across thick carpet, his M4 at the ready.

The lights clicked on as Rojas sprinted across the tile and not two seconds later an explosion from behind sent drywall, beams, and concrete dropping into the subterranean garage where he stored his antique cars. It took him but a single glance to assess what was happening: His attackers had blown a hole in the ceiling and a rope appeared. They were coming down.

Rojas hustled over to the vault on the left side of the basement and got to work on the access panel, struggling for breath. He typed in the code, did the fingerprint scan, then realized he had to remove his mask for the retinal scan. He took a deep breath, held it, then tugged up the mask and placed his eye in the correct spot. The laser flashed. Then he inserted his finger in the tube for the blood sample.

As the first soldier appeared on the rope, Rojas withdrew a pistol from his trench coat pocket and fired, causing the soldier to drop to the floor and seek cover behind Rojas's vintage Ferrari 166 Inter.

A second soldier started down, and Rojas shifted away from the panel and waited as the vault door thumped and hissed open. He hustled into the vault, then took a breath, figuring the air inside might be clean. It was. But he couldn't close the door—a fail-safe prevented him from being locked inside.

He rushed on through the hundreds of pieces of art, rows of furniture, cases of books, and boxes and display cases of firearms, along with a vinyl record collection numbering 10,000 that had each album stored in its own plastic case. Sofia had loved that collection and sometimes spent hours leafing through it. He reached the back wall, where stood two large racks from which hung more of his Turkish rugs, along with a Persian silk piece from the sixteenth century that he'd bought from Christie's for 4.45 million U.S. dollars, making it one of the most expensive rugs in the world.

He shifted the racks aside to reveal a metal door set into the wall with a rotary combination lock. He rolled the dial. The combination was set to the date of his wedding anniversary. The lock thumped, and he lifted the small handle, tugging the door toward him.

He was beginning to panic now, to envision himself being caught and having to explain it all to Miguel. He'd never told Miguel how his brother Esteban had been killed, how that shotgun had felt in his hands, and how desperately he'd wanted revenge; he had never told him how hard he'd struggled to build his businesses, how many risks he'd taken, never told him about how many sleepless nights he'd endured so that he could give the boy anything he dreamed of, anything. But it wouldn't matter. All the time in the world, all the explaining, and all the apologies wouldn't change the fact that the lie was death.

And a piece of Jorge Rojas would die this evening.

Gunfire from just outside the vault chilled him back to the moment.

Then it struck him: Where was Alexsi? Had they already captured her?

The lights switched on as Rojas pushed into the rectangular room, no wider than three meters and about fifteen meters long. On both sides stood boltless steel shelving racks buckling under the weight of cash, American dollars, millions and millions of American dollars, perhaps five hundred million or more—Rojas wasn't even sure himself.

Glimpsing that much money in one place was enough to strike anyone inert, the cash bundled and stacked faceup to form brick-and-mortar walls of mottled green. Rojas had once mused that the bills were the pages of some spectacularly long narrative chronicling his life and that no, they were *not* tainted by blood. At the far end of the vault were more racks loaded with crates of firearms and more ammunition—not antiques or collectibles like those found in the outer vaults, but police killers and the IEDs given to him by Samad's people, which had been smuggled up from Colombia. A concrete archway lay at the very end, and beyond it, the tunnel leading out toward the garage on the hillside. The tunnel's walls had been reinforced with pressure-treated wood, then filled in with cinder blocks, rebar, and concrete. It was the kind of passageway Rojas wished he could build between Juárez and the United States, even more sophisticated than the one Castillo had been forced to destroy.

He started for the archway and the tunnel beyond.

But at the far end of the room behind him, a soldier appeared, leveling his rifle.

Valley View Apartments
Laurel Canyon Boulevard
Studio City, California

Samad was sitting up in bed, the soft glow of his cell phone casting long shadows across the ceiling. Talwar, Niazi, and the rest of the Los Angeles team were sleeping in the other rooms. Rahmani was supposed to call him at any moment so he could report on their practice run, and Samad wished the old man would make that call because he felt entirely drained, his eyes already narrowed to slits. What they were about to do—the complexity and audacity of it all, the sheer will it took—was a lot to bear. He would never admit openly to feeling any guilt, but the nearer they got to that fateful moment, the sharper, the deeper, his reservations became.

His father was the problem. That old picture spoke to him, told him that this was not what Allah wanted, that killing innocent civilians was not Allah's will, and that the infidels should be taught the error of their ways, not murdered because of them. That old picture reminded Samad of the day his father had given him a bag filled with chocolate. *"Where did you get it?"* Samad had asked. *"From an American missionary. The Americans want to help us."*

Samad squeezed shut his eyes and balled his hands into fists, digging his nails deeply into his skin, as though he could purge the guilt from his body, sweat it out like a fever. He needed to meditate, to pray more deeply to Allah and ask for his peace. He glanced over to his Qur'an:

> *O Messenger, rouse the Believers to the fight. If there are twenty amongst you, patient and persevering, they will vanquish two hundred: if a hundred, they will vanquish a thousand of the Unbelievers: for these are a people without understanding.*

The phone vibrated, startling him. "Yes, Mullah Rahmani, I am here."

"And all is well?"

"God is great. Our run went perfectly, and I heard back from the other teams. No problems."

"Excellent. I have another bit of news I thought I'd share. I made a deal with the Sinaloa Cartel. Even though Zúñiga was killed, his successor, who is also his brother-in-law, has promised me the same arrangement we had with Rojas—but even better, because he's put us in contact with the Gulf Cartel in order to double our shipments. We don't need the Juárez Cartel anymore. I never liked Señor Rojas's attitude."

"He was not very agreeable when I spoke to him."

"No matter now. I will talk to you tomorrow, Samad. Rest easy, rest well. *Allahu Akbar.*"

Rojas Mansion
Cuernavaca, Mexico
56 Miles South of Mexico City

Moore had chased the figure down the stairs, through the basement, and toward the pair of vaults. But then he'd taken fire from someone behind him, and that had left him pinned down, just behind the open vault door, with no clear way to swing around and get inside the vault.

He chanced a look out, spied the guy across the basement, hunkered down near one of the cars. As the guy lifted his head, revealing the black eye patch beneath his gas mask, Moore opened up on him, a solid three-round burst that drove him scrambling for better cover.

With a chance to move, Moore rose up from his haunches, about to sprint into the vault. Three more of Soto's men were in the basement with him, as evidenced by the shots they now traded with the one-eyed Castillo, and Moore called to Marina-Two to have those men focus all their attention on that man. "Make sure they know I'm in the vault," he added.

As Soto's men sent a barrage of fire in Castillo's direction, Moore swung around and rushed forward, sweeping the corners, the crevices, every spot near or around a piece of furniture or behind a rug where one of them could be hidden. It was a vault. How far could he go? But then there it was, just ahead, past the racks of carpets, another door with a combination lock, slightly ajar.

His heart raced. To hell with it. He ripped off his gas mask, needing all of his senses now. The air was good, or at least it seemed so for now. He'd trained extensively with various forms of gases, beginning way back in boot camp inside the Confidence Chamber and continuing on through SEAL training. He'd been exposed both with a mask and without. Red eyes and vomiting were often the results of a successful evolution. At least his increased lung capacity gave him an advantage. He took a deep breath, held it, and—

Pulled open and rolled around the door. He swung himself inside, his gaze probing.

It all hit him at once: the racks, the stacks of money, the guns and boxes of ammo at the far end, and the concrete entrance to a tunnel . . .

Then another image struck like an electrical current that made him gasp—it was Rojas brandishing an AK-47.

Reacting much faster than Moore had anticipated, Rojas threw himself to the floor beside one of the gun racks and got off a full automatic salvo.

Two rounds hammered into Moore's left breast, knocking him back toward one of the money racks, his breath gone, his return fire going wide and hammering into the wall of cash until he could cease fire.

Rojas hit the ground, one elbow crashing hard, and he lost his grip on the rifle.

Moore caught his balance and hunkered down to squint ahead, where Rojas was about to lift his AK-47, but he stopped, realizing that Moore had him—no time, no chance. He raised one palm, then the other.

"Get up!" Moore ordered.

Rojas rose, leaving his rifle on the floor. With hands still raised, he padded in bare feet toward Moore.

So this was the richest man in all of Mexico, surrounded by the spoils of the war he had waged on Mexico, on the United States, and on the rest of the world. He built hospitals and schools, even as the cancer of his empire spread through those same schoolyards. He was a saint, all right, his white robes now bloody, his pockets lined with the sorrows of millions. And, of course, he was so self-absorbed that he had no idea how many people had died because of him.

But Moore knew at least a few of them, their ghosts at his shoulders, their deaths in vain were it not for this moment, this night.

Rojas began shaking his head and glaring. "Your pathetic little raid? All of this? Do you think it means anything? You'll arrest me, and I'll walk away."

"I know," said Moore, releasing his rifle and drawing one of his Glocks, a round already chambered. He lifted the gun to Rojas's head. "I'm not here to arrest you."

Castillo was lying against one of Rojas's antique cars, the 1963 Corvette to be precise, dying from a gunshot wound to the neck when he heard a shot go off from inside the vault. He removed his mask and his eye patch and began to pray for God to take his soul. It had been a good life, and he'd suspected that the end would be like this. If you lived by the bullet then you should die by the bullet. He only wished he knew if Señor Rojas had escaped. If he could die knowing that much was true, then he would leave this earth with a grin after he took in his last breath. He owed Jorge Rojas everything.

During the raid, Soto's men had successfully captured the chef, several other servants, and a woman identified as Alexsi, Rojas's girlfriend. Once the house had been secured, Towers, who was wearing a sling, joined Moore as they climbed into one of the civilian cars left parked around the corner for their escape. "It's too bad you had to shoot him . . ."

Towers lifted his brow, prying for details.

Moore glanced away and climbed into the driver's seat.

"Let's go before the circus arrives. We need to pick up Sonia and get to the airport."

Misión del Sol
Resort and Spa
Cuernavaca, Mexico

Miguel heard the knock on their door, and when he looked up, Sonia, wearing her robe, was already answering it. She allowed two men dressed in slacks and dark jackets to enter, then she flicked on a light. He squinted into the glare.

"Sonia, what the hell? Who're these guys?"

She came over to the bed and raised her palms. "Just relax. These guys are part of my team."

"Your team?"

She took a deep breath, her gaze wandering as though she was groping for words. In fact, she was. "Look, it's all about your father. It's always been about him."

He bolted from the bed, started toward her, but one of the men approached and glowered at him.

"Sonia, what is this?"

"This is me saying good-bye. And that I'm sorry. You're still a young man with a great future, despite everything your father has done. You should know that."

He began to tremble, to lose his breath. "Who are you?"

Her voice turned cool, steely, strangely professional. "Obviously I'm not who you think I am. And neither is your father. You were right about him."

"I was?"

"I have to go. You won't see me ever again." She tossed him his cell phone. "Take care, Miguel."

"Sonia?"

She started toward the door with the two men.

"Sonia, what the fuck is this?"

She didn't look back.

"SONIA, DON'T LEAVE! YOU CAN'T LEAVE!"

One of the men turned back and pointed a finger. "You stay here," he warned. "Until after we've left."

He shut the door after himself, leaving Miguel standing there, in shock, as his mind rewound through everything Sonia had ever said to him, through the millions of lies.

41

IMPACT

Gulfstream III
En Route to San Diego, California
0230 Local Time

THE AGENCY WANTED Moore and Sonia out of there immediately, and Towers received the same directive from his BORTAC senior administrators. While the operation had been a success, Soto, along with seven of his men, had been killed. The Black Hawk pilots and crew chiefs were also lost. Terrible news, but these were men who had known the risks and accepted them.

Sonia was a bit shaken when they'd picked her up at the hotel, but within five minutes she was talking rapidly and thanking Moore for saving her back in San Juan Chamula.

"And yes," she said, "I do owe you coffee."

"And I will collect," he said with a wink.

Once on the plane, she folded her arms over her chest and buried herself in her seat, losing herself in her smartphone. Moore appreciated the sacrifices she had made, giving all of herself to Miguel in order to get close to Rojas, a man who had so well protected himself that her mission had become nearly impossible. She was young, though remarkably professional, having understood the ramifications of what she was doing and the toll it would take on her emotions. Her level of commitment had never wavered, and early on, she had seen that her mission could lead to familial collateral damage: Rojas had condemned his son to years of investigations and probes. Who was going to believe that Miguel Rojas didn't know what his father was doing? Sonia could not come to his aid. There was no way the CIA would compromise itself and allow her to testify in any court, open or closed. She might be allowed to testify in a "closed" session before a congressional intelligence committee, but that would never help Miguel. She knew this, knew the full extent of her betrayal. Her strength thoroughly impressed Moore.

Towers had allowed the Mexican medics to bandage him up, and they'd stopped the bleeding, but as soon as he and Moore arrived in San Diego, he was going to the hospital for some additional care. He needed X-rays, an MRI, and stitches, since the exit wound on his shoulder was not pretty, but he insisted on having that work done back in San Diego. And so he was resting easy at Moore's side.

For his part, Moore had only a few bruises on his chest, new additions to a collection that had been growing since the start of the operation. With his computer balanced on his lap, he watched the Mexican news coverage of the raid on Rojas's mansion and snickered over how the media billed it as the "shocking discovery of a secret life led by one of the world's wealthiest men." As they'd planned, the Mexican Navy was given credit for the raid with no mention of American assistance. Moore couldn't believe it, but the Mexican authorities had already allowed the media to get footage of the vaults. The walls of money were long gone, having already been "taken care of" by the FES troops. The Mexican government was no doubt torn between being grateful and being furious over a rogue FES mission that had received no clearance from anyone but had turned into a remarkable find and a great public-relations story of the Mexican president's war on drugs.

Meanwhile, the Associated Press had picked up another story, of a government raid on the jungle warehouse of Juan Ramón Ballesteros, reputed leader of one of Colombia's most productive and profitable cocaine cartels, with direct ties to the Juárez Cartel of Mexico (as revealed to them earlier by Dante Corrales). Ballesteros had, quite surprisingly, been captured alive, and Moore accessed a CIA report to learn that fellow agents had been the ones leading the raid on Ballesteros's camp. *Hooyah*. Another small battle won.

True to his word, Towers handed over the name of every corrupt Federal Police officer that Gómez had given them, twenty-two names in all, including a surprising if not depressing revelation: The secretary of public security in the federal cabinet was also on Rojas's payroll. The names were not only delivered to the Federal Police but deliberately leaked to the media and e-mailed to the president of Mexico himself. Rioting of the kind that Gloria Vega had described outside the Delicias station would soon occur all over Juárez and in cities throughout Mexico, as local officers demanded the ousting of their corrupt bosses. Towers had said he wanted to force the issue, and, oh, yes, they were forcing it, all right. Gómez, who believed he was getting a plea bargain, would be extradited to the United States to face conspiracy-to-murder charges and everything else the attorneys could throw at him. Small battle number two won . . .

Turncoat *sicario* Dante Corrales was going to be placed in the witness protection program as he continued to name names and help tear apart the cartel. His intel regarding the cartel's connections in Afghanistan and Pakistan was, however, dated, with the leads he'd given them on Rahmani's whereabouts yesterday's news, according to Moore's colleagues operating in the region. Moore had already sent a text message to Wazir to see if he'd learned anything more about the Hand of Fatima pendant and the group of Taliban that Moore so firmly believed had entered the United States. The Agency still had no leads on Gallagher's whereabouts (he'd obviously had his shoulder beacon surgically removed), although he had been identified as the man who'd hired the kid to paint the police cars. As a field agent, Gallagher had been trained to find people who didn't want to be found and was an expert at dropping off the grid himself. Over the years, he'd studied all the different methods people used to conceal themselves—and he'd learned which ones had worked and which had not. Finding him would cost money, time, assets, and, Moore contended, a feverish obsession.

Sometime later, Moore fell asleep and was awakened by the single attendant who asked that he sit up and fasten his seat belt.

San Diego, California
0405 Local Time

Once on the ground, Sonia said she was catching another flight back to Langley, where she'd be debriefed by her people.

"You did a great job," Moore told her. "I mean it."

She smiled tightly. "Thank you."

Moore drove Towers over to Sharp Memorial Hospital, a level 1 trauma center. When the nurses learned that Towers was a law enforcement officer, they treated him like royalty, and he was seen by a doctor within ten minutes. They told Moore their timing was fortunate. In a few hours, all of the rush-hour car accident victims would begin pouring in—just another day at a trauma center in a big city.

While seated in the waiting room, Moore read an e-mail from Slater's assistant, who said they were hoping to schedule a video conference later in the day. Moore had already spoken at length with his bosses during the plane ride back.

As he was about to doze off yet again, a gunshot echoed as though through mountains. Moore cursed and shuddered awake. That wasn't a gunshot, but his phone was vibrating: a call from Wazir. Moore rose and stepped out of the waiting room and into the hallway. "How are you, my friend?"

"I know it is early there, but I had to call. I thought I would leave you a message."

"What's wrong?"

"Some of the informants your men recruited have brought trouble. Another drone launched missiles yesterday, killing one of my best sources of information. You need to stop this."

"I'll make a call as soon as we're finished."

"I can't help you if you don't help me. Your agency is directing the strikes on the people I need most."

"Wazir, I understand that."

"Good."

"Do you have anything for me?"

"Bad news. A group of seventeen men entered the United States through a tunnel between Mexicali and Calexico, just as you feared. Samad, the man who is Rahmani's fist, is with them, along with two of his lieutenants, Talwar and Niazi. Samad has been known to wear the Hand of Fatima."

Moore balled his hand into a fist and held back the curses. "I need everything you can get on those men, all seventeen of them. And I need to know where Samad and Rahmani are . . . right now."

"I'm already working on that. Rahmani is here, but he keeps moving, and as I said, it's getting very dangerous for me. Stop the drone attacks. Tell your people to back off so I can work for you."

"I will."

Moore immediately called Slater, who was en route to his office. Moore conveyed what Wazir had said and added, "I need you to stop the drone attacks. Let 'em run recon, but no bombing. Not now."

"I need actionable intel."

"You won't get it if you kill my sources. I just got confirmation. Samad's already here. He's got a team. Gallagher helped him."

"I'll get with DHS and see if they're willing to step up some operations and raise the terror alert status."

Specific government activities related to specific threat levels were not fully revealed to the public, and often the Agency was not made aware of every other department's activities (no surprise there), given that deep-cover operations like Sonia's were not disclosed to the rest of the Agency itself. Certain measures had already been challenged in court as being illegal, and the courts had yet to rule on many of those issues, even as the current system suffered accusations of being politically manipulated (threat levels being raised before elections, et cetera).

Moore thanked Slater, then added, "It's imperative now that we hold fire, all right? My guy Wazir is a good man, the best guy I've got. He'll help us find these bastards. Just hold fire."

Slater hesitated at first, then said, "Keep me informed on how Towers is doing. I've got a full plate today, but I'll talk to you later."

7-Eleven Convenience Store
Near San Diego International Airport

Kashif Aslam, a forty-one-year-old Pakistani immigrant, dreamed of one day owning his own 7-Eleven, but for now he managed the store on Reynard Way, barely a mile from the airport. By popular demand from a small group of Pakistanis living in the immediate area, Aslam started selling *pakora*s, a Pakistani finger-food snack consisting of potato or onion or cauliflower deep-fried in a chickpea batter. Each morning his wife would get up early to make the batter, alternating between the potato, onion, and cauliflower, and Aslam would bring the *pakora*s to work and complete the fritters in the store's deep fryer. The snacks were such a success that the owner began paying Aslam for all the supplies and for his wife's labor.

After six years of managing the same location, Aslam was very familiar with all of his local customers, especially his fellow Pakistanis. Just before noon, three strangers in their early twenties had come in and rejoiced over the fritters. They were all countrymen, who had spoken in Urdu and had cleaned him out of every last *pakora*. Of course they had roused his curiosity. Aslam had asked them how they'd heard about him and the snacks, and they said that they had a friend who worked at the airport, but they had, oddly enough, been unable to give him a name, saying it was another friend who'd made contact. That could very well be true, but there was something troublesome about these men, their nervous reaction when he'd asked, their unwillingness to discuss how long they'd been in the country and exactly where they were from in Pakistan. Aslam decided to eavesdrop on their conversation outside the store, where they'd stood, eating heartily. He pretended to be taking out the trash, walking around the back toward the big Dumpster, when he'd heard one of them talking about flight numbers and flight patterns.

Aslam was a true believer in America; the country had been very good to him, his wife, and their six daughters. He did not want any trouble, and, more important, he did not want anything to interfere with his new life and promising future.

While he couldn't prove anything, Aslam thought the men might be criminals—smugglers perhaps—or in the country illegally, and he did not want the authorities to associate him or the store in any way with them. He did not want them coming back. They were driving a dark red Nissan compact car, and Aslam had been careful to record their tag number. After they'd left, he'd called the police and reported the incident to one of two officers who had come to take his statement. Then, thirty minutes later, a man who identified himself as Peter Zarick, an FBI agent, arrived to interview him. He said they would follow up on the tag number and assured him that he would not be associated with them in any way.

"What happens now?" he asked the man before he left.

"My boss will pass this information on to all the other agencies."

"That's very good," said Aslam. "Because I don't want any trouble for anyone."

———

FBI Agent Peter Zarick got in his car and drove away from the 7-Eleven. When he got back to the field office, he'd turn in his 302 report to Meyers, the special agent in charge, who would fax it to Virginia, to the National Counterterrorism Center. The NCTC hosted three daily secure video teleconferences (SVTCs) and maintained constant voice and electronic contact with major intelligence and counterterrorism community players and foreign partners.

Ever since that BOLO (Be On the Lookout) alert had gone out for terrorists in Calexico, and the field office had learned that a fellow agent, Michael Ansara, had been killed, Zarick had been working his tail off, canvassing the area for any leads— and this was the first good one they had. He could barely contain himself when he reached the Field Intelligence Group Office on Aero Drive. He charged out of his car and ran.

DEA Office of Diversion Control
San Diego, California

By two p.m. Moore and Towers had left the hospital and returned to the conference room. Towers was feeling great after having his shoulder and arm treated. The GSW (gunshot wound) had appeared a lot worse than it actually was, and the doctor had spent some time telling Towers just how lucky he'd been, that he could have had a collapsed lung and so on. They wanted to give him a sling, but he'd refused. Moore had been around many operators who'd been shot, and sometimes even the meanest badasses turned into crying thumb-suckers when they were injured, but Towers was a tough and obviously thick-skinned bastard. He'd wanted no sympathy or special treatment, only a chicken sandwich with french fries, so they'd hit the drive-thru of a KFC. Moore had ordered the same, and while they ate, they watched CNN to see if it had picked up anything else on the Rojas story. At the same time, Moore scanned the intel gathered thus far on the hunt for Samad and his group. The trail ended abruptly at the Calexico airport. They'd checked all the records of all the flights from all the airports within the range of a variety of aircraft. It was needle-in-a-haystack time, and as Towers had pointed out, the FAA had docs for only about two-thirds of all small planes. Witnesses were few and far between, and even if the group had been sighted, Moore figured they'd disguised themselves as migrant workers, who were a common sight and always on the move.

Part of Moore wanted to believe that Samad and his group were just sleepers, that their mission was to live secretly in the United States for years until they would be called into action, and that would give him and the Agency the time they needed for the hunt . . . and the kill. He could reassure himself with that, but in the next thought he'd imagine what they'd been carrying in those rectangular packs: rifles, RPGs, missile launchers, and, God forbid, nukes? Of course, the Agency's analysts—in conjunction with more than a dozen other agencies, including DHS, NEST (the Nuclear Emergency Support Team), the FBI, and Interpol—were scouring the planet for evidence of recent arms sales, especially between the Taliban in Waziristan and the Pakistan Army. After dozens of false leads, the trail in that regard had gone cold, and Moore suddenly cursed aloud.

"Take it easy, bro," Towers said. He reached into his breast pocket and produced a plastic prescription bottle. "You want a painkiller?"

Moore just gave him a look.

At about 4:45 p.m., Moore received an e-mail that took him aback. Maqsud Kayani, the commander of that Pakistan patrol boat and nephew of the late Colonel Saadat Khodai, had written to share some important information he'd been given via an ISI agent who'd been a friend of his uncle's. The ISI had recently questioned a group of Taliban sympathizers up in Waziristan, one of whom revealed that his brother was on some kind of mission in the United States. The more ironic or perhaps fateful part of the e-mail followed:

The brother was in San Diego.

```
I want you to know that my uncle was a
brave man who understood exactly what he was
doing, and I'm hoping this information will
help you catch the men who murdered him.
```

Moore shared the e-mail with Towers, who nearly fell out of his chair as he spotted something on his own computer screen. "We got a good lead from the Bureau, right here on the 302. Three guys at a 7-Eleven, all from Pakistan. Guy who reported them was from Pakistan, too. He got a tag number."

"They run it?"

"Yeah, came from a rental car place near the airport. Guy who took it fits the description of any one of the 7-Eleven guys. Looks like his ID was fake, though, and so was his address—whoa, whoa, whoa, hold on now. Holy shit."

"What?" Moore demanded.

"Airport security just called. They spotted the car in the cell-phone lot on North Harbor. They have orders not to approach."

Moore burst to his feet. "Let's go!"

They were out the door in seconds, practically leaping into their SUV, with Moore at the wheel and Towers on his cell phone, talking to a guy named Meyers at the Bureau who already had his Special Weapons and Tactics (SWAT) unit en route.

"Tell them to hold back!" hollered Towers. "We don't want them running. Keep them back!"

Moore had the airport programmed into the windshield-mounted GPS, so the unit began showing and calling out the turns: west on Viewridge toward Balboa, hang a left, get on to I-15, then merge later on with I-8. Freeway driving during rush hour left him white-knuckling his way around slower-moving vehicles. The airport was about fourteen miles away, a twenty-minute drive without traffic, but once they got onto the San Diego Freeway to head south, the ribbons of brake lights and hoods gleaming in the sun stretched to the horizon.

And that's when Moore took to the shoulder and hauled ass, leaving a cloud of debris in their wake. They rumbled as long as they could over fast-food garbage and pieces of tractor-trailer tires until they were forced to weave back into traffic to make their next exit.

Los Angeles International Airport (LAX)
Cell-Phone Waiting Lot
9011 Airport Boulevard

Samad's mouth had gone dry as they pulled into the lot. He checked his watch: 5:29 p.m. local time. He glanced over to Niazi, seated in the van's passenger seat. The young man's eyes grew wider, and he licked his lips like a snow leopard before the kill. Samad craned his head back to Talwar, who had the Anza propped on his shoulder and was praying quietly. The van's engine thrummed, and Samad tapped a button, lowering his window to breathe in the cooler evening air.

He reached into his pocket and unwrapped a piece of chocolate. He examined it as though it were a precious gem before popping it into his mouth.

The piece of paper lying across his lap, the one Rahmani referred to as the target report, had cell-phone numbers hand-written beside each of the cities:

Los Angeles (LAX)

Flt#: US Airways 2965

Dest: New York, NY (JFK)

Departure: June 6, 5:40 p.m. Pacific Time

Boeing 757, twin-engine jet

202 passengers, 8 crew

San Diego (SAN)

Flt#: Southwest Airlines SWA1378

Dest: Houston, TX (HOU)

Departure: June 6, 5:41 p.m. Pacific Time

Boeing 737-700, twin-engine jet

149 passengers, 6 crew

Phoenix (PHX)

Flt#: US Airways 155

Dest: Minneapolis, MN (MSP)

Departure: June 6, 6:44 p.m. Mountain Time

Boeing 767-400ER

304 passengers, 10 crew

Tucson (TUS)

Flt#: Southwest Airlines SWA694

Dest: Chicago, IL (MDW)

Departure: June 6, 6:45 p.m. Mountain Time

Boeing 737-300, twin-engine jet

150 passengers, 8 crew

El Paso (ELP)
Flt#: Continental 545
Dest: Boston, MA (BOS)
Departure: June 6, 7:41 p.m. Central Time
Boeing 737-300
150 passengers, 8 crew

San Antonio (SAT)
Flt#: SkyWest Airlines OO5429
Dest: Los Angeles, CA (LAX)
Departure: June 6, 7:40 p.m. Central Time
Canadian CRJ900LR, twin-jet (tail)
76 passengers, 4 crew

The planes would be lifting off within minutes of one another, and all of Samad's crews had finished checking in to say that their equipment was ready and that all of their flights were running on time, despite some earlier concerns about summer storms. Samad no longer had any uncertainties. He'd realized that even if he gave up, walked away, guided by the guilt imposed upon him by the memory of his dead father, that Talwar and Niazi would go on without him, that the others would go on without him. There was no stopping the jihad. He would die a fool and a coward. Thus before leaving for the mission, he had lit a match and had burned the photograph of his father, had left the ashes in the bathroom sink. They said their afternoon prayer, and then Samad had driven away from the apartment with narrow eyes and a clenched fist.

An airport police car cruised through the lot, the officers searching for unattended vehicles. Samad lifted his cell phone and pretended to speak. As he'd seen before, the other drivers were entirely consumed by their electronic devices, and there was an eerie calm that settled over the lot, broken momentarily by the next flight thundering on by.

5:36 p.m.

Samad brought up the iPhone app as their secondary source of identifying their target plane. He'd come to discover there was a thirty-second delay in the information the app gave him, but that didn't matter. All Talwar needed to do was sight the target, and the missile would do the rest.

5:37 p.m.

The seconds were minutes, the minutes hours, as his pulse began to race. The sky had turned a bluish yellow, streaked by beams of the setting sun, with only a few finger clouds to the east. They would have a spectacular and unobstructed view of the launch.

His phone vibrated. And there they were: the text-message reports from their team inside the airport.

US Airways Flight 155
Phoenix to Minneapolis
6:42 p.m. Mountain Time

At the age of sixteen, Dan Burleson had soloed in a Cessna 150 over Modesto, California. He was flying planes before he had a driver's license. He'd saved all of his lawn-cutting money for two years to take flying lessons. He'd grown up in the Salinas Valley and had been mesmerized by the crop-duster pilots swooping down to deliver their cargo. He knew that's what he wanted to do. For the next three decades he pursued his passion for flying, spraying cotton fields in Georgia, serving as an airborne traffic reporter in Florida, and flying banking cargo and medical specimens out of the Southeast. He piloted single-engine planes, Cessna 210 Centurions, and twin-engine cargo planes, Beechcraft Baron 58s. He'd experienced every conceivable equipment failure imaginable, flying on one engine and nearly crashing when his plane was flipped over during a storm. He could hear the rivets popping and felt certain he was going to die.

All of which was to say that Mr. Dan Burleson was not your average commercial airline passenger. He had a keen interest in what was happening in the cockpit and could tell you when the pilots were switching command to the flight computer to literally take over the plane during the climb out to altitude. The pilot would input turns and altitude directions via keyboard tabulation or by rotating a dial to the direction desired. For example, Airport Traffic Control might call with "Delta 1234, turn right to 180 degrees." The pilot would rotate a dial on the FMS (Flight Management System) to 180, and the plane would start turning in that direction to meet that instruction received from ATC while the plane was being controlled by the FMS computer. Every time he flew, Dan would sit there imagining what was happening in the cockpit. Call it force of habit.

On this particular evening, he was seated in 21J, the exit

row, with the window at his right shoulder. At over six-feet-five and three hundred pounds, he never had much choice in seat selection. Exit row was the name of the game. He was on his way to Minneapolis for a weeklong fishing trip with two high school buddies who promised him trophy-sized smallmouth bass. The wife had given Dan the okay, and his grown son, who'd been invited, had been forced to work instead.

They were taxiing along toward the runway, and Dan leaned back and glanced across the aisle: a college-aged girl was reading a textbook with the word *Aesthetics* in the title, and beside her, a dark-skinned young man, perhaps Indian or Middle Eastern, sat quietly, his head lowered, his eyes closed. He looked scared. *Pussy.*

"Please slide your tray tables to their upright position . . ."

"Yeah, yeah," Dan said with a groan.

San Diego International Airport (SAN)
Cell-Phone Waiting Lot
North Harbor Drive

The fifty-space San Park cell-phone lot was located across a tree-lined drive from the Coast Guard Station's main gate and its rows of tiled-roof buildings. The lot was a rectangular strip of pavement with a single row of angled parking spaces set along tall rows of shrubs and a chain-link fence, beyond which stood hangars and other airport service facilities.

"Meyers split up his people. He's got six across the street at the Coast Guard Station, and he's got another four getting up on the roofs of the hangars to the north," said Towers. "The red Nissan is parked at the far end, south side. We're the team moving in."

"Not you, just me," said Moore, pulling into the lot and taking the nearest spot to their right beside a yellow Park-n-Ride van with dark tinted windows.

"I'm good," argued Towers. "I'm coming."

Moore winced. "You're the boss, boss." He unzipped his jacket so he'd have quick access to his shoulder holster, then hustled out of the SUV, keeping close to the shrubs, Towers tight to his shadow. A few SWAT team operators crawled catlike up the backside of the Coast Guard Station's roof. Moore caught movement up on the roofs of the hangars to their right, and for just a second he saw a head pop up, then vanish. These SWAT unit guys were hard-core assaulters, breachers, and sniper/observers, outfitted for war with Kevlar helmets, goggles, bulletproof vests, MOLLE (Modular Lightweight Load-carrying Equipment) gear buckling with attached equipment pouches, and H&K MP5 submachine guns—the standard-issue rifles for everyone but the snipers, who fielded the Precision Arms .308-caliber sniper rifle. One of Moore's buddies from SEAL Team 8 had left the Navy to become an FBI SWAT team member, and he'd schooled Moore in their weapons, tactics, techniques, and procedures. He'd even tried to recruit Moore, who at the time was being heavily courted by the CIA. The point was, Moore felt comfortable supported by these determined and highly trained operators.

The sign posted at the lot's entrance warned of a one-hour time limit and that vehicles must remain running—this to discourage long-term parking and loitering, and to create a sense of urgency in drivers all paying exorbitant fuel prices.

Consequently, as Moore and Towers approached the brick-red Nissan Versa, he saw immediately that the car was empty, its engine off. His shoulders shrank. The men hurried forward, and in frustration Moore rapped a fist on the driver's-side window.

Two SWAT team operators, along with a third man, middle-aged, gray sideburns, came around the corner and jogged toward them. The only tactical gear this older man wore was a vest and a helmet.

"Towers? Moore?" he called. "I'm Meyers. We empty here or what?"

Moore whirled around, studying the lot, his gaze panning the long row of cars and empty spaces, like ones and zeros, bits and bytes. Why would these guys leave a car in the cell-phone lot? Were they coming back for it within the hour? Were they concerned that they'd get towed? Where were they now?

He was just checking his watch, 5:42 p.m., when the back door of the yellow Park-n-Ride van beside their SUV slammed open, and out stepped a man wearing jeans, a plaid shirt, and a black balaclava concealing his face. He was shouldering a missile launcher.

Two more similarly dressed men burst out behind him, carrying machine guns.

The launcher guy rushed back toward Harbor Drive, positioning himself between the street and a tree to his left. He lifted his weapon into the air—

And there it was, his target, a Southwest twin-engine jet roaring into the sky, its blue-and-red fuselage glinting as the landing gear began folding away.

Moore observed this in the span of two breaths before he screamed, "The van!"

As he charged toward the group, the snipers across the street at the Coast Guard Station opened fire, hitting one of the terrorists brandishing a machine gun while his partner whirled and directed fire toward the rooftops across the street. The first guy's head jerked to the right, and a fountain of blood, flesh, and pieces of skull arced in the air.

Moore focused on the launcher guy, running and firing, striking the guy in the arm, the chest, the leg, as the terrorist lost his balance, turned—and a white-hot flash swelled from the launcher's barrel, which had drifted down toward the rows of parked cars.

With a gasp, Moore threw himself onto the grass median to his right as the missile raced across the lot and banked hard, finding the nearest heat source: the idling engine of the terrorists' own yellow van. The missile's warhead contained HE-fragmentation, the high explosive detonating on impact with the van's hood despite the minimum-distance arming sequence. Jagged pieces of steel, plastic, and glass flew in all directions as the van lifted six feet off the ground, the blast wave knocking Moore's SUV onto its side and doing likewise to the car on the other side of the van. At the same time, the van's gas tank ruptured, sending a pool of burning fuel spreading outward as the vehicle crashed back onto the ground with an echoing thud and a clatter of more glass. The stench of that burning fuel and the black smoke rising in thick clouds caught the attention of drivers out on the highway, and as Moore clambered to his feet, a taxi plowed into the back of a limousine, bumpers crunching. With ringing ears, and squinting against the smoke burning his eyes, Moore rushed to the launcher guy, who now lay on the ground, clutching his wounds, the green Anza launcher still hot and smoking, abandoned near his leg.

Moore dropped to his knees beside the man. He grabbed the guy by the shirt collar, ripped off his balaclava, and spoke through his teeth in Urdu: "Where's Samad?"

The guy just looked at him, his eyes full of red veins, his breathing more labored.

"WHERE IS HE?" Moore screamed.

Shouting erupted around him—the SWAT unit converging and trying to rescue someone from the car that had been blown over.

Towers hustled over to the other two terrorists, one lying supine on the pavement, the other on his side.

The launcher guy's eyes went vague; then his head fell limp. Moore cursed and shoved him back to the ground. He groaned his way up to his feet. "This was just one team!" he shouted to Towers. "Just one! There could be more!"

Los Angeles International Airport (LAX)
Cell-Phone Waiting Lot
9011 Airport Boulevard

Samad smiled tightly.

Every airport in the entire world was about to be shut down, nearly fifty thousand of them.

Every pilot in the sky, every last one of them, was about to receive orders to land immediately—

Even the fateful six, who would, of course, be unable to comply with those instructions.

Los Angeles, San Diego, Phoenix, Tucson, El Paso, and San Antonio . . . all major American cities whose first responders would confront sheer horrors unlike any they'd experienced before, airports whose TSA employees were about to realize that their "layers of security" policies had been ineffectual, that Rahmani's teams knew exactly how to act so as not to alert the behavior-detection officers. With flawless documents and nothing suspicious in their luggage, they'd been allowed on-board. Airport security teams, police, and local law enforcement authorities would be reminded that they could not secure the ground beneath so many flight paths.

Most of all, the American public—the infidels who polluted the holy lands, who endorsed leaders of injustice and oppression, and who rejected the truth—would turn their heads skyward and bear witness to Allah's power and might, fully alive before their eyes.

Samad opened his door and got out. He held the iPhone

up to the airliner in the distance, which was cutting through the sky with a deep and breath-robbing rumble. Confirmation.

He returned to the van, pulled on his balaclava, received the AK-47 handed to him by Niazi, then cried, *"Yalla!"* and swung around and wrenched open the van's back door.

Talwar climbed out with the Anza on his shoulder while Niazi came around, holding the second missile.

The woman in the Nissan Pathfinder with the flag of Puerto Rico hanging from her rearview mirror glanced up from her cell phone as Samad raised his rifle at her and Talwar turned to sight the airliner.

They were seconds away from launch, and while others in the lot began to look up from their phones, not a one of them made a move to get out of his or her car. They sat there, sheep, while Talwar counted aloud, *"Thalatha! Ithnain! Wahid!"*

The MK III tore away from the launcher, leaving a dense exhaust cloud in its wake. Before Samad could take another breath, Talwar and Niazi had counted down again, and Niazi was helping his comrade reload the weapon.

Torn between watching the missile's glowing trajectory and covering his men, Samad shifted around the van once more, swinging the weapon wildly on the cars in a show of force. The sheep began to react: mouths falling open, utter shock reaching their eyes.

Samad glanced back at the plane, at the ribbon of exhaust sewn across the sky, at the missile's white-hot engine a second before—

Impact!

42

DEVASTATION

Tucson International Airport (TUS)
Cell-Phone Waiting Lot
East Airport Drive
6:46 p.m. Mountain Time

Joe Dominguez was at the airport to pick up his cousin Ricky, who was flying in from Orlando to spend a week's vacation. Dominguez was twenty-four, an admittedly scrawny kid who made up for it with a keen wit and argumentative nature. He was the only son of Mexican immigrants who'd come legally into the United States back in the late 1970s. Both parents had eventually become citizens. Joe's father was a framer and drywall installer with a crew of ten who worked for a half-dozen commercial homebuilders in the Tucson metropolitan area. His mother had started her own maid service when he was a boy, and she now managed more than forty employees who cleaned both commercial and residential properties; they even had their own fleet of cars. Meanwhile, Joe had finished high school with little desire to attend "regular" college and had instead moved temporarily to Southern California, where he'd enrolled in Ford Motor Company's ASSET (Automotive Student Service Educational Training) program to get his AA degree and become a certified Ford Automotive Technician. After two long years of taking courses in engine control systems, brakes, steering/suspensions, transmissions, and fuel and emission control systems, he'd graduated with a 3.3 GPA. He returned home to Tucson, where he'd been hired by Holmes Tuttle Ford Lincoln Mercury. He loved being a grease monkey and had eventually saved up enough money to buy his dream ride: a black Ford F-250 FX4 pickup truck with six-inch lift kit and BFGoodrich Mud-Terrain T/A KM2 tires. His friends referred to the truck as the "black beast," and those brave enough to come along for a ride found they needed either a ladder or good flexibility to climb into the cab. Sure, the truck intimidated the girls he dated, but he wasn't looking for timid women, anyway. He wanted an adventurous girl. He was still looking.

As he sat there, the diesel engine thrumming, the radio set low so he could hear Ricky's call, he did a double take at the three men getting out of their Hampton Inn shuttle van parked across the lot in the next row of angled spaces. They were dressed like Mexicans but were taller, and all three wore black ski masks. While two guys argued with each other, a third went around the back to open the rear doors.

The two arguing broke off, and one pointed to the sky, where a Southwest jet was just lifting off.

Then the other guy reached past the van's open side door and handed his partner a rifle with a curved magazine, an AK-47.

Joe Dominguez blinked. Hard.

Now both guys had rifles and joined the third guy, who lifted to his shoulder a green missile launcher like the kind Dominguez had seen in Schwarzenegger movies. The launcher man swung his weapon toward the climbing airliner while the two riflemen swept their barrels across the rows of cars, covering him.

The cell-phone lot was packed, and a quick glance to his left revealed that the woman waiting in her small sedan was pointing at the men and yelling something at the teenage girl seated beside her.

This, Dominguez needed to remind himself, was not a daydream. These *motherfuckers*—because that's what they were—planned to shoot down that plane!

His heart raced as instincts took over. He threw the truck in gear, jammed his snakeskin boot down on the accelerator pedal, and took the black beast forward with a great roar and cloud of diesel exhaust. He steered directly for the guy with the launcher, covering the distance between them in three seconds.

The other two bastards reacted immediately with gunfire. Dominguez ducked behind the wheel as rounds punched through his windshield. First came a thump, then a much louder crash as he plowed into the back of the shuttle van. He stole a look up—

The other two, who'd gotten out of the way, fired once more into his truck, bullets pinging off the doors. He ducked again and let out a scream.

Then . . . more gunfire from outside. Different guns. He chanced a look through his side window, saw two men with pistols, one wearing a black cowboy hat, running straight at the terrorists and emptying their magazines. Dominguez, a registered gun owner himself, finally remembered that fact and reached into the center console of his truck. He dug out his Beretta, worked the safety, chambered a round, then jumped out of his truck.

He crouched down near the front wheel, and there beneath his engine lay the missile-launcher guy. He'd cracked his head open on the pavement but was still alive, groaning softly.

Gunfire continued popping, and in the fray, Dominguez watched as the terrorist glanced up at him, then reached toward his waist.

Dominguez cursed and fired a single round into his head.

"We're clear, we're clear!" someone shouted behind him. "They're all down!"

He craned his neck, and the man wearing the cowboy hat was hovering over him. His gray beard was closely cropped, and the diamond earring in his left ear seemed to match the twinkle in his eye. His collar was bound by a bolo tie featuring a longhorn steer head with turquoise eyes. "I saw what you did," he said. "That got my attention. I just can't believe it."

The cowboy proffered his hand, and Dominguez took it. He stepped away from the truck, then glanced back at his pride and joy.

Holy shit. The black beast was riddled with bullet holes. He gasped and began to feel a pinching sensation in his left arm. He pushed up his sleeve and noticed a cut across his biceps and a piece of skin flapping.

"Damn, son, you got grazed! I've never seen one that close!"

Dominguez didn't know what was happening, but as he touched the wound he began to feel nauseated, and then it hit. He'd almost died. He leaned over and threw up . . .

"Aw, that's all right, boy, you let it all out."

Sirens lifted in the distance.

And from inside the truck, his cell phone rang. Ricky . . .

US Airways Flight 155
Phoenix to Minneapolis

Mr. Dan Burleson had settled in to enjoy the terrific roar and awe-inspiring vibration of the Pratt & Whitney turbofan engines when three events occurred in succession.

First, they left the runway without incident and the fasten-seat-belt sign remained lit.

Second, the scared-looking guy beside the college girl suddenly threw off his seat belt and literally climbed over the girl, stomping on her lap, to get into the aisle.

Third—as Dan thought, *What the fuck?*—the guy began screaming for people to turn their electronic devices back on and video-record him. He raised his voice even more as some shocked passengers lifted their cell-phone cameras. A fiery light came into his eyes, and he spoke in a strange lilt, the words heavily accented but clear enough:

"People of America, this message is for you. The jihad has returned to your soil because we are free men who do not sleep under oppression. We are here by the grace of Allah to fight you infidels, to purge you from our Holy Lands, and to remind you that the false prophets in your White House who wage war against us to keep their corporations busy are responsible for your deaths. This is the recompense for unbelievers who attack Allah. This is the truth. *Allahu Akbar!*"

As one of the flight attendants who'd been buckled in at the front of the aircraft came rushing down the aisle, the crazy guy whirled, reached into his pocket, and produced his cell phone, which he held tightly in one hand, allowing it to jut out from the bottom of his fist like some pathetic knife. He reared back and ran toward the approaching attendant, a lithe blonde no more than five feet tall who couldn't have weighed more than 110 pounds.

Well, fuck this shit, Dan thought. He threw off his seat belt and bolted up into the aisle, charging after the guy, as two more flight attendants appeared behind the first.

And that's when the plane shook violently, as though it'd passed into a powerful downburst. A flash of light came through the windows near Dan's seat, and he flicked a quick glance back. Smoke and flames were whipping from beneath the wing, and worse: Most of the engine was now gone.

Meanwhile, the punk terrorist in the aisle was only a few seconds away from attacking the flight attendant.

Los Angeles International Airport (LAX)
Cell-Phone Waiting Lot
9011 Airport Boulevard

A few of the cars farther away from the van began to turn around and try to exit the lot, tires squealing a moment before two of them crashed into each other, blocking one exit.

Samad fired a warning salvo into the air as a fat Hispanic guy with a beard that seemed to have been drawn in marker on his face shouted at him.

Behind Samad, Niazi was helping Talwar load the second missile, and without delay—their count going exactly as planned—Talwar fired again.

The airliner had already taken the first hit. Its engine had exploded and was issuing a long trail of smoke as the plane rolled toward the damaged side.

Three, two, one, and praise Allah, the second missile, which Samad thought might take out the other engine, homed in on the hottest heat source, the first engine still on fire.

It was simply unbelievable to watch the MK III cut a secondary path through the first missile's smoke trail, a tiny spot of light growing fainter for a second until a magnificent flash, like the first impact.

Because the plane had rolled, this second strike tore up

through the flaming engine, blasting apart the wing. Part of it hung on for a second, then ripped off and boomeranged away beneath fountains of flaming and sparking debris.

Samad was enthralled by the image, unable to move, until the man who'd been yelling at him regained his attention. The guy had gotten out of his car and drawn a handgun. At that, Samad gasped and opened fire, full automatic, hammering the guy back into his low-rider car, blood spraying across the roof and windows.

And then, as quickly as it all happened, it was over. Samad leapt into the back of the van, where Talwar closed the door after him. Niazi was at the wheel now, and they sped away, riding up across the grass along the lot's perimeter, then bounding over the sidewalk and bouncing onto the street. They raced up to the first corner and turned sharply. Once there, they slowed with the traffic so as not to distinguish their vehicle from any others. They headed toward the parking garage five minutes away, where the second car and driver were waiting.

If only they had time to watch the airliner crash, but he'd assured his men that they'd be able to watch it over and over on TV, and that in the years to come, cable channels would create documentaries detailing the genius and audacity of their attack.

"Praise God, can you believe that?" cried Talwar, glancing up through the windshield, trying to watch the airliner's trajectory as it now began to dive inverted toward the ground at about a forty-five-degree angle.

"Today is a great day," cried Niazi.

Samad agreed, but he couldn't help wishing that he hadn't burned that photograph of his father.

110 Harbor Freeway Southbound
Los Angeles, California

Abe Fernandez cursed as the guy in front of him jammed on his brakes. It was too late. Fernandez plowed into the back of the guy, who was driving a piece-of-shit old Camry. But then some asshole smashed into the rear bumper of Fernandez's small pickup, and they were all piling up, one after another. He screamed, turned down the radio, and pulled his car over to the shoulder, his front bumper still attached to the other guy's car.

Growing up in downtown Los Angeles had allowed Fernandez to see a lot in his short life of nineteen years: car accidents, shootings, drug deals, high-speed chases . . .

But he had never witnessed anything like this.

He realized why everyone was stopping, why everyone was crashing, because in the sky to the west came a surreal sight.

He blinked hard. Not a dream. Or a nightmare.

A giant commercial airplane, US Airways, with its blue tailfin and pristine white fuselage, was missing a large portion of one wing, rolling out of control, and streaking directly toward them. What sounded like metal actually screaming and the plane's remaining engine joining in made Fernandez's jaw drop. In his next breath he smelled the jet fuel.

Reflexively, he threw open his door and started running back along the freeway, along with dozens and dozens of other drivers, the panic reaching their mouths, the cries of hysteria sending chills down Fernandez's spine as he felt the heat of the aircraft's approach.

He charged past a kid wearing an Abercrombie & Fitch T-shirt who was videoing the airliner with his iPhone, as though it were all happening on YouTube and he weren't about to be killed. The kid didn't move as Fernandez screamed at him, nearly knocked him over, and when he looked back, the airliner—upside down, dark liquids streaming from its torn wing, its single engine now coughing, struck the freeway at about a thirty-degree angle.

There was nowhere to go. Fernandez just stopped, faced the massive nose of the plane, and couldn't believe that this was the way he would die.

The plane exploded not fifty feet in front of him, the wind knocking him to the asphalt before the fires came roaring. He took a breath. No air. And then the plane was on him.

Gilbert Lindsay Community Center
East 42nd Place
Los Angeles, California

Barclay Jones was ten years old and loved going to the rec center. He was part of the after-school club, and his mom paid fifteen bucks a day so that he could play baseball with a pretty cool bunch of guys. He also got snacks and homework help and tutoring. There were a couple of bullies he didn't like at the center, but sometimes their moms couldn't afford to pay the money and they didn't come.

Barclay stepped up to the plate and was ready to hit a home run like one of his Baseball Hall of Fame favorites, Cal Ripken, Jr., who used to be called Iron Man back in the days when he played.

However, before the first pitch to him was thrown, a booming came from the distance. He frowned and lowered his bat, as the pitcher turned to his left and Barclay turned to his right. Now the booming sounded louder and louder, and just above the trees that formed a row behind right field came a strange line of black smoke rising high into the air, like the smoke from an old train chugging down the tracks.

The booming was louder now, and weird sounds like cars crashing and buildings smashing all at the same time got scary loud, and Barclay began to pant.

Something crashed through the trees, and it was only in that last second that he knew what it was, the tail section of a giant plane that looked as though it had tumbled along the ground, picking up pieces of buildings and trees and even what might be some people along the way.

Just after the tail came a rush of fire so loud that Barclay covered his ears and started to run toward the third-base line, as did every other player on the field. Barclay watched as the tail section came slicing across the field, and one by one his friends vanished beneath the gigantic, flaming steel. He screamed and called for his mother.

San Diego International Airport (SAN)
Cell-Phone Waiting Lot
North Harbor Drive

Moore and Towers were still on scene at the cell-phone lot, and the news coming in was changing by the second, rapid-fire and fragmented. Reports of missiles being launched from the ground . . . witnesses saying they filmed a crew in Los Angeles jumping out of a van and firing on a plane . . . more witnesses saying they saw something very similar in San Antonio.

Panic. Pandemonium. Moore watched a news feed on his smartphone with an on-air anchor having to leave her seat because she began crying . . .

People in New York and Chicago were reporting that they thought they saw missiles fired at planes taking off from their airports . . .

A police officer in Phoenix said he witnessed a missile rise up from the ground to strike a plane taking off . . . He'd recorded the video with his phone, had e-mailed it to his local news station.

And there it was, a white-hot streak on Moore's phone screen, rising like a firefly to strike the airliner.

"How did you get such a good picture of this?" the anchor asked. "It all happened so fast."

"My daughter wanted me to take some videos of planes taking off and landing for a school project. I just came down here when I got off work. It's a coincidence that's making me sick."

US Airways Flight 155
Phoenix to Minneapolis

Before the screaming man could strike the tiny flight attendant with his cell phone, Dan Burleson came up behind him and wrapped one of his powerful arms beneath the man's chin while simultaneously seizing the man's arm and drawing it behind his back with such force that he heard the man's shoulder popping.

The guy let out an ear-shattering cry as Dan dragged him back and away from the attendant, saying, "I got him! I got him!" If there was a federal air marshal onboard, Dan didn't see him . . .

At the same time that Dan seized the guy, the plane began to roll, and Dan knew that the pilots would have to compensate for the missing engine. Dan dragged himself backward with the terrorist in hand until he got near his seat and collapsed into it, still gripping the thug by the throat. He did not make a conscious decision to increase his grip. The man struggled against him, and Dan only reacted. He gritted his teeth and fought to remain in his seat as the single engine thundered up and the passengers continued to cry and scream. An elderly black woman two seats ahead got to her feet and shouted, "Y'all be quiet and let Jesus do his work here!"

And that's when Dan realized that maybe Jesus had begun his work, because the terrorist was no longer moving and the pilots had finally leveled out. Dan relaxed his grip on the man and just sat there, listening, as the pilots ramped the engine to full power. They'd already no doubt cut off the fuel supply to the damaged engine and had rotated the dials on the transponder to read 7700, the Air Traffic Control (ATC) code for EMERGENCY. Flight controllers had noticed the brightening of the plane's radar signature on their screens and were receiving audible alarms of the emergency. No radio contact would be necessary. Those pilots were too busy attending to the aircraft to give a second thought about talking to ATC.

The flight attendant who was about to be attacked staggered her way to him and looked at the terrorist.

"Is he dead?"

Dan shrugged, but he felt pretty sure he had choked the guy to death.

She widened her eyes, started to say something, changed her mind, then said, "You have to buckle up! Now!"

Dan shoved the guy into the seat next to his, then buckled up as he was told.

The college girl, whose face was now stained with tears, looked over at him and nodded.

San Diego International Airport (SAN)
Cell-Phone Waiting Lot
North Harbor Drive

Moore and Towers were standing near the open back door of an SUV, watching a live news feed on a laptop supplied by SAC Meyers. Moore glanced down at his hand; it was shaking.

The incidents appeared to be moving from west to east. The West Coast news was in full swing, and their reaction time in airing news was much faster. Moore had already watched footage captured by a KTLA news helicopter of the incredible and surreal damage in Los Angeles, the long line of destruction carved across the city as the plane had struck the freeway, then dropped down to plow through the densely populated section of West 41st and West 42nd Streets, destroying homes, bars, bargain stores, fish markets, and anything else in its way. The tail section had been catapulted off the freeway at an even higher velocity than the rest of the plane and had crashed into a recreation center, where, reports said, more than twenty children had been killed.

"Moore," Towers called, lowering his phone. "They just tried to hit Tucson, but a group of civilians took them out. And I just heard they hit El Paso and San Antonio. That's six so far. It's a full-on terrorist attack. Nine-eleven all over again."

Moore cursed and glanced at the three bodies of the terrorists being zipped up while the fire department crew continued foaming down the area.

US Airways Flight 155
Phoenix to Minneapolis

If Dan Burleson had to bet on it, he'd say the pilots were trying to decide if they thought they could initiate a turn and make it back to the airport. The more likely situation was that they would land at the best possible off-airport site. It all depended on whether or not they thought they had enough power to keep the plane level. If they attempted to turn without sufficient power, they'd very quickly lose altitude. Pilots of single-engine aircraft were instructed to never, ever, attempt to return to the runway, because they would lose too much altitude to effect the turnaround. Case in point: On January 15, 2009, Captain Chesley Sullenberger was in command of US Airways Flight 1549 en route from La Guardia to Charlotte. He had lifted off and flown through a flock of birds, resulting in the loss of both engines. He knew he'd lose precious altitude if he started a turnaround with no engines producing power, and determined that his best course of action was to ditch in the river. His actions had saved the lives of the crew and every passenger on board.

They could blame the birds for that near disaster, but Dan felt certain that Mr. Allahu Akbar in the seat next to him, along with his buddies, was responsible for their present dilemma.

"Ladies and gentlemen, this is Captain Ethan Whitman. As most of you already know, we've lost an engine but plan to make our turn and head back to the airport. We have every confidence that we'll be able to set the aircraft down on the runway. Those noises you just heard were the gear going down and now we're about to initiate our all-important turn back to Phoenix. Despite our confidence regarding the landing, we will still initiate crash-landing procedures and want to insist that you remain calm and allow the attendants to do their jobs. Listen to what they say and comply immediately for your own safety and the safety of those around you. Thank you."

Not five seconds later, the aircraft began to turn.

Bring us home, boys, Dan thought. *Bring us home.*

United States Coast Guard Station
San Diego, California

Moore, Towers, and a few of Meyers's FBI agents had gone across the street and spoken to the Coast Guard Station's commanding officer, John Dzamba, who'd already sent out a dozen of his personnel to help control the scene and keep traffic moving. They borrowed a conference room equipped with big-screen TVs, and there Moore paced and watched the screens with a mixture of horror and disbelief, while Towers got online to see what intel the other agencies were gathering.

Nearly every television network in the United States of America was interrupting its regularly scheduled programming to bring word about the multiple missile attacks on airliners heading toward the East from the West Coast. The local San Diego news stations' anchors began speculating on more attacks that might happen in the Midwest and at airports along the East Coast as flights everywhere were being grounded and air traffic controllers were doing their best to take those planes away from highly volatile areas such as the oil refineries near Newark, New Jersey, and other heavily populated areas. As a matter of fact, in Newark, flights from Europe would be diverted to Nova Scotia/Newfoundland as they had been on 9/11. And likewise as had occurred on 9/11, rumors and false reports continued to run rampant.

Slater and O'Hara finally got on a video conference that Slater said could last no more than two minutes because they were understandably swamped.

"The nuke teams are already converging on the major cities," said O'Hara.

"And we've got the NSA's computers monitoring cell phones for key words like flight numbers, Middle Eastern accents and phrases. Your man Samad might try to give his boss Rahmani a report, and if he does, then we'll work on triangulating his location."

"These guys are too smart for that. The only way to get him is HUMINT," said Moore. "Boots on the ground. People who know where Samad is going. He's got help. Sleepers everywhere, safe houses. They know how to hide—and if they still got Gallagher helping them, then he's taught them all our TTPs."

"We've got a team hunting for him," said Slater. "And they will find him."

O'Hara chimed in: "Towers, we've got the go-ahead to keep you on this, because your JTF is already set up for interagency ops. You'll team up with some new agents from the FBI, DEA, and I've got a TSA guy we need to get onboard. I assume you're well enough to keep working?"

"Hell, yeah, sir," said Towers.

Moore began to shake his head. "The answers aren't here. They're back there. In the mountains. In Waziristan. Did you call off the air strikes for me?"

"Still working on it," said Slater.

Moore held back a curse. "Please work harder. *Sir*."

After the call, Moore went into the bathroom. He had the dry heaves and just hung his head over the toilet for a few minutes. When he returned to the conference room, he found a fresh cup of coffee waiting for him.

Towers gave him a sympathetic look. "Hey, man, there's no way in hell we could've known this shit would go down. We signed on to take out a cartel. Our timing sucked. Period. But we still did our jobs."

They both glanced back at the flat screen, now showing live video of the plane in Phoenix landing at the airport, one engine still smoking. The gear hit the tarmac in a picture-perfect landing.

But then the broadcast was interrupted once more, by live images of a plane coming down toward Interstate 10 outside San Antonio.

"Oh my God," Moore said with a gasp.

Both engines were out, and it was all the pilot could do to keep the aircraft level. The gear was down, but then he suddenly lost more altitude.

The highway was jammed with building rush-hour traffic, and drivers attempted to pull off to the shoulder, but they were hardly in time.

Two hundred feet. One hundred. The main gear hit the ground but then collided with several cars before the forward gear suddenly slammed down with such a force that the wheels just snapped off, sending the plane skidding forward and through more cars, which were bulldozed out of the way and sent tumbling through the air like Matchbox toys. The fuselage split apart, just forward of the wings, and that first section broke off and went spinning off the highway, while the rest of the jet began to slow as it continued crashing through more and more cars, dense black smoke rising in its wake.

The newspeople were now crying on the air, and Towers was saying, "There'll be survivors for sure. Some people will walk away from that."

Moore tore his fingers through his hair, then tugged out his smartphone and sent off a text message to Wazir.

MUST TALK ASAP. URGENT.

43

THE MORE THINGS CHANGE

DEA Office of Diversion Control
San Diego, California

MOORE AND TOWERS had hitched a ride back with Meyers and his agents, who'd dropped them off at the DEA office. Video taken by a woman waiting at LAX's cell-phone lot showed three terrorists standing near a DirecTV satellite van. They wore jeans and flannel shirts like migrant workers, with balaclavas concealing their faces. Gigi Rasmussen was a nineteen-year-old USC freshman who'd started her recording with the launch of the second missile, the killing of a civilian who'd challenged the terrorists, and then their departure, all narrated by her as she gasped and repeatedly chanted "ohmygod" throughout the entire sequence. She'd sold the video to CNN, but the Agency had managed to stop its airing in the interest of national security, although Moore knew it'd eventually be released to the public. The missile launcher was identified as an Anza, the missile presumably an MK III, the same type used by the guys in San Diego. The Agency could now focus its searches for weapons deals on that specific ordnance, but even a cursory scan of the MANPADS' specs told Moore enough: The weapon's place of origin was Pakistan, and the MK III missiles were the Chinese version of the American Stinger. These were the types of weapons the Taliban might have access to and train with in Waziristan.

Moore reviewed every photo they had on file of Mullah Abdul Samad and zoomed in on the man's eyes in each photograph. Then he compared those eyes to a still image he'd captured from the video. He rapped a knuckle on the screen and told Towers to look for himself.

"Damn, that could be him. And hey, they found what was left of the van at a Johnny Park on 111th Street. They burned it up. No weapons. No witnesses. You know why? Because they killed all the employees there. Gagged and taped them up, then stabbed them."

Moore shook his head in disgust. "Mark my words, if they find any DNA at all, it'll match what we got off the pendant. Samad led the team in L.A. I'll bet my life on it."

Towers considered that, then his expression grew odd. "There's one other thing. Apparently these scumbags like chocolate. They found wrappers all over the floor mats. Foil survived the fire."

"Maybe they'll get some good samples off of those, but you know what's scaring me now? The thought of how many sleepers they had helping them . . ." Moore flicked his glance up to the television.

All planes were on the ground now. FEMA teams were on the way. Roadblocks and checkpoints were going up within a one-hundred-mile radius of the six major airports where the incidents had occurred. Samad and his men must have accounted for those. Had they escaped before the checkpoints had gone up? Or would they remain within the secured zone for a few days or even a few weeks?

Meanwhile, the entire country was holding its collective breath, waiting to see what else might happen—chemical, biological, or nuclear—as the terrible, *terrible* images continued flashing across screens. People in Times Square had crowded into the streets and stood like zombies, their necks craned up to the towering images of charred landscape, scars across the soil and the fabric of the nation.

Six planes had been targeted on June 6. Two airliners whose engines had been struck by missiles had landed safely: Phoenix and El Paso. The Los Angeles flight had crashed, killing all passengers, crew, and hundreds of civilians on the ground. The Tucson flight proceeded without incident after a young kid named Joe Dominguez ran over one of the terrorists with his jacked-up truck. The San Antonio flight had crash-landed, with survivors being pulled alive from that wreck. The death tolls were mounting.

By nine p.m., the President of the United States was addressing the nation and quoting liberally from George W. Bush's address on that fateful Tuesday in September 2001:

"The search is under way for those who are behind these evil acts. I've directed the full resources of our intelligence and law enforcement communities to find those responsible and bring them to justice. We will make no distinction between the terrorists who committed these acts and those who harbor them."

"So if you're Samad, where do you go?" asked Towers. "Michigan? Canada? Or the other direction . . . back into Mexico?"

"If he slips across either border we can still legally pursue him," Moore said.

"You think that's his plan?"

"Actually, I think he's going to lay low. He's got a safe house somewhere in L.A. He's there right now. Probably some little apartment in the valley."

"Well, if he doesn't make a break for one of the borders now, he'll have a hell of time after this."

"Yeah, so it's one thing or the other. He's racing toward the border right now, or he'll just sit tight till things cool off. Then he'll make his move to wherever his final destination is."

"Back to Pakistan?"

"Nah, too dangerous for that. We don't have much on him, but we know he's got friends in Zahedan and Dubai. We need to get his face out there. Some neighborhood kid could ID him."

"Sit tight, bro. When that DNA comes back from the van, I think your boys in Langley might be willing to go public."

"They'd better be. So . . . there's no way I can sleep. Let's go up to L.A."

Towers took a long pull on his coffee, nodded, and said, "It's been one hell of a night."

Phoenix Sky Harbor International Airport
Terminal 4, Concourse D

Dan Burleson squinted against the blinding lights and the cameras directed at him and the rest of the passengers as they entered the terminal, having just completed the inflatable-slide exit from the plane made infamous by a JetBlue flight attendant who, after being harassed by a passenger, had quit his job and subsequently exited the plane in the same fashion, in what some called the most epic resignation ever. Before exiting the plane, Dan and the others had been told that they would need to be quarantined and questioned briefly by federal investigators. Doctors would also be available, and vouchers to make up for the flight would be issued. The flight attendant who'd nearly been attacked had clutched Dan's hand before he exited the plane and said, "Thank you."

He'd blushed.

As they moved through the crowd of media held back by airport security guards, the black lady who'd told everyone to shut up lifted her voice to the crowd: "Jesus did his work tonight! And he gave us this great man right here! This hero who saved us from the terrorist on our plane!"

She pointed directly at Dan, who winced and waved and

tried to move as quickly as he could past the throng as camera lights now went off like fireworks. He had a feeling that by morning, he'd be sitting in numerous TV studios and giving interviews about something that had never occurred to him as heroism. He wanted to believe that anyone in his position would have done the same thing, that there were still Good Samaritans left in this world. That's all there was to it.

And, alas, the smallmouth bass would have to wait.

University Medical Center
Tucson, Arizona

Joe Dominguez had been examined by the doctor, his arm stitched up, and then he'd been questioned by the local Tucson police and by two guys from the FBI, who must have asked him one thousand questions in just one hour.

His parents came down to the hospital, and after he was released, two cops said they would "help" get him back to his parents' car. He didn't understand what that meant until the automatic doors opened and they went outside—

Into a crowd of reporters, probably ten or fifteen of them, with cameramen and lights—and the sight of those cameras balanced on the shoulders of those men gave Dominguez a flashback to the moment, even as digital cameras began to flash. A reporter he recognized from the local news thrust her microphone into his face and said, "Joe, we know you were a hero out there, taking down the terrorists. Can you tell us what happened?"

"Uh, I wish I could, but they told me not to say anything right now."

"But it's true that you ran over the guys with your truck, then shot one of them in the head, right? We've talked to other witnesses who've told us that."

Dominguez looked back at his father, who shook his head vigorously: *Don't talk!*

"Uh, I can't say anything. But if they tell me that I can, then, you know, hey, I'll tell you all about it."

"What does it feel like to be a hero?" shouted another reporter.

Before he could respond, the police forced back the reporters and steered Joe and his parents through the breach. By the time they reached his father's battered white pickup truck, he was exhausted.

And his father was crying.

"Dad, what's wrong?"

"Nothing," his father said, glancing away, embarrassed. "I'm just so proud of you."

Johnny Park
111th Street
Los Angeles, California

About two and a half hours later, Moore and Towers were in Los Angeles, talking with the incident commander inside the parking garage.

Another of the CIA's mobile labs had arrived to assist the

FBI's forensic teams. Moore spoke to the techs, who said they were using the new rapid DNA analysis platform, the same one they'd used on the pendant back in San Diego.

By morning he had his answer: The DNA on the foil wrappers they'd found matched what had been on the pendant.

U.S. Embassy
Islamabad, Pakistan
One Week Later

Photographs of Samad, Talwar, Niazi, and Rahmani had been released to the world. The Agency had been denying any knowledge of exactly how the terrorists had passed into the country, and the talking heads were in their glory, with hundreds of hours of television programming easily filled by their speculation and arguments about better securing America's borders and how the Department of Homeland Security, despite all the budget increases and measurable improvements, had failed the nation. TSA screeners were more adept at discovering transvestites and breast implants than would-be terrorists—so said the pundits. The comptroller general of the United States, the head of the GAO (Government Accountability Office), was being questioned about a recent performance audit of the DHS in which he stated that the DHS was not making its operations transparent enough for Congress to be sure the department was working effectively, efficiently, and economically, in view of its massive annual budget. The GAO would once again exercise its broad statutory right to the department's records in an attempt to pinpoint where the failures had taken place. Moore could only hope that public pressure didn't take the investigation to the CIA, to Calexico, to a border tunnel that had been controlled by the Juárez Cartel and exploited by terrorists, to a man assigned to shut down that cartel.

Once again American flags were being raised over homes throughout America, and those who'd been largely apathetic about their patriotism suddenly found it once more. Cries in Congress for a military response like the one seen after 9/11 got citizens enraged and protesting for an overwhelming response. Thousands rallied on Capitol Hill. Gun sales increased tenfold. Mosques were bombed and looted.

Then, on the seventh day after the terror strike, a victory was reported in the tribal lands of Pakistan: Mullah Omar Rahmani was, according to Moore's colleagues, dead, killed by a Hellfire missile launched from one of the CIA's Predator drones. His death was the only good news to reach the American people since the attack. The hunt for the other terrorists was ongoing and thus far unsuccessful, despite thousands of man-hours and tens of thousands of leads.

The President gave a press conference to confirm that the "mastermind" behind the airliner attacks had been killed—and country-music stars were already releasing new songs about how America kicks ass.

Moore hardly celebrated Rahmani's demise. He had not heard back from Wazir, and the old man's silence deeply troubled him and robbed the so-called good news of any pleasure.

He told Slater and O'Hara that he would travel to Pakistan himself to ID Rahmani's body; it was something he had to do. At the same time, he would try to reestablish contact with Wazir. He also reminded his bosses that killing Rahmani might have made it impossible to find the others. While he didn't like it, Moore understood why his request to have the drones stand down had been denied. The American people wanted blood, and the Agency had been under extreme pressure to give it to them. The days of the Colosseum had returned.

Moore had flown into Islamabad and thought he'd first stop at the embassy to surprise Leslie. He'd learned through a mutual friend that she'd been transferred from the embassy in Kabul back to the one in Islamabad, where they'd first met.

He caught her in the parking lot as she was heading out for lunch.

"Oh my God," she said, then lowered her glasses to stare over the rim. "Am I dreaming?"

"No, I am."

She shoved him hard in the shoulder. "That's cheesy, and you, uh, look pretty good. You clean up well. I like the haircut. It reminds me that we should do more to strengthen our bilateral relationship."

"You mean we should get something straight between us?"

"That's inappropriate."

"I'd like to get inappropriate with you."

She took a deep breath and turned away.

"What?"

"What do you mean 'What?' What did you expect? I gave them my two weeks' notice. I'm leaving at the end of the week, going back to the U.S."

He threw his hands up, knowing how much she'd put into the career. "Why?"

"Because this isn't for me anymore. I thought a transfer back to Islamabad would make a difference, but it hasn't. The only thing that made it fun and exciting was you."

"No, no, no. You need to slow down. Let's go over to Club 21 like old times. They still got the best beer in this town."

"The only beer in this town."

He moved to her, put his hand beneath her chin. "I owed you a real good-bye—not that awkward, uh, whatever that was on the phone, and that's why I came back. If this made it worse, then I'm just an idiot, but I didn't want to leave it like that. I felt terrible."

"You did?"

He nodded, and two rounds of beers later, he dropped her off at the embassy, and there was a moment where he held her hand, squeezed it tightly, and said, "You're going to have a great life."

Miran Shah
North Waziristan
Near the Afghan Border

Before driving up to North Waziristan, Moore stopped off at Forward Operating Base Chapman, one of the CIA's key facilities in Afghanistan, located near the eastern city of Khost. Chapman was the site of the infamous suicide attack that, on December 30, 2009, killed seven CIA operatives, including the chief of the base. The Agency's primary mission at that time was to gather HUMINT for drone attacks against targets located within the tribal lands, and those attacks had incited retaliation from the Taliban operating across the border. The attack was one of the most lethal ever carried out against the CIA. Moore knew three of the dead men and had spoken on the phone with all the others. He'd walked around in a daze for about a week afterward. It was, for everyone, a devastating loss.

Rahmani's body—or what was left of it—had been transferred there, and while the torso had been shredded by the bombs, his face had remained somewhat intact. Moore was probably imagining it, but it almost seemed that he'd died with a sardonic grin on his face.

Moore arrived in Miran Shah in the late afternoon. The dust and squalor and antiquated influences of Western culture struck him once more. This time, however, without Rana as his driver, he was aggressively stopped by four guards, members of the Army who were pleased to show him the business ends of their AK-47s. Frowning, one of them shouldered his weapon and shook his finger at Moore. "I remember you."

"I remember you, too," Moore lied. "I'm heading up to see Wazir."

The guards looked strangely at one another, and then the one who remembered Moore said, "ID, please."

Moore waited while the man inspected the document.

"Okay," he said, returning the ID. "Where is your young friend?"

Moore averted his gaze. No reason to lie now. "He died."

"Sorry."

The guards lowered their rifles, and he was waved on. Moore followed the dirt road, remembering the turn to the right and the ascent through the foothills. He pulled up near the two brick homes with satellite dishes on their roofs and the collection of tents rising behind them. The goats and cows were shifting in their pens behind, and in the valley below were dozens of farmers working the fields. He had never smelled air so clean.

An old man came out, leaving the door open behind him, and Moore did a double take. This man wore black robes and a matching vest, but his beard was much shorter than Wazir's. Two more men appeared—soldiers with rifles pointed at Moore. He shut down the engine and stepped out.

"Who are you?" asked the old man.

"My name is Khattak. I've come to see Wazir."

"Wazir?" The old man faced his guards, then gestured for them to return to the house.

"Is something wrong?" Moore asked.

The old man made a face. "I'll take you to see him." He started around the house and past the tents, working his way along the animal pens and through a serpentine path toward the hillside beyond. Moore followed in silence.

"So, you are a friend?" the old man finally asked as they mounted the hill.

"Yes. And you?"

"Oh, yes. Wazir and I fought the Soviets together."

Moore took a deep breath and hoped against fate that his suspicions weren't true. "What is your name?"

"Abdullah Yusuff Rana."

Moore stopped walking and turned back toward the valley. This was Rana's grandfather and the reason why young Rana had known Wazir all of his life. Moore wanted very badly to tell the old man that he knew his grandson, that the boy had worked bravely for him, given his life for what he believed in, and that Moore owed him everything.

"Do you see something?" the old man asked.

Moore shook his head. "Just beautiful up here."

The older Rana shrugged and led him farther up the hill, where near the top lay a deep crater with pulverized stone lying in curious lines and fanning out in all directions. Off to the left was a rectangular mound lying in the shade of three tall trees. A grave.

Rana pointed. "Do you want me to leave you alone?"

Moore tried to breathe. Tried. "What happened?"

"I thought you knew."

Moore shook his head vigorously.

Rana looked to the sky. "Wazir liked to come up here to

read and meditate. The drone flew over and dropped the bomb on him. As far as we are concerned, he was a martyr, buried in the clothes he died in, lying on his side and facing Mecca, and it was Allah's will that he died in his most favorite place." Rana closed his eyes and added in Arabic, *"Inna Lillahi wa Inna ileyhi Raj'oon."*

Truly we belong to Allah, and truly to Him shall we return.

"I will leave you alone," said Rana, heading back the way they'd come.

Moore stepped over to the grave site. He'd been planning to take Wazir up on his offer:

"When you're ready to talk, come back to me. I want to hear your story. I'm an old man. I'm a good listener."

I'm sorry, Wazir. You did everything you could for me, and I got you killed. I came here looking for answers. Now I won't get any. I wanted to tell you about the most difficult thing I've done in my life. Do you know what it is? Just trying to forgive myself. I don't know how.

Moore rubbed the corners of his eyes, then started back down the hillside. The breeze caught his hair, and he thought he could hear the old man's voice in his ear, but it was only the rustle of leaves.

Samad and the rest of those evil bastards would escape because of big bureaucracies and impatience and actionable intelligence that excused murder. The more things changed, the more they stayed the same.

When he reached the front of the house, Rana was waiting for him and said, "Please stay for the evening meal."

It would be rude for Moore to decline, but he was too depressed to do much more than leave.

A tug came at his sleeve. It was the boy who'd helped Wazir serve them stew. He was Wazir's great-grandson, Moore remembered, maybe eight or nine years old. Between his thumb and forefinger was a slip of yellow lined paper folded in half. "My great-grandfather said if you came when he wasn't home, I should give this to you."

44

COLD-TRAILING

CIA Safe House
Saidpur Village
Islamabad, Pakistan

THE ENTIRE WORLD'S intelligence and law enforcement assets were hunting for Samad and his men, and Moore had been handed an address on a slip of paper that could very well be the most significant clue anyone had.

However, that information gave him pause.

If he turned it over to the Agency, and they in turn released that intel to all agencies worldwide, the hyper-alert Samad with contacts everywhere would vanish before they ever arrived.

So with the paper tucked tightly into his pocket, Moore had come to the old safe house. It was a bittersweet return. He reflected on the many conversations he'd had with Rana as they'd sat on the balcony among the Margallah Hills, the lights of Islamabad flickering in the distance. He could almost hear the kid's voice: *"What's wrong, Money? You look really tense now."*

And he was, while he waited impatiently for all the connections of the video conference he'd set up for himself, Slater, O'Hara, and Towers.

Once everyone was online, he abandoned all pleasantries and hit them immediately with the news. "I've got a credible lead on Samad. It comes from Wazir, and I trust it. I'm flying out tonight."

"You know where Samad is?" asked O'Hara.

"I might."

"Then let's get a team together," said Slater. "How many guys you need? Ten? Twelve?"

Moore shook his head. "Look, if he's on the run, he's traveling with his two lieutenants. That's it. Maybe Gallagher's helping them, I don't know. Point is, Towers and I got this."

"You're pitching a two-man show? Are you kidding me?" asked O'Hara, raising his voice.

"No, sir. I'm not."

O'Hara leaned toward the camera. "We need to capture this guy alive—because we're hearing he'll take over for Rahmani, and that means he's already got significant operational intelligence. We also assume he knows where the rest of the missile teams are, and not a one of those guys has been captured. Make no mistake: Samad is the Highest-Value Target in the world right now."

"Sir, with all due respect, the importance of the target

does not necessarily dictate the size and scope of the operation. If my lead is solid, our target is already out of the U.S., and if you saddle me with a team to go down there, we're harder to move, harder to hide, and we make a lot more noise. If the operation goes south, you've got an increased likelihood of witnesses, bodies, and yes, you've been there, done that. Towers and I will barely make a ripple. You go in there with big guns, and our guy will be long gone."

O'Hara sighed. "So you want to go down there. Exactly where is that?"

"I've got an address in Mexico—and given what you've just said, it's not only imperative that we take Samad alive but that we're able to question him without political interference."

Slater cleared his throat and weighed in. "Moore, if you and Towers get this bastard, I don't want any other agencies involved. I don't want the administration involved—no one, that is, until we've had our time with him."

"We're on the same page. So we're talking about rendition."

"Gentlemen, whoa, whoa, whoa. Slow down," said O'Hara. "I can neither confirm nor deny I've heard any of this, and I'll need to step out at this time." He rose, giving them a hard look and a thumbs-up.

"We understand," said Slater.

After 9/11, approximately three thousand suspected terrorist prisoners were captured and imprisoned by the CIA, an act known as "extraordinary rendition." These prisoners were transferred around the world to top-secret detention centers known as "black sites," many of them in Europe. The Council of Europe and a majority of the European Union parliament claimed that these prisoners were tortured and that both the United States and British governments were well aware of the entire operation. A more recent Executive Order signed by the President of the United States opposed rendition torture.

Consequently, O'Hara was excusing himself because he needed deniability. He would not knowingly order Moore to capture Samad then have him transferred to a black site for torture. The United States government did not engage in acts of torture, did not transfer people to places where officials knew they'd be tortured, and black sites no longer existed.

On the other hand, Slater was thankfully still living in the past. He lifted his voice: "You capture that bastard, and I'll work with you all the way."

"Then here's the deal," said Moore. "No teams, no other U.S. forces involved. We keep the administration clean. Just Towers and I. No witnesses. You let us hunt Samad down our way—and then you'll get your rendition, and we'll get what we need out of that miserable fuck, no matter what it takes. Otherwise, Washington gets involved, he's moved into military jurisdiction . . . and even if Samad never sees the inside of a courtroom and rots away at Gitmo, he'll never be put in a position to tell us what we want. We get him, we get what we need, then we stage some fake capture and turn him over to the administration and let them play with him—after we've already bled him dry. My point is, if we don't have this all planned first, then capturing him is a waste of time. His intel is worth more than his life."

"Wow," said Towers with a gasp. "Wow."

"Mr. Towers, you sure you want in?" asked Slater. "This could get ugly, as in career-ending ugly."

Towers snorted and checked his watch. "I'm sorry, sir, I don't have time to talk. I need to catch a plane."

"Call me on your way to the airport," said Moore. Towers broke his connection, leaving Moore and Slater alone.

"I asked him, and I'll ask you," began Slater. "You sure you want to do this?"

"Yeah. Just work with me and don't change your mind. Don't bow to the pressure. And don't forget about all the blood, sweat, and tears we've shed trying to flush out these bastards. If Samad can help us disrupt their operations, then it's worth it." Moore's gaze went distant. "I used to sit out here on this balcony, talking to Rana about doing just that. So let's finish what we started."

Puerto Penasco/Rocky Point
Sonora, Mexico

The gated and security-patrolled beachfront community of Las Conchas was on mainland Mexico's west coast, overlooking the Gulf of California, and was about four hundred miles west of Ciudad Juárez. The address Wazir had given his great-grandson was for an estate comprising three separate living areas, with three kitchens, eleven bedrooms, and twelve baths. The home was on the market for $2.7 million, and, according to the real estate site that Moore had accessed, it offered 180-degree ocean-front vistas. The home belonged to Mr. David Almonte Borja.

And with just a little more research, Moore learned that Borja was, in fact, Ernesto Zúñiga's brother-in-law and, according to Dante Corrales, the most likely heir to the Sinaloa Cartel.

But here was the kicker: Just forty-eight hours prior, Borja had been taken into custody by Federal Police inspectors and was being held in Mexico City on murder, conspiracy to commit murder, and drug-smuggling charges. The timing of his arrest was not entirely coincidental; Federal Police Inspector Alberto Gómez had named two colleagues who had, in turn, given up many more details regarding Borja and his relationship to the cartel.

That Las Conchas had its own security force made accessing the community even easier. Moore and Towers met with the security company's owner, who understood the English alphabet very well: CIA.

The owner said that according to his guards, no one had been in the house since Borja had been arrested. Had the real estate agent shown the home to anyone? They didn't think so. Multimillion-dollar homes seldom drew a lot of traffic, and were shown by appointment only after the potential buyer had been prequalified.

"Give your guards the night off with pay," Moore told the man. "We'll cover it."

"Okay."

They left him and went to see the real estate agent, an

elegant woman in her late fifties who bore a striking resemblance to the movie star Sophia Loren. She was equally cooperative and somewhat depressed because she'd learned of Borja's arrest and would lose a major commission. She gave them the code to the lockbox on the front door and the code to disarm the security system. Moore would not have minded picking the lock; there were few companies on the planet who could machine their parts to near flawless tolerances and still make money, which of course kept locksmiths, thieves, and spies in business.

With the Agency's satellites focused on the home, Moore and Towers, wearing security guard uniforms, drove their golf cart into the driveway at five p.m. local time. Towers went around the side of the house to check on the power: Still on.

Moore plugged in the code on the lockbox, removed the key, and worked the lock. The main building had three security keypads: one in the entrance foyer, one in the garage, and another in the master bedroom. The door opened. No warning tone to indicate the alarm was about to go off or beeping to indicate the door had simply been opened. There was no sound at all, as though the alarm had not only been turned off but dismantled. Moore was right. The keypad's status light was unlit. Wires had been cut. *Odd.*

They moved quietly inside, across mosaic tile that formed a zodiac wheel in the center of the grand foyer. This main house was still fully furnished in a fusion of contemporary and Southwest designs, which was to say that everything looked damned expensive to Moore. From somewhere within came the faint sound of a television.

Moore gave Towers a hand signal. Towers nodded and held back. He was recovering well from his shoulder and arm wounds, but it'd be another year before he entered his next Ironman competition. Moore clutched his suppressed Glock with both hands and took point.

A hallway ahead. A mirror on the wall, television images flashing in that mirror. He took two more steps. The bedroom door to the left was open. He smelled food . . . Meat? Chicken? He wasn't sure. He glanced to his right, back into the mirror, and froze. He looked back at Towers, emphatic: *Don't fucking move!* Then he faced the mirror once more, calculating distances, his own reaction time, how quickly he thought his opponent might move. He'd call on muscle memory and sheer aggression honed by years of fieldwork.

He finished plotting his advance, rehearsed it in his mind's eye, and knew that if he thought about it anymore, he'd get the shakes. *Time to move.*

A toilet flushed. The master bathroom lay just inside the suite, and a woman's voice came from within: "I'm so drunk now!"

Moore flicked a look back at Towers, pointed, and mouthed the command: *You get her.*

And then Moore bolted into the bedroom, where on the other side of the broad room sat a most familiar man in his boxer shorts and with a bag of tortilla chips balanced in his lap.

Bashir Wassouf—aka Bobby Gallagher—arguably one of

the most ruthless traitors in the history of the United States of America, gaped at the man standing in his bedroom.

Gallagher had a Beretta sitting on the table beside his recliner. Moore had already seen it and had anticipated which hand the traitor might use to grab it. Gallagher's mere presence suggested that he didn't know Borja had been arrested—a grave error on his part.

He was already reaching for his pistol as Moore shouted, "Hold it!"

At nearly the same time, the girl screamed and cursed behind them. Towers hollered at her to freeze.

In the next heartbeat, Gallagher ignored Moore's command and snatched up his gun.

Expecting to be shot, Moore fired first, hitting Gallagher in the shoulder, then putting a second round in his leg, but it was already too late.

Gallagher had the Beretta in his mouth.

"No, no, no, no!" Moore screamed, lunging toward the man as the shot rang out.

Within the next hour, the local police arrived, the woman (a prostitute) was taken into custody, and Moore and Towers tore apart the entire estate.

Sitting atop a nightstand in one of the back bedrooms were eleven Hershey's Kisses wrappers rolled into eleven silver balls.

Ministerial Federal Police Headquarters
Mexico City

Six hours later, Moore and Towers were sitting in their rental car in the parking lot, about to go inside to question Borja. They had nothing to lose. Gallagher had taken Samad's location to his grave. The only other living witnesses were three of the six terrorists who'd boarded the planes, and they'd all repeated the same story: They knew only their mission, nothing else, and Moore tended to believe that, because the Taliban most often used compartmentalized cells. One terrorist was pulled from the wreckage of the San Antonio flight and had been so badly burned on his face and neck that he couldn't have talked even if he had wanted to.

But Borja . . . He had to know something. He was involved with Gallagher. Samad had left those Hershey's Kisses wrappers at his house. The connection was there. He couldn't deny that anymore.

Moore spoke to Slater, who agreed. A deal must be brokered.

Borja was much younger than expected—mid-thirties, perhaps—with a shaved head and enough tattoos to earn him the admiration of most *sicarios*. But when he'd opened his mouth, his cadence, diction, and inflections were those of a well-educated businessman, and that was auspicious, because they were about to get down to some serious business.

The interrogation room smelled like bleach. Apparently,

the last guy who'd been questioned there had been, according to the police, "sloppy."

Moore narrowed his gaze on Borja and began abruptly: "Gallagher's dead. He killed himself at your house in Las Conchas."

Borja folded his arms over his chest. "Who?"

"All right, let me explain this very carefully. You're going to jail for the rest of your life. I'm willing to help broker a deal between our two governments. If you know anything about where Samad is, you tell me. And if you're telling the truth, I get you full amnesty. Clean fucking slate. You walk away. Let me say that again very slowly . . . You . . . *walk* . . . *away*."

"Who's Samad?"

Towers interrupted Moore by sliding over his laptop so that Moore could glimpse the screen. Their colleagues at Fort Meade had come through once again: cell-phone calls between Borja and Rahmani picked up by the NSA's satellites, the evidence finally collected and confirmed only hours ago.

"You were talking to Rahmani, too, huh?" Moore asked. "There's no point in lying now. We know."

Borja rolled his eyes.

"Were you helping Samad escape?"

Borja leaned forward on his chair. "If you're going to get me full amnesty, I want it in writing from the government. I want my lawyers to go over it to make sure it's legitimate."

"Okay, but that'll take time. And I'm sure our buddy is on the move. I promise you, you give me what I want and I get Samad, you're free."

"I'm not going to believe one fucking gringo."

Moore rose. "Your choice." He turned to Towers. "Let's go . . . Start extradition papers. We'll deal with this asshole in the States." They headed for the door.

Borja slid back his chair and stood, his hands still cuffed behind his back. "Wait!"

Gulfstream III
En Route to Goldson International Airport
Belize

Borja, like any good heir to a Mexican drug cartel, feared extradition to the United States more than the wrath of his own government, and so his shoulders had slumped and his mouth had worked to spin the yarn of how he'd been commissioned by Rahmani to form a new smuggling alliance and how he'd been charged with helping Samad and two of his lieutenants to reach a safe house in San José, Costa Rica. Samad and his men had been hidden in Borja's vacation home, where they'd remained until just the previous night. They'd been flown in one of Borja's private planes to Goldson International, then driven out into the jungle to a safe house on the New River Lagoon in Belize. Borja said the house was used by mules moving Colombian cocaine into the vacation areas of Cozumel and Cancún, where the coke was sold primarily to American college students. Lovely. Borja had hired a Guatemalan pilot with an R44 Raven single-engine helicopter to pick them up and fly them down to Costa Rica, with one refueling stop in Nicaragua.

Moore questioned the man about every detail, including the type of helicopter being used, the name of the pilot, the pilot's phone number, everything and anything.

For once, their timing might be favorable. Samad and his men were scheduled to be picked up at midnight, local time, and the chopper was going to set down in one of the clearings near the ruins of Lamanai (a word that meant submerged crocodile in the Mayan language). The Mask Temple, High Temple, and Temple of the Jaguar Masks were frequented by tourists during the day but closed in the evenings. The safe house was about nine miles south down the river, and Samad and his men were supposed to take one of several Zodiacs up to the rendezvous point. Borja had given Samad two bodyguards, so Moore and Towers were expecting a party of five.

They would move in on the safe house as a team of two, but Slater was already working on some creative backup forces for them, should the need arise. He'd already arranged for weapons and transport.

Moore's watch read 9:12 p.m. local time when they landed at Goldson International Airport, just north of Belize City. The plane was met by two vehicles: a four-wheel-drive Jeep Wrangler and another vehicle, a local taxi.

"Welcome to the armpit of the Caribbean," Towers said, lifting his shirt against the stifling humidity.

Moore snorted. "You've been here before."

A young man no more than twenty-two, with a crew cut and dressed in black T-shirt and khaki pants, hurried out of the cab, opened the trunk, and tossed a big duffel bag into the back of the Wrangler, even as the Jeep's driver, a man who could be the first man's brother, left the Jeep and hurried into the back of the cab. Moore approached.

"You're all set here, sir," the kid said, his British accent unmistakable. "Night-vision goggles on the front seat. Garmin GPS has been programmed. Just listen to the nice lady with the sexy voice, and she'll tell you how to get there."

Moore shook the kid's hand. "Thank you."

"It's not over yet, right?" He thrust a satellite phone into Moore's hand.

Moore nodded and hopped into the Jeep, with Towers coming around the other side.

"Great service around here," he said.

Moore threw the Jeep in gear. "I was just trying to impress you, boss."

"I'm duly impressed." Towers tapped a couple of buttons on the GPS, and the sexy lady with the British accent told them they had 30.41 miles to their destination. "Now, then, I've just got one more question: What if Borja lied?"

"You mean we get to the safe house and no one's home? They're already gone or they weren't there in the first place?"

"Yeah."

"I just checked before we got off the plane. The National Reconnaissance Office has had eyes on the house since we called it in. NASA and a whole group of universities are always using satellites to map the ruins here, so the NRO's got access to quite a few sources. They already spotted two individuals out on the dock. They're there. And remember: Borja knows he doesn't get shit if we don't get Samad. That punk in jail is our number-one fan."

The sexy GPS lady told them to take the left fork in the road, which Moore did, and they bounced over several potholes and continued on, the headlights pushing out through the swirling bugs toward the narrow passage, the power poles like those grave markers in San Juan Chamula. The dense jungle occasionally grew alive with the shimmering eyes of troops of baboons watching them from the trees. They had to go through a police checkpoint, but the officers there had already been informed of their presence by their British contacts and waved them through.

When they reached the sign for the Howler Monkey Resort, Moore donned the night-vision goggles and switched off the headlights to cover the last eight miles to the house. After they passed the main lodge and cabins, the road grew a little more rutted and uneven, and Moore veered twice around dead turtles taken out by other motorists, although they had yet to see another car.

While it felt like he and Towers were alone, thousands of miles from home and driving deeper into the Belizean jungle, Slater, along with analysts in the counterterrorism and counterintelligence centers, was at this very moment monitoring them, reporting their every move, and he and the analysts were holding their collective breaths.

He and Towers drove on in silence, each man mentally preparing for the raid to come. Moore wondered if Towers was a religious man, or maybe he chalked it all up to fate or a merciless universe. For his part, Moore thought in more simple terms: It was time to say thank you to all the people who'd made the ultimate sacrifice. It was time to capture this bastard Samad and do it for them, in their name.

And yes, the trail had finally grown warm. Very warm.

Within one mile of the safe house, Moore pulled off the road, threw the Jeep into park, and turned off the engine. He and Towers looked at each other, banged fists, then climbed out.

It took a few seconds before Moore realized that his boss was humming a familiar rock-and-roll anthem: Guns N' Roses' "Welcome to the Jungle." Moore smiled weakly as he wrenched open the Jeep's tailgate, and they got to work.

45

THE WATER WAS
THEIR HOME

New River Lagoon
Central Belize

FTER MOORE AND TOWERS had gone through the duffel bag, had changed into their black cargo pants and shirts, and had donned their Kevlar vests, web gear, and balaclavas, Towers scrutinized the weapons they'd been provided. The inventory included two bolt-action sniper rifles—the L115A3 (.338) with Schmidt and Bender scopes and five-round magazines—a couple of Browning 9x19-millimeter Parabellum semiautomatic pistols, a very sweet pair of Steiner 395 binoculars, and two Fairbairn-Sykes fighting knives with double edges and ring grips.

Towers held up his blade. "These Royal Marines have some nice toys."

Moore agreed, and it was fortunate that 45 Commando, a battalion-sized unit of the Royal Marines, frequently had platoons training in the area. Slater had arranged to use them as a backup force. All the Brits knew was that Towers and Moore were CIA agents hunting down some drug smugglers and that they might need a little muscle. The Brits would be happy to oblige.

Moore held up the satellite phone. "Those guys are just a phone call away."

"Let's hope we don't need them," said Towers.

They slid into their backpacks, then started off, both wearing NVGs against the utter darkness. The grunts, chirps, and rustling noises coming from the jungle beside them were not the most reassuring sounds, and if they were accosted by, say, a baboon, howler monkey, or something, ahem, worse, it was not the animal that Moore feared so much as the racket created by such an encounter.

Consequently, they kept to the edge of the jungle, off the road but not too far, thankful the Brits had included bug spray against the mosquitoes, doctor flies, and chiggers. New operators would call their seasoned colleagues wimps for worrying about bugs, but Moore had been taught in both the SEALs and the CIA that an annoying itch could cause a distraction—and cost you your life.

His brow was already damp with sweat, and he tasted the salt on his lips by the time they reached the water's edge, where the ground turned muddy and unstable, and roots breached the surface like varicose veins. He led Towers to a stand of trumpet trees, where they dropped to their haunches. He warned Towers to avoid touching the trees, because they were home to wasplike ants called pseudomyrmex. The ants felt vibration and would swarm to attack invaders with painful stings.

About thirty meters north stood the house, no more than a thousand square feet constructed on two-meter-high stilts, with a small porch beneath a gabled tin roof and windows covered by heavy wooden shutters for full privacy. There were no vehicles in sight. The wooden dock was barely ten meters long, with a pair of Zodiacs tied to the north side. Each boat with inflatable tubes around the sides was equipped with an outboard motor and could carry three to five passengers. A trail that the late Michael Ansara would have described as an "excellent single track" for mountain biking wove away from the road behind them and up toward the house. Another path wide enough for a four-wheel-drive cut through the jungle to the north and linked back to the main road. Were they back in the States, a house like this would be mistaken for a fishing camp, not a drug-smuggling way station.

Moore's watch read 10:44 p.m.

He wrenched off the NVGs and the balaclava in order to wipe more sweat from his face. Towers cursed and did likewise, then he took up the binoculars and scanned the dock. He regarded Moore with an urgent expression and handed over the binoculars.

A man had come out onto the dock with a small kerosene lantern. He was carrying a plastic five-gallon jug of gasoline. He might be one of the *sicarios* that Borja had assigned to Samad.

Hell, it could be Samad himself. Moore couldn't be sure, even after zooming in.

The man, bare-chested and wearing a pair of tan shorts, climbed carefully into one of the Zodiacs and proceeded to fill the outboard's external fuel tank seated just beneath the motor.

O'Hara had been adamant: Take Samad alive.

So they'd put gas grenades on their wish list, and the Royal Marines had come through with a dozen, along with two gas masks that they'd stowed in the packs. Kick in the door, throw in the grenades, gas them out, stand back, and capture them.

But Moore now saw an opportunity too good to ignore.

"I'll take this guy, then I'll meet you around back. We move a lot faster now."

"You sure?"

Moore nodded.

With Towers's help, he stripped quickly out of his gear and vest, and was down to his skivvies and belt holster within thirty seconds. Instead of taking one of the pistols the Brits had given them, he chose his Glock 17, which he'd packed upon hearing they were jungle-bound. The pistol was equipped with maritime spring cups for use in water environments. The cups were placed within the firing-pin assembly to ensure that water passed by the firing pin within the firing-pin channel. This prevented the creation of a hydraulic force that could slow the firing pin and cause light primer strikes. The NATO spec ammo Moore used had waterproof sealed primers and case mouths, which of course further increased the weapon's reliability.

With the Glock holstered at his side, he grabbed the combat knife and slid like one more predator beneath the ink-black water.

The river felt warm and thick in his palms; the vegetation growing from the bottom (which might have been hydrilla; he wasn't sure) scraped across his bare feet. He estimated the river's depth at just eight or nine feet in this section. He swam silently, guided by the kerosene lantern light shining down on the waves ahead. Yes, this was home. This was where Carmichael lived forever . . .

It was only as he neared the dock that he remembered the crocodiles.

He shuddered and came up beneath the second Zodiac, his exit from the water silent, his breath slowly released. Their man was in the first boat, docked farthest out. Moore peered furtively around the boat's hull. The guy was one of Borja's *sicarios*, mid-twenties, lanky, with a few tribal tattoos slashing across his shoulder blades. Samad and his men would not have tattoos; they were forbidden in Islam.

After his container made a louder chugging noise, the *sicario* stopped filling the tank, checked the fuel level, then lifted the plastic container once more.

Moore looked back at the house: all quiet, save for the almost electric hum of thousands of insects.

He submerged and swam back around the Zodiac, getting himself in position.

So the plan, formulated anew, was to take out this guy and fall back to the house. He and Towers would have one fewer guy to deal with and could still smoke 'em out. However, as he'd warned Towers, they had to be fast so gas boy wouldn't be missed.

Moore held the combat knife in a reverse grip, the blade jutting from the bottom of his fist. Three, two, one, he kicked hard and came out of the water, slid one arm around the man's waist while plunging the blade into his chest and dragging him over the side—and it all needed to happen before the guy yelled, because Moore couldn't reach his mouth.

Every consideration had been taken. The blade's tip was sharp, and it had good cutting edges. Moore had discovered the hard way that if you cut an artery with a dull blade, it tended to contract and stop bleeding. A cleanly severed main artery resulted in loss of consciousness and death. Furthermore, holding the man underwater would cause his heart to race, and death would come even sooner.

The snatch itself had gone off perfectly, textbook. Moore could go up to Rhode Island and give lectures about it at the Naval War College. The guy had gone over the side with only a gasp and a barely perceptible groan. Even the splash wasn't very loud, as Moore had eased him down into the water rather than jerking him.

But in that second, as the water rushed over Moore's face and he gritted his teeth and sucked in air—that second when every muscle in his body had tensed—he spied from the corner of his eye the back door of the house opening and a figure appearing in silhouette.

That individual had seen a man rise from the water and drag his colleague over the side. And it was all Moore could do to hold the struggling man beneath the water while shaking against the fear that the alarm had just gone off.

His heart red-zoned immediately.

He wanted to scream. They were *fucked*!

One task at a time. First, he willed himself into a moment of calm as he continued choking the man, who abruptly stopped thrashing.

As he released the guy, the first salvo of gunfire tore into the river, the shots punching just behind him as he now swam down toward the dock's pilings and kept tight to them, on the inside beneath the dock.

Then came another salvo, and another, full automatic-weapons fire hosing down a 180-degree line around the dock, the muffled thumping painfully familiar. Still tight to the piling, Moore ascended until his mouth broke water, and he took in a long breath. *Bring down the heart rate. And* think . . .

Towers's sniper rifle thundered from the tree line, and a man up on the dock hit the planks with a double thud, wailing in Spanish. A wounding round, to be sure. Towers knew what he was doing, but he'd also given up his location and would be slower to return fire with that bolt-action rifle.

More footfalls now. Louder. The dock vibrated. AK-47 fire popped again, two weapons. Towers's gun replied with a formidable crack, then fell silent against an onslaught of withering fire.

A third AK added its voice to the first two.

Then, a break . . .

"Talwar? Niazi? In the boat, now!"

Moore could barely contain himself. That was him, Samad,

speaking in Arabic and standing on the dock above Moore's head. And there was Moore, in the water, armed with a knife and a pistol. Three versus one. Were the object to kill Samad, he would push out from beneath the dock and surprise attack. Again, he willed himself back into a state of calm. His impatience had already cost them too much. *Hold position. Wait.*

The Zodiac bobbed up and down as the men climbed aboard, and one of them turned the key on the outboard. The engine started immediately.

Moore couldn't disable the engine without being spotted and drawing their point-blank fire, but maybe he could sink the boat before they knew what was happening . . .

While the Zodiac had a rigid fiberglass hull, it still had synthetic rubber tubes constructed in separate sections, six or more chambers, he estimated. The rubber was actually a plastomer bound to a dense polyester cloth and tougher to damage than plain old rubber, but that didn't mean Moore wouldn't try.

He pushed off the piling, submerged again, and swam up beside the Zodiac while the motor was still idling. He took the knife and plunged it into the first compartment. The air hissed loudly and sent a steady rush of bubbles into the river. He swam under the boat as the men reacted and thrust his knife up once more, stabbing another section.

The fifty-horsepower engine throttled up, and Moore dove quickly to avoid being hit by the skeg or shredded by the propeller. As the boat passed overhead, he turned, swam hard for the surface, came up, and drew his pistol, lifting it over the waves and targeting the back tubes of the boat, firing once, twice, before the man at the outboard lifted a pistol and squeezed off two rounds. Moore threw himself back under the water, kicking hard for the dock.

By the time he began pulling himself up onto the dock, Towers was sprinting toward him, carrying all their gear. "What the fuck?" was all he shouted.

"Second Zodiac!" Moore answered.

Towers threw the backpacks and rifles into the boat and climbed aboard. "Keys! No keys!"

The guy Towers had hit still lay on the dock in a pool of blood and clutching his hip. Moore dropped to his knees beside the man. "Keys for the boat?"

The man just looked at him, all teeth and agony.

Moore went through his pockets. Nothing. *Back in the house? Should he go check? No time.*

Wait. The guy in the water. He looked up. The body was floating facedown. Moore ran to the edge of the dock and dove in, swimming out to the corpse. This guy had probably put the keys in the first outboard. There was nothing to say that he didn't have the keys to the second one still in his pocket.

Moore reached him, felt the man's pockets, found the keys, and dug them out. He swam back to the Zodiac and tossed the keys to his partner, who fumbled to get them in the outboard.

"Good to go!" Towers announced.

Moore reached up, and Towers hauled him into the Zodiac. While Towers started the engine, Moore threw off the line. The engine thrummed, and they sped away from the dock as Towers used one hand to tug on his night-vision goggles.

"They've got a good lead on us," Towers said, pointing ahead as they dropped into the first Zodiac's dissolving wake. "And I got a good look . . . and that is *them*! Samad is wearing a gray or tan T-shirt. The other guys are wearing black."

"I heard him call to his men." Moore was fighting for breath, trembling badly, the adrenaline overwhelming him as he riffled through his pack and produced the satellite phone. He thumbed it on and scrolled to the call log. There was only one contact saved there: BOOTNECK FIVE.

He hit the button, waited.

"This is Bootneck Five," came a distinctly British voice.

"Hey, this is River Team," Moore said. "Our package is on the move. They're heading north in a Zodiac toward the rendezvous point. We're in pursuit. We need your intercept at the rendezvous."

"No problem, River Team. We were hoping for your call. I'll contact you once we're in position."

"Thanks, bro."

"You'll thank us all later with a pint, mate."

"My pleasure." Moore returned the phone to his backpack, then sat up and readjusted his grip on the Glock, testing out his firing position from his seat. The wind was whipping over them now, and from the shoreline came pinpricks of light that became darker forms as they approached.

"Hey, did you check fuel?" Towers called.

"Shit, no." Moore leaned down and rapped a knuckle on the plastic gas tank. Hollow. He dove for a small pocket on his backpack and produced a penlight, which he directed on the plastic so he could see the shadow line of fuel. *Oh, shit . . . not good news.* And that's why the first guy had come out to fill the tank.

"You think we'll make it?" asked Towers.

"Full-throttle. Just keep going." Moore estimated their speed at nearly thirty knots, all they could bleed out of the little outboard. He reached down and pulled on his own NVGs, the world transformed from layers of gray, dark blue, and black to glowing green and white. He focused his attention ahead, and there, in the distance, he spotted the Zodiac with three ribbons of whitewater fluttering behind.

A gunshot ricocheted off the side of their outboard.

"Get down!" Moore ordered, throwing himself on top of his backpack.

Towers ducked but had to keep his hand on the tiller. Moore tugged off his NVGs and grabbed one of the sniper rifles. Three more pops sounded above the din of outboards, and a hissing came from the front portside of their boat. Moore crawled up toward the bow, propped his elbows on the tubes, and settled down with the rifle. He sighted the back of the Zodiac, but between all the bouncing of their craft and the target, an accurate shot was impossible. If he gambled and the shot went wide and struck Samad in the head . . . He cursed and turned back to Towers. "I can't get a bead. Can we get any closer?"

"I'm trying!"

Moore leaned over, set down the rifle, and tugged out his

Glock. Samad had probably called ahead to their pilot for an early pickup. The pilot's cell phone was already being monitored by the NSA, so the second he got that call, Moore's people would know. A quick check of his smartphone confirmed that. Text message from Slater: Chopper called. He's en route to the ruins and rendezvous.

But so was a Sea King Mk4 helicopter carrying up to twenty-seven Royal Marines who would fast-rope into the rendezvous point and secure it. However, if Samad spotted that helo, he and his boys could ditch early and make a run for it into the jungle. The fool could get himself killed if he did that.

Moore checked their GPS position on his smartphone, the signal from his shoulder chip being received and routed to the Agency's satellites and that information being shot back down to him for a position accurate to within three meters. They were about five miles up the river now, with about four miles to go, which translated into less than ten minutes boat time.

They heard the whomping first, followed by the distant flashes of the helo's lights. No, it wasn't the Guatemalan pilot but the Royal Marines, coming in loud, as though announced by trumpets, and if Samad didn't see that bird far ahead, then he had his head under the water. *Shit*.

Behind Moore, the outboard sputtered, and then he felt it—the bow lowering toward the waves as they slowed, the tube growing softer as more air jetted out.

Samad's Zodiac was less than fifty meters away. They'd slowed, too, the boat's pilot distracted by the oncoming helicopter, which, perhaps, confused him. They were expecting a small chopper but were getting a big one. Moore hadn't considered that.

As the outboard chugged even more loudly, sucking on fumes now, Moore cursed again and looked back at Towers, who said, "Up to the Marines now, I guess, huh? They got orders to take them alive, I hope?"

"Those orders don't mean shit. If they're fired upon, they will fire back. I only wanted them as a roadblock."

A more high-pitched thumping from the northeast joined the deeper baritone of the Marines' chopper, and Moore lifted his binoculars to spy the tiny R44 whirlybird whose twin-bladed rotor sat atop a dorsal-fin–like platform. The helo could carry a pilot and three passengers, and that's exactly what its pilot intended to do.

But how would the Guatemalan react to soldiers fast-roping into his intended landing zone? He'd haul ass out of there. And Samad would see that, too.

Moore panned down with the binoculars and focused on Samad's Zodiac. The man himself was pointing up at the second helicopter, then gesticulating wildly for his man at the tiller to pull over, across the river.

When his man failed to react, Samad himself seized the tiller, and the Zodiac cut hard to the right toward the shoreline, and that's when the portside tubing struck something in the water. The boat fishtailed suddenly as the outboard was struck and lifted partially out of the water. The violent impact threw Samad and one of his men across the Zodiac—

And over the side. Into the water. The guy at the tiller, who'd been white-knuckling that handle even as Samad had taken over, shouted and broke into a wide arc, trying to wheel around. Moore saw it now—a fallen tree all but an inch or so submerged and nearly invisible in the darkness. Samad's pilot had run right over it.

Moore stole a look back. Their outboard was down to a gurgle. He took up the sniper rifle, even as Towers released the tiller and lifted his own gun, working the bolt to prepare for his next shot.

The engine quit. They were gliding now toward the other Zodiac and the men in the water. Twenty meters. From the corner of his eye Moore saw movement along the shoreline. Splashes. Glowing eyes. The man in the Zodiac spotted him, thrust out his pistol—but not before Moore sighted his head and took the first shot.

While the pilot might have been a valuable prisoner, keeping him alive decreased Moore's chances of capturing Samad. They needed to isolate the target. The man's head snapped back, and he slumped near the outboard. Pilotless, the Zodiac now drove straight for the shoreline.

Samad and the other guy, either Talwar or Niazi, swam back toward the boat, both hollering and well aware they were not alone in the water. While Samad struggled forward, his partner let out a horrific cry before vanishing beneath the waves.

Towers took the butt of his rifle and used it like an oar, trying to steer them closer to the other boat. Ten meters now.

The water moved again.

And Moore spotted the first enormous shadow coming up behind Samad and fired twice. The shadow jerked left and disappeared.

Samad, a man who'd been raised in the mountains and desert, was hardly a good swimmer, and in his panic, he began to hyperventilate and go under.

Towers fired at another shadow just to the left of Samad, and Moore realized what he had to do.

He dropped the rifle, checked to make sure his Glock was still holstered at his side, then dove into the water.

Meanwhile, Towers took up both pistols and began firing all around Samad, trying to create a screen around him. Then he widened his fire as Moore came up and swam hard toward the man.

"Just calm down," Moore told Samad in Arabic. "I'll get you out."

Samad did not answer and continued thrashing and gasping for air. If Moore got too close, he could be knocked out, so he drew up slowly, then, seeing a chance, he darted closer and grabbed one of Samad's wrists as Towers glided up to them in the Zodiac.

"Come on, the boat's right here," Moore barked.

He jerked Samad forward, past him, then shoved the guy up toward the Zodiac, where Towers seized one of the handles on the hull and used the other to haul Samad aboard. As the man collapsed onto the deck, his clean-shaven face and head glistening with water, Towers drew his pistol and said, "*Allahu Akbar.*"

Samad glared at him.

Moore breathed the sigh of a lifetime. They'd done it. He clutched the Zodiac with one hand and just hung there for a few seconds, the tears threatening to fall. He wasn't sure how he felt: overjoyed one second, wanting to commit murder the next, and those conflicting emotions overwhelmed him. For the moment, all was right with the world, and he wished Frank Carmichael were there to see it. The water was their home, be it an ocean, a river, the bottom of a pool.

Towers had already tossed a pair of handcuffs to Samad and ordered that he bind his wrists behind his back, which he did. "Hey, I can't help you up," he told Moore. "I'm covering him."

"No problem, buddy. I'll be right there."

The satellite phone began to ring.

Moore whirled and faced the Zodiac, reaching up to pull himself into the boat. The water moved strangely.

And in the next pair of seconds, Moore freed his Glock from its holster, shoved the pistol into the water, and jerked the trigger.

Epilogue

BLACK COFFEE

Starbucks
McLean, Virginia
Two Weeks Later

T HE STARBUCKS in Old Dominion Center, known as the Chesterbrook store, was a stand-alone building with a fireplace on the second floor. It was one of three Starbucks near the George H. W. Bush Center for Central Intelligence, and the lines were sometimes out the door during the morning rush. Moore was not fond of waiting fifteen minutes for a five-dollar cup of coffee, and so he'd told her to meet him there at four p.m., during the slower time, when the blenders and cappuccino machines weren't humming quite as often. He sat in a chair near the entrance, creating profiles of the people around him and those ordering at the counter. He summed up their entire lives within seconds, where they'd grown up, where they'd gone to school, whether or not they hated their jobs, and how much money they made. He assigned them sexual orientation, marital status, and political affiliation. Being a keen observer was a prerequisite for his line of work, but the game now had nothing to do with that and everything to do with calming down.

Every part of his body still hurt, and he'd mentioned that to Towers, who said he'd only been shot up by some drug-smuggling thugs, which was pretty much routine for a BORTAC guy. Their last handshake at the airport in San Diego had carried with it the heart and soul of the entire joint task force. Even Towers had choked up. Moore vowed to stay in touch with the man. A good man.

With a groan, Moore checked his phone again. This is what you got for being fifteen minutes early—extra time to let the nerves run wild. SEALs were not late. Ever. Well, there was no message to cancel and blow him off. She was still coming. He imagined her floating through the glass doors in a short dress, heels, and wearing a delicate diamond necklace. So European. So incredibly sexy. Her voice like a musical instrument from another century.

"Mr. Moore?"

He glanced up, not into the eyes of a beautiful woman but into the frown of an unshaven face, dark features, and curly black hair. The guy was about Moore's age, handsome but not arrogantly so.

"Who are you?" Moore asked.

"Dominic Caruso."

Moore sighed. Slater had called Moore earlier in the week to say this guy Caruso wanted to talk to him, that he was a "good guy," and that Moore should "trust him." Slater had been unwilling to say anything else, and Moore couldn't pull up much on the guy, save for the fact that he'd been a fibbie but had left the Bureau. There was nothing after that. Moore was supposed to call Caruso to set up a meeting as a favor to Slater, but despite Slater's reassurances, Moore hardly trusted the stranger, and there was no way in hell he'd volunteer information about any of his operations.

Caruso proffered his hand; Moore ignored it. "Do you think we can go somewhere more private to talk?" Caruso asked.

Moore tried and failed to hide his disgust. "How'd you find me?"

"You told Slater you'd be here. He told me what you look like."

"I guess he's one of your fans. Unfortunately, I'm not."

"You will be."

"Look, this isn't a good time. I'm, uh, supposed to meet someone right now, and she's much prettier than you."

"I understand. I just need a little information."

"And what do you plan to do with it?"

Caruso smiled guiltily.

"Who do you work for?" Moore asked.

Caruso opened his mouth, seemed to think better of it, then said quickly, "I'm sorry I bothered you. We'll be in touch again." He gave Moore a brusque nod and left.

What the hell was that? Moore thought.

He was about to call Slater when his coffee date entered, wearing a wrinkled sweatshirt, jeans, and jogging shoes. His shoulders slumped, if only a little. The dark hair was pulled back to reveal those spectacular cheekbones.

It's only coffee, he reminded himself.

She saw him, gave a tentative wave, then beamed as she approached. "Hey, there. Glad you're finally letting me pay you back." Her English was very good, but the accent made it sound even better, older, like she was in her thirties and much closer to his age.

They shook hands, hers a delicate piece of silk, his a leathery talon. "The timing worked out," he said. "Which is no small miracle."

She nodded, and he crossed over to the counter with her and ordered. He took her for a latte girl. She ordered a venti coffee, black. He was impressed and ordered the same. She held up her debit card and mouthed the words *Thank you*.

"You're very welcome. There's a fireplace upstairs."

"It's still summer."

"Yeah, but it's a gas fireplace, and they keep it lit all year. It's really nice."

On the second floor they dropped onto a leather sofa, set their coffee cups on the table, then stared for a long moment at the fire and the pairs of college kids from Marymount seated around them, their heads buried in their computers as they barely looked over to grab their drinks.

"Were you ever that serious?" Her voice came softly, so that no one else could overhear.

"I wasn't serious till I got in the Navy."

"And now you're really intense."

He grinned and reached for his coffee. "So how much do you know?"

"More than you think."

"I'm talking about Samad."

"I was talking about you."

"No, really, you should've seen the look on his face when he saw the plane in Belize."

"What do you mean?"

"We got some help from the Israelis to fly him out. El Al plane. Big Star of David on the tail. He went nuts, like we were pouring holy water on him."

"We don't have a black site in Israel, do we?"

He grinned. "Black sites? I don't know what you're talking about."

She smirked. "So where'd we take him? I haven't found anything, and no one's talking. I mean, they haven't even gone public yet. It's crazy."

"To be honest, I have no idea where he is now. Kogălniceanu in Romania, Stare Kiejkuty in Poland, and Diego Garcia are all a no-go. Too many outsider eyes and ears. Hell, they could have him on a boat. We've done that before."

"Rumor is the President's Special Task Force wasn't even notified, meaning there are only about a dozen people in the world who know what happened."

Moore agreed and, of course, wouldn't be entirely honest with her, either. "With all the bullshit we've had to go through since nine-eleven, they want to make sure we do this thing right—lest the media starts wailing about how Samad was taken to a secret CIA prison and tortured."

"So as it stands, Samad is being interrogated at an undisclosed location, and some people on the Hill want us to believe this undermines the public's trust in our justice system."

"What do you think?"

"I think you should have killed the motherfucker when you had the chance."

"Wow."

"I'm surprised you didn't."

"I thought about it—but he's got intel we need."

"So . . . did you read my file?"

He cocked a brow at her. "If I say no, you'll accuse me of lying. If I say yes, you'll call me a stalker."

She sipped her coffee. "I don't care if you did. My parents won't talk to me anymore because of the choice I made. My father still believes Rojas was a great man. You know we spent two years putting that together."

"I don't pretend to know how you feel about it."

She nodded and tugged out her cell phone, as if to change the subject. "Hmmm, let's see what I have here on you. I was surprised you got lured away from the DIA and resigned your commission. You were supposed to get the Navy Cross and they downgraded it to a Silver Star."

"I don't talk about that, except to say that by then the Navy and I were ready to part company. I'll always be a SEAL, but the politics were getting a little too hot for me. I had some other things going on, too."

"They sent you to The Point, though, huh? I've requested to train there three times. Denied three times. Which, of course, is bullshit."

The Harvey Point Defense Testing Activity facility in Elizabeth City, North Carolina, was a little-known CIA school dedicated to hard-core paramilitary ops training. Those boys at The Point thought they were some badasses, but Moore breezed through that training and showed them a thing or two about shooting, moving, and communicating, SEAL-style.

"You don't want to go to The Point."

"Why not? Because I'm a *girl*?"

"Because what you do with the political action group is much more clever and dangerous. I couldn't do it. Those meatheads over there couldn't do it."

Her gaze seemed to focus on infinity. "I'm finding it very hard to . . . I just don't know if this is . . ."

"What's the hardest thing you've ever done in your life?"

"Are you nuts? *This* . . ."

"Sitting here with me?"

She reached over and punched him. "I mean all the lies. I mean letting down my guard and really living the entire lie. I started dreaming that his father wasn't a criminal and actually thinking about a life with Miguel."

"We all have our moments of weakness."

She bit her lip. "I'll never forgive myself for what I did to him. He was a beautiful man." She blushed and glanced away, trying to hide tears.

"That's okay. It hurts now, but eventually the sting will go away."

"You really think so?"

He raised his brows. "Yes."

"What about you? The hardest thing you've ever done?"

Moore hesitated, and then he told her in an even voice that eventually cracked. And when the tears came, he was not embarrassed because for the first time ever, they felt good.

She slid over to him and tucked her head into his shoulder. "These people here? Everyone out there? They have no idea what it takes to keep them safe."

"Don't resent them for that."

"I can't help it."

"You just need a vacation."

"I just finished a vacation. And I still feel terrible."

"Maybe you need a new boyfriend."

She lifted her head and looked at him. "Oh, yeah?"

"Yeah, you know, to get your mind off things." He adopted his best innocent-schoolboy look.

"I see. Then I have a question—have you ever been to Spain?"

Tom Clancy

RAINBOW SIX

Newly named head of an élite multinational task force, John Clark faces the
world's greatest fear: international terrorism. And following each terrifying new
outbreak – the ghosts from his own past.

The challenge of a new mission is just what Clark needs, but the opportunities
come faster than he expected. Hostage-taking at a Swiss bank. The kidnapping
of an international trader. Carnage at a theme park in Spain. Each incident seems
separate, yet the timing disturbs Clark.

Is there a connection? Is he being tested? Or is there a bigger threat out there, from
terrorists so extreme that no government is ready to admit their existence?

'The action scenes are superlative, and the complex, multi-stranded narrative is
orchestrated with Bach-like precision' *Evening Standard*

TOM CLANCY

THE BEAR AND THE DRAGON

President Jack Ryan faces a crisis unlike any he has ever known.

Being President isn't getting any easier. Not only is there trouble at home, but the Asian economy is collapsing, and now, in an already unstable Russia, someone may have tried to assassinate the chairman of the SVR (formerly the KGB) with a rocket-propelled grenade. Even more disturbing are the possible motives of the assassins – are they political, criminal or personal? Or, Ryan wonders, is something far more dangerous going on?

While the Russians investigate, and some of Ryan's most trusted people head for Moscow, forces in China are moving ahead with a plan of truly audacious scope. Tired of the arrogance of the West and eager to fulfil their destiny, they are taking matters into their own hands. If they succeed, the world will never be the same. If they fail . . . the consequences may be unthinkable.

'Exhilarating . . . No other novelist is giving so full a picture of modern conflict' *Sunday Times*

TOM CLANCY

RED RABBIT

Jack Ryan. The early CIA days . . .

When young Jack Ryan joins the CIA as an analyst he is thrust into a world of political intrigue and conspiracy. Stationed in England, he quickly finds himself debriefing a Soviet defector with an extraordinary story to tell: senior Russian officials are plotting to assassinate Pope John Paul II. The CIA novice must forget his inexperience and rely on all his wits to firstly discover the details of the plot – and then prevent its execution. For it is not just the Pope's life that is at stake, but also the stability of the Western world . . .

'There's hardly another thriller writer alive who can fuel an adrenaline surge the way Clancy can. His plots tear along as though the world were about to end' *Daily Mail*

TOM CLANCY

THE TEETH OF THE TIGER

'If you want to kick the tiger in his ass, you'd better have a plan for dealing with his teeth'

Just before Jack Ryan stepped down as US President, he created a secret organization designed to operate in areas where the CIA and FBI couldn't go – able to use any and all means to neutralize terrorists who threatened America. Now his son, Jack Ryan, Jr, is part of that organization and he's on the front line when a group of Islamic terrorists backed up by Columbian drug smugglers strike at the heart of American society. With no conventional way to hit back at the shadowy ringleaders, it's left to Jack Ryan, Jr to take on the terrorists the only way he knows how . . .

'Incredibly addictive . . . 400 tightly woven, adrenalin-fuelled pages' *Daily Mail*